THE QUINN BROTHERS

Nora Roberts

Series

Irish Born Trilogy

BORN IN FIRE
BORN IN ICE
BORN IN SHAME

Dream Trilogy

DARING TO DREAM
HOLDING THE DREAM
FINDING THE DREAM

Chesapeake Bay Saga

SEA SWEPT
RISING TIDES
INNER HARBOR
CHESAPEAKE BLUE

Gallaghers of Ardmore Trilogy

JEWELS OF THE SUN
TEARS OF THE MOON
HEART OF THE SEA

Three Sisters Island Trilogy

DANCE UPON THE AIR
HEAVEN AND EARTH
FACE THE FIRE

Key Trilogy

KEY OF LIGHT
KEY OF KNOWLEDGE
KEY OF VALOR

In the Garden Trilogy

BLUE DAHLIA
BLACK ROSE
RED LILY

Circle Trilogy

MORRIGAN'S CROSS
DANCE OF THE GODS
VALLEY OF SILENCE

Sign of Seven Trilogy

BLOOD BROTHERS
THE HOLLOW
THE PAGAN STONE

Bride Quartet

VISION IN WHITE
BED OF ROSES
SAVOR THE MOMENT
HAPPY EVER AFTER

The Inn BoonsBoro Trilogy

THE NEXT ALWAYS
THE LAST BOYFRIEND
THE PERFECT HOPE

The Cousins O'Dwyer Trilogy

DARK WITCH
SHADOW SPELL
BLOOD MAGICK

The Guardians Trilogy

STARS OF FORTUNE
BAY OF SIGHS
ISLAND OF GLASS

Nora Roberts & J. D. Robb

REMEMBER WHEN

J. D. Robb

NAKED IN DEATH
GLORY IN DEATH
IMMORTAL IN DEATH
RAPTURE IN DEATH
CEREMONY IN DEATH
VENGEANCE IN DEATH
HOLIDAY IN DEATH
CONSPIRACY IN DEATH
LOYALTY IN DEATH
WITNESS IN DEATH
JUDGMENT IN DEATH
BETRAYAL IN DEATH
SEDUCTION IN DEATH
REUNION IN DEATH
PURITY IN DEATH
PORTRAIT IN DEATH
IMITATION IN DEATH
DIVIDED IN DEATH
VISIONS IN DEATH
SURVIVOR IN DEATH
ORIGIN IN DEATH
MEMORY IN DEATH
BORN IN DEATH
INNOCENT IN DEATH
CREATION IN DEATH
STRANGERS IN DEATH
SALVATION IN DEATH
PROMISES IN DEATH
KINDRED IN DEATH
FANTASY IN DEATH
INDULGENCE IN DEATH
TREACHERY IN DEATH
NEW YORK TO DALLAS
CELEBRITY IN DEATH
DELUSION IN DEATH
CALCULATED IN DEATH
THANKLESS IN DEATH
CONCEALED IN DEATH
FESTIVE IN DEATH
OBSESSION IN DEATH
DEVOTED IN DEATH
BROTHERHOOD IN DEATH
APPRENTICE IN DEATH

NORA ROBERTS

THE QUINN BROTHERS

JOVE
New York

A JOVE BOOK
Published by Berkley
An imprint of Penguin Random House LLC
375 Hudson Street, New York, New York 10014

Copyright © 2006 by Nora Roberts
Sea Swept copyright © 1998 by Nora Roberts
Rising Tides copyright © 1998 by Nora Roberts

A JOVE BOOK and BERKLEY are registered trademarks and the B colophon is a trademark of Penguin Random House LLC.

ISBN: 9780425208144

The Library of Congress has catalogued the Berkley
trade edition of this book as follows:

Roberts, Nora.
[Sea swept]
The Quinn Brothers / Nora Roberts
p.   cm.
Contents: Sea swept — Rising tides.
ISBN 0-425-20814-1
1. Chesapeake Bay Region (Md. and Va.)—Fiction.   2. Eastern Shore (Md. and Va.)—
Fiction.   3. Boatbuilding—Fiction.   4. Brothers—Fiction.   5. Adoptees—Fiction.
I. Roberts, Nora. Rising Tides   II. Title.
PS3568.O243S43   2006
813'.54—dc22
2005053600

Berkley trade edition / January 2006
Jove trade edition / April 2018

Printed in the United States of America
13   15   17   19   21   20   18   16   14   12

Cover design © Rita Frangie
Cover photo of New England house on Cape Cod © ideeone / Getty Images
Book design by Tiffany Estreicher

CONTENTS

SEA SWEPT

For Mary Blayney
of the warm and generous heart

PROLOGUE

Cameron Quinn wasn't quite drunk. He could get there if he put his mind to it, but at the moment he preferred the nice comfortable buzz of the nearly there. He liked to think it was just the two-steps-short-of-sloppy state that was holding his luck steady.

He believed absolutely in the ebb and flow of luck, and right now his was flowing fast and hot. Just the day before, he'd raced his hydrofoil to victory in the world championship, edging out the competition by the point of the bow and breaking the standing record for time and speed.

He had the glory, and the hefty purse, and he'd taken both over to Monte Carlo to see how they held up.

They held up just dandy.

A few hands of baccarat, a couple of rolls of the dice, the turn of a card, and his wallet weighed heavier. Between the paparazzi and a reporter from *Sports Illustrated*, the glory showed no signs of dimming either.

Fortune continued to smile—no, make that leer, Cameron thought—by turning him toward that little jewel in the Med at the same time that popular magazine was wrapping its swimsuit-edition shoot.

And the leggiest of those long-stemmed gifts from God had turned her high-summer blue eyes on him, tipped her full, pouty lips up in an invitational smile a blind man could have spotted, and opted to stay on a few days longer.

And she'd made it clear that with very little effort, he could get a whole lot luckier.

Champagne, generous casinos, mindless, no-strings sex. Yes indeed, Cameron mused, luck was definitely being his kind of lady.

When they stepped out of the casino into the balmy March night, one of the ubiquitous paparazzi leaped out, snapping frantically. The woman pouted—it was, after all, her trademark look—but gave her endless mane of ribbon-straight silvery-blond hair an artful toss and shifted her killer body expertly. Her red-is-the-color-of-sin dress, barely thicker than a coat of paint, made an abrupt halt just south of the Gates of Paradise.

Cameron just grinned.

"They're such pests," she said with a hint of a lisp or a French accent. Cameron was never sure which. She sighed, testing the strength of that thin silk, and let Cameron guide her down the moon-dappled street. "Every place I look is a camera. I'm so weary of being viewed as an object for the pleasure of men."

Oh, yeah, right, he mused. And because he figured the pair of them were as shallow as a dry creek after a drought, he laughed and turned her into his arms. "Why don't we give him something to splash on page one, sugar?"

He brought his mouth down to hers. The taste of her tickled his hormones, engaged his imagination, and made him grateful their hotel was only two blocks away.

She skimmed her fingers up into his hair. She liked a man with plenty of hair, and his was full and thick and as dark as the night around them. His body was hard, all tough muscle and lean, disciplined lines. She was very choosy about the body of a potential lover, and his more than met her strict requirements.

His hands were just a bit rougher than she liked. Not the pressure or movement of them—that was lovely—but the texture. They were a working man's hands, but she was willing to overlook their lack of class because of their skill.

His face was intriguing. Not pretty. She would never be coupled, much less allow herself to be photographed, with a man prettier than she. There was a toughness about his face, a hardness that had to do with more than tanned skin tight over bones. It was in the eyes, she thought as she laughed lightly and wiggled free. They were gray, more the color of flint than smoke, and they held secrets.

She enjoyed a man with secrets, as none of them were able to keep them from her for long.

"You're a bad boy, Cameron." The accent was on the last syllable. She tapped a finger against his mouth, a mouth that held no softness whatsoever.

"So I've always been told—" He had to think for a moment as her name skimmed along the edges of his memory. "Martine."

"Maybe, tonight, I'll let you be bad."

"I'm counting on it, sweetie." He turned toward the hotel, slanted a glance over. At six feet, she was nearly eye to eye with him. "My suite or yours?"

"Yours." She all but purred it. "Perhaps if you order up another bottle of champagne, I'll let you try to seduce me."

Cameron cocked an eyebrow, asked for his key at the desk. "I'll need a bottle of Cristal, two glasses, and one red rose," he told the clerk while keeping his eyes on Martine. "Right away."

"Yes, Monsieur Quinn, I'll take care of it."

"A rose." She fluttered at him as they walked to the elevator. "How romantic."

"Oh, did you want one too?" Her puzzled smile warned him humor wasn't going to be her strong point. So they'd forget the laughs and conversation, he decided, and shoot straight for the bottom line.

The minute the elevator doors closed them in, he pulled her against him and met that sulky mouth with his own. He was hungry. He'd been too busy, too focused on his boat, too angled in on the race to take any time for recreation. He wanted soft skin, fragrant skin, curves, generous curves. A woman, any woman, as long as she was willing, experienced, and knew the boundary lines.

That made Martine perfect.

She let out a moan that wasn't altogether feigned for his benefit, then arched her throat for his nipping teeth. "You go fast."

He slid his hand down the silk, up again. "That's how I make my living. Going fast. Every time. Every way."

Still holding her, he circled out of the elevator, down the corridor to his rooms. Her heart was rapping hard against his, her breath catching, and her hands . . . well, he figured she knew just what she was doing with them.

So much for seduction.

He unlocked the door, shoved it open, then closed it by bracing Martine against it. He pushed the two string-width straps off her shoulders and with his eyes on hers helped himself to those magnificent breasts.

He decided her plastic surgeon deserved a medal.

"You want slow?"

Yes, the texture of his hands was rough, but God, exciting. She brought one mile-long leg up, wrapped it around his waist. He had to give her full marks for a sense of balance. "I want now."

"Good. Me too." He reached up under her excuse for a skirt and ripped away the whisper of lace beneath. Her eyes went wide, her breath thickened.

"Animal. Beast." And she fastened her teeth in his throat.

Even as he reached for his fly, the knock sounded discreetly on the door behind her head. Every ounce of blood had drained out of his head to below his belt. "Christ, service can't be that good here. Leave it outside," he demanded and prepared to take the magnificent Martine against the door.

"Monsieur Quinn, I beg your pardon. A fax just came for you. It was marked urgent."

"Tell him to go away." Martine wrapped a hand around him like a clamp. "Tell him to go to hell and fuck me."

"Hold on. I mean," he continued, unwrapping her fingers before his eyes could cross. "Wait just a minute." He shifted her behind the door, took a second to be sure he was zipped, then opened it.

"I'm sorry to disturb—"

"No problem. Thanks." Cameron dug in his pocket for a bill, didn't bother to check the denomination, and traded it for the envelope. Before the clerk could babble over the amount of the tip, Cameron shut the door in his face.

Martine gave that famous head toss again. "You're more interested in a silly fax than me. Than this." With an expert hand, she tugged the dress down, wiggling free of it like a snake shedding skin.

Cameron decided whatever she'd paid for that body, it had been worth every penny. "No, believe me, baby, I'm not. This'll just take a second." He ripped the envelope open before he could give in to the urge to ball it up, toss it over his shoulder, and dive headlong into all that female glory.

Then he read the message and his world, his life, his heart stopped.

"Oh, Jesus. Goddamn." All the wine cheerfully consumed throughout the evening swam giddily in his head, churned in his stomach, turned his knees to water. He had to lean back against the door to steady himself before reading it again.

Cam, damn it, why haven't you returned a call? We've been trying to reach you for hours. Dad's in the hospital. It's bad, as bad as it gets. No time for details. We're losing him fast. Hurry. Phillip.

Cameron lifted a hand—one that had held the wheel of dozens of boats, planes, cars that raced, one that could show a woman shuddery glimpses of heaven. And the hand shook as he dragged it through his hair.

"I have to go home."

"You are home." Martine decided to give him another chance and stepped forward to rub her body over his.

"No, I have to go." He nudged her aside and headed for the phone. "You have to go. I need to make some calls."

"You think you can tell me to go?"

"Sorry. Rain check." His mind just wouldn't engage. Absently he pulled bills out of his pocket with one hand, picked up the phone with the other. "Cab fare," he said, forgetting she was booked in the same hotel.

"Pig!" Naked and furious, she launched herself at him. If he had been steady, he'd have dodged the blow. But the slap connected, and the quick swipe. His ears rang, his cheek stung, and his patience snapped.

Cameron simply locked his arms around her, revolted when she took that as a sexual overture, and carted her to the door. He took the time to scoop up her dress, then tossed both the woman and the silk into the hall.

Her shriek rattled the teeth in his head as he threw the bolt. "I'll kill you. You pig! You bastard! I'll kill you for this. Who do you think you are? You're nothing! Nothing!"

He left Martine screaming and pounding at the door and went into the bedroom to throw a few necessities into a bag.

It looked like luck had just taken the nastiest of turns.

ONE

Cam called in markers, pulled strings, begged favors, and threw money in a dozen directions. Hooking transportation from Monaco to Maryland's Eastern Shore at one o'clock in the morning wasn't an easy matter.

He drove to Nice, bulleting down the winding coastal highway to a small airstrip where a friend had agreed to fly him to Paris—for the nominal fee of a thousand American dollars. In Paris he chartered a plane, for half again the going rate, and spent the hours over the Atlantic in a blur of fatigue and gnawing fear.

He arrived at Washington Dulles Airport in Virginia at just after six A.M. eastern standard time. The rental car was waiting, so he began the drive to the Chesapeake Bay in the dark chill of predawn.

By the time he hit the bridge crossing the bay, the sun was up and bright, sparkling off the water, glinting off boats already out for the day's catch. Cam had spent a good part of his life sailing on the bay, on the rivers and inlets of this part of the world. The man he was racing to see had shown him much more than port and starboard. Whatever he had, whatever he'd done that he could take pride in, he owed to Raymond Quinn.

He'd been thirteen and racing toward hell when Ray and Stella Quinn had plucked him out of the system. His juvenile record was already a textbook study of the roots of the career criminal.

Robbery, breaking and entering, underage drinking, truancy, assault, vandalism, malicious mischief. He'd done as he'd pleased and even then had often enjoyed long runs of luck where he hadn't been caught. But the luckiest moment of his life had been being caught.

Thirteen years old, skinny as a rail, and still wearing the bruises from the last beating his father had administered. They'd been out of beer. What was a father to do?

On that hot summer night with the blood still drying on his face, Cam had promised himself he was never going back to that run-down trailer, to that life, to the man the system kept tossing him back to. He was going somewhere, anywhere. Maybe California, maybe Mexico.

His dreams had been big even if his vision, courtesy of a blackened eye, was blurry. He had fifty-six dollars and some loose change, the clothes on his back, and a piss-poor attitude. What he needed, he decided, was transportation.

He copped a ride in the cargo car of a train heading out of Baltimore. He didn't know where it was going and didn't care as long as it was away. Huddled in the dark, his body weeping at every bump, he promised himself he'd kill or he'd die before he went back.

When he crept off the train, he smelled water and fish, and he wished to God he'd thought to grab some food somewhere. His stomach was screamingly empty. Dizzy and disoriented, he began to walk.

There wasn't much there. A two-bit little town that had rolled up its streets for the night. Boats bumping at sagging docks. If his mind had been clear, he might have considered breaking into one of the shops that lined the waterfront, but it didn't occur to him until he had passed through town and found himself skirting a marsh.

The marsh's shadows and sounds gave him the willies. The sun was beginning to break through the eastern sky, turning those muddy flats and that high, wet grass gold. A huge white bird rose up, making Cam's heart skip. He'd never seen a heron before, and he thought it looked like something out of a book, a made-up one.

But the wings flashed, and the bird soared. For reasons he couldn't name, he followed it along the edge of the marsh until it disappeared into thick trees.

He lost track of how far and what direction, but instinct told him to keep to a narrow country road where he could easily tuck himself into the high grass or behind a tree if a black-and-white cruised by.

He badly wanted to find shelter, somewhere he could curl up and sleep, sleep away the pangs of hunger and the greasy nausea. As the sun rose higher, the air grew thick with heat. His shirt stuck to his back; his feet began to weep.

He saw the car first, a glossy white 'Vette, all power and grace, sitting like a grand prize in the misty light of dawn. There was a pickup beside it, rusted, rugged and ridiculously rural beside the arrogant sophistication of the car.

Cam crouched down behind a lushly blooming hydrangea and studied it. Lusted after it.

The son of a bitch would get him to Mexico, all right, and anywhere else he wanted to go. Shit, the way a machine like that would move, he'd be halfway there before anybody knew it was gone.

He shifted, blinked hard to clear his wavering vision, and stared at the house. It always amazed him that people lived so neatly. In tidy houses with painted shutters, flowers and trimmed bushes in the yard. Rockers on the front porch, screens on the windows. The house seemed huge to him, a modern white palace with soft blue trim.

They'd be rich, he decided, as resentment ground in his stomach along with hunger. They could afford fancy houses and fancy cars and fancy lives. And a part of him, a part nurtured by a man who lived on hate and Budweiser, wanted to destroy, to beat all the bushes flat, to break all the shiny windows and gouge the pretty painted wood to splinters.

He wanted to hurt them somehow for having everything while he had nothing. But as he rose, the bitter fury wavered into sick dizziness. He clamped down on it, clenching his teeth until they, too, ached, but his head cleared.

Let the rich bastards sleep, he thought. He'd just relieve them of the hot car. Wasn't even locked, he noted and snorted at their ignorance as he eased the door open. One of the more useful skills his father had passed on to him was how to hot-wire a car quickly and quietly. Such a skill came in very handy when a man made the best part of his living selling stolen cars to chop shops.

Cam leaned in, shimmied under the wheel, and got to work.

"It takes balls to steal a man's car right out of his own driveway."

Before Cam could react, even so much as swear, a hand hooked into the back of his jeans and hauled him up and out. He swung out, and his bunched fist seemed to bounce off rock.

He got his first look at the Mighty Quinn. The man was huge, at least six-five and built like the offensive line of the Baltimore Colts. His face was weathered and wide, with a thick shock of blond hair that glinted with silver surrounding it. His eyes were piercingly blue and hotly annoyed.

Then they narrowed.

It didn't take much to hold the boy in place. He couldn't have weighed a hundred pounds, Quinn thought, if he'd fished the kid out of the bay. His face was filthy and badly battered. One eye was nearly swollen shut, while the other, dark slate gray, held a bitterness no child should feel. There was blood dried on the mouth that managed to sneer despite it.

Pity and anger stirred in him, but he kept his grip firm. This rabbit, he knew, would run.

"Looks like you came out on the wrong end of the tussle, son."

"Get your fucking hands off me. I wasn't doing nothing."

Ray merely lifted a brow. "You were in my wife's new car at just past seven on a Saturday morning."

"I was just looking for some loose change. What's the big fucking deal?"

"You don't want to get in the habit of overusing the word 'fuck' as an adjective. You'll miss the vast variety of its uses."

The mildly tutorial tone was well over Cam's head. "Look, Jack, I was just hoping for a couple bucks in quarters. You wouldn't miss it."

"No, but Stella would have dearly missed this car if you'd finished hot-wiring it. And my name isn't Jack. It's Ray. Now, the way I figure it you've got a couple of choices. Let's outline number one: I haul your sorry butt into the house and call the cops. How do you feel about doing the next few years in a juvenile facility for badasses?"

Whatever color Cam had left in his face drained away. His empty stomach heaved, his palms suddenly covered in sweat. He couldn't stand a cage. Was sure he would die in a cage. "I said I wasn't stealing the goddamn car. It's a four-speed. How the hell am I supposed to drive a four-speed?"

"Oh, I have a feeling you'd manage just fine." Ray puffed out his cheeks, considered, blew out air. "Now, choice number two—"

"Ray! What are you doing out there with that boy?"

Ray glanced toward the porch, where a woman with wild red hair and a ratty blue robe stood with her hands on her hips.

"Just discussing some life choices. He was stealing your car."

"Well, for heaven's sake!"

"Somebody beat the crap out of him. Recently, I'd say."

"Well." Stella Quinn's sigh could be heard clearly across the dewy green lawn. "Bring him in and I'll take a look at him. Hell of a way to start the morning. Hell of a way. No, you get inside there, idiot dog. Fine one you are, never one bark when my car's being stolen."

"My wife, Stella." Ray's smile spread and glowed. "She just gave you choice number two. Hungry?"

The voice was buzzing in Cam's head. A dog was barking in high, delighted yips from miles and miles away. Birds sang shrilly and much too close by. His skin went brutally hot, then brutally cold. And he went blind.

"Steady there, son. I'll get you."

He fell into the oily black and never heard Ray's quiet oath.

When he woke, he was lying on a firm mattress in a room where the breeze ruffled the sheer curtains and carried in the scent of flowers and water. Humiliation and panic rose up in him. Even as he tried to sit up, hands held him down.

"Just lie still a minute."

He saw the long, thin face of the woman who leaned over him, poking, prodding. There were thousands of gold freckles over it, which for some reason he found fascinating. Her eyes were dark green and frowning. Her mouth was set in a thin, serious line. She'd scraped back her hair, and she smelled faintly of dusting powder.

Cam realized abruptly that he'd been stripped down to his tattered Jockeys. The humiliation and panic exploded.

"Get the hell away from me." His voice came out in a croak of terror, infuriating him.

"Relax now. Relax. I'm a doctor. Look at me." Stella leaned her face closer. "Look at me now. Tell me your name."

His heart thundered in his chest. "John."

"Smith, I imagine," she said dryly. "Well, if you have the presence of mind to lie, you're not doing too badly." She shined a light in his eyes, grunted. "I'd say you've got yourself a mild concussion. How many times have you passed out since you were beat up?"

"That was the first." He felt himself coloring under her unblinking stare and struggled not to squirm. "I think. I'm not sure. I have to go."

"Yes, you do. To the hospital."

"No." Terror gave him the strength to grab her arm before she could rise. If he ended up in the hospital, there would be questions. With questions came cops. With cops came the social workers. And somehow, before it was over, he'd end up back in that trailer that stank of stale beer and piss with a man who found his greatest relief in pounding on a boy half his size.

"I'm not going to any hospital. I'm not. Just give me my clothes. I've got some money. I'll pay you for the trouble. I have to go."

She sighed again. "Tell me your name. Your real one."

"Cam. Cameron."

"Cam, who did this to you?"

"I don't—"

"Don't lie to me," she snapped.

And he couldn't. His fear was too huge, and his head was starting to throb so fiercely he could barely stop the whimper. "My father."

"Why?"

"Because he likes to."

Stella pressed her fingers against her eyes, then lowered her hands and looked out of the window. She could see the water, blue as summer, the trees, thick with leaves, and the sky, cloudless and lovely. And in such a fine world, she thought, there were parents who beat their children because they liked to. Because they could. Because they were there.

"All right, we'll take this one step at a time. You've been dizzy, experienced blurred vision."

Cautious, Cam nodded. "Maybe some. But I haven't eaten in a while."

"Ray's down taking care of that. Better in the kitchen than me. Your ribs are bruised, but they're not broken. The eye's the worst of it," she murmured, touching a gentle finger to the swelling. "We can treat that here. We'll clean you up and doctor you and see how you do. I am a doctor," she told him again, and smiled as her hand, blissfully cool, smoothed his hair back. "A pediatrician."

"That's a kid doctor."

"You still qualify, tough guy. If I don't like how you do, you're going in for X-rays." She reached into her bag for antiseptic. "This is going to sting a little."

He winced, sucked in his breath as she began to treat his face. "Why are you doing this?"

She couldn't stop herself. With her free hand she brushed back a messy shock of his dark hair. "Because I like to."

⟪⟫

They'd kept him. It had been as simple as that, Cam thought now. Or so it had seemed to him at the time. He hadn't realized until years later how much work, effort, and money they'd invested in first fostering, then adopting him. They'd given him their home, their name, and everything worthwhile in his life.

They'd lost Stella nearly eight years ago to a cancer that had snuck into her body and eaten away at it. Some of the light had gone out of that house on the outskirts of the little water town of St. Christopher's, and out of Ray, out of Cam, and out of the two other lost boys they'd made their own.

Cam had gone racing—anything, anywhere. Now he was racing home to the only man he'd ever considered his father.

He'd been to this hospital countless times. When his mother had been on staff, and then when she'd been in treatment for the thing that killed her.

He walked in now, punchy and panicked, and asked for Raymond Quinn at the admissions desk.

"He's in Intensive Care. Family only."

"I'm his son." Cameron turned away and headed for the elevator. He didn't have to be told what floor. He knew too well.

He saw Phillip the moment the doors opened onto ICU. "How bad?"

Phillip handed over one of the two cups of coffee he held. His face was pale with fatigue, his normally well-groomed tawny hair tousled by his hands. His long, somewhat angelic face was roughened by stubble, and his eyes, a pale golden brown, shadowed with exhaustion.

"I wasn't sure you'd make it. It's bad, Cam. Christ, I've got to sit down a minute."

He stepped into a small waiting area, and dropped into a chair. The can of Coke in the pocket of his tailored suit clunked. For a moment he stared blindly at the morning show running brightly on the TV screen.

"What happened?" Cam demanded. "Where is he? What do the doctors say?"

"He was heading home from Baltimore. At least Ethan thinks he'd gone to Baltimore. For something. He hit a telephone pole. Dead on." He pressed the heel of his hand to his heart because it ached every time he pictured it. "They say maybe he had a heart attack or a stroke and lost control, but they're not sure yet. He was driving fast. Too fast."

He had to close his eyes because his stomach kept trying to jump into his throat. "Too fast," he repeated. "It took them nearly an hour to cut him out of the wreck. Nearly an hour. The paramedics said he was conscious on and off. It was just a couple miles from here."

He remembered the Coke in his pocket, opened the can, and drank. He kept trying to block the image out of his head, to concentrate on the now, and the what happened next. "They got ahold of Ethan pretty quick," Phillip continued. "When he got here Dad was in surgery. He's in a coma now." He looked up, met his brother's eyes. "They don't expect him to come out of it."

"That's bullshit. He's strong as an ox."

"They said . . ." Phillip closed his eyes again. His head felt empty, and he had to search for every thought. "Massive trauma. Brain damage. Internal injuries. He's on life support. The surgeon . . . he . . . Dad's a registered organ donor."

"Fuck that." Cam's voice was low and furious.

"Do you think I want to consider it?" Phillip rose now, a tall, rangy man in a wrinkled thousand-dollar suit. "They said it's a matter of hours at most. The machines are keeping him breathing. Goddamn it, Cam, you know how Mom and Dad talked about this when she got sick. No extreme measures. They made living wills, and we're ignoring his because . . . because we can't stand not to."

"You want to pull the plug?" Cam reached out, grabbed Phillip by the lapels. "You want to pull the goddamn plug on him?"

Weary and sick at heart, Phillip shook his head. "I'd rather cut my hand off. I don't want to lose him any more than you do. You'd better see for yourself."

He turned, led the way down the corridor, where the scent was hopeless-ness not quite masked by antiseptics. They moved through double doors, past a nurse's station, past small glass-fronted rooms where machines beeped and hope hung stubbornly on.

Ethan was sitting in a chair by the bed when they walked in. His big, calloused hand was through the guard and covering Ray's. His tall, wiry body was bent over, as if he'd been talking to the unconscious man in the bed beside him. He stood up slowly and, with eyes bruised from lack of sleep, studied Cam.

"So, you decided to put in an appearance. Strike up the band."

"I got here as soon as I could." He didn't want to admit it, didn't want to believe it. The man, the old, terrifyingly frail man, lying in the narrow bed, was his father. Ray Quinn was huge, strong, invincible. But the man with his father's face was shrunken, pale, and still as death.

"Dad." He moved to the side of the bed, leaned down close. "It's Cam. I'm here." He waited, somehow sure it would take only that for his father's eyes to open, to wink slyly.

But there was no movement, and no sound except the monotonous beep of the machines.

"I want to talk to his doctor."

"Garcia." Ethan scrubbed his hands over his face, back into his sun-bleached hair. "The brain cutter Mom used to call Magic Hands. The nurse'll page him."

Cam straightened, and for the first time he noticed the boy curled up asleep in a chair in the corner. "Who's the kid?"

"The latest of Ray Quinn's lost boys." Ethan managed a small smile. Normally it would have softened his serious face, warmed the patient blue eyes. "He told you about him. Seth. Dad took him on about three months ago." He started to say more but caught Phillip's warning look and shrugged. "We'll get into that later."

Phillip stood at the foot of the bed, rocking back and forth on his heels. "So how was Monte Carlo?" At Cam's blank stare, he shrugged his shoul-der. It was a gesture all three of them used in lieu of words. "The nurse said that we should talk to him, to each other. That maybe he can . . . They don't know for sure."

"It was fine." Cam sat and mirrored Ethan by reaching for Ray's hand through the bed guard. Because the hand was limp and lifeless, he held it gently and willed it to squeeze his own. "I won a bundle in the casinos and had a very hot French model in my suite when your fax came through." He shifted, spoke directly to Ray. "You should have seen her. She was incredi-ble. Legs up to her ears, gorgeous man-made breasts."

"Did she have a face?" Ethan asked dryly.

"One that went just fine with the body. I tell you, she was a killer. And when I said I had to leave, she got just a little bitchy." He tapped his face where the scratches scored his cheek. "I had to toss her out of the room into the hall before she tore me to ribbons. But I did remember to toss her dress out after her."

"She was naked?" Phillip wanted to know.

"As a jay."

Phillip grinned, then had his first laugh in nearly twenty hours. "God, leave it to you." He laid his hand over Ray's foot, needing the connection. "He'll love that story."

In the corner, Seth pretended to be asleep. He'd heard Cam come in. He knew who he was. Ray had talked about Cameron a lot. He had two thick scrapbooks filled to busting with clippings and articles and photos of his races and exploits.

He didn't look so tough and important now, Seth decided. The guy looked sick and pale and hollow-eyed. He'd make up his own mind about what he thought of Cameron Quinn.

He liked Ethan well enough. Though the man'd work your butt raw if you went out oystering or clamming with him. He didn't preach all the time, and he'd never once delivered a blow or a backhand even when Seth had made mistakes. And he fit Seth's ten-year-old view of a sailor pretty well.

Rugged, tanned, thick curling hair with streaks of blond in the brown, hard muscles, salty talk. Yeah, Seth liked him well enough.

He didn't mind Phillip. He was usually all pressed and polished. Seth figured the guy must have six million ties, though he couldn't imagine why a man would want even one. But Phillip had some sort of fancy job in a fancy office in Baltimore. Advertising. Coming up with slick ideas to sell things to people who probably didn't need them anyway.

Seth figured it was a pretty cool way to run a con.

Now Cam. He was the one who went for the flash, who lived on the edge and took the risks. No, he didn't look so tough, he didn't look like such a badass.

Then Cam turned his head, and his eyes locked on to Seth's. Held there, unblinking and direct until Seth felt his stomach quiver. To escape, he simply closed his eyes and imagined himself back at the house by the water, throwing sticks for the clumsy puppy Ray called Foolish.

Knowing the boy was awake and aware of his gaze, Cam continued to study him. Good-looking kid, he decided, with a mop of sandy hair and a body that was just starting to go gangly. If he grew into his feet, he'd be a tall one before he was finished sprouting. He had a kiss-my-ass chin, Cam observed, and a sulky mouth. In the pretense of sleep, he managed to look harmless as a puppy and just about as cute.

But the eyes . . . Cam had recognized that edge in them, that animal wariness. He'd seen it often enough in the mirror. He hadn't been able to make out the color, but they'd been dark. Blue or brown, he imagined.

"Shouldn't we park the kid somewhere else?"

Ethan glanced over. "He's fine here. Nobody to leave him with anyhow. On his own he'd just look for trouble."

Cam shrugged, looked away, and forgot him. "I want to talk to Garcia. They've got to have test results, or something. He drives like a pro, so if he had a heart attack or a stroke . . ." His voice trailed off—it was simply too much to contemplate. "We need to know. Standing around here isn't helping."

"You need to do something," Ethan said, his soft voice a sign of suppressed temper, "you go on and do it. Being here counts." He stared at his brother across Ray's unconscious form. "It's always what counted."

"Some of us didn't want to dredge for oysters or spend our lives checking crab pots," Cam shot back. "They gave us a life and expected us to do what we wanted with it."

"So you did what you wanted."

"We all did," Phillip put in. "If something was wrong with Dad the last few months, Ethan, you should have told us."

"How the hell was I supposed to know?" But he had known something, just hadn't been able to put his finger on it. And had let it slide. That ate at him now as he sat listening to the machines that kept his father breathing.

"Because you were there," Cam told him.

"Yeah, I was there. And you weren't—not for years."

"And if I'd stayed on St. Chris he wouldn't have run into a damn telephone pole? Christ." Cam dragged his hands through his hair. "That makes sense."

"If you'd been around. If either of you had, he wouldn't have tried to do so much on his own. Every time I turned around he was up on a damn ladder, or pushing a wheelbarrow, or painting his boat. And he's still teaching three days a week at the college, tutoring, grading papers. He's almost seventy, for Christ's sake."

"He's only sixty-seven." Phillip felt a hard, ice-edged chill claw through him. "And he's always been healthy as a team of horses."

"Not lately he hasn't. He's been losing weight and looking tired and worn-out. You saw it for yourself."

"All right, all right." Phillip scrubbed his hands over his face, felt the scrape of a day's growth of beard. "So maybe he should have been slowing down a little. Taking on the kid was probably too much, but there wasn't any talking him out of it."

"Always squabbling."

The voice, weak and slurred, caused all three men to jolt to attention.

"Dad." Ethan leaned forward first, his heart fluttering in his chest.

"I'll get the doctor."

"No. Stay," Ray mumbled before Phillip could rush out of the room. It was a hideous effort, this coming back, even for a moment. And Ray understood he had moments only. Already his mind and body seemed separate things, though he could feel the pressure of hands on his hands, hear the sound of his sons' voices, and the fear and anger in them.

He was tired, oh, God, so tired. And he wanted Stella. But before he left, he had one last duty.

"Here." The lids seemed to weigh several pounds apiece, but he forced his eyes to open, struggled to focus. His sons, he thought, three wonderful gifts of fate. He'd done his best by them, tried to show them how to become men. Now he needed them for one more. Needed them to stay a unit without him and tend the child.

"The boy." Even the words had weight. It made him wince to push them from mind to lips. "The boy's mine. Yours now. Keep the boy, whatever happens, you see to him. Cam. You'll understand him best." The big hand, once so strong and vital, tried desperately to squeeze. "Your word on it."

"We'll take care of him." At that moment, Cam would have promised to drag down the moon and stars. "We'll take care of him until you're on your feet again."

"Ethan." Ray sucked in another breath that wheezed through the respirator. "He'll need your patience, your heart. You're a fine waterman because of them."

"Don't worry about Seth. We'll look after him."

"Phillip."

"Right here." He moved closer, bending low. "We're all right here."

"Such good brains. You'll figure how to make it all work. Don't let the boy go. You're brothers. Remember you're brothers. So proud of you. All of you. Quinns." He smiled a little, and stopped fighting. "You have to let me go now."

"I'm getting the doctor." Panicked, Phillip rushed out of the room while Cam and Ethan tried to will their father back to consciousness.

No one noticed the boy who stayed curled in the chair, his eyes squeezed tightly shut against hot tears.

TWO

They came alone and in crowds to wake and to bury Ray Quinn. He'd been more than a resident of the dot on the map known as St. Christopher's. He'd been teacher and friend and confidant. In years when the oyster crop was lean, he'd helped organize fund-raisers or had suddenly found dozens of odd jobs that needed to be done to tide the watermen over a hard winter.

If a student was struggling, Ray found a way to carve out an extra hour for a one-on-one. His literature classes at the university had always been filled, and it was rare for one to forget Professor Quinn.

He'd believed in community, and that belief had been both strong and supple in deed. He had realized that most vital of humanities. He had touched lives.

And he had raised three boys that no one had wanted into men.

They had left his gravesite buried in flowers and tears. So when the whispering and wondering began, it was most often hushed quickly. Few wanted to hear any gossip that reflected poorly on Ray Quinn. Or so they said, even as their ears twitched to catch the murmurs.

Sexual scandals, adultery, illegitimate child. Suicide.

Ridiculous. Impossible. Most said so and meant it. But others leaned a bit closer to catch every whisper, knit their brows, and passed the rumor from lip to ear.

Cam heard none of the whispers. His grief was so huge, so monstrous, he could barely hear his own black thoughts. When his mother had died, he'd handled it. He'd been prepared for it, had watched her suffer and had prayed for it to end. But this loss had been too quick, too arbitrary, and there was no cancer to blame for it.

There were too many people in the house, people who wanted to offer sympathy or share memories. He didn't want their memories, couldn't face them until he'd dealt with his own.

He sat alone on the dock that he'd helped Ray repair a dozen times over the years. Beside him was the pretty twenty-four-foot sloop they'd all sailed in countless times. Cam remembered the rig Ray had had that first summer—a little Sunfish, an aluminum catboat that had looked about as big as a cork to Cam.

And how patiently Ray had taught him how to sail, how to handle the rigging, how to tack. The thrill, Cam thought now, of the first time Ray had let him handle the tiller.

It had been a life-altering experience for a boy who'd grown up on hard streets—salty air in his face, wind snapping the white canvas, the speed and freedom of gliding over water. But most of all, it had been the trust. Here, Ray had said, see what you can do with her.

Maybe it had been that one moment, on that hazy afternoon when the leaves were so full and green and the sun already a white-hot ball behind the mist, that had turned the boy toward the man he was now.

And Ray had done it with a grin.

He heard the footsteps on the dock but didn't turn. He continued to look out over the water as Phillip stood beside him.

"Most everybody's gone."

"Good."

Phillip slipped his hands into his pockets. "They came for Dad. He'd have appreciated it."

"Yeah." Tired, Cam pressed his fingers to his eyes, let them drop. "He would have. I ran out of things to say and ways to say them."

"Yeah." Though he made his living with clever words, Phillip understood exactly. He took a moment to enjoy the silence. The breeze off the water had a bit of a bite, and that was a relief after the crowded house, overheated with bodies. "Grace is cleaning up in the kitchen. Seth's giving her a hand. I think he's got a case on her."

"She looks good." Cam struggled to shift his mind to someone else. Anything else. "Hard to imagine her with a kid of her own. She's divorced, right?"

"A year or two ago. He took off right before little Aubrey was born." Phillip blew out a breath between his teeth. "We've got some things to deal with, Cam."

Cam recognized the tone, and the tone meant it was time for business. Resentment bubbled up instantly. "I was thinking of taking a sail. There's a good wind today."

"You can sail later."

Cam turned his head, face bland. "I can sail now."

"There's a rumor going around that Dad committed suicide."

Cam's face went blank, then filled with red-hot rage. "What the fuck is this?" he demanded as he shot to his feet.

There, Phillip thought with dark satisfaction, that got your attention. "There's some speculation that he aimed for the pole."

"That's just pure bullshit. Who the hell's saying that?"

"It's going around—and some of it's rooting. It has to do with Seth."

"What has to do with Seth?" Cam began to pace, long, furious strides up and down the narrow dock. "What, do they think he was crazy for taking the kid on? Hell, he was crazy for taking any of us on, but what does that have to do with an accident?"

"There's some talk brewing that Seth is his son. By blood."

That stopped Cam dead in his tracks. "Mom couldn't have kids."

"I know that."

Fury pounded in his chest, a hammer on steel. "You're saying that he cheated on her? That he went off with some other woman and got a kid? Jesus Christ, Phil."

"I'm not saying it."

Cam stepped closer until they were face-to-face. "What the hell are you saying?"

"I'm telling you what I heard," Phillip said evenly, "so we can deal with it."

"If you had any balls you'd have decked whoever said it in their lying mouth."

"Like you want to deck me now. Is that your way of handling it? Just beat on it until it goes away?" With his own temper bubbling, Phillip shoved Cam back an inch. "He was my father too, goddamn it. You were the first, but you weren't the only."

"Then why the hell weren't you standing up for him instead of listening to that garbage? Afraid to get your hands dirty? Ruin your manicure? If you weren't such a damn pussy, you'd have—"

Phillip's fist shot out, caught Cam neatly on the jaw. There was enough force behind the punch to snap Cam's head back, send him staggering for a foot or two. But he regained his balance quickly enough. With eyes dark and eager, he nodded. "Well, then, come on."

Hot blood roaring in his head, Phillip started to strip off his jacket. Attack came swiftly, quietly, and from behind. He barely had time to curse before he was sailing off the dock and into the water.

Phillip surfaced, spat, and shoved the wet hair out of his eyes. "Son of a bitch. You son of a bitch."

Ethan had his thumbs tucked in his front pockets now and studied his brother as Phillip treaded water. "Cool off," he suggested mildly.

"This suit is Hugo Boss," Phillip managed as he kicked toward the dock.

"That don't mean shit to me." Ethan glanced over at Cam. "Mean anything to you?"

"Means he's going to have a hell of a dry-cleaning bill."

"You, too," Ethan said and shoved Cam off the dock. "This isn't the time or place to go punching each other. So when the pair of you haul your butts out and dry off, we'll talk this through. I sent Seth on with Grace for a while."

Eyes narrowed, Cam skimmed his hair back with his fingers. "So you're in charge all of a sudden."

"Looks to me like I'm the only one who kept his head above water." With this, Ethan turned and sauntered back toward the house.

Together Cam and Phillip gripped the edge of the dock. They exchanged one long, hard look before Cam sighed. "We'll throw him in later," he said.

Accepting the apology, Phillip nodded. He pulled himself up on the dock and sat, dragging off his ruined silk tie. "I loved him too. As much as you did. As much as anyone could."

"Yeah." Cam yanked off his shoes. "I can't stand it." It was a hard admission from a man who'd chosen to live on the edge. "I didn't want to be there today. I didn't want to stand there and watch them put him in the ground."

"You were there. That's all that would have mattered to him."

Cam peeled off his socks, his tie, his jacket, felt the chill of early spring. "Who told you about—who said those things about Dad?"

"Grace. She's been hearing talk and thought it best that we knew what was being said. She told Ethan and me this morning. And she cried." Phillip lifted a brow. "Still think I should have decked her?"

Cam heaved his ruined shoes onto the lawn. "I want to know who started this, and why."

"Have you looked at Seth, Cam?"

The wind was getting into his bones. That was why he suddenly wanted to shudder. "Sure I looked at him." Cam turned, headed for the house.

"Take a closer look," Phillip murmured.

⁂

When Cam walked into the kitchen twenty minutes later, warm and dry in a sweater and jeans, Ethan had coffee hot and whiskey ready.

It was a big, family-style kitchen with a long wooden table in the center. The white countertops showed a bit of age, the wear and tear of use. There'd been talk a few years back of replacing the aging stove. Then Stella had gotten sick, and that had been the end of that.

There was a big, shallow bowl on the table that Ethan had made in his junior year in high school wood shop. It had sat there since the day he'd brought it home, and was often filled with letters and notes and household flotsam rather than the fruit it had been designed for. Three wide, curtainless windows ranged along the back wall, opening the room up to the yard and the water beyond it.

The cabinet doors were glass-fronted, and the dishes inside plain white stoneware, meticulously arranged. As would be, Cam thought, the contents of all the drawers. Stella had insisted on that. When she wanted a spoon, by God, she didn't want to search for one.

But the refrigerator was covered with photos and newspaper clippings, notes, postcards, children's drawings, all haphazardly affixed with multicolored magnets.

It gave his heart a hitch to step into that room and know his parents wouldn't ever again be there.

"Coffee's strong," Ethan commented. "So's the whiskey. Take your choice."

"I'll have both." Cam poured a mug, added a shot of Johnnie Walker to the coffee, then sat. "You want to take a swing at me, too?"

"I did. May again." Ethan decided he wanted his whiskey alone and neat. And poured a double. "Don't much feel like it now." He stood by the window, looking out, the untouched whiskey in his hand. "Maybe I still think you should have been here more the last few years. Maybe you couldn't be. It doesn't seem to matter now."

"I'm not a waterman, Ethan. I do what I'm good at. That's what they expected."

"Yeah." He couldn't imagine the need to run from the place that was home, and sanctuary. And love. But there was no point in questioning it, or in holding on to resentments. Or, he admitted, casting blame. "The place needs some work."

"I noticed."

"I should have made more time to come around and see to things. You always figure there's going to be plenty of time to go around, then there's not. The back steps are rotting out, need replacing. I kept meaning to." He turned as Phillip came into the room. "Grace has to work tonight, so she can't keep Seth occupied for more than a couple hours. You lay it out, Phil. It'll take me too long."

"All right." Phillip poured coffee, left the whiskey alone. Rather than sit, he leaned back against the counter. "It seems a woman came to see Dad a few months back. She went to the college, caused a little trouble that nobody paid much attention to at the time."

"What kind of trouble?"

"Caused a scene in his office, a lot of shouting and crying on her part. Then she went to see the dean and tried to file sexual molestation charges against Dad."

"That's a crock."

"The dean apparently thought so, too." Phillip poured a second cup of coffee and this time brought it to the table. "She claimed Dad had harassed and molested her while she was a student. But there was no record of her ever being a student at the college. Then she said she'd just been auditing his class because she couldn't afford full tuition. But nobody could verify that either. Dad's rep stood up to it, and it seemed to go away."

"He was pretty shaken," Ethan put in. "He wouldn't talk to me about it. Wouldn't talk to anybody. Then he went away for about a week. Told me he was going down to Florida to do some fishing. He came back with Seth."

"You're trying to tell me people think the kid's his? For Christ's sake, that he had something going on with this bimbo who waits, what, ten, twelve years to complain about it?"

"Nobody thought too much of it then," Phillip put in. "He had a history of bringing strays home. But then there was the money."

"What money?"

"He wrote checks, one for ten thousand dollars, another for five, and another for ten over the last three months. All to Gloria DeLauter. Somebody at the bank noticed and mumbled to somebody else, because Gloria De-Lauter was the name of the woman who'd tried to hang him up on the sexual misconduct charges."

"Why the hell didn't somebody tell me what was going on around here?"

"I didn't find out about the money until a few weeks ago." Ethan stared down into his whiskey, then decided it would do him more good inside than out. He downed it, hissed once. "When I asked him about it, he just told me the boy was what was important. Not to worry. As soon as everything was settled he'd explain. He asked me for some time, and he looked so . . . defenseless. You don't know what it was like, seeing him scared and old and fragile. You didn't see him, you weren't here to see him. So I waited." Whiskey and guilt paired with resentment and grief to burn a hole inside him. "And I was wrong."

Shaken, Cam pushed back from the table. "You think he was paying blackmail. That he diddled some student a dozen years ago and knocked her up? And now he was paying so she'd keep quiet. So she'd hand over the kid for him to raise?"

"I'm telling you what was, and what I know." Ethan's voice was even, his eyes steady. "Not what I think."

"I don't know what I think," Phillip said quietly. "But I know Seth's got his eyes. You only have to look at him, Cam."

"No way he fucked with a student. And no way he cheated on Mom."

"I don't want to believe it." Phillip set down his mug. "But he was human. He could have made a mistake." One of them had to be realistic, and he decided he was elected. "If he did, I'm not going to condemn him for it. What we have to do is figure out how to do what he asked. We have to find a way to keep Seth. I can find out if he started adoption proceedings. They couldn't be final yet. We're going to need a lawyer."

"I want to find out more about this Gloria DeLauter." Deliberately, Cam unclenched his fists before he could use them on something, or someone. "I want to know who the hell she is. Where the hell she is."

"Up to you." Phillip shrugged his shoulders. "Personally, I don't want to get near her."

"What's this suicide crap?"

Phillip and Ethan exchanged a look, then Ethan rose and walked to a kitchen drawer. He pulled it open, took out a large sealed bag. It hurt him to hold it, and he saw by the way Cam's eyes darkened that Cam recognized the worn green enameled shamrock key ring as their father's.

"This is what was inside the car after the accident." He opened it, took out an envelope. The white paper was stained with dried blood. "I guess somebody—one of the cops, the tow truck operator, maybe one of the paramedics—looked inside and read the letter, and they didn't trouble to keep it to themselves. It's from her." Ethan tapped out the letter, held it out to Cam. "DeLauter. The postmark's Baltimore."

"He was coming back from Baltimore." With dread, Cam unfolded the letter. The handwriting was a large, loopy scrawl.

Quinn, I'm tired of playing nickel and dime. You want the kid so bad, then it's time to pay for him. Meet me where you picked him up. We'll make it Monday morning. The block's pretty quiet then. Eleven o'clock. Bring a hundred and fifty thousand, in cash. Cash money, Quinn, and no discounts. You don't come through with every penny, I'm taking the kid back. Remember, I can pull the plug on the adoption any time I want. A hundred and fifty grand's a pretty good bargain for a good-looking boy like Seth. Bring the money and I'm gone. You've got my word on it. Gloria

"She was selling him," Cam murmured. "Like he was a—" He stopped himself, looked up sharply at Ethan as he remembered. Ethan had once been sold as well, by his own mother, to men who preferred young boys. "I'm sorry, Ethan."

"I live with it," he said simply. "Mom and Dad made sure I could. She's not going to get Seth back. Whatever it takes, she won't get her hands on him."

"We don't know if he paid her?"

"He emptied his bank account here," Phillip put in. "From what I can tell—and I haven't gone over his papers in detail yet—he closed out his regular savings, cashed in his CDs. He only had a day to get the cash. That would have come to about a hundred thousand. I don't know if he had fifty more—if he had time to liquidate it if he did."

"She wouldn't have gone away. He'd have known that." Cam put the letter down, wiped his hands on his jeans as if to clean them. "So people are whispering that he killed himself in what—shame, panic, despair? He wouldn't have left the kid alone."

"He didn't." Ethan moved to the coffeepot. "He left him with us."

"How the hell are we supposed to keep him?" Cam sat again. "Who's going to let us adopt anybody?"

"We'll find a way." Ethan poured coffee, added enough sugar to make Phillip wince in reaction. "He's ours now."

"What the hell are we going to do with him?"

"Put him in school, put a roof over his head, food in his belly, and try to give him something of what we were given." He brought the pot over, topped off Cam's coffee. "You got an argument?"

"Couple dozen, but none of them get past the fact that we gave our word."

"We agree on that, anyway." Frowning, Phillip drummed his fingers on the table. "But we've left out one pretty vital point. None of us knows what Seth's going to have to say about it. He might not want to stay here. He might not want to stay with us."

"You're just looking to complicate things, as usual," Cam complained. "Why wouldn't he?"

"Because he doesn't know you, he barely knows me." Phillip lifted his cup and gestured. "The only one he's spent any time with is Ethan."

"Didn't spend all that much with me," Ethan admitted. "I took him out on the boat a few times. He's got a quick mind, good hands. Doesn't have much to say for himself, but when he does, he's got a mouth on him. He's spent some time with Grace. She doesn't seem to mind him."

"Dad wanted him to stay," Cam stated with a shrug. "He stays." He glanced over at the sound of a horn tooting three quick beeps.

"That'll be Grace dropping him back off on her way to Shiney's Pub."

"Shiney's?" Cam's brows shot up. "What's she doing down at Shiney's?"

"Making a living, I expect," Ethan returned.

"Oh, yeah." A slow grin spread. "Does he still have his waitresses dress in those little skirts with the bows on the butt and the black fishnet stockings?"

"He does," Phillip said with a long, wistful sigh. "He does indeed."

"Grace would fill out one of those outfits pretty well, I'd imagine."

"She does." Phillip smiled. "She does indeed."

"Maybe I'll just mosey down to Shiney's later."

"Grace isn't one of your French models." Ethan pushed back from the table, took his mug and his annoyance to the sink. "Back off."

"Whoa." Behind Ethan's back, Cam wiggled his brows at Phillip. "Backing off, bro. Didn't know you had your eye aimed in that particular direction."

"I don't. She's a mother, for Christ's sake."

"I had a really fine time with the mother of two in Cancun last winter," Cam remembered. "Her ex was swimming in oil—olive oil—and all she got in the divorce settlement was a Mexican villa, a couple of cars, some trinkets, art, and two million. I spent a memorable week consoling her. And the kids were cute—from a distance. With their nanny."

"You're such a humanitarian, Cam," Phillip told him.

"Don't I know it."

They heard the front door slam and looked at each other. "Well, who talks to him?" Phillip wanted to know.

"I'm no good at that kind of stuff." Ethan was already edging toward the back door. "And I've got to go feed my dog."

"Coward," Cam muttered as the door shut at Ethan's back.

"You bet. Me, too." Phillip was up and moving. "You get first crack. I've got those papers to go through."

"Wait just a damn minute—"

But Phillip was gone, and cheerfully telling Seth that Cameron wanted to talk to him. When Seth came to the kitchen door, the puppy scrambling at his heels, he saw Cam scowling as he poured more whiskey in his coffee.

Seth stuck his hands in his pockets and lifted his chin. He didn't want to be there, didn't want to talk to anybody. At Grace's he'd been able to just sit on her little stoop, be alone with his thoughts. Even when she'd come out for a little while and sat beside him with Aubrey on her knee, she'd let him be.

Because she understood he'd wanted to be quiet.

Now he had to deal with the man. He wasn't afraid of big hands and hard eyes. Wouldn't—couldn't—let himself be afraid. He wouldn't care that

they were going to kick him loose, toss him back like one of the runt fish
Ethan pulled out of the bay.

He could take care of himself. He wasn't worried.

His heart scrambled in his chest like a mouse in a cage.

"What?" The single word was ripe with defiance and challenge. Seth
stood, his legs locked, and waited for a reaction.

Cam only continued to frown and sip his doctored coffee. With one
hand, he absently stroked the puppy, who was trying valiantly to climb into
his lap. He saw a scrawny boy wearing jeans still stiff and obviously new, a
screw-you sneer, and Ray Quinn's eyes. "Sit down."

"I can stand."

"I didn't ask you what you could do, I told you to sit down."

On cue, Foolish obediently plopped his fat butt on the floor and grinned.
But boy and man stared at each other. The boy gave way first. It was the
quick jerk of the shoulders that had Cam setting his mug down with a click.
It was a Quinn gesture, through and through. Cam took a moment to settle,
tried to gather his thoughts. But they remained scattered and elusive. What
the hell was he supposed to say to the boy?

"You get anything to eat?"

Seth watched him warily from under girlishly thick lashes. "Yeah, there
was stuff."

"Ah, Ray, did he talk to you about . . . things. Plans for you?"

The shoulders jerked again. "I don't know."

"He was working on adopting you, making it legal. You knew about
that."

"He's dead."

"Yeah." Cam picked up his coffee again, let the pain roll through. "He's
dead."

"I'm going to Florida," Seth burst out as the idea slammed into his
mind.

Cam sipped coffee, angled his head as if mildly interested. "Oh, yeah?"

"I got some money. I figured I'd leave in the morning, catch a bus south.
You can't stop me."

"Sure I can." More comfortable now, Cam leaned back in his chair.
"I'm bigger than you. What do you plan to do in Florida?"

"I can get work. I can do lots of things."

"Pick some pockets, sleep on the beach."

"Maybe."

Cam nodded. That had been his plan when his destination had been
Mexico. For the first time he thought he might be able to connect with the
boy after all. "I guess you can't drive yet."

"I could if I had to."

"Harder to boost a car these days unless you've got some experience. And you need to be mobile to keep ahead of the cops. Florida's a bad idea."

"That's where I'm going." Seth set his jaw.

"No, it isn't."

"You're not sending me back." Seth lurched up from the chair, his thin frame vibrating with fear and rage. The sudden move and shout sent the puppy racing fearfully from the room. "You got no hold over me, you can't make me go back."

"Back where?"

"To her. I'll go right now. I'll get my stuff and I'm gone. And if you think you can stop me, you're full of shit."

Cam recognized the stance—braced for a blow but ready to fight back. "She knock you around?"

"That's none of your fucking business."

"Ray made it my fucking business. You head for the door," he added as Seth shifted to the balls of his feet, "I'll just haul you back." Cam only sighed when Seth made his dash.

Even as he caught him three feet before the front door, he had to give Seth credit for speed. And when he caught the boy around the waist, took the backhanded fist on his already tender jaw, he gave him credit for strength.

"Get your goddamn hands off me, you son of a bitch. I'll kill you if you touch me."

Grimly, Cam dragged Seth into the living room, pushed him into a chair, and held him there with their faces close. If it had just been anger he saw in the boy's eyes, or defiance, he wouldn't have cared. But what he saw was raw terror.

"You got balls, kid. Now try to develop some brains to go with them. If I want sex, I want a woman. Understand me?"

He couldn't speak. All he'd known when that hard, muscled arm had wrapped around him was that this time he wouldn't be able to escape. This time he wouldn't be able to fight free and run.

"There's nobody here who's going to touch you like that. Ever." Without realizing it, Cam had gentled his voice. His eyes remained dark, but the hardness was gone. "If I lay hands on you, the worst it means is I might try to knock some sense into you. You got that?"

"I don't want you to touch me," Seth managed. His breath was gone. Panic sweat slicked his skin like oil. "I don't like being touched."

"Okay, fine. You sit where I put you." Cam eased back, then pulled over a footstool and sat. Since Foolish was now shivering in terror, Cam plucked him up and dumped him in Seth's lap. "We got a problem," Cam began, and prayed for inspiration on how to handle it. "I can't watch you twenty-four hours a day. And if I could, I'm damned if I would. You take off for Florida, I'm going to have to go find you and haul you back. That's really going to piss me off."

Because the dog was there, Seth stroked him, gaining comfort while giving it. "What do you care where I go?"

"I can't say I do. But Ray did. So you're going to have to stay."

"Stay?" It was an option Seth had never considered. Certainly hadn't allowed himself to believe. "Here? When you sell the house—"

"Who's selling the house?"

"I—" Seth broke off, decided he was saying too much. "People figured you would."

"People figured wrong. Nobody's selling this house." It surprised Cam just how firm his feelings were on that particular point. "I don't know how we're going to manage it yet. I'm still working on that. But in the meantime, you'd better get this into your head. You're staying put." Which meant, Cam realized with a jolt, so was he.

It appeared his luck was still running bad.

"We're stuck with each other, kid, for the next little while."

THREE

Cam figured this had to be the weirdest week of his life. He should have been in Italy, prepping for the motocross he'd planned to treat himself to. Most of his clothes and his boat were in Monte Carlo, his car was in Nice, his motorcycle in Rome.

And he was in St. Chris, babysitting a ten-year-old with a bad attitude. He hoped to Christ the kid was in school where he belonged. They'd had a battle royal over that little item that morning. But then, they were at war over most everything.

Kitchen duty, curfews, laundry, television picks. Cam shook his head as he pried off the rotting treads on the back steps. He'd swear the boy would square up for a bout if you said good morning.

And maybe he wasn't doing a fabulous job as guardian, but damn it, he was doing his best. He had the tension headache to prove it. And mostly, he was on his own. Phillip had promised weekends, and that was something. But it also left five hideous days between. Ethan made a point of coming by and staying a few hours every evening after he pulled in the day's catch.

But that left the days.

Cam would have traded his immortal soul for a week in Martinique. Hot sand and hotter women. Cold beer and no hassles. Instead he was doing laundry, learning the mysteries of microwave cooking, and trying to keep tabs on a boy who seemed hell-bent on making life miserable.

"You were the same way."

"Hell I was. I wouldn't have lived to see twelve if I'd been that big an idiot."

"Most of that first year Stella and I used to lie in bed at night and wonder if you'd still be here in the morning."

"At least there were two of you. And . . ."

Cam's hand went limp on the hammer. His fingers simply gave way until it thudded on the ground beside him. There in the old, creaking rocker on the back porch sat Ray Quinn. His face was wide and smiling, his hair a tousled white mane that grew long and full. He wore his favored gray fishing pants, a faded gray T-shirt with a red crab across the chest. His feet were bare.

"Dad?" Cam's head spun once, sickly, then his heart burst with joy. He leaped to his feet.

"You didn't think I'd leave you fumbling through this alone, did you?"

"But—" Cam shut his eyes. He was hallucinating, he realized. It was stress and fatigue, grief tossed in.

"I always tried to teach you that life's full of surprises and miracles. I wanted you to open your mind not just to possibilities, Cam, but to impossibilities."

"Ghosts? God!"

"Why not?" The idea seemed to cheer Ray immensely as he let loose with one of his deep, rumbling laughs. "Read your literature, son. It's full of them."

"Can't be," Cam mumbled to himself.

"I'm sitting right here, so it looks like it can. I left too many things unfinished around here. It's up to you and your brothers now, but who says I can't give you a little help now and again?"

"Help. Yeah, I'm going to need some serious help. Starting with a psychiatrist." Before his legs gave out on him, Cam picked his way through the broken stairs and sat down on the edge of the porch.

"You're not crazy, Cam, just confused."

Cam took a steadying breath and turned his head to study the man who lazily rocked in the old wooden chair. The Mighty Quinn, he thought while the air whooshed out of his lungs. He looked solid and real. He looked, Cam decided, there.

"If you're really here, tell me about the boy. Is he yours?"

"He's yours now. Yours and Ethan's and Phillip's."

"That's not enough."

"Of course it is. I'm counting on each of you. Ethan takes things as they come and makes the best of them. Phillip wraps his mind around details and ties them up. You push at everything until it works your way. The boy needs all three of you. Seth's what's important. You're all what's important."

"I don't know what to do with him," Cam said impatiently. "I don't know what to do with myself."

"Figure out one, you'll figure out the other."

"Damn it, tell me what happened. Tell me what's going on."

"That's not why I'm here. I can't tell you if I've seen Elvis either." Ray grinned when Cam let out a short, helpless laugh. "I believe in you, Cam. Don't give up on Seth. Don't give up on yourself."

"I don't know how to do this."

"Fix the steps," Ray said with a wink. "It's a start."

"The hell with the steps," Cam began, but he was alone again with the sound of singing birds and gently lapping water. "Losing my mind," he murmured, rubbing an unsteady hand over his face. "Losing my goddamn mind."

And rising, he went back to fix the steps.

Anna Spinelli had the radio blasting. Aretha Franklin was wailing out of her million-dollar pipes, demanding respect. Anna was wailing along with her, deliriously thrilled with her spanking-new car.

She'd worked her butt off, budgeted and juggled funds to afford the down payment and the monthly installments. And as far as she was concerned it would be worth every carton of yogurt she ate rather than a real meal.

Despite the chilly spring air, she'd have preferred to have the top down as she sped along the country roads. But it wouldn't have looked professional to arrive windblown. Above all else, it was essential to appear and behave in a professional manner.

She'd chosen a plain and proper navy suit and white blouse for this home visit. What she wore under it was nobody's business but her own. Her affection for silk strained her ever beleaguered budget, but life was for living, after all.

She'd fought her long, curling black hair into a tidy bun at the nape of her neck. She thought it made her look a bit more mature and dignified. Too often when she wore her hair down she was dismissed as a hot number rather than a serious-minded social worker.

Her skin was pale gold, thanks to her Italian heritage. Her eyes, big and dark and almond-shaped. Her mouth was full, with a ripe bottom lip. The bones in her face were strong and prominent, her nose long and straight. She wore little makeup during business hours, wary of drawing the wrong kind of attention.

She was twenty-eight years old, devoted to her work, satisfied with the single life, and pleased that she'd been able to settle in the pretty town of Princess Anne.

She'd had enough of the city.

As she drove between long, flat fields of row crops with the scent of water a hint on the breeze through her window, she dreamed of one day moving to such a place. Country lanes and tractors. A view of the bay and boats.

She'd need to save up, to plan, but one day she hoped to manage to buy a little house outside of town. The commute wouldn't be so hard, not when driving was one of her greatest personal pleasures.

The CD player shifted, the Queen of Soul to Beethoven. Anna began to hum the "Ode to Joy."

She was glad the Quinn case had been assigned to her. It was so interesting. She only wished she'd had the chance to meet Raymond and Stella Quinn. It would take very special people to adopt three half-grown and troubled boys and make it work.

But they were gone, and now Seth DeLauter was her concern. Obviously the adoption proceedings couldn't go forward. Three single men—one living in Baltimore, one in St. Chris, and the other wherever he chose to at the moment. Well, Anna mused, it didn't appear to be the best environment for the child. In any case, it was doubtful they would want guardianship.

So Seth DeLauter would be absorbed back into the system. Anna intended to do her best by him.

When she spotted the house through the greening leaves, she stopped the car. Deliberately she turned the radio down to a dignified volume, then checked her face and hair in the rearview mirror. Shifting back into first, she drove the last few yards at a leisurely pace and turned slowly into the drive.

Her first thought was that it was a pretty house in a lovely setting. So quiet and peaceful, she mused. It could have used a fresh coat of paint, and the yard needed tending, but the slight air of disrepair only added to the hominess.

A boy would be happy here, she thought. Anyone would. It was a shame he'd have to be taken away from it. She sighed a little, knowing too well that fate had its whims. Taking her briefcase, she got out of the car.

She hitched her jacket to make certain it fell in line. She wore it a bit loose, so it wouldn't showcase distracting curves. She started toward the front door, noting that the perennial beds flanking the steps were beginning to pop.

She really needed to learn more about flowers; she made a mental note to check out a few gardening books from the library.

She heard the hammering and hesitated, then in her practical low heels cut across the lawn toward the back of the house.

He was kneeling on the ground when she caught sight of him. A black T-shirt tucked into snug and faded denim. From a purely female outlook, it was impossible not to react and approve of him. Muscles—the long and lean sort—rippled as he pounded a nail into wood with enough anger, Anna mused, enough force, to send vibrations of both into the air to simmer.

Phillip Quinn? she wondered. The advertising executive. Highly doubtful. Cameron Quinn, the globe-trotting risk-taker? Hardly.

So this must be Ethan, the waterman. She fixed a polite smile on her face and started forward. "Mr. Quinn."

His head came up. With the hammer still gripped in his hand, he turned until she saw his face. Oh, yes, the anger was there, she realized, full-blown and lethal. And the face itself was more compelling and certainly tougher than she'd been prepared for.

Some Native American blood, perhaps, she decided, would account for those sharp bones and bronzed skin. His hair was a true black, untidy and long enough to fall over his collar. His eyes were anything but friendly, the color of bitter storms.

On a personal level, she found the package outrageously sexy. On a professional one, she knew the look of an alley brawler when she saw one, and decided on the spot that whichever Quinn this was, he was a man to be careful with.

He took his time studying her. His first thought was that legs like that deserved a better showcase than a drab navy skirt and ugly black shoes. His second was that when a woman had eyes that big, that brown, that beautiful, she probably got whatever she wanted without saying a word.

He set the hammer down and rose. "I'm Quinn."

"I'm Anna Spinelli." She kept the smile in place as she walked forward, hand extended. "Which Quinn are you?"

"Cameron." He'd expected a soft hand because of the eyes, because of the husky purr of her voice, but it was firm. "What can I do for you?"

"I'm Seth DeLauter's caseworker."

His interest evaporated, and his spine stiffened. "Seth's in school."

"I'd hope so. I'd like to speak with you about the situation, Mr. Quinn."

"My brother Phillip's handling the legal details."

She arched a brow, determined to keep the small polite smile in place. "Is he here?"

"No."

"Well, then, if I could have a few moments of your time. I assume you're living here, at least temporarily."

"So what?"

She didn't bother to sigh. Too many people saw a social worker as the enemy. She'd done so once herself. "My concern is Seth, Mr. Quinn. Now we can discuss this, or I can simply move forward with the procedure for his removal from this home and into approved foster care."

"It'd be a mistake to try that, Miz Spinelli. Seth isn't going anywhere."

Her back went up at the way he drawled out her name. "Seth DeLauter

is a minor. The private adoption your father was implementing wasn't finalized, and there is some question about its validity. At this point, Mr. Quinn,
you have no legal connection to him."

"You don't want me to tell you what you can do with your legal connection, do you, Miz Spinelli?" With some satisfaction he watched those big,
dark eyes flash. "I didn't think so. I can resist. Seth's my brother." The saying of it left him shaken. With a jerk of his shoulder, he turned. "I need a
beer."

She stood for a moment after the screen door slammed. When it came to
her work, she simply didn't permit herself to lose her temper. She breathed
in, breathed out three times before climbing the half-repaired steps and going into the house.

"Mr. Quinn—"

"Still here?" He twisted the top off a Harp. "Want a beer?"

"No. Mr. Quinn—"

"I don't like social workers."

"You're joking." She allowed herself to flutter her lashes at him. "I never
would have guessed."

His lips twitched before he lifted the bottle to them. "Nothing personal."

"Of course not. I don't like rude, arrogant men. That's nothing personal
either. Now, are you ready to discuss Seth's welfare, or should I simply come
back with the proper paperwork and the cops?"

She would, Cam decided after another study. She might have been given
a face suitable for painting, but she wasn't a pushover. "You try that, and the
kid's going to bolt. You'd pick him up sooner or later, and he'd end up in
juvie—then he'd end up in a cell. Your system isn't going to help him, Miz
Spinelli."

"But you can?"

"Maybe." He frowned into his beer. "My father would have." When he
looked up again, there were emotions storming in his eyes that pulled at her.
"Do you believe in the sanctity of a deathbed promise?"

"Yes," she said before she could stop herself.

"The day my father died I promised him—we promised him—that we'd
keep Seth with us. Nothing and no one is going to make me break my word.
Not you, not your system, not a dozen cops."

The situation here wasn't what she'd expected to find. So she would
reevaluate. "I'd like to sit down," Anna said after a moment.

"Go ahead."

She pulled out a chair at the table. There were dishes in the sink, she
noted, and the faint smell of whatever had been burnt for dinner the night

before. But to her that only meant someone was trying to feed a young boy. "Do you intend to apply for legal guardianship?"

"We—"

"You, Mr. Quinn," she interrupted. "I'm asking you if that is your intention." She waited, watching the doubts and resistance sweep over his face.

"Then I guess it is. Yeah." God help them all, he thought. "If that's what it takes."

"Do you intend to live in this house, with Seth, on a permanent basis?"

"Permanent?" It was perhaps the only truly frightening word in his life. "Now I have to sit down." He did so, then pinched the bridge of his nose between his thumb and forefinger to relieve some of the pressure. "Christ. How about we use 'for the foreseeable future' instead of 'permanent'?"

She folded her hands on the edge of the table. She didn't doubt his sincerity, would have applauded him for his intentions. But . . . "You have no idea what you're thinking of taking on."

"You're wrong. I do, and it scares the hell out of me."

She nodded, considering the answer a point in his favor. "What makes you think you would be a better guardian for a ten-year-old boy, a boy I believe you've known for less than two weeks, than a screened and approved foster home?"

"Because I understand him. I've been him—or part of him. And because this is where he belongs."

"Let me lay out some of the bigger obstacles to what you're planning. You're a single man with no permanent address and without a steady income."

"I've got a house right here. I've got money."

"Whose name is the house in, Mr. Quinn?" She only nodded when his brows knit. "I imagine you have no idea."

"Phillip will."

"Good for Phillip. And I'm sure you have some money, Mr. Quinn, but I'm speaking of steady employment. Going around the world racing various forms of transportation isn't stable employment."

"It pays just fine."

"Have you considered the risk to life and limb of your chosen lifestyle when you propose to take on a responsibility like this? Believe me, the court will. What if something happens to you when you're trying to break land and speed records?"

"I know what I'm doing. Besides, there are three of us."

"Only one of you lives in this house where Seth will live."

"So?"

"And the one who does isn't a respected college professor with the experience of raising three sons."

"That doesn't mean I can't handle it."

"No, Mr. Quinn," she said patiently, "but it is a major obstacle to legal guardianship."

"What if we all did?"

"Excuse me?"

"What if we all lived here? What if my brothers moved in?" What a damn mess, Cam thought, but he kept going. "What if I got a . . ." Now he had to take a deep swallow of beer, knowing the word would stick in his throat. "A job," he managed.

She stared at him. "You'd be willing to change your life so dramatically?"

"Ray and Stella Quinn changed my life."

Her face softened, making Cam blink in surprise as her generous mouth curved in a smile, as her eyes seemed to go darker and deeper. When her hand reached out, closed lightly over his, he stared down at it, surprised by a quick jolt of what was surely pure lust.

"When I was driving here, I was wishing I could have met them. I thought they must have been remarkable people. Now I'm sure of it." Then she drew back. "I'll need to speak with Seth, and with your brothers. What time does Seth get home from school?"

"What time?" Cam glanced at the kitchen clock without a clue. "It's sort of . . . flexible."

"You'll want to do better than that if this gets as far as a formal home study. I'll go by the school and see him. Your brother Ethan." She rose. "Would I find him at home?"

"Not at this time of day. He'll be bringing in his catch before five."

She glanced at her watch, gauged her time. "All right, and I'll contact your other brother in Baltimore." From her briefcase she took a neat leather notebook. "Now, can you give me names and addresses of some neighbors. People who know you and Seth and who would stand for your character. The good side of your character, that is."

"I could probably come up with a few."

"That's a start. I'll do some research here, Mr. Quinn. If it's in Seth's best interest to remain in your home, under your care, I'll do everything I can to help you." She angled her head. "If I reach the opinion that it's in his best interest to be taken out of your home, and out of your care, then I'll fight you tooth and nail to make that happen."

Cam rose as well. "Then I guess we understand each other."

"Not by a long shot. But you've got to start somewhere."

The minute she was out of the house, Cam was on the phone. By the time he'd been passed through a secretary and an assistant and reached Phillip, his temper had spilled over.

"There was a goddamn social worker here."

"I told you to expect that."

"No, you didn't."

"Yes, I did. You don't listen. I've got a friend of mine—a lawyer—working on the guardianship. Seth's mother took a hike; as far as we can tell, she's not in Baltimore."

"I don't give a damn where the mother is. The social worker was making noises about taking Seth."

"The lawyer's putting through a temporary guardianship. It takes time, Cam."

"We may not have time." He shut his eyes, tried to think past the anger. "Or maybe I bought us some. Who owns the house now?"

"We do. Dad left it—well, everything—to the three of us."

"Fine, good. Because you're about to change locations. You're going to need to pack up those designer suits of yours, pal, and get your butt down here. We're going to be living together again."

"Like hell."

"And I've got to get a goddamn job. I'm going to expect you by seven tonight. Bring dinner. I'm sick to death of cooking."

It gave him some satisfaction to hang up on Phillip's vigorous cursing.

Anna found Seth sullen and smart-mouthed and snotty. And liked him immediately. The principal had given her permission to take him out of class and use a corner of the empty cafeteria as a makeshift office.

"It would be easier if you'd tell me what you think and feel, and what you want."

"Why should you give a damn?"

"They pay me to."

Seth shrugged and continued to draw patterns on the table with his finger. "I think you should mind your own business, I feel bored, and I want you to go away."

"Well, that's enough about me," Anna said and had the pleasure of seeing Seth struggle to suppress a smile. "Let's talk about you. Are you happy living with Mr. Quinn?"

"It's a cool house."

"Yes, I liked it. What about Mr. Quinn?"

"He thinks he knows everything. Thinks he's a BFD because he's been all over the world. He sure as hell can't cook, let me tell you."

She left her pen on the table and folded her hands over her notebook. He was much too thin, she thought. "Do you go hungry?"

"He ends up going to get pizza or burgers. Pitiful. I mean what's it take to work a microwave?"

"Maybe you should do the cooking."

"Like he'd ask me. The other night he blows up the potatoes. Forgets to poke holes in them, you know, and bam!" Seth forgot to sneer, laughing out loud instead. "What a mess! He swore a streak then, man, oh, man."

"So the kitchen isn't his area of expertise." But, Anna decided, he was trying.

"You're telling me. He's better off when he's going around hammering things or fiddling with that cool-ass car. Did you see that 'Vette? Cam said it was his mom's and she had it for like ever. Drives like a rocket, too. Ray kept it in the garage. Guess he didn't want to get it out."

"Do you miss him? Ray?"

The shoulder shrugged again, and Seth's gaze dropped. "He was cool. But he was old and when you get old you die. That's the way it is."

"What about Ethan and Phillip?"

"They're okay. I like going out on the boats. If I didn't have school, I could work for Ethan. He said I pulled my weight."

"Do you want to stay with them, Seth?"

"I got no place to go, do I?"

"There's always a choice, and I'm here to help you find the one that works best for you. If you know where your mother is—"

"I don't know." His voice rose, his head snapped up. His eyes darkened to nearly navy against a pale face. "And I don't want to know. You try to send me back there, you'll never find me."

"Did she hurt you?" Anna waited a beat, then nodded when he only stared at her. "All right, we'll leave that alone for now. There are couples and families who are willing and able to take children into their home, to care for them, to give them a good life."

"They don't want me, do they?" The tears wanted to come. He'd be damned if he'd let them. Instead his eyes went hot and burning dry. "He said I could stay, but it was a lie. Just another fucking lie."

"No." She grabbed Seth's hand before he could leap up. "No, they do want you. As a matter of fact, Mr. Quinn—Cameron—was very angry with me for suggesting you should go into another home. I'm only trying to find out what you want. And I think you just told me. If living with the Quinns is what you want, and what's best for you, I want to help you to get that."

"Ray said I could stay. He said I'd never have to go back. He promised."

"If I can, I'll try to help him keep that promise."

Four

Since there seemed to be nothing cold to drink in the house but beer, carbonated soft drinks, and some suspicious-looking milk, Ethan put the kettle on to boil. He'd brew up some tea, ice it, and enjoy a tall glass out on the porch while evening moseyed in.

He was in hour fourteen of his day and ready to relax.

Which wasn't going to be easy, he decided while he hunted up tea bags and overheard Cam and Seth holding some new pissing match in the living room. He figured they must enjoy sniping at each other or they wouldn't spend so much time at it.

For himself, he wanted a quiet hour, a decent meal, then one of the two cigars he allowed himself per day. The way things sounded, he didn't think the quiet hour was going to make the agenda.

As he dumped tea bags in the boiling water, he heard feet stomping up the stairs, followed by the bullet-sharp sound of a slamming door.

"The kid's driving me bat-shit," Cam complained as he stalked into the kitchen. "You can't say boo to him without him squaring up for a fight."

"Mm-hmm."

"Argumentative, smart-mouthed, troublemaker." Feeling grossly put upon, Cam snagged a beer from the fridge.

"Must be like looking in a mirror."

"Like hell."

"Don't know what I was thinking of. You're such a peaceable soul." Moving at his own relaxed pace, Ethan bent down to search out an old glass pitcher. "Let's see, you were just about fourteen when I came along. First thing you did was pick a fight so you'd have the excuse to bloody my nose."

For the first time in hours, Cam felt a grin spread. "That was just a welcome-to-the-family tap. Besides, you gave me a hell of a black eye as a thank-you."

"There was that. Kid's too smart to try to punch you," Ethan continued and began to dump generous scoops of sugar into the pitcher. "So he razzes you instead. He sure as hell's got your attention, doesn't he?"

It was irritating because it was true. "You got him pegged so neatly, why don't you take him on?"

"Because I'm on the water every morning at dawn. Kid like that needs supervision." That, Ethan thought, was his story and he'd stick to it through all the tortures of hell. "Of the three of us, you're the only one not working."

"I'm going to have to fix that," Cam muttered.

"Oh, yeah?" With a mild snort, Ethan finished making the tea. "That'll be the day."

"The day's coming up fast. Social worker was here today."

Ethan grunted, let the implications turn over in his mind. "What'd she want?"

"To check us out. She's going to be talking to you, too. And Phillip. Already talked to Seth—which is what I was trying to diplomatically ask him about when he started foaming at the mouth again."

Cam frowned now, thinking more of Anna Spinelli of the great legs and tidy briefcase than of Seth. "If we don't pass, she's going to work on pulling him."

"He isn't going anywhere."

"That's what I said." He dragged his hand through his hair again, which for some reason reminded him he'd meant to get a haircut. In Rome. Seth wasn't the only one not going anywhere. "But, bro, we're about to make some serious adjustments around here."

"Things are fine as they are." Ethan filled a glass with ice and poured tea over it so that it crackled.

"Easy for you to say." Cam stepped out on the porch, let the screen door slap shut behind him. He walked to the rail, watched Ethan's sleek Chesapeake Bay retriever, Simon, play tag and tumble with the fat puppy. Upstairs, Seth had obviously decided to seek revenge by turning his radio up to earsplitting. Screaming headbanger rock blasted through the windows.

Cam's jaw twitched. He'd be damned if he'd tell the kid to turn it down. Too clichéd, too terrifyingly adult a response. He sipped his beer, struggled to loosen the knots in his shoulders, and concentrated on the way the lowering sun tossed white diamonds onto the water.

The wind was coming up so that the marsh grass waved like a field of

Kansas wheat. The drake of a pair of ducks that had set up house where the water bent at the edge of the trees flew by quacking.

Lucy, I'm home, was all Cam could think, and it nearly made him smile again.

Under the roar of music he heard the gentle rhythmic creak of the rocker. Beer fountained from the lip of the bottle when he whirled. Ethan stopped rocking and stared at him.

"What?" he demanded. "Christ, Cam, you look like you've seen a ghost."

"Nothing." Cam swiped a hand over his face, then carefully lowered himself to the porch so he could lean back against the post. "Nothing," he repeated, but set the beer aside. "I'm a little edgy."

"Usually are if you stay in one place more than a week."

"Don't climb up my back, Ethan."

"Just a comment." And because Cam looked exhausted and pale, Ethan reached in the breast pocket of his shirt, took out two cigars. It wouldn't hurt to change his smoke-after-dinner routine. "Cigar?"

Cam sighed. "Yeah, why not?" Rather than move, he let Ethan light the first and pass it to him. Leaning back again, he blew a few lazy smoke rings. When the music shut off abruptly, he felt he'd achieved a small personal victory.

For the next ten minutes, there wasn't a sound but the lap of water, the call of birds, and the talk of the breeze. The sun dropped lower, turning the western sky into a soft, rosy haze that bled into the water and blurred the horizon. Shadows deepened.

It was like Ethan, Cam mused, to ask no questions. To sit in silence and wait. To understand the need for quiet. He'd nearly forgotten that admirable trait of his brother's. And maybe, Cam admitted, he'd nearly forgotten how much he loved the brother Ray and Stella had given him.

But even remembering, he wasn't sure what to do about it.

"See you fixed the steps," Ethan commented when he judged Cam was relaxing again.

"Yeah. The place could use a coat of paint, too."

"We'll have to get to that."

They were going to have to get to a lot of things, Cam thought. But the quiet creak of the rocker kept taking his mind back to that afternoon. "Have you ever had a dream while you were wide awake?" He could ask because it was Ethan, and Ethan would think and consider.

After setting the nearly empty glass on the porch beside the rocker, Ethan studied his cigar. "Well . . . I guess I have. The mind likes to wander when you let it."

It could have been that, Cam told himself. His mind had wandered—maybe even gotten lost for a bit. That could have been why he'd thought he saw his father rocking on the porch. The conversation? Wishful thinking, he decided. That was all.

"Remember how Dad used to bring his fiddle out here? Hot summer nights he'd sit where you're sitting and play for hours. He had such big hands."

"He could sure make that fiddle sing."

"You picked it up pretty well."

Ethan shrugged, puffed lazily on his cigar. "Some."

"You ought to take it. He'd have wanted you to have it."

Ethan shifted his quiet eyes, locked them on Cam's. Neither spoke for a moment, nor had to. "I guess I will, but not right yet. I'm not ready."

"Yeah." Cam blew out smoke again.

"You still got the guitar they gave you that Christmas?"

"I left it here. Didn't want it banging around with me." Cam looked at his fingers, flexed them as though he were about to lay them on the strings. "Guess I haven't played in more than a year."

"Maybe we should try Seth on some instrument. Mom used to swear playing a tune pumped out the aggression." He turned his head as the dogs began to bark and race around the side of the house. "Expecting somebody?"

"Phillip."

Ethan's brows lifted. "Thought he wasn't coming down till Friday."

"Let's just call this a family emergency." Cam tapped out the stub of the cigar before he rose. "I hope to Christ he brought some decent food and none of that fancy pea pod crap he likes to eat."

Phillip strode into the kitchen balancing a large bag on top of a jumbo bucket of chicken and shooting out waves of irritation. He dumped the food on the table, skimmed a hand through his hair, and scowled at his brothers.

"I'm here," he snapped as they came through the back door. "What's the damn problem?"

"We're hungry," Cam said easily, and peeling the top from the bucket, he grabbed a drumstick. "You got dirt on your 'I'm an executive' pants there, Phil."

"Goddamn it." Furious now, Phillip brushed impatiently at the pawprints on his slacks. "When are you going to teach that idiot dog not to jump on people?"

"You cart around fried chicken, dog's going to see if he can get a piece. Makes him smart if you ask me." Unoffended, Ethan went to a cupboard for plates.

"You get fries?" Cam poked in the bag, snagged one. "Cold. Somebody better nuke these. If I do it they'll blow up or disintegrate."

"I'll do it. Get something to dish up that cole slaw."

Phillip took a breath, then one more. The drive down from Baltimore was long, and the traffic had been ugly. "When you two girls have finished playing house, maybe you'll tell me why I broke a date with a very hot-looking CPA—the third date by the way, which was dinner at her place with the definite possibility of sex afterward—and instead just spent a couple hours in miserable traffic to deliver a fucking bucket of chicken to a couple of boobs."

"First off, I'm tired of cooking." Cam heaped cole slaw on his plate and took a biscuit. "And even more tired of tossing out what I've cooked because even the pup—who drinks out of the toilet with regularity—won't touch it. But that's only the surface."

He took another hefty bite of chicken as he walked to the doorway and shouted for Seth. "The kid needs to be here. We're all in this."

"Fine. Great." Phillip dropped into a chair, tugged at his tie.

"No use sulking because your accountant isn't going to be running your figures tonight, pal." Ethan offered him a friendly smile and a plate.

"Tax season's heating up." With a sigh, Phillip scooped out slaw. "I'll be lucky to get a warm look from her until after April fifteenth. And I was so close."

"None of us is likely to be getting much action for the next little while." Cam jerked a head as Seth's feet pounded down the stairs. "The patter of little feet plays hell with the sex life."

Cam tucked away the urge for another beer and settled on iced tea as Seth stepped into the kitchen. The boy scanned the room, his nose twitching at the scent of spicy chicken, but he didn't dive into the bucket as he would have liked to.

"What's the deal?" he demanded and tucked his hands in his pockets while his stomach yearned.

"Family meeting," Cam announced. "With food. Sit." He took a chair himself as Ethan put the freshly buzzed fries on the table. "Sit," Cam repeated when Seth stayed where he was. "If you're not hungry you can just listen."

"I could eat." Seth sauntered over to the table, slid into a chair. "It's got to be better than the crud you've been trying to pass off as food."

"You know," Ethan said in his mild drawl before Cam could snarl, "seems to me I'd be grateful if somebody tried to put together a hot meal for me from time to time. Even if it was crud." With his eyes on Seth, Ethan tipped down the bucket, contemplated his choices. "Especially if that some-body was doing the best he could."

Because it was Ethan, Seth flushed, squirmed, then shrugged as he plucked out a fat breast. "Nobody asked him to cook."

"All the more reason. Might work better if you took turns."

"He doesn't think I can do anything." Seth sneered over at Cam. "So I don't."

"You know, it's tempting to toss this little fish back into the pond." Cam dumped salt on his fries and struggled to hold on to a simmering temper. "I could be in Aruba this time tomorrow."

"So go." Seth's eyes flashed up, full of anger and defiance. "Go wherever the hell you want as long as it's out of my face. I don't need you."

"Smart-mouthed little brat. I've had it." Cam had a long reach and used it now to shoot a hand across the table and pluck Seth out of his chair. Even as Phillip opened his mouth to protest, Ethan shook his head.

"You think I've enjoyed spending the last two weeks babysitting some snot-nosed monster with a piss-poor attitude? I've put my life on hold to deal with you."

"Big deal." Seth had turned sheet-white and was ready for the blow he was sure would come. But he wouldn't back down. "All you do is run around collecting trophies and screwing women. Go back where you came from and keep doing it. I don't give a shit."

Cam watched the edges of his own vision turn red. Fury and frustration hissed in his blood like a snake primed to strike.

He saw his father's hands at the end of his arms. Not Ray's, but the man who had used those hands on him with such casual violence through-out his childhood. Before he did something unforgivable, he dropped Seth back into his chair. His voice was quiet now, and the room vibrated with his control.

"If you think I'm staying for you, you're wrong. I'm staying for Ray. Have you got any idea where the system will toss you if one of us decides you're not worth the trouble?"

Foster homes, Seth thought. Strangers. Or worse, *her*. Because his legs were trembling badly, he locked his feet around the legs of his chair. "You don't care what they do with me."

"That's just one more thing you're wrong about," Cam said evenly. "You don't want to be grateful, fine. I don't want your goddamn gratitude. But you'll start showing some respect, and you'll start showing it now. It's not just me who's going to be hounding your sorry ass, pal. It's the three of us."

Cam sat down again, waited for his composure to solidify. "The social worker who was here today—Spinelli, Anna Spinelli—has some concerns about the environment."

"What's wrong with the environment?" Ethan wanted to know. The nasty little altercation had cleared the air, he decided. Now they could get to the details. "It's a good, solid house, a nice area. School's good, crime's low."

"I got the impression *I'm* the environment. At the moment, I'm the only one here, supervising things."

"The three of us will go down as guardians," Phillip pointed out. He poured a glass of iced tea and set it casually next to the hand Seth had fisted on the table. He imagined the boy's throat would be burning dry right about now. "I checked with the lawyer after you called. The preliminary paperwork should go through by the end of the week. There'll be a probationary period—regular home studies and meetings, evaluations. But unless there's a serious objection, it doesn't look like a problem."

"Spinelli's a problem." Cam refused to let the altercation spoil his appetite and reached for more chicken. "Classic do-gooder. Great legs, serious mind. I know she talked to the kid, but he's not inclined to share their conversation, so I'll share mine. She had doubts about my qualifications as guardian. Single man, no steady means of employment, no permanent residence."

"There are three of us." Phillip frowned and poked at his slaw. A trickle of guilt was working through, and he didn't care for it.

"Which I pointed out. Miz Spinelli of the gorgeous Italian eyes countered with the sad fact that I happen to be the only one of the three of us actually living here with the kid. And it was tactfully implied that of the three of us I'm the least likely candidate for guardian. So I tossed out the idea of all of us living here."

"What do you mean 'living here'?" Phillip dropped his fork. "I work in Baltimore. I've got a condo. How the hell am I supposed to live here and work there?"

"That'll be a problem," Cam agreed. "Bigger one will be how you'll fit all your clothes into that closet in your old room."

While Phillip tried to choke out a response, Ethan tapped a finger on the edge of the table. He thought of his small, and to him perfect, house. The quiet and solitude of it. And he saw the way Seth stared down at his plate with dark, baffled eyes. "How long you figure it would take?"

"I don't know." Cam dragged both hands back through his hair. "Six months, maybe a year."

"A year." All Phillip could do was close his eyes. "Jesus."

"You talk to the lawyer about it," Cam suggested. "See what's what. But we present a united front to Social Services or they're going to pull him. And I've got to find work."

"Work." Phillip's misery dissolved in a grin. "You? Doing what? There aren't any racetracks in St. Chris. And the Chesapeake, God bless her, sure ain't the Med."

"I'll find something. Steady doesn't mean fancy. I'm not looking at something I'll need an Armani suit for."

He was wrong, Cam realized. This damn business *was* going to spoil his appetite. "The way I figure it, Spinelli's going to be back tomorrow, the next day at the latest. We have to hammer this out, and it has to look like we know what the hell we're doing."

"I'll take my vacation time early." Phillip bid farewell to the two weeks he'd planned to spend in the Caribbean. "That buys us a couple of weeks. I can work with the lawyer, deal with the social worker."

"I'll deal with her." Cam smiled a little. "I liked the looks of her, and I ought to get some perks out of this. Of course, all this depends on what the kid said to her today."

"I told her I wanted to stay," Seth mumbled. Tears were raw in his stomach. The food sat untouched on his plate. "Ray said I could. He said I could stay here. He said he'd fix it so I could."

"And we're what's left of him." Cam waited until Seth lifted his gaze. "So we'll fix it."

⌇

Later, when the moon was up and the dark water was slashed by its luminous white beam, Phillip stood on the dock. The air was cold now, the damp wind carrying the raw edge of the winter that fought not to yield to spring.

It suited his mood.

There was a war raging inside him between conscience and ambition. In two short weeks, the life he had planned out, plotted meticulously, and implemented with deliberation and simple hard work had shattered.

Now, still numb with grief for his father, he was being asked to transplant himself, to compromise those careful plans.

He'd been thirteen when Ray and Stella Quinn took him in. Most of those years he'd spent on the street, dodging the system. He was an accomplished thief, an enthusiastic brawler who used drugs and liquor to dull the ugliness. The projects of Baltimore were his turf, and when a drive-by shooting left him bleeding on those streets, he was prepared to die. To simply end it.

Indeed, the life he'd led up to the point when he wound up in a gutter choked with garbage ended that night. He lived, and for reasons he never understood, the Quinns wanted him. They opened a thousand fascinating doors for him. And no matter how often, how defiantly he tried to slam them shut again, they didn't allow it.

They gave him choices, and hope, and a family. They offered him a chance for an education that had saved his soul. He used what they'd given him to make himself into the man he was. He studied and worked, and he buried that miserable boy deep.

His position at Innovations, the top advertising firm in the metropolitan area, was solid. No one doubted that Phillip Quinn was on the fast track to the top. And no one who knew the man who wore the elegant tailored suits, who could order a meal in perfect French and always knew the proper wine, would have believed he had once bartered his body for the price of a dime bag.

He had pride in that, perhaps too much pride, but he considered it his testament to the Quinns.

There was enough of that selfish, self-serving boy still inside him to rebel at the thought of giving up one inch of it. But there was too much of the man Ray and Stella had molded to consider doing otherwise.

Somehow he had to find the compromise.

He turned, looked back at the house. The upstairs was dark. Seth was in bed by now, Phillip mused. He didn't have a clue how he felt about the boy. He recognized him, understood him, and he supposed resented just a bit those parts of himself he saw in young Seth DeLauter.

Was he Ray Quinn's son?

There, Phillip thought as his teeth clenched—more resentment at even the possibility of it. Had the man he'd all but worshiped for more than half his life really fallen off his pedestal, succumbed to temptation, betrayed wife and family?

And if he had, how could he have turned his back on his own blood? How could this man who had made strangers his own ignore for more than a decade a son who'd come from his own body?

We've got enough problems, Phillip reminded himself. The first was to keep a promise. To keep the boy.

He walked back, using the back porch light to guide him. Cam sat on the steps, Ethan in the rocker.

"I'll go back into Baltimore in the morning," Phillip announced. "I'll see what the lawyer can firm up. You said the social worker was named Spinelli?"

"Yeah." Cam nursed a cup of black coffee. "Anna Spinelli."

"She'd be county, probably out of Princess Anne. I'll pass that on." Details, he thought. He'd concentrate on the facts. "The way I see it, we're going to have to come off as three model citizens. I already pass." Phillip smiled thinly. "The two of you are going to have to work on your act."

"I told Spinelli I'd get a job." Even the thought of it disgusted Cam.

"I'd hold off on that awhile." This came from Ethan, who rocked quietly in the shadows. "I got an idea. I want to think on it awhile more. Seems to me," he went on, "that with Phil and me around, both of us working, you could be running the house."

"Oh, Jesus" was all Cam could manage.

"It goes like this." Ethan paused, rocked, continued. "You'd be what they'd call primary caregiver. You're available if the school calls with a problem, if Seth gets sick or whatever."

"Makes sense," Phillip agreed and, feeling better, he grinned at Cam. "You're Mommy."

"Fuck you."

"That's no way for Mommy to talk."

"If you think I'm going to be stuck washing your dirty socks and swabbing the toilet, you wasted that fine education you're so proud of."

"Just temporarily," Ethan said, though he enjoyed the image of his brother wearing an apron and hunting up cobwebs with a feather duster. "We'll work out shifts. Seth ought to have some regular chores too. We always did. But it's going to fall to you for the next few days anyway, while Phillip figures out how we handle the legal end and I see how I can juggle my time."

"I've got business of my own to deal with." The coffee was beginning to burn a hole in his gut, but Cam drank it down anyway. "My stuff's scattered all over Europe."

"Well, Seth's in school all day, isn't he?" Absently Ethan reached down to stroke the dog snoring beside his chair.

"Fine. Great." Cam gave up. "You," he said, pointing at Phillip, "bring some groceries back with you. We're out of damn near everything. And Ethan can throw whatever you bring together into a meal. Everybody makes their own bed, goddamn it. I'm not a maid."

"What about breakfast?" Phillip said dryly. "You're not going to send your men off in the morning without a hot meal, are you?"

Cam eyed him balefully. "You're enjoying this, aren't you?"

"Might as well." He sat on the steps beside Cam, leaned back on his elbows. "Somebody ought to talk to Seth about cleaning up his language."

"Oh, yeah." Cam merely snorted. "That'll work."

"He swears that way in front of the neighbors, the social worker, his teachers, it's going to give a bad impression. How's his schoolwork anyway?"

"How the hell should I know?"

"Now, Mother—" Phillip grunted, then laughed when Cam's elbow jabbed his ribs.

"Keep it up and you're going to end up with another ruined suit, ace."

"Let me change and we can go a couple rounds. Or better yet . . ." Phillip arched a brow, slid his gaze over toward Ethan, then back to Cam.

Approving the plan, Cam scratched his chin, set down his empty cup. They shot off the steps in tandem, so fast that Ethan barely had a chance to blink.

His fist shot out, was blocked, and he was hauled out of the chair by armpits and ankles, cursing all the way. Simon leaped up to bark delightedly and raced circles around the men who hauled his struggling master off the porch.

Inside the kitchen, the pup wiggled madly and yipped in answer. To keep him close, Seth pulled off a chunk of the chicken he'd come down to forage and dropped it on the floor. While Foolish gobbled, Seth watched in puzzled amazement as the silhouettes headed for the dock.

He'd come down to fill his empty belly. He was used to moving quietly. He'd stuffed his mouth with chicken and listened to the men talk.

They acted like they were going to let him stay. Even when they didn't know he was there to hear, they talked as if it was a simple fact. At least for now, he decided, until they forgot they'd made a promise, or no longer cared.

He knew promises didn't mean squat.

Except Ray's. He'd believed Ray. But then he'd gone and died and ruined everything. Still, every night he spent in this house, between clean sheets with the puppy curled beside him, was an escape. Whenever they decided to ditch him, he'd be ready to run.

Because he'd die before he went back to where he'd been before Ray Quinn.

The pup was nosing at the door, drawn by the sound of laughter and barking and the shouts. Seth fed him more chicken to distract him.

He wanted to go out too, to run across the lawn and join in that laughter, that fun . . . that family. But he knew he wouldn't be welcome. They'd stop and they'd stare at him as if they wondered where the hell he'd come from and what the hell they were supposed to do about it.

Then they'd tell him to get back to bed.

Oh, God, he wanted to stay. He just wanted to be here. Seth pressed his face against the screen, yearning with all his heart to belong.

When he heard Ethan's long, laughing oath, the loud splash that followed it, and the roars of male satisfaction that came next, he grinned.

And he stayed there, grinning even as a tear escaped and trickled unnoticed down his cheek.

FIVE

Anna got in to work early. Odds were her supervisor would already be at her desk. You could always count on Marilou Johnston to be at her desk or within hailing distance.

Marilou was a woman Anna both admired and respected. When she needed advice, there was no one whose opinion she valued more.

When she poked her head around the open office door, Anna smiled a little. As expected, Marilou was there, buried behind the files and paperwork on her cluttered desk. She was a small woman, barely topping five feet. She wore her hair close-cropped for convenience as much as style. Her face was smooth, like polished ebony, and the expression on it could remain composed even during the worst crises.

A calm center was how Anna often thought of Marilou. Though how she could be calm when her life was filled with a demanding career, two teenage boys, and a house that Anna had seen for herself was constantly crowded with people was beyond her.

Anna often thought she wanted to be Marilou Johnston when she grew up.

"Got a minute?"

"Sure do." Marilou's voice was quick and lively, ripe with that Southern Shore accent that caught words between a drawl and a twang. She waved Anna to a chair with one hand and fiddled with the round gold ball in her left ear. "The Quinn-DeLauter case?"

"Right the first time. There were a couple of faxes waiting for me yesterday from the Quinns' lawyer. A Baltimore firm."

"What did our Baltimore lawyer have to say?"

"The gist of it is they're pursuing guardianship. He'll be pushing through a petition to the court. They're very serious about keeping Seth De-Lauter in their home and under their care."

"And?"

"It's an unusual situation, Marilou. Up 'til now I've only spoken with one of the brothers. The one who lived in Europe until recently."

"Cameron? Impressions?"

"He certainly makes one." And because Marilou was also a friend, Anna allowed herself a grin and a roll of her eyes. "A treat to look at. I came across him when he was repairing the back porch steps. I can't say he looked like a happy man, but he was certainly a determined one. There's a lot of anger there, and a lot of grief. What impressed me the most—"

"Other than his looks?"

"Other than his looks," Anna agreed with a chuckle, "was the fact that he never questioned keeping Seth. It was simply fact. He called Seth his brother. He meant it. I'm not sure he knows exactly how he feels about it, but he meant it."

She went on, while Marilou listened without comment, detailing the conversation, Cam's willingness to change his life, and his lifestyle, his concerns that Seth would bolt if he were taken out of the home.

"And," she continued, "after speaking with Seth, I tend to agree with him."

"You think the boy's a runner?"

"When I suggested foster care, he became angry, resentful. And afraid. If he feels threatened, he'll run." She thought of all the children who ended up on the mean streets of inner cities, homeless, desperate. She thought of what they did to survive. And she thought of how many didn't survive at all.

It was her job to keep this one child, this one boy, safe.

"He wants to stay there, Marilou. Maybe he needs to. His feelings about his mother are very strong, and very negative. I suspect abuse, but he's not ready to discuss it. At least not with me."

"Is there any word on the mother's whereabouts?"

"No. We have no idea where she is, or what she'll do. She signed papers allowing Ray Quinn to begin adoption proceedings, but he died before they were finalized. If she comes back and wants her son . . ." Anna shook her head. "The Quinns would have a fight on their hands."

"You sound as though you'd be in their corner."

"I'm in Seth's," Anna said firmly. "And I'm going to stay there. I spoke with his teachers." She pulled out a file as she spoke. "I have my report on that. I'm going back today to speak with some of the neighbors, and hopefully to meet with all three of the Quinns. It may be possible to stop the temporary guardianship until I complete the initial study, but I'm inclined against it. That boy needs stability. He needs to feel wanted. And even if the Quinns only want him because of a promise, it's more than he's had before, I believe."

Marilou took the file, set it aside. "I assigned this case to you because you don't look just at the surface. And I sent you in cold because I wanted your take. Now I'll tell you what I know about the Quinns."

"You know them?"

"Anna, I was born and raised on the Shore." She smiled, beautifully. It was a simple fact, but one she had great pride in. "Ray Quinn was one of my professors at college. I admired him tremendously. When I had my two boys, Stella Quinn was their pediatrician until we moved to Princess Anne. We adored her."

"When I was driving out there yesterday I kept wishing I'd had the chance to meet them."

"They were exceptional people," Marilou said simply. "Ordinary, even simple in some ways. And exceptional. Here's a case in point," she added, leaning back in her chair. "I graduated from college sixteen years ago. The three Quinns were teenagers. You heard stories now and again. Maybe they were a little wild, and people wondered why Ray and Stella had taken on half-grown men with bad tendencies. I was pregnant with Johnny, my first, working my butt off to get my degree, and help my husband, Ben, pay the rent. He was working two jobs. We wanted a better life for ourselves, and we sure as hell wanted one for the baby I was carrying."

She paused, turned the double picture frame on her desk to a closer angle so that she could see her two young men smile out at her. "I wondered too. Figured they were crazy, or just playing at being Samaritans. Professor Quinn called me into his office one day. I'd missed a couple of classes. Had the worst case of morning sickness known to woman."

It still made her grimace. "I swear I don't understand how some women reminisce over that kind of thing. In any case, I thought he was going to recommend me dropping his class, which meant losing the credits toward my degree. With me an inch away—an inch away and I would be the first in my family with a college degree. I was ready to fight. Instead, he wanted to know what he could do to help. I was speechless."

She smiled, remembering, then beamed over at Anna. "You know how impersonal college can be—the huge lectures where a student is just one more face in the crowd. But he'd noticed me. And he'd taken the time to find out something about my situation. I burst into tears. Hormones," she said with a wry grin. "Well, he patted my hand, gave me some tissues, and let me cry it out. I was on a scholarship, and if my grades dropped or I blew a class,

I could lose it. I only had one more semester. He said for me not to worry, we'd work it all out, and I was going to get my degree. He started talking, about this and that, to calm me down. He was telling me some story about teaching his son to drive. Made me laugh. It wasn't until later, I realized he hadn't been talking about one of the boys he'd taken in. Because that's not what they were to him. They were his."

A sucker for a happy ending, Anna sighed. "And you got your degree."

"He made sure I did. I owe him for that. Which is why I didn't tell you about this until you'd formed some impressions of your own. As for the three Quinns, I don't really know them. I've seen them at two funerals. Saw Seth DeLauter with them at Professor Quinn's. For personal reasons I'd like to see them have a chance to be a family. But . . ." She laid her hands palm to palm. "The best interest of the boy comes before that—and the structure of the system. You're thorough, Anna, and you believe in structure and in the system. Professor Quinn would have wanted what's best for Seth, and to re- pay an old debt, I gave him you."

Anna blew out a long breath. "No pressure, huh?"

"Pressure's all we've got around here." As if on cue, her phone began to ring. "And the clock's running."

Anna rose. "I'd better get to work, then. Looks like I'll be in the field most of today."

I t was nearly one P.M. when Anna pulled up in the Quinns' drive. She'd managed to conduct interviews with three of the five names Cam had given her the day before, and she hoped to expand on that before too much more time passed.

Her call to Phillip Quinn's office in Baltimore had given her the infor- mation that he was on leave for the next two weeks. She was hoping she would find him here and be able to file an impression of another Quinn.

But it was the pup who greeted her. He barked ferociously even as he backed rapidly away from her. Anna watched with amusement as he peed on himself in terror. With a laugh, she crouched down, held out a hand.

"Come on, cutie, I won't hurt you. Aren't you sweet, aren't you pretty?" She kept murmuring to him until he bellied over to sniff her hand, then rolled over in ecstasy as she scratched him.

"For all you know, he's got fleas and rabies."

Anna glanced up and saw Cam in the front doorway. "For all I know, so do you."

With a snort of a laugh and his hands tucked in his pockets, he came out on the porch. It was a brown suit today, he noted. For the life of him he couldn't figure why she'd pick such a dull color. "I guess you're willing to risk it, since you're back. Didn't expect you so soon."

"A boy's welfare is at stake, Mr. Quinn. I don't believe in taking my time under the circumstances."

Obviously charmed by her voice, the puppy leaped up and bathed her face. The giggle escaped before she could stop it—a sound that made Cam raise his eyebrows—and defending herself from the puppy's eager tongue, she rose. Tugged down her jacket. And her dignity.

"May I come in?"

"Why not?" This time he waited for her, even opened the door and let her go in ahead of him.

She saw a large and fairly tidy living area. The furniture showed some wear but appeared comfortable and colorful. The spinet in the corner caught her eye. "Do you play?"

"Not really." Without realizing it, Cam ran a hand over the wood. He didn't notice that his fingers left streaks in the dust. "My mother did, and Phillip's got an ear for it."

"I tried to reach your brother Phillip at his office this morning."

"He's out buying groceries." Because he was pleased to have won that battle, Cam smiled a little. "He's going to be living here . . . for the foreseeable future. Ethan, too."

"You work fast."

"A boy's welfare is at stake," he said, echoing her.

Anna nodded. At a distant rumble of thunder, she glanced outside, frowned. The light was dimming, and the wind beginning to kick. "I'd like to discuss Seth with you." She shifted her briefcase, glanced at a chair.

"Is this going to take long?"

"I couldn't say."

"Then let's do it in the kitchen. I want coffee."

"Fine."

She followed him, using the time to study the house. It was just neat enough to make her wonder if Cam had been expecting her. They passed a den where the dust was layered over tables, the couch was covered with newspapers, and shoes littered the floor.

Missed that, didn't you? she thought with a smirk. But she found it endearing.

Then she heard his quick and vicious oath and nearly jumped out of her practical shoes.

"Goddamn it. Shit. What the hell is this? What next? Jesus Christ." He was already sloshing through the water and suds flowing over the kitchen floor to slap at the dishwasher.

Anna stepped back to avoid the flood. "I'd turn that off if I were you."

"Yeah, yeah, yeah. Now I've got to take the bitch apart." He dragged the door open. An ocean of snowy-white suds spewed out.

Anna bit the inside of her cheek, cleared her throat. "Ah, what kind of soap did you use?"

"Dish soap." Vibrating with frustration, he yanked a bucket out from under the sink.

"Dish*washer* soap or dish-washing soap?"

"What the hell's the difference?" Furious, he started to bail. Outside, the rain began to fall in hard, driving sheets.

"This." Keeping her face admirably sober, she gestured to the river running over the floor. "This is the difference. If you use the liquid for hand-washing dishes in a dishwasher, this is the inevitable result."

He straightened, the bucket in his hand, and a look of such pained irritation on his face, she couldn't hold back the laugh. "Sorry, sorry. Look, turn around."

"Why?"

"Because I'm not willing to ruin my shoes or my hose. So turn around while I take them off and I'll give you a hand."

"Yeah." Pathetically grateful, he turned his back, and even did his best not to imagine her peeling off her stockings. His best wasn't quite good enough, but it was the effort that counted. "Ethan handled most of the kitchen chores when we were growing up. I did my share, but it doesn't seem to have stuck with me."

"You seem to be out of your element." She tucked her hose neatly in her shoes, set them aside. "Get me a mop. I'll swab, you get the coffee."

He opened a long, narrow closet and handed her a string mop. "I appreciate it."

Her legs, he noted as he sloshed over for mugs, didn't need hose. They were a pale and fascinating gold in color, and smooth as silk. When she bent over, he ran his tongue over his teeth. He'd had no idea a woman with a mop would be quite so . . . attractive.

It's so amazingly pleasant, he realized, to be here, with the rain drumming, the wind howling, and a pretty, barefoot woman keeping him kitchen company. "You seem to be in your element," he commented, then grinned when she turned her head and eyed him balefully. "I'm not saying it's woman's work. My mother would have skinned me for the thought. I'm just saying you seem to know what you're doing."

As she'd worked her way through college cleaning houses, she knew very well. "I can handle a mop, Mr. Quinn."

"Since you're mopping my kitchen floor, you ought to make it Cam."

"About Seth—"

"Yeah, about Seth. Do you mind if I sit down?"

"Go ahead." She caught herself before she began to hum. The mindless chore, the rain, the isolation were just a tad too relaxing. "I'm sure you know I spoke with him yesterday."

"Yeah, and I know he told you he wanted to stay here."

"He did, and it's in my report. I also spoke with his teachers. How much do you know about his schoolwork?"

Cam shifted. "I haven't had a lot of time to get into that yet."

"Mmm-hmm. When he was first enrolled, he had some trouble with the other students. Fistfights. He broke one boy's nose."

Good for him, Cam thought with a surprising tug of pride, but he did his best to look disapproving. "Who started it?"

"That's not the point. However, your father handled the situation. At this point I'm told that Seth keeps mostly to himself. He doesn't participate in class, which is another problem. He rarely turns in his homework assignments, and those he does bother to turn in are most often sloppily done."

Cam felt a new headache begin to brew. "So the kid's not a scholar—"

"On the contrary." Anna straightened up, leaned on the mop. "If he participated even marginally in class, and if his assignments were done and turned in on time, he would be a straight A student. He's a solid B student as it is."

"So what's the problem?"

Anna closed her eyes a moment. "The problem is that Seth's IQ and evaluation tests are incredibly high. The child is brilliant."

Though he had his doubts about that, Cam nodded. "So, that's a good thing. And he's getting decent grades and staying out of trouble."

"Okay." She would try this a different way. "Suppose you were in a Formula One race—"

"Been there," he said with wistful reminiscence. "Done that."

"Right, and you had the finest, fastest, hottest car in the field."

"Yeah." He sighed. "I did."

"But you never tested its full capabilities, you never went full-out, you never punched it on the turns or popped it into fifth and poured down the straights."

His brow lifted. "You follow racing?"

"No, but I drive a car."

"Nice car, too. What have you had it up to?"

Eighty-eight, she thought with secret glee, but she would never admit it. "I consider a car transportation," she said, lying primly. "Not a toy."

"No reason it can't be both. Why don't I take you out in the 'Vette? Now that's a fine mode of entertaining transportation."

While she would have loved to indulge in the fantasy of sliding behind the wheel of that sleek white bullet, she had a point to make. "Try to stick with the analogy here. You're racing a superior machine. If you didn't drive that car the way it was meant to be driven, you'd be wasting its potential, and maybe you'd still finish in the money, but you wouldn't win."

He got her point, but couldn't help grinning. "I usually won."

Anna shook her head. "Seth," she said with admirable patience. "We're talking about Seth. He's socially stunted, and he defies authority consistently. He's regularly given in-school suspension. He needs supervision here at home when it comes to this area of his life. You're going to have to take an active roll in his schoolwork and his behavior."

"Seems to me a kid gets B's he ought to be left the hell alone." But he held up a hand before she could speak. "Potential. I had potential drummed into my head by the best. We'll work on it."

"Good." She went back to mopping. "I had communications from your lawyer in regard to the guardianship. It's likely you'll be granted that, at least temporarily. But you can expect regular spot checks from Social Services."

"Meaning you."

"Meaning me."

Cam paused a moment. "Do you do windows?"

She couldn't help it, she laughed as she dumped sudsy water into the sink. "I've also talked to some of your neighbors and will talk to more." She turned back. "From this point on, your life's an open book for me."

He rose, took the mop, and to please himself stood just an inch closer than was polite. "You let me know when you get to a chapter that interests you, on a personal level."

Her heart gave two hard knocks against her ribs. A dangerous man, she thought, on a personal level. "I don't have time for much fiction."

She started to step back, but he took her hand. "I like you, Miz Spinelli. I haven't figured out why, but I do."

"That should make our association simpler."

"Wrong." He skimmed his thumb over the back of her hand. "It's going to make it complicated. But I don't mind complications. And it's about time my luck started back on an upswing. You like Italian food?"

"With a name like Spinelli?"

He grinned. "Right. I could use a quiet meal in a decent restaurant with a pretty woman. How about tonight?"

"I don't see any reason why you shouldn't have a quiet meal in a decent restaurant with a pretty woman tonight." Deliberately, she eased her hand free. "But if you're asking me for a date, the answer's no. First, it wouldn't be smart; second, I'm booked."

"Damn it, Cam, didn't you hear me honking?"

Anna turned and saw a soaking wet and bitterly angry man cart two heaping bags of groceries into the room. He was tall, bronzed, and very nearly beautiful. And spitting mad.

Phillip shook the hair out of his eyes and focused on Anna. The shift of expression was quick and smooth—from snarling to charming in the space of a single heartbeat.

"Hello. Sorry." He dumped the bags on the table and smiled at her. "Didn't know Cam had company." He spied the bucket, the mop held between them, and leaped to the wrong conclusion. "I didn't know he was going to hire domestic help. But thank God." Phillip grabbed her hand, kissed it. "I already adore you."

"My brother Phillip," Cam said dryly. "This is Anna Spinelli, with Social Services. You can take your Ferragamo out of your mouth now, Phil."

The charm didn't shift or fade. "Ms. Spinelli. It's nice to meet you. Our lawyer's been in touch, I believe."

"Yes, he has. Mr. Quinn tells me you'll be living here now."

"I told you to call me Cam." He walked to the stove to top off his coffee. "It's going to be confusing if you're calling all of us Mr. Quinn." Cam heard the rattle at the back door and got out another mug. "Especially now," he said as the door burst open and let in a dripping dog and man.

"Christ, this bitch blew in fast." Even as Ethan dragged off his slicker, the dog set his feet and shook furiously. Anna only winced as water sprayed her suit. "Barely smelled her before—"

He spotted Anna and automatically pulled off his soaked cap, then scooped a hand through his damp, curling hair. Seeing woman, bucket, mop, he thought guiltily about his muddy boots. "Ma'am."

"My other brother, Ethan." Cam handed Ethan a steaming cup of coffee. "This is the social worker your dog's just sprayed water and dog hair all over."

"Sorry. Simon, go sit."

"It's all right," Cam went on. "Foolish already slobbered all over her, and Phillip just got finished hitting on her."

Anna smiled blandly. "I thought you were hitting on me."

"I asked you to dinner," Cam corrected. "If I'd been hitting on you, I wouldn't have been subtle." Cam sipped his coffee. "Well, now you know all the players."

She felt outnumbered, and more than a little unprofessional standing there in the dimly lit kitchen in her bare feet, facing three big and outrageously handsome men. In defense, she pulled out every scrap of dignity and reached for a chair.

"Gentlemen, shall we sit down? This seems to be an ideal time to discuss how you plan to care for Seth." She angled her head at Cam. "For the foreseeable future."

⌒

"Well," Phillip said an hour later. "I think we pulled that off."

Cam stood at the front door, watching the neat little sports car drive away in the thinning rain. "She's got our number," Cam muttered. "She doesn't miss a trick."

"I liked her." Ethan stretched out in the big wing chair and let the puppy climb into his lap. "Get your mind out of the sewer, Cam," he suggested when Cam snickered. "I mean I liked her. She's smart, and she's professional, but she's not cold. Seems like a woman who cares."

"And she's got great legs," Phillip added. "But regardless of all that, she's going to note down every time we screw up. Right now, I figure we've got the upper hand. We've got the kid, and he wants to stay. His mother's run off to God knows where and isn't making any noises—at the moment. But if pretty Anna Spinelli talks to too many people around St. Chris, she's going to start hearing the rumors."

He dipped his hands in his pockets and started to pace. "I don't know if they're going to count against us or not."

"They're just rumors," Ethan said.

"Yeah, but they're ugly. We've got a good shot at keeping Seth because of Dad's reputation. That reputation gets smeared, and we'll have battles to fight on several fronts."

"Anyone tries to smear Dad's rep, they're going to get more than a fight."

Phillip turned to Cam. "That's just what we have to avoid. If we start going around kicking ass, it's only going to make things worse."

"So you be the diplomat." Cam shrugged and sat on the arm of the sofa. "I'll kick ass."

"I'd say we're better off dealing with what is than what might be." Thoughtfully, Ethan stroked the puppy. "I've been thinking about the situation. It's going to be rough for Phillip to live here and commute back and forth to Baltimore. Sooner rather than later, Cam's going to get fed up with playing house."

"Sooner's already here."

"I was thinking we could pay Grace to do some of the housework. Maybe a couple days a week."

"Now that's an idea I can get behind one hundred percent." Cam dropped onto the sofa.

"Trouble with that is it leaves you with nothing much to do. The idea is for the three of us to be here, share responsibility for Seth. That's what the lawyer says, that's what the social worker says."

"I said I'd find work."

"What are you going to do?" Phillip asked. "Pump gas? Shuck oysters? You'd put up with that for a couple of days."

Cam leaned forward. "I can stick. Can you? Odds are, after the first week of commuting, you'll be calling from Baltimore with excuses about why you can't make it back. Why don't you stay here and try pumping gas or shucking oysters for a while?"

The argument was inevitable. In minutes they were both up and nose to nose. It took several attempts before Ethan's voice got through. Cam stepped back and with a puzzled frown turned. "What?"

"I said I think we ought to try building boats."

"Building boats?" Cam shook his head. "For what?"

"For business." Ethan took out a cigar, but ran it through his fingers rather than lighting it. His mother hadn't allowed smoking in the house. "We got a lot of tourists coming down this way in the last few years. And a lot more people moving down to get out of the city. They like to rent boats. They like to own boats. Last year I built one in my spare time for this guy out of D.C. Little fourteen-foot skiff. Called me a couple months ago to see if I'd be interested in building him another one. Wants a bigger boat, with a sleep cabin and galley."

Ethan tucked the cigar back in his pocket. "I've been thinking on it. It'd take me months to do it alone, in my spare time."

"You want us to help you build a boat?" Phillip pressed his fingers to his eyes.

"Not one boat. I'm talking about going into business."

"I'm in business," Phillip muttered. "I'm in advertising."

"And we'd be needing somebody who knew about that kind of thing if we were starting a business. Boat building's got a history in this area, but nobody's doing it anymore on St. Chris."

Phillip sat. "Did it occur to you that there might be a reason for that?"

"Yeah, it occurred to me. And I thought about it, and I figure it's because nobody's taking the chance. I'm talking wooden boats. Sailing vessels. A specialty. And we already got one client."

Cam rubbed his chin. "Hell, Ethan, I haven't done that kind of work seriously since we built your skipjack. That's been—Jesus—almost ten years."

"And she's holding, isn't she? So we did a good job with her. It's a gamble," he added, knowing that single word was the way to Cam's heart.

"We've got money for start-up costs," Cam murmured, warming up to the idea.

"How do you know?" Phillip demanded. "You don't have a clue how much money you need for start-up costs."

"You'll figure it out." A roll of the dice, Cam thought. He liked nothing better. "Christ knows, I'd rather be swinging a hammer than a damn vacuum hose. I'm in."

"Just like that?" Phillip threw up his hands. "Without a thought to overhead, profit and loss, licenses, taxes, insurance. Where the hell are you going to set up shop? How're you going to run the business end?"

"That's not my problem," Cam said with a grin. "That would be yours."

"I have a job. In Baltimore."

"I had a life," Cam said simply, "in Europe."

Phillip paced away, back, away again. Trapped, was all he could think. "I'll do what I can to get things started. This could be a huge mistake, and it's going to cost a lot of money. And you'd both better consider that the social worker might take a dim view of us starting a risky business at this point. I'm not giving up my job. At least that's one steady income."

"I'll talk to her about it," Cam decided on impulse. "See how she reacts. You'll talk to Grace about pitching in around the house?" he asked Ethan.

"Yeah, I'll go down to the pub and run it by her."

"Fine. That leaves you to deal with Seth tonight." He smiled thinly at Phillip. "Make sure he does his homework."

"Oh, God."

"Now that that's settled," Cam eased back, "who's cooking dinner?"

SIX

Tracking down Anna Spinelli was the perfect excuse to escape the post-dinner chaos at home. It meant the dishes were someone else's problem—and that he couldn't be pulled into the homework argument that had just begun to heat up between Phillip and Seth.

In fact, as far as Cam was concerned, a rainy evening drive to Princess Anne was high entertainment. And that was pretty pitiful for a man who'd grown accustomed to jetting from Paris to Rome.

He tried not to think about it.

He'd arranged to have his hydrofoil stored, his clothes packed up and sent. He had yet to have his car shipped over, though. It was just a bit too permanent a commitment. But between the time spent repairing steps and doing laundry, he'd entertained himself by tuning up and tinkering with his mother's prized 'Vette.

It gave him a great deal of pleasure to drive it—so much that he accepted the speeding ticket he collected just outside of Princess Anne without complaint.

The town wasn't the hive of activity it had been during the eighteenth and nineteenth centuries when tobacco had been king and wealth poured into the area. But it was pretty enough, Cam supposed, with the old homes restored and preserved, the streets clean and quiet. Now that tourism was becoming the newest deity for the Shore, the charm and grace of historic towns were a huge economic draw.

Anna's apartment was less than half a mile from the offices of Social Services. Easy walking distance to work, to the courts. Shopping was convenient. He imagined she'd chosen the old Victorian house for those reasons as well as for the ambience.

The building was tucked behind big trees, their branches now hazed with new leaves. The walkway was cracked but flanked by daffodils that were ready to pop out with sunny yellow. Steps led to a covered veranda. The plaque beside the door stated that the house was on the historic register.

The door itself was unlocked and led Cam into a hallway. The wood floor was a bit worn, but someone had troubled to polish it to a dull gleam. The mail slots on the wall were brass, again polished, and indicated that the building had been converted to four apartments. A. Spinelli occupied 2B.

Cam trooped up the creaking stairs to the second floor. The hallway was more narrow here, the lights dimmer. The only sound he heard was the muffled echo of what sounded like a riotous sitcom from the television of 2A.

He knocked on Anna's door and waited. Then he knocked again, tucked his hands in his pockets, and scowled. He'd expected her to be home. He'd never considered otherwise. It was nearly nine o'clock, a weeknight, and she was a civil servant.

She should have been quietly at home, reading a book or filling out forms and reports. That was how practical career women spent their evenings—though he hoped eventually to show her a more entertaining way to pass the time.

Probably at some women's club meeting, he decided, annoyed with her. He searched the pockets of his black leather bomber jacket for a scrap of paper and was about to disturb 2A in hopes of borrowing something to write on and with when he heard the quick, rhythmic click that an experienced man recognized as a woman's high heels against wood.

He glanced down the hall, pleased that his luck had changed.

He barely noticed that his jaw dropped.

The woman who walked toward him was built like a man's darkest fantasy. And she was generous enough to showcase that killer body in a snug electric-blue dress scooped low at the breasts and cut high on the thighs. It left nothing—and everything to a male's imagination.

The click of heels on wood was courtesy of ice pick heels in the same shocking color, which turned her legs into endless fascination.

Her hair, dewy with rain, curled madly to her shoulders, a thick ebony mane that brought images of gypsies and campfire sex to mind. Her mouth was red and wet, her eyes huge and dark. The scent of her reached him ten seconds before she did and delivered a breathtaking punch straight to the loins.

She said nothing, only narrowed those amazing eyes, cocked one glorious hip, and waited.

"Well." He had to work on getting his breath back. "I guess you've never heard the one about hiding your light under a bushel."

"I've heard it." She was furious to find him on her doorstep, furious that

she was without her professional armor. And even more furious that he'd
been on her mind throughout the evening a great deal more than her date.
"What do you want, Mr. Quinn?"

Now he grinned, fast and sharp as a wolf baring fangs. "That's a loaded
question at the moment, Miz Spinelli."

"Don't be ordinary, Quinn. You've avoided that so far."

"I promise you, I don't have a single ordinary thought in my mind." Unable to resist, he reached out to toy with the ends of her hair. "Where ya
been, Anna?"

"Look, it's well after business hours, and my personal life isn't—" She
broke off, struggled not to curse or moan as the door across the hall opened.

"You're back from your date, Anna."

"Yes, Mrs. Hardelman."

The woman of about seventy was wrapped in a pink chenille robe and
peered over the glasses perched on her nose. Heat and canned laughter
poured out into the hall. She beamed at Cam, the smile lighting her pleasant
face. "Oh, he's much better-looking than the last one."

"Thanks." Cam stepped over and smiled back. "Does she have a lot of
them?"

"Oh, they come and they go." Mrs. Hardelman chuckled and fluffed at
her thin white hair. "She never keeps them."

Cam leaned companionably on the doorjamb, enjoying the sounds of
frustration Anna made behind him. "Guess she hasn't found one worth
keeping yet. She sure is pretty."

"And such a nice girl. She picks up things at the market for us if Sister
and I aren't feeling up to going out. Always offers to drive us to church on
Sunday. And when my Petie died, Anna took care of the burial herself."

Mrs. Hardelman looked over at Anna with such affection and sweetness,
Anna could only sigh. "You're missing your show, Mrs. Hardelman."

"Oh, yes." She glanced back into the apartment, where the television
blasted. "I do love my comedies. You come back now," she told Cam and
gently closed the door.

And because Anna was perfectly aware that her neighbor wouldn't be
able to resist peeping through the security hole hoping to catch a romantic
good-night kiss, she dug out her keys.

"You might as well come in since you're here."

"Thanks." He crossed the hall, waiting while she unlocked her door.
"You buried your neighbor's husband."

"Her parakeet," Anna corrected. "Petie was a bird. She and her sister
have both been widows for about twenty years. And all I did was get a shoe
box and dig a hole out back next to a rosebush."

He brushed a hand over her hair again as she pushed the door open. "It meant something to her."

"Watch your hands, Quinn," she warned and flicked on the lights.

To indicate that he was willing to oblige, he held them out, then tucked them into his pockets while he studied the room. Soft, deep cushions, bright, bold colors. He decided the choices meant she had a deep-rooted sensual side.

He liked to think that.

The room was spacious, and she'd furnished it sparingly. The sofa was big and plush enough for sleeping, but there was only a wide upholstered chair and two tables to keep it company.

Yet she'd covered the walls with art. Prints, posters, pen-and-ink sketches. They were of places rather than people, and many of the scenes he recognized. The narrow streets of Rome, the wild cliffs of western Ireland, the classy little cafes of Paris.

"I've been here." He tapped the frame of the Paris cafe.

"How nice for you." She said it dryly, trying not to resent the fact that her pictures were the only way she could afford to travel. For now. "Now, what are you doing here?"

"I wanted to talk to you about—" He made the mistake of turning, looking at her again. She was obviously a very annoyed woman, but it only added to her appeal. Her eyes and mouth were sulky, her body braced in challenge. "Christ, you're a looker, Anna. I was attracted to you before—I imagine you caught that—but . . . who knew?"

She didn't want to be flattered. She certainly didn't want her heartbeat to pick up speed and lose its steady rhythm. But it was difficult to control either reaction when a man like Cameron Quinn was standing there looking at her as if he'd like to start nibbling at any single part of her body and keep going till he'd devoured it all.

She took a careful breath. "You wanted to talk to me about . . . ?" she prompted.

"The kid, stuff. How about some coffee? That's civilized, right?" He decided to test them both by walking to her. "I figure you expect me to act civilized. I'm willing to give it a shot."

She brooded a moment, then pivoted on those sexy blue heels. Cam appreciated the rear view, rolled his eyes toward heaven, then followed her to the spotless counter that separated living room and kitchen. He leaned on it, pleased that the location gave him a perfect view of her legs.

Then he heard the electric rumble and caught the amazing scent of fresh coffee. "You grind your own beans?"

"If you're going to make coffee, you might as well make good coffee."

"Yeah." He closed his eyes to better appreciate the aroma. "Oh, yeah. Do I have to marry you to get you to make my coffee every day, or can we just live together?"

She looked over her shoulder, lifted her brows at his wide, winning grin, then got back to the task at hand.

"I bet you've used that look to shut men down with enormous success. But me, I like it. So where were you tonight?"

"I had a date."

He moved around the counter. The kitchen area was small, no more than a narrow passageway. He liked being close enough so that her scent mixed with the smell of coffee. "Early evening," he commented.

"It was going to be." She felt the hair on the back of her neck prickle. He was too damn close. Instinctively she employed her usual method with men who crowded her space. She rammed her elbow into his gut.

"Practiced move," he murmured and, rubbing his stomach, backed off an inch. "Do you ever have to use it in your social worker mode?"

"Rarely. How do you want your coffee?"

"Strong and black."

She set it to brew, turned around, and bumped solidly into him. Her radar, she decided as his hands came up to take her arms, had definitely been off. Or, she was forced to admit, she'd ignored it because she'd wondered how they might fit.

Well, now she knew.

He deliberately kept his eyes on her face, didn't let them dip down to the small gold cross nestled between her breasts. He wasn't particularly devout, but he was afraid he would go to hell for having lascivious thoughts about the framework for a religious symbol.

Besides, he liked her face.

"Quinn," she said with a long, irritated sigh. "Back off."

"You dropped the *Mister* Quinn. Does that mean we're pals?"

Because he smiled when he said it, and because he did step back, she found herself chuckling. "Jury's still out."

"I like the way you smell, Anna. Lusty, provocative. Challenging. Of course, I like the way Miz Spinelli smells, too. Quiet and practical and subtle."

"All right . . . Cam." She turned, took out two pretty, deep cups from the cupboard. "Let's stop dancing and agree that we're attracted to each other."

"I was hoping once we agreed to that we'd start dancing."

"Wrong." She tossed her hair back and poured coffee. "I'm Seth's caseworker. You're proposing to be his guardian. It would be incredibly unwise for either of us to act on a physical attraction."

He picked up the cup, leaned back against the counter. "I don't know

about you, but I love doing stuff that's unwise. Especially if it feels good."
He brought the cup to his lips, then smiled slowly. "And I bet acting on that physical attraction would feel damn good."

"It's fortunate that I happen to be very wise." With a mirroring smile, she leaned back on the opposite counter. "Now, you wanted to discuss Seth—and stuff, as I believe you put it."

Seth, the rest of his brothers, and the situation had gone completely out of his mind. He supposed he'd used it as an excuse to see her. That was something to consider later. "I have to admit, coming into Princess Anne to talk to you was a great reason to escape. I was about to get stuck with dish duty, and Phil and the kid were already into round one on the homework issue."

"I'm glad someone's dealing with his schoolwork. And why don't you ever refer to Seth by his name?"

"I do. Sure I do."

"No, not as a rule." She cocked her head. "Is that a habit of yours, Cameron, to avoid the personal contact of names with people you don't intend to have an important or permanent relationship with?"

Her point, he was forced to admit, was a good one but he lifted a brow. "I use your name."

He saw her blink, heard her sigh, then she waved the issue away. "What about Seth?"

"It's not about him, directly. Except I figure we're starting to divvy things up more evenhandedly. Phil's the best to keep on him—keep on Seth," he corrected with emphasis, "about school because for some reason Phil actually liked school. And we decided to get somebody to come in and deal with most of the housework a couple of days a week."

She still had a picture of him standing in a puddle of suds with a look of baffled fury on his face. Her lips wanted badly to twitch into a smile. "You'll be happier."

"I hope never to see another vacuum cleaner bag. Ever had one rip on you?" He shuddered deliberately and made her laugh. "Anyhow, Ethan had this brainstorm. I'm at loose ends, Phillip needs something to occupy him if he's going to be staying here—though he figures on commuting to Baltimore for now. So we're going into business."

"Into business? What kind of business?"

"Boat building."

She lowered her cup. "You're going to build boats?"

"I've built plenty—so has Ethan. And actually, though Phil went over to the suit-and-tie life, he's done some himself. The three of us worked on the skipjack that Ethan still sails."

"That's fine for recreation, for personal use, for a hobby. But to consider starting a business, a risky one, at the very time when you're trying to take on a minor dependent . . ."

"He won't go hungry. For Christ's sake, Ethan holds his own on the bay, and Phil's got that desk job in Baltimore. I could get busywork, but what's the point?"

"I'm only pointing out that a venture of this nature would consume a great deal of money and time, particularly during the first months. Stability—"

"Isn't every damn thing." Annoyed, he set his coffee down and began to pace. "Shouldn't the kid learn there's more to life than nine-to-fiving it? That there can be choices, that you can take a chance? How good is it for him if I'm stuck in that house dusting furniture and hating every goddamn minute of it? Ethan's already got one client, and if Ethan brought this up you can believe he's weighed it from every angle. Nobody thinks things through as much as he does."

"And since you felt you wanted to discuss this with me, I'm simply trying to do the same. Weigh it from every angle."

"And you think it would be better if I went out and got some nice, stable, time-clock job that brings in a nice, stable, time-clock paycheck every week." He stopped in front of her. "Is that the kind of man who appeals to you? The kind who reports in at nine five days a week, who takes you out to dinner on a rainy night and lets you get away at a reasonable hour without even trying to convince you to take off what there is of that dress?"

She took a minute, reminding herself it wouldn't solve anything if both of them lost the battle with temper. "What appeals to me, what I wear, and how I choose to spend my evenings aren't the issues here. As Seth's caseworker, I'm concerned that his home life be as stable and happy as possible."

"Why should me building boats make him unhappy?"

"My question regarding this idea of yours is whether your attention will be taken away from him and turned toward this new business. A business that you would, I imagine, find exciting, challenging, and interesting, at least for a time."

His eyes narrowed. "You just don't think I can stick, do you?"

"That's yet to be proved. But I do think you'll try. What worries me is that you're not trying for Seth, you're trying for your father. For your parents. I don't think that's a count against you, Cam," she said more gently. "But it's not a point in Seth's favor."

How the hell did you argue with a woman who insisted on dotting every *i*? he wondered. "So you think he's better off with strangers?"

"No, I think he's better off with you and your brothers." She smiled, satisfied that she had shut him up for the moment. "And that's what went into my report. This idea of starting a boat-building business is something new to think about, and I hope none of you intends to rush into it."

"Do you sail?"

"No, I've never tried it. Why?"

"I'd never been on a boat in my life until Ray Quinn took me out."

Because he remembered how those eyes of hers could warm with compassion, he decided to tell her how it had been for him. "I was scared to death, but too tough to admit it. I'd only been with them a few days, never figured I'd stay. He took me out on this little Sunfish he had back then. Told me the air would do me good."

All he had to do was think, and the image of that morning came clear as sunlight in his head. "My father was a big man. The Mighty Quinn. Built like a bull. I knew that little boat was going to tip over, and I'd probably drown, but he had a way of getting you to do things."

Love, Anna thought. It was pure and simple love in his voice. It attracted her, she admitted, every bit as much as that toughly handsome face. "Could you swim?"

"No—but I still hated it that he made me wear a PFD. Personal flotation device," he explained. "Life jacket. Figured it was for sissies."

"You'd rather have drowned?"

"Hell, no, but I had to make him think so. Anyway, I sat in the stern, my stomach clutched. I was wearing these sunglasses my mother—Stella," he corrected, for she'd been Stella then—"had dug up somewhere because my eye was pretty banged up and the sunlight hurt."

He'd been beaten, abused, neglected, she remembered, when the Quinns had found him. Her heart went out to the little boy. "You must have been terrified."

"Down to the bone, but I'd have choked on my tongue before I'd have admitted it. He must have known that," Cam said quietly. "He always knew what was in my head. It was hot, and the humidity was up so that every time you took a breath it was like swallowing water. He said it would be cooler when we moved out of the gut and onto the river, but I didn't believe him. I figured we'd just sit there and fry. The boat didn't even have a motor. Christ, he laughed when I said that. He told me we had something better than a motor."

He'd forgotten his coffee, and even the point of the story drifted away in the memory. "We headed out across the water, slow and easy at first, the boat rocked when we turned into the bend, and I figured that was it. Game over. This heron came out of the trees. I'd seen it once before. At least I like to think it was the same one. It winged right over the boat, wings spread to trap the air. And then we caught the wind and that little sail filled. We started to fly. He turned around and grinned at me. I didn't even know I was grinning back until I split my lip open again. I'd never felt like that before in my life. Not once."

Without thinking, he lifted his hand and tucked her hair behind her ear. "Not once in my life."

"It changed you." She knew that single moments, both simple and dramatic, could alter courses forever.

"It started to. A boat on the water, and people who were giving me a chance. It wasn't much more complicated than that. It doesn't have to be that much more complicated here. We'll have the kid swing the hammer, put some sweat and effort into building a boat. If it's going to be a Quinn operation, that includes him."

Her smile came quickly, fully, and to his surprise, she patted him on the cheek. "That last part said it all. It's a gamble. I'm not sure if it's the time or the place for one, but . . . it should be interesting to watch."

"Is that what you're going to do?" He eased forward, nudging her back against the counter. "Watch me?"

"I don't intend to take my eyes off you—on a professional level—until I'm assured that you and your brothers provide Seth with the proper home and guardianship."

"Fair enough." He moved in just a little closer, just a fraction till two well-toned bodies brushed. "And how about on a personal level?"

She weakened enough to let her gaze skim down, linger. His mouth was definitely tempting—dangerous and very close. "Keeping my eyes on you on a personal level isn't a hardship. A mistake, maybe—but not a hardship."

"I always figure if you're going to make a mistake . . ." He put his hands on the counter, caging her. "Make it a big one. What do you say, Anna?" He dipped his head a little lower, hovered.

She tried to think, to consider the consequences. But there were times when needs, desire, and lust simply overpowered logic. "Hell," she muttered and, cupping her hand at the back of his neck, dragged his mouth down on hers.

It was exactly as she wanted. Hungry and fierce and mindless. His mouth was hot, and it was hard, and it was almost heathen as he crushed down to devour hers. She gave in to it, gave all to it, a moment's madness where body ruled mind and blood roared over reason.

And the thrill snapped through her like a whip, sharp, painful, and with a quick, shocking burn.

"Christ." His breath was gone, his mind was reeling. Reflexively, his hands dug into the counter before he jerked them away and filled them with her.

Whatever he'd expected, whatever he'd imagined didn't come close to the volcano that had so suddenly erupted in his arms. He dragged a hand through her hair, the wild, curling mass of it, fisted it there, then plundered as if his life depended on it.

"Can't," she managed, but her arms wound around him, banded around him until it seemed his heart wasn't merely thundering against hers but inside hers. Her moan was a rumble of desperate, delirious pleasure that sounded in her throat exactly where his teeth nipped, then scraped, then dug greedily into flesh.

The counter bit into her back, her fingers bit into his hips as she dragged him closer. Oh, God, she wanted contact, friction, more. She found his mouth with hers again, plunged blindly into the next kiss.

Just one more, she promised herself, meeting, matching his reckless demand.

Her scent seduced his senses. Her name was a murmur on his lips, a whisper in his mind. Her body was a glorious banquet melded to his. No woman had ever filled him so quickly, so completely, so utterly to the exclusion of all else.

"Let me." It was a plea, and he'd never in his life begged for a woman. "For God's sake, Anna, let me have you." His hands ran up her legs, those endless thighs. "Now."

She wanted. It would be so easy to take, and be taken. But easy, she knew, was rarely right.

"No. Not now." Regret smothered her even as she lifted her hands to frame his face. For a moment longer, her mouth stayed on his. "Not yet. Not like this."

Her eyes were dark, clouded. He knew enough of a woman's pleasures and his own skills to believe he could make them go blind. "It's perfect like this."

"The timing's wrong, the circumstances. Wait." Someone had to move, she decided. To break that contact. She sidestepped, let out a shaky breath. She closed her eyes, lifted a hand to hold him off. "Well," she managed after another moment, "that was insane."

He took the hand she'd raised, brought it to his lips and nipped his teeth into her forefinger. "Who needs sanity?"

"I do." She nearly managed a genuine smile as she tugged her hand free. "Not that I don't regret that deeply at this moment, but I do need it. Wow." She drew in another long breath, pushed her hands up through her hair. "Cameron. You're every bit as potent as I expected."

"I haven't even started."

The smile widened. "I bet. I just bet." She eased back a little more, picked up her rapidly cooling coffee. "I don't know as that episode's going to make either one of us sleep easier tonight, but it was bound to happen." She angled her head when his eyes narrowed. "What?"

"Most women, especially in your position, would make excuses."

"For what?" She lifted a shoulder and promised herself her system would level again eventually. "That was as much my doing as yours. I wondered what it might be like to get my hands on you from the first time I saw you."

Cam decided he might never be the same again. "I think I'm crazy about you."

"No, you're not." She laughed and handed him his coffee. "You're intrigued, you're attracted, you've got a good healthy case of lust, but those are entirely different matters. And you don't even know me."

"I want to." He let out a short laugh. "And that's a big surprise to me. I don't usually care one way or the other."

"I'm flattered. I'm not sure if that's a tribute to your charm or my own stupidity, but I'm flattered. But—"

"Damn, I knew that was coming."

"But," she repeated and set her cup in the sink. "Seth is my priority. He has to be." The warmth that was both compassion and understanding came into her eyes, and it touched something in him that was buried under that healthy lust. "And he should be yours. I hope I'm around if and when that happens."

"I'm doing everything I can think of."

"I know you are. And you're doing more than most would." She touched his arm briefly, then moved away. "I have a feeling you've got more inside you yet. But . . ."

"There it is again."

"You'd better go now."

He wanted to stay, even if it was just to stand there and talk to her, to be. "I haven't finished my coffee."

"It's cold. And it's getting late." She glanced toward the window where raindrops ran like tears. "And the rain makes me wonder about things I shouldn't be wondering about."

He winced. "I don't suppose you said that to make me suffer."

"Sure I did." She laughed again and moved to the door, opened it wide to make her point. "If I'm going to, why shouldn't you?"

"Oh, I like you, Anna Spinelli. You're a woman after my own heart."

"You're not interested in a woman going for your heart," she said as he crossed the room. "You want one who's after your body."

"See, we're getting to know each other already."

"Good night." She didn't evade when he pulled her in for another kiss as he walked out the door. Evading would have been a pretense, and she wasn't one to delude herself.

So she met the kiss with teasing heat and honest enthusiasm. Then she shut the door in his face.

And then she leaned back against it weakly.

Potent? That wasn't the half of it. Her pulse was likely to stay on overdrive for hours. Maybe days.

She wished she didn't feel so damn happy about it.

SEVEN

Cam was scowling at a basket full of pink socks and Jockey shorts when the phone rang. He knew damn well the socks and underwear had been white—or close to it—when he'd dumped them in the machine. Now they were Easter-egg pink.

Maybe they just looked that way because they were wet.

He pulled them out to stuff them in the dryer, saw the red sock hiding among the pink. And bared his teeth.

Phillip, he vowed, was a dead man.

"Fuck it." He dumped them inside, slapped the dryer on what he hoped was broil and went to answer the phone.

He remembered, just in time, to turn down the little portable TV tucked in the corner of the counter. It wasn't as if he was actually watching it, it certainly wasn't that he was paying any attention at all to the passion and betrayals of the late-morning soap opera.

He'd just switched it on for the noise.

"Quinn. What?"

"Hey, Cam. Took some doing to track you down, hoss. Tod Bardette here."

Cam reached into an open bag of Oreos on the counter and took out a handful. "How's it going, Tod?"

"Well, I have to tell you it's going pretty damn good. I've been spending some time anchored off the Great Barrier Reef."

"Nice spot," Cam muttered over a cookie. Then his brows shot up as an impossibly gorgeous woman tumbled into bed with a ridiculously handsome man on the tiny screen across the kitchen.

Maybe there was something to this daytime TV after all.

"It'll do. Heard you kicked ass in the Med a few weeks ago."

A few weeks? Cam thought while he munched on a second cookie. Surely it had been a few years ago that he'd flown across the finish line in his hydrofoil. Blue water, speed, cheering crowds, and money to burn.

Now he was lucky if he found enough milk in the fridge to wash down a stale Oreo.

"Yeah, that's what I heard too."

Tod gave a rich chuckle. "Well, the offer to buy that toy from you still holds. But I got another proposition coming at you."

Tod Bardette always had another proposition coming at you. He was the rich son of a rich father from East Texas who used the world as his playground. And he was boat happy. He raced them, sponsored races, bought and sold them. And collected wives, trophies, and his share of the purse with smooth regularity.

Cam had always felt Tod's luck had run hot since conception. Since it never hurt to listen—and the bedroom scene had just been displaced by a commercial featuring a giant toilet brush, he switched off the set.

"I'm always ready to hear one."

"I'm setting up a crew for La Coupe Internationale."

"The One-Ton Cup?" Cam felt his juices begin to flow, and he lost all interest in cookies and milk. The international race was a giant in the sailing world. Five legs, he thought, the final one an ocean race of three hundred grueling miles.

"You got it. You know the Aussies took the cup last year, so it's being held down here in Australia. I want to whip their butts, and I've got a honey of a boat. She's fast, hoss. With the right crew she'll bring the cup back to the U S of A. I need a skipper. I want the best. I want you. How soon can you get Down Under?"

Give me five minutes. That's what he wanted to say. He could have a bag packed in one, hop a plane and be on his way. For men who raced, it was one of life's golden opportunities. Even as he opened his mouth, his gaze landed on the rocker outside the kitchen window.

So he closed his eyes, listened resentfully to the hum of the pink socks drying in the utility room behind him.

"I have to pass, Tod. I can't get away now."

"Lookie here, I'm willing to give you some time to put your affairs—pun intended," he said with a snorting laugh, "in order. Take a couple weeks. If you've got another offer, I'll beat it."

"I can't do it. I've got—" Laundry to do? A kid to raise? Damn if he was going to humiliate himself with that piece of information. "My brothers and I started a business," he said on impulse. "I've got a commitment here."

"A business." This time Tod's laugh was long and delighted. "You? Don't pull my leg so hard, it hurts."

Now Cam's eyes narrowed. He didn't doubt Tod Bardette of East Texas would be joined by others of his friends and acquaintances in laughing at the idea of Cameron Quinn, businessman.

"We're building boats," he said between his teeth. "Here on the Eastern Shore. Wooden boats. Custom jobs," he added, determined to play it to the hilt. "One of a kinds. In six months, you'll be paying me top dollar to design and build you a boat by Quinn. Since we're old friends, I'll try to squeeze you in."

"Boats." The interest in Tod's voice picked up. "Well now, you know how to sail them, guess maybe you'd know how to build them."

"There's no maybe about it."

"That's an interesting enterprise, but come on, Cam, you're not a businessman. You're not going to stay stuck on some pretty little bay in Maryland eating crabs and nailing planks. You know I'll make this race worth your while. Money, fame, and fortune." And he chuckled. "After we win, you can go back and put a couple of little sloops together."

He could handle it, Cam promised himself. He could handle the insults, the frustration of not being able to pack and go as he chose. What he wouldn't do was give Bardette the satisfaction of knowing he was ruffled. "You're going to have to find another skipper. But if you want to buy a boat, give me a call."

"If you actually get one finished, give me a call." A sigh came through the receiver. "You're missing the chance of a lifetime here. You change your mind in the next couple hours, get in touch. But I need to nail down my crew this week. Talk to you."

And Cam was listening to a dial tone.

He didn't hurl the receiver through the window. He wanted to, considered it, then figured he'd be the one sweeping up the glass, so what would be the point?

So he hung up the phone, with careful deliberation. He even took a deep breath. And if whatever he'd put in the washing machine hadn't chosen that moment to spin out of balance and send the machine hopping, he wouldn't have slammed his fist into the wall.

"I thought for a minute there you were going to pull it off."

He whirled, and saw his father sitting at the kitchen table, chuckling. "Oh, God, this caps it."

"Why don't you get some ice for your knuckles?"

"It's all right." Cam glanced down at them. A couple of scrapes. And the sharp pain was a good hold on reality. "I thought about this, Dad. Really thought about it. I just don't believe you're here."

Ray continued to smile. "You're here, Cam. That's what matters. It was tough turning down a race like that. I'm grateful to you. I'm proud of you."

"Bardette said he had a honey of a boat. With his money behind it . . ." Cam pressed his hands on the counter and stared out the window toward the quiet water. "I could win that bastard. I captained a crew to second in the Little America's Cup five years ago, and I took the Chicago-Mackinac last year."

"You're a fine sailor, Cam."

"Yeah." He curled his fingers into fists. "What the hell am I doing here? If this keeps up I'm going to get hooked on soap operas. I'll start thinking Lilac and Lance are not only real people but close personal friends. I'll start obsessing that my whites aren't white enough. I'll clip coupons and collect recipes and go the rest of the way out of my fucking mind."

"I'm surprised at you, thinking of tending a home in those terms." Ray's voice was sharp now, with disappointment around the edges. "Making a home, caring for family is important work. The most important work there is."

"It's not my work."

"It seems it is now. I'm sorry for that."

Cam turned back. If you were going to have a conversation with a hallucination, you might as well look at it. "For what? For dying on me?"

"Well, that was pretty inconvenient all around."

He would have laughed, the comment and the ironic tone were so typically Ray Quinn. But he had to get out what was nibbling at his mind. "Some people are saying you aimed for the pole."

Ray's smile faded, and his eyes turned sober and sad. "Do you believe that?"

"No." Cam let out a breath. "No, I don't believe that."

"Life's a gift. It doesn't always fit comfortably, but it's precious. I wouldn't have hurt you and your brothers by throwing mine away."

"I know that," Cam murmured. "It helps to hear you say it, but I know that."

"Maybe I could have stopped things. Maybe I could have done things differently." He sighed and turned the gold wedding band around and around on his finger. "But I didn't. It's up to you now, you and Ethan and Phillip. There was a reason the three of you came to me and Stella. A reason the three of you came together. I always believed that. Now I know it."

"And what about the kid?"

"Seth's place is here. He needs you. He's in trouble right now, and he needs you to remember what it was like to be where he is."

"What do you mean, he's in trouble?"

Ray smiled a little. "Answer the phone," he suggested seconds before it rang.

And then he was gone.

"I've got to start getting more sleep," Cam decided, then yanked the receiver off the hook. "Yeah, yeah."

"Hello? Mr. Quinn?"

"Right. This is Cameron Quinn."

"Mr. Quinn, this is Abigail Moorefield, vice principal of St. Christopher Middle School."

Cam felt his stomach sink to his toes. "Uh-huh."

"I'm afraid there's been some trouble here. I have Seth DeLauter in my office."

"What kind of trouble?"

"Seth was in a fight with another student. He's being suspended. Mr. Quinn, I'd appreciate it if you could come to my office so matters can be explained to you and you can take Seth home."

"Great. Wonderful." At his wits' end, Cam dragged a hand through his hair. "On my way."

The school hadn't changed much, Cam noted, since he'd done time there. The first morning he'd passed through those heavy front doors, Stella Quinn had all but dragged him.

He was nearly eighteen years older now, and no more enthusiastic.

The floors were faded linoleum, the light bright from wide windows. And the smell was of contraband candy and kid sweat.

Cam jammed his hands in his pockets and headed for the administration offices. He knew the way. After all, he'd beaten a path to those offices countless times during his stay at St. Chris Middle.

It wasn't the same old eagle-eyed secretary manning the desk in the outer room. This one was younger, perkier, and beamed smiles all over him. "May I help you?" she asked in a bouncing voice.

"I'm here to post bail for Seth DeLauter."

She blinked at that, and her smile turned puzzled. "I beg your pardon?"

"Cameron Quinn to see the VP."

"Oh, you mean Mrs. Moorefield. Yes, she's expecting you. Second door down the little hallway there. On the right." Her phone rang and she plucked it up. "Good morning," she sang, "St. Christopher's Middle School. This is Kathy speaking."

Cam decided he preferred the battle-ax who had guarded the offices in his day to this terminally pert newcomer. Even as he started toward the door, his back went up, his jaw set—and his palms went damp.

Some things, he supposed, never changed.

Mrs. Moorefield was sitting behind her desk, calmly entering data into a computer. Cam thought her fingers moved efficiently. And the movement suited her. She was neat and trim, probably early fifties. Her hair was short and sleek and light brown, her face composed and quietly attractive.

Her gold wedding band caught the light as her fingers moved over the keys. The only other jewelry she wore were simple gold shells at her ears.

Across the room, Seth was slumped in a chair, staring up at the ceiling. Trying to look bored, Cam assumed, but coming off as sulky. Kid needed a haircut, he realized and wondered who was supposed to deal with that. He was wearing jeans frayed to strings at the cuffs, a jersey two sizes too big, and incredibly dirty high-tops.

It looked perfectly normal to Cam.

He rapped on the doorjamb. Both the vice principal and Seth glanced over, with two dramatically different expressions. Mrs. Moorefield smiled in polite welcome. Seth sneered.

"Mr. Quinn."

"Yeah." Then he remembered he was supposed to be here as a responsible guardian. "I hope we can straighten this out, Mrs. Moorefield." He stuck his own polite smile into place as he stepped to her desk and offered a hand.

"I appreciate your coming in so quickly. When we have to take regrettable disciplinary action such as this against a student, we want the parents or responsible parties to have the opportunity to understand the situation. Please, Mr. Quinn, sit down."

"What is the situation?" Cam took his seat and found he didn't like it any more than he used to.

"I'm afraid Seth physically attacked another student this morning between classes. The other boy is being treated by the school nurse, and his parents have been informed."

Cam lifted a brow. "So where are they?"

"Both of Robert's parents are at work at the moment. But in any case—"

"Why?"

Her smile returned, small, attentive, questioning. "Why, Mr. Quinn?"

"Why did Seth slug Robert?"

Mrs. Moorefield sighed. "I understand you've only recently taken over as Seth's guardian, so you may not be aware that this isn't the first time he's fought with other students."

"I know about it. I'm asking about this incident."

"Very well." She folded her hands. "According to Robert, Seth demanded that Robert give him a dollar, and when Robert refused to pay him, Seth attacked him. At this point," she added, shifting her gaze to Seth, "Seth has neither confirmed nor denied. School policy requires that students be suspended for three days as a disciplinary action when involved in a fight on school premises."

"Okay." Cam rose, but when Seth started to get up, he pointed a finger. "Stay," he ordered, then crouched until they were eye to eye. "You try to shake this kid down?"

Seth jerked a shoulder. "That's what he says."

"You slugged him."

"Yeah, I slugged him. Went for the nose," he added with a thin smile, and shoved at the straw-colored hair that flopped into his eyes. "It hurts more."

"Why'd you do it?"

"Maybe I didn't like his fat face."

With his patience as frayed as Seth's jeans, Cam gripped Seth by the shoulders. When Seth winced and hissed in a breath, alarm bells went off. Before Seth could evade him, Cam tugged the arm of the oversized jersey down. Nasty little bruises—knuckle rappers, Cam would have called them— ran from Seth's shoulder to his elbow.

"Get off me." His face heated with shame, Seth squirmed, but Cam merely shifted him. Scrapes were scored high on Seth's back, red and raw.

"Hold still." Cam moved his grip and laid his hands on the arms of the chair. His eyes stayed on Seth. "You tell me what went down. And don't even think about lying to me."

"I don't want to talk about it."

"I didn't ask you what you wanted. I'm telling you to spill it. Or," he said, lowering his voice so only Seth could hear, "are you going to let that punk get away clean?"

Seth opened his mouth, closed it again. He had to set his jaw so it wouldn't wobble. "He was pissed off. We had this history test the other day and I aced it. An idiot could've gotten an ace, but he's less than an idiot and he flunked. So he kept hassling me, dogged me down the hall, jabbing at me. I walked away because I'm sick to death of ISS."

"Of what?"

Seth rolled his eyes. "In-School Suspension. It's boring. I didn't want to do more time, so I walked. But he kept jabbing and calling me names. Egghead, teacher's pet, and all that shit. Didn't let it bother me. But then he shoved me back against the lockers and he said I was just a son of a whore and everybody knew it, so I decked him."

Shamed and sick, he jerked a defiant shoulder. "So I get a three-day vacation. Big deal."

Cam nodded and rose. When he turned around his eyes were nearly black with fury. "You're not suspending this kid for defending himself against an ignorant bully. And if you try, I'll go over your head to the Board of Education."

Shocked to the core, Seth stared up at Cam. Nobody had ever stood up for him. He'd never expected anyone to stand up for him.

"Mr. Quinn—"

"Nobody calls my brother a son of a whore, Mrs. Moorefield. And if you don't have a school policy against vicious name-calling and harassment, you damn well should. So I'm telling you, you better take another look at this situation. And you better rethink just who gets suspended here. *And* you can tell little Robert's parents that if they don't want their kid crying over a bloody nose, they better teach him some manners."

She took a moment before speaking. She'd been teaching and counseling children for nearly thirty years. What she saw on Seth's face at that moment was hope, stunned and wary, but hope nonetheless. It was a look she didn't want to extinguish.

"Mr. Quinn, you can be certain that I will investigate this matter further. I wasn't aware that Seth had been injured. If you'd like to take him down to the nurse while I speak with Robert and . . . others—"

"I can take care of him."

"As you wish. I'll hold the suspension in abeyance until I've satisfied myself with the facts."

"You do that, Mrs. Moorefield. But I'm satisfied with the facts. Now I'm taking Seth home for the rest of the day. He's had enough."

"I agree with you."

The child hadn't looked shaken when he'd come into her office, she thought. He'd looked cocky. He hadn't looked shaken when she'd told him to sit down and called his home. He'd looked belligerent.

But he looked shaken now, finally, with his eyes wide and stunned and his hands gripping the arms of the chair. The thin, hard shield he'd kept tight around him, a shield neither she nor any of his teachers had been able to so much as scratch, appeared to be deeply dented.

Now, she decided, they would see what they could do for him.

"If you will bring Seth into school in the morning and meet with me here, we'll resolve the matter."

"We'll be here. Let's go," he said to Seth and headed out.

As they walked down the hall toward the front doors, their footsteps echoed hollowly. Cam glanced down, noted that Seth was staring at his shoes.

"Still gives me the creeps," he said.

Seth shoved at the door. "What?"

"The way it sounds when you take the long walk to the VP's office."

Seth snorted, hunched his shoulders and kept walking. His stomach felt as if a thousand butterflies had gone to war inside it.

The American flag on the pole near the parking lot snapped in the wind. From an open window behind them, the pathetically off-key sounds of a mid-morning music class clamored. The elementary school was separated from the middle by a narrow swatch of grass and a few sad-looking evergreen bushes.

Across the small outdoor track stood the brown brick of the high school. It seemed smaller now, Cam noted, almost quaint, and not at all like the prison he'd once imagined it to be.

He remembered leaning lazily against the hood of his first secondhand car in the parking lot and watching girls. Walking through those noisy hallways from class to class, and watching girls. Sitting in the butt-numbing chairs during brain-numbing classes. And watching girls.

The fact that his high school experience came back to him in a parade of varying female forms made him almost sentimental.

Then a bell rang shrilly, and the noise level through the open windows behind him erupted. Sentiment dried up quickly. Thank God, was all he could think, that chapter of his life was over.

But it wasn't over for the kid, he remembered. And since he was here, he could try to help him through it. They opened opposite doors of the 'Vette, and Cam paused, waited for their eyes to meet. "So, do you figure you broke the asshole's nose?"

A glimmer of a smile worked around Seth's mouth. "Maybe."

"Good." Cam got in, slammed the door. "Going for the nose is fine, but if you don't want a lot of blood messing things up, go for the belly. A good, solid short arm punch to the gut won't leave as much evidence."

Seth considered the advice. "I wanted to see him bleed."

"Well, you make your choices in life. Pretty good day for a sail," he decided as he started the engine. "Might as well."

"I guess." Seth picked at the knee of his jeans. Someone had stood up for him, was all his confused mind could think. Had believed him, defended him, and taken his part. His arm hurt, his shoulders ached, but someone had taken his part. "Thanks," he muttered.

"No problem. You mess with one Quinn, you mess with them all." He glanced over as he drove out of the lot and saw Seth staring at him. "That's how it shakes down. Anyway, let's get some burgers or something to take on the boat."

"Yeah, I could eat." Seth swiped a hand under his nose. "Got a dollar?"

When Cam laughed and punched the accelerator it was one of the best moments of Seth's life.

T he wind was out of the southwest and steady so that the marsh grasses waved lazily. The sky was clear and cheerfully blue, the perfect frame for the heron that rose up, out of the waving grass over the glinting water, then down like a flashing white kite to catch an early lunch.

On impulse, Cam had tossed some fishing gear into the boat. With any luck they'd have fried fish for dinner.

Seth already knew more about sailing than Cam had expected. He shouldn't have been surprised by it, he realized. Anna had said the boy had a quick mind, and Ethan would have taught him well, and patiently.

When he saw how easily Seth handled the lines, he trusted him to trim the jib. The sails caught the wind, and Cam found speed.

God, he had missed it. The rush, the power, the control. It poured through him, clearing his mind of worries, obligations, disappointments, even grief. Water below and sky above, and his hands on the helm coaxing the wind, daring it, tricking it into giving more.

Behind him, Seth grinned and caught himself just before he yelled out in delight. He'd never gone so fast. With Ray it had been slow and steady, with Ethan work and wonder. But this was a wild, free ride, rising and falling with the waves, shooting like a long white bullet to anywhere.

The wind nearly took his cap, so he turned the bill backward so the breeze wouldn't catch it and flip it away.

They skimmed across the shoreline, passed the waterfront docks that were the hub of St. Chris before they finally slowed. An old skipjack no longer in use was docked there, a symbol to the waterman's way of life.

The men and women who harvested the bay brought their day's catch there. Flounder and sea trout and rockfish at this time of year, and . . .

"What's the date?" Cam demanded as he glanced over his shoulder.

"Like the thirty-first." Seth shoved up his wraparound sunglasses and stared at the dock. He was hoping for a glimpse of Grace. He wanted to wave to someone he knew.

"Crab season starts tomorrow. Hot damn. Guarantee you tomorrow Ethan brings home a bushel of beauties. We'll eat like kings. You like crabs, right?"

"I dunno."

"What do you mean you don't know?" Cam popped the top of a Coke and guzzled. "Haven't you had crab before?"

"No."

"You'd better prepare your mouth for a treat, then, kid, because you'll have it tomorrow."

Mirroring Cam's move, Seth reached for a soft drink himself. "Nothing you cook's a treat."

It was said with a grin and received with one. "I can do crab just fine. Nothing to it. Boiling water, lots of spices, then you pop those snapping bastards into the pot—"

"Alive?"

"It's the only way."

"That's sick."

Cam merely shifted his stance. "They aren't alive for long. Then they're dinner. Add a six-pack of beer and you got a feast. Another few weeks, and we're talking softshell blues. You plop 'em between a couple pieces of bread and bite in."

This time Seth actually felt his stomach roll. "Not me."

"Too squeamish?"

"Too civilized."

"Shit. Sometimes on Saturday in the summer Mom and Dad used to bring us down to the docks. We'd get us some softshell crab sandwiches, a tub of peanut oil fries, and watch the tourists try to figure out what to eat. Laughed our asses off."

The memory made him suddenly sad, and he tried to shake off the mood. "Sometimes we sailed down like this. Or we'd cruise down to the river and fish. Mom wasn't much on fishing, so she'd swim, then she'd head to shore and sit on the bank and read."

"Why didn't she just stay home?"

"She liked to sail," Cam said softly. "And she liked being there."

"Ray said she got sick."

"Yeah, she got sick." Cam blew out a breath. She had been the only woman he'd ever loved, the only woman he'd ever lost. The missing of her could still creep up and cut him off at the knees.

"Come about," he ordered. "Let's head down the Annemessex and see if anything's biting."

It didn't occur to either of them that the three hours they spent on the water was the most peaceful interlude either had experienced in weeks.

And when they returned home with six fat striped bass in the cooler, they were for the first time in total harmony.

"Know how to clean them?" Cam asked.

"Maybe." Ray had taught him, but Seth was no fool. "I caught four of the six, that ought to mean you clean them."

"That's the beauty of being boss," Cam began, then stopped dead when he saw sheets snapping on the ancient clothesline. He hadn't seen anything hanging out on the line since his mother had gotten sick. For a moment he was afraid he was having another hallucination, and his mouth went dry.

Then the back door opened, and Grace Monroe stepped out on the porch.

"Hey, Grace!"

It was the first time Cam had heard Seth's voice raised in happiness and pure boyish pleasure. It surprised him enough to make him look over sharply, then nearly drop the cooler on his foot as Seth let go of his end and dashed forward.

"Hey, there." She had a warm voice that contrasted with cool looks. She was tall and slim, with long limbs she'd once dreamed of using as a dancer.

But Grace had learned to put most of her dreams aside.

Her hair was boyishly short, and that was for convenience. She didn't have the time or energy to worry about style. It was a dark, honey blond that was often streaked with paler color during the summer. Her eyes were a quiet green and all too often had shadows dogging them.

But her smile was pure and sunny and never failed to light up her face, or to set the dimple just beside her mouth winking.

A pretty woman, Cam thought, with the face of a pixie and the voice of a siren. It amazed him that men weren't throwing themselves at her feet.

The boy all but did, Cam noted, surprised when Seth just about ran into her open arms. He hugged and was hugged—this prickly kid who didn't like to be touched. Then he flushed and stepped back and began to play with the puppy, who'd followed Grace out of the house.

"Afternoon, Cam." Grace shielded her eyes from the sun with the flat of her hand. "Ethan came by the pub last night and said y'all could use a hand around here."

"You're taking over the housework."

"Well, I can give you three hours two days a week until—"

She got no further, for Cam dumped the cooler, took the steps three at a time, and grabbed her into a loud, enthusiastic kiss. It set Seth's teeth on edge to see it, even as Grace stuttered and laughed.

"That's nice," she managed, "but you're still going to have to pay me."

"Name your price. I adore you." He snatched her hands and planted more kisses there. "My life for you."

"I can see I'm going to be appreciated around here—and needed. I've got those pink socks soaking in some diluted bleach. Might do the trick."

"The red sock was Phil's. He's responsible. I mean, what reasonable guy even owns a pair of red socks?"

"We'll talk more about sorting laundry—and checking pockets. Someone's little black book went through the last cycle."

"Shit." He caught her arched-brow look down at the boy and cleared his throat. "Sorry. I guess it was mine."

"I made some lemonade, and I was going to put a casserole together, but it looks like you may have caught your supper."

"Tonight's, but we could do with a casserole too."

"Okay. Ethan wasn't really clear about what you'd need or want done. Maybe we should go over things."

"Darling, you do whatever you think we need, and it'll be more than we can ever repay."

She'd already seen that for herself. Pink underwear, she mused, dust an inch thick on one table and unidentified substances sticking to another. And the stove? God only knew when it had last been cleaned.

It was good to be needed, she thought. Good to know just what had to be done. "We'll take it as it goes, then. I may have to bring the baby along sometimes. Julie minds her at night when I'm working at the pub, but I can't always find somebody to take her otherwise. She's a good girl."

"I can help you watch her," Seth offered. "I get home from school at three-thirty."

"Since when?" Cam wanted to know, and Seth shrugged.

"When I don't have ISS."

"Aubrey loves playing with you. I've got another hour here today," she said because she was a woman constantly forced to budget time. "So I'll make up that casserole and put it in the freezer. All you have to do is heat it up when you want it. I'll leave you a list of cleaning supplies you're low on, or I can pick them up for you if you like."

"Pick them up for us?" Cam could have knelt at her feet. "Want a raise?"

She laughed and started back inside. "Seth, you see that that pup stays out of the fish guts. He'll smell for a week otherwise."

"Okay, sure. I'll be finished in a few minutes and I'll be in." He stood up, then stepped off the porch so Grace wouldn't hear him through the door. Manfully, he sized up Cam. "You're not going to start poking at her, are you?"

"Poking at her?" He was blank for a moment, then shook his head. "For God's sake." Hefting the ice chest, he started around the side of the house to the fish-cleaning table. "I've known Grace half my life, and I don't poke at every woman I see."

"Okay, then."

It was the boy's tone that made Cam run his tongue around his teeth as he set the cooler down. Possessive, proprietary, and satisfied. "So . . . you got your eye on her yourself, huh?"

Seth colored a little, opened the drawer for the fish scaler. "I just look out for her, that's all."

"She sure is pretty," Cam said lightly and had the pleasure of seeing Seth's eyes flash with jealousy. "But as it happens I'm poking at another woman right now, and it gets sticky if you try that with more than one at a time. And this particular female is going to take a lot of convincing."

EIGHT

He decided to get started on poking at Anna. Since she was on his mind, Cam left Seth to deal with the last couple of fish on his own and wandered inside. He made appreciative noises at whatever Grace was putting together over at the stove, then wandered upstairs.

He'd have a little more privacy on the phone in his room. And Anna's business card was in his pocket.

At the door to his room, he stopped and could have wept with gratitude. Since his bed was freshly made, the plain green spread professionally smoothed, the pillows plumped, he knew some of the sheets hanging out on the line were his.

Tonight he would sleep on fresh, clean sheets he hadn't even had to launder. It made the prospect of sleeping alone a little more tolerable.

The surface of his old oak dresser wasn't just dust-free. It gleamed. The bookshelves that still held most of his trophies and some of his favorite novels had been tidied, and the overstuffed chair he'd taken to using as a catchall was now empty. He hadn't a clue where she'd put his things, but he imagined he'd find them in their logical place.

He supposed he'd gotten spoiled living in hotels over the last few years, but it did his heart good to walk into his bedroom and not see a half a dozen testy little chores waiting for attention.

Things where looking up, so he plopped down on the bed, stretched out, and reached for the phone.

"Anna Spinelli." Her voice was low, professionally neutral. He closed his eyes to better fantasize how she looked. He liked the idea of imagining her behind some bureaucratic desk wearing that tight little blue number she'd had on the night before.

"Miz Spinelli. How do you feel about crabs?"

"Ah . . ."

"Let me rephrase that." He scooted down until he was nearly flat and realized he could be asleep in five minutes without really trying. "How do you feel about eating steamed crabs?"

"I feel favorable."

"Good. How about tomorrow night?"

"Cameron—"

"Here," he specified. "At the house. The house that's never empty. Tomorrow's the first day of crab season. Ethan'll bring home a bushel. We'll cook them up. You can see how the Quinns—what would you call it?—relate, interact. See how Seth's getting along—acclimating to this particular home environment."

"That's very good."

"Hey, I've dealt with social workers before. Of course, never one who wore blue high heels, but . . ."

"I was off the clock," she reminded him. "However, I think dinner might be a workable idea. What time?"

"Six-thirty or thereabouts." He heard the flap of papers and found himself slightly annoyed that she was checking her calendar.

"All right, I can do that. Six-thirty."

She sounded entirely too much like a social worker making an appointment to suit him. "You alone in there?"

"In my office? Yes, at the moment. Why?"

"Just wondering. I've been wondering about you on and off all day. Why don't you let me come into town and get you tomorrow, then I could drive you home. We could stop and—I'd say climb into the backseat, but the 'Vette doesn't have one. Still, I think we could manage."

"I'm sure we could. Which is why I'll drive myself down."

"I'm going to have to get my hands on you again."

"I don't doubt that's going to happen. Eventually. In the meantime—"

"I want you."

"I know."

Because her voice had thickened and didn't sound quite so prim, he smiled. "Why don't I tell you just what I'd like to do to you? I can go step by step. You can even take notes in your little book for future reference."

"I . . . think we'd better postpone that. Though I may be interested in discussing it at another time. I'm afraid I have an appointment in a few minutes. I'll see you and your family tomorrow evening."

"Give me ten minutes alone with you, Anna." He whispered it. "Ten minutes to touch you."

"I—we can try for that time frame tomorrow. I have to go. Good-bye."

" 'Bye." Pleased that he'd rattled her, he slid the phone back on the hook and let himself drift off into a well-deserved nap.

◌◍

He was awakened just over an hour later by the slamming of the front door and Phillip's raised and furious voice.

"Home, sweet home," Cam muttered and rolled out of bed. He stumbled to the door and down the hall to the steps. He was a lousy napper, and whenever he indulged he woke up groggy, irritable, and in desperate need of coffee.

By the time he got downstairs, Phillip was in the kitchen uncorking a bottle of wine. "Where the hell is everybody?" Phillip demanded.

"I dunno. Get out of my way." Rubbing one hand over his face, Cam poured the dregs of the pot into a mug, stuck the mug in the microwave, and punched numbers at random.

"I've been informed by the insurance company that they're holding the claim until such time as an investigation is complete."

Cam stared at the microwave, willing those endless two minutes to pass so he could gulp caffeine. His bleary brain took in insurance, claim, investigation, and couldn't correlate the terms. "Huh?"

"Pull yourself together, damn it." Phillip gave him an impatient shove. "They won't process Dad's policy because they suspect suicide."

"That's bullshit. He told me he didn't kill himself."

"Oh, really?" Sick and furious, Phillip still managed to raise an ironic eyebrow. "Did you have this conversation with him before or after he died?"

Cam caught himself, but very nearly flushed. Instead he cursed again and yanked open the microwave door. "I mean, there's no way he would have, and they're just stalling because they don't want to pay off."

"The point is, they're not paying off at this time. Their investigator's been talking to people, and some of those people were apparently delighted to tell him the seamier details of the situation. And they know about the letter from Seth's mother—the payments Dad made to her."

"So." He sipped coffee, scalded the roof of his mouth, and swore. "Hell with it. Let them keep their fucking blood money."

"It's not as simple as that. Number one is if they don't pay, it goes down that Dad committed suicide. Is that what you want?"

"No." Cam pinched the bridge of his nose to try to relieve some of the pressure that was building. He'd lived most of his life without headaches, and now it seemed he was plagued with them.

"Which means we'd have to accept their conclusions, or we'd have to take them to court to prove he didn't, and it'd be one hell of a public mess."

Struggling to calm himself, Phillip sipped his wine. "Either way it smears his name. I think we're going to have to find this woman—Gloria DeLauter—after all. We have to clear this up."

"What makes you think finding her and talking to her is going to clear this up?"

"We have to get the truth out of her."

"How, through torture?" Not that it didn't have its appeal. "Besides, the kid's scared of her," Cam added. "She comes around, she could screw up the guardianship."

"And if she doesn't come around we might never know the truth, all of the truth." He needed to know it, Phillip thought, so he could begin to accept it.

"Here's the truth as I see it." Cam slammed his mug down. "This woman was looking for an easy mark and figured she'd found one. Dad fell for the kid, wanted to help him. So he went to bat for him, just the way he did for us, and she kept hitting him up for more. I figure he was upset coming home that day, worried, distracted. He was driving too fast, misjudged, lost control, whatever. That's all there is to it."

"Life's not as simple as you live it, Cam. You don't just start in one spot, then finish in the other as fast as you can. Curves and detours and road-blocks. You better start thinking about them."

"Why? That's all you ever think about, and it seems to me we've ended up in exactly the same place."

Phillip let out a sigh. It was hard to argue with that, so he decided a second glass of wine was in order. "Whatever you think, we've got a mess on our hands and we're going to have to deal with it. Where's Seth?"

"I don't know where he is. Around."

"Christ, Cam, around where? You're supposed to keep an eye on him."

"I've had my eye on him all damn day. He's around." He walked to the back door, scanned the yard, scowled when he didn't see Seth. "Probably around front, or taking a walk or something. I'm not keeping the kid on a leash."

"This time of day he should be doing his homework. You've only got to watch out for him on your own a couple of hours after school."

"It didn't work out that way today. There was a little holiday from school."

"He hooked? You let him hook when we've got Social Services sniffing around?"

"No, he didn't hook." Disgusted, Cam turned back. "Some little jerk at school kept razzing him, poked bruises all over him and called him a son of a whore."

Phillip's stance shifted immediately, from mild annoyance to righteous fury. His gilt eyes glittered, his mouth thinned. "What little jerk? Who the hell is he?"

"Some fat-faced kid named Robert. Seth slugged him, and they said they were going to suspend him for it."

"Hell they are. Who the hell's principal now, some Nazi?"

Cam had to smile. When push came to shove, you could always count on Phillip. "She didn't seem to be. After I went down and we got the whole story out of Seth, she shifted ground some. I'm taking him back in tomorrow for another little conference."

Now Phillip grinned, wide and wicked. "You? Cameron Kick-Ass Quinn is going in for a parent conference at the middle school. Oh, to be a fly on the wall!"

"You won't have to be, because you're coming too."

Phillip swallowed wine hastily before he choked. "What do you mean, I'm coming?"

"And so's Ethan," Cam decided on the spot. "We're all going. United front. Yeah, that's just the way it's going to be."

"I've got an appointment—"

"Break it. There's the kid." He spotted Seth coming out of the woods with Foolish beside him. "He's just been fooling around with the dog. Ethan ought to be along any minute, and I'm tagging him for this deal."

Phillip scowled into his wine. "I hate it when you're right. We all go."

"It should be a fun morning." Satisfied, Cam gave Phillip a friendly punch on the arm. "We're the big guys this time. And when we win this little battle with authority, we can celebrate tomorrow night—with a bushel of crabs."

Phillip's mood lightened. "April Fool's Day. Crab season opens. Oh, yeah."

"We got fresh fish tonight—I caught it, you cook it. I want a shower." Cam rolled his shoulders. "Miz Spinelli's coming to dinner tomorrow."

"Uh-huh, well, you—what?" Phillip whirled as Cam started out of the room. "You asked the social worker to dinner? Here?"

"That's right. Told you I like her looks."

Phillip could only close his eyes. "For God's sake, you're hitting on the social worker."

"She's hitting on me, too." Cam flashed a grin. "I like it."

"Cam, not to put down your warped idea of romance, but use your head. We've got this problem with the insurance company. And we've got a problem with Seth at school. How's that's going to play to Social Services?"

"We don't tell them about the first, and we give them the straight story on the second. I think that's going to go over just fine with Miz Spinelli. She's going to love it that the three of us went in to stand for Seth."

Phillip opened his mouth, reconsidered, and nodded. "You're right. That's good." Then as new thoughts began to play, he angled his head. "Maybe you could use your . . . influence on her to get her to move this case study along, get the system out of our hair."

Cam said nothing for a moment, surprised at how angry even the suggestion of it made him. So his voice was quiet. "I'm not using anything on her, and it's going to stay that way. One situation has nothing to do with the other. That's staying that way too."

When Cam strode off, Phillip pursed his lips. Well, he thought, wasn't that interesting?

A s Ethan guided his boat toward the dock, he spotted Seth in the yard. Beside Ethan, Simon gave a high, happy bark. Ethan ruffled his fur. "Yeah, fella, almost home now."

While he worked the sails, Ethan watched the boy toss sticks for the pup. There had always been a dog in this yard to chase sticks or balls, to wrestle in the grass with. He remembered Dumbo, the sweet-faced retriever he'd fallen madly in love with when he'd come to the Quinns.

He'd been the first dog to play with, to be comforted by, in Ethan's life. From Dumbo he'd learned the meaning of unconditional love, had certainly trusted the dog long before he'd trusted Ray and Stella Quinn or the boys who would become his brothers.

He imagined Seth felt much the same. You could always depend on your dog.

When he'd come here all those years ago, damaged in body and soul, he had no hope that his life would really change. Promises, reassurances, decent meals, and decent people meant nothing to him. So he'd considered ending that life.

The water had drawn him even then. He imagined himself walking out into it, drifting out until it was over his head. He didn't know how to swim then, so it would have been simple. Just sinking down and down and down until there was nothing.

But the night he'd slipped out to do it, the dog had come with him. Licking his hand, pressing that warm, furry body against his legs. And Dumbo had brought him a stick, tail wagging, big brown eyes hopeful. The first time, Ethan threw the stick high and far and in fury. But Dumbo chased it happily and brought it back. Tail wagging.

He threw it again, then again, then dozens of times. Then he simply sat down on the grass, and in the moonlight cried his heart out, clutching the dog like a lifeline.

The need to end it had passed.

A dog, Ethan thought now as he rubbed a hand over Simon's head, could be a glorious thing.

He saw Seth turn, catch sight of the boat. There was the briefest of hesitations, then the boy lifted a hand in greeting and with the pup raced to the dock.

"Secure the lines, mate."

"Aye, aye." Seth handled the lines Ethan tossed out competently enough, slipping the loop over the post. "Cam said how you'd be bringing crabs tomorrow."

"Did he?" Ethan smiled a little, pushed back his fielder's cap. Thick brown hair tickled the collar of his work-stained shirt. "Go on, boy," he murmured to the dog, who was sitting, vibrating in place as he waited for the command to abandon ship. With a celebrational bark, Simon leaped into the water and swam to shore. "As it turns out, he's right. Winter wasn't too hard and the water's warming up. We'll pull in plenty. Should be a good day."

Leaning over the side, he pulled up a crab pot that dangled from the dock. "No winter hair."

"Hair, why would there be hair in an old chicken wire box?"

"Pot. It's a crab pot. If I pulled this up and it was hairy—full of blond seaweed—it'd mean the water was too cold yet for crabs. Seen them that way, nearly into May, if there's been a bad winter. That kind of spring, it's hard to make a living on the water."

"But not this spring, because the water's warm enough for crabs."

"Seems to be. You can bait this pot later—chicken necks or fish parts do the job fine—and in the morning we may just find us a couple of crabs sulking inside. They fall for it every time."

Seth knelt down, wanting a closer look. "That's pretty stupid. They look like big ugly bugs, so I guess they're bug-dumb."

"Just more hungry than smart, I'd say."

"And Cam says you boil them alive. No way I'm eating those."

"Suit yourself. Me, I figure on going through about two dozen come tomorrow night." He let the pot slip back into the water, then leaped expertly from boat to dock.

"Grace was here. She cleaned the house and stuff."

"Yeah?" He imagined the house would smell lightly of lemon. Grace's house always did.

"Cam kissed her, right on the mouth."

Ethan stopped walking, looked down at Seth's face. "What?"

"Smackaroo. It made her laugh. It was like a joke, I guess."

"Like a joke, sure." He shrugged and ignored the hard, sick ball in his gut. None of his business who Grace kissed. Nothing to do with him. But he found his jaw clenched when Cam, hair dripping, stepped out on the back porch.

"How's the crab business looking?"

"It'll do," Ethan said shortly.

Cam lifted his brows at the tone. "What, did one crawl out of the pot early and up your butt?"

"I want a shower and a beer." Ethan moved past him and into the house.

"Woman's coming for dinner tomorrow."

That stopped Ethan again, and he turned, keeping the screen door between them. "Who?"

"Anna Spinelli."

"Shit," was Ethan's only comment as he walked away.

"Why's she coming? What does she want?" Panic rose up inside Seth like a fountain and spewed out in his voice before he could stop it.

"She's coming because I asked her, and she wants a crab dinner." Cam tucked his thumbs in his pockets, rocked back on his heels. Why the hell was he the one who always had to handle this white-faced fear? "I figure she wants to see if all we do around here is fart and scratch and spit. We can probably hold off on that for one evening. You gotta remember to put the toilet seat down, though. Women really hate when you don't. They make it a social and political statement if you leave it up. Go figure."

Some of the tension eased out of Seth's face. "So, she's just, like, coming to see if we're slobs. And Grace cleaned everything up and you're not cooking, so it's mostly okay."

"It'll be more than mostly if you watch that foul mouth of yours."

"Yours is just as foul."

"Yeah, but you're shorter than I am. And I don't intend to ask you to pass the fucking potatoes in front of her."

Seth snorted at that, and his rock-hard shoulders relaxed. "Are you going to tell her about that shit in school today?"

Cam blew out a breath. "Practice finding an alternate word for 'shit,' just for tomorrow night. Yeah, I'm going to tell her what happened in school. And I'm telling her that Phil and Ethan and I went in with you tomorrow to deal with it."

This time all Seth could do was blink. "All of you? You're all going?"

"That's right. Like I said, you mess with one Quinn, you mess with them all."

It shocked and appalled and terrified them both when tears sprang to

Seth's eyes. They swam there for a moment, blurring that deep, bright blue. Instantly both of them stuck their hands in their pockets and turned away.

"I have to do . . . something," Cam said, groping. "You go . . . wash your hands or whatever. We'll be eating pretty soon."

Just as he worked up the nerve to turn, intending to lay a hand on Seth's shoulder, to say something that would undoubtedly make them both feel like idiots, the boy darted inside and rushed through the kitchen.

Cam pressed his fingers to his eyes, massaged his temples, dropped his arms. "Jesus, I've got to get back to a race where I know what I'm doing." He took a step toward the door, then shook his head and walked quickly away from it. He didn't want to go inside with all that emotion, all that need, swirling in the air.

God, what he wanted was his freedom back, to wake up and find it had all been a dream. Better, to wake up in some huge, anonymous hotel bed in some exotic city with a hot, naked woman beside him.

But when he tried to picture it, the bed was the same one he slept in now, and the woman was Anna.

As a substitute it wasn't such a bad deal, but . . . it didn't make the rest of it go away. He glanced up at the windows of the second floor as he walked around the house. The kid was up there, pulling himself together. And he was out here, trying to do the same thing.

The look the kid had shot him, Cam thought, just before things got sloppy. It had stirred up his gut. He'd have sworn he'd seen trust there, and a pathetic, almost desperate gratitude that both humbled and terrified him.

What the hell was he going to do with it? And when things settled down and he could pick up his own life again . . . That had to happen, he assured himself. Had to. He couldn't stay in charge like this. Couldn't be expected to live like this forever. He had places to go, races to run, risks to take.

Once they had everything under control, once they did what needed to be done for the kid and got this business Ethan wanted established, he'd be free to come and go as he pleased again.

A few more months, he decided, maybe a year, then he was out of here. No one could possibly expect more from him.

Not even himself.

NINE

Vice Principal Moorefield studied the three men who stood like a well-mortared wall in her office. The outward appearance would never indicate they were brothers. One wore a trim gray suit and perfectly knotted tie, another a black shirt and jeans, and the third faded khakis and a wrinkled denim work shirt.

But she could see that at the moment they were as united as triplets in the womb.

"I realize you have busy schedules. I appreciate all of you coming in this morning."

"We want to get this straightened out, Mrs. Moorefield." Phillip kept a mild, negotiating smile on his face. "Seth needs to be in school."

"I agree. After Seth's statement yesterday, I did some checking. It does appear as though Robert instigated the incident. There does seem to be some question over the motivation. The matter of the petty extortion—"

Cam held up a hand. "Seth, did you tell this Robert character to give you a dollar?"

"Nah." Seth tucked his thumbs in his front pockets, as he'd seen Cam do. "I don't need his money. I don't even talk to him unless he gets in my face."

Cam looked back at Mrs. Moorefield. "Seth says he aced that test and Robert flunked. Is that right?"

The vice principal folded her hands on her desk. "Yes. The test papers were handed back yesterday just before the end of class, and Seth received the highest grade. Now—"

"Seems to me," Ethan interrupted in a quiet voice, "that Seth told you straight, then. Excuse me, ma'am, but if the other boy lied about some of it, could be he's lying about all of it. Seth says the boy came after him, and he did. He said it was about this test, so I figure it is."

"I've considered that, and I tend to agree with you, Mr. Quinn. I've spoken with Robert's mother. She's no happier than you are about this incident, or about the fact that both boys are to be suspended."

"You're not suspending Seth." Cam planted his feet. "Not over this—not without a fight."

"I understand how you feel. However, blows were exchanged. Physical violence can't be permitted here."

"I'd agree with you, Mrs. Moorefield, under most circumstances." Phillip laid a hand on Cam's arm to prevent him from stepping forward. "However, Seth was being physically and verbally attacked. He defended himself. There should have been a teacher monitoring the hallway during the change of classes. He should have been able to depend on an adult, on the system to protect him. Why didn't one come forward to do so?"

Moorefield puffed out her cheeks, blew out a breath. "That's a reasonable question, Mr. Quinn. I won't start weeping to you about budget cuts, but it's impossible, with a staff of our size, to monitor all the children at all times."

"I sympathize with your problem, but Seth shouldn't have to pay for it."

"There's been a rough time recently," Ethan put in. "I don't figure that kicking the boy out of school for a couple days is going to help him any. Education's supposed to be more than learning—leastways that's how we were taught. It's supposed to help build your character and help teach you how to get on in the world. If it tells you that you get booted for doing what you had to, for standing up for yourself, then something's wrong with the system."

"You punish him the same way you punish the boy who started it," Cam said, "you're telling him there's not much difference between right and wrong. That's not the kind of school I want my brother in."

Moorefield steepled her hands, looked over the tips of her fingers at the three men, then down at Seth. "Your evaluation tests were excellent, and your grades are well above average. However, your teachers say you rarely turn in homework assignments and even more rarely participate in class discussion."

"We're dealing with the homework." Cam gave Seth a subtle nudge. "Right?"

"Yeah, I guess. I don't see why—"

"You don't have to see." Cam cut him off with one lowering glance. "You just have to do it. We can't sit in the classroom with him and make him open his mouth, but he'll turn in his homework."

"I imagine he will," she murmured. "This is what I'll agree to do. Seth, because I believe you, you won't be suspended. But you will go on a thirty-day probation. If there are no more disruptive incidents, and your teachers report that you have improved your at-home-assignment record—we'll put this matter aside. However, your first homework assignment comes now and from me. You have one week to write a five-hundred-word essay on the violence in our society and the need for peaceful resolutions to problems."

"Oh, man—"

"Shut up," Cam ordered mildly. "That's fair," he said to Mrs. Moorefield. "We appreciate it."

☙

"That wasn't so bad." Phillip stepped back into the sunlight and rolled his shoulders.

"Speak for yourself." Ethan snugged his cap back on his head. "I was sweating bullets. I don't want to have to do that again in this lifetime. Drop me off at the waterfront. I can get a ride out to the boat. Jim's working her, and he ought to have pulled in a nice mess of crabs by now."

"Just make sure you bring us home our share." Cam piled into Phillip's shiny navy blue Land Rover. "And don't forget we've got company coming."

"Not going to forget," Ethan mumbled. "Principals in the morning, social workers in the evening. Christ Jesus. Every time you turn around, you have to talk to somebody."

"I intend to keep Miz Spinelli occupied."

Ethan turned around to look at Cam. "You just can't leave females alone, can you?"

"What would be the point? They're here."

Ethan only sighed. "Somebody better pick up more beer."

☙

Cam volunteered to get the beer late that afternoon. It wasn't altruism. He didn't think he could stand listening to Phillip another five minutes. Going to the market was the best way to get out of the house and away from the tension while Phillip drafted and perfected a letter to the insurance company on his snazzy little laptop computer.

"Get some salad stuff while you're out," Phillip shouted, causing Cam to turn back and poke his head in the kitchen where Phillip was typing away at the table.

"What do you mean, salad stuff?"

"Field greens—for God's sake, don't come back here with a head of iceberg and a couple of tasteless hothouse tomatoes. I made up a nice vinaigrette the other day, but there's not a damn thing around here to put it on. Get some plum tomatoes if they look decent."

"What the hell do we need all that for?"

Phillip sighed and stopped typing. "First, because we want to live long and healthy lives, and second, because you invited a woman to dinner—a woman who's going to look at how we deal with Seth's nutritional needs."

"Then you go to the goddamn store."

"Fine. You write this goddamn letter."

He'd rather be burned alive. "Field greens, for sweet Christ's sake."

"And get some sourdough bread. And we're nearly out of milk. Since I'm going to be bringing my juicer the next time I get back to Baltimore, pick up some fresh fruit, some carrots, zucchini. I'll just make a list."

"Hold it, hold it." Cam felt the controls slipping out of his hands and struggled to shift his grip. "I'm just going for beer."

"Whole wheat bagels," Phillip muttered, busily writing.

Thirty minutes later, Cam found himself pondering the produce section of the grocery store. What the hell was the difference between green leaf and romaine lettuce, and why should he care? In defense, he began loading the cart at random.

Since that worked for him, he did the same thing through the aisles. By the time he reached checkout, he had two carts, overflowing with cans, boxes, bottles, and bags.

"My goodness, you must be having a party."

"Big appetites," he told the checkout clerk, and after a quick search of his brain pegged her. "How's it going, Mrs. Wilson?"

"Oh, fair enough." She ran items expertly over the belt and scanner and into bags, her quick, red-tipped fingers moving like lightning. "Too pretty a day to be stuck inside here, I can tell you that. I get off in an hour and I'm going out chicken-necking with my grandson."

"We're counting on having crab for dinner ourselves. Probably should have bought some chicken necks for the pot off our dock."

"Ethan'll keep you supplied, I imagine. I'm awful sorry about Ray," she added. "Didn't really get to tell you so after the funeral. We're sure going to miss him. He used to come in here once or twice a week after Stella passed, buy himself a pile of those microwave meals. I'd tell him, 'Ray, you got to do better for yourself than that. A man needs a good slab of meat now and then.' But it's a hard thing cooking for one when you're used to family."

"Yeah." It was all Cam could say. He'd been family, and he hadn't been there.

"Always had some story to tell about one of you boys. Showed me pictures and things from foreign newspapers on you. Racing here, racing there. And I'd say, 'Ray, how do you know if the boy won or not when it's written in I-talian or Fran-say?' We'd just laugh."

She checked the weight on a bag of apples, keyed them in. "How's that young boy? What's his name, now? Sam?"

"Seth," Cam murmured. "He's fine."

"Good-looking boy. I said to Mr. Wilson when Ray brought him home, 'That's Ray Quinn for you, always keeping his door open.' Don't know how a man of his age expected to handle a boy like that, but if anybody could, Ray Quinn could. He and Stella handled the three of you."

Because she smiled and winked, he smiled back. "They did. We tried to give them plenty to handle."

"I expect they loved every minute of it. And I expect the boy, Seth, was company for Ray after y'all grew up and lit out. I want you to know I don't hold with what some people are saying. No, I don't."

Her mouth thinned as she rang up three jumbo boxes of cold cereal. With a cluck of her tongue and a shake of her head, she continued. "I tell them straight to their face if they do that nasty gossiping in my hearing that if they had a Christian bone in their body, they'd mind their tongues."

Her eyes glittered with fury and loyalty. "Don't you pay any mind to that talk, Cameron, no mind at all. Why the idea that Ray would have had truck with that woman, that the boy was his by blood. Not one decent mind's going to believe that, or that he'd run into that pole on purpose. Makes me just sick to hear it."

It was making Cam sick now. He wished to God he'd never come in the store. "Some people believe lies, Mrs. Wilson. Some people would rather believe them."

"That they do." She nodded her head twice, sharply. "And even if they don't, they like to spread them around. I want you to know that Mr. Wilson and me considered Ray and Stella good friends and good people. Anybody says something I don't like about them around me's going to get their ears boxed."

He had to smile. "As I remember, you were good at that."

She laughed now, a kind of happy hoot. "Boxed yours that time you came sniffing too close to my Caroline. Don't think I didn't know what you were after, boy."

"Caroline was the prettiest girl in tenth grade."

"She's still a picture. It's her boy I'm going chicken-necking with. He'll be four this summer. And she's carrying her second into the sixth month now. Time does go right by."

It seemed it did, Cam thought when he was back at home and hauling bags of groceries into the house. He knew Mrs. Wilson had meant everything she'd said for the best, but she had certainly managed to depress him.

If someone who'd been a staunch friend of his parents was being told such filthy lies, they were spreading more quickly, and more thickly, than he'd imagined. How long could they be ignored before denials had to be given and a stand taken?

Now he was afraid they would have no choice but to take Phillip's advice and find Seth's mother.

The kid was going to hate that, Cam knew. And what would happen to the trust he'd seen swimming in Seth's eyes?

"Guess you want a hand with that stuff." Phillip stepped into the kitchen. "I was on the phone. The lawyer. Temporary guardianship's a lock. There's step one anyway."

"Great." He started to relay the conversation in the grocery store, then decided to let it ride for the night. Goddamn it, they'd won two battles that day. He wasn't going to see the rest of the evening spoiled by wagging tongues.

"More out in the car," he told Phillip.

"More what?"

"Bags."

"More?" Phillip stared at the half dozen loaded brown bags. "Jesus, Cam, I didn't have more than twenty items on that list."

"So I added to it." He pulled a box out, tossed it on the counter. "Nobody's going to go hungry around here for a while."

"You bought Twinkies? *Twinkies?* Are you one of the people who believe that white stuff inside them is one of the four major food groups?"

"The kid'll probably go for them."

"Sure he will. You can pay his next dentist bill."

His temper dangerously close to the edge, Cam whirled around. "Look, pal, he who goes to the store buys what he damn well pleases. That's a new rule around here. Now do you want to get that stuff out of the car or let it fucking rot?"

Phillip only lifted a brow. "Since shopping for food puts you in such a cheery mood, I'll take that little chore from now on. And we'd better start a household fund to draw from for day-to-day incidentals."

"Fine." Cam waved him away. "You do that."

When Phillip walked out, Cam began to stuff boxes and cans wherever they fit. He would let somebody else worry about organizing. In fact, he'd let anybody else worry about it. He was done for a while.

He started out, and when he hit the front door saw that Seth had arrived home. Phillip was passing him bags, and the two of them were talking as if they hadn't a care in the world.

So, he'd go out the back, he decided, let the two of them handle things for a couple of hours. As he turned, the puppy yipped at him, then squatted and peed on the rug.

"I suppose you expect me to clean that up." When Foolish wagged his tail and let his tongue loll, all Cam could do was close his eyes.

"I still say the essay's a raw deal," Seth complained as he walked into the house. "That kind of stuff's crap. And I don't see why—"

"You'll do it." Cam pulled the bag out of Seth's arms. "And I don't want to hear any bitching about it. You can get started right after you clean up the mess your dog just made on the rug."

"My dog? He's not mine."

"He is now, and you better make sure he's housebroken all the way or he stays outside."

He stalked off toward the kitchen, with Phillip, who was trying desperately not to laugh, following.

Seth stood where he was, staring down at Foolish. "Dumb dog," he murmured, and when he crouched down, the puppy launched himself into Seth's arms, where he was welcomed with a fierce hug. "You're my dog now."

⟨⊞⟩

Anna told herself she would and could be perfectly professional for the evening. She'd cleared the informal visit with Marilou, just to keep it official. And the truth was, she wanted to see Seth again. Every bit as much as she wanted to see Cam.

Different reasons, certainly, and perhaps different parts of her, but she wanted to see them both. She could handle both sides of her heart, and her mind. She'd always been able to separate areas of her life and conduct them all in a satisfactory manner.

This situation wouldn't be any different.

Verdi soared out of her speakers, wild and passionate. She rolled her window up just enough that the breeze didn't disturb her hair. She hoped the Quinns would allow her a few moments alone with Seth, so she could judge for herself, without influence, how he was feeling.

She hoped she could steal a few moments alone with Cam, so she could judge for herself how she was feeling.

Itchy, she admitted. Needy.

But it wasn't always necessary, or possible to act on feelings, however strong they might be. If, after seeing him again, she felt it best for all concerned to take a large step back, she would do so.

She had no doubt the man had an iron will. But so did Anna Spinelli. She would match herself against Cameron Quinn in that respect any day. And she could win.

Even as she reassured herself of that one single fact, Anna pulled her spiffy little car into the drive.

And Cam walked out onto the porch.

They stayed where they were for just a moment, eyeing each other. When he came off the porch and onto the walk, that hard body tucked into snug black, that dark hair unruly, those smoky eyes unreadable, her heart took one helpless spin and landed with a thud.

She wanted that tough-looking mouth on her, those rough-palmed hands on her. She wanted that all-male body pinning hers to a mattress, moving with the speed that was so much a part of his life. It was idiotic to deny it.

But she'd handle him, Anna promised herself. She only hoped she could handle herself.

She stepped out, wearing a prim, boxy suit the color of a bird's nest. Her hair was pulled up and back and ruthlessly controlled. Her unpainted lips curved in a polite, somewhat distant smile, and she carried her briefcase.

For reasons that baffled him, Cam had precisely the same reaction he'd had when she'd clipped down her hallway on stiletto heels that rainy night. Instant and raging lust.

When he started toward her, she angled her head, just a little, just enough to send the warning signal. The hands-off sign was clear as a shout.

But he leaned forward a bit when he reached her, sniffed at her hair. "You did that on purpose."

"Did what on purpose?"

"Wore the don't-touch suit and the sex goddess perfume at the same time just to drive me crazy."

"Listen to the suit, Quinn. Dream about the perfume." She started past him, then looked down coolly when his hand clamped over her arm. "You're not listening."

"I like to play games as much as the next guy, Anna." He tugged until she turned and they were again face-to-face. "But you may have picked a bad time for this one."

There was something in his eyes, she realized, something along with desire, annoyance. And because she recognized it as unhappiness, she softened. "Has something happened? What's wrong?"

"What's right?" he tossed back.

She put a hand over the one still clamped to her arm and squeezed lightly. "Rough day?"

"Yes. No. Hell." Giving up, he let her go and leaned back on the hood of her car. It was a testimony to her compassion that she was able to stifle a wince. She'd just had it washed and waxed. "There was this thing at school this morning."

"Thing?"

"You'll probably get some official report or something about it, so I want to give you our side personally."

"Uh-oh, sides. Well, let's hear it."

So he told her, found himself heating up again when he got to the point where he'd seen the bruises on Seth's arm, and ended up pushing himself off the car and stalking around it as he finished the story of how it had been resolved.

"You did very well," Anna murmured, nearly laughing when he stopped and stared at her suspiciously. "Of course hitting the other boy wasn't the answer, but—"

"I think it was a damn good answer."

"I realize that, and we'll just let it go for now. My point is, you did the responsible and the supportive thing. You went down, you listened, you convinced Seth to tell you the truth, and then you stood up for him. I doubt he was expecting you to."

"Why shouldn't I—why wouldn't I? He was right."

"Believe me, not everyone goes to bat for their children."

"He's not my kid. He's my brother."

"Not everyone goes to bat for his brother," she corrected. "The three of you going in this morning was exactly right, and again unfortunately more than everyone would do. It's a corner turned for all of you, and I suspect you understand that. Is that what's upset you?"

"No, that's piddly. Other things, doesn't matter." He could hardly tell her about the investigation into his father's death or the village gossip over it at this precarious point. Nor did he think it would count in their favor if he confessed he was feeling trapped and dreaming of escape.

"How's Seth taking it?"

"He's cool with it." Cam shrugged a shoulder. "We went sailing yesterday, did some fishing. Blew off the day."

She smiled again, and this time her heart was in it. "I'd hoped I'd be around to see it happening. You're starting to fall for him."

"What are you talking about?"

"You're starting to care about him. Personally. He's beginning to be more than an obligation, a promise to be kept. He matters to you."

"I said I'd take care of him. That's what I'm doing."

"He matters to you," she repeated. "That's what's worrying you, Cam. What happens if you start caring too much. And how do you stop it from happening."

He looked at her, the way the sun dropped down in the sky at her back, the way her eyes stayed warm and dark on his. Maybe he was worrying, he admitted, and not just about his shifting feelings for Seth. "I finish what I start, Anna. And I don't walk away from my family. Looks like the kid qualifies there. But I'm a selfish son of a bitch. Ask anybody."

"Some things I prefer to find out for myself. Now am I getting a crab dinner or not?"

"Ethan ought to have the pot going by now." He moved forward as if to lead her inside. Then, judging the moment when she relaxed, he yanked her into his arms and caught her up in a hot, heart-hammering kiss.

"See, that was for me," he murmured when they were both breathless and quivering. "Want it, take it. I warned you I was selfish."

Anna eased back, calmly adjusted her now rumpled jacket, ran a hand over her hair to assure herself it was in place. "Sorry, but I'm afraid I enjoyed that every bit as much as you did. So it doesn't qualify as a selfish act."

He laughed even as his pulse scrambled. "Let me try it again. I can pull it off this time."

"I'll take a rain check. I want my dinner." With that, she sauntered up the steps, knocked briefly, and slipped into the house.

Cam just stood where he was, grinning. This was a woman, he thought, who was going to make this episode of his life a memorable one.

By the time Cam made his way inside and to the kitchen, Anna was already chatting with Phillip and accepting a glass of wine.

"You drink beer with crabs," Cam told her and got one out of the fridge for himself.

"I don't seem to be eating any at the moment. And Phillip assures me this is a very nice wine." She sipped, considered, and smiled. "He's absolutely right."

"It's one of my favorite whites." Since she'd approved, Phillip topped off her glass. "Smooth, buttery, and not overpowering."

"Phil's a wine snob." Cam twisted off the top and lifted the bottle of Harp to his lips. "But we let him live here anyway."

"And how is that working out?" She wondered if they realized how male the house seemed. Tidy as a pin, yes, but without even a whiff of female. "It must be odd adjusting to the three of you in the same household again."

"Well, we haven't killed each other." Cam bared his teeth in a smile at his brother. "Yet."

With a laugh she walked to the window. "And where is Seth?"

"He's with Ethan," Phillip told her. "They're doing the crabs around at the pit."

"The pit?"

"Around the side." Cam took her hand and tugged her toward the door. "Mom wouldn't let us cook crab in the house. She might have been a doctor, but she could be squeamish. Didn't like to watch." He drew her off the porch and down the steps as he spoke. "Dad had this brick pit around the side of the house. Fell down my first summer. He didn't know much about laying bricks. But we rebuilt it."

When they stepped around the corner, she saw Ethan and Seth standing by a huge kettle over an open fire in a lopsided brick-sided pit. Smoke billowed, and from a big steel barrel on the ground came the scraping and clattering of claws.

Anna looked from barrel to kettle and back again. "You know what, I think I can be a bit squeamish myself."

She stepped back, turned to the view of the water. She didn't even mind that Cam laughed at her, especially when she heard Seth's voice raised in desperate excitement.

"Are you dumping them in now? Oh, man, shit, that is so *gross*."

"I told him to watch his mouth tonight, but he doesn't know you're here yet."

She only shook her head. "He sounds very normal." She winced a little when she heard a clatter and Seth's wild exclamation of delight and disgust. "And I'd think what's happening around the corner is just barbaric enough to thrill him." Her hand lifted quickly, protectively, to her hair when she felt a tug.

"I like it down." Cam tossed the pin he'd pulled out aside.

"I want it up," she said mildly and began to walk toward the water.

"I bet we're going to knock heads about all kinds of things." He sipped his beer and sent her a sidelong look as they walked. "Ought to keep it all interesting."

"I doubt either of us will be bored. Seth comes first, Cam. I mean that." She paused, listened to the musical lap of water against the hull of the boats, the sloping shoreline. Topping one of the markers was a huge nest. Buoys bobbed in the tide.

"I can help him, and it's unlikely we'll always agree on what's right for him. It'll be essential to keep that issue completely separate when we end up in bed."

He was grateful he hadn't taken another sip from the bottle. No doubt in his mind he'd have choked on it. "I can do that."

She lifted her head as an egret soared by, and wondered if the nest belonged to her. "When I'm certain I can, we'll use my bed. My apartment's more private than your house."

He rubbed a hand over his stomach in a futile attempt to calm himself. "Lady, you're right up front, aren't you?"

"What's the point in being otherwise? We're grown-ups, unattached." She shot him a look—a flick of the lashes, an arch of a brow. "But if you're the type who'd prefer me to pretend reluctance until seduction, sorry."

"No, I'm all right with it this way." If he didn't overheat and explode in the meantime. "No games, no pretenses, no promises. . . . Where the hell do you come from?" he finished, fascinated.

"Pittsburgh," she said easily and started back toward the house.

"That's not what I meant."

"I know. But if you intend to sleep with me, you should have some interest in the basic facts. No games, no pretenses, no promises. That's fine. But I don't have sex with strangers."

He put a hand on her arm before she wandered too close to the house. He wanted another moment alone. "Okay, what are the basic facts?"

"I'm twenty-eight, single, of Italian descent. My mother . . . died when I was twelve and I was raised primarily by my grandparents."

"In Pittsburgh."

"That's right. They're wonderful—old-fashioned, energetic, loving. I can make a terrific red sauce from scratch—the recipe's been passed down in my family for generations. I moved to D.C. right after college, worked there and did some graduate studies. But Washington didn't suit me."

"Too political?"

"Yes, and too urban. I was looking for something a little different, so I ended up down here."

Cam glanced around the quiet yard, the quiet water. "It's different from D.C., all right."

"I like it. I also like horror novels, sappy movies, and any kind of music except jazz. I read magazines from back to front and don't know why, and though I'm comfortable with all sorts of people, I don't particularly like large social functions."

She stopped, considered. They would see, she decided, how much more he'd want to find out. "I think that's enough for now, and my glass is nearly empty."

"You're nothing like my first impression of you."

"No? I think you're exactly like mine of you."

"Do you speak Italian?"

"Fluently."

He leaned forward and murmured a highly charged and sexually explicit suggestion in her ear. Some women might have slapped his face, others might have giggled, some certainly would have blushed. Anna merely made a humming sound in her throat.

"Your accent's mediocre, but your imagination is exceptional." She gave his arm a light pat. "Be sure to ask me again—some other time."

"Damn right I will," Cam muttered, and watched her smile in an easy, open manner at Seth as he came barreling around the corner of the house.

"Hello, Seth."

He skidded to a halt. That wary and distant look came into his eyes. His shoulders hunched. "Yeah, hi. Ethan says we can eat anytime."

"Good, I'm starved." Though she knew he was braced against her, she kept walking toward him. "I hear you went sailing yesterday."

Seth's gaze slid by her, locked accusingly on Cam's. "Yeah. So?"

"I've never been." She said it quickly, sensing that Cam's indrawn breath was the signal for a sharp reminder of manners. "Cam offered to let me tag along with you sometime."

"It's his boat." Then catching the dark scowl on Cam's face, Seth shrugged. "Sure, that'd be cool. I'm supposed to go get a ton of newspaper to spread on the porch. That's the way you eat crabs."

"Right." Before he could dash off, she bent down and whispered in his ear. "Good thing for us Cam didn't cook them."

That got a snicker out of him and a quick, fleeting grin before he turned and ran inside.

TEN

She wasn't so bad. For a social worker. Seth came to this thoughtful conclusion about Anna after he'd retreated to his room, ostensibly to work
on his anti-violence essay. He was drawing pictures instead, quick little
sketches of faces. He had a stupid week to write the stupid thing, didn't he?
Wouldn't take more than a couple of hours once he got down to doing it.
Which was a raw deal all around, but better than letting fat-faced Robert get
him suspended.

He could still close his eyes and bring up the image of all three of the
Quinns standing in the principal's office. All three of them standing beside
him and facing down the all-powerful Moorefield. It was so . . . cool, he decided and began to doodle the moment in his notebook.

There . . . there was Phillip in his fancy suit with his hair just right and
his kind of narrow face. He looked like one of the magazine ads, Seth
thought, the ones that sold stuff only rich guys could buy.

Next he sketched in Ethan, all serious-faced, Seth mused, his hair a little
shaggy even though Seth remembered how he'd combed it just before they'd
gone into the school. He looked exactly like what he was. The kind of guy
who made his living and lived his life outdoors.

And there was Cam, rough and tough with that light of mean in his eyes.
Thumbs hooked in the front pockets of his jeans. Yeah, that was it, Seth decided. He most always stood like that when he was ticked off. Even in the
rough sketch he came across as someone who'd done most everything and
planned to do a whole lot more.

Last he sketched in himself, trying to see what others would see. His
shoulders were too thin and bony, he thought with some disappointment.
But they wouldn't always be. His face was too thin for his eyes, but it would

fill out too. One day he'd be taller, and stronger, and he wouldn't look like such a puny kid.

But he'd kept his head up, hadn't he? He hadn't been afraid of anything. And he didn't look like he'd just wandered into the picture. He looked—almost—like he belonged there.

Mess with one Quinn, mess with them all. That's what Cam had said—and he must have meant it. But he wasn't a Quinn, Seth thought, frowning as he held up the sketch to study details. Or maybe he was, he just didn't know. It hadn't mattered to him if Ray Quinn had been his father like some people said. All that had mattered was that he was away from *her*.

It hadn't mattered who his father was. Still didn't, he assured himself. He just didn't give a rat's ass. All he wanted was to stay here, right here.

Nobody had used the back of their hand or their fists on him for months now. Nobody got blitzed out on drugs and laid around so long and so still he thought they were dead. Secretly hoped they were. No flabby guys with sweaty hands tried to grope him.

He wasn't even going to think about that.

Eating crabs had been pretty cool, too. Good and messy, he remembered with a grin. You got to eat them with your hands. The social worker didn't act all prim and girly about it either. She just took off her jacket and rolled up her sleeves. It didn't seem like she was watching to see if he burped or scratched his butt or anything.

She'd laughed a lot, he remembered. He wasn't used to women laughing a lot when they weren't coked up. And that was a different kind of laughing, Seth knew. Miss Spinelli's wasn't wild and hard and desperate. It was low and, well, smooth, he supposed.

Nobody'd told him he couldn't have more, either. Man, he'd bet he ate a hundred of those ugly suckers. He didn't even mind eating the salad, though he pretended he did.

He hadn't had that gnawing, sick feeling in his stomach that was desperate hunger for a long time now, so long he might have forgotten the sensation. But he hadn't forgotten. He hadn't forgotten anything.

He'd worried some that the social worker would want to pull him back in, but she seemed pretty okay to him. And he saw her sneaking little bits of crab and bread to Foolish, so she couldn't be all bad.

But he'd have liked her better if she was a waitress or something like Grace.

When the light knock sounded on his door, Seth slapped the notebook closed on his sketches and quickly opened another, where the first dozen words of his five-hundred-word essay were scrawled.

"Yeah?"

Anna poked her head in. "Hi. Can I come in a minute?"

It was weird being asked, and he wondered if she would just turn around and go if he said no. But he shrugged. "I guess."

"I have to leave soon," she began, taking a quick survey of the room. A twin bed, inexpertly made, a sturdy dresser and desk, a wall of shelves that held a few books, a portable stereo that looked very new, and a pair of binoculars that didn't. There were white miniblinds at the windows and a pale-green paint on the walls.

It needed junk, she thought. A boy's junk. Ancient broken toys, posters tacked to the walls. But the puppy snoring in the corner was a very good start.

"This is nice." She wandered to the window. "You've got a good view, water and trees. You get to watch the birds. I bought a book on local water-fowl when I moved here from D.C. so I could figure out what was what. It must be nice to see egrets every day."

"I guess."

"I like it here. It's hard not to, huh?"

He shrugged his shoulders, took the cautious route. "It's okay. I got no problems with it."

She turned, glanced down at his notebook. "The dreaded essay?"

"I started it." Defensively, he pulled the notebook closer—and knocked the other one to the floor. Before he could snatch it up, Anna crouched to pick it up herself.

"Oh, look at this!" It had fallen open to a sketch of the puppy, just his face, straight on, and she thought the artist had captured that sweet and silly expression perfectly. "Did you sketch this?"

"It's no big deal. I'm working on the damn essay, aren't I?"

She might have sighed over his response, but she was too charmed by the sketch. "It's wonderful. It looks just like him." Her fingers itched to turn the pages, to see who else Seth might have drawn. But she resisted and set the notebook down. "I can't draw a decent stick man."

"It's nothing. Just fooling around."

"Well, if you don't want it, maybe I could have it?"

He thought it might be a trick. After all, she had her jacket back on, was carrying her briefcase. She looked like Social Services again rather than the woman who'd rolled up her sleeves and laughed over steamed crabs. "What for?"

"I can't have pets in my apartment. Just as well," she added. "It wouldn't be fair to keep one closed in all day while I'm at work, but . . ." Then she smiled and glanced over at the sleeping puppy. "I really like dogs.

When I can afford a house and a yard, I'm going to have a couple of them. But until then, I have to play with other people's pets."

It seemed odd to him. In Seth's mind adults ruled—often with an iron hand. Did what they wanted when they wanted. "Why don't you just move someplace else?"

"The place I've got is close to work, the rent's reasonable." She looked toward the window again, to the stretch of land and water. Both were deep with shadows as night moved in. "It has to do until I can manage to get the house and yard." She wandered to the window, drawn to that quiet view. The first star winked to life in the eastern sky. She nearly made a wish. "Somewhere near the water. Like this. Anyway . . ."

She turned back and sat on the side of the bed facing him. "I just wanted to come up before I left, see if there's anything you wanted to talk about, or any questions you wanted to ask me."

"No. Nothing."

"Okay." She hadn't really expected him to talk to her freely. Yet. "Maybe you'd like to know what I see here, what I think." She took his shoulder jerk as assent. "I see a houseful of guys who are trying to figure out how to live with each other and make it work. Four very different men who are bumping up against each other. And I think they're going to make some mistakes, and most certainly irritate each other and disagree. But I also think they'll work it out—eventually. Because they all want to," she added with an easy smile. "In their own ways they all want the same thing."

She rose and took a card out of her briefcase. "You can call me whenever you want. I put my home number on the back. I don't see any reason for me to come back—in an official capacity—for a while. But I may come back for a puppy fix. Good luck with the essay."

When she started for the door, Seth went with impulse and tore the sketch of Foolish out of his notebook. "You can have this if you want."

"Really?" She took the page, beamed at it. "God, he's cute. Thanks." He jerked back when she bent to kiss his cheek, but she brushed her lips across it lightly, then straightened. She stepped back, ordering herself to keep an emotional distance. "Say good night to Foolish for me."

Anna slipped the sketch in her briefcase as she walked downstairs. Phillip was noodling at the piano, his fingers carelessly picking out some bluesy number. It was another skill she envied. It was a constant disappointment to her that she had no talent.

Ethan was nowhere to be seen, and Cam was restlessly pacing the living room.

She thought that might be a very typical overview of all three men.

Phillip elegantly whiling away the time, Ethan off on some solitary pursuit. And Cam working off excess energy.

With the boy up in his room, drawing his pictures and thinking his thoughts.

Cam glanced up, and when their eyes locked, the ball of heat slammed into her gut.

"Gentlemen, thank you for a wonderful meal."

Phillip rose and held out a hand to take hers. "We have to thank you. It's been too long since we had a beautiful woman to dinner. I hope you'll come back."

Oh, he's a smooth one, she decided. "I'd like that. Tell Ethan he's a genius with a crab. Good night, Cam."

"I'll walk you out."

She'd counted on it. "First thing," she said when they stepped outside. "From what I can see, Seth's welfare is being seen to. He has proper supervision, a good home, support with his school life. He could certainly use some new shoes, but I don't imagine there's a boy of ten who couldn't."

"Shoes? What's wrong with his shoes?"

"Regardless," she said, turning to him when they reached her car. "All of you still have adjustments to make, and there's no doubt he's a very troubled child. I suspect he was abused, physically and perhaps sexually."

"I figured that out for myself," Cam said shortly. "It won't happen here."

"I know that." She laid a hand on his arm. "If I had a single doubt in that area he wouldn't be here. Cam, he needs professional counseling. You all do."

"Counseling? That's crap. We don't need to pour our guts out to some underpaid county shrink."

"Many underpaid county shrinks are very good at their job," she said dryly. "Since I have a degree in psychology myself, I could be considered an underpaid county shrink, and I'm good at mine."

"Fine. You're talking to him, you're talking to me. We've been counseled."

"Don't be difficult." Her voice was deliberately mild because she knew it would spark a flash of annoyance in his eyes. It was only fair, she thought, as he'd annoyed her.

"I'm not being difficult. I've cooperated with you from the get-go."

More or less, she mused, and continuing to be fair, admitted it was more than she'd expected. "You've made a solid start here, but a professional counselor will help all of you get beneath the surface and deal with the root of the problems."

"We don't have any problems."

She hadn't expected such hard-line resistance to such a basic step, but realized she should have. "Of course you do. Seth's afraid to be touched."

"He's not afraid to let Grace touch him."

"Grace?" Anna pursed her lips in thought. "Grace Monroe, from the list you gave me?"

"Yeah, she's doing the housework now, and the kid's nuts about her. Might even have a little crush."

"That's good, that's healthy. But it's only a start. When a child's been abused, it leaves scars."

What the hell were they talking about this for? he thought impatiently. Why were they talking about shrinks and digging at old wounds when all he'd wanted was a few minutes of easy flirtation with a pretty woman?

"My old man beat the hell out of me. So what? I survived." He hated remembering it, hated standing in the shadow of the house that had been his sanctuary and remembering. "The kid's mother knocked him around. Well, she's not going to get the chance to do it again. That chapter's closed."

"It's never closed," Anna said patiently. "Whatever new chapter you start always has some basis in the one that came before. I'm recommending counseling to you now, and I'm going to recommend it in my report."

"Go ahead." He couldn't explain why it infuriated him even to think about it. He only knew he'd be damned if he would ask himself or any of his brothers to open those long-locked doors again. "You recommend whatever you want. Doesn't mean we have to do it."

"You have to do what's best for Seth."

"How the hell do you know what's best?"

"It's my job," she said coolly now, because her blood was starting to boil.

"Your job? You got a college degree and a bunch of forms. We're the ones who lived it, who are living it. You haven't been there. You don't know anything about it, what it's like to get your face smashed in and not be able to stop it. To have some bureaucratic jerk from the county who doesn't know dick decide what happens to your life."

Didn't know? She thought of the dark, deserted road, the terror. The pain and the screams. Can't be personal, she reminded herself, though her stomach clutched and fluttered. "Your opinion of my profession has been crystal-clear since our first meeting."

"That's right, but I cooperated. I filled you in, and all of us took steps to make this work." His thumbs went into his front pockets in a gesture Seth would have recognized. "It's never quite enough, though. There's always something else."

"If there weren't something else," she returned, "you wouldn't be so angry."

"Of course I'm angry. We've been working our butts off here. I just turned down the biggest race of my career. I've got a kid on my hands who looks at me one minute as if I'm the enemy and the next as if I'm his salvation. Jesus Christ."

"And it's harder to be his salvation than his enemy."

Bull's-eye, he thought with growing resentment. How the hell did she know so much? "I'm telling you, the best thing for the kid, for all of us, is to be left alone. He needs shoes, I'll get him goddamn shoes."

"And what are you going to do about the fact that he's afraid to be touched, even in the most casual way, by you or your brothers? Are you going to buy his fear away?"

"He'll get over it." Cam was dug in now and refused to allow her to pry him out.

"Get over it?" A sudden fury had her almost stuttering out the words. Then they poured out in a hot stream that made the flash of pain in her eyes all the more poignant. "Because you want him to? Because you tell him to? Do you know what it's like to live with that kind of terror? That kind of shame? To have it bottled up inside you and have little drops of that poison spill out even when someone you love wants to hold you?"

She ripped open her car door, tossed her briefcase in. "I do. I know exactly." He grabbed her arm before she could get into the car. "Get your hand off me."

"Wait a minute."

"I said get your hand off me."

Because she was trembling, he did. Somewhere during the argument she'd gone from being professionally irritated to being personally enraged. He hadn't seen the shift.

"Anna, I'm not going to let you get behind the wheel of this car when you're this churned up. I lost someone I cared about recently, and I'm not going to let it happen again."

"I'm fine." Though she bit off the words, she followed them up by a long, steadying breath. "I'm perfectly capable of driving home. If you want to discuss the possibility of counseling rationally, you can call my office for an appointment."

"Why don't we take a walk? Both of us can cool off."

"I'm perfectly cool." She slipped into her car, nearly slammed the door on his fingers. "You might take one, though, right off the dock."

He cursed when she drove away. Briefly considered chasing her down, pulling her out of the car and demanding that they finish the damn stupid argument. His next thought was to stalk back into the house and forget it. Forget her.

But he remembered the wounded look that had come into her eyes, the way her voice had sounded when she'd said she knew what it was like to be afraid, to be ashamed.

Someone had hurt her, he realized. And at that moment everything else faded to the background.

A nna slammed the door of her apartment, yanked off her shoes, and heaved them across the room. Her temper was not the type that flashed and boiled, then cooled. It was a simmering thing that bubbled and brewed, then spewed over.

The drive home hadn't calmed her down at all; it had merely given her rising emotions enough time to reach a peak.

She tossed her briefcase on the sofa, stripped off her suit jacket, and threw it on top. Ignorant, hardheaded, narrow-minded man. She fisted her hands and rapped them against her own temples. What had made her think she could get through to him? What had made her think she wanted to?

When she heard the knock on her door, she bared her teeth. She expected her across-the-hall neighbor wanted to exchange some little bit of news or gossip.

She wasn't in the mood.

Determined to ignore it until she could be civilized, she began yanking pins out of her hair.

The knock came again, louder now. "Come on, Anna. Open the damn door."

Now she could only stare as shock and fury made her ears ring. The man had followed her home? He'd had the *nerve* to come all the way to her door and expect to be welcomed inside?

He probably thought she'd be so consumed with lust that she'd jump him and have wild sex on the living room floor. Well, he was in for a surprise of his own.

She strode to the door, yanked it open. "You son of a bitch."

Cam took one look at her flushed and furious face, the wild, tumbling hair, the eyes that sparkled with vengeance, and decided it was undoubtedly perverse to find that arousing.

But what could he do about it?

He glanced down at her clenched fist. "Go ahead," he invited. "But if you belt me you'll have to write a five-hundred-word essay on violence in our society."

She made a low, threatening sound in her throat and tried to slam the door in his face. He was quick enough to slap a hand on it, strong enough to put his weight against it and hold it open. "I wanted to make sure you got home all right," he began as they struggled with the door. "And since I was in the neighborhood, I thought I should come up."

"I want you to go away. Very far away. In fact, I want you to go all the way to hell."

"I get that, but before I take the trip, give me five minutes."

"I've already given you what I now consider entirely too much of my time."

"So what's five more minutes?" To settle it, he braced the door open with one hand—which she found infuriating—and stepped inside.

"If it wasn't for Seth, I'd call the cops right now and have your butt tossed in jail."

He nodded. He'd dealt with his share of furious women and knew there was a time to be careful. "Yeah, I get that too. Listen—"

"I don't have to listen to you." Using the flat of her hand, she shoved him hard in the chest. "You're insulting and you're hardheaded and you're *wrong*, so I don't have to listen to you."

"I'm not wrong," he tossed back. "*You're* wrong. I know—"

"Every damn thing," she interrupted. "You drop in from bouncing around all over the world playing hotshot daredevil, and suddenly you know everything about what's best for a ten-year-old boy you've known barely a month."

"I was not playing at being a hotshot daredevil. I was making a career out of it!" He erupted, his purpose of conciliation and peacemaking shattering to bits. "A goddamn good one. And I do know what's best for the kid. I'm the one who's been there day and night. You spend a couple of hours with him and figure you got a better handle on it. That's just bullshit."

"It's my job to have a handle on it."

"Then you should know that every situation is different. Maybe it works for some people to spill their guts to a stranger and have their dreams analyzed." He'd worked it out carefully, logically on the way over. He was determined to be absolutely reasonable. "Nothing wrong with that, if it's what does it for you. But you can't rubber-stamp this. You have to look at the circumstances and the personalities here and, you know, make adjustments."

She couldn't get her breathing under control, so she finally stopped trying. "I don't rubber-stamp the people I'm chosen to help. I study and I evaluate, and goddamn you, I care. I am not some bureaucratic jerk who doesn't know dick. I'm a trained caseworker with over six years' experience, and I got that training and that experience because I know exactly what it's like to be on the other side, to be hurt and scared and alone and helpless. And no one whose case is assigned to me is just a name on a form."

Her voice broke, shocking her to silence. Quickly she stepped back, pressing one hand to her mouth, holding the other up to signal him away. She felt it rising inside her, knew she wouldn't be able to stop it. "Get out," she managed. "Get out of here now."

"Don't do that." Panic closed his throat as the first hot tears spilled down her cheeks. Furious women he understood and could deal with. The ones who wept destroyed him. "Time out. Foul. Jesus, don't do that."

"Just leave me alone." She turned away, thinking only of escape, but he wrapped his arms around her, buried his face in her hair.

"I'm sorry, I'm sorry, I'm sorry." He'd have apologized for anything, everything, if only to put them back on even ground. "I was wrong. I was out of line, whatever you said. Don't cry, baby." He turned her around, holding her close. He pressed his lips to her forehead, her temple. His hands stroked her hair, her back.

Then his mouth was on hers, gently at first, to comfort and soothe while he continued to murmur mindless pleas and promises. But her arms lifted, wrapped around his neck, her body pressed into his, and her lips parted, heated.

The change happened quickly and he was lost in her, drowning in her. The hand that had stroked gently through her hair now tangled in it, fisted as the kiss rushed toward searing.

Take me away, was all she could think. Don't let me reason, don't let me think. Just take me. She wanted his hands on her, his mouth on her, she wanted to feel her muscles quiver with need under his fingers. With that strong, half-wild taste of his filling her, she could let everything go.

She trembled against him, shuddered in his arms, and the sound she made against his desperate mouth might have been a whimper. He jerked back as if he'd been stung, and though his hands weren't completely steady he kept them on her arms, and kept her at arm's length.

"That wasn't—" He had to stop, give himself a minute. His mind was mush and was unlikely to clear if she continued to look at him with those dark, damp eyes that were clouded with passion. "I don't believe I'm going to say this, but this isn't a good idea." He ran his hands up and down her arms as he struggled to hold on to control. "You're upset, probably not thinking . . ." He could still taste her, and the flavor on his tongue had outrageous hunger stirring in his belly. "Christ, I need a drink."

Annoyed with both of them, she swiped the back of her hand over her cheek to dry it. "I'll make coffee."

"I wasn't talking about coffee."

"I know, but if we're going to be sensible, let's stick with coffee."

She stepped into the kitchen area and kept herself busy with the homey process of grinding beans and brewing. Every nerve in her body was on edge. Every need she'd ever had or imagined having was brutally aroused.

"If we'd finished that, Anna, you might have thought I used the situation."

She nodded, continued to fix coffee. "Or I would have wondered if I had. Either way, bad idea. It's important to me never to mix sex and guilt." She looked at him then, quietly, levelly. "It's vital to me."

And he knew. Knowing, he suffered both helpless rage and helpless pity. "Christ, Anna. When?"

"When I was twelve."

"I'm sorry." It made him sick, in his gut, in his heart. "I'm sorry," he said again, inadequately. "You don't have to talk about it."

"That's where we disagree. Talking about it is finally what saved me." And he would listen, she thought. And he would know her. "My mother and I had gone to Philadelphia for the day. I wanted to see the Liberty Bell because we were studying about the Revolutionary War in school. We had this clunker of a car. We drove over, saw the sights. We ate ice cream and bought souvenirs."

"Anna—"

Her head whipped up, a direct challenge. "Are you afraid to hear it?"

"Maybe." He raked a hand through his hair. Maybe he was afraid to hear it, afraid of what it would change between them. Another roll of the dice, he thought, then looked at her, waiting patiently. And he understood he needed to know. "Go ahead."

Turning, she chose cups from the cabinet. "It was just the two of us. It always had been. She'd gotten pregnant when she was sixteen and would never say who the father was. Having me complicated her life enormously and must have brought her a great deal of shame and hardship. My grandparents were very religious, very old school." Anna laughed a little. "Very Italian. They didn't cut my mother out of their lives, but my sense was that it made her uncomfortable to have more than a peripheral part in them. So we had an apartment about a quarter the size of this one."

She brought the pot to the counter, poured the rich, dark coffee. "It was in April, on a Saturday. She'd taken off work so we could go. We had the best day, and we stayed later than we'd planned because we were having fun. I was half asleep on the ride back, and she must have made a wrong turn. I know we got lost, but she just joked about it. The car broke down. Smoke started pouring out from under the hood. She pulled over to the side and we got out. Just started giggling. What a mess, what a fix."

He knew what was coming, and it sickened him. "Maybe you should sit down."

"No, I'm all right. She thought it was the radiator needing water," Anna continued. Her eyes unfocused as she looked back. She could remember how warm it had been, how quiet, and how the moon had drifted in and out of smoky-looking clouds. "We were going to hike back to the closest house and see if we could get some help. A car came along, stopped. There were two men inside, and one of them leaned out and asked us if we had a problem."

She lifted her coffee, sipped. Her hands were steady now. She could say it all again and live through it all again. "I remember the way her hand squeezed mine, clamped down so hard it hurt. I realized later that she was afraid. They were drunk. She said something about just walking down to her brother's house, that we were fine, but they got out of the car. She pushed me behind her. When the first one grabbed her, she yelled at me to run. But I couldn't. I couldn't move. He was laughing and pawing at her, and she was fighting him. And when he dragged her off the road and pushed her down, I ran up and tried to pull him off. But of course I couldn't, and the other man yanked me off and tore my shirt."

A defenseless woman and a helpless child. Cam's hands fisted at his sides as both rage and impotence coursed through him. He wanted to go back to that night, that deserted road, and use them viciously.

"He kept laughing," Anna said quietly. "I saw his face very clearly for a moment or two. Like it was frozen in front of my eyes. I kept hearing my mother screaming, begging them not to hurt me. He was raping her, I could hear him raping her, but she kept begging them to leave me alone. And she must have seen that that wasn't going to happen, and she fought harder. I could hear the man hitting her, yelling at her to shut up. It didn't seem real, even when he was raping me it didn't seem like it could be real. Just an awful dream that went on and on and on.

"When they were finished, they stumbled back to their car and drove away. They just left us there. My mother was unconscious. He'd beaten her badly. I didn't know what to do. They said I went into shock, but I don't remember anything until I was in the hospital. My mother never regained consciousness. She was in a coma for two days, then she died."

"Anna, I don't know what to say to you. What can be said to you."

"I didn't tell you for your sympathy," she said. "She was twenty-seven, a year younger than I am now. It was a long time ago, but you don't forget. It never goes away completely. And I remember everything that happened that night, everything I did afterward—after I went to live with my grandparents. I did everything I could to hurt them, to hurt myself. That was my way of dealing with what had happened to me. I refused counseling," she told him coolly. "I wasn't going to talk to some thin-faced, dried-up shrink. Instead I picked fights, looked for trouble, found it. I had indiscriminate sex, used drugs, ran away from home, and butted up against the social workers and the system."

She picked up the jacket she'd stripped off earlier and folded it neatly now. "I hated everyone, myself most of all. I was the one who had wanted to go to Philadelphia. I was the reason we were there. If I hadn't been with her, she would have gotten away."

"No." He wanted to touch her but was afraid to. Not because she seemed fragile—she didn't. She seemed impossibly strong. "No, you weren't to blame for any of it."

"I felt the blame. And the more I felt it, the more I struck out at everyone and everything around me."

"Sometimes it's all you can do," he murmured. "Fight back, run wild, until you get it all out."

"Sometimes there's nothing to fight, and nowhere to run. For three years I used what had happened that night to do whatever I chose." She looked at Cam again with a quick, ironic lift and fall of brow. "I didn't choose well. I thought I was a pretty tough cookie when I ended up in juvie. But my case-worker was tougher. She pushed and she prodded and she hounded me. Because she refused to give up on me, she got through. And because my grandparents refused to give up on me, I got through."

Carefully, she laid the jacket back over the arm of the sofa. "It could have been different. I could have stayed just one more failed statistic in the system. But I didn't."

He thought it was amazing that she had turned a horror into such strength. She was amazing for choosing work that would have to remind her daily of what had ripped her life apart. "And you decided to pay it back. To go into the kind of work that had turned you around."

"I knew I could help. And yes, I owed a debt, the same way you feel you owe one. I survived," she said, looking him dead in the eyes again, "but sur-vival isn't enough. It wasn't enough for me, or for you. And it won't be enough for Seth."

"One thing at a time," he murmured. "I want to know if they caught the bastards."

"No." She'd long ago learned to accept and to live with that. "It was weeks before I was coherent enough to make a statement. They never caught them. The system doesn't always work, but I've learned, and I believe, it does its best."

"I've never thought so, and this doesn't change my mind." He started to reach out, hesitated, then tucked his hand into his pocket. "I'm sorry I hurt you. That I said things that made you remember."

"It's always there," she told him. "You cope and you put it aside for long periods of time. It comes back now and again, because it never really goes away."

"Did you have counseling?"

"Eventually, yes. I—" She broke off, sighed. "All right, I'm not saying counseling works miracles, Cam. I'm telling you it can be helpful, it can be healing. I needed it, and when I was finally ready to use that help, I was better."

"Let's do this." He did touch her now, just laid a hand over hers on the counter. "We'll leave it as an option. Let's see how things go . . . all around."

"See how things go." She sighed, too tired to argue. Her head ached, and her body felt hollowed out and fragile. "I agree with that, but I'll still recommend counseling in my report."

"Don't forget the shoes," he said dryly and was vastly relieved when she laughed.

"I won't have to mention them, because I know you'll have him at the store by the weekend."

"We could call it a compromise. I seem to be getting better at them lately."

"Then you must have been incredibly obstinate before."

"I think the word my parents used was 'bullheaded.' "

"It's comforting to be understood." She looked down at the hand covering hers. "If you asked to stay, I couldn't say no."

"I want to stay. I want you. But I can't ask tonight. Bad timing all around."

She understood how some men felt about a woman who'd been sexually attacked. Her stomach seized into hard knots. But it was best to know. "Is it because I was raped?"

He wouldn't let it be. He refused to allow what had happened to her affect what would happen between them. "It's because you couldn't say no tonight and tomorrow you might be sorry you didn't."

Surprised, she looked up at him again. "You're never quite what I expect you to be."

He wasn't quite what he expected either, not lately. "This thing here. Whatever it is, isn't quite what I expected it to be. How about a Saturday night date?"

"I have a date Saturday." Her lips curved slowly. The knots in her stomach had loosened. She hadn't even been aware of it. "But I'll break it."

"Seven o'clock." He leaned across the counter, kissed her, lingered over it, kissed her again. "I'm going to want to finish this."

"So am I."

"Well." He heaved a sigh and started for the door while he was sure he could. "That's going to make the drive home easier."

He paused, turned around to look at her. "You said you survived, Anna, but you didn't. You triumphed. Everything about you is a testament to courage and strength." When she stared at him, obviously stunned, he smiled a little. "You didn't get either from a social worker or a counselor. They just helped you figure out how to use it. I figure you got it from your mother. She must have been a hell of a woman."

"She was," Anna murmured, near tears again.

"So are you." Cam closed the door quietly behind him.

He decided he would take his time driving home. He had a lot to think about.

ELEVEN

Pretty Saturday mornings in the spring were not meant to be spent indoors or on crowded streets. To Ethan they were meant to be spent on the water. The idea of shopping—actually shopping—was very close to terrifying.

"Don't see why we all have to do this."

Because he'd gotten to the Jeep first, Cam rode in front. He turned his head to spare Ethan a glance. "Because we're all in this. The old Claremont barn's for rent, right? We need a place if we're going to build boats. We have to make the deal."

"Insanity," was all Phillip had to say as he turned down Market Street in St. Chris.

"Can't go into business if you don't have a place of business," Cam returned. He found that single fact inarguably logical. "So we take a look at it, make the deal with Claremont, and get started."

"Licenses, taxes, materials. Orders, for God's sake," Phillip began. "Tools, advertising, phone lines, fax lines, bookkeeping."

"So take care of it." Cam shrugged carelessly. "Soon as we sign the lease and get the kid his shoes, you can do whatever comes next."

"*I* can do it?" Phillip complained at the same time Seth muttered he didn't need any damn shoes.

"Ethan got our first order, I found out about the building. You take care of the paperwork. And you're getting the damn shoes," he told Seth.

"I don't know how come you're the boss of everybody."

Cam could only manage a short, grim laugh. "Me either."

The Claremont building wasn't really a barn, but it was as big as one. In the mid-1700s it had been a tobacco warehouse. After the Revolutionary War, the British ships no longer sailed to St. Chris carrying their wide variety of goods. Businesses that had boomed went bankrupt.

The revival in the late 1800s grew directly from the bay. With improved methods of canning and packing, the national market for oysters opened up and St. Chris once again prospered. And the old tobacco warehouse was refitted as a packinghouse.

Then the oyster beds played out, and the building became a glorified storage shed. Over the last fifty years it had been empty as often as it was filled.

From the outside it was unpretentious. Sun- and weather-faded brick, thumb-size holes in the mortar. A sagging old roof that was desperately in need of reshingling. What windows it could boast were small and stingy. Most were broken, all were filthy.

"Oh, yeah, this looks promising." Already disgusted, Phillip parked in the pitted lot at the side of the building.

"We need space," Cam reminded him. "It doesn't have to be pretty."

"Good thing, because this doesn't come close to pretty."

A bit more interested now, Ethan climbed out. He walked up to the closest window, used the bandanna from his back pocket to rub off most of the grime so he could peer through. "It's a good space. Got cargo doors at the back, a dock. Needs a little work."

"A little?" Phillip stared in over Ethan's shoulder. "Floor's rotting out. It's got to be infested with vermin. Probably termites and rodents."

"Probably be a good idea to mention that to Claremont," Ethan decided. "Keep the rent down." Hearing the tinkle of glass breaking, he saw that Cam had just put his elbow through an already cracked window. "Guess we're going inside."

"Breaking and entering." Phillip only shook his head. "That's a good start."

Cam flipped the pathetic lock on the window and shoved it up. "It was already broken. Give me a minute." He boosted himself inside, disappeared.

"Cool," Seth decided, and before a word could be spoken he climbed inside too.

"Nice example we're setting for him." Phillip ran a hand over his face and wished fervently he'd never given up smoking.

"Well, think of it this way. You could have picked the locks. But you didn't."

"Right. Listen, Ethan, we've got to think about this. There's no reason why you can't—we can't—build that first boat at your place. Once we start renting buildings, filing for tax numbers, we're committed."

"What's the worst that can happen? We waste some time and some money. I figure I've got enough of both." He heard the mix of Cam's and

Seth's laughter echoing inside. "And maybe we'll have some fun while we're at it."

He started around to the front door, knowing Phillip would grumble but follow.

"I saw a rat," Seth said in pure delight when Cam shoved the front door open. "It was awesome."

"Rats." Phillip studied the dim space grimly before stepping inside. "Lovely."

"We'll have to get us a couple of she-cats," Ethan decided. "They're meaner than toms."

He looked up, scanning the high ceiling. Water damage showed clearly in the open rafters. There was a loft, but the steps leading up to it were broken. Rot, and very likely rats, had eaten at the scarred wood floor.

It would require a great deal of cleaning out and repair, but the space was generous. He began to allow himself to dream.

The smell of wood under the saw, the tang of tongue oil, the slap of hammer on nail, the glint of brass, the squeak of rigging. He could already see the way the sun would slant in through new, clean windows onto the skeleton of a sloop.

"Throw up some walls, I guess, for an office," Cam was saying. Seth dashed here and there, exploring and exclaiming. "We'll have to draw up plans or something."

"This place is a heap," Phillip pointed out.

"Yeah, so it'll come cheap. We put a couple thousand into fixing it up—"

"Better to have it bulldozed and start over."

"Phil, try to control that wild optimism." Cam turned to Ethan. "What do you think?"

"It'll do."

"It'll do what?" Phillip threw up his hands. "Fall down around our ears?" At that moment a spider—which Phillip estimated to be about the size of a Chihuahua—crawled over the toe of his shoe. "Get me a gun," he muttered.

Cam only laughed and slapped him on the back. "Let's go see Claremont."

Stuart Claremont was a little man with hard eyes and a dissatisfied mouth. The little chunks of St. Christopher that he owned were most often left to fall into disrepair. If his tenants complained loudly enough, he occasionally, and grudgingly, tinkered with plumbing or heat or patched a roof.

But he believed in saving his pennies for a rainy day. In Claremont's mind, it never rained quite hard enough to part with a cent.

Still, his house on Oyster Shell Lane was a showplace. As anyone in St. Chris could tell you, his wife, Nancy, could nag the ears off a turnip. And she ruled that roost.

The wall-to-wall carpet was thick and soft, the walls prettily papered. Fussy curtains were ruthlessly coordinated with fussy upholstery. Magazines lay in military lines over a gleaming cherry wood coffee table that matched gleaming cherry wood end tables that matched gleaming cherry wood occasional tables.

Nothing was out of place in the Claremont house. Each room looked like a picture from a magazine. Like the picture, Cam mused, and not at all like life.

"So, you're interested in the barn." With a stretched-out grin that hid his teeth, Claremont ushered them all into his den. It was decorated in English baronial style. The dark paneling was accented with hunting prints. There were deep-cushioned leather chairs in a port wine shade, a desk with brass fittings, and a brick fireplace converted to gas.

The big-screen television seemed both out of place and typical.

"Mildly," Phillip told him. It had been agreed on the drive over that Phillip would handle the negotiations. "We've just started to look around for space."

"Terrific old place." Claremont sat down behind his desk and gestured them to chairs. "Lots of history."

"I'm sure, but we're not interested in history in this case. There seems to be a lot of rot."

"A bit." Claremont waved that away with one short-fingered hand. "You live round here, what can you expect? You boys thinking of starting some business or other?"

"We're considering it. We're in the talking-about-it stages."

"Uh-huh." Claremont didn't think so, or the three of them wouldn't be sitting on the other side of his desk. As he considered just how much rent he could pry out of them for what he considered an irritating weight around his neck, he looked at Seth. "Well, we'll talk about it, then. Maybe the boy here wants to go outside."

"No, he doesn't," Cam said without a smile. "We're all talking about it."

"If that's the way you want it." So, Claremont thought, that's the way it was. He could hardly wait to tell Nancy. Why, he'd had a good, close-up look at the kid now, and a half-blind idiot could see Ray Quinn in those eyes. Saint Ray, he thought sourly. It looked like the mighty had fallen, yes sir. And he was going to enjoy letting people know what was what.

"I'm looking for a five-year lease," he told Phillip, correctly judging who would be handling the business end.

"We're looking for one year at this point, with an option for seven. Of course, we'd expect certain repairs to be completed before we took occupancy."

"Repairs." Claremont leaned back in his chair. "Hah. That place is solid as a rock."

"And we'd require termite inspection and treatment. Regular maintenance would, of course, be our responsibility."

"Ain't no damn bugs in that place."

"Well, then." Phillip smiled easily. "You'd only have to arrange for the inspection. What are you asking for in rent?"

Because he was annoyed, and because he'd always despised Ray Quinn, Claremont bumped up his figure. "Two thousand a month."

"Two—" Before Cam could choke out his pithy opinion, Phillip rose. "No point in wasting your time, then. We appreciate you seeing us."

"Hold it, hold it." Claremont chuckled, fought off the little tug of panic at having a deal slip through his grasping fingers so quickly. "Didn't say that wasn't negotiable. After all, I knew your daddy . . ." He aimed that tight-lipped smile directly at Seth. "Knew him more than twenty-five years. I wouldn't feel right if I didn't give his . . . boys a little break."

"Fine." Phillip settled down again, resisted rubbing his hands together. He forgot all his objections to the overall plan in his delight in the art of the deal. "Let's negotiate."

"What the hell have I done?" Thirty minutes later, Phillip sat in his Jeep, methodically rapping his head against the steering wheel.

"A damn good job, I'd say." Ethan patted him on the shoulder. He'd reached the Jeep ahead of Cam this time and had taken winner's point in the front seat. "Cut his opening price in half, got him to agree to paying for most of the repairs if we do them ourselves, and confused him enough to have him go for the what-was-it—rent control clause if we take the seven-year option."

"The place is a dump. We're going to pay twelve thousand dollars a year—not including utilities and maintenance—for a pit."

"Yeah, but now it's our pit." Pleased, Cam stretched out his legs—or tried. "Pull that seat up some, Ethan, I'm jammed back here."

"Nope. Maybe you should drop me back by the place. I can start figuring things, and I can get a lift home later."

"We're going shopping," Cam reminded him.

"I don't need any damn shoes," Seth said again, but in reflex rather than annoyance.

"You're getting damn shoes, and you're getting a damn haircut while we're at it, and we're all going to the damn mall."

"I'd rather get hit with a brick than go to the mall on a Saturday." Ethan hunched down in his seat, pulled the brim of his cap low over his eyes. He couldn't bear to think about it.

"When you start working in that death trap," Phillip told him, "you'll likely be hit with a ton of them."

"If I have to get a haircut, everybody's getting one."

Cam glanced briefly at Seth's mutinous face. "You think this is a democracy? Shit. Grab some reality, kid. You're ten."

"You could use one." Phillip met Cam's eyes in the rearview mirror as he drove north out of St. Chris. "Your hair's longer than his."

"Shut up, Phil. Ethan, goddamn it, pull your seat up."

"I hate the mall." In defiance, Ethan stretched his own legs out and tipped the back of his seat down a notch. "It's full of people. Pete the barber's still got his place on Market Street."

"Yeah, and everybody who walks out of it looks like Beaver Cleaver." Frustrated, Cam gave the back of Ethan's seat a solid kick.

"Keep your feet off my upholstery," Phillip warned. "Or you'll walk to the damn mall."

"Tell him to give me some room."

"If I have to get shoes, I get to pick them out. You don't have any say in it."

"If I'm paying for the shoes, you'll wear what I tell you and like it."

"I'll buy the stinking shoes myself. I got twenty dollars."

Cam snorted out a laugh. "Try to get a grip on that reality again, pal. You can't buy decent socks for twenty these days."

"You can if you don't have to have some fancy designer label on them," Ethan tossed in. "This ain't Paris."

"You haven't bought decent shoes in ten years," Cam threw back. "And if you don't pull up that frigging seat, I'm going to—"

"Cut it out!" Phillip exploded. "Cut it out right now or I swear I'm going to pull over and knock your heads together. Oh, my God." He took one hand off the wheel to drag it down his face. "I sound like Mom. Forget it. Just forget it. Kill each other. I'll dump the bodies in the mall parking lot and drive to Mexico. I'll learn how to weave mats and sell them on the beach at Cozumel. It'll be quiet, it'll be peaceful. I'll change my name to Raoul, and no one will know I was ever related to a bunch of fools."

Seth scratched his belly and turned to Cam. "Does he always talk like that?"

"Yeah, mostly. Sometimes he's going to be Pierre and live in a garret in Paris, but it's the same thing."

"Weird," was Seth's only comment. He pulled a piece of bubble gum out of his pocket, unwrapped it, and popped it into his mouth. Getting new shoes was turning into an adventure.

∾

It would have stopped at shoes if Cam hadn't noticed that the seat of Seth's jeans was nearly worn through. Not that he thought that was a big deal, he assured himself. But it was probably best, since they were there anyway, to pick up a couple of pairs of jeans.

He had no doubt that if Seth hadn't bitched so much about trying on jeans, he himself wouldn't have felt compelled to push on to shirts, to shorts, to a windbreaker. And somehow they'd ended up with three ball caps, an Orioles sweatshirt, and a glow-in-the-dark Frisbee.

When he tried to think back to exactly where he'd taken that first wrong turn, it all became a blur of clothes racks, complaining voices, and cash registers churning.

The dogs greeted them with wild and desperate enthusiasm the minute they pulled into the drive. This would have been endearing but for the fact that the pair of them reeked of dead fish.

With much cursing and shoving and threats, the humans escaped into the house, shutting the dogs with their hurt feelings outside. The phone was ringing.

"Somebody get that," Cam pleaded. "Seth, take this junk upstairs, then go give those stinking dogs a bath."

"Both of them?" The thought thrilled him, but he thought it best to complain. "How come I have to do it?"

"Because I said so." Oh, he hated falling back on something that lame, and that adult. "The hose is around back. God, I want a beer."

But because he lacked the energy even for that, he dropped into the closest chair and stared glassy-eyed at nothing. If he had to face that mall again in this life, he promised himself, he would just shoot himself in the head and be done with it.

"That was Anna," Phillip told him as he wandered back into the living room.

"Anna? Saturday night." He couldn't stop the groan. "I need a transfusion."

"She said to tell you she'd take care of dinner."

"Good, fine. I've got to pull myself together. The kid's yours and Ethan's for tonight."

"He's Ethan's," Phillip corrected. "I've got a date myself." But he sank into a chair and closed his eyes. "It's not even five o'clock and all I want to do is crawl into bed and oblivion. How do people do this?"

"He's got enough clothes to last him a year. If we only have to do it once a year, how bad can it be?"

Phillip opened one eye. "He's got spring and summer clothes. What happens when fall gets here? Sweaters, coats, boots. And he's bound to outgrow every damn thing we bought today."

"We can't allow that to happen. There must be a pill or something we can give him. And maybe he's got a coat already."

"He came pretty much with the clothes on his back. Dad didn't get a package deal this time either."

"Okay, we'll think about that later. Lots later." Cam pressed his fingers to his eyes. "You saw the way Claremont looked at him, didn't you? That nasty little gleam in his beady little eyes."

"I saw it. He'll talk, and he'll say what he wants to say. Nothing we can do about it."

"You think the kid knows anything, one way or the other?"

"I don't know what Seth knows. I can't get a handle on him. But I'm going to look into investigators on Monday. Check on tracking down the mother."

"Asking for trouble."

"We've already got trouble. The only way to deal with it is to gather information. If it turns out that Seth's a Quinn by blood, then we deal with that."

"Dad wouldn't have hurt Mom that way. Marriage wasn't just a thing to them. It was *the* thing. And they were solid."

"If he'd slipped, he'd have told her." That Phillip firmly believed. "And they'd have worked it out. That part of their lives wasn't our business, and it wouldn't be our business now but for Seth."

"He wouldn't have slipped," Cam murmured, determined to believe it. "I'll tell you one thing I got from them. You get married, you make that promise, that's it. I figure that's why the three of us are still on the single side of life."

"Maybe. But we can't ignore the talk, the suspicions. And if the insurance company balks on paying off Dad's policy, it's going to put all four of us in a bind. Especially since we just signed a lease for that hellhole."

"We'll be okay. Luck's starting to move in our direction."

"Oh?" Phil asked as Cam rose. "How do you figure that?"

"Because I'm about to spend the evening with one of the sexiest women on the planet. And I intend to get very lucky." He glanced back as he started up the stairs. "Don't wait up, bro."

When he stepped into his bedroom, Cam heard the commotion from the backyard. He walked to the window and looked down on Seth and the dogs. Simon was sitting stoically while Seth soaped him down. Foolish raced in mad circles, barking in excitement and terror at the hose that was pouring out water where it had been carelessly tossed on the grass.

Of course, the kid was wearing his brand-new shoes, which were now soaking wet and muddy. He was laughing like a loon.

He hadn't known the boy could laugh like that, Cam realized as he kept watching. He hadn't known he could look like that, unreservedly happy and young and silly.

Simon stood up, gave a long, violent shake that sent water and soap flying. Backing up, Seth slipped in the wet grass and tumbled onto his back. He continued to howl with laughter as both dogs pounced on him. They wrestled over the water and mud and soap until the three of them were soaked and filthy.

Upstairs Cam just stood watching with a mile-wide grin on his face.

The image popped in his head when he headed down the hallway to Anna's apartment. He wanted to be able to tell her about it over dinner. He wanted to share it—and he thought it would certainly soften her every bit as much as a quiet meal in a candlelit restaurant.

The roses he'd picked up on the way weren't going to hurt either. He sniffed them himself. If he was any judge of the female mind and heart, he'd bet his full stake that Anna Spinelli had a weak spot for yellow roses.

Before he could knock on Anna's door, the door across the hall swung open. "Hello, there, you must be the new boyfriend."

"Hi, Mrs. Hardelman. We met a few days ago."

"No, we didn't. You met Sister."

"Oh." He smiled cautiously. She looked exactly like the woman who had popped out of that door before, even down to the pink chenille robe. "Well . . . how's it going?"

"You brought her flowers. She'll like that. My beaux used to bring me flowers, and my Henry, God rest his soul, brought me lilacs every May. You think lilacs next month, young man, if Anna lets you keep coming around. Most of them she scoots along, but maybe she'll keep you."

"Yeah." He managed to smile even as his heart stopped at the words "keep you." "Maybe." On impulse he pulled one of the roses out and gave it to her with a neat little flourish.

"Oh!" A girlish blush rose pink on her wrinkled face. "Oh, my goodness." Her eyes gleamed with pleasure as she sniffed it. "How lovely. How sweet. Why, if I were forty years younger, I'd fight Anna for you." She winked flirtatiously. "And I'd win."

"No contest." He flashed her a return wink and a grin. "Ah, say hi to . . . Sister."

"You have a nice time tonight. You go dancing," she added as she shut the door.

"Good idea." And chuckling to himself, Cam knocked.

When she answered, looking sexy enough to gobble up in three quick bites, he decided the dance should begin immediately. He snatched her up, whirled her around to the throbbing, elemental beat of classic Bruce Springsteen and the E Street Band. Then he dipped her as she laughed and stumbled.

"Well, hello." Enjoying the quick dizziness, she chuckled. "Let me up. You've got me off balance."

"That's just where I want you. Off balance." He lowered his mouth to hers in a molten kiss that melted every bone in her body. With her head spinning, she clutched at his shoulders.

"Door's still open," she managed and flailed out with a hand to slam it shut.

"Good thinking." He brought her up slowly, inch by inch, his mouth still nibbling busily on hers. "Your neighbor said I should take you dancing."

"Oh." She was surprised steam wasn't pumping out of her pores. "Is that what that was?"

"That was just a sample." He caught her bottom lip between his teeth, tugged, released. "Wanna tango, Anna?"

"I think we'd better sit this one out." But she pressed a hand to her heart to hold it in place as she eased out of his arms. "You brought me flowers." She buried her face in them as she took them from him. "Figured I was a sucker for rosebuds, did you?"

"Yeah."

"You're right." She laughed over the blooms. "I'll put them in water. You can pour us some wine. I've got it breathing on the counter. Glasses are right there."

"Okay. I—" He looked over, saw a shiny pot steaming on the stove, a platter of antipasto on the counter. "What's all this?"

"Dinner." She crouched down at a kitchen cupboard to locate a vase. "Didn't Phillip give you my message?"

"I thought when you told him you'd take care of it, you meant you had someplace you wanted to go and you'd make the reservations." He plucked a stuffed mushroom off the platter, sampled it, and sighed in pure sensory delight. "I didn't think you'd be cooking for me."

"I like to cook," she said easily as she filled a pale pink vase with water. "And I wanted to be alone with you."

He swallowed quickly. "Hard to argue with that. What are we having?"

"Linguini, with the famous Spinelli family red sauce."

She turned to take the glass of Merlot he'd poured for her. Her face was just a little flushed from the kitchen heat. The dress she'd chosen was the color of ripe peaches and molded her curves like a lover's hands. Her hair was down and curling madly, and her lips were painted nearly the same color as the wine she sipped.

Cam decided if they were to have more than a three-second conversation before he grabbed her again, he'd better stay on the opposite side of the counter.

"It smells incredible."

"It tastes better."

Her pulse was hammering everywhere at once. The way he'd looked at her, just that one long, intense, and measuring stare before he smiled, had brought out her need, a low and nagging ache of need, throbbing incessantly. On an impulse she reached back and turned the flame under the pot off. Keeping her eyes on Cam's, she walked around the counter.

"So do I," she told him. She set her glass aside, then took his, placed it on the counter. She shook her hair back, tipped her face up to his, smiled slowly. "Try me."

TWELVE

His blood was already pounding, a hard, primal beat, as he took a step forward. He looked into her eyes, wanting to see every shift and flicker of emotion. "I'm going to want to do more than try. So be sure."

Sometimes, she thought, you had to go with your instincts, with your cravings. At that moment hers, all of hers, centered on him. "You wouldn't be here tonight if I wasn't."

With a slow curving of lips, she reached up and twined his hair around her finger. She could handle him. She was sure of it.

He put his hands on her hips. This was no pencil-slim model with a body like a boy, but a woman. And he wanted her. He smiled back. He could handle her. He was sure of it. "You like to gamble, Anna?"

"Now and then."

"Let's roll the dice."

He brought her against him in one hard jerk, one that made her breath catch and release an instant before his mouth was on hers. The kiss was quickly desperate, quickly ravenous, tongues tangling, teeth nipping. The little feral purrs that sounded in her throat went straight to his head like hot whiskey.

She tugged his shirt free of his waistband, then her hands shot under. Flesh and muscle, she needed to feel it. With a hum of pleasure she kneaded and scraped and stroked until that flesh seemed to burn under her fingers, and those muscles hardened like iron.

She wanted those muscles, that strength pitted against her own.

He fumbled at the back of her dress, searching for a zipper, and she laughed breathlessly with her mouth at his throat. "It doesn't have a zipper." She closed her teeth over his jaw and didn't bother to be gentle. "You have to . . . peel it off."

"Jesus." He tugged the snug, stretchy material off her shoulder and replaced it with teeth as the craving for the taste of flesh, her flesh, overwhelmed him.

They circled like dancers, though their pace outdistanced the dreamy strains of the Chopin prelude that had replaced the Boss. He toed off his shoes. She rushed open the buttons of his shirt. His head was swimming as they bumped into the bedroom door. She laughed again, but the sound slipped toward a moan when he yanked the dress down to her waist, when those eyes of smoked steel streaked down, when he lowered his head and began to devour the flesh above the black lace edge of her bra.

His tongue slid under, teasing and tasting until her knees were loose and her head full of flashing lights and colors. She'd known he could do this to her, take her to that teetering edge of reason and insanity. She'd wanted him to. More, she'd wanted to take him there with her.

The wanting was huge, ruthlessly keen, recklessly primitive. And for now, for both of them, it was all that mattered.

Murmuring mindlessly, she dragged off his shirt and dug her nails into the hard ridge of his shoulders. His chest was broad and firm, the flesh hot and smooth under her roaming hands. There were scars, under the shoulder, along the ribs. The body, she thought, of a risk-taker, of a man who played to win.

With a quick and expert flick of his fingers, he opened the front hook and let her breasts fill his greedy hands. She was magnificent. Golden skin and lush curves. He thought her body almost impossibly perfect. Yet it was erotically real, soft and firm and smooth and fragrant. He wanted to bury himself in her, but when she tugged at the button of his slacks, he shook his head.

"Uh-uh. I want you in bed." He brought her hands up until they circled his neck, brought his mouth down until the kiss was savage and stunning. "I want you under me, over me, wrapped around me."

She kicked off one shoe, balancing herself as they swayed toward the bed. "I want you inside me." Kicked off the other as they tumbled to the mattress.

She rolled over him first, straddling him. The light was nearly gone. Only a pale wash from the setting sun slipped through the windows. Shadows shifted. Her lips were hungry, restless, racing over his face, his throat. Though she had wanted men before, now there was a ferocious and primal greed sweeping through her that she'd never experienced. She would take him, was all she could think, take what she wanted and ease this almost unbearable need.

When she arched back and her upper body was silhouetted in that fragile light, the breath clogged in his lungs. He wanted with an urgency he couldn't remember feeling for anything or anyone else. The desire to take, to possess, to own, surged violently in his already raging blood.

He reared up, gripping her hair in one hand, yanking her head back to expose that long column of throat to his mouth. He could have anything with her. Would have everything.

He was rougher than he meant to be as he pushed her back on the bed. His breath was already heaving as he locked his hands with hers. Her eyes were dark and gleaming—the kind of eyes, he thought, for a man to drown in. Her hair a tangled mass of black silk against the deep bronze of the spread. The scent of her was more than a provocative invitation. It was a smoldering demand.

Take me, it seemed to say. If you dare.

"I could eat you alive," he murmured and once more crushed his mouth to hers.

He held her down, knowing that if she wrestled free it would be over too soon. Fast, God, yes, he wanted fast, but he didn't want it to end. He thought he could live his life right here in this bed with Anna's quivering body under his.

Her hands flexed under his, her body arched when he drew the tip of her breast into his mouth. He could feel her heartbeat stumble as he used teeth, tongue, lips to taste, to pleasure them both.

When he'd filled himself on her, fed himself on her, he released her hands to touch, and be touched.

They rolled over the bed, groping, tugging at the clothes that remained between them. Their breath was quick and labored, punctuated by half gasps and low moans that spoke of turbulent thrills and dark delights. Sensation slid over sensation, building trembling layers toward delirium. She shuddered under his hands, nearly wept, as each new lash of pleasure whipped through her, each sharp and separate.

She fought to bring him the same barbed and edgy ache.

His hand closed over her, and she was hot and wet and ready. Her body arched, her nails bit into his back as her system exploded to peak.

Then they went mad.

She would remember only a battle for more. And more. Still more. Wild animal sex, a craving to mate. Seeking hands slid off damp flesh, hungry mouth sought hungry mouth. She came again, and her cry of release was a half sob of both triumph and helplessness.

The light was gone, but he could still see her. The glint of those dark eyes, the generous shape of that beautiful mouth. The blood roared in his head, in his heart, in his loins. He could think only *now* and drove himself hard and deep inside her.

His vision grayed, his mind reeled. They remained poised for a shivering moment, joined, mated. He wasn't even aware that his hands sought hers, that their fingers locked into fists.

Then they began to move, a race now full of speed and urgency. There was the good, healthy sound of damp flesh slapping against damp flesh. Their gazes met and held. He watched her eyes go blind and opaque as she crested, he heard the moan tear from her lips an instant before he closed his over hers to swallow the sound.

Her hips pumped like pistons, urging him on, driving him closer to his own jagged brink. He hammered himself into her, holding on to the edge by his fingertips. Watching her, watching her while the need for release clawed viciously at his gut. Then her body went taut, a drawn bow of shock and pleasure.

It was her scream he swallowed as he let himself fall.

∞

He couldn't possibly move. Cam was certain that if someone held a gun to his head at that moment, he would simply lie there and take the bullet. At least he'd die a satisfied man.

He couldn't think of a better place to be than stretched out over Anna's curvy body, with his face buried in her hair. And if he stayed there long enough, he might get his second wind.

The music had changed again. When his mind cleared enough for him to tune in to it, he recognized Paul Simon's clever twists of lyrics and melody. He nearly drifted off as he was invited to call the singer Al.

"If you fall asleep on top of me, I'm going to have to hurt you."

He drummed up the energy to smile. "I'm not going to sleep. I'm thinking about making love to you again."

"Oh." She stroked her hands down his back to his hips. "Are you?"

"Yeah. Just give me a couple of minutes."

"I'd be glad to. If I could breathe."

"Oh." Lazily he propped himself on his elbows and looked down at her. "Sorry."

She only grinned. "No, you're not. You're smug. But so am I, so that's okay."

"It was great sex."

"It was great sex," she agreed. "Now I'm going to finish dinner. We'll need fuel if we're going to try that again."

Both delighted and baffled, he shook his head. "You're a fascinating woman, Anna. No games, no pretenses. Looking the way you do, you could have men jumping through hoops."

She gave him a little shove so she could wiggle free. "What makes you think I haven't? You're exactly where I wanted you, aren't you?" Smiling, she rose and walked naked to the closet.

"That's a hell of a body you've got there, Miz Spinelli."

She glanced over her shoulder as she wrapped herself in a short red robe. "Same to you, Quinn."

She headed out to the kitchen, humming to herself as she turned the heat back on under the sauce, filled a pot with water for the pasta. Lord, it was lovely, she thought, to feel so loose, so limber, so liberated. However reckless it might be for her to take Cameron Quinn as a lover, the results were worth every risk.

He'd made her aware of every inch of her body, and every inch of his. He made her feel painfully alive. And best of all, she mused as she took out the bread she wanted to toast lightly, he seemed to understand her.

It was one thing to be wanted by a man, to be satisfied by a man. But it warmed her heart to be liked by the man who desired her.

She turned and picked up her wine just as Cam came out of the bedroom. He'd pulled on his slacks but hadn't bothered to hook them. Anna sipped slowly while she studied him over the rim of her glass. Broad shoulders, hard chest, the waist that tapered to narrow hips and long legs. Oh, yes, he had a terrific body.

And for now it was all hers.

She lifted a pepper from the tray and held it up to his lips.

"It's got bite," Cam said as the heat filled his mouth.

"Um-hmm. I like . . . bite." She picked up his wine and handed it to him. "Hungry?"

"As a matter of fact."

"It won't be long." And because she recognized the look in his eye, she slipped around the counter to stir her sauce. "The water's nearly on the boil."

"You know what they say about a watched pot," he began and started around the counter after her. It was the sketch on the refrigerator that distracted him from his half-formed plan to wrestle her to the kitchen floor. "Hey, that looks just like Foolish."

"It is Foolish. Seth drew it."

"Get out!" He hooked a thumb in his pocket as he took a closer study. "Really? It's damn good, isn't it? I didn't know the kid could draw."

"You would, if you spent more time with him."

"I spend time with him every day," Cam muttered. "He doesn't tell me dick." Cam didn't know where the vague annoyance had come from, but he didn't care for it. "How'd you get this out of him?"

"I asked," she said simply, and slid linguini into the boiling water.

Cam shifted on his feet. "Look, I'm doing the best I can with the kid."

"I didn't say you weren't. I just think you'll do better—with a little more practice and a little more effort."

She pushed her hair back. She hadn't meant to get into this. Her relationship with Cam was supposed to have two separate compartments, without their contents getting mixed up together. "You're doing a good job. I mean that. But you've got a long way to go, Cam, in gaining his trust, his affection. Giving your own. He's an obligation you're fulfilling, and that's admirable. But he's also a young boy. He needs love. You have feelings for him. I've seen them." She smiled over at him. "You just don't know what to do with them yet."

Cam scowled at the sketch. "So now I'm supposed to talk to him about drawing dogs?"

Anna sighed, then turned to frame Cam's face in her hands. "Just talk to him. You're a good man with a good heart. The rest will come."

Annoyed again, he gripped her wrists. He couldn't have said why the quiet understanding in her voice, the amused compassion in her eyes made him nervous. "I'm not a good man." His grip tightened just enough to make her eyes narrow. "I'm selfish, impatient. I go for the thrills because that's what suits me. Paying your debts doesn't have anything to do with having a good heart. I'm a son of a bitch, and I like it that way."

She merely arched a brow. "It's always wise to know yourself."

He felt a little flutter of panic in his throat and ignored it. "I'll probably hurt you before we're done."

Anna tilted her head. "Maybe I'll hurt you first. Willing to risk it?"

He didn't know whether to laugh or swear and ended up pulling her into his arms for a smoldering kiss. "Let's eat in bed."

"That was the plan," she told him.

The pasta was cold by the time they got to it, but that didn't stop them from eating ravenously.

They sat cross-legged on her bed, knees bumping, and ate in the glow of the half dozen candles she'd lighted. Cam shoveled in linguini and closed his eyes in pure sensory pleasure. "Goddamn, this is good."

Anna wound pasta expertly around her fork and bit. "You should taste my lasagna."

"I'm counting on it." Relaxed and lazy, he broke a piece of the crusty bread she'd put into a wicker basket and handed half to her.

Her bedroom, he'd noted, was different from the rest of the apartment. Here she hadn't gone for the practical, for the streamlined. The bed itself was a wide pool covered in soft rose sheets and a slick satin duvet in rich bronze. The headboard was a romantic arch of wrought iron, curvy and frivolous and plumped now with a dozen fat, colorful pillows.

The dresser he pegged as an antique, a heavy old piece of mahogany refinished to a rosy gleam. It was covered with pretty little bottles and bowls and a silver-backed brush. The mirror over it was a long oval.

There was a mahogany lady's vanity with a skirted stool and glinting brass handles. For some reason he'd always found that particular type of furniture incredibly sexy.

A copper urn was filled with tall, fussy flowers, the walls were crowded with art, and the windows framed in the same rich bronze as the spread.

This, he thought idly, was Anna's room. The rest of the apartment was still Miz Spinelli's. The practical and the sensual. Both suited her.

He reached over the side of the bed to the floor, where he'd put the bottle of wine. He topped off her glass.

"Trying to get me drunk?"

He flashed a grin at her. Her hair was tangled, the robe loose enough to have one shoulder curving free. Her big dark eyes seemed to laugh at both of them. "Don't have to—but it might be interesting anyway."

She smiled, shrugged and drank. "Why don't you tell me about your day?"

"Today?" He gave a mock shudder. "Nightmare time."

"Really." She twirled more pasta, fed it to him. "Details."

"Shopping. Shoes. Hideous." When she laughed, he felt the smile split his face. God, she had a great laugh. "I made Ethan and Phillip go with me. No way I was facing that alone. We had to practically handcuff the kid to get him to go. You'd think I was fitting him for a straitjacket instead of new high-tops."

"Too many men don't appreciate the joys, challenges, and nuances of shopping."

"Next time, you go. Anyway, I had my eye on this building on the waterfront. We checked it out before we headed to the mall. It'll do the job."

"What job?"

"The business. Boat building."

Anna set her fork down. "You're serious about that."

"Dead serious. The place'll do. It needs some work, but the rent's in line—especially since we're strong-arming the landlord into paying for most of the basic repairs."

"You want to build boats."

"It'll get me out of the house, keep me off the streets." When she didn't smile back, he shrugged his shoulder. "Yeah, I think I could get into it. For now, anyway. We'll do this one for the client Ethan's already got lined up, see how it goes from there."

"I take it you signed a lease."

"That's right. Why putz around?"

"Some might say caution, consideration, details."

"I leave the caution and consideration to Ethan, the details to Phillip. If it doesn't work, all we've lost is a few bucks and a little time."

Odd how that prickly temper suited him, she mused. It went so well with those dark, damn-it-all looks. "And if it does work," she added. "Have you thought of that?"

"What do you mean?"

"If it works, you'll have taken on another commitment. It's getting to be a habit." She laughed now, at the expression of annoyance and surprise on his face. "It's going to be fun to ask you how you feel about all this in six months or so." She leaned forward and kissed him lightly. "How about some dessert?"

The nagging worry the word "commitment" had brought on faded back as her lips rubbed over his. "Whatcha got?"

"Cannoli," she told him as she set their plates on the floor.

"Sounds good."

"Or—" Watching him, she unbelted her robe, let it slide off her shoulders. "Me."

"Sounds better," he said and let her pull him to her.

✥

It was just after three when Seth heard the car pull into the drive. He'd been asleep but having dreams. Bad ones, where he was back in one of those smelly rooms where the walls were stained and thinner than his drawing paper, and every sound carried through them.

Sex noises—grunts and groans and creaking mattresses—his mother's nasty laugh when she was coked up. It made him sweat, having those dreams. Sometimes she would come in to where he was trying to find comfort and sleep on the musty sofa. If her mood was good, she would laugh and give him smothering hugs, waking him out of a fitful sleep into the smells and sounds of the world she'd dragged him into.

If her mood was bad, she would curse and slap and often end up sitting on the floor crying wildly.

Either way made for one more miserable night.

But worse, hundreds of times worse, was when one of the men she'd taken to bed slipped out, crept across the cramped room, and touched him.

It hadn't happened often, and waking up screaming and swinging drove them off. But the fear lived inside him like a red-hot demon. He'd learned to sleep on the floor behind the sofa whenever she had a man around.

But this time Seth hadn't waked from nightmare to worse. He fought his way out of the sweaty dream and found himself on clean sheets, with a snoring puppy curled beside him.

He cried a little, because he was alone and there was no one to see. Then he snuggled closer to Foolish, comforted by the soft fur and steady heartbeat. The sound of the car coming in stopped him from drifting back to sleep.

His first thought was *cops!* They'd come to get him, to haul him away. Then he told himself, even as his heart jumped up to pound in his throat, that he was being a baby. Still, he crept out of bed, padded silently to the window to look.

He had a hiding place picked out if one was needed.

It was the 'Vette. Seth told himself he'd have recognized the sound of its engine if he hadn't been half asleep. He saw Cam get out, heard the soft, cheerful whistling.

Been out poking at some woman, Seth decided with a sneer. Grown-ups were so predictable. When he remembered that Cam was supposed to have dinner with the social worker that night, his eyes went wide, his jaw dropped.

Man, oh, man, he thought. Cam was bouncing on Miss Spinelli. That was so . . . weird. So weird, he realized he didn't know how he felt about it. One thing for sure, he realized as Cam whistled his way to the door—Cam felt just fine and dandy about it.

When he heard the front door close, he snuck to his own bedroom door. He wanted to get a quick peek, but at the sound of feet coming up the stairs he dived back into bed. Just in case.

The puppy whimpered, began to stir, and Seth slammed his eyes shut as the door opened.

When the footsteps came slowly, quietly toward the bed, his heart began to pound in his chest. What would he do? he thought in a sick panic. God, what could he do? Foolish's tail began to thump on the bed as Seth cringed and waited for the worst.

"Guess you think this is a pretty good deal, lazing around half the day, getting your belly filled, having a nice soft bed at night," Cam murmured.

His voice was slightly slurred from lack of sleep, but to Seth it sounded like drugs or liquor. He struggled to keep his breathing slow and steady while his heartbeat pounded like a jackhammer against his ribs, in his head.

"Yeah, you fell into roses, didn't you? And didn't have to do a thing to earn it. Goofy-looking dog." Seth nearly blinked, realizing Cam was speaking to Foolish and not him. "It'll be his problem, won't it, when you're grown and take up more of the bed than he does."

Cautious, Seth slitted his eyes open just enough so he could see through his lashes. He saw Cam's hand come down, give Foolish a quick, careless stroke. Then the tangled sheets and blanket came up, smoothed over his shoulders. That same hand gave Seth's head a quick and careless stroke.

When the door closed again, Seth waited thirty full seconds before daring to open his eyes. He looked straight into Foolish's face. The pup seemed to be grinning at him as though they'd gotten away with something. Grinning back, Seth draped an arm around the pup's pudgy body.

"I guess it is a pretty good deal, huh, boy?" he whispered.

In agreement, Foolish licked Seth's face, then yawning hugely, settled down to sleep again.

This time, when Seth dropped off to sleep, there were no sweaty dreams to haunt him.

THIRTEEN

"You're awfully damn happy these days."
Cam acknowledged Phillip's pithy comment with a shrug and kept on whistling while he worked. They were making decent progress on what Cam jokingly thought of as their shipyard. It was hard, sweaty, filthy work.

And every time Cam compared it to laundry detail, he praised God.

Though what windows weren't broken were open wide, the air still carried a vague chemical scent. At Phillip's insistence they'd bought a batch of insect bombs and blasted the place with killing fog. When it cleared, the death toll was heavy. It took nearly a half a day just to clear out the corpses.

Replacement windows were slated to be delivered that day. Claremont had bitched bitterly about the expense—despite the deal he got on them because his brother-in-law managed the lumber company in Cambridge and had sold them to him at cost. He'd been only slightly mollified that the Quinns would rip out the old windows and install the new ones, saving him from hiring laborers.

If the fact that the improvements to the building would spike the potential resale value pleased him, he kept that small delight to himself.

They'd pried or punched out rotted boards and hauled them outside to a steadily growing pile of discards. The metal banister of the stairs leading up to the overhead loft was rusted through, so they yanked it out. Claremont was able to finesse the proper permits, so they were tossing up a couple of walls to close in what would be a bathroom.

Because Cam considered this kind of work a hobby, one he enjoyed, and he came home most nights to a clean house and had a pretty woman willing to tango with him whenever time and circumstances permitted, he figured he had a right to be happy.

Hell, the kid had even been doing his homework—most of the time. He had turned in the much-despised essay and was halfway through his probation without incident.

Cam figured his luck had been running hot and strong for the past couple of weeks.

As far as Phillip was concerned, it had been the worst two weeks of his life. He had barely spent any time in his apartment, had lost his favorite pair of Magli loafers to the gnawing puppy teeth of Foolish, hadn't seen the inside of a single four-star restaurant, and hadn't so much as sniffed a woman.

Unless he counted Mrs. Wilson at the supermarket, and he damn well didn't.

Instead, he was handling and juggling and bouncing details that no one else so much as thought about, getting blisters on his hands swinging a hammer, and spending his evenings wondering what had happened to life as he'd known it.

The fact that he knew Cam was getting regular sex fried the hell out of him.

When the board he lifted gifted him with a fat splinter in the thumb, he swore ripely. "Why the hell didn't we hire carpenters?"

"Because, as keeper of our magic funds, you pointed out it's cheaper this way. And Claremont gave us the first month's rent free if we did it ourselves." Cam took the board himself, placed it, and began to hammer in the next stud. "You said it was a good deal."

Gritting his teeth, he yanked out the splinter, sucked on his aching thumb. "I was insane at the time."

Phillip stepped back, hands on his hips above his tool belt, and surveyed the area. It was filthy. Dirt, sawdust, piles of refuse, stacks of lumber, sheets of plastic. This was not his life, he thought again, as the sound of Cam's hammer thudded in time with the gritty rock beat of Bob Seger that pumped out of the radio.

"I must have been insane. This place is a dump."

"Yep."

"Setting up this idiotic business is going to devour our capital."

"No doubt about it."

"We'll go under in six months."

"Could be."

Phillip scowled and reached down for the jug of iced tea. "You don't give a good damn."

"If it bombs, it bombs." Cam tucked his hammer back in his belt, took out his measuring tape. "We're no worse off. But if it makes it, if it just bumps along for a while, we'll have what we need."

"Which is?"

Cam picked up the next board, eyeballed it along its length, then set it over the sawhorses. "A business—which Ethan can run after the dust settles. He gets himself a couple of part-timers—off-season watermen—he builds three or four boats a year to keep it afloat."

He paused long enough to mark the board, run the saw. Dust flew and the noise was awesome. Cam set the power saw aside, hefted the board into place. "I'll give him a hand now and then, you'll keep track of the money end. But it ought to give us room to move some. I can get in a few races a year, you can get back to bilking the consumer with jazzy ads." He pulled out his hammer. "Everybody's happy."

Phillip cocked his head, scratched his chin. "You've been thinking."

"That's right."

"When do you figure this slide back to normality's going to happen?"

Cam swiped at the sweat on his forehead with the back of his hand. "The faster we get this place up and running, the faster we get the first boat done."

"Which explains why you've been busting your ass, and mine. Then what?"

"I've got enough contacts to line up a second job, even a third." He thought of Tod Bardette—the bastard—even now priming a crew for the One-Ton Cup. Yeah, he could finesse Bardette into a boat by Quinn. And there were others, plenty of others, who would pay and pay well. "I figure my main contribution to this enterprise is contacts. Six months," he said. "We can handle six months."

"I'm going back to work Monday," Phillip told him, braced for a fight. "I've got to. I'm flexing time so I'll only be in Baltimore Monday through Thursday. It's the best I can do."

Cam considered. "Okay. I don't have a problem with that. But you'll be busting ass on weekends."

For six months, Phillip thought. More or less. Then he hissed out a breath. "One factor you haven't worked into your plan. Seth."

"What about him? He'll be here. He's got a place to live. I'm going to use the house as a base."

"And when you're off breaking records and female hearts in Monte Carlo?"

Cam scowled and rapped the hammer harder than necessary on the head of the nail. "He doesn't want to be in my damn pocket all the time. You guys'll be around when I'm not. The kid's going to be taken care of."

"And if the mother comes back? They haven't been able to find her. Nothing. I'd feel better if we knew where she is and what she's up to."

"I'm not thinking about her. She's out of the picture." Has to be, Cam insisted, remembering the look of pasty-faced terror on Seth's face. "She's not going to mess with us."

"I'd like to know where she is," Phillip said again. "And what the hell she was to Dad."

Cam put it out of his mind. His way of handling loose ends was to knot them up together and forget about them. The immediate problem, as he saw it, was getting the building in shape, ordering equipment, tools, supplies. If the business was a means to an end, it had to begin.

Every day he worked on the building was one day closer to escape. Every dollar he poured into supplies and equipment was an investment in the future. His future.

He was keeping his promise, he told himself. His way.

With the sun beating down on his back and a faded blue bandanna tied around his head, he ripped broken shingles off the roof. Ethan and Phillip were working behind him, replacing shingles. Seth appeared to be having a fine time winging the discarded ones from roof to ground, and a satisfying pile was forming below.

It was a cool place to be as far as Seth was concerned. Up on the roof with the sun beating down and the occasional gull flying by. You could see just about everything from up here. The town, with its straight streets and square yards. The old trees popping up out of the grass. The flowers were okay, too. From up here they were just blobs and dots of color. Someone was mowing, and the sound carried up to him like a distant hum.

He could see the waterfront, with the boats at dock or cruising along the water. A couple of kids were sailing a little skiff with blue sails, and because he envied them, he looked away toward the docks.

There were people, shopping or strolling or eating lunch at one of the outdoor tables with umbrellas. Tourists were watching the show the crab pickers put on. He liked to sneer at the tourists; when he did, he didn't envy the boys in their neat little boat quite so much.

He wished he had the binoculars Ray had given him so he could see even farther. He wished he could sit up here sometime with his sketchbook.

Everything looked so . . . clean from up here. The sky and water both so blue, the grass and leaves so green. You could smell the water if you took a good sniff—and maybe that was hot dogs grilling.

The scent made his stomach growl with hunger. He shifted a little and looked at Cam out of the corner of his eye. Man, he wished he had muscles like that. With muscles like that you could do anything and nobody could stop you. If a guy had muscles like that he would never have to be afraid of anything, anyone, ever in his whole life.

Testing his own biceps with his finger, he was far from satisfied. He thought maybe if he got to use tools, he could harden them up.

"You said I could pull some of them off," Seth reminded him.

"Later."

"You said later before."

"I'm saying it again." It was hot, nasty, tedious work, and Cam wanted it over as much as he wanted to breathe. He'd already sweated through his T-shirt and pulled it off. His back gleamed damp and his throat was desert-dry. He pried off another square and watched Seth send it soaring. "You throwing them in the same place?"

"That's what you said to do."

He eyed the boy. Seth's hair stuck out from under an Orioles fielder's cap that Cam had ended up buying him when they went to a game the week before. Now that he thought of it, Cam didn't think he'd seen the kid without the cap since he got it.

The ball game had been an impulse, he thought now, just one of those things. But it had given him a sharp tug to see the way Seth's eyes had gone huge at the sight of Camden Yards. How he'd sat there, a hot dog clutched and forgotten in his hand as he watched every movement on the field.

And it had made Cam laugh when Seth's serious and firm opinion had been "It looks like shit on TV compared to this."

He watched Seth send another shingle flying and wondered if he should teach the kid how to field a ball. Instantly, the fact that he had had the thought irritated him. "You're not looking where you're throwing them."

"I know where they're going. If you don't like how I do it, you can throw them down yourself. You said I could pull some off."

Not worth it, Cam told himself. Not worth the effort to argue. "Fine, you want to rip shingles off the damn roof. Here, look, see how I'm doing this? You use the claw of the hammer and—"

"I've been watching you for an hour. It doesn't take brains to rip off shingles."

"Fine," Cam said between his teeth. "You do it." He shoved the hammer into Seth's eager hand. "I'm going down. I need a drink."

Cam went nimbly down the ladder, trying to assure himself that all ten-year-old boys were snotty assholes. And the more shingles the kid ripped free, the fewer there would be for him to do himself. If he survived the day, he had another Saturday night date with Anna. He wanted to make the most of it.

Now there was a woman, he thought as he grabbed the jug of ice water and glugged some down. Damn near the perfect woman. Though it occasionally gave him an uneasy feeling in the gut to think of her that way, it was tough to find the flaws.

Beautiful, smart, sexy. That great laugh she let loose so often. Those gorgeous, warm, understanding eyes. The wild spirit of adventure tucked into the practical public servant suits.

And she could cook.

He chuckled to himself and pulled out another bandanna to mop his face.

Why, if he was the settling-down type, he would snatch her right up. Get a ring on her finger, say the I-do's, and tuck her into his house—his bed—on a permanent basis.

Hot meals, hot sex.

Conversation. Laughter. Slow smiles to wake you up in the morning. Shared looks that said more than dozens of words.

When he caught himself staring into space, the jug dangling from his fingers and a stupid grin on his face, he shook himself hard. Let out a long breath.

The sun had baked his brain, he decided. Permanent wasn't his style. Never had been. And marriage—the word made him shudder—was for other people.

Thank God Anna wasn't looking for any more than he was. A nice, easy, no strings, no frills relationship suited them both.

To ensure that his mind didn't go hot again, he dumped frigid water over his head. Six months, he promised himself as he started back outside. Six months and he would start easing himself back into his own world. Competition, speed, glittery parties, and women who were only looking for a fast ride.

When the thought of it fell flat, when the image of it all left him hollow inside, he swore. It was what he wanted, goddamn it. What he knew. Where he belonged. He wasn't cut out to spend his life building boats for other people to sail, raising a kid and worrying about matching socks.

Sure, maybe he'd teach the kid how to field a grounder or a pop fly, but that was no big deal. Maybe Anna Spinelli was firmly hooked in his brain, but that didn't have to be a big deal either.

He needed room, he needed freedom.

He needed to race.

His thoughts were boiling as he stepped outside. The aluminum extension ladder nearly crashed on top of him. His hot oath and the muffled scream overhead sounded as one.

When he looked up, his heart simply stopped beating.

Seth dangled from his fingertips from the broken frame of a window twenty feet above. In the space of a trio of heartbeats, Cam saw the pattern on the bottom of the new high-tops, the dangling laces, the droopy socks. Before he could draw the first breath, both Ethan and Phillip were leaning over the roof and struggling to reach Seth.

"You hold on," Ethan shouted. "Hear me?"

"Can't." Panic made Seth's voice thin, and very, very young. "Slipping."

"We can't reach him from here." Phillip's voice was deadly calm, but his eyes as they stared down at Cam's were bright with fear. "Put the ladder up. Quick."

He made the decision in seconds, though it seemed like the rest of his life. Cam gauged the time it would take to haul the ladder into place, to climb up or climb down to where Seth hung. Too long, was all he could think, and he moved to stand directly under Seth.

"You let go, Seth. Just let go. I'll catch you."

"No. I can't." His fingers were raw and bleeding and nearly gave way as he shook his head fiercely. Panic skittered up his spine like hungry mice. "You won't."

"Yes, you can. I will. Close your eyes and just let go. I'm here." Cam planted his legs apart and ignored his own trembling heart. "I'm right here."

"I'm scared."

"Me, too. Let go. Do it!" he said so sharply that Seth's fingers released on instinct.

It seemed as though he fell forever, endlessly. Sweat poured down Cam's face. Air refused to come into Seth's lungs. Though his eyes stung from sun and salt, Cam never took them off the boy. His arms were there, braced and ready as Seth tumbled into them.

Cam heard the explosion of breath, his, Seth's, he didn't know which as they both fell heavily. Cam used his body to cushion the boy, took the hard ground on his bare back. But in an instant, he was up on his knees. He spun Seth around and plastered the boy against him.

"Christ! Oh, Christ!"

"Is he all right?" Ethan shouted from above.

"Yeah. I don't know. Are you okay?"

"I think. Yeah." He was shaking badly, his teeth chattering, and when Cam loosened his hold enough to look into his face he saw deathly pale skin and huge, glassy eyes. He sat down on the ground, pulled Seth into his lap, and pushed the boy's head between his knees.

"Just shaken up," he called to his brothers.

"Nice catch." Phillip sat back on the roof, rubbed his hands over his

clammy face, and figured his heart rate would get back to normal in another
year or two. "Jesus, Ethan, what was I thinking of, sending that kid down
for water?"

"Not your fault." Hoping to steady both of them, Ethan squeezed
Phillip's shoulder. "Nobody's fault. He's okay. We're okay." He looked
down again, intended to tell Cam to get the ladder. But what he saw was the
man holding on to the boy, his cheek pressed to the top of the boy's hair.

The ladder could wait.

"Just breathe," Cam ordered. "Just take it slow. You got the wind
knocked out of you, that's all."

"I'm okay." But he kept his eyes closed, terrified that he would throw up
now and totally humiliate himself. His fingers were burning, but he was
afraid to look. When it finally sank in that he was being held, and held close,
it wasn't sick panic, it wasn't shuddering disgust that raced through him.

It was gratitude, and a sweet, almost desperate relief.

Cam closed his eyes as well. And it was a mistake. He saw Seth falling
again, falling and falling, but this time he wasn't quick enough, or strong
enough. He wasn't there at all.

Fear bent under fury. He whirled Seth around until their faces were close
and shook him. "What the hell were you doing? What were you thinking of?
You idiot, you could have broken your neck."

"I was just—" His voice hitched, mortifying him. "I was only—I didn't
know. My shoe was untied. I must've stepped wrong. I only . . ."

But the rest of the words were muffled against Cam's hard, sweaty chest
as he was pulled close again. He could feel the rapid beat of Cam's heart,
hear it thunder under his ear. And he closed his eyes again. And slowly, test-
ingly, his arms crept around to hold.

"It's all right," Cam murmured, ordering himself to calm down.
"Wasn't your fault. You scared the shit out of me."

His hands were trembling, Cam realized. He was making a fool of himself. Deliberately, he pulled Seth back and grinned. "So, how was the ride?"

Seth managed a weak smile. "I guess it was pretty cool."

"Death-defying." Because they were both feeling awkward, they eased
back slowly, warily. "Good thing you're puny yet. You had any weight on
you, you might have knocked me out cold."

"Shit," Seth said, because he couldn't think of anything else.

"Messed up your hands some." Cam frowned consideringly at the
bloody, torn fingertips. "Guess we better get the rest of the crew down and
fix you up."

"It's nothing." It hurt like fire.

"No use having you bleed to death." Because his hands still weren't quite steady, Cam made quick work of lifting the ladder into place. "Go on in and get the first aid kit," he ordered. "Looks like Phil was on the mark when he made us buy the damn thing. We might as well use it on you."

After he watched Seth go inside, out of sight, Cam simply lowered his brow to the side of the ladder. His stomach continued to jump, and a headache he hadn't been aware of until that instant roared through his temples like a freight train.

"You okay?" Ethan put a hand on Cam's shoulder the minute he was on the ground.

"I've got no spit. My spit's dried clean up. Never been so fucking scared."

"That makes three of us." Phillip glanced around. Because his knees were still wobbly, he sat on one of the rungs of the ladder. "How bad are his hands? Does he need a doctor?"

"Fingers are ripped up some. It's not too bad." At the sound of a car pulling into the loose-gravel lot, he turned to see who it was. And his jittery stomach sank. "Oh, perfect. Sexy social worker at three o'clock."

"What's she doing here?" Ethan pulled his cap down lower on his head. He hated having women around when he was sweaty.

"I don't know. We have a date tonight, but not until seven. She's going to have some damn female thing to say about us having the kid up there in the first place."

"So we won't tell her," Phillip murmured even as he shot Anna a charming, welcoming smile. "Well, this brightens the day. Nothing better than to see a beautiful woman after a tough morning's work."

"Gentlemen." She only smiled when Phillip took her hand and brought it to his lips. Amusement rippled through her. Three men, three brothers, three reactions. Phillip's polished welcome, Ethan's vaguely embarrassed nod, and Cam's irritated scowl.

And there was no doubt each and every one of them looked outrageously male and appealing in sweat and tool belts.

"I hope you don't mind. I wanted to see the building, and I did come bearing gifts. There's a picnic hamper in my car—men food," she added. "For anyone who'd like a lunch break."

"That was nice of you. Appreciate it." Ethan shifted his feet. "I'll go fetch it out of your car."

"Thanks." She surveyed the building, tipped down her round-lensed wire-rimmed sunglasses, studied it again. All she could think was that she was glad she'd dressed casually for this impromptu visit, in roomy jeans and a T-shirt. There was no way to go in there, she imagined, and come out clean. "So this is it."

"The start of our empire," Phillip began, having just figured out that he could take her on a tour around the outside and give Cam enough time to clean Seth up—and shut him up—when the boy came out.

The color was back in his face—which was filthy with sweat, dirt, and the blood that he'd smeared on his cheeks from his fingers. His white Just Do It T-shirt was in the same condition. He carried the first aid kit like a banner.

Alarm shot into Anna's eyes. She was rushing toward Seth, taking him gently by the shoulders before either Cam or Phillip could think of a reasonable story. "Oh, honey, you're hurt. What happened?"

"Nothing," Cam began. "He just—"

"I fell off the roof," Seth piped up. He'd calmed down while he was inside and had gone from being weak-kneed to wildly proud.

"Fell off the—" Shocked to numbness, Anna instinctively began to check for broken bones. Seth stiffened, then squirmed, but she continued grimly until she was satisfied. "My God. What are you doing walking around?" She turned her head long enough to aim a furious glare at Cam. "Have you called an ambulance?"

"He doesn't need a damn ambulance. It's just like a woman to fall to pieces."

"Fall to pieces." Keeping a protective hand on Seth's shoulder, she whirled on them. "Fall to pieces! The three of you are standing around here like a herd of baboons. The child could have internal injuries. He's bleeding."

"Just my fingers." Seth held them out, admiring them. Man, was he going to be the hot topic in school come Monday! "I slipped off the ladder coming down, but I caught myself on the window frame up there." He pointed it out helpfully, while Anna's head spun from the height. "And Cam told me to let go and he'd catch me, and I did and he did."

"Damn kid won't say two words half the time," Cam muttered to Phillip. "The other half he won't shut the hell up. He's fine," he said, lifting his voice. "Just knocked the wind out of him."

She didn't bother to respond, only sent him one long, fulminating look before turning back to smile at Seth. "Why don't I take a look at your hands, honey? We'll clean them up and see if you need stitches." She lifted her chin, but the shaded glasses didn't quite conceal the heat in her eyes. "Then I'd like to speak with you, Cameron."

"I bet you would," he mumbled as she led Seth toward her car.

Seth found he didn't mind being babied a bit. It was a new experience to have a woman fuss over a little blood. Her hands were gentle, her voice soothing. And if his fingers throbbed and stung, it was a small price to pay for what now seemed a glorious adventure.

"It was a long way down," he told her.

"Yes, I know." Thinking of it only made the ball of anger in her stomach harden. "You must have been terrified."

"I was only scared for a minute." He bit the inside of his cheek so he wouldn't whimper as she carefully bandaged his wounds. "Some kids would've screamed like a girl and wet their pants."

He wasn't sure if he'd screamed or not—that part was a blur—but he'd checked his jeans and knew he was okay there. "And Cam, he was pissed off. You'd think I kicked the damn ladder out from under me on purpose."

Her head came up. "He yelled at you?"

He started to expand on that, but there was something about her eyes that made it hard to tell an out-and-out lie. "For a minute. Mostly he just got goofy about it. You'd think I'd had my arm whacked off the way he was carrying on, patting on me and stuff."

He shrugged, but remembered the warm glow in his gut at being held close, safe, tight. "Some guys, you know? They can't take a little blood."

Her smile softened, and she reached up to brush his hair back. "Yeah, I know. Well, you're in pretty good shape for a guy who likes to dive off roofs. Don't do it again, okay?"

"Once was enough."

"Glad to hear it. There's fried chicken in the hamper—unless they've eaten it all."

"Yeah. Man, I could eat a dozen pieces." He started to race off, then felt a tug on his conscience. It was another rare sensation, and it caused him to turn back and meet her eyes. "Cam said he'd catch me, and he did. He was cool."

Then he ran toward the building, shouting for Ethan to save him some damn chicken.

Anna only sighed. She sat there on the side of the passenger seat while she put the first aid kit back in order. When the shadow fell across her, she continued to tidy up. She could smell him, sweat, man, the faint undertones of the soap from his morning shower. She knew his scent so well now—and the way it would mix with her own—that she could have picked him out of a roomful of men had she been handcuffed and blindfolded.

And though it was certainly true that she'd been curious about the building, it was really only a handy excuse to drive over from Princess Anne to see him.

"I don't suppose there's any point in me telling you that boys Seth's age shouldn't be going up and down extension ladders unsupervised."

"I don't suppose there is."

"Or that boys his age are careless, often awkward, and clumsy."

"He's not clumsy," Cam said with some heat. "He's agile as a monkey. Of course," he added with a sneer in his voice, "the rest of us are baboons, so that fits."

She closed the first aid kit, rose, and handed it to him. "Apparently," she agreed. "However, accidents happen, no matter how careful you are, no matter how hard you try to prevent them. That's why they're accidents."

She looked at his face. The irritation was still there, she noted—with her, with circumstances. And oh, that underlying anger that never seemed to fade completely away was very, very close to the surface.

"So," she said softly, "how many years of your life did that little event shave off?"

He let out a breath. "A couple of decades. But the kid handled himself."

He turned a little, to look back toward the building. It was then that Anna saw the smears of blood on his back. Smears, she realized after her heart's first leap, that had come from Seth's hands. The boy had been held, she thought. And the boy had held on.

Cam turned back, caught her smiling. "What?"

"Nothing. Well, since I'm here, and you're all eating my food, I think I'm entitled to a tour."

"How much of this business are you going to have to put in one of your reports?"

"I'm not on the clock," she told him, more sharply than she intended. "I thought I was coming to pay a visit to friends."

"I didn't mean it that way, Anna."

"Really?" She stepped around the car door and slammed it shut at her back. Damn it, she had come to see him, to be with him, not to fit in an unannounced home visit. "What I will put in my next report, unless I see something to the contrary, is that it's my opinion that Seth is bonding with his guardians and they with him. I'll make sure you get a copy. I'll take a rain check on the tour. You can get the hamper back to me at your convenience."

She thought it was a great exit as exits went, striding around the car while she tossed off her lines. Her temper was flaring but just under control. Then he grabbed her as she reached for the car door and spoiled it.

She whirled around swinging, but her fist slid off his damp chest and ruined the impact. "Hands off."

"Where are you going? Just hold it a minute."

"I don't have to hold anything, and I don't want you holding me." She shoved at him with both hands. "God, you're filthy!"

"If you'd just be still and listen—"

"To what? You don't think I get it? You don't think I've clued in to what you saw, what you thought when I pulled up. 'Oh, hell, here comes the social worker? Close ranks, boys.' " She jerked back. "Well, fuck you."

He could have denied it, could have taken the I-don't-know-what-you're-talking-about approach and done an expert job of it. But her eyes had the same effect on him as they'd had on Seth. They wouldn't let his tongue wrap itself around a decent lie.

"Okay, you're right. It was knee-jerk."

"At least you have the decency to be honest." The depth of the hurt infuriated her as much as it surprised her.

"I don't know what you're so frosted about."

"Don't you?" She tossed back her hair. "Then I'll tell you. I looked at you and saw a man who also happens to be my lover. You looked at me and saw a symbol of a system you don't trust or respect. Now that that's cleared up, get out of my way."

"I'm sorry." He dragged the bandanna off because his head was splitting. "You're right again, and I'm sorry."

"So am I." She started to open the car door.

"Will you give me a damn minute here?" Instead of reaching for her again, he dragged his hands through his hair. It wasn't the impatient tone that stopped her, but the weariness of the gesture.

"All right." She let go of the door handle. "You've got a minute."

He didn't think there was another woman on the planet he'd explained himself to more than the one watching him now with a faint frown. "We were all a little shaken up right then. The timing couldn't have been worse. Goddamn it, my hands were still shaking."

He hated to admit that—hated it. To gather some control, he turned away, paced off, paced back. "I was in a wreck once. About three years ago. Grand Prix. Hit the chute, misjudged, went into a hell of a spin. The car was breaking apart around me. The worst fear is invisible fire. Vapors catching hold. I had this flash of myself burned to a crisp. Just for an instant, but it was vivid."

He balled the bandanna up in his hand, then pulled it out smooth. "I'm telling you, Anna, I swear to you, standing under that kid and watching his shoelaces dangle was worse. Hell of a lot worse."

How could she hold on to her anger? And why couldn't he see that he had such a huge well of love to give if he would only let himself dip into it freely? He'd said that he would probably hurt her, but she hadn't known it would come so soon, or from this direction.

She hadn't been looking in the right direction. She hadn't known she was falling in love with him.

"I can't do this," she said, half to herself, and wrapped her hands around her arms to warm them. The chill penetrated, even though she stood in streaming sun. How many steps had she taken toward love, she wondered, and how many could she take back to save herself? "I don't know what I was thinking of. Being involved with you on a personal level only complicates our mutual interest in the child."

"Don't back off from me, Anna." He experienced another level of fear now, one he'd never felt before. "So we take a few wrong steps. We get the balance back. We're good together."

"We're good in bed," she said and blinked when she saw what might have been hurt flash in his eyes.

"Only?"

"No," she said slowly as he stepped toward her, "not only. But—"

"I've got something for you inside me, Anna." He forgot his hands were grimy and laid them on her shoulders. "I haven't used it up yet. This thing with you, it's one of the first times I haven't wanted to rush to the finish line."

They would still get there, she realized. She would have to be prepared for him to reach that line, and cross it, ahead of her. "Don't mix up who I am and what I am," she told him quietly. "You have to be honest with me, or the rest of it means nothing."

"I've been more up front with you than I've ever been with a woman before. And I know who you are."

"All right." She laid a hand on his cheek when he bent to kiss her. "We'll see what happens next."

FOURTEEN

It was a good spring afternoon. Balmy air, fine wind, and just enough cloud cover to filter the sun and keep it from baking your flesh down to your bones. When Ethan guided his workboat into dock, the waterfront was busy with tourists who'd come to see the watermen work and the busy fingers of the crab pickers fly.

He had reached his quota early, which suited him fine. The water tanks under the faded striped awning of his boat were crawling with annoyed crabs that would find their way into the pot by nightfall. He would turn in his catch and leave his mate to diddle with the engine. It was running just a tad rough. He planned to take himself over to the building to see how the plumbing was coming.

He was itching to have it done, and Ethan Quinn wasn't a man who itched for much—at least, he didn't allow himself to think he did. But the boat building enterprise was a little private dream that he'd nurtured for some time now. He thought it was about ripe.

Simon let out one sharp, happy woof as the boat bumped the pilings. Even as Ethan prepared to secure the lines, there were hands reaching for them. Hands he recognized before he lifted his gaze to the face. Long, pretty hands that wore no rings or polish.

"I've got it, Ethan."

He looked up and smiled at Grace. "Appreciate it. What're you doing on the docks midday?"

"Picking crabs. Betsy was feeling off this morning, so they were short a pair of hands. My mother wanted Aubrey for a couple of hours anyway."

"You ought to take some time for yourself, Grace."

"Oh . . ." She secured the lines expertly, then straightened to run a hand through her short cap of hair. "One of these days. Did y'all finish up that ham casserole I made the other day?"

"Fought over the last bite. It was great. Thanks." Now that he'd about run out of easy conversation and was standing on the dock beside her, he didn't know what to do with his hands. To compensate, he scratched Simon's head. "We pulled in a nice catch today."

"So I see." But her smile didn't reach her eyes, and she was gnawing on her lip. A sure sign, Ethan thought, that what was on Grace's mind was trouble.

"Is there a problem?"

"I hate to take up your time when you're busy, Ethan." Her eyes scanned the docks. "Could you walk with me a minute?"

"Sure. I could use something cold. Jim, you handle things from here all right?"

"You got it, Cap'n."

With the dog trotting between them, Ethan tucked his hands in his pockets. He nodded when a familiar voice called out a greeting, barely noticed the quick fingers of the crab pickers, who put on quite a show while they worked. He noticed the smells because he was so fond of them—water, fish, salt in the air. And the subtle notes of Grace's soap and shampoo.

"Ethan, I don't want to cause you or your family any grief."

"You couldn't, Grace."

"You may already know. It just bothers me so much. I just hate it so much." Her voice lowered, sizzling with a temper that Ethan knew was rare. He saw that her face was set, her mouth grim, and he decided to forgo that cold drink and lead her farther away from the docks.

"You better tell me, get it off your mind."

"And put it on yours," she said with a sigh. She hated to do it. Ethan was always there if you had trouble or needed a shoulder. Once she'd wished he would offer her more than a shoulder . . . but she'd learned to accept the way things were.

"It's best that you know," she said, half to herself. "You can't deal with things unless you know. There's an investigator for the insurance company talking to people, asking questions about your father, about Seth too."

Ethan laid a hand on her arm briefly. They were far enough away from the docks, from the storefronts and the jangle of traffic. He'd thought they were done with that. "What kind of questions?"

"About your daddy's state of mind the last few weeks before his accident. About him bringing Seth home. He came to see me this morning, first thing. I thought it was better to talk to him than not." She looked at Ethan, relieved when he nodded. "I told him Ray Quinn was one of the finest men I've ever known—and gave him a piece of my mind about going around trying to pick up nasty gossip."

Because Ethan smiled at that, her lips curved. "Well, he made me so mad. Claims he's only doing his job, and his manner's mild as skim milk. But it bothered me, especially when he asked if I knew anything about Seth's mother or where he'd come from. I told him I didn't and that it didn't matter. Seth was where he was supposed to be, and that was that. I hope I did the right thing."

"You did just fine."

Her eyes were the color of stormy seas now, as emotions churned through her. "Ethan, I know it'll hurt if some people talk, if some of them say things they've got no business saying. It doesn't mean anything," she continued and took his hands in hers. "Not to anyone who knows your family."

"We'll get through it." He gave her hands a quick squeeze, then didn't know if he should hold on to them or let go. "I'm glad you told me." He let go. But he kept looking at her face, looked so long that the color began to rise in her cheeks. "You're not getting enough sleep," he said. "Your eyes are tired."

"Oh." Embarrassed, annoyed, she brushed her fingertips under them. Why was it the man only seemed to notice if something was wrong with her? "Aubrey was a little fussy last night. I've got to get back," she said quickly and gave the patient Simon a quick rub. "I'll be by the house tomorrow to clean."

She hurried off, thinking hopelessly that a man who only noticed when you looked tired or troubled would never pay you any mind as a woman.

But Ethan watched her walk away and thought she was too damn pretty to work herself like a mule.

The inspector's name was Mackensie, and he was making the rounds. So far, his notes contained descriptions of a man who was a saint with a halo as wide and bright as the sun. A selfless Samaritan of a man who not only loved his neighbors but cheerfully bore their burdens, who had with his faithful wife beside him saved large chunks of humanity and kept the world safe for democracy.

His other notations termed Raymond Quinn a pompous, interfering, holier-than-thou despot, who collected bad young boys like other men collected stamps and used them to provide him with slave labor, an ego balm, and possibly prurient sexual favors.

Though Mackensie had to admit the latter was more interesting, that view had come from only a scattered few.

Being a man of details and caution, he realized that the truth probably lay somewhere in between the saint and the sinner.

His purpose wasn't to canonize or condemn one Raymond Quinn, policy number 005-678-LQ2. It was simply to gather facts, and those facts would determine whether the claim against that policy would be paid or disputed.

Either way, Mackensie got paid for his time and his efforts.

He'd stopped off and grabbed a sandwich at a little grease spot called Bay Side Eats. He had a weakness for grease, bad coffee, and waitresses with names like Lulubelle.

It was why, at age fifty-eight, he was twenty pounds overweight—twenty-five if he didn't tip the scale a few notches back from zero before he stepped on it—had a chronic case of indigestion, and was twice divorced.

He was also balding and had bunions, and an eyetooth that ached like a bitch in heat. Mackensie knew he was no physical prize, but he knew his job, had thirty-two years with True Life Insurance, and kept records as clean as a nun's heart.

He pulled his Ford Taurus into the pitted gravel lot beside the building. His last contact, a little worm named Claremont, had given him directions. He would find Cameron Quinn there, Claremont had told him with a tight-lipped smile.

Mackensie had disliked the man after five minutes in his company. The inspector had worked with people long enough to recognize greed, envy, and simple malice even when they were layered over with charm. Claremont didn't have any layers that Mackensie had noticed. He was all smarm.

He belched up a memory of the dill pickle relish he'd indulged in at lunch, shook his head, and thumbed out his hourly dose of Zantac. There was a pickup truck in the lot, an aging sedan, and a spiffy classic Corvette.

Mackensie liked the looks of the 'Vette, though he wouldn't have gotten behind the wheel of one of those death traps for love or money. No, indeed. But he admired it anyway as he hauled himself out of his car.

He could admire the looks of the man as well, he mused, when a pair of them stepped out of the building. Not the older one with the red-checked shirt and clip-on tie. Paper pusher, he decided—he was good at recognizing types.

The younger one was too lean, too hungry, too sharp-eyed to spend much time pushing papers. If he didn't work with his hands, Mackensie thought, he could. And he looked like a man who knew what he wanted—and found a way to make it so.

If this was Cameron Quinn, Mackensie decided that Ray Quinn had had his hands full while he was alive.

Cam spotted Mackensie when he walked the plumbing inspector out. He was feeling pretty good about the progress. He figured it would take another week to complete the bathroom, but he and Ethan could do without that little convenience that much longer.

He wanted to get started, and since the wiring was done and that, too, had passed inspection, there was no need to wait.

He tagged Mackensie as some sort of paper jockey. Jiggling his memory, he tried to recall if he had another appointment set up, but he didn't think so. Selling something, he imagined, as Mackensie and the inspector passed each other.

The man had a briefcase, Cam noted wearily. When people carried a briefcase it meant there was something inside they wanted to take out.

"You'd be Mr. Quinn," Mackensie said, his voice affable, his eyes measuring.

"I would."

"I'm Mackensie, True Life Insurance."

"We've got insurance." Or he was nearly sure they did. "My brother Phillip handles those kinds of details." Then it clicked, and Cam's stance shifted from relaxed to on guard. "True Life?"

"That's the one. I'm an investigator for the company. We need to clear up some questions before your claim on your father's policy can be settled."

"He's dead," Cam said flatly. "Isn't that the question, Mackensie?"

"I'm sorry for your loss."

"I imagine the insurance company's sorry it has to shell out. As far as I'm concerned, my father paid in to that policy in good faith. The trick is you have to die to win. He died."

It was warm in the sun, and the pastrami on rye with spicy mustard wasn't settling well. Mackensie blew out a breath. "There's some question about the accident."

"Car meets telephone pole. Telephone pole wins. Trust me, I do a lot of driving."

Mackensie nodded. Under other circumstances he might have appreciated Cam's no-bullshit tone. "You'd be aware that the policy has a suicide clause."

"My father didn't commit suicide, Mackensie. And since you weren't in the car with him at the time, it's going to be tough for you to prove otherwise."

"Your father was under a great deal of stress, emotional upheaval."

Cam snorted. "My father raised three badasses and taught a bunch of snot-nosed college kids. He had a great deal of stress and emotional upheaval all his life."

"And he'd taken on a fourth."

"That's right." Cam tucked his thumbs in his front pockets, and his stance became a silent challenge. "That doesn't have anything to do with you or your company."

"As it bears on the circumstances of your father's accident. There's a question of possible blackmail, and certainly a threat to his reputation. I have a copy of the letter found in his car at the scene."

When Mackensie opened his briefcase, Cam took a step forward. "I've seen the letter. All it means is there's a woman out there with the maternal instincts of a rabid alley cat. You try to say that Ray Quinn smashed into that pole because he was afraid of some two-bit bitch, I'll bury your insurance company."

Fury he thought he'd already passed through sprang back, full-blown and fang-sharp. "I don't give a good goddamn about the money. We can make our own money. True Life wants to welsh on the deal, that's my brother's area—and the lawyer's. But you or anybody else messes with my father's rep, you'll deal with me."

The man was a good twenty-five years younger, Mackensie calculated, tough as a brick and mad as a starving wolf. He decided it would be best all round if he changed tactics. "Mr. Quinn, I have no interest or desire to smear your father's reputation. True Life's a good company, I've worked for them most of my life." He tried a winning smile. "This is just routine."

"I don't like your routine."

"I can understand that. The gray area here is the accident itself. The medical reports confirm that your father was in good physical shape. There's no evidence of a heart attack, a stroke, any physical reason that would have caused him to lose control of his car. A single-car accident, an empty stretch of road on a dry, clear day. The accident-reconstruction expert's findings were inconclusive."

"That's your problem." Cam spotted Seth walking down the road from the direction of school. And there, he thought, is mine. "I can't help you with it. But I can tell you that my father faced his problems, square on. He never took the easy way. I've got work to do." Leaving it at that, Cam turned away and walked toward Seth.

Mackensie rubbed eyes that were tearing up from the sunlight. Quinn might have thought he'd added nothing to the report, but he was wrong. If nothing else, Mackensie could be sure the Quinns would fight for their claim to the bitter end. If not for the money, for the memory.

"Who's that guy?" Seth asked as he watched Mackensie head back to his car.

"Some insurance quack." Cam nodded down the street where two boys loitered a half a block away. "Who're those guys?"

Seth gave a careless glance over his shoulder, followed it with a shrug. "I don't know. Just kids from school. They're nobody."

"They hassling you?"

"Nah. Are we going up on the roof?"

"Roof's done," Cam murmured and watched with some amusement as the two boys wandered closer, trying and failing to look disinterested. "Hey, you kids."

"What're you doing?" Seth hissed, mortified.

"Relax. Come on over here," Cam ordered as both boys froze like statues.

"What the hell are you calling them over for? They're just jerks from school."

"I could use some jerk labor," Cam said mildly. It had also occurred to him that Seth could use some companions of his own age. He waited while Seth squirmed and the two boys held a fast, whispering consultation. It ended with the taller of the two squaring his shoulders and swaggering down the road on his battered Nikes.

"We weren't doing anything," the boy said, his tone of defiance slightly spoiled by a lisp from a missing tooth.

"I could see that. You want to do something?"

The boy slid his eyes to the younger kid, then over to Seth, then cautiously up to Cam's face. "Maybe."

"You got a name?"

"Sure. I'm Danny. This is my kid brother, Will. I turned eleven last week. He's only nine."

"I'll be ten in ten months," Will stated and rapped his brother in the ribs with his elbow.

"He still goes to elementary," Danny put in with a sneer, which he generously shared with Seth. "Baby school."

"I'm not a baby."

As Will's fist was already clenched and lifted, Cam took hold of it, then lightly squeezed his upper arm. "Seems strong enough to me."

"I'm plenty strong," Will told him, then grinned with the charm of an angelic host.

"We'll see about that. See all this crap piled up around here? Old shingles, tar paper, trash?" Cam surveyed the area himself. "You see that Dumpster over there? The crap goes in the Dumpster, you get five bucks."

"Each?" Danny piped up, his hazel eyes glinting in a freckled face.

"Don't make me laugh, kid. But you'll get a two-dollar bonus if you do it without me having to come out and break up any fights." He jerked a thumb at Seth. "He's in charge."

The minute Cam left them alone, Danny turned to Seth. They sized each other up in narrow-eyed silence. "I saw you punch Robert."

Seth shifted his balance evenly. It would be two against one, he calculated, but he was prepared to fight. "So what?"

"It was cool," was all Danny said and began to pick up torn shingles.

Will grinned happily up into Seth's face. "Robert is a big, fat fart, and Danny said when you socked him he bled and bled."

Seth found himself grinning back. "Like a stuck pig."

"Oink, oink," Will said, delighted. "We can buy ice cream with the money up at Crawford's."

"Yeah . . . maybe." Seth started to gather up trash, with Will cheerfully dogging his heels.

Anna wasn't having a good day. She'd started out the morning running her last pair of hose before she even got out her front door. She was out of bagels, and yogurt, and, she admitted, almost every damn thing, because she'd been spending too much time with Cam or thinking about Cam to keep to her usual marketing routine.

When she stopped off to mail a letter to her grandparents, she chipped a nail on the mailbox. Her phone was already ringing when she walked into her office at eight-thirty, and the hysterical woman on the other end was demanding to know why she had yet to receive her medical card.

She calmed the woman down, assured her she would see to the matter personally. Then, simply because she was there, the switchboard passed through a whining old man who insisted his neighbors were child abusers because they allowed their offspring to watch television every night of the week.

"Television," he told her, "is the tool of the Communist left. Nothing but sex and murder, sex and murder, and subliminal messages. I read all about them."

"I'm going to look into this, Mr. Bigby," she promised and opened her top drawer, where she kept her aspirin.

"You'd better. I tried the cops, but they don't do nothing. Those kids're doomed. Going to need to deprogram them."

"Thank you for bringing this to our attention."

"My duty as an American."

"You bet," Anna muttered after he'd hung up.

Knowing that she was due in family court at two that afternoon, she booted up her computer, intending to call up the file to review her reports and notes. When the message flashed across her screen that her program had committed an illegal act, she didn't bother to scream. She simply sat back, closed her eyes, and accepted that it was going to be a lousy day.

It got worse.

She knew her testimony in court was key. The Higgins case file had come across her desk nearly a year ago. The three children, ages eight, six, and four, had all been physically and emotionally abused. The wife, barely twenty-five, was a textbook case of the battered spouse. She'd left her husband countless times over the years, but she always went back.

Six months before, Anna had worked hard and long to get her and her children into a shelter. The woman had stayed less than thirty-six hours before changing her mind. Though Anna's heart ached for her, it had come down to the welfare of the children.

Their pinched faces, the bruises, the fear—and worse, the dull acceptance in their eyes—tormented her. They were in foster care with a couple who was generous enough and strong enough to take all of them. And seeing those foster parents flanking the three damaged boys, she vowed she would do everything in her power to keep them there.

"Counseling was recommended in January of last year when this case first came to my attention," Anna stated from the witness stand. "Both family and individual. The recommendation was not taken. Nor was it taken in May of that same year when Mrs. Higgins was hospitalized with a dislocated jaw and other injuries, or in September when Michael Higgins, the eldest boy, suffered a broken hand. In November of that year Mrs. Higgins and her two oldest sons were all treated in ER for various injuries. I was notified and assisted Mrs. Higgins and her children in securing a place in a women's shelter. She did not remain there two full days."

"You've been caseworker of record on this matter for more than a year." The lawyer stood in front of her, knowing from experience it wasn't necessary to guide her testimony.

"Yes, more than a year." And she felt the failure keenly.

"What is the current status?"

"On February sixth of this year, a police unit responding to the call from a neighbor found Mr. Higgins under the influence of alcohol. Mrs. Higgins was reported as hysterical and required medical treatment for facial bruises and lacerations. Curtis, the youngest child, had a broken arm. Mr. Higgins was taken into custody. At that time, as I was the caseworker of record, I was notified."

"Did you see Mrs. Higgins and the children on that day?" the lawyer asked her.

"Yes. I drove to the hospital. I spoke with Mrs. Higgins. She claimed that Curtis had fallen down the stairs. Due to the nature of his injuries, and the history of the case, I didn't believe her. The attending physician in ER shared my opinion. The children were taken into foster care, where they have remained since that date."

She continued to answer questions about the status of the case file and the children themselves. Once, she drew a smile out of the middle boy when she spoke of the T-ball team he'd been able to join.

Then Anna prepared herself for the irritation and tedium of cross-examination.

"Are you aware that Mr. Higgins has voluntarily entered an alcohol rehabilitation program?"

Anna spared one glance at the Higginses' pro bono lawyer, then looked directly into the father's eyes. "I'm aware that over the past year, Mr. Higgins has claimed to have entered a rehabilitation program no less than three times."

She saw the hate and fury darken his face. *Let him hate me*, she thought. She'd be damned if he would lay hands on those children again. "I'm aware that he's never completed a program."

"Alcoholism is a disease, Ms. Spinelli. Mr. Higgins is now seeking treatment for his illness. You would agree that Mrs. Higgins has been a victim of her husband's illness?"

"I would agree that she has suffered both physically and emotionally at his hands."

"And can you possibly believe that she should suffer further, lose her children and they her? Can you possibly believe that the court should take these three little boys away from their mother?"

The choice, Anna thought, was hers. The man who beat her and terrorized their children, or the health and safety of those children. "I believe she will suffer further, until she makes the decision to change her circumstances. And it's my professional opinion that Mrs. Higgins is incapable of caring for herself, much less her children, at this time."

"Both Mr. and Mrs. Higgins now have steady employment," the lawyer continued. "Mrs. Higgins has stated, under oath, that she and her husband are reconciled and continuing to work on their marital difficulties. Separating the family will, as she stated, only cause emotional pain for all involved."

"I know she believes that." Her steady look at Mrs. Higgins was compassionate, but her voice was firm. "I believe that there are three children whose welfare and safety are at stake. I'm aware of the medical reports, the psychiatric reports, the police reports. In the past fifteen months, these three children have been treated in the emergency room a combined total of eleven times."

She looked at the lawyer now, wondering how he could stand in a court of law and fight for what was surely the destruction of three young boys. "I'm aware that a four-year-old boy's arm was snapped like a twig. I strongly recommend that these children remain in licensed and supervised foster care to ensure their physical and emotional safety."

"No charges have been filed against Mr. Higgins."

"No, no charges have been filed." Anna shifted her gaze to the mother, let it rest on that tired face. "That's just another crime," she murmured.

When she was finished, Anna passed by the Higginses without a glance. But behind the rail, little Curtis reached out for her hand. "Do you have a lollipop?" he whispered, making her smile.

She made a habit of carrying them for him. He had a weakness for cherry Tootsie Roll Pops. "Maybe I do. Let's see."

She was reaching into her purse when the explosion came from behind her. "Get your hands off what's mine, you bitch."

As she started to turn, Higgins hit her full force, knocking her sprawling and sending Curtis to the floor with her in a heap of screams and wails. Her head rang like church bells and stars dazzled her eyes. She could hear screams and curses as she managed to push herself up to her hands and knees.

Her cheek ached fiercely where it had connected with the seat of a wooden chair. Her palms sang from skidding on the tile floor. And damn it, the new hose she had bought to replace the ones she'd run were torn at the knees.

"Hold still," Marilou ordered. She was crouched in Anna's office, grimly doctoring the scrapes.

"I'm all right." Indeed, the injuries were minor. "It was worth it. That little demonstration in open court ensures that he won't get near those kids for quite a while."

"You worry me, Anna." Marilou looked up with those dark, gleaming eyes. "I'd almost think you enjoyed being tackled by that two-hundred-pound putz."

"I enjoyed the results. Ouch, Marilou." She blew out a breath as her supervisor rose to examine the bruise on Anna's cheek. "I enjoyed filing charges for assault, and most of all I enjoyed seeing those kids go home with their foster family."

"A good day's work?" With a shake of her head, Marilou stepped back. "It worries me, too, that you let yourself get too close."

"You can't help from a distance. So much of what we do is just paperwork, Marilou. Forms and procedures. But every now and again you get to do something—even if it's only getting tackled by a two-hundred-pound putz. And it's worth it."

"If you care too much, you end up with more than a couple of bruises and a skinned knee."

"If you don't care enough, you should find another line of work."

Marilou blew out a breath. It was difficult to argue when she felt exactly the same way. "Go home, Anna."

"I've got another hour on the clock."

"Go home. Consider it combat pay."

"Since you put it that way. I could use the hour. I don't have anything in the house to eat. If you hear any more on—" She broke off and looked up at the knock on her doorjamb. Her eyes widened. "Cameron."

"Miz Spinelli, I wonder if you have a minute to—" His smile of greeting transformed into a snarl. The light in his eyes turned hot and sharp as a flaming sword. "What the hell happened to you?" He was in the room like a shot, filling it, nearly barreling over Marilou to get to Anna. "Who the hell hit you?"

"No one, exactly, I was—"

Instead of giving her a chance to finish, he whirled on Marilou. Torn between fascination and amusement, Marilou backed up a step and held her hands up, palms out. "Not me, champ. I only browbeat my staff. Never lay a finger on them."

"There was a ruckus in court, that's all." Struggling to be brisk and professional despite her bare legs and feet, Anna rose. "Marilou, this is Cameron Quinn. Cameron, Marilou Johnston, my supervisor."

"It's a pleasure to meet you, even under the circumstances." Marilou held out a hand. "I was a student of your father's a million years ago. I quite simply adored him."

"Yeah, thanks. Who hit you?" he demanded again of Anna.

"Someone who is even now on the wrong side of a locked cell." Quickly, Anna worked her bare feet back into her low-heeled pumps. "Marilou, I'm going to take you up on the hour off." Her only thought now was to get Cam out, away from Marilou's curious and all-too-observant eyes. "Cameron, if you need to speak with me about Seth, you could give me a ride home." She slipped on her dove-gray jacket, smoothed it into place. "It's not far. I'll buy you a cup of coffee."

"Fine. Sure." When he caught her chin in his hand, a tug-of-war of pleasure and alarm raged inside her. "We'll talk."

"I'll see you tomorrow, Marilou."

"Oh, yes." Marilou smiled easily while Anna hurriedly gathered her briefcase. "We'll talk, too."

FIFTEEN

Anna kept her mouth firmly shut until they were out of the building and safely alone in the parking lot. "Cam, for God's sake."

"For God's sake, what?"

"This is where I work." She stopped at his car, turned to face him. "Where I work, remember? You can't come storming into my office like an outraged lover."

He took her chin in hand again, leaned his face close. "I *am* an outraged lover, and I want the name of the son of a bitch who put his hands on you."

She wouldn't allow herself to be thrilled by the violence sparking around him. It would be, she reminded herself as her stomach gave a delicious little hop, completely unprofessional.

"The person in question is being dealt with by the proper authorities. And you're not allowed to be a lover, outraged or otherwise, during business hours."

"Yeah? Try and stop me," he challenged and leading with his temper, crushed his mouth to hers.

She wiggled for a moment. Anyone could peek out an office window and see. The kiss was too hot, too heady for a daylight embrace in an office parking lot.

The kiss was also too hot, too heady to resist. She gave in to it, to him, to herself, and wrapped her arms around him. "Will you cut it out?" she said against his mouth.

"No."

"Okay, then, let's take this indoors."

"Good idea." With his mouth still on hers, he reached back to open the car door.

"I can't get in until you let me go."

"Good point." He released her, then surprised her by gently, tenderly brushing his lips over the bruise on her cheek. "Does it hurt?"

Her heart was still flopping. "Maybe a little." She got inside, deliberately reaching for her seat belt, keeping her moves efficient and casual.

"What happened?" he asked as he slid in beside her.

"Abusive father of three, wife beater, didn't care for my testimony in family court today. He shoved me. I had my back turned or he'd have gotten a hard knee to the groin, but as it was I was off balance. Did a nosedive—which would have been embarrassing but for the fact that he's now in lockup and the kids are with their foster family."

"And the wife?"

"I can't help her." Anna let her aching head fall back. "You have to pick your battles."

He said nothing to that. He'd been thinking the same thing. It was why he'd decided to dump three kids on Ethan and come to see her. He'd made up his mind to tell her about the insurance investigation, the speculations about Seth's connection to his father, the search that Phillip had instigated for Seth's mother.

He'd decided to tell her everything, to ask her advice, to get her take. Now he found himself wondering if that was the wisest course—for her, for him, for Seth.

It would wait, he told himself, and rationalized his postponement: she'd had a rough time, needed a little attention.

"So, do you get knocked around much in your line of work?"

"Hmm? No." She laughed a little as he pulled up in front of her building. "Now and again somebody takes a swing or throws something at you, but mostly it's just verbal abuse."

"Fun job."

"It has its moments." She took his hand, walked alongside him. "Did you know that television is the tool of the Communist left?"

"I hadn't heard that."

"I'm here to tell you." She used her key to check her mail slot, gathered letters and bills and a fashion magazine. "*Sesame Street* is just a front."

"I always suspected that big yellow bird."

"Nah, he's just a shill. The frog's the mastermind." She put her finger to her lips as they approached her door. They snuck in together like kids hooking school. "I just didn't want to have the sisters fussing over me."

"Mind if I do?"

"That depends on your definition of fussing."

"We'll start here." He slipped his arms around her waist, touched his lips to hers.

"I suppose I could tolerate that." She helped him deepen the kiss. "What are you doing here, Cam?"

"I had a lot on my mind." His lips brushed over the bruise again, then lower, to her jawline. "You, mostly. I wanted to see you, be with you, talk to you. Make love to you."

Her lips curved against his. "All at the same time."

"Why not? I did have this thought about taking you out to dinner . . . but now I'm thinking maybe we could order pizza."

"Perfect." She said it with a sigh. "Why don't you pour us some wine, and I'll change?"

"There's this other thing." He worked his way over to her ear. "Something I've been wanting to do. I've been wondering what it would be like to get Miz Spinelli out of one of her dedicated-public-servant suits."

"Have you?"

"Since the first time I saw you."

She smiled wickedly. "Now's your chance."

"I was hoping you'd say that." He brought his mouth back to hers, hungrier now, more possessive. This time her sigh caught on a trembling gasp as he jerked her jacket off her shoulders and trapped her arms. "I'm wanting the hell out of you. Day and night."

Her voice was throaty now, dark with need. "I guess that makes it handy, since I want the hell out of you too."

"It doesn't scare you?"

"Nothing about you and me scares me."

"And what if I said I want you to let me do anything I want to you? Everything?"

Her heart fluttered to her throat, but her eyes stayed steady. "I'd say who's stopping you?"

With desire dark and dangerous in his eyes, he skimmed his gaze down, then back to her face. "I wonder what Miz Spinelli wears under these prim little blouses."

"I don't think a man like you is going to let a few buttons keep him from finding out."

"You're right." He shifted his hands from her jacket to the crisply pressed cotton of her blouse. And ripped. He watched her eyes go wide and shocked. And aroused. "If you want me to stop, I will. I won't do anything you don't want."

He'd torn her blouse. And it had thrilled her. He waited, watching, for her to say stop or go. And it thrilled her even more. She understood she hadn't been completely truthful when she'd told him nothing about them scared her. She was afraid of what might be happening to her heart.

But here, in physical love, she knew she could match him.

"I want everything. All."

His blood leaped. Still, he kept his touch light, teasing, running the back of his hand above the slick white material of her demi-cut bra. "Miz Spinelli." He drawled it while his fingers slipped beneath the polished satin to rub against her stiffened nipple. "How much can you take?"

His light tugs had heat spiraling through her system. Already the air was thick. "I think we're about to find out."

Slowly, his eyes on her face, he backed her against the wall. "Let's start here. Brace yourself," he murmured, and his hand shot under her skirt and tore aside the lacy swatch she wore beneath. Her breath exploded out, and she nearly laughed. Then he plunged his fingers into her, lancing that hard, rough shock of pleasure through her unprepared system. The orgasm ripped through her, emptying her mind, stealing her breath. When her knees gave way, he simply held her against the wall.

"Take more." He was desperate to watch her take more, to see the shocked excitement capture her face, to see those gorgeous eyes go wild and blind.

She gripped his shoulders for balance. With her head tipped back he could see the pulse in her throat beat madly and was compelled to taste just there. She moaned against him, moved against him, her breath hitching when he yanked the jacket and what was left of her blouse away.

She was helpless, staggered. The assault on her senses left her limbs shuddering and her heart hammering. She said his name, tried to, but it caught on a gasp as he spun her around. Her damp palms pressed to the wall.

He tore at the button of her skirt. She felt it give way, shivering as the material slid over her hips and pooled at her feet. His hands were on her breasts, molding, sliding from satin to flesh and back again. Then he tore that as well, and she gloried in the sound of the delicate material rending.

His teeth nipped into her shoulder. And his hands—oh, his hands were everywhere, driving her toward madness, then beyond. Rough palms against smooth skin, clever fingers pressing, sliding.

The breath that had torn ragged through her lips began to slow. Pleasure was thick, and midnight dark. She felt herself slipping into some erotic half-world where there was only sensation.

Slick, stunning, and sinful.

The wall was smooth and cool; his hands were not. The contrasts were unbearably arousing.

When he spun her around again, her eyes were dazzled by the sunlight. He was still fully dressed and she was naked. She found it exquisitely erotic, and could say nothing as he slowly lifted her arms above her head, bracketed her wrists with one hand.

Watching her, he combed his hand roughly through her hair to scatter pins. "I want more." He could barely speak. "Tell me you want more."

"Yes, I want more."

He pressed his body to hers, soft cotton, rough denim against damp flesh. And the kiss he took from her left her mind spinning.

Then his mouth went to work on her quivering body.

He wanted all the tastes of her, the dark honey of her mouth, the damp silk of her breasts. There was the creamy taste of her belly, the polished satin of her thighs.

Then the heat, the furnace flood of it as he licked his way between them.

Everything. All, was all he could think. Then more.

Her hands gripped his hair, pressing his face closer as she climbed to peak. It was her cry, the half scream, that broke the final link on his control. It had to be now.

He freed himself, then pressed against her. "I need to fill you." He panted the words out. "I want you to watch me when I do."

He drove into her where they stood, and their twin groans tangled in the air.

Afterward, he carried her to bed, lay down beside her. She curled up against him like a child, a gesture he found surprisingly sweet. He watched her sleep, thirty minutes, then a hour. He couldn't stop touching her—a hand through her hair, fingertips over the bruise on her face, a stroke over the curve of her shoulder.

Had he said he had something inside of him for her? He began to worry just what that something might be. He'd never felt compelled to stay with a woman after sex. Had never felt the need to just look at her while she slept, or to touch only for the sake of touching and not to arouse.

He wondered what odd and slippery level they'd reached.

Then she stirred, sighed, and her eyes fluttered open and focused on him. When she smiled, his heart quite simply turned over in his chest.

"Hi. Did I fall asleep?"

"Looked like it to me." He searched for some glib remark, something light and frivolous, but all he could find to say was her name. "Anna." And he lowered his mouth to hers. Tenderly, softly, lovingly.

The sleep had cleared from her eyes when he drew away, but he couldn't read them. She breathed in once, slowly, then out again. "What was that?"

"Damned if I know." Both of them eased back cautiously. "I think we'd better order that pizza."

Relief and disappointment warred inside her. Anna put all her effort into supporting the relief. "Good idea. The number's right next to the kitchen phone. If you don't mind calling it in, I'd like to grab a quick shower, get some clothes on."

"All right." With casual intimacy he stroked a hand over her hip. "What do you want on it?"

"All I can get." She waited while he laughed and was pleased that he rolled out of bed first. She needed another minute.

"I'll pour the wine."

"Terrific." The minute she was alone, she turned her face into the pillow and let out a muffled scream of frustration. Steps back? she thought, furious with herself. Where did she get the idiotic idea she could take a few steps back? She was over her head in love with him.

My fault, she reminded herself, my problem. Sitting up, she pressed a hand to her traitorous heart. And my little secret, she decided.

<hr>

She felt better when she was dressed and had a light shield of makeup in place. She'd given herself a good talking-to in the shower. Maybe she was in love with him. It didn't have to be a bad thing. People fell in and out of love all the time, and the wise ones, the steady ones, enjoyed the ride.

She could be wise and steady.

She certainly wasn't looking for happily ever after, a white knight, a Prince Charming. Anna had outgrown fairy tales long ago, and all of her innocence had cemented into reality on the side of a deserted road at the age of twelve.

She'd learned to make herself happy because for too many years following the rape it had seemed she was helpless to do anything but make herself and everyone near her miserable.

She'd survived the worst. There was no doubt she could survive a slightly dented heart.

In any case, she'd never been in love before—she had skirted around it, breezed over it, wriggled under it, but had never before run headlong into it. It could be a marvelous adventure, certainly a learning experience.

And any woman who found herself a lover like Cameron Quinn had plenty of blessings to count.

So she was smiling when she came into the living room and found Cam, sipping wine, staring at the cover of her latest fashion magazine. He'd put music on. Eric Clapton was pleading with Laylah.

When she came up behind him and pecked a kiss on the back of his neck, she didn't expect his jolt of surprise.

It was guilt, plain and simple, and he hated it. He nearly bobbled the wine and had to fight to keep his face composed.

The pouty face on the cover of the magazine in his hand was a certain long-stemmed French model named Martine.

"Didn't mean to startle you." She raised an eyebrow as she looked at the magazine in his hands. "Absorbed with this summer's new pastels, were you?"

"Just passing the time. Pizza should be along in a minute." He started to set the magazine down, wanted sincerely to bury it under the sofa cushions, but she was nipping it out of his hand.

"I used to hate her."

His throat was uncomfortably dry. "Huh?"

"Well, not Martine the Magnificent exactly. Models like her. Slim and blond and perfect. I was always too round and too brunette. This," she added, giving her wet, curling hair a tug, "made me insane as a teenager. I tried everything imaginable to straighten it."

"I love your hair." He wished she'd turn the damn magazine facedown. "You're twice as beautiful as she is. There's no comparison."

Her smile came quick and warm around the edges. "That's very sweet."

"I mean it." He said it almost desperately—but thought it best not to add that he'd seen both of them naked and knew what he was talking about.

"Very sweet. Still, I wanted so badly to be slim and blond and hipless."

"You're real." He couldn't stop himself. He took the magazine and tossed it over his shoulder. "She's not."

"That's one way to put it." Enjoying herself, she cocked her head. "Seems to me you race-around-the-world types usually go for the supermodels—they look so good draped over a man's arm."

"I barely know her."

"Who?"

Jesus, he was losing it. "Anybody. There's the pizza," he said with great relief. "Your wine's on the counter. I'll get the food."

"Fine." Without a clue as to what was suddenly making him so edgy, she wandered to the kitchen for her drink.

Cam saw that the magazine had fallen faceup so it appeared that Martine was aiming those killer blue eyes right at him. It brought back the memory of a scored cheek and a spitting female. He cast a wary glance at Anna. It wasn't an experience he cared to repeat.

As he paid the delivery boy, Anna took the wine out to her tiny balcony. "It's a nice evening. Let's eat out here."

She had a couple of chairs and a small folding table set out. Pink geraniums and white impatiens sprang cheerfully out of clay pots.

"If I ever manage to save enough for a house, I want a porch. A big one. Like you have." She went back in for plates and napkins. "And a garden. One of these days I'm going to learn something about flowers."

"A house, garden, porches." More comfortable out in the air, he settled down. "I pictured you as a town girl."

"I always have been. I'm not sure suburbia would suit me. Fences with neighbors just over them. Too much like apartment living, I'd think, without the privacy and convenience." She slid a loaded slice of pizza onto her plate. "But I'd like to give home owning a shot—somewhere in the country. Eventually. The problem is, I can't seem to stick to a budget."

"You?" He helped himself. "Miz Spinelli seems so practical."

"She tries. My grandparents were very frugal, had to be. I was raised to watch my pennies." She took a bite and drew in a deep, appreciative breath before speaking over a mouthful of cheese and sauce. "Mostly I watch them roll away."

"What's your weakness?"

"Primarily?" She sighed. "Clothes."

He looked over his shoulder, through the door to her clothes, heaped in a tattered pile on the floor. "I think I owe you a blouse . . . and a skirt, not to mention the underwear."

She laughed lustily. "I suppose you do." She stretched out, comfortable in pale-blue leggings and an oversized white T-shirt. "This was such a hideous day. I'm glad you came by and changed it."

"Why don't you come home with me?"

"What?"

Where the hell had that come from? he wondered. The thought hadn't even been in his mind when the words popped out of his mouth. But it must have been, somewhere. "For the weekend," he added. "Spend this weekend at the house."

She brought her pizza back to her lips, bit in carefully. "I don't think that would be wise. There's an impressionable young boy in your home."

"He knows what the hell's going on," he began, then caught the look—the Miz Spinelli look—in her eye. "Okay, I'll sleep on the sofa downstairs. You can lock the bedroom door."

Her lips quirked. "Where do you keep the key?"

"This weekend I'll be keeping it in my pocket. But my point is," he continued when she laughed, "you can have the bedroom. On a professional level it'll give you some time with the kid. He's coming along, Anna. And I want to take you sailing."

"I'll come over Saturday and we can go sailing."

"Come Friday night." He took her hand, brought her knuckles to his lips. "Stay till Sunday."

"I'll think about it," she murmured and drew her hand away. Romantic gestures were going to undo her. "And I think if you're going to have a houseguest, you should check with your brothers. They might not care to have a woman underfoot for a weekend."

"They love women. Especially women who cook."

"Ah, so now I'm supposed to cook."

"Maybe just one little pot of linguini. Or a dish of lasagna."

She smiled and took another slice of pizza. "I'll think about it," she said again. "Now tell me about Seth."

"He made a couple of buddies today."

"Really? Terrific."

Her eyes lit with such pleasure and interest, he couldn't help himself. "Yeah, I had them all up on the roof, practiced catching them as they fell off."

Her mouth fell open, then shut again on a scowl. "Very funny, Quinn."

"Gotcha. A kid from Seth's class and his kid brother. I bought them for five bucks as slave labor. Then they wheedled an invite out to the house for dinner, so I stuck Ethan with them."

She rolled her eyes. "You left Ethan alone with three young boys?"

"He can handle it. I did for a couple of hours this afternoon." And, he recalled, it hadn't been so bad. "All he has to do is feed them and make sure they don't kill each other. Their mother's picking them up at seven-thirty. Sandy McLean—well, Sandy Miller now. I went to school with her."

He shook his head, amazed and baffled. "Two kids and a minivan. Never would've figured that for Sandy."

"People change," she murmured, surprised at how much she envied Sandy Miller and her minivan. "Or they weren't precisely what we imagined them to be in the first place."

"I guess. Her kids are pistols."

Because he said it with such easy good humor, she smiled again. "Well, now I see why you popped up at my office. You wanted to escape the madness."

"Yeah, but mostly I just wanted to rip your clothes off." He took another slice himself. "I did both."

And, he thought, as he sipped his wine and watched the sun go down with Anna beside him, he felt damn good about it.

SIXTEEN

Drawing wasn't Ethan's strong point. With the other boats he'd built, he'd worked off very rough sketches and detailed measurements. For the first boat for this client, he'd fashioned a lofting platform and had found working from it was easier and more precise.

The skiff he'd built and sold had been a basic model, with a few tweaks of his own added. He'd been able to see the completed project in his mind easily enough and had no trouble envisioning side or interior views.

But he understood that the beginnings of a business required all the forms Phillip had told him to sign and needed something more formal, more professional. They would want to develop a reputation for skill and quality quickly if they expected to stay afloat.

So he'd spent countless hours in the evenings at his desk struggling over the blueprints and drawings of their first job.

When he unrolled his completed sketches on the kitchen table, he was both pleased and proud of his work. "This," he said, holding down the top corners, "is what I had in mind."

Cam looked over Ethan's shoulder, sipped the beer he'd just opened, grunted. "I guess that's supposed to be a boat."

Insulted but not particularly surprised by the comment, Ethan scowled. "I'd like to see you do better, Rembrandt."

Cam shrugged, sat. Upon closer, more neutral study, he admitted he couldn't. But that didn't make the drawing of the sloop look any more like a boat. "I guess it doesn't matter much, as long as we don't show your art project to the client." He pushed the sketch aside and got down to the blueprints. Here, Ethan's thoughtful precision and patience showed through. "Okay, now we're talking. You want to go with smooth-lap construction."

"It's expensive," Ethan began, "but it's got advantages. He'll have a strong, fast boat when we're finished."

"I've been in on a few," Cam murmured. "You've got to be good at it."

"We'll be good at it."

Cam had to grin. "Yeah."

"The thing is . . ." As a matter of pride, Ethan nudged the sketch of the completed boat back over. "It takes skill and precision to smooth-lap a boat. Anybody who knows boats recognizes that. This guy, he's a Sunday sailor, doesn't know more than basic port and starboard—he's just got money. But he hangs with people who know boats."

"And so we use him to build a rep," Cam finished. "Good thinking." He studied the figures, the drawings, the views. It would be a honey, he mused. All they had to do was build it. "We could build a lift model."

"We could."

Building a lift model was an old and respected stage of boat building. Boards of equal thickness would be pegged together and shaped to the desired hull form. Then the model could be taken apart so that the shape of the mold frames could be determined. Then the builders would trace the shape of the planks, or lifts, in their proper relation to one another.

"We could start the lofting," Cam mused.

"I figured we could start work on that tonight and continue tomorrow."

That meant drawing the full-sized shape of the hull on a platform in the shop. It would be detailed, showing the mold sections—and those sections would be tested by drawing in the longitudinal curves, waterlines.

"Yeah, why wait?" Cam glanced up as Seth wandered in to raid the refrigerator. "Though it would be better if we had somebody who could draw worth diddly," he said casually and pretended not to notice Seth's sudden interest.

"As long as we have the measurements, and the work's first class, it doesn't matter." Defending his work, Ethan smoothed a hand over his rendition of the boat.

"Just be nicer if we could show the client something jazzy." Cam lifted a shoulder. "Phillip would call it marketing."

"I don't care what Phillip would call it." The stubborn line began to form between Ethan's eyebrows, a sure sign that he was about to dig in his heels. "The client's satisfied with my other work, and he's not going to be critiquing a drawing. He wants a damn boat, not a picture for his wall."

"I was just thinking . . ." Cam let it hang as Ethan, obviously irritated, rose to get his own beer. "Lots of times in the boatyards I've known, people come around, hang out. They like to watch boats being built—especially the people who don't know squat about boat building but think they do. You could pick up customers that way."

"So?" Ethan popped the top and drank. "I don't care if people want to watch us rabbeting laps." He did, of course, but he didn't expect it would come to that.

"It'd be interesting, I was thinking, if we had good framed sketches on the walls. Boats we've built."

"We haven't built any damn boats yet."

"Your skipjack," Cam pointed out. "The workboat. The one you already did for our first client. And I put in a lot of time on a two-masted schooner up in Maine a few years ago, and a snazzy little skiff in Bristol."

Ethan sipped again, considering. "Maybe it would look good, but I'm not voting to hire some artist to paint pictures. We've got an equipment list to work out, and Phil's got to finish fiddling with the contract for *this* boat."

"Just a thought." Cam turned. Seth was still standing in front of the wide-open refrigerator. "Want a menu, kid?"

Seth jolted, then grabbed the first thing that came to hand. The carton of blueberry yogurt wasn't what he'd had in mind for a snack, but he was too embarrassed to put it back. Stuck with what he considered Phillip's health crap, he got out a spoon.

"I got stuff to do," he muttered and hurried out.

"Ten bucks says he feeds that to the dog," Cam said lightly and wondered how long it would take Seth to start drawing boats.

He had a detailed and somewhat romantic sketch of Ethan's skipjack done by morning. He didn't need Phillip's presence in the kitchen to remind him it was Friday. The day before freedom. Ethan was already gone, sailing out to check crab pots and rebait. Though Seth had tried to plot how to catch all three of them together, he simply hadn't been able to figure out how to delay Ethan's dawn departure. But two out of three, he thought as he passed the table where Cam was brooding silently over his morning coffee, wasn't bad.

It took at least two cups of coffee before any man in the Quinn household communicated with more than grunts. Seth was already used to that, so he said nothing as he set down his backpack. He had his sketchbook, with his finger wedged between the pages. He dropped it on the table as if it didn't matter to him in the least, then, with his heart skipping, rummaged through the cupboards for cereal.

Cam saw the sketch immediately. Smiling into his coffee, he said nothing. He was considering the toast he'd managed to burn when Seth came to the table with a box and a bowl. "That damn toaster's defective."

"You turned it up to high again," Phillip told him and finished beating his egg-white-and-chive omelette.

"I don't think so. How many eggs are you scrambling there?"

"I'm not scrambling any." Phillip slid the eggs into the omelette pan he'd brought from his own kitchen. "Make your own."

Jeez, was the guy blind or what? Seth wondered. He poured milk on his cereal and gently nudged the sketchbook an inch closer to Cam.

"It wouldn't kill you to add a couple more while you're doing it." Cam broke off a piece of the charcoaled toast. He had almost learned to like it that way. "I made the coffee."

"The sludge," Phillip corrected. "Let's not get delusions of grandeur."

Cam sighed lustily, then rose to get a bowl. He picked up the cereal box that sat beside Seth's open sketchbook. He could all but hear the boy grind his teeth as he sat back down and poured. "Probably going to have company this weekend."

Phillip concentrated on browning the omelette to perfection. "Who?"

"Anna." Cam slopped milk into his bowl. "I'm going to take her sailing, and I think I've got her talked into cooking dinner."

All the guy could think about was girls and filling his gut, Seth decided in disgust. He used his elbow to shove the sketch pad closer. Cam never glanced up from his cereal bowl.

When he saw Phillip slide the omelette from pan to plate, he judged it time to make his move. Seth's face was a study in agonized fury. "What's this?" Cam said absently, cocking his head to view the sketch that was by now all but under his nose.

Seth nearly rolled his eyes. It was about damn time. "Nothing," he muttered, and gleefully kept eating.

"Looks like Ethan's boat." Cam picked up his coffee, glanced at Phillip. "Doesn't it?"

Phillip stood, sampling the first bite of his breakfast, approving it. "Yeah. It's a good drawing." Curious, he looked at Seth. "You do it?"

"I was just fooling around." The flush of pride was creeping up his neck and leaving his stomach jittery.

"I work with guys who can't draw this well." Phillip gave Seth an absent pat on the shoulder. "Nice work."

"No big deal," Seth said with a shrug as the thrill burst through him.

"Funny, Ethan and I were just talking about using sketches of boats in the boatyard. You know, Phil, like advertising our work."

Phillip settled down to his eggs, but lifted a brow in both surprise and approval. "You thought of that? Color me amazed. Good idea." He studied the sketch more closely as he worked it through. "Frame it rough, keep the edges of the sketch raw. It should look working-man, not fancy."

Cam made a sound in his throat, as if he were mulling it over. "One sketch won't make much of a statement." He frowned at Seth. "I guess you couldn't do a few more, like of Ethan's workboat? Or if I got some pictures of a couple of the boats I've worked on?"

"I dunno." Seth fought to keep the excitement out of his voice. He nearly succeeded in keeping his eyes bored when they met Cam's, but little lights of pleasure danced in them. "Maybe."

It didn't take Phillip long to clue in. Catching the drift, he reached for his coffee and nodded. "Could make a nice statement. Clients who came in would see different boats we've done. It'd be good to have a drawing of the one you're starting on."

Cam snorted. "Ethan's got a pathetic sketch. Looks like a kindergarten project. Don't know what can be done about it." Then he looked at Seth, narrowed his eyes. "Maybe you can take a look at it."

Seth felt laughter bubble up in his throat and gamely swallowed it. "I suppose."

"Great. You got about ninety seconds to make the bus, kid, or you're walking to school."

"Shit." Seth scrambled up, grabbed his backpack, and took off in a flurry of pounding sneakers.

When the front door slammed, Phillip sat back. "Nice work, Cam."

"I have my moments."

"Every now and again. How'd you know the kid could draw?"

"He gave Anna a picture he'd done of the pup."

"Hmm. So what's the deal with her?"

"Deal?" Cam went back to his pitiful toast and tried not to envy Phillip his eggs.

"Spending the weekend, sailing, cooking dinner. Haven't seen you sniffing around any other woman since she came on the scene." Phillip grinned into his coffee. "Sounds serious. Almost . . . domestic."

"Get a grip." Cam's stomach took an uncomfortable little lurch. "We're just enjoying each other."

"I don't know. She looks like the picket-fence type to me."

Cam snorted. "Career woman. She's smart, she's ambitious, and she's not looking for complications." She wanted a house in the country, Cam remembered, near the water, with a yard where she could plant flowers.

"Women always look for complications," Phillip said positively. "Better watch your step."

"I know where I'm going, and how to get there."

"That's what they all say."

⟪⟫

A nna was doing her best not to look for, or find, complications. It was one of the reasons she'd decided against seeing Cameron on Friday night. She made work her excuse and compromised by telling him she'd be at his house bright and early Saturday morning for a sail. When he wheedled, she weakened and promised to make lasagna.

The part of her that gained so much pleasure from watching others eat what she'd prepared herself came from her grandmother. Anna believed that was something to be proud of.

Though she didn't commit to spending the night, they both realized it was understood.

She took the evening for herself, changing out of her suit and into baggy sweats. She put some of her favorite music on, nestling Billie Holiday between Verdi and Cream. She poured a glass of good red wine and watched the sun set.

It was time, she knew, long past time, to do some clear thinking, some objective analyzing. She'd known Cameron Quinn only a matter of weeks, yet she'd allowed herself to become more involved with him than with any other man who'd touched her life.

This level of involvement hadn't been in her plans. She usually planned so well. Steps she took, both professionally and personally, were always carefully thought out. She knew that was a protective action, one she had decided upon coolly and at an early age. If she thought about where each step was leading or could lead, held back on impulse, and depended on intellect, it was much harder to make a mistake.

She felt she'd made too many mistakes years before. If she had continued along the path she blindly raced down after losing her innocence and her mother, she would have been doomed.

She'd had to learn not to blame herself for the things she had done during that dark part of her life, not to wallow in guilt for the hurt she'd caused the people who loved her. Guilt was a negative emotion. Anna preferred positive actions, results, direction.

What she had chosen and accomplished had been for her grandparents, for her mother, and for that terrified child curled on the side of a dark road.

It had taken time, a long healing time, before it came to her that while she'd lost her mother, her grandparents had lost their only child. A daughter they loved. Despite their grief, they opened their home to Anna; despite her destructive actions, their hearts never faltered.

Eventually she learned to accept the loss, the horrors she'd experienced. More, she learned to accept that everything she had done for the two years following that night was the result of a wounded soul. She was fortunate to have people love her enough to help her heal.

When she found her way again, she promised herself that she would never be reckless again.

Impulse was saved for foolish things. Spending sprees, long, fast drives to nowhere. It had become so important to her that she remain basically practical, motivated, and rational that she had buried that reckless bent of her heart. Now, she thought, it was that same heart that had led her to this.

Loving Cameron Quinn was ridiculously reckless. And she knew it was going to cost her.

But her emotions were her own responsibility, she decided. That was something she had learned the hard way. She would handle them, and she would survive them.

But it was just so odd, she admitted, and leaned against the open patio door to catch the early-evening breeze. She'd always believed that if she ever experienced love, she would be aware of every stage of it. She'd hoped to enjoy it—the gradual slide she'd imagined, the mutual awareness of deepening feelings.

But there had been no gradual slide, no gentle fall with Cam. It was one fast, hard tumble. One moment, she felt attraction, interest, enjoyment. Then it seemed she no more than blinked before she was headlong in love.

She imagined it would scare him to death—as he was racing for the hills. The image made her laugh a little. They were well matched there, she decided. She would like to do some fast running in the opposite direction herself. She'd been prepared for an affair but far from ready for a love affair.

So analyze, she ordered herself. What was it about him that made the difference? His looks? On a little hum of pleasure, she closed her eyes. There was little doubt that's what had gained her attention initially. What woman wouldn't look twice, then look again at those dangerous, dark looks? The restless steel-colored eyes, the firm mouth that was equally appealing in a grin or a snarl. His body was the perfect female fantasy of tough muscle, rough hands, and lean lines.

Naturally she'd been attracted. And his quick mind had intrigued her. So had his arrogance, she admitted—though it was a lowering thought. But it was his heart that had changed everything. Oh, she hadn't expected that generous heart—recklessly generous. He had so much to give and was so unaware of it.

He thought himself selfish, hard-bitten, even cold. And she imagined he could be. But where it counted most, he was warm and giving. She didn't think he was fully aware of how much he was offering Seth or how their relationship was changing.

She sincerely doubted he fully understood that he loved the boy. And Anna realized it was that blind spot in Cam to his own goodness that had undone her.

She supposed, when it came down to it, falling in love with him had actually been sensible.

Staying in love with him would be disastrous. She would have to work on that.

The phone rang, distracting her. Carrying her wine, she walked back in and picked up the portable on the coffee table. "Hello."

"Miz Spinelli. Working?"

She couldn't stop the smile. "Working something out, yes." An aria soared out of her stereo as she sat down, propped her feet on the coffee table. "You?"

"Ethan and I have a little something we'll fiddle with tonight yet. Then I'm not even going to think about work until Monday."

He had a portable phone himself and had wandered outside, where he might find some privacy. It was Seth's turn to do the dinner dishes, and he heard another plate hit the floor with a crash. "They're calling for fair weather tomorrow."

"Are they? That's handy."

"You could still drive up tonight."

It was tempting, but she'd already given in to too many impulses where he was concerned. "I'll be there early enough in the morning."

"I don't suppose you have a bikini. A red one."

She tucked her tongue in her cheek. "No, I don't . . . mine's blue."

He waited a beat. "Don't forget to pack."

"If I pack—if I stay—I keep the key to the bedroom door."

"You're so strict." He watched an egret sail over the water and into a nest atop a marker. Making for home, he thought, settling in.

"Just cautious, Quinn. And very smart. How's the building coming?"

"Along," he murmured. He liked hearing her voice, feeling the moist air move, watching the evening slide gentle as a kiss over water and trees. "I'll show you when you're here."

He wanted to show her Seth's sketch. He'd framed it himself that afternoon and wanted to share it with . . . someone who mattered. "We'll probably get started on the first boat next week."

"Really? That quick?"

"Why wait? It's time to put our money down and see how the dice fall. I've been feeling lucky lately." From the house behind him he heard the puppy bark madly, followed by Simon's deeper tones. Then Phillip's voice, raised in a half shout, half laugh and echoed by the rarely heard sound of Seth's giggle.

It made him turn, stare at the house. The back door opened, and the two canine forms bulleted out, tumbling over each other as they reached the steps. And there, framed in the doorway with the kitchen light washing through, was the boy, grinning.

Whatever pulled at Cam's heart pulled hard. For a moment, just one wild moment, he thought he heard the creak of the porch rocker and his father's low chuckle.

"Jesus, it's weird," he murmured.

The connection began to waver and crackle as he walked. "What?"

"Everything." He found himself gripping the phone tighter, yearning for her with a wild, almost desperate desire. "You should be here. I miss you."

"I can't hear you."

He realized he'd been stepping away from the house, a kind of knee-jerk denial of the sensation of being drawn in.

Coming home. Settling in.

With a shake of his head, he walked back until the connection cleared, and thanked God for the vagaries of technology. "I said . . . what are you wearing?"

She laughed softly, looked down at her baggy, practical sweats. "Why, nothing much," she purred, and both of them fell into the ease of phone flirting with various sensations of relief.

⬤

A short time later, Cam set the phone on the porch steps and wandered down to the dock. Water lapped gently against the hull of the boat. Night birds were stirring, and the deep two-toned call of an owl in the woods beyond led the chorus. The sea was ink-dark under the fragile light of a thumbnail moon.

There was work to do. He knew Ethan would be waiting for him. But he needed to sit there by the water for a moment. To sit in the quiet while stars winked on and the owl called endlessly, patiently, for its mate.

He didn't jump when he saw the movement beside him. He was getting used to it. He couldn't count the times he'd sat on this same dock under this same sky with his father. It occurred to him that it was probably a little different to sit here with his father's ghost, but what the hell. Nothing about his life was the same as it once had been.

"I knew you were here," Cam said quietly.

"I like to keep an eye on things." Ray, dressed in fishermen's pants and a short-sleeved sweatshirt that Cam remembered had once been bright blue, dangled a line in the water. "Been a while since I did any night fishing."

Cameron decided that if Ray pulled up a wriggling catfish, it would most likely send him over the thin edge of sanity. "How close an eye?" he asked, thinking of Anna and just what the two of them did in the dark.

Ray chuckled. "I always respected my boys' privacy, Cam. Don't you worry about that. She sure is a looker," he said lightly. "She tries to cover it up when she's working, but a man with a good eye can see through it. You always had a good eye for the ladies."

"How about you?" Cam hated himself for asking. It was such a peaceful night, such a perfect one. But he never knew how long these visitations—hallucinations, whatever they were—would last. He had to ask. "How was your eye for the ladies, Dad?"

"Sharp enough—landed on your mother, didn't it?" And Ray sighed. "I never touched another woman after I made my vows to Stella, Cam. I looked, I appreciated, I enjoyed, but I never touched."

"You have to tell me about Seth."

"I can't. It's not the way it has to be. You did a good thing by the boy, making him a part of the business you're starting by using his drawings. He needs to feel that he's a part of things. I wish I'd had more time with him, with all of you. But that's not the way it has to be either."

"Dad—"

"You know what I miss, Cam? The silliest things. Watching the three of you argue over something. There were times when your mother and I thought you'd bicker us crazy, but I miss that now. And early-morning fishing when the sun just starts to burn off the mist over the water. I miss teaching. I miss seeing that look on a student's face when something you say, just one thing, clicks and opens the mind. I miss pretty girls in summer dresses and lying in bed at three o'clock in the morning listening to rain on the roof."

Then he turned his head and smiled. His eyes were as bright and brilliantly blue as the sweatshirt had once been. "You should appreciate those things while you have them, but you never do. Not all the way. Too busy living. Now and again, you should try to stop to appreciate the little things. They'll build up if you do."

"I've got a little more on my mind than rain on the roof right now."

"I know. You've got a mess on your hands, but you're sorting it. You've still got to figure out what you want, and what you need, and what's inside you. You've got more in there than you think."

"I want answers. I need answers."

"You'll find them," Ray said complacently. "When you slow down."

"Tell me this. Do Ethan and Phillip know you're . . . here?"

"They will." Ray smiled again. "When it's time for it. It should be a nice day for sailing tomorrow. Enjoy the little things," he said and faded away.

SEVENTEEN

He was watching for her. Cam figured it was just one more first in his life. He'd never watched and waited for a woman that he could recall. Even as a teenager, they had come to him. Calling on the phone, wandering by the house, loitering near his locker at school. He supposed he'd gotten used to it. Spoiled by it.

He had never faced the typical male terror of asking for that first date. He'd been asked out when he was fifteen by the luscious Allyson Brentt. An older woman of sixteen. She even picked him up at his front door in her daddy's '72 Chevy Impala. He wasn't sure how he felt about being driven around by a girl. Until Allyson had parked on Blue Crab Drive and suggested they make use of the backseat.

He didn't mind that a bit.

Losing his virginity to pretty, fast-handed Allyson at fifteen was a sweaty and delightful experience. And Cam had never looked back.

He liked women, liked everything about them—even the annoying parts. It was what made them female, and he figured men got the best part of the deal. They got to look, they got to touch and smell. And unless they were complete morons, they could usually wriggle out of those soft arms and move on to the next ones without too much trouble.

He'd never been a moron.

But he watched for Anna, and waited for her. And wondered what it was about her that made him not quite so anxious to wriggle.

Maybe it was the lack of pressure, he mused as he wandered away from the dock toward the side of the house to listen for her car. Again. It could be the very lack of any expectations. She was joyfully sexual, and she didn't seem to expect a lot of romantic trappings. She'd come from a painful childhood, yet she'd gotten past the damage and made herself into something strong and whole.

He admired that.

The way she could, and did, play up or play down her looks fascinated him. That duality kept him wondering who she would be. And yet both parts of her fit so smoothly together, a man could barely see the seam.

The more he thought about her, the more he wanted her.

"What're you doing?"

He nearly jumped out of his skin when Seth came up behind him. He'd been staring at the road, all but willing Anna to pull into the drive. Now he jammed his hands in his pockets, mortified.

"Nothing, just walking around."

"You weren't walking," Seth pointed out.

"Because I'd stopped. Now I'm walking again. See?"

Seth rolled his eyes at Cam's back, then caught up with him. "What am I supposed to do?"

Cam feigned intense interest in the candy-red tulips sunning themselves along the edge of the house. "About what?"

"Stuff. Ethan's out on the workboat and Phillip's closed up in the office doing computer stuff."

"So?" He leaned down to tug up a weed—at least he thought it was a weed. Where the hell was she? "Where are those kids you've been hanging with?"

"They had to go to the store and have lunch with their grandmother." Seth sneered on principle. "I don't have anything to do. It's boring."

"Well, go . . . clean your room or something."

"Come on."

"Jesus, what am I, your social director? Is the TV broken?"

"Nothing on Saturday mornings but kid shit."

"You *are* a kid," Cam pointed out and heard the sound of an approaching car with vast relief. "Teach that brain-dead dog of yours some tricks."

"He's not brain-dead." Instantly insulted, Seth turned and whistled for the pup. "Watch." Foolish raced up, carrying what appeared to be a can of beer in his mouth.

"Yeah, chewing on aluminum. That's brilliant. Look, I don't—" But Cam broke off when Seth snapped a finger, pointed, and Foolish plopped his butt on the ground.

"He does it on voice command, too," Seth said matter-of-factly as he rubbed Foolish's head in reward. "But I've got him responding to hand signals." He held a hand out, and Foolish gamely lifted a paw.

"That's pretty good." Pride and surprise mixed in his voice. "How long did it take you to teach him that?"

"Just a couple hours here and there."

All three watched as Anna pulled into the drive. Foolish was the first to rush to greet her.

"He doesn't do real good with Stay yet," Seth confided. "But we haven't worked on it long."

He didn't do real good with Down, either. The minute Anna stepped out of the car Foolish was leaping and yipping, his tongue lashing out joyfully to lick everywhere.

Cam figured the dog had the right idea. He'd have liked to jump on her and start licking himself. She wore jeans that were faded to a soft, pale blue and a lipstick-red top tucked into the waistband. It was a simple outfit that borrowed from the practical and the siren.

And made Cam's mouth water.

"She looks different with her hair down," Seth commented.

"Yeah." He wanted his hands on it, on her. And that was that.

She was crouched down, purring at the puppy, who had flopped adoringly on his back to have his belly rubbed. Her head came up, and even with the shaded glasses, Cam could see her eyes widen in awareness, then shift warningly to the child who walked behind him.

Ignoring the signal, he hauled her to her feet, gave her one good yank that made her stumble over the pup and against him, and closed his mouth over her sputtering protest.

It was like being swallowed by the sun, was all she could think. The heat was huge and had reached flash point before she could draw the first breath. Need, restless and greedy, pumped out of him and slammed into her at alarming speed. The wild drumming of a woodpecker hunting breakfast echoed through the still air and matched the frantic beat of her heart. All she could do was hold on until he'd devoured enough of what he wanted from her to satisfy him.

When he eased her back, those clever lips curved—a smug look she was sure she would resent when her head settled back on her shoulders again. "Morning, Anna."

"Good morning." She cleared her throat, stepped back, and made herself look over at Seth. He appeared to be more bored than shocked, so she worked up a smile for him. "Good morning, Seth."

"Yeah, hi."

"Your dog's growing into his feet." Because she needed the distraction, she looked down at Foolish and held out a hand. He planted his rump and lifted a paw, charming her. "Oh, aren't you smart?" She crouched again, shook his paw, tugged his ears. "What else can you do?"

"We're working on a couple of things." Foolish had just run through his entire repertoire, but Seth didn't want to say so.

"You make a good team. I've got some groceries in the car," she said casually. "Makings for dinner. Give me a hand?"

"Yeah, all right." He shot a resentful look at Cam. "I've got nothing else to do."

"We're going sailing, aren't we?" She said it brightly, amused when she saw Cam's mouth fall open and Seth look at her with sharp, interested eyes.

"Am I going?"

"Of course." She turned, opened the car door, then handed him a bag. "As soon as we put this stuff away. I hope I'm a quick learner. I know next to nothing about boats."

Cheered, Seth settled bags on each hip. "Nothing to it. But you should have a hat." With this, he carted his bags toward the house.

"I was figuring on it being just you and me," Cam told her. And he'd had a nice fantasy going about slipping into some quiet bend of the river and making rocky love to her in the bottom of the boat.

"Were you?" She took out a small overnight bag, pushed it into his hands. "I'm sure it'll be great fun with the three of us."

She closed her car door, patted Cam's cheek, then sauntered into the house behind Seth.

⟳

It turned out to be the four of them. Seth insisted on taking Foolish, and with Anna backing him all the way, they outvoted Cam.

It was tough to stay annoyed when his crew was so damn cheerful. Foolish sat on a bench, wearing an ancient doggie life jacket that had belonged to one of Ray and Stella's numerous dogs, and barked happily at waves and birds.

Seth, already munching on one of the sandwiches from the cooler, dutifully explained to Anna the mystery of the rigging.

She looked so damned cute, Cam thought, with one of his old and battered Orioles caps on her head, watching studiously as Seth identified each line.

He maneuvered through the channels, motoring between markers at an easy speed, working through what the locals called Little Neck River into Tangier Sound and toward the bay.

There was a light chop, and Cam glanced back to see how Anna would weather it. She was kneeling in the stern, leaning over the rail, but he saw with a grin that it wasn't because of a queasy stomach. Her smile was huge, her finger pointing eagerly as she caught sight of the clumps of trees and spreading marshes of Smith Island.

He called for Seth to hoist sail.

It was a moment Anna would never forget. City life hadn't prepared her for the sounds, the motion, the sight of white sails rising, snapping in the wind, then filling with it.

For a moment the boat seemed to fly, with the wind slapping her cheeks and filling the canvas to bursting. Water churned in their wake and she tasted salt.

She wanted to watch everything at once, the waves rising from blue-green water, the sea of white canvas above, the stretches and bumps of land. And the man and boy who worked so smoothly, so competently, with barely a word passing between them.

They sailed past what Seth identified as a crab shanty. It was no more than a fragile shack of beaten and weathered gray wood stilted out of the water and attached to a rickety dock. The orange floats that marked the crab pots dotted the surface. She watched a workboat rocking in the tide as a waterman—a picture in his faded pants, battered cap, and white boots—hauled up a chicken wire cage.

He paused in his work long enough to touch the brim of his cap in greeting before tossing two snapping crabs into his water tank.

Life on the water, Anna thought and watched the workboat putt toward the next float.

"That's Little Donnie," Seth told her. "Ethan says they call him that even though he's grown up because his father's Big Donnie. Weird."

Anna laughed. It had looked to her as if Little Donnie was pushing two hundred pounds. "I guess that's the way it is when you live in a small community. It must be wonderful to live and work on the water that way."

Seth lifted a shoulder. "It's okay. But I'd rather just sail."

When she lifted her face to the wind, she decided he had a point. Just sail—fast and free, with the boat rising and falling, the gulls wheeling overhead. Cam looked so natural at the wheel, she thought, with his long legs planted apart to accommodate the roll of the boat, his hands firm, his dark hair flying. When he turned his head, was it any wonder her heart jumped? When he held out a hand, was it any wonder she rose and walked cautiously over the unfamiliar deck to take it.

"Want the wheel?"

Desperately. "Better not," she said, trying to be practical. "I don't know what I'm doing."

"I do." He tugged her in front of him, put his hands over hers. "That's Pocomoke," he told her, nodding toward a narrow channel. "If you want to slow down, we can head that way, dodge some crab pots."

The wind slapped playfully at her face. She watched a gull swoop toward the surface of the water, skim it, then rise up calling in that sharp cry that sounded like a laughing scream. The hell with practicalities. "I don't want to slow down."

She heard him laugh above her ear. "Atta girl."

"Where are we heading? What are we doing?"

"Heading south, southwest. Sailing to the luff," he told her. "On the edge of the wind."

"On the edge? It feels like we're in the middle of it. I didn't know we could go so fast. It's wonderful."

"Good. Hold on a minute."

To her shock, he stepped back and called to Seth to help him make some adjustments to the sails. As her hands white-knuckled on the wheel, she heard them laughing. She heard the creak of the masts, the shiver of the canvas as it turned. If anything, she thought the boat picked up speed. She tried to relax. After all, there was nothing but water ahead of them.

She could see to the right—starboard, she corrected herself—a small motorboat cruising out of one of the many rivers and channels. Too far away, she judged, for any traffic jams or accidents.

Just as she had herself convinced she could do the job without incident, the boat tilted. She muffled a scream and nearly whipped the wheel in the opposite direction of the tilt, but Cam's hands closed over hers again and held it steady.

"We're going over!"

"Nah. We're heeled in nicely. More speed."

Her heart stayed in her throat. "You left me at the wheel."

"Sails needed trimming. The kid knows how to work the sheets. Ethan's taught him a lot, and he catches on quick. He's a damn good sailor."

"But you left me at the wheel," she repeated.

"You did fine." He brushed an absent kiss on the top of her head. "That's Tangier Island up ahead. We'll go around it, then head north. There's some quiet spots on the Little Choptank. We'll hit there about lunchtime."

They didn't appear to be capsizing, she thought with a steadying breath. And since she hadn't run them aground, she relaxed enough to lean back against him.

She planted her feet apart, as Cam did, and let her body balance with the motion of the boat. Her newest ambition was to have a little sloop, skiff, whatever it was called, when she finally got that house on the water.

She would have the Quinn brothers build it for her, she decided, dreaming. "If I had a boat, I'd do this every chance I got."

"We'll have to teach you the basics. Before long we'll have you trapezing."

"What? Swinging from the mast in a spangled leotard?"

The image had its appeal. "Not quite. You use a rig—a trapeze—and you hang out over the water."

"For fun?"

"Well, I like it," he said with a laugh. "It's for speed, balancing power."

"Hanging out over the water," she mused, glancing to port. "I might like it too."

He let her work the jib, under Seth's watchful eye. She liked the feel of the line in her hand and knowing she was in charge—more or less—of the billowing white sheet. They rounded the little sandy spit of Tangier Island, and she was treated to the quick maneuvering of tacking, jibbing, the teamwork necessary to maintain speed while changing course.

Cam had stripped down to denim cutoffs, and his skin gleamed with sun and sweat and water. If her hands ached a little from the unfamiliar work, she didn't complain. Instead she got a foolish thrill when Cam told her she was a pretty good crew.

They had lunch on Hudson Creek off the Little Choptank River, near a broken-down wharf with only the birds and the lap of water for company. The sun was bright in a clear blue sky, and the temperature had soared into the eighties to give a hint of the summer that was still weeks away.

To the accompaniment of music on the radio, they took a cooling swim. Foolish paddled joyfully while Seth dived beneath the mirrorlike surface and swam like a wild dolphin.

"He's having the time of his life," Anna murmured. A layer of the sulky, defiant, angry boy she'd first interviewed was being washed away. She wondered if he knew it.

"Then I guess I can't be too annoyed that you insisted on his coming along."

She smiled. She'd bundled her hair on top of her head in a vain attempt to keep it dry. With the way Seth and the puppy were splashing, nothing was dry. "You don't really mind. And you'd never have had that smooth of a sail without him on board."

"True enough, but there's something to be said for a rough sail." He parted the water in front of him, then slid his arms around her.

Anna gripped his shoulders in automatic defense. "No dunking."

"Would I do anything that predictable?" His eyes were smoky with laughter. "Especially when this is more fun." He tilted his head and kissed her.

Their lips were wet and slippery, and Anna's pulse thrummed at the sensation of his mouth sliding over hers, then capturing, then taking. The cool water seemed to grow warmer as their legs tangled. She was weightless, sighing as she floated into the kiss.

Then she was underwater.

She surfaced sputtering, shaking wet hair out of her eyes. The first thing she heard was Seth's laughter. The first thing she saw was Cam's grin.

"It was irresistible," he claimed, then swallowed water himself as she flipped onto her stomach and kicked it into his face.

"You're next," she warned Seth, who was so stunned at the idea of an adult playing with him that she caught him easily and wrestled him under.

He struggled, spat out water, swallowed more when he laughed. "Hey, I didn't do anything."

"You laughed. Besides, as I see it, you guys work as a team. It was probably your idea."

"No way." He wiggled free, then got the bright idea to dive and pull her under the surface by the ankle.

It was a pitched battle, and when they were exhausted, they agreed to call it a draw. It was only then that they noticed Cam was no longer in the water but sitting comfortably on the side of the boat eating a sandwich.

"What are you doing up there?" Anna called out while she pushed her sopping-wet hair back.

"Watching the show." He washed the ham and cheese down with Pepsi. "A couple of goons."

"Goons?" She slid her eyes toward Seth, and in tacit agreement the foes became a unit. "I only see one goon around here, how about you?"

"Just one," he agreed as they swam slowly toward the boat.

Any idiot could have seen what they had in mind. Cam nearly lifted his legs out of reach, then he decided what the hell and let them pull him back into the water with an impressive splash.

It would be hours before it occurred to Seth that Anna and Cam had both had their hands on him. And he hadn't been scared at all.

After the boat was docked, the sails dropped, the decks swabbed, Anna rolled up her metaphorical sleeves and got to work in the kitchen. It was her mission to give the Quinn men a meal they wouldn't soon forget. She might have been a novice sailor, but here she was an expert.

"It smells like glory," Phillip told her when he wandered in.

"It'll taste better." She built the layers of her lasagna with an artist's flair. "Old family recipe."

"They're the best," he agreed. "We've got my father's secret waffle batter recipe. I'll have to whip you up some in the morning."

"I'd like that." She glanced up to smile at him and noted what she thought was worry in his eyes. "Everything all right?"

"Sure. Just some leftover tangles from work." It had nothing to do with work, but with the latest report from the private investigator he'd hired. Seth's mother had been spotted in Norfolk—and that was entirely too close. "Need any help in here?"

"Everything's under control." She finished off her casserole with a thin layer of mozzarella before popping it in the oven. "You might want to try the wine."

Absently Phillip picked up the bottle breathing on the counter. And instantly his interest was piqued. "Nebbiolo, the best of the Italian reds."

"I think so, and I can promise my lasagna's a match for it."

Phillip grinned as he poured two glasses. His eyes were a golden brown that for some reason made Anna think of archangels. "Anna, my love, why don't you toss Cam over and run away with me?"

"Because I'd hunt you both down and kill you," Cam stated as he stepped into the kitchen. "Back off from my woman, bro, before I hurt you." Though it was said lightly, Cam wasn't entirely sure he was joking. And he wasn't entirely pleased to feel the hot little spurt of jealousy.

He wasn't the jealous type.

"He doesn't know a Barolo from a Chianti," Phillip told her as he got down another glass. "You're better off with me."

"Goodness," she said in a passable imitation of their below-the-Mason-Dixon-line drawl, "I just love being fought over by strong men. And here comes one more," she added as Ethan stepped through the back door. "You want to duel for me too, Ethan?"

He blinked and scratched his head. Women confused him, but he was pretty sure there was a joke coming on. "Did you make whatever's cooking in there?"

"With my own little hands," she assured him.

"I'll go get my gun."

When she laughed, he shot her a quick smile, then ducked out of the room to shower off the day's work.

"Jesus, Ethan nearly flirted with a woman." Amazed, Phillip lifted his glass in a toast. "We're going to have to keep you around, Anna."

"If someone will set the table while I put the salad together, I might hang around long enough to let you sample my cannoli."

Cam and Phillip eyed each other. "Whose turn is it?" Cam demanded.

"Not mine. It must be yours."

"No way. I did it yesterday." They studied each other another moment, then both turned to the door and yelled for Seth.

Anna only shook her head. Younger brothers, she supposed, were meant to be abused in such matters.

She knew the meal was a success when Seth gobbled up a third helping. He'd lost that alley-cat boniness, she noted. And the pallor. Perhaps his eyes were still occasionally wary, peeking out under his lashes as if searching for the blow that he'd learned too young to expect. But more often, Anna thought, there was humor in his eyes. He was a bright boy who was discovering how to be amused by people.

His language was rough, and she didn't expect there would be a great deal of improvement in it as long as he lived in a household of men. Though she did see that Cam booted him lightly under the table now and again when he swore too often.

They were making it work. She'd had strong doubts in the beginning that three grown men, well set in their ways, would find a way of adjusting, of making room. And especially of opening their hearts to a boy who had been thrust upon them.

But they were making it work. When she wrote her report on the Quinn case the following week, she was going to state that Seth DeLauter was home, exactly where he belonged.

It would take time for the guardianship to move from temporary to permanent, but she would add her weight. Nothing warmed her heart quite so deeply as seeing the way Seth looked over at Cam after another under-the-table kick and grinned exactly like a ten-year-old boy caught sinning.

He would make a terrific father, she thought. Just rough enough around the edges to make it fun. He'd be the type to cart a child around on his shoulders, to wrestle in the yard. She could almost see it—the handsome dark-haired little boy, the pretty rosy-cheeked girl.

"You're in the wrong business," Phillip told her as he pushed back from the table and considered loosening his belt.

She blinked, caught daydreaming, and very nearly flushed. "I am?"

"You should own a restaurant. Any time you want to shift gears in that direction, I'll be the first in line to invest." He rose, intending to make use of his cappuccino maker to complement her dessert, and answered the phone on the first ring.

At the sound of the husky female voice with a sexy Italian accent, he raised his eyebrows. "He's right here." Phillip ran his tongue over his teeth and held out the phone to Cam. "It's for you, pal."

Cam took the phone, and after one purring sentence in his ear, almost placed the voice. "Hi, sugar," he said, searching for a name. *"Come va?"*

Because he did indeed love his brother, Phillip tried his best to distract Anna. "I just picked up this machine about six months ago," he told her, holding her chair so she would rise—and perhaps move out of earshot. "It's a beaut."

"Really?" She wasn't the least bit interested in the working of some fancy coffee machine. Not when she'd heard just how smoothly Cam had greeted his obviously female caller. When she heard him laugh, her teeth went on edge.

It didn't occur to Cam to muffle his voice or censor the content. He'd finally put a name with the voice—Sophia of the curvy body and bedroom eyes—and was chatting lightly about mutual acquaintances. She liked racing—all manner of racing—and was a hot, sleek bullet in bed.

"No, I had to take a pass on the rest of the season this year," he told her. "I don't know when I'll get back to Rome. You'll be the first, *bella*," he answered when she asked if he would call her when he did. "Sure, I remember—the little trattoria near the Trevi Fountain. Absolutely."

He leaned back against the counter. Her voice brought back memories. Not of her particularly, as he could barely get a clear image of her face in his head. But of Rome itself, the busy, narrow streets, the smells, the sounds, the rush.

The races.

"What?" Her question about his Porsche jerked him back to the present time and place. "Yeah, I've got it garaged in Nice until . . ."

He trailed off, his thoughts scattering as she asked him if he would consider selling it. She had a friend, she told him. Carlo. He remembered Carlo, didn't he? Carlo wondered if Cam would be interested in selling the car, since he was staying so long in the States.

"I haven't thought about it." Sell the car? A little lance of panic stabbed him. It would be like admitting he wasn't going back. Not just to Europe but to his life.

She was speaking quickly, persuasively, her Italian and English mixing and confusing him. He had her number, *si?* And could call her anytime. She would tell Carlo he was thinking about it. They were all missing Cam. Rome was so *noioso* without him. She had heard he had said no to a big race in Australia and was afraid it must be a woman holding him. Had he finally fallen for a woman?

"Yes, no—" His head was spinning. "It's complicated, sweetie. But I'll be in touch." Then she made him laugh one more time when she whispered a suggestion on how they might spend his first night back in Rome. "I'll be sure to keep that in mind. Darling, how could I forget? Yeah. *Ciao*."

Phillip was busily foaming milk and trying with the air of a desperate man to engage Anna in conversation about types of coffee beans. Ethan, with the instinct of a survivor, had already deserted the kitchen. And Seth simply sat, crumbling a heel of garlic bread for Foolish, who hid under the table.

Oblivious, Cam raised a suspicious eyebrow at the cappuccino machine. "I'll stick with regular coffee," he began and smiled when Anna walked up to him. "I remember your cannoli from—" And the air whooshed out of his lungs as she plowed a fist into his gut. Before he could suck it back in, she strode past him and outside with a slap of the screen door.

"What?" Rubbing his stomach, Cam goggled at Phillip. "Jesus, what did you say to her?"

"You're such a jerk," Phillip muttered and deftly poured the first cup.

"She looked really pissed," Seth commented and sniffed the air. "Can I try some of that junk you're making?"

"Sure." Phillip made up a latte, heavy on the milk, while Cam headed outside.

Cam caught up to Anna on the dock, where she stood fuming, her arms folded over her chest. "What the hell was that for?"

"Oh, I don't know, Cam. For the hell of it." She whirled around to face him, her eyes blazing in the starlight. "Women are peculiar creatures. They get annoyed when the man they're supposed to be with flirts over the phone, right in their damn face, with some Italian bimbo."

The light dawned, but to his credit he barely winced. "Come on, sugar—"

He broke off, unsure whether he was amused or frightened when she lifted a fist. "Don't you call me sugar. You use my name. Do you think I'm an idiot? Sugar, sweetie, honey pie—that's what you say when you can't even remember the name of the woman who's underneath you in bed."

"Wait a damn minute."

"No, *you* wait a damn minute. Do you have any idea how *insulting* it is to stand there and hear you make a date to meet your Italian squeeze in Rome when my lasagna's barely settled in your stomach?"

Worse, she thought, much, much worse, he'd done it seconds after she'd been building foolish castles in the air of him with children. Their children. Oh, it was mortifying. Infuriating.

"I wasn't making a date," he began, then paused, fascinated, while a stream of impressive Italian curses poured out of her mouth. "You didn't learn those from your grandparents." When she bared her teeth and hissed, he couldn't stop the smile. "You're jealous."

"It's not a matter of jealousy. It's a matter of courtesy." She tossed her head and tried to calm down. She was only embarrassing herself more with the outburst, she realized. But by damn, she wasn't finished yet. "You're a free agent, Cameron, and so am I. No pretenses, no promises, fine. But I won't tolerate you having phone sex while I'm standing in the same room."

"It wasn't phone sex, it was a conversation."

"The little trattoria by the Trevi Fountain?" she said, coolly now. "How could I forget? You'll be the first? You want to have some Italian *zucchero*, Cam, that's your business. But don't you ever do it in my face again."

She took a breath, then held up a hand before he could speak. "I'm sorry I hit you."

He gauged her mood. Ruffled, but calming. "No, you're not."

"Okay, I'm not. You deserved it."

"It didn't mean anything, Anna."

Yes, she thought wearily, it did. To her it meant a great deal. And that was her own fault, her own small disaster. "It was rude."

"Manners never were my strong point. I'm not interested in her. I can't even remember her face."

Anna angled her head. "Do you honestly think a statement like that goes to your credit?"

What the hell did she want him to say? he wondered with a quick, impatient hiss of breath. Sometimes, he supposed, the truth was best. "It's your face, Anna, that I can't get out of my mind."

She sighed. "Now you're trying to distract me."

"Is it working?"

"Maybe." Her emotions, she reminded herself, her problem. "Let's just agree that even casual relationships have lines that shouldn't be crossed."

He wasn't sure "casual" was the word to describe what was between them. But at the moment whatever made her happy suited him. "Okay. Starting now you're the only Italian bimbo I flirt with." Her bland, unsmiling stare made him grin. "It was terrific lasagna. None of my other bimbos could cook."

She slid her gaze to the water, back to his face. Then cocked her head consideringly. Cam was pretty sure he saw the beginnings of humor in her eyes. "We'd both end up in there," he told her. "But I don't mind if you don't."

"I suppose, all in all, I'd rather stay dry." She glanced toward the house when music slipped through the windows and into the air. "Who plays the violin?"

"That's Ethan." It was a quick and lively jig, one of their parents' favorites. The piano joined in, made him smile. "And that's Phillip."

"What do you play?"

"A little guitar."

"I'd like to hear." In a gesture of peace, she held out a hand. He took it, drawing her closer, taking her fingers to his lips.

"You're the one I want, Anna. You're the one I think of."

For now, she thought, and let him slide her into his arms. Now was all that had to matter.

EIGHTEEN

Anna wasn't sure how she felt about seeing Cam frown in concentration as he tuned up a battered old Gibson guitar. It was a piece of him she hadn't counted on.

It surprised her, pleased her, to see how smoothly, how easily the three men had slid into a song. Strong voices, she mused, quick and clever fingers. Teamwork once again. And unbroken family ties.

Without a doubt there had been many evenings such as this in their lives. She could imagine the three of them, years younger, melding their tunes, with the two people who had given them the music, and the purpose, and the family, sitting in the room with them.

She took that image, and the music, upstairs with her when she finally went to bed. To Cam's bed.

Reminding herself there was a child in the house, she locked the door— in case Cam came tiptoeing up from his makeshift bed on the sofa down- stairs. And she told herself she wouldn't unlock it if he came tapping. No matter how sexy he'd looked strumming that old guitar to life.

Most of the tunes had been old Irish ballads and pub songs that she'd been unfamiliar with. She found them sad and heart-wrenching even when the tune beneath the words was lively. They mixed in some rock, and sneered at Seth when he suggested they play something from this century.

It had been sweet, Anna thought as she undressed. They would never think of it that way, and would likely be horrified that anyone else did. But sweet was how she'd seen it. Four males—four brothers—not of the blood but of the heart. It was easy to see how well they understood each other, and how they had come to just not accept the child but to include him.

When Seth commented that violins were for girls and wusses, Ethan merely smiled and went into a hot lick designed to capture Seth's interest and imagination. And Ethan's dry comment—*let's see a wuss do that*—earned a shrug and a grin from Seth.

When Seth had fallen asleep, they'd just left him there, sprawled on the rug with the puppy's head pillowed on his butt. Another belonging, in Anna's mind.

She slipped into her nightshirt and picked up her hairbrush. This house was an easy place to feel belonging. Big, simple rooms, lived-in furniture, noisy plumbing. She caught a few female touches that hadn't been there before. A gleam to the furniture, the odd vase of spring flowers. Compliments of the housekeeper, Anna imagined, which probably went largely unnoticed by the occupants.

If it were her house, she wouldn't change much, she decided, dreaming again as she ran the brush through her hair. Maybe spruce up some of the colors, add a bit of dash here and there with thick throw pillows and splashier flowers. She would definitely want to expand the gardens. She'd been doing some reading on perennials—what worked best in sun, what thrived in shade. There was a nice spot where the trees began to take over from the yard. She thought lily of the valley, some hostas, and periwinkles would do well there and add some interest.

Wouldn't it be lovely, she reflected, to while away a Saturday morning, digging in the earth, crowding pretty bedding plants together, planning the flow of colors and textures and heights?

And to watch them grow and spread and bloom, year after year.

A movement outside the window caught her eye in the mirror. Her heart sprang into her throat as she saw the shadow move behind the dark glass. As the window crept up, she turned slowly, holding the brush like a weapon.

And Cam stepped over the sill. "Hi." He had enjoyed watching her brush her hair, hated to see her stop. "Brought you something."

He held out a clutch of wild violets, which she tried to eye suspiciously. "Just how did you get up here?"

"Climbed." He stepped forward, she stepped back.

"Climbed what?"

"Up the side of the house mostly. Used to be able to shimmy up and down the gutter, but I weighed less then." He came closer, she moved back.

"That was clever of you. What if you'd fallen?"

He'd climbed sheer rock faces in Montana, Mexico, and France, but he smiled winningly at her concern. "You'd have felt sorry for me?"

"I don't think so." Since he had maneuvered his way to arm's length, she reached out and snatched the slightly crushed flowers. "Thanks for the violets. Good night."

Interesting, he decided. Her voice and her expression were prim despite the fact that she was standing there in nothing more than a long white T-shirt. For some reason he found the plain and practical cotton ridiculously sexy. It appeared he was finally going to get the chance to seduce her.

"I couldn't sleep." He reached over, hit the light switch, and left only the small bedside lamp burning warm and gold.

"You didn't try very long," she said, flicking the switch back on again.

"Seemed like hours." He lifted a hand to trace a finger lightly up her arm from wrist to elbow. Her skin was dusky, golden against the pure white of the nightshirt. "All I could think about was you. Beautiful Anna," he said softly, "with the Italian eyes."

Her toes seemed to curl in response to that skimming finger, which moved now to trace her jawline. Her heart was fluttering. No, it was her stomach. No, it was everything. "Cam, there's a young boy in the house."

"Who's dead asleep." His fingers dipped to her throat, tested the rapid pulse beating there. "Snoring on the living room rug."

"You should have carried him up to bed."

"Why?"

"Because . . ." There had to be a good reason, but how was she supposed to think clearly when he was looking at her, those flint-gray eyes so focused, so intense on her face? "You planned this," she said weakly.

"Not exactly. I thought I would have to talk you into going for a walk in the woods after the house quieted down. And then I would make love to you outside." He took her hand, turned it palm up, and pressed his lips to the center. "In the starlight. But rain's coming in."

"Rain?" She glanced toward the window and saw the curtains billowing in the freshening wind. When she looked back he was closer, and his arms were around her, those broad-palmed, clever hands stroking up her back.

"And I want you in bed. My bed." He tipped his head to nibble kisses along her jaw, then just under it where the skin was soft as water. "I want you, Anna. Day and night."

"Tomorrow," she began.

"Tonight. Tomorrow." And the word "always" was on the edge of his mind when his mouth found hers.

She made a small sound that might have been distress when his tongue slipped through her parted lips to deepen the kiss. It went deeper, still deeper until she had no choice but to let herself sink. The pretty little flowers drifted to the floor as her fingers went limp.

He had kissed her like this only once before, with such unspeakable tenderness that it stripped her soul bare. If she could have formed words, she would have babbled out her love for him. But her knees were jelly, her heart lost, and words were beyond her.

He barely touched her, just those hands light on her back while his mouth drank from hers—and destroyed her.

"It's not a race this time." He heard himself murmur the words but wasn't sure if he spoke to himself or to her. All he knew was he wanted slow, painfully slow, endlessly slow, so that he could savor every moment, every move, every moan.

He reached out, dimmed the lights. "I want this spot," he whispered and let his mouth journey along the fragile skin just under her jaw again. "And this one." To the slender column of her throat, where her scent was warm and smoky.

When he stepped back and tugged his shirt over his head, she took a breath. She would get her feet back under her, she thought, and offer back some of what he was giving her. She reached for him, rose on her toes until their eyes and mouths lined up.

But he kissed her temples, her brow, her eyes when they fluttered closed. "I love looking at you," he told her. He took the hem of her nightshirt in his fingers and lifted it, inch by inch. "All of you. Even when you're not around, I have a picture of you in my head."

When her nightshirt was pooled on the floor, he kept his eyes on her face, lifted her into his arms. Felt her tremble.

And he knew, in one breath-stealing flash, that he had never wanted another woman the way he wanted Anna. This time when he laid her on the bed, it was he who sank mindlessly into the kiss.

He didn't have to order his hands to be gentle, to go slowly. He didn't have to hold back an urge to plunder. Not when she sighed so softly under his touch, not when she moved so fluidly beneath his hands, not when she gave so completely before he could ask.

He explored her with a kind of wonder, as if it were the first time. The first woman, the first need. Somehow it was new, this longing to linger. To sip instead of gulp. To glide instead of race. When her hands roamed over him, his skin quivered and warmed.

Neither of them heard the first soft patters of rain or the low, poignant moan of the wind.

She rose to peak on one long, shimmering wave. Floated down again breathing out his name.

Pleasure was liquid, soft as morning dew, wide as a dark sea. She could feel it sliding through her, shifting, spreading, taking her up on another high, curving crest where only he existed.

She pressed her mouth to his throat, his shoulder, would have absorbed him into her skin if she'd known a way. No one had ever taken her away so completely. And when she framed his face, brought his mouth to hers and poured all she was into the kiss, she knew he was with her. Absolutely hers.

When he filled her, it was only one more link. She opened, took him, and gave. They moved together slowly, breath tangling, gazes locked. Moved together silkily, rhythms matched to draw out every ounce of pleasure.

It built, dizzying and dazzling so that her lips curved even as her eyes swam. "Kiss me," she demanded on one last, trembling breath.

So their mouths met, clung, as that last sweeping wave swamped them.

He didn't speak, didn't dare, when her hands slid limply from his back to the bed. He felt as if he'd tumbled off a cliff and fallen hard on his heart. Now his heart was swollen, exposed. And it was hers.

If this was love, it scared the hell out of him.

But he couldn't move, couldn't let her go. She felt so good, so right beneath him. His body was weak, sated, and his mind close to empty. It was only his heart that trembled and pumped.

He would worry about it later.

Saying nothing, nothing at all, he shifted, drew her close, possessively close, to his side, and let the rain lull him to sleep.

Anna awoke with the sun shooting into her eyes and was stunned to find herself wrapped up in Cam. His arms had a good strong hold on her, and hers were snug around him. Their legs were tangled, with her right hooked over his hip like an anchor.

If her mind had been clear it might have occurred to her that while they both assumed their affair was casual, even sophisticated, in sleep they'd both known better.

She slid her leg down, hoping to unknot their limbs, but he only shifted and anchored hers more firmly.

"Cam." She whispered it, feeling foolish and guilty, and when she received no response, wriggled and spoke more firmly. "Cameron, wake up."

He grunted, snuggled closer, and muttered something into her hair.

She sighed and, deciding she had no choice, lifted the leg that was caught between his until her knee pressed firmly against his crotch. Then she gave it a quick nudge.

That got his eyes open.

"Whoa! What?"

"Wake up."

"I'm awake." And his just-open eyes were all but crossed. "Would you mind moving your . . ." When the pressure eased off, he let out the breath he'd been holding. "Thanks."

"You've got to go." She was back to whispering. "You shouldn't have stayed in here all night."

"Why not?" he whispered back. "It's my bed."

"You know what I'm talking about," she hissed. "One of your brothers could get up any minute."

He exerted himself to lift his head a couple of inches and peer at the clock on the opposite nightstand. "It's after seven. Ethan's already up, has probably emptied his first crab pot. And why are we whispering?"

"Because you're not supposed to be here."

"I live here." A sleepy smile moved over his face. "Damn, you're pretty when you're all rumpled and embarrassed. I guess I have to have you again."

"Stop it." She nearly giggled, until his hand snuck around to cup her breast. "Not now."

"We're here now, naked and everything. And you're all soft and warm." He nuzzled his way to her neck.

"Don't you start."

"Too late. I'm already into the first lap."

And indeed when he shifted, she understood that the starting gun had already sounded. He was inside her in one easy move, and it was so smooth, so natural, so lovely, she could only sigh.

"No moaning," he said with a chuckle at her ear. "You'll wake up my brothers."

She snorted out a laugh and, caught between amusement and arousal, shoved and rolled until she straddled him. He looked sleepy, and dangerous, and exciting. A little breathless, she braced her hands on either side of his head. She bent down and sucked his bottom lip into her mouth.

"Okay, smart guy, let's see who moans first."

And arching back, she began to ride.

Afterward, they decided it was a tie.

She made him climb out the window, which he claimed was ridiculous. But it made her feel a little less decadent. The house was quiet when she came downstairs, freshly showered and comfortable in olive-drab cotton slacks and a camp shirt. Seth was still sleeping on the rug. Foolish stood guard on the floor.

At the sight of Anna, the pup scrambled up, whining pitifully as he followed her into the kitchen. She assumed it was either an empty stomach or a full bladder. When she opened the back door, he shot out like a bullet and proved it was the latter by peeing copiously on an azalea just struggling into bloom.

Birds were singing with full, joyful throats. Dew sparkled on the grass— and the grass needed mowing. There was still a light mist on the water, but it was burning off quickly, like blown smoke, and through it she could see little diamond sparks of sunlight on calm water.

The air was fresh from the night's rain, and the leaves seemed greener, fuller than they had only a day before.

She built a little fantasy that included steaming coffee and a walk down to the dock. By the time she'd taken the first step toward brewing the coffee, Cam came in through the hallway door.

He hadn't shaved, she noted, and found that the stubble of beard suited her image of a lazy Sunday morning in the country. He lifted a brow.

She got two mugs out of the cupboard, then lifted hers. "Good morning, Cameron."

"Good morning, Anna." Deciding to play along, he walked over and gave her a chaste kiss. "How did you sleep?"

"Very well, and you?"

"Like a log." He wound a lock of her hair around his finger. "It wasn't too quiet for you?"

"Quiet?"

"City girl, country silence."

"Oh. No, I liked it. In fact, I don't think I've ever slept better."

They were grinning at each other when Seth stumbled in, rubbing his eyes. "Have we got anything to eat?"

Cam kept his gaze locked on Anna's. "Phillip ran his mouth about making waffles. Go wake him up."

"Waffles? Cool." He ran off, his bare feet slapping on the wood floor.

"Phillip's not going to appreciate that," Anna commented.

"He's the one who started the waffle rumor."

"I could make them."

"You made dinner. We take turns around here. To avoid chaos. And the shedding of blood." A loud and nasty thud sounded over their heads and made Cam grin. "Why don't we pour that coffee and take a walk out of the line of fire?"

"I was thinking the same thing."

On impulse, he grabbed a fishing pole. "Hold this." A hunt through the fridge netted him a small round of Phillip's Brie.

"I thought we were having waffles."

"We are. This is bait." He tucked the cheese in his pocket and picked up his coffee.

"You use Brie for bait?"

"You use what's handy. A fish is going to bite, it'll bite on damn near anything." He handed her a mug of coffee. "Let's see what we can catch."

"I don't know how to fish," she said as they headed out.

"Nothing to it. You drown a worm—or in this case some fancy cheese— and see what happens."

"Then why do guys go off with all that expensive, complicated gear and those funny hats?"

"Just trappings. We're not talking dry fly-fishing here. We're just dropping a line. If we can't pull up a couple of cats by the time Phillip's got waffles on the table, I've really lost my touch."

"Cats?" For one stunning moment, she was absolutely horrified. "You don't use cats as bait."

He blinked at her, saw that she was perfectly serious, then roared with laughter. "Sure we do. You catch 'em by the tail, skin their bellies, and drop them in." He took pity on her only because she went deathly pale. But it didn't stop him from laughing. "Catfish, honey. We're going to bring up some catfish before breakfast."

"Very funny." She sniffed and started walking again. "Catfish are really ugly. I've seen pictures."

"You're telling me you've never eaten catfish?"

"Why in the world would I?" A little miffed, she sat on the side of the dock, feet dangling, and cupped her mug in both hands.

"Fry them fresh and fry them right, and you've never tasted better. Toss in some hush puppies, a couple ears of sweet corn, and you've got yourself a feast."

She eyed him as he settled beside her and began to bait his hook with Brie. His chin was stubbled, his hair untidy, his feet bare. "Fried catfish and hush puppies? This from the reckless Cameron Quinn, the man who races through the waters, roads, and the hearts of Europe. I don't think your little pastry from Rome would recognize you."

He grimaced and dropped his line in the water. "We're not going to get into that again, are we?"

"No." She laughed and leaned over to kiss his cheek. "I almost don't recognize you myself. But I kind of like it."

He handed her the pole. "You don't exactly look like the sober and dedicated public servant yourself this morning, Miz Spinelli."

"I take Sundays off. What do I do if I catch a fish?"

"Reel it in."

"How?"

"We'll worry about that when it happens." He leaned over to pull up the crab pot tied to the near piling. The two annoyed-looking jimmies inside made him grin. "At least we won't starve tonight."

The snapping claws had Anna lifting her feet slightly higher above the water. But she was content to sit there, sipping coffee, watching the morning bloom. When Mama Duck and her six fuzzy babies swam by, she had what Cam considered a typical city girl reaction.

"Oh, look! Look, baby ducks. Aren't they cute?"

"We get a nest down there in the bend near the edge of the woods most every year." And because she was looking so dreamy-eyed, he couldn't resist. "Makes for good hunting over the winter."

"Hunting what?" she murmured, charmed and already imagining what it would be like to hold one of those puffy ducklings in her hand. Then her eyes popped wide, horrified. "You shoot the little ducks?"

"Well, they're bigger by then." He had never shot a duck or anything else in his life. "You can sit right here and drop a couple before breakfast."

"You should be ashamed."

"Your city's showing."

"I'd call it my humanity. If they were my ducks, no one would shoot them." His quick grin had her narrowing her eyes. "You were just trying to get a rise out of me."

"It worked. You look so cute when you're outraged." He kissed her cheek to mollify her. "My mother's heart was too soft to allow hunting. Fishing never bothered her. She said that was more of an even match. And she hated guns."

"What was she like?"

"She was . . . steady," he decided. "It was hard to rock her. Once you did, she had a kick-ass temper, but it was tough to get it going. She loved her work, loved the kids. She had a lot of soft spots. She'd cry at movies or over books, and she couldn't even watch when we cleaned fish. But when there was trouble, she was a rock."

He'd taken Anna's hand without realizing it, lacing their fingers. "When I came here I was beat up pretty bad. She fixed me up. I kept thinking I'd take off as soon as I was steady on my feet again. I kept telling myself these people were a couple of assholes. I could rob them blind and take off anytime I wanted. I was going to Mexico."

"But you didn't take off," Anna said quietly.

"I fell in love with her. It was the day I got back from my first sail with Dad. This world had opened up for me. I was a little scared of it, but there it was. He went inside to grade some papers, I think. I was making bitching noises about having to wear that stupid life jacket, and just general bullshit. She took me by the hand and pulled me right into the water. She said then I'd better learn to swim. And she taught me. I fell in love with her about ten feet out from this dock. You couldn't have dragged me away from here."

Moved, Anna lifted their joined hands to her cheek. "I wish I'd had the chance to meet her. To meet both of them."

He shifted, suddenly realizing that he had told her a story he'd never shared with anyone. And he remembered the way he'd sat here the night before, talking to his father. "Do you, ah, believe that people come back?"

"From?"

"You know, ghosts, spirits, *Twilight Zone* stuff?"

"I don't not believe it," she said after a moment. "After my mother died, there were times when I could smell her perfume. Just out of the blue, out of the air, this scent that was so . . . her. Maybe it was real, maybe it was my imagination, but it helped me. That's what counts, I suppose."

"Yeah, but—"

"Oh!" She nearly dropped the pole when she felt the tug. "Something's on here! Take it!"

"Uh-uh. You caught it." He decided the distraction was for the best. Another minute or two, he might have made a total fool of himself and told her everything. He reached over to steady the pole. "Reel it in some, then let it play out. That's it. No, don't jerk, just slow and steady."

"It feels big." Her heart was thudding between her ears. "Really big."

"They always do. You got it now, just keep bringing it in." He rose to get the net that always hung over the edge of the dock. "Bring her up, up and out."

Anna leaned back, eyes half shut. They popped wide when the fish came flashing and wriggling out of the water and into the sunlight. "Oh, my God."

"Don't drop the pole, for God's sake." Shaking with laughter, Cam gripped her shoulder before she could pitch herself into the water. Leaning forward, he netted the flopping catfish. "Nice one."

"What do I do? What do I do now?"

Expertly Cam freed fish from hook, then to her horror handed her the full net. "Hang on to it."

"Don't leave me with this thing." She took one squinting look, saw whiskers and fishy eyes—and shut her own. "Cam, come back here and take this ugly thing."

He set the widemouthed pail he'd just filled with water on the dock, took the net, and flopped the catch into it. "City girl."

She let out a long breath of relief. "Maybe." She peeped into the pail. "Ugh. Throw it back. It's hideous."

"Not on your life. It's a four-pounder easy."

When she refused to take the pole a second time, he sacrificed the rest of his brother's Brie and settled down to catch the rest of that night's supper himself.

∝∾

The reception that her morning's work received from Seth changed her attitude. Impressing a small boy by catching an indisputably ugly and possibly gourmand fish was a new kind of triumph. By the time she was driving with Cam to the boatyard, she'd decided one of her next projects would be to read up on the art of fishing.

"I think, with the proper bait, I could catch something much more attractive than a catfish."

"Want to go dig up some night crawlers next weekend?"

She tipped down her sunglasses. "Are those what they sound like?"

"You bet."

She tipped them back up. "I don't think so. I think I'd prefer using those pretty feathers and whatnot." She glanced at him again. "So, do you know your father's secret waffle recipe?"

"Nope. He didn't trust me with it. He figured out pretty fast that I was a disaster in the kitchen."

"What kind of bribe would work best on Phillip?"

"You couldn't worm it out of him with a Hermes tie. It only gets passed down to a Quinn."

They'd see about that, she decided, and tapped her fingers on her knee. She continued tapping them when he pulled into the lot beside the old brick building. She wasn't sure what reaction he expected from her. As far as she could see, there was little change here. The trash had been picked up, the broken windows replaced, but the building still looked ancient and deserted.

"You cleaned up." It seemed like a safe response, and it appeared to satisfy him as they got out of opposite doors of the car.

"The dock's going to need some work," he commented. "Phillip ought to be able to handle it." He took out keys, as shiny as the new lock on the front door. "I guess we need a sign or something," he said half to himself as he unlocked the dead bolts. When he opened the door, Anna caught the scent of sawdust, mustiness, and stale coffee. But the polite smile she'd fixed on her face widened in surprise as she stepped inside.

He flicked on lights and made her blink. They were brilliant overhead, hanging from the rafters and unshaded. The newly repaired floor had been swept clean—or nearly so. Bare drywall angled out on the near side to form a partition. The stairs had been replaced, the banister of plain wood oiled. The loft overhead still looked dangerous, but she began to see the potential.

She saw pulleys and wenches, enormous power tools with wicked teeth, a metal chest with many drawers that she assumed held baffling tools. New steel locks glinted on the wide doors leading to the dock.

"This is wonderful, Cam. You do work fast."

"Speed's my business." He said it lightly, but it pleased him to see that she was genuinely impressed.

"You had to work like dogs to get this much done." Though she wanted to see everything, it was the huge platform in the center of the building that pulled her forward. Drawn on it in dark pencil or chalk were curves and lines and angles.

"I don't understand this." Fascinated, she circled around it. "Is this supposed to be a boat?"

"It is a boat. The boat. It's lofting. You draw the hull, full size. The mold section, transverse forms. Then you test them out by sketching in some longitudinal curves—like the sheer. Some of the waterlines."

He was on his knees on the platform as he spoke, using his hands to show her. And still leaving her in the dark.

But it didn't matter whether she understood the technique he described or not. She understood him. He might not realize it yet, but he had fallen in love with this place, and with the work he would do here.

"We need to add the bow lines, and the diagonals. We may want to use this design again, and this is the only way to reproduce it with real accuracy. It's a damn good design. I'm going to want to add in the structural details, full size. The more detail, the better."

He looked up and saw her smiling at him, swinging her sunglasses by the earpiece. "Sorry. You don't know what the hell I'm talking about."

"I think it's wonderful. I mean it. You're building more than boats here."

Faintly embarrassed, he got to his feet. "Boats is the idea." He jumped nimbly off the platform. "Come take a look at these."

He caught her hand, led her to the opposite walls. There were two framed sketches now, one of Ethan's beloved skipjack and the other of the boat yet to be built.

"Seth did them." The pride in his voice was just there. He didn't even notice it. "He's the only one of us who can really draw worth a damn. Phil's adequate, but the kid is just great. He's doing Ethan's workboat next, then the sloop. I've got to get some pictures of a couple of boats I worked on so he can copy them. We'll hang them all in here—and add drawings of the others we build. Kind of like a gallery. A trademark."

There were tears in her eyes when she turned and wrapped her arms around him. Her fierce grip surprised him, but he returned it.

"More than boats," she murmured, then drew back to frame his face in her hands. "It's wonderful," she said again and pulled his mouth down to hers.

The kiss swarmed through him, swamped him, staggered him. Everything about her, about them, spun around in his heart. Questions, dozens of them, buzzed like bees in his head. And the answer, the single answer to all of them, was nearly within his reach.

He said her name, just once, then drew her unsteadily away. He had to look at her, really look, but nothing about him seemed quite on balance.

"Anna," he said again. "Wait a minute."

Before he could get a firm grip on the answer, before he could get his feet back under him again, the door creaked open, letting in sunlight.

"Excuse me, folks," Mackensie said pleasantly. "I saw the car out front."

NINETEEN

Cam's first reaction was pure annoyance. Something was happening here, something monumental, and he didn't want any interruptions.

"We're not open for business, Mackensie." He kept his grip on Anna's arms firm and turned his back to the man he considered no more than a paper-pushing pest.

"Didn't think you were." With his voice still mild and friendly, Mackensie wandered in. In his line of work he rarely received a warm welcome. "Door was unlocked. Well, this is going to be quite a place."

He was a Harry Homemaker at heart, and the sight of all those spanking-new power tools stirred the juices. "Got yourself some top-grade equipment here."

"You want a boat, come back tomorrow and we'll talk."

"I get seasick," Mackensie confessed with a quick grimace. "Can't even stand on a dock without getting queasy."

"That's tough. Go away."

"But I sure do admire the looks of boats. Can't say I ever gave much thought to what went into building them. That's some band saw over there. Must've set you back some."

This time Cam did turn, the fury in his eyes as dangerous as a cocked gun. "It's my business how I spend my money."

Baffled by the exchange, Anna laid a hand on Cam's arm. She wasn't surprised that he was being rude—she'd seen him be rude before—but the snap and hiss of his anger over what appeared to be no more than a nuisance puzzled her.

If this is the way he intends to treat potential clients, she thought, he might as well close the doors now.

Before she could think of the proper calming words, Cam shook her off. "What the hell do you want now?"

"Just a couple of questions." He nodded politely to Anna. "Ma'am. Larry Mackensie, claim investigator for True Life Insurance."

In the dark, Anna automatically accepted the hand he held out. "Mr. Mackensie. I'm Anna Spinelli."

Mackensie did a quick flip through his mental file. It took only a moment for him to tag her as Seth DeLauter's caseworker. As she had come on the scene after the death of the insured, he'd had no need to contact her, but she was in his records. And the cozy little scene he'd walked in on told him she was pretty tight with at least one of the Quinns. He wasn't sure if or how that little bit of information would apply, but he would just make a note of it.

"Pleased to meet you."

"If you two have business to discuss," Anna began, "I'll just wait outside."

"I don't have anything to discuss with him, now or later. Go file your report, Mackensie. We're done."

"Just about. I figured you'd like to know I'll be heading back to the home office. Got a lot of mixed results on my interviews, Mr. Quinn. Not much of what you'd call hard facts, though." He glanced toward the band saw again, wished fleetingly he could afford one like it. "There's the letter that was found in your father's car—that goes to state of mind. Single-car accident, driver a physically fit man, no traces of alcohol or drugs." He lifted his shoulders. "Then there's the fact that the insured increased his policy and added a beneficiary shortly before the accident. The company looks hard at that kind of thing."

"You go ahead and look." Cam's voice had lowered, like the warning growl of an attack dog. "But not here. Not in my place."

"Just letting you know how things stand. Starting a new business," Mackensie said conversationally, "takes a good chunk of capital. You been planning this for long?"

Cam sprang quickly, had Mackensie by the lapels and up on the toes of his shiny, lace-up shoes. "You son of a bitch."

"Cam, stop it!" The order was quick and sharp, and Anna punctuated it by stepping forward and shoving a hand on each man's chest. She thought it was like moving between a wolf and a bull, but she held her ground. "Mr. Mackensie, I think you'd better go now."

"On my way." His voice was steady enough, despite the cold sweat that had pooled at the base of his neck and was even now dripping down his spine. "It's just details, Mr. Quinn. The company pays me to gather the details."

But it didn't pay him, he reminded himself as he walked outside where he could gulp in air, to be beaten to a pulp by a furious beneficiary.

"Bastard, fucking bastard." Cam desperately wanted to hit something, anything, but there was too much empty air. "Does he really think my father plowed into a telephone pole so I could start building boats? I should have decked him. Goddamn it. First they say he did it because he couldn't face the scandal, now it's because he wanted us to have a pile of money. The hell with their dead money. They didn't know him. They don't know any of us."

Anna let him rant, let him prowl around the building looking for something to damage. Her heart was frozen in her chest. Suicide was suspected, she thought numbly. An investigation was in place.

And Cam had known, must have known all along.

"That was a claim investigator from the company who holds your father's life insurance policy?"

"That was a fucking moron." Cam whirled, more oaths stinging his tongue. Then he saw her face—set and entirely too cool. "It's nothing. Just a hassle. Let's get out of here."

"It's suspected that your father committed suicide."

"He didn't kill himself."

She held up a hand. She had to keep the hurt buried for now and lead with the practical. "You've spoken with Mackensie before. And I assume you—your lawyer at any rate—has been in contact with the insurance company about this matter for some time."

"Phillip's handling it."

"You knew, but you didn't tell me."

"It has nothing to do with you."

No, she realized, it wasn't possible to keep all the hurt buried. "I see." That was personal, she reminded herself. She would deal with that later. "And as to how it affects Seth?"

Fury sprang up again, clawed at his throat. "He doesn't know anything about it."

"If you actually believe that, you're deluding yourself. Gossip runs thick in small towns, close communities. And young boys hear a great deal."

It was the caseworker now, Cam thought with rising resentment. She might as well be carrying her briefcase and wearing one of her dumpy suits. "Gossip's all it is. It doesn't matter."

"On the contrary, gossip can be very damaging. You'd be wiser to be open with him, to be honest. Though that seems to be difficult for you."

"Don't twist this around on me, Anna. It's goddamn insurance. It's nothing."

"It's your father," she corrected. "His reputation. I don't imagine there's much that means more to you." She drew a deep breath. "But as you said, it's nothing to do with me on a personal level. I think we're finished here."

"Wait a minute." He stepped in front of her, blocking her exit. He had the sinking feeling that if she walked, she meant to walk a lot farther than his car.

"Why? So you can explain? It's family business? I'm not family. You're absolutely right." It amazed her that her voice was so calm, so detached, so utterly reasonable when she was boiling inside. "And I imagine you felt it best to hold the matter back from Seth's caseworker. Much wiser to show her only the positive angles, lock up any negatives."

"My father didn't kill himself. I don't have to defend him to you, or anyone."

"No, you don't. And I'd never ask you to." She stepped around him and started for the door. He caught her before she reached it, but she'd expected that and turned calmly. "There's no point in arguing, Cam, when essentially we agree."

"There's no point in you being pissed off," he shot back. "We're handling the insurance company. We're handling the gossip about Seth being his love child, for Christ's sake."

"What?" Stunned, she pressed a hand to her head. "There's speculation that Seth is your father's illegitimate son?"

"It's nothing but bull and small minds," Cam replied.

"My God, have you considered, even for a moment, what it could do to Seth to hear that kind of talk? Have you considered, even for a moment, that this was something I needed to know in order to evaluate, in order to help Seth properly?"

His thumbs went into his pockets. "Yeah, I considered it—and I didn't tell you. Because we're handling it. We're talking about my father here."

"We're also talking about a minor child in your care."

"He is in my care," Cam said evenly. "And that's the point. I'm doing what I thought was best all around. I didn't tell you about the insurance thing or about the gossip because they're both lies."

"Perhaps they are, but by not telling me, you lied."

"I wasn't going to go around feeding anybody this crap that the kid was my father's bastard."

She nodded slowly. "Well, take it from some other man's bastard, it doesn't make Seth less of a person."

"I didn't mean it like that," he began and reached out for her. But she stepped away. "Don't do that." He exploded with it and grabbed her arms. "Don't back off from me. For Christ's sake, Anna, my life has turned inside out in the past couple of months, and I don't know how long it's going to be before I can turn it back around. I've got the kid to worry about, the business, you. Mackensie's coming around, people are speculating about my father's morals over the fresh fruit at the supermarket, Seth's bitch of a mother's down in Norfolk—"

"Wait." She didn't move away this time, she yanked away. "Seth's mother has contacted you?"

"No. No." Jesus, his brain was on fire. "We hired a detective to track her down. Phillip figured we'd be better off knowing where she is, what she's up to."

"I see." Her heart broke in two halves, one for the woman, one for the professional. Both sides bled. "And she's in Norfolk, but you didn't bother to tell me that either."

"No, I didn't tell you." He'd backed himself into this corner, Cam realized. And there was no way out. "We only know she was there a couple of days ago."

"Social Services would expect to be notified of this information."

He kept his eyes on hers, nodded slowly. "I guess they just were. My mistake."

There was a line between them now, she realized, very thick and very darkly drawn. "Obviously you don't think very much of me—or of yourself, for that matter. Let me explain something to you. However I may be feeling about you on a personal level at this moment, it's my professional opinion that you and your brothers are the right guardians for Seth."

"Okay, so—"

"I will have to take this information I've just learned into consideration," she continued. "It will have to be documented."

"All that's going to do is screw things up for the kid." He hated the fact that his stomach clenched at the thought. Hated the idea that he might see that look of white-faced fear on Seth's face again. "I'm not going to let some sick gossip mess things up for him."

"Well, on that we can agree." She'd gotten her wish on one level, Anna realized. She'd been around to see how much Seth would come to matter to him. Just long enough, she thought hollowly.

"It's my professional opinion that Seth is well cared for both physically and emotionally." Her voice was brisk now, professional. "He's happy and is beginning to feel secure. Added to that is the fact that he loves you, and you love him, though neither one of you may fully realize it. I still believe counseling would benefit all of you, and that, too, will go into my report and recommendation when the court rules on permanent guardianship. As I told you from the beginning, my concern—my primary concern—is the best welfare of the child."

She was solidly behind them, Cam realized. And would have been no matter what he'd told her. Or hadn't told her. Guilt struck him a sharp, backhanded blow.

"I was never less than honest with you," she said before he could speak.

"Damn it, Anna—"

"I'm not through," she said coolly. "I have no doubt that you'll see Seth is well settled, and that this new business is secure before—as you put it—you turn your life back around. Which I assume means picking up your racing career in Europe. You'll have to find a way to juggle your needs, but that's not my concern. But there may come a time when the guardianship is contested, if indeed Seth's mother makes her way back here. At that time, the case file will be reevaluated. If he remains happy and well cared for under your guardianship, I'll do whatever I can to see to it that he remains with you. I'm on his side, which appears to put me on yours. That's all."

Shame layered onto guilt, with a sprinkling of relief between. "Anna, I know how much you've done. I'm grateful."

She shook her head when he lifted a hand. "I'm not feeling very friendly toward you at the moment. I don't want to be touched."

"Fine. I won't touch you. Let's find somewhere to sit down and talk the rest of this out."

"I thought we just had."

"Now you're being stubborn."

"No, now I'm being realistic. You slept with me, but you didn't trust me. The fact that I was honest with you and you weren't with me is my problem. The fact that I went to bed with a man who saw me as an enjoyment on one hand and an obstacle on the other is my mistake."

"That's not the way it was." His temper began to rise again, pumped by a slick panic. "That's not the way it is."

"It's the way I see it. Now I need to take some time and see how I feel about that. I'd appreciate it if you'd drive me back to my car."

She turned and walked away.

✣

He preferred fire to ice, but he couldn't break through the frigid shield she'd wrapped around her temper. It scared him, a sensation that he didn't appreciate. She was perfectly polite, even friendly, to Seth and Phillip when she returned to the house to gather her things.

She was perfectly polite to Cam—so polite that he imagined he would feel the chill of it for days.

He told himself it didn't matter. She'd get over it. She was just in a snit because he hadn't bared his soul, shared all the intimate details of his life with her. It was a woman thing.

After all, women had invented the cold shoulder just to make men feel like slugs.

He would give her a couple of days, he decided. Let her stew. Let her come to her senses. Then he would take her flowers.

"She's ticked off at you," Seth commented as Cam stood by the front door staring out.

"What do you know?"

"She's ticked off," Seth repeated, entertaining himself with his sketchbook while sitting cross-legged on the front porch. "She didn't let you kiss her good-bye, and you're all the time locking lips."

"Shut up."

"What'd you do?"

"I didn't do anything." Cam kicked the door open and stomped out. "She's just being female."

"You did something." Seth eyed him owlishly. "She's not a jerk."

"She'll get over it." Cam dropped down into the rocker. He wasn't going to worry about it. He never worried about women.

He lost his appetite. How was he supposed to eat fried fish without remembering how he and Anna had sat on the dock that morning?

He couldn't sleep. How was he supposed to sleep in his own bed without remembering how they'd made love on those same sheets?

He couldn't concentrate on work. How was he supposed to detail diagonals without remembering how she'd beamed at him when he showed her the lofting platform?

By mid-morning, he gave up and drove to Princess Anne. But he didn't take her flowers. Now *he* was ticked off.

He strode through the reception area, straight back into her office. Then fumed when he found it empty. Typical, was all he could think. His luck had turned all bad.

"Mr. Quinn." Marilou stood in the doorway, her hands folded. "Is there something I can do for you?"

"I'm looking for Anna—Ms. Spinelli."

"I'm sorry, she's not available."

"I'll wait."

"It'll be a long one. She won't be in until next week."

"Next week?" His narrowed eyes reminded Marilou of steel sharpened to the killing point. "What do you mean, she won't be in?"

"Ms. Spinelli is taking the week off." And Marilou figured the reason for it was even now boring holes through her with furious gray eyes. She'd thought the same when Anna had dropped off her report that morning and requested the time. "I'm familiar with the case file, if there's something I can do."

"No, it's personal. Where did she go?"

"I can't give you that information, Mr. Quinn, but you're free to leave a message, either a written one or one on her voice mail. Of course, if she checks in, I'll be happy to tell her you'd like to speak with her."

"Yeah, thanks."

He couldn't get out fast enough. She was probably in her apartment, he decided as he hopped back in his car. Sulking. So he would let her yell at him, get it all out of her system. Then he'd nudge her along to bed so they could put this ridiculous little episode behind them.

He ignored the nerves dancing in his stomach as he walked down the hall to her apartment. He knocked briskly, then tucked his hands into his pockets. He knocked louder, banged his fist on the door.

"Damn it, Anna. Open up. This is stupid. I saw your car out front."

The door behind him creaked open. One of the sisters peered out. The jingling sound of a morning game show filled the hallway. "She not in there, Anna's Young Man."

"Her car's out front," he said.

"She took a cab."

He bit back an oath, pasted on a charming smile, and walked across the hall. "Where to?"

"To the train station—or maybe it was the airport." She beamed up at him. Really, he was such a handsome boy. "She said she'd be gone for a few days. She promised to call to make sure Sister and I were getting on. Such a sweet girl, thinking of us when she's on vacation."

"Vacation to . . ."

"Did she say?" The woman bit her lip and her eyes unfocused in thought. "I don't think she mentioned it. She was in an awful hurry, but she stopped by just the same so we wouldn't be worried. She's such a considerate girl."

"Yeah." The sweet, considerate girl had left him high and dry.

⌘

She'd had no business flying to Pittsburgh; the airfare had eaten a large hole in her budget. But she'd wanted to get there. Had needed to get there. The minute she walked into her grandparents' cramped row house, half her burden lifted.

"Anna Louisa!" Theresa Spinelli was a tiny, slim woman with steel-gray hair ruthlessly waved, a face that fell into dozens of comfortable wrinkles, and a smile as wide as the Mediterranean Sea. Anna had to bend low to be clasped and kissed. "Al, Al, our bambina's home."

"It's good to be home, Nana."

Alberto Spinelli hurried to the door. He was a foot taller than his wife's tidy five-three, with a broad chest and a spare tire that pressed cozily against Anna as they embraced. His hair was thin and white, his eyes dark and merry behind his thick glasses.

He all but carried her into the living room, where they could begin to fuss over her in earnest.

They spoke rapidly, and in a mix of Italian and English. Food was the first order of business. Theresa always thought her baby was starving. After they'd plied her with minestrone, and fresh bread and an enormous cube of tiramisu, Theresa was almost satisfied that her chick wouldn't perish of malnutrition.

"Now." Al sat back, puffing to life one of his thick cigars. "You'll tell us why you're here."

"Do I need a reason to come home?" Struggling to relax fully, Anna stretched out in one of a pair of ancient wing chairs. It had been recovered, she knew, countless times. Just now it was in a gay striped pattern, but the cushion still gave way beneath her butt like butter.

"You called three days ago. You didn't say you were coming home."

"It was an impulse. I've been swamped at work, up to my ears. I'm tired and wanted a break. I wanted to come home and eat Nana's cooking for a while."

It was true enough, if not the whole truth. She didn't think it would be wise to tell her doting grandparents that she'd walked into an affair, eyes wide open, and ended up with her heart broken.

"You work too hard," Theresa said. "Al, don't I tell you the girl works too hard?"

"She likes to work hard. She likes to use her brain. It's a good brain. Me, I've got a good brain, too, and I say she's not here just to eat your manicotti."

"Are we having manicotti for dinner?" Anna beamed, knowing it wouldn't distract them for long. They'd seen her through the worst, stuck by her when she'd done her best to hurt them, and herself. And they knew her.

"I started the sauce the minute you called to say you were coming. Al, don't nag the girl."

"I'm not nagging, I'm asking."

Theresa rolled her eyes. "If you have such a good brain in that big head of yours, you'd know it's a boy that sent her running home. Is he Italian?" Theresa demanded, fixing Anna with those bright bird eyes.

And she had to laugh. God, it was good to be home. "I have no idea, but he loves my red sauce."

"Then he's got good taste. Why don't you bring him home, let us get a look at him?"

"Because we're having some problems, and I need to work them out."

"Work them out?" Theresa waved a hand. "How do you work them out when you're here and he's not? Is he good-looking?"

"Gorgeous."

"Does he have work?" Al wanted to know.

"He's starting his own business—with his brothers."

"Good, he knows family." Theresa nodded, pleased. "You bring him next time, we'll see for ourselves."

"All right," she said because it was easier to agree than to explain. "I'm going to go unpack."

"He's hurt her heart," Theresa murmured when Anna left the room.

Al reached over and patted her hand. "It's a strong heart."

⁂

Anna took her time, hanging her clothes in the closet, folding them into the drawers of the old dresser she'd used as a child. The room was so much the same. The wallpaper had faded a bit. She remembered that her grandfather had hung it himself, to brighten the room when she'd come to live with them.

And she'd hated the pretty roses on the wall because they looked so fresh and alive, and everything inside her was dead.

But the roses were still there, a little older but still there. As were her grandparents. She sat on the bed, hearing the familiar creak of springs.

The familiar, the comforting, the secure.

That, she admitted, was what she wanted. Home, children, routine—with the surprises that family always provided thrown in. To some, she supposed, it would have sounded ordinary. At one time, she had told herself the same thing.

But she knew better now. Home, marriage, family. There was nothing ordinary there. The three elements formed a unit that was unique and precious.

She wanted, needed that, for herself.

Maybe she had been playing games after all. Maybe she hadn't been completely honest. Not with Cam, and not with herself. She hadn't tried to trap him into her dreams, but underneath it all, hadn't she begun to hope he'd share them? She'd maintained a front of casual, no-strings sex, but her heart had been reckless enough to yearn for more.

Maybe she deserved to have it broken.

The hell she did, she thought, springing up. She'd been making it enough, she'd accepted the limitations of their relationship. And still, he hadn't trusted her. That she wouldn't tolerate.

Damned if she'd take the blame for this, she decided, and stalking to the streaked mirror over her dresser, she began to freshen her makeup.

She would have what she wanted one day. A strong man who loved her, respected her, *and* trusted her. She would have a man who saw her as a partner, not as the enemy. She'd have that home in the country near the water, and children of her own, and a goddamn stupid dog if she wanted. She would have it all.

It just wouldn't be with Cameron Quinn.

If anything, she should thank him for opening her eyes, not only to the flaws in their so-called relationship but to her own needs and desires.

She would rather choke.

TWENTY

A week could be a long time, Cam discovered. Particularly when you had a great deal stuck in your craw that you couldn't spit out.

It helped that he'd been able to pick fights with both Phillip and Ethan. But it wasn't quite the same as having a showdown with Anna.

It helped, too, that beginning work on the hull of the boat took so much of his time and concentration. He couldn't afford to think about her when he was planking.

He thought of her anyway.

He'd had a few bad moments imagining her running around on some Caribbean beach—in that little bikini—and having some overmuscled, over-tanned type rubbing sunscreen on her back and buying her mai tais.

Then he'd told himself that she'd gone off somewhere to lick her imaginary wounds and was probably in some hotel room, drapes drawn, sniffing into a hankie.

But that image didn't make him feel any better.

When he got home from a full Saturday at the boatyard, he was ready for a beer. Maybe two. He and Ethan headed straight for the refrigerator and had already popped tops when Phillip came in.

"Seth isn't with you?"

"Over at Danny's." Cam guzzled from the bottle to wash the sawdust out of his throat. "Sandy's dropping him off later."

"Good." Phillip got a beer for himself. "Sit down."

"What?"

"I got a letter from the insurance company this morning." Phillip pulled out a chair. "The gist is, they're stalling. They used a bunch of legal terms, cited clauses, but the upshot is they're casting doubt on cause of death and are continuing to investigate."

"Fuck that. Cheapscate bastards just don't want to shell out." Annoyed, Cam kicked out a chair—and wished with all his heart it had been Mackensie.

"I talked to our lawyer," Phil continued, grimacing. "He may start rethinking our friendship if I keep calling him on weekends. He says we have some choices. We can sit tight, let the insurance company continue its investigation, or we can file suit against them for nonpayment of claim."

"Let them keep their fucking money, I don't want it anyway."

"No." Ethan spoke quietly in the echo of Cam's outburst. He continued to brood into his beer, shaking his head. "It's not right. Dad paid the premiums, year after year. He added to the policy for Seth. It's not right that they don't pay. And if they don't pay, it's going to go down somewhere that he killed himself. That's not right either. They've been doing all the pushing up to now," he added and raised his somber eyes. "Let's push back."

"If it ends up going to court," Phillip warned him, "it could get messy."

"So we turn away from a fight because it could get messy?" For the first time, amusement flickered over Ethan's face. "Well, fuck that."

"Cam?"

Cam sipped again. "I've been wanting a good fight for a while. I guess this is it."

"Then we're agreed. We'll have the papers drawn up next week, and we'll go after their asses." Revved and ready, Phillip lifted his bottle. "Here's to a good fight."

"Here's to winning," Cam corrected.

"I'm for that. It's going to cost us some," Phillip added. "Filing fees, legal fees. Most of the capital we've pooled is sunk into the business." He blew out a breath. "I guess we need another pool."

With less regret than he'd expected, Cam thought of his beloved Porsche waiting patiently for him in Nice. Just a car, he told himself. Just a damn car. "I can get my hands on some fresh cash. It'll take a couple of days."

"I can sell my house." Ethan shrugged his shoulders. "I've had some people asking about it, and it's just sitting there."

"No." The thought of it twisted in Cam's gut. "You're not selling your house. Rent it out. We'll get through this."

"I've got some stocks." Phillip sighed and waved good-bye to a chunk of his growing portfolio. "I'll tell my broker to cash them in. We'll open a joint account next week—the Quinn Legal Defense Fund."

The three of them managed weak smiles.

"The kid ought to know," Ethan said after a moment. "If we're going to take this to the wall, he ought to know what's going on."

Cam looked up in time to see both of his brothers' eyes focus on him. "Oh, come on. Why does it have to be me?"

"You're the oldest." Phillip grinned at him. "Besides, it'll take your mind off Anna."

"I'm not brooding about her—or any woman."

"Been edgy and broody all week," Ethan mumbled. "Making me nuts."

"Who asked you? We had a little disagreement, that's all. I'm giving her time to simmer down."

"Seems to me she'd simmered down to frozen the last time I saw her." Phillip examined his beer. "That was a week ago."

"It's my business how I handle a woman."

"Sure is. But let me know when you're done with her, will you? She's—"

Phillip broke off when Cam all but leaped over the table and grabbed him by the throat. Beer bottles flew and shattered on the floor.

Resigned, Ethan raked his hand through his hair, scattering drops of spilled beer. Cam and Phillip were on the floor, pounding hell out of each other. He got himself a fresh beer before filling a pitcher with cold water.

His work boots crunched over broken glass, which he kicked out of the way in hopes that he wouldn't have to run anybody to the hospital for stitches. With malice toward neither, he emptied the pitcher on both his brothers.

It got their attention.

Phillip's lip was split, Cam's ribs throbbed, and both of them were bleeding from rolling around on broken glass. Drenched and panting, they eyed each other warily. Gingerly, Phillip wiped a knuckle over his bloody lip.

"Sorry. Bad joke. I didn't know things were serious between you."

"I never said they were serious."

Phillip laughed, then winced as his lip wept. "Brother, did you ever. I guess I never figured you'd be the first of us to fall in love with a woman."

The stomach that Phillip's fists had abused jittered wildly. "Who said I'm in love with her?"

"You didn't punch me in the face because you're in like." He looked down at his pleated slacks. "Shit. Do you know how hard it is to get blood-stains out of a cotton blend?" He rose, held out a hand to Cam. "She's a ter-rific lady," he said as he hauled Cam to his feet. "Hope you work it out."

"I don't have to work out anything," Cam said desperately. "You're way off here."

"If you say so. I'm going to get cleaned up."

He headed out, limping only a little.

"I ain't mopping the damn floor," Ethan stated, "because your glands got in an uproar."

"He started it," Cam muttered, not caring how ridiculous it sounded.

"No, I figure you did, with whatever you did to piss Anna off." Ethan opened the broom closet, took out a mop, and tossed it to Cam. "Now I guess you got to clean it up."

He slipped out the back door.

"The two of you think you know so goddamn much." Furious, he kicked a chair over on his way to fetch a bucket. "I ought to know what's going on in my own life. Insanity, that's what. I should be in Australia, prepping for the race of my life, that's where I should be."

He dragged the mop through water, beer, glass, and blood, muttering to himself. "Australia's just where I'd be if I had any sense left. Damn woman's complicating things. Better off just cutting loose there."

He kicked over another chair because it felt good, then shook shards of glass from the mop into the bucket.

"Who had a fight?" Seth wanted to know.

Cam turned and narrowed his eyes at the boy standing in the doorway. "I kicked Phillip's ass."

"What for?"

"Because I wanted to."

With a nod, Seth walked around the puddle and got a Pepsi out of the fridge. "If you kicked his ass, how come you're bleeding?"

"Maybe I like to bleed." He finished mopping up while the boy stood watching him. "What's your problem?" Cam demanded.

"I got no problem."

Cam shoved the bucket aside with his foot. The least Phillip could do was empty it somewhere. He went to the sink and bad-temperedly picked glass out of his arm. Then he got out the whiskey, righted a chair, and sat down with the bottle and a glass.

He saw Seth's eyes slide over the bottle and away. Deliberately Cam poured two fingers of Johnnie Walker into a glass. "Not everybody who drinks gets drunk," he said. "Not everybody who gets drunk—as I may decide to do—knocks kids around."

"Don't know why anybody drinks that shit anyway."

Cam knocked back the whiskey. "Because we're weak, and stupid, and it feels good at the time."

"Are you going to Australia?"

Cam poured another shot. "Doesn't look like it."

"I don't care if you go. I don't care where the hell you go." The underlying fury in the boy's voice surprised them both. Flushing, Seth turned and raced out the door.

Well, hell, Cam thought and shoved the whiskey aside. He pushed away from the table and hit the door as Seth streaked across the yard to the woods.

"Hold it!" When that didn't slow the boy down, Cam put some mean into it. "Goddamn it, I said hold it!"

This time Seth skidded to a halt. When he turned around, they stared at each other across the expanse of grass, temper and nerves vibrating from them in all but visible waves.

"Get your butt back over here. Now."

He came, fists clenched, chin jutting out. They both knew he had nowhere to run. "I don't need you."

"Oh, the hell you don't. I ought to kick your ass for being stupid. Everybody says you've got some genius brain in there, but if you ask me you're dumb as dirt. Now sit down. There," he added, jabbing a finger at the steps. "And if you don't do what I tell you when I tell you, I might just kick your ass after all."

"You don't scare me," Seth said, but he sat.

"I scare you white, and that gives me the hammer." Cam sat as well, watched the puppy come crawling toward them on his belly. And I scare little dogs too, he thought in disgust. "I'm not going anywhere," he began.

"I said I don't care."

"Fine, but I'm telling you anyway. I figured I would, once everything settled down. I told myself I would. I guess I needed to. Never figured on coming back here to stay."

"Then why don't you go?"

Cam gave him a halfhearted boot on the top of his head with the heel of one hand. "Why don't you shut up until I say what I have to say?"

The painless smack and impatient order were more comforting to Seth than a thousand promises.

"I've been coming to the fact that I've been running long enough. I liked what I was doing while I was doing it, but I guess I'm pretty well finished with it. It looks like I've got a place here, and a business here, maybe a woman here," he murmured, thinking of Anna.

"So you're staying to work and poke at a girl."

"Those are damn good reasons for hanging in one place. Then there's you." Cam leaned back on the upper steps, bracing with his elbows. "I can't say I cared much for you when I first came back. There's that crappy attitude of yours, and you're ugly, but you kind of grow on a guy."

Immensely cheered, Seth snickered. "You're uglier."

"I'm bigger, I'm entitled. So I guess I'll hang around to see if you get any prettier as time goes on."

"I didn't really want you to go," Seth said under his breath after a long moment. It was the closest he could get to speaking his heart.

"I know." Cam sighed. "Now that we've got that settled, we've got this other thing. Nothing to worry about, it's just some legal bullshit. Phil and the lawyer'll handle most of it, but there might be some talk. You shouldn't pay any attention to it if you hear it."

"What kind of talk?"

"Some people—some idiots—think Dad aimed for that pole. Killed himself."

"Yeah, and now this asshole from the insurance company's asking questions."

Cam hissed out a breath. He knew he should probably tell the kid not to call adults assholes, but there were bigger issues here. "You knew that?"

"Sure, it goes around. He talked to Danny and Will's mother. Danny said she gave him an earful. She didn't like some guy coming around asking questions about Ray. That butthead Chuck up at the Dairy Queen told the detective guy that Ray was screwing around with his students, then had a crisis of conscience and killed himself."

"Crisis of conscience." Jesus, where did the kid come up with this stuff? "Chuck Kimball? He always was a butthead. Word is he got caught cheating on a lit exam and got booted out of college. And it seems to me Phillip beat the crap out of him once. Can't remember why, though."

"He's got a face like a carp."

Cam laughed. "Yeah, I guess he does. Dad—Ray—never touched a student, Seth."

"He was square with me." And that counted for everything. "My mother . . ."

"Go ahead," Cam prompted.

"She told me he was my father. But another time she said this other guy was, and once when she was really loaded she said my old man was some guy named Keith Richards."

Cam couldn't help it, the laugh just popped out. "Jesus, now she's hitting on the Stones?"

"Who?"

"I'll see to your music education later."

"I don't know if Ray was my father." Seth looked up. "She's a liar, so I don't go with anything she said, but he took me. I know he gave her money, a lot of it. I don't know if he'd have told me if he was. He said there were things we had to talk about, but he had stuff to work out first. I know you don't want him to be."

It couldn't matter, Cam realized. Not anymore. "Do you want him to be?"

"He was decent," the boy said so simply that Cam draped an arm around his shoulders. And Seth leaned against him.

"Yeah, he was."

Everything had changed. Everything was different. And he was desperate to tell her. Cam knew his life had turned on its axis yet again. And somehow he'd ended up exactly where he needed to be.

The only thing missing was Anna.

He took a chance and drove to her apartment. It was Saturday night, he thought. She was due back at work on Monday. She was a practical woman and would want to take Sunday to catch up, sort her laundry, answer her mail. Whatever.

If she wasn't home, he was going to by God sit on her doorstep until she got there.

But when she answered his knock and stood there looking so fresh, so gorgeous, he was caught off balance.

Anna, on the other hand, had prepared for this meeting all week. She knew exactly how she would handle it. "Cam, this is a surprise. You just caught me."

"Caught you?" he said stupidly.

"Yes, but I've got a few minutes. Would you like to come in?"

"Yeah, I—where the hell have you been?"

She lifted her brows. "Excuse me?"

"You took off, out of the blue."

"I wouldn't say that. I arranged leave from work, checked in with my neighbors, had my plants watered while I was gone. I was hardly abducted by aliens, I simply took a few days of personal time. Do you want some coffee?"

"No." Okay, he thought, she was going to keep playing it cool. He could do that. "I want to talk to you."

"That's good, because I want to talk to you, too. How's Seth?"

"He's fine. Really. We got a lot of things ironed out. Just today—"

"What have you done to your arm?"

Impatient, he glanced down at the raw nicks and scrapes. "Nothing. It's nothing. Listen, Anna—"

"Why don't you sit down? I'd really like to apologize if I was hard on you last weekend."

"Apologize?" Well, that was more like it. Willing to be forgiving, he sat on the sofa. "Why don't we just forget it? I've got a lot to tell you."

"I'd really like to clear this up." Smiling pleasantly, she sat across from him. "I suppose we were both in a difficult position. A great deal of that was my fault. Becoming involved with you was a calculated risk. But I was attracted and didn't weigh the potential problems as carefully as I should have. Obviously something like last weekend's disagreement was bound to happen. And as we both have Seth's interests at heart, and will continue to, I would hate for us to be at odds."

"Good, then we won't." He reached for her hand, but she evaded his gesture and merely patted his.

"Now that that's settled, you really have to excuse me. I hate to rush you along, Cam, but I have a date."

"A what?"

"A date." She glanced at the watch on her wrist. "Shortly, as it happens, and I have to change."

Very slowly he got to his feet. "You have a date? Tonight? What the hell is that supposed to mean?"

"What it generally does." She blinked twice, as if confused, then let her eyes fill with apology. "Oh, I'm sorry. I thought we both understood that we'd ended the . . . well, the more personal aspect of our relationship. I assumed it was clear that it wasn't working out for either of us."

It felt as though someone had blown past his guard and rammed an iron fist into his solar plexus. "Look, if you're still pissed off—"

"Do I look pissed off?" she asked coolly.

"No." He stared at her, shaking his head while his stomach did a quick pitch and roll. "No, you don't. You're dumping me."

"Don't be melodramatic. We're simply ending an affair that both of us entered freely and without promises or expectations. It was good while it lasted, really good. I'd hate to spoil that. Now as far as our professional relationship goes, I've told you that I'll do all I can to support your permanent guardianship of Seth. However, I do expect you to be more forthcoming with information from now on. I'll also be happy to consult with you or advise you on any area of that guardianship. You and your brothers are doing a marvelous job with him."

He waited, certain there would be more. "That's it?"

"I can't think of anything else—and I am a little pressed for time."

"You're pressed for time." She'd just stabbed him dead center of the heart, and she was pressed for time. "That's too damn bad, because I'm not finished."

"I'm sorry if your ego's bruised."

"Yeah, my ego's bruised. I got a lot of bruises right now. How the hell can you stand there and brush me off after what we had together?"

"We had great sex. I'm not denying it. We're just not going to have it any longer."

"Sex?" He grabbed her arms and shook her, and had the small satisfaction of seeing a flash of anger heat through the chill in her eyes. "That's all it was for you?"

"That's what it was for both of us." It wasn't going the way she'd planned. She'd expected him to be angry and storm out. Or to be relieved that she'd backed away first and walk away whistling. But he wasn't supposed to confront her like this. "Let go of me."

"The hell I will. I've been half crazy for you to get back. You turned my life upside down, and I'll be damned if you'll just stroll away because you're through with me."

"We're through with each other. I don't want you anymore, and it's your bad luck I said it first. Now take your hands off me."

He released her as if her skin had burned his palms. There'd been a hitch in her voice, a suspicious one. "What makes you think I'd have said it at all?"

"We don't want the same things. We were going nowhere, and I'm not going to keep heading there, no matter how I feel about you."

"How do you feel about me?"

"Tired of you!" she shouted. "Tired of me, tired of us. Sick and tired of telling myself fun and games could be enough. Well, it's not. Not nearly, and I want you out."

He felt the temper and panic that had gripped him ease back into delight. "You're in love with me, aren't you?"

He'd never seen a woman go from simmer to boil so fast. And seeing it, he wondered why it had taken him so long to realize he adored her. She whirled, grabbed a lamp, and hurled it.

He gave her credit for aim and gave thanks that he was light on his feet, as the base whistled by his head before it crashed into the wall.

"You arrogant, conceited, cold-blooded son of a bitch." She grabbed a vase now, a new one she'd bought on the way home to cheer herself up. She let it fly.

"Jesus, Anna." It was admiration, pure and simple, that burst through him as he was forced to catch the vase before it smashed into his face. "You must be nuts about me."

"I despise you." She looked frantically for something else to throw at him and snagged a bowl of fruit off the kitchen counter. The fruit went first. Apples. "Loathe you." Pears. "Hate you." Bananas. "I can't believe I ever let you touch me." Then the bowl. But she was more clever this time, feinted first, then heaved in the direction of his dodge.

The stoneware caught him just above the ear and had stars spinning in front of his eyes.

"Okay, game over." He made a dive for her, caught her around the waist. His already abused body suffered from kicks and punches, but he hauled her to the couch and held her down. "Get ahold of yourself before you kill me."

"I want to kill you," she said between gritted teeth.

"Believe me, I get the picture."

"You don't get anything." She bucked under him and sent his system into a tangled mess of lust and laughter. Sensing both, she reared up and bit him, hard.

"Ouch. Goddamn it. Okay, that's it." He dragged her up and threw her over his shoulder. "You still packed? Tells me she's got a damn date. Like hell she does. Tells me we're finished. What bullshit." He marched her into the bedroom, saw her bag on the bed, and grabbed it.

"What are you doing? Put me down. Put that down."

"I'm not letting loose of either until we're in Vegas."

"Vegas? Las Vegas?" She thudded both fists on his back. "I'm not going anywhere with you, much less Vegas."

"That's exactly where we're going. It's the quickest place to get married, and I'm in a hurry."

"And how the hell do you expect to get me on a plane when I'm screaming my lungs out? I'll have you in jail in five minutes flat."

At his wits' end because she was inflicting considerable damage, he dumped her at the front door and held her arms. "We're getting married, and that's the end of it."

"You can just—" Her body sagged, and her head reeled. "Married?" The word finally pierced her temper. "You don't want to get married."

"Believe me, I've been rethinking the idea since you beaned me with the fruit bowl. Now, are you going to come along reasonably, or do I have to sedate you?"

"Please let me go."

"Anna." He lowered his brow to hers. "Don't ask me to do that, because I don't think I can live without you. Take a chance, roll the dice. Come with me."

"You're angry and you're hurt," she said shakily. "And you think rushing off to Vegas to have some wild, plastic-coated instant marriage is going to fix everything."

He framed her face, gently now. Tears were shimmering in her eyes, and he knew he'd be on his knees if she let them spill over. "You can't tell me you don't love me. I won't believe you."

"Oh, I'm in love with you, Cam, but I'll survive it. There are things I need. I had to be honest with myself and admit that. You broke my heart."

"I know." He pressed his lips to her forehead. "I know I did. I was shortsighted, I was selfish, I was stupid. And damn it, I was scared. Of me, of you, of everything that was going on around me. I messed it up, and now you don't want to give me another chance."

"It's not a matter of chances. It's a matter of being practical enough to admit that we want different things."

"I finally figured out today what it is I want. Tell me what you want."

"I want a home."

He had one for her, he thought.

"I want marriage."

Hadn't he just asked her?

"I want children."

"How many?"

Her tears dried up, and she shoved at him. "It isn't a joke."

"I'm not joking. I was thinking two with an option for three." His mouth quirked at the look of blank-eyed shock on her face. "There, now *you're* getting scared because you're beginning to realize I'm serious."

"You—you're going back to Rome, or wherever, as soon as you can."

"*We* can go to Rome, or wherever, on our honeymoon. We're not taking the kid. I draw the line there. I might like to get in a couple of races from time to time. Just to keep my hand in. But basically I'm in the boat building business. Of course, it might go belly-up. Then you'd be stuck with a house-husband who really hates housework."

She wanted to press her fingers to her temples, but he still had her by the arms. "I can't think."

"Good. Just listen. You cut a hole in me when you left, Anna. I wouldn't admit it, but it was there. Big and empty."

He rested his brow on hers for a moment. "You know what I did today? I worked on building a boat. And it felt good. I came home, the only home I've ever had, and it felt right. Had a family meeting and decided that we'd take on the insurance company and do what's right for our father. By the way, I've been talking to him."

She couldn't stop staring at him, even though her head was reeling. "What? Who?"

"My father. Had some conversations with him—three of them—since he died. He looks good."

Her breath was clogged right at the base of her throat. "Cam."

"Yeah, yeah," he said with a quick grin. "I need counseling. We can talk about that later—didn't mean to get off the track. I was telling you what I did today, right?"

Very slowly she nodded. "Yes."

"Okay, after the meeting, Phil made some smart remark, so I punched him, and we beat on each other for a bit. That felt good too. Then I talked to Seth about the things I should have talked to him about before, and I listened to him the way I should have listened before, then we just sat for a while. That felt good, Anna, and it felt right."

Her lips curved. "I'm glad."

"There's more. I knew when I was sitting there that that was where I wanted to be, needed to be. Only one thing was missing, and that was you. So I came to find you and take you back." He pressed his lips gently to her forehead. "To take you home, Anna."

"I think I want to sit down."

"No, I want your knees weak when I tell you I love you. Are you ready?"

"Oh, God."

"I've been real careful never to tell a woman I loved her—except my mother. I didn't tell her often enough. Take a chance on me, Anna, and I'll tell you as often as you can stand hearing it."

She hitched in a breath. "I'm not getting married in Vegas."

"Spoilsport." He watched her lips bow up before he closed his over them. And the taste of her soothed every ache in his body and soul. "God, I missed you. Don't go away again."

"It brought you to your senses." She wrapped her arms tight around him. And it felt good, she thought giddily. It felt right. "Oh, Cam, I want to hear it, right now."

"I love you. It feels so damn perfect loving you. I can't believe I wasted so much time."

"Less than three months," she reminded him.

"Too much time. But we'll make it up."

"I want you to take me home," she murmured. "After."

He eased back, cocked his head. "After what?" Then he made her laugh by lifting her into his arms.

He picked his way through the wreckage, kicked a very sad-looking banana out of the way. "You know, I can't figure out why I used to think marriage would be boring."

"Ours won't be." She kissed his bruised head. It was still bleeding a little. "Promise."

RISING TIDES

*For the witty and delightful Christine Dorsey
Yes, Chris, I mean you.*

PROLOGUE

Ethan climbed out of his dreams and rolled out of bed. It was still dark, but he habitually started his day before night yielded to dawn. It suited him, the quiet, the simple routine, the hard work that would follow.

He'd never forgotten to be grateful that he'd been able to make this choice and have this life. Though the people responsible for giving him both the choice and the life were dead, for Ethan, the pretty house on the water still echoed with their voices. He would often find himself glancing up from his lone breakfast in the kitchen expecting to see his mother shuffle in, yawning, her red hair a wild tangle from sleep, her eyes half blind with it.

And though she'd been gone nearly seven years, there was a comfort in that homey morning image.

It was more painful to think of the man who had become his father. Raymond Quinn's death was still too fresh after a mere three months for there to be comfort. And the circumstances surrounding it were both ugly and unexplained. His death had come in a single-car accident in broad daylight on a dry road, on a March day that had only hinted of spring. The car was traveling fast, with its driver unable—or unwilling—to control it on a curve. Tests had proven that there had been no physical reason for Ray to crash into the telephone pole.

But there was evidence of an emotional reason, and that lay heavy on Ethan's heart.

Ethan thought of it as he readied himself for the day—giving his hair, still damp from the shower, a cursory swipe with his comb, which did nothing to tame the thick waves of sun-bleached brown. He shaved in the foggy mirror, his quiet blue eyes sober as he scraped lather and a night's worth of beard from a tanned, bony face that held secrets he rarely chose to share.

There was a scar that rode along the left of his jawline—courtesy of his oldest brother and patiently stitched up by his mother. It had been fortunate, Ethan thought as he rubbed a thumb absently over the faded line, that their mother had been a doctor. One of her three sons was usually in need of first aid.

Ray and Stella had taken them in, three half-grown boys, all wild, all damaged, all strangers. And had made them a family.

Then months before his death, Ray had taken in another.

Seth DeLauter belonged to them now. Ethan never questioned it. Others did, he knew. There was talk buzzing through the little town of St. Christopher's that Seth was not just another of Ray Quinn's strays but his illegitimate son. A child conceived with another woman while his wife was still alive. A younger woman.

Ethan could ignore the talk, but it was impossible to ignore the fact that ten-year-old Seth looked at you with Ray Quinn's eyes.

There were shadows in those eyes that Ethan also recognized. The wounded recognized the wounded. He knew that Seth's life, before Ray had taken him on, had been a nightmare. He'd lived through one himself.

The kid was safe now, Ethan thought as he pulled on baggy cotton pants and a faded work shirt. He was a Quinn now, even if the legalities hadn't been completely worked out. They had Phillip to deal with that. Ethan figured his detail-mad brother would handle that end of things with the lawyer. And he knew that Cameron, the eldest of the Quinn boys, had managed to form a tenuous bond with Seth.

Fumbled his way to it, Ethan thought with a half smile. It had been like watching two angry tomcats spit and claw. Now that Cam had married the pretty social worker, things might just settle down some.

Ethan preferred a settled life.

They had battles yet, with the insurance company refusing to honor Ray's policy because there was suspicion of suicide. Ethan's stomach clutched, and he took a moment to will himself relaxed again. His father would never have killed himself. The Mighty Quinn had always faced his problems and had taught his sons to do the same.

But it was a cloud over the family that refused to blow away. There were others, too. The sudden appearance in St. Christopher's of Seth's mother and her accusations of sexual molestation, made to the dean of the college where Ray had taught English literature. That hadn't held—there'd been too many lies, too many shifts in her story. But there was no denying that his father had been shaken. There was no denying that shortly after Gloria DeLauter had left St. Chris again, Ray had gone away, too.

And he'd returned with the boy.

Then there was the letter found in the car after Ray's accident. An obvious blackmail threat from the DeLauter woman. There was the fact that Ray had given her money, a great deal of money.

Now she had disappeared again. Ethan wanted her to stay gone, but he knew the talk wouldn't stop until all the answers were clear.

Nothing he could do about it, Ethan reminded himself. He stepped out into the hall, gave a quick knock on the door opposite his. Seth's groan was followed by a sleepy mutter, then an annoyed curse. Ethan kept going, heading downstairs. He had no doubt that Seth would bitch again about getting up so early. But with Cam and Anna in Italy on their honeymoon, and Phillip in Baltimore until the weekend, it was Ethan's job to get the boy up, to get him headed over to a friend's house to stay until it was time to leave for school.

Crabbing season was in full swing, and a waterman's day started before the sun. So until Cam and Anna returned, so did Seth's.

The house was silent and dark, but he moved through it easily. He had a house of his own now, but part of the deal in gaining guardianship of Seth had been for the three brothers to live under the same roof and share the responsibilities.

Ethan didn't mind responsibilities, but he missed his little house, his privacy and the ease of what had been his life.

He flicked on the lights in the kitchen. It had been Seth's turn to clean it up after dinner the evening before, and Ethan noted that he'd done a half-assed job. Ignoring the cluttered and sticky surface of the table, he moved directly to the stove.

Simon, his dog, stretched lazily out of his curl. His tail thumped on the floor. Ethan set the coffee to brew, greeting the retriever with an absent scratch on the head.

The dream was coming back to him now, the one he'd been caught in just before waking. He and his father, out on the workboat checking crab pots. Just the two of them. The sun had been blinding bright and hot, the water mirror-clear and still. It had been so vivid, he thought now, even the smells of water and fish and sweat.

His father's voice, so well remembered, had carried over the sounds of engine and gulls.

"I knew you'd look after Seth, the three of you."

"You didn't have to die to test that out." There was resentment in Ethan's tone, an underlying anger he hadn't allowed himself to admit while awake.

"It wasn't what I had in mind, either," Ray said lightly, culling crabs from the pot under the float that Ethan had gaffed. His thick orange fisherman's gloves glowed in the sun. "You can trust me on that. You got some good steamers here and plenty of sooks."

Ethan glanced at the wire pot full of crabs, automatically noting size and number. But it wasn't the catch that mattered, not here, not now. "You want me to trust you, but you don't explain."

Ray glanced back, tipping up the bright-red cap he wore over his dramatic silver mane. The wind tugged at his hair, teased the caricature of John Steinbeck gracing his loose T-shirt into rippling over his broad chest. The great American writer held a sign claiming he would work for food, but he didn't look too happy about it.

In contrast, Ray Quinn glowed with health and energy, ruddy cheeks where deep creases only seemed to celebrate a full and contented mood of a vigorous man in his sixties with years yet to live.

"You've got to find your own way, your own answers." Ray smiled at Ethan out of brilliantly blue eyes, and Ethan could see the creases deepen around them. "It means more that way. I'm proud of you."

Ethan felt his throat burn, his heart squeeze. Routinely he rebaited the pot, then watched the orange floats bob on the water. "For what?"

"For being. Just for being Ethan."

"I should've come around more. I shouldn't have left you alone so much."

"That's a crock." Now Ray's voice was both irritated and impatient. "I wasn't some old invalid. It's going to piss me off if you think that way, blame yourself for not looking after me, for Christ's sake. Same way you wanted to blame Cam for going off to live in Europe—and even Phillip for going off to Baltimore. Healthy birds leave the nest. Your mother and I raised healthy birds."

Before Ethan could speak, Ray raised a hand. It was such a typical gesture, the professor making a point and refusing interruption, that Ethan had to smile. "You missed them. That's why you wanted to be mad at them. They left, you stayed, and you missed having them around. Well, you've got them back now, don't you?"

"Looks that way."

"And you've got yourself a pretty sister-in-law, the beginnings of a boat-building business, and this . . ." Ray gestured to take in the water, the bobbing floats, the tall, glossily wet eelgrass on the verge where a lone egret stood like a marble pillar. "And inside you, you've got something Seth needs. Patience. Maybe too much of it in some areas."

"What's that supposed to mean?"

Ray sighed gustily. "There's something you don't have, Ethan, that you need. You've been waiting around and making excuses to yourself and doing not a damn thing to get it. You don't make a move soon, you're going to lose it again."

"What?" Ethan shrugged and maneuvered the boat to the next float. "I've got everything I need, and what I want."

"Don't ask yourself what, ask yourself who." Ray clucked his tongue, then gave his son a quick shoulder shake. "Wake up, Ethan."

And he had awakened, with the odd sensation of that big, familiar hand on his shoulder.

But, he thought as he brooded over his first cup of coffee, he still didn't have the answers.

ONE

"Got us some nice peelers here, Cap'n." Jim Bodine culled crabs from the pot, tossing the marketable catch in the tank. He didn't mind the snapping claws—and had the scars on his thick hands to prove it. He wore the traditional gloves of his profession, but as any waterman could tell you, they wore out quick. And if there was a hole in them, by God, a crab would find it.

He worked steadily, his legs braced wide for balance on the rocking boat, his dark eyes squinting in a face weathered with age and sun and living. He might have been taken for fifty or eighty, and Jim didn't much care which end you stuck him in.

He always called Ethan Cap'n, and rarely said more than one declarative sentence at a time.

Ethan altered course toward the next pot, his right hand nudging the steering stick that most watermen used rather than a wheel. At the same time, he operated the throttle and gear levels with his left. There were constant small adjustments to be made with every foot of progress up the line of traps.

The Chesapeake Bay could be generous when she chose, but she liked to be tricky and make you work for her bounty.

Ethan knew the Bay as well as he knew himself. Often he thought he knew it better—the fickle moods and movements of the continent's largest estuary. For two hundred miles it flowed from north to south, yet it measured only four miles across where it brushed by Annapolis and thirty at the mouth of the Potomac River. St. Christopher's sat snug on Maryland's southern Eastern Shore, depending on its generosity, cursing it for its caprices.

Ethan's waters, his home waters, were edged with marshland, strung with flatland rivers with sharp shoulders that shimmered through thickets of gum and oak.

It was a world of tidal creeks and sudden shallows, where wild celery and widgeongrass rooted.

It had become his world, with its changing seasons, sudden storms, and always, always, the sounds and scents of the water.

Timing it, he grabbed his gaffing pole and in a practiced motion as smooth as a dance hooked the pot line and drew it into the pot puller.

In seconds, the pot rose out of the water, streaming with weed and pieces of old bait and crowded with crabs.

He saw the bright-red pincers of the full-grown females, or sooks, and the scowling eyes of the jimmies.

"Right smart of crabs," was all Jim had to say as he went to work, heaving the pot aboard as if it weighed ounces rather than pounds.

The water was rough today, and Ethan could smell a storm coming in. He worked the controls with his knees when he needed his hands for other tasks. And eyed the clouds beginning to boil together in the far western sky.

Time enough, he judged, to move down the line of traps in the gut of the bay and see how many more crabs had crawled into the pots. He knew Jim was hurting some for cash—and he needed all he could come by himself to keep afloat the fledgling boatbuilding business he and his brothers had started.

Time enough, he thought again, as Jim rebaited a pot with thawing fish parts and tossed it overboard. In leapfrog fashion, Ethan gaffed the next buoy.

Ethan's sleek Chesapeake Bay retriever, Simon, stood, front paws on the gunwale, tongue lolling. Like his master, he was rarely happier than when out on the water.

They worked in tandem, and in near silence, communicating with grunts, shrugs, and the occasional oath. The work was a comfort, since the crabs were plentiful. There were years when they weren't, years when it seemed the winter had killed them off or the waters would never warm up enough to tempt them to swim.

In those years, the watermen suffered. Unless they had another source of income. Ethan intended to have one, building boats.

The first boat by Quinn was nearly finished. And a little beauty it was, Ethan thought. Cameron had a second client on the line—some rich guy from Cam's racing days—so they would start another before long. Ethan never doubted that his brother would reel the money in.

They'd do it, he told himself, however doubtful and full of complaints Phillip was.

He glanced up at the sun, gauged the time—and the clouds sailing slowly, steadily eastward.

"We'll take them in, Jim."

They'd been eight hours on the water, a short day. But Jim didn't complain. He knew it wasn't so much the oncoming storm that had Ethan piloting the boat back up the gut. "Boy's home from school by now," he said.

"Yeah." And though Seth was self-sufficient enough to stay home alone for a time in the afternoon, Ethan didn't like to tempt fate. A boy of ten, and with Seth's temperament, was a magnet for trouble.

When Cam returned from Europe in a couple of weeks, they would juggle Seth between them. But for now the boy was Ethan's responsibility.

The water in the Bay kicked, turning gunmetal gray now to mirror the sky, but neither men nor dog worried about the rocky ride as the boat crept up the steep fronts of the waves, then slid back down into the troughs. Simon stood at the bow now, head lifted, his ears blowing back in the wind, grinning his doggie grin. Ethan had built the workboat himself, and he knew she would do. As confident as the dog, Jim moved to the protection of the awning and, cupping his hands, lit a cigarette.

The waterfront of St. Chris was alive with tourists. The early days of June lured them out of the city, tempted them to drive from the suburbs of D.C. and Baltimore. He imagined they thought of the little town of St. Christopher's as quaint, with its narrow streets and clapboard houses and tiny shops. They liked to watch the crab pickers' fingers fly, and eat the flaky crab cakes or tell their friends they'd had a bowl of she-crab soup. They stayed in the bed-and-breakfasts—St. Chris was the proud home of no less than four—and they spent their money in the restaurants and gift shops.

Ethan didn't mind them. During the times when the Bay was stingy, tourism kept the town alive. And he thought there would come a time when some of those same tourists might decide that having a hand-built wooden sailboat was their heart's desire.

The wind picked up as Ethan moored at the dock. Jim jumped nimbly out to secure lines, his short legs and squat body giving him the look of a leaping frog wearing white rubber boots and a grease-smeared gimme cap.

At Ethan's careless hand signal, Simon plopped his butt down and stayed in the boat while the men worked to unload the day's catch and the wind made the boat's sun-faded green awning dance. Ethan watched Pete Monroe walk toward them, his iron-gray hair crushed under a battered billed hat, his stocky body outfitted in baggy khakis and a red checked shirt.

"Good catch today, Ethan."

Ethan smiled. He liked Mr. Monroe well enough, though the man had a bone-deep stingy streak. He ran Monroe's Crab House with a tightly closed fist. But, as far as Ethan could tell, every man's son who ran a picking plant complained about profits.

Ethan pushed his own cap back, scratched the nape of his neck where sweat and damp hair tickled. "Good enough."

"You're in early today."

"Storm's coming."

Monroe nodded. Already his crab pickers who had been working under the shade of striped awnings were preparing to move inside. Rain would drive the tourists inside as well, he knew, to drink coffee or eat ice cream sundaes. Since he was half owner of the Bayside Eats, he didn't mind.

"Looks like you got about seventy bushels there."

Ethan let his smile widen. Some might have said there was a hint of the pirate in the look. Ethan wouldn't have been insulted, but he'd have been surprised. "Closer to ninety, I'd say." He knew the market price, to the penny, but understood they would, as always, negotiate. He took out his negotiating cigar, lit it, and got to work.

The first fat drops of rain began to fall as he motored toward home. He figured he'd gotten a fair price for his crabs—his eighty-seven bushels of crabs. If the rest of the summer was as good, he was going to consider dropping another hundred pots next year, maybe hiring on a part-time crew.

Oystering on the Bay wasn't what it had been, not since parasites had killed off so many. That made the winters hard. A few good crabbing seasons were what he needed to dump the lion's share of the profits into the new business—and to help pay the lawyer's fee. His mouth tightened at that thought as he rode out the swells toward home.

They shouldn't need a damn lawyer. They shouldn't have to pay some slick-suited talker to clear their father's good name. It wouldn't stop the whispers around town anyway. Those would only stop when people found something juicier to chew on than Ray Quinn's life and death.

And the boy, Ethan mused, staring out over the water that trembled under the steady pelting of rain. There were some who liked to whisper about the boy who looked back at them with Ray Quinn's dark-blue eyes.

He didn't mind for himself. As far as Ethan was concerned people could wag their tongues about him until they fell out of their flapping mouths. But he minded, deeply, that anyone would speak a dark word about the man he'd loved with every beat of his heart.

So he would work his fingers numb to pay the lawyer. And he would do whatever it took to guard the child.

Thunder shook the sky, booming off the water like cannon fire. The light went dim as dusk, and those dark clouds burst wide to pour out solid sheets of rain. Still he didn't hurry as he docked at his home pier. A little more wet, to his mind, wouldn't kill him.

As if in agreement with the sentiment, Simon leaped out to swim to
shore while Ethan secured the lines. He gathered up his lunch pail, and with
his waterman's boots thwacking wetly against the dock, headed for home.

He removed the boots on the back porch. His mother had scalded his
skin often enough in his youth about tracking mud for the habit to stick to
the man. Still, he didn't think anything of letting the wet dog nose in the
door ahead of him.

Until he saw the gleaming floor and counters.

Shit, was all he could think as he studied the pawprints and heard Simon's
happy bark of greeting. There was a squeal, more barking, then laughter.

"You're soaking wet!" The female voice was low and smooth and
amused. It was also very firm and made Ethan wince with guilt. "Out, Simon! Out you go. You just dry off on the front porch."

There was another squeal, baby giggles, and the accompanying laughter
of a young boy. The gang's all here, Ethan thought, rubbing rain from his
hair. The minute he heard footsteps heading in his direction, he made a beeline for the broom closet and a mop.

He didn't often move fast, but he could when he had to.

"Oh, Ethan." Grace Monroe stood with her hands on her narrow hips,
looking from him to the pawprints on her just-waxed floor.

"I'll get it. Sorry." He could see that the mop was still damp and decided
it was best not to look at her directly. "Wasn't thinking," he muttered, filling
a bucket at the sink. "Didn't know you were coming by today."

"Oh, so you let wet dogs run through the house and dirty up the floors
when I'm not coming by?"

He jerked a shoulder. "Floor was dirty when I left this morning, didn't
figure a little wet would hurt it any." Then he relaxed a little. It always
seemed to take him a few minutes to relax around Grace these days. "But if
I'd known you were here to skin me over it, I'd have left him on the porch."

He was grinning when he turned, and she let out a sigh.

"Oh, give me the mop. I'll do it."

"Nope. My dog, my mess. I heard Aubrey."

Absently Grace leaned on the doorjamb. She was tired, but that wasn't
unusual. She had put in eight hours that day, too. And she would put in another four at Shiney's Pub that night serving drinks.

Some nights when she crawled into bed she would have sworn she heard
her feet crying.

"Seth's minding her for me. I had to switch my days. Mrs. Lynley called
this morning and asked if I'd shift doing her house till tomorrow because her
mother-in-law called her from D.C. and invited herself down to dinner. Mrs.
Lynley claims her mother-in-law is a woman who looks at a speck of dust

like it's a sin against God and man. I didn't think you'd mind if I did y'all to-day instead of tomorrow."

"You fit us in whenever you can manage it, Grace, and we're grateful."

He was watching her from under his lashes as he mopped. He'd always thought she was a pretty thing. Like a palomino—all gold and long-legged. She chopped her hair off short as a boy's, but he liked the way it sat on her head, like a shiny cap with fringes.

She was as thin as one of those million-dollar models, but he knew Grace's long, lean form wasn't for fashion. She'd been a gangling, skinny kid, as he recalled. She'd have been about seven or eight when he'd first come to St. Chris and the Quinns. He supposed she was twenty-couple now—and "skinny" wasn't exactly the word for her anymore.

She was like a willow slip, he thought, very nearly flushing.

She smiled at him, and her mermaid-green eyes warmed, faint dimples flirting in her cheeks. For reasons she couldn't name, she found it entertaining to see such a healthy male specimen wielding a mop.

"Did you have a good day, Ethan?"

"Good enough." He did a thorough job with the floor. He was a thorough man. Then he went to the sink again to rinse bucket and mop. "Sold a mess of crabs to your daddy."

At the mention of her father, Grace's smile dimmed a little. There was distance between them, had been since she'd become pregnant with Aubrey and had married Jack Casey, the man her father had called "that no-account grease monkey from upstate."

Her father had turned out to be right about Jack. The man had left her high and dry a month before Aubrey was born. And he'd taken her savings, her car, and most of her self-respect with him.

But she'd gotten through it, Grace reminded herself. And she was doing just fine. She would keep right on doing fine, on her own, without a single penny from her family—if she had to work herself to death to do it.

She heard Aubrey laugh again, a long, rolling gut laugh, and her resentment vanished. She had everything that mattered. It was all tied up in a bright-eyed, curly-headed little angel just in the next room.

"I'll make you up some dinner before I go."

Ethan turned back, took another look at her. She was getting some sun, and it looked good on her. Warmed her skin. She had a long face that went with the long body—though the chin tended to be stubborn. A man could take a glance and he would see a long, cool blonde—a pretty body, a face that made you want to look just a little longer.

And if you did, you'd see shadows under the big green eyes and weariness around the soft mouth.

"You don't have to do that, Grace. You ought to go on home and relax a while. You're on at Shiney's tonight, aren't you?"

"I've got time—and I promised Seth sloppy joes. It won't take me long." She shifted as Ethan continued to stare at her. She'd long ago accepted that those long, thoughtful looks from him would stir her blood. Just another of life's little problems, she supposed. "What?" she demanded, and rubbed a hand over her cheek as if expecting to find a smudge.

"Nothing. Well, if you're going to cook, you ought to hang around and help us eat it."

"I'd like that." She relaxed again and moved forward to take the bucket and mop from him and put them away herself. "Aubrey loves being here with you and Seth. Why don't you go on in with them? I've got some laundry to finish up, then I'll start dinner."

"I'll give you a hand."

"No, you won't." It was another point of pride for her. They paid her, she did the work. All the work. "Go on in the front room—and be sure to ask Seth about the math test he got back today."

"How'd he do?"

"Another A." She winked and shooed Ethan away. Seth had such a sharp brain, she thought as she headed into the laundry room, off the kitchen. If she'd had a better head for figures, for practical matters when she'd been younger, she wouldn't have dreamed her way through school.

She'd have learned a skill, a real one, not just serving drinks and tending house or picking crabs. She'd have had a career to fall back on when she found herself alone and pregnant, with all her hopes of running off to New York to be a dancer dashed like glass on brick.

It had been a silly dream anyway, she told herself, unloading the dryer and shifting the wet clothes from the washer into it. Pie in the sky, her mama would say. But the fact was, growing up, there had only been two things she'd wanted. The dance, and Ethan Quinn.

She'd never gotten either.

She sighed a little, holding the warm, smooth sheet she took from the basket to her cheek. Ethan's sheet—she'd taken it off his bed that day. She'd been able to smell him on it then, and maybe, for just a minute or two, she'd let herself dream a little of what it might have been like if he'd wanted her, if she had slept with him on those sheets, in his house.

But dreaming didn't get the work done, or pay the rent, or buy the things her little girl needed.

Briskly she began to fold the sheets, laying them neatly on the rumbling dryer. There was no shame in earning her keep by cleaning houses or serving drinks. She was good at both, in any case. She was useful, and she was needed. That was good enough.

She certainly hadn't been useful or needed by the man she was married to so briefly. If they'd loved each other, really loved each other, it would have been different. For her it had been a desperate need to belong to someone, to be wanted and desired as a woman. For Jack . . . Grace shook her head. She honestly didn't know what she had been for Jack.

An attraction, she supposed, that had resulted in conception. She knew he believed he'd done the honorable thing by taking her to the courthouse and standing with her in front of the justice of the peace on that chilly fall day and exchanging vows.

He had never mistreated her. He had never gotten mean drunk and knocked her around the way she knew some men did wives they didn't want. He didn't go sniffing after other women—at least not that she knew about. But she'd seen, as Aubrey grew inside her and her belly rounded, she'd seen the look of panic come into his eyes.

Then one day he was simply gone without a word.

The worst of it was, Grace thought now, she'd been relieved.

If Jack had done anything for her, it was to force her to grow up, to take charge. And what he'd given her was worth more than the stars.

She put the folded laundry in a basket, hitched the basket on her hip, and walked into the front room.

There was her treasure, her curly blond hair bouncing, her pretty, rosy-cheeked face alight with joy as she sat on Ethan's lap and babbled at him.

At two, Aubrey Monroe resembled a Botticelli angel, all rose and gilt, with bright-green eyes and dimples denting her cheeks. Little kitten teeth and long-fingered hands. Though he could decipher only half her chatter, Ethan nodded soberly.

"And what did Foolish do then?" he asked as he figured out she was telling him some story about Seth's puppy.

"Licked my face." Her eyes laughing, she took both hands and ran them up over her cheeks. "All over." Grinning, she cupped her hands on Ethan's face and fell into a game she liked to play with him. "Ouch!" She giggled, rubbed his face again. "Beard."

Obliging, he skimmed his knuckles over her smooth cheek, then jerked his hand back. "Ouch. You've got one, too."

"No! You."

"No." He pulled her close and planted noisy kisses on her cheeks while she wriggled in delight. "You."

Screaming with laughter now, she wiggled away and dived for the boy sprawled on the floor. "Seth beard." She covered his cheek with sloppy kisses. Manhood demanded that he wince.

"Jeez, Aub, give me a break." To distract her, he picked up one of her toy cars and ran it lightly down her arm. "You're a racetrack."

Her eyes beamed with the thrill of a new game. Snatching the car, she ran it, not quite so gently, over any part of Seth she could reach.

Ethan only grinned. "You started it, pal," he told Seth when Aubrey walked over Seth's thigh to reach his other shoulder.

"It's better than getting slobbered on," Seth claimed, but his arm came up to keep Aubrey from tumbling to the floor.

For a few moments, Grace simply stood and watched. The man, relaxed in the big wing chair and grinning down at the children. The children themselves, their heads close—one delicate and covered with gold curls, the other with a shaggy mop shades and shades deeper.

The little lost boy, she thought, and her heart went out to him as it had from the first day she'd seen him. He'd found his way home.

Her precious girl. When Aubrey had been only a fluttering in her womb, Grace had promised to cherish, to protect, and to enjoy her. She would always have a home.

And the man who had once been a lost boy, who had slipped into her girlish dreams years before and had never really slipped out again. He had made a home.

The rain drummed on the roof, the television was a low, unimportant murmur. Dogs slept on the front porch, and the moist wind blew through the screen door.

And she yearned where she knew she had no business yearning—to set down the basket of laundry, to go over and climb into Ethan's lap. To be welcomed there, even expected there. To close her eyes, for just a little while, and be part of it all.

Instead she retreated, finding herself unable to step into that quiet, lazy ease. She went back to the kitchen, where the overhead lights were bright and just a little hard. There, she set the basket on the table and began to gather what she needed to make dinner.

When Ethan came in a few moments later to hunt up a beer, she had meat browning, potatoes frying in peanut oil, and a salad under way.

"Smells great." He stood awkwardly for a minute. He wasn't used to having someone cook for him—not for years—and then not a woman. His father had been at home in the kitchen, but his mother . . . They'd always joked that whenever she cooked, they needed all her medical skills to survive the meal.

"It'll be ready in half an hour or so. I hope you don't mind eating early. I've got to get Aubrey home and bathed and then change for work."

"I never mind eating, especially when I'm not doing the cooking. And the fact is, I want to get to the boatyard for a couple hours tonight."

"Oh." She looked back, blowing at her bangs. "You should have told me. I'd have hurried things up."

"This pace works for me." He took a pull from the bottle. "You want a drink or something?"

"No, I'm fine. I was going to use that salad dressing Phillip made up. It looks so much prettier than the store-bought."

The rain was letting up, petering out into slow, drizzling drops with watery sunlight struggling to break through. Grace glanced toward the window. She was always hoping to see a rainbow. "Anna's flowers are doing well," she commented. "The rain's good for them."

"Saves me from dragging out the hose. She'd have my head if they died on her while she's gone."

"Wouldn't blame her. She worked so hard getting them planted before the wedding." Grace worked quickly, competently as she spoke. Draining crisp potatoes, adding more to the sizzling oil. "It was such a beautiful wedding," she went on as she mixed sauce for the meat in a bowl.

"Came off all right. We got lucky with the weather."

"Oh, it couldn't have rained that day. It would have been a sin." She could see it all again, so clearly. The green of the grass in the backyard, the sparkling of water. The flowers Anna had planted glowing with color—and the ones she'd bought spilling out of pots and bowls alongside the white runner that the bride had walked down to meet her groom.

A white dress billowing, the thin veil only accentuating the dark, deliriously happy eyes. Chairs had been filled with friends and family. Anna's grandparents had both wept. And Cam—rough-and-tumble Cameron Quinn—had looked at his bride as if he'd just been given the keys to heaven.

A backyard wedding, Grace thought now. Sweet, simple, romantic. Perfect.

"She's the most beautiful woman I've ever seen." Grace said it with a sigh that was only lightly touched with envy. "So dark and exotic."

"She suits Cam."

"They looked like movie stars, all polished and glossy." She smiled to herself as she stirred spicy sauce into the meat. "When you and Phillip played that waltz for their first dance, it was the most romantic thing I've ever seen." She sighed again as she finished putting the salad together. "And now they're in Rome. I can hardly imagine it."

"They called yesterday morning to catch me before I left. They said they're having a good time."

She laughed at that, a rippling, smoky sound that seemed to cruise along his skin. "Honeymooning in Rome? It would be hard not to." She started to scoop out more potatoes and swore lightly as oil popped and splattered on the side of her hand. "Damn." Even as she was lifting the slight burn to her mouth to soothe it, Ethan leaped forward and grabbed her hand.

"Did it get you?" He saw the pinkening skin and pulled her to the sink. "Run some cold water on it."

"It's nothing. It's just a little burn. Happens all the time."

"It wouldn't if you were more careful." His brows were knitted, his hand gripping her fingers firmly to keep her hand under the stream of water. "Does it hurt?"

"No." She couldn't feel anything but his hand on her fingers and her own heart thundering in her chest. Knowing she'd make a fool of herself any moment, she tried to pull free. "It's nothing, Ethan. Don't fuss."

"You need some salve on it." He started to reach up into the cupboard to find some, and his head lifted. His eyes met hers. He stood there, the water running, both of their hands trapped under the chilly fall of it.

He tried never to stand quite so close to her, not so close that he could see those little gold dust flecks in her eyes. Because he would start to think about them, to wonder about them. Then he'd have to remind himself that this was Grace, the girl he'd watched grow up. The woman who was Aubrey's mother. A neighbor who considered him a trusted friend.

"You need to take better care of yourself." His voice was rough as the words worked their way through a throat that had gone dust-dry. She smelled of lemons.

"I'm fine." She was dying, somewhere between giddy pleasure and utter despair. He was holding her hand as if it were as fragile as spun glass. And he was frowning at her as if she were slightly less sensible than her two-year-old daughter. "The potatoes are going to burn, Ethan."

"Oh. Well." Mortified because he'd been thinking—just for a second—that her mouth might taste as soft as it looked, he jerked back, fumbling now for the tube of salve. His heart was jumping, and he hated the sensation. He preferred things calm and easy. "Put some of this on it anyway." He laid it on the counter and backed up. "I'll . . . get the kids washed up for dinner."

He scooped up the laundry basket on his way and was gone.

With deliberate movements, Grace shut the water off, then turned and rescued her fries. Satisfied with the progress of the meal, she picked up the salve and smoothed a little on the reddened splotch on her hand before tidily replacing the tube in the cupboard.

Then she leaned on the sink, looked out the window.

But she couldn't find a rainbow in the sky.

Two

There was nothing like a Saturday—unless it was the Saturday leading up to the last week of school and into summer vacation. That, of course, was all the Saturdays of your life rolled into one big shiny ball.

Saturday meant spending the day out on the workboat with Ethan and Jim instead of in a classroom. It meant hard work and hot sun and cold drinks. Man stuff. With his eyes shaded under the bill of his Orioles cap and the really cool sunglasses he'd bought on a trip to the mall, Seth shot out the gaff to drag in the next marker buoy. His young muscles bunched under his *X-Files* T-shirt, which assured him that the truth was out there.

He watched Jim work—tilt the pot and unhook the oyster-can-lid stopper to the bait box on the bottom of the pot. Shake out the old bait, Seth noted and see the seagulls dive and scream like maniacs. Cool. Now get a good solid hold on that pot, turn it over, and shake it like crazy so the crabs in the upstairs section fall out into the washtub waiting for them. Seth figured he could do all that—if he really wanted to. He wasn't afraid of a bunch of stupid crabs just because they looked like big mutant bugs from Venus and had claws that tended to snap and pinch.

Instead, his job was to rebait the pot with a couple handfuls of disgusting fish parts, do the stopper, check to make sure there were no snags in the line. Eyeball the distance between markers and if everything looked good, toss the pot overboard. Splash!

Then he got to toss out the gaff for the next buoy.

He knew how to tell the sooks from the jimmies now. Jim said the girl crabs painted their fingernails because their pincers were red. It was wild the way the patterns on the underbellies looked like sex parts. Anybody could see that the guy crabs had this long T shape there that looked just like a dick.

Jim had shown him a couple of crabs mating, too—he called them doublers—and that was just too much. The guy crab just climbed aboard the girl, tucked her under him, and swam around like that for days.

Seth figured they had to like it.

Ethan had said the crabs were married, and when Seth had snickered, he lifted a brow. Seth had found himself intrigued enough to go to the school library and read up on crabs. And he thought he understood, sort of, what Ethan meant. The guy protected the girl by keeping her under him because she could only mate when she was in her last molt and her shell was soft, so she was vulnerable. Even after they'd done it, he kept carrying her like that until her shell was hard again. And she was only going to mate once, so it was like getting married.

He thought of how Cam and Miss Spinelli—Anna, he reminded himself, he got to call her Anna now—had gotten married. Lots of the women got all leaky, and the guys laughed and joked. Everybody made such a big deal out of it with flowers and music and tons of food. He didn't get it. It seemed to him getting married just meant you got to have sex whenever you wanted and nobody got snotty about it.

But it had been cool. He'd never been to anything like it. Even though Cam had dragged him out to the mall and made him try on suits, it was mostly okay.

Maybe sometimes he worried about how it was going to change things, just when he was getting used to the way things were. There was going to be a woman in the house now. He liked Anna okay. She'd played square with him even though she was a social worker. But she was still a female.

Like his mother.

Seth clamped down on that thought. If he thought about his mother, if he thought about the life he'd had with her—the men, the drugs, the dirty little rooms—it would spoil the day.

He hadn't had enough sunny days in his ten years to risk ruining one.

"You taking a nap there, Seth?"

Ethan's mild voice snapped Seth back to the moment. He blinked, saw the sun glinting off the water, the orange floats bobbing. "Just thinking," Seth muttered and quickly pulled in another buoy.

"Me, I don't do much thinking." Jim set the trap on the gunwale and began culling crabs. His leathered face creased in grins. "Gives you brain fever."

"Shit," Seth said, leaning over to study the catch. "That one's starting to molt."

Jim grunted, held up a crab with a shell cracking along the back. "This buster'll be somebody's soft-shell sandwich by tomorrow." He winked at Seth as he tossed the crab into the tank. "Maybe mine."

Foolish, who was still young enough to deserve the name, sniffed at the trap, inciting a quick and ugly crab riot. As claws snapped, the pup leaped back with a yelp.

"That there dog." Jim shook with laughter. "He don't have to worry about no brain fever."

Even when they'd taken the day's catch to the waterfront, emptied the tank, and dropped Jim off, the day wasn't over. Ethan stepped back from the controls. "We've got to go into the boatyard. You want to take her in?"

Though Seth's eyes were shielded by the dark sunglasses, Ethan imagined that their expression matched the boy's dropped jaw. It only amused him when Seth jerked a shoulder as if such things were an everyday occurrence.

"Sure. No problem." With sweaty palms, Seth took the helm.

Ethan stood by, hands casually tucked in his back pockets, eyes alert. There was plenty of water traffic. A pretty weekend afternoon drew the recreational sailors to the Bay. But they didn't have far to go, and the kid had to learn sometime. You couldn't live in St. Chris and not know how to pilot a workboat.

"A little to starboard," he told Seth. "See that skiff there? Sunday sailor, and he's going to cut right across your bow if you keep this heading."

Seth narrowed his eyes, studied the boat and the people on deck. He snorted. "That's because he's paying more attention to that girl in the bikini than to the wind."

"Well, she looks fine in the bikini."

"I don't see what's the big deal about breasts."

To his credit, Ethan didn't laugh out loud, but nodded soberly. "I guess part of that's because we don't have them."

"I sure don't want any."

"Give it a couple of years," Ethan murmured under the cover of the engine noise. And the thought of that made him wince. What the hell were they going to do when the kid hit puberty? Somebody was going to have to talk to him about . . . things. He knew Seth already had too much sexual knowledge, but it was all the dark and sticky sort. The same sort he himself had known about at much too early an age.

One of them was going to have to explain how things should be, could be—and before too much more time passed.

He hoped to hell it wasn't going to have to be him.

He caught sight of the boatyard, the old brick building, the spanking new dock he and his brothers had built. Pride rippled through him. Maybe it didn't look like much with its pitted bricks and patched roof, but they were making something out of it. The windows were dusty, but they were new and unbroken.

"Cut back on the throttle. Take her in slow." Absently Ethan put a hand over Seth's on the controls. He felt the boy stiffen, then relax. He still had a problem with being touched unexpectedly, Ethan noted. But it was passing. "That's the way, just a bit more to starboard."

When the boat bumped gently against the pilings, Ethan jumped onto the pier to secure lines. "Nice job." At his nod, Simon, all but quivering with anticipation, leaped overboard. Yipping frantically, Foolish clambered onto the gunwale, hesitated, then followed.

"Hand me up the cooler, Seth."

Grunting only a little, Seth hefted it. "Maybe I could pilot the boat sometime when we're crabbing."

"Maybe." Ethan waited for the boy to scramble safely onto the pier before heading to the rear cargo doors of the building.

They were already open wide and the soul-stirring sound of Ray Charles flowed out through them. Ethan set the cooler down just inside the doors and put his hands on his hips.

The hull was finished. Cam had put in dog's hours to get that much done before he left for his honeymoon. They'd planked it, rabbeting the edges so that they would lap, yet remain smooth at the seams.

The two of them had completed the steam-bent framing, using pencil lines as guides and "walking" each frame carefully into place with slow, steady pressure. The hull was solid. There would be no splits in a Quinn boat's planking.

The design was primarily Ethan's with a few adjustments here and there of Cam's. The hull was an arc-bottom, expensive to construct but with the virtues of stability and speed. Ethan knew his client.

He'd designed the shape of the bow with this in mind and had decided on a cruiser bow, attractive and, again, good for speed, buoyant. The stern was a counterdesign of moderate length, providing an overhang that would make the boat's length greater than her waterline length.

It was a sleek, appealing look. Ethan understood that his client was every bit as concerned with appearance as he was with basic seaworthiness.

He'd used Seth for grunt labor when it was time to coat the interior with the fifty-fifty mix of hot linseed oil and turpentine. It was sweaty work, guaranteed to cause a few burns despite caution and gloves. Still, the boy had held up fine.

From where he stood, Ethan could study the sheerline, the outline at the top edge of the hull. He'd gone with a flattened sheerline to ensure a roomier, drier craft with good headroom below. His client liked to take friends and family out for a sail.

The man had insisted on teak, though Ethan had told him pine or cedar would have done the job well enough for hull planking. The man had money to spend on his hobby, Ethan thought now—and money to spend on status. But he had to admit, the teak looked wonderful.

His brother Phillip was working on the decking. Stripped to the waist in defense against the heat and humidity, his dark bronze hair protected by a black cap without team name or emblem and worn bill to the back, he was screwing the deck planks into place. Every few seconds, the hard, high-pitched buzz of the electric driver competed with Ray Charles's creamy tenor.

"How's it going?" Ethan called over the din.

Phillip's head came up. His martyred-angel's face was damp with sweat, his golden-brown eyes annoyed. He'd just been reminding himself that he was an advertising executive, for God's sake, not a carpenter.

"It's hotter than a summer in hell in here and it's only June. We've got to get some fans in here. You got anything cold, or at least wet, in that cooler? I ran out of liquids an hour ago."

"Turn on the tap in the john and you get water," Ethan said mildly as he bent to take a cold soft drink from the cooler. "It's a new technology."

"Christ knows what's in that tap water." Phillip caught the can Ethan tossed him and grimaced at the label. "At least they tell you what chemicals they load in here."

"Sorry, we drank all the Evian. You know how Jim is about his designer water. Can't get enough of it."

"Screw you," Phillip said, but without heat. He glugged the chilly Pepsi, then raised a brow when Ethan came up to inspect his work.

"Nice job."

"Gee, thanks, boss. Can I have a raise?"

"Sure, double what you're getting now. Seth's the math whiz. What's zip times zip, Seth?"

"Double zip," Seth said with a quick grin. His fingers itched to try out the electric screwdriver. So far, nobody would let him touch it or any of the other power tools.

"Well, now I can afford that cruise to Tahiti."

"Why don't you grab a shower—unless you object to washing with tap water, too. I can take over here."

It was tempting. Phillip was grimy, sweaty, and miserably hot. He would cheerfully have killed three strangers for one cold glass of Pouilly-Fuisse. But he knew Ethan had been up since before dawn and had already put in what any normal person would consider a full day.

"I can handle a couple more hours."

"Fine." It was exactly the response Ethan had expected. Phillip tended to bitch, but he never let you down. "I think we can get this deck knocked out before we call it a day."

"Can I—"

"No," Ethan and Phillip said together, anticipating Seth's question.

"Why the hell not?" he demanded. "I'm not stupid. I won't shoot anybody with a stupid screw or anything."

"Because we like to play with it." Phillip smiled. "And we're bigger than you. Here." He reached into his back pocket, pulled out his wallet and found a five. "Go on down to Crawford's and get me some bottled water. If you don't whine about it, you can get some ice cream with the change."

Seth didn't whine, but he did mutter about being used like a slave as he called his dog and headed out.

"We ought to show him how to use the tools when we have more time," Ethan commented. "He's got good hands."

"Yeah, but I wanted him out. I didn't have the chance to tell you last night. The detective tracked Gloria DeLauter as far as Nags Head."

"She's heading south, then." He lifted his gaze to Phillip's. "He pin her yet?"

"No, she moves around a lot, and she's using cash. A lot of cash." His mouth tightened. "She's got plenty to toss around since Dad paid her a bundle for Seth."

"Doesn't look like she's interested in coming back here."

"I'd say she's got as much interest in that kid as a rabid alley cat has in a dead kitten." His own mother had been the same, Phillip remembered, when she'd been around at all. He had never met Gloria DeLauter, but he knew her. Despised her.

"If we don't find her," Phillip added, rolling the cold can over his forehead, "we're never going to get to the truth about Dad, or Seth."

Ethan nodded. He knew Phillip was on a mission here, and knew he was most likely right. But he wondered, much too often for comfort, what they would do when they had the truth.

⟨∾⟩

Ethan's plans after a fourteen-hour workday were to take an endless shower and drink a cold beer. He did both, simultaneously. They'd gotten take-out subs for dinner, and he had his on the back porch alone, in the soft quiet of early twilight. Inside, Seth and Phillip were arguing over which video to watch first. Arnold Schwarzenegger was doing battle with Kevin Costner.

Ethan had already placed his bets on Arnold.

They had an unspoken agreement that Phillip would take responsibility for Seth on Saturday nights. It gave Ethan a choice for the evening. He could go in and join them, as he sometimes did for these movie fests. He could go up and settle in with a book, as he often preferred to do. He could go out, as he rarely did.

Before his father had died so suddenly and life had changed for all of them, Ethan had lived in his own little house, with his own quiet routine. He still missed it, though he tried not to resent the young couple who were now renting it from him. They loved the coziness of it and told him so often. The small rooms with their tall windows, the little covered porch, the shady privacy of the trees that sheltered it, and the gentle lap of water against shore.

He loved it, too. With Cam married and Anna moving in, he might have been able to slip out again. But the rental money was needed now. And, more important, he'd given his word. He would live here until all the legal battles were waged and won and Seth was permanently theirs.

He rocked, listening to the night birds begin to call. And must have dozed because the dream came, and came clearly.

"You always were more of a loner than the others," Ray commented. He sat on the porch rail, turned slightly so he could look out to the water if he chose. His hair was shiny as a silver coin in the half light, blowing free in the steady breeze. "Always liked to go off by yourself to think your thoughts and work out your troubles."

"I knew I could always come to you or Mom. I just liked to have a handle on things first."

"How about now?" Ray shifted to face Ethan directly.

"I don't know. Maybe I haven't gotten a good handle on it yet. Seth's settling in. He's easier with us. The first few weeks, I kept expecting him to rabbit off. Losing you hurt him almost as much as it did us. Maybe just as much, because he'd just started to believe things were okay for him."

"It was bad, the way he had to live before I brought him here. Still, it wasn't as bad as what you'd faced, Ethan, and you got through."

"Almost didn't." Ethan took out one of his cigars, took his time lighting it. "Sometimes it still comes back on me. Pain and shame. And the sweaty fear of knowing what's going to happen." He shrugged it off. "Seth's a little younger than I was. I think he's already shed some of it. As long as he doesn't have to deal with his mother again."

"He'll have to deal with her eventually, but he won't be alone. That's the difference. You'll all stand by him. You always stood by each other."

Ray smiled, his big, wide face creasing everywhere at once. "What are you doing sitting out here alone on a Saturday night, Ethan? I swear, boy, you worry me."

"Had a long day."

"When I was your age, I put in long days and longer nights. You just turned thirty, for Christ's sake. Porch sitting on a warm Saturday night in June is for old men. Go on, take a drive. See where you end up." He winked. "I bet we both know where that's likely to be."

The sudden blare of automatic gunfire and screams made Ethan jerk in his chair. He blinked and stared hard at the porch rail. There was no one there. Of course there was no one there, he told himself with a quick shake. He'd nodded off for a minute, that was all, and the movie action in the living room had wakened him.

But when he glanced down, he saw the glowing cigar in his hand. Baffled, he simply stared at it. Had he actually taken it out of his pocket and lit it in his sleep? That was ridiculous, absurd. He must have done it before he'd drifted off, the habit so automatic that his mind just didn't register the moves.

Still, why had he fallen asleep when he didn't feel the least bit tired? In fact, he felt restless and edgy and too alert.

He rose, rubbing the back of his neck, stretching his legs on a pacing journey up and down the porch. He should just go in and settle down with the movie, some popcorn, and another beer. Even as he reached for the screen door, he swore.

He wasn't in the mood for Saturday night at the movies. He would just take a drive and see where he ended up.

⚉

Grace's feet were numb all the way to the ankles. The cursed high heels that were part of her cocktail waitress uniform were killers. It wasn't so bad on a weekday evening when you had time now and then to step out of them or even sit for a few minutes. But Shiney's Pub always hopped on Saturday night—and so did she.

She carted her tray of empty glasses and full ashtrays to the bar, efficiently unloading as she called out her order to the bartender. "Two house whites, two drafts, a gin and tonic, and a club soda with lime."

She had to pitch her voice over the crowd noise and what was loosely called music from the three-piece band Shiney had hired. The music was always lousy at the pub, because Shiney wouldn't shell out the money for decent musicians.

But no one seemed to care.

The stingy dance floor was bumper to bumper with dancers, and the band took this as a sign to boost the volume.

Grace's head was ringing like steel bells, and her back was beginning to throb in time with the bass.

Her order complete, she carried the tray through the narrow spaces between tables and hoped that the group of young tourists in trendy clothes would be decent tippers.

She served them with a smile, nodded at the signal to run a tab, and followed the hail to the next table.

Her break was still ten minutes away. It might as well have been ten years.

"Hey, there, Gracie."

"How's it going, Curtis, Bobbie." She'd gone to school with them in the dim, distant past. Now they worked for her father, packing seafood. "Usual?"

"Yeah, a couple of drafts." Curtis gave Grace his usual—a quick pat on her bow-clad butt. She'd learned not to worry about it. From him it was a harmless enough gesture, even a show of affectionate support. Some of the outlanders who dropped in had hands a great deal less harmless. "How's that pretty girl of yours?"

Grace smiled, understanding that this was one of the reasons she tolerated his pats. He always asked about Aubrey. "Getting prettier every day." She saw another hand pop up from a nearby table. "I'll get you those beers in just a minute."

She was carting a tray full of mugs, bowls of beer nuts, and glasses when Ethan walked in. She nearly bobbled it. He never came into the pub on Saturday night. Sometimes he dropped in for a quiet beer midweek, but never when the place was crowded and noisy.

He should have looked the same as every second man in the place. His jeans were faded but clean, a plain white T-shirt tucked into them, his work boots ancient and scuffed. But he didn't look the same as other men—and never had to Grace.

Maybe it was the lean and rangy body that moved as easily as a dancer through the narrow spaces. Innate grace, she mused, the kind that can't be taught, and still so blatantly male. He always looked as though he was walking the deck of a ship.

It could have been his face, so bony and rugged and somewhere just at the edges of handsome. Or the eyes, always so clear and thoughtful, so serious that it seemed to take them a few seconds to catch up whenever his mouth curved.

She served her drinks, pocketed money, took more orders. And watched out of the corner of her eye as he squeezed into a standing spot at the bar directly beside the order station.

She forgot all about her much-desired break.

"Three drafts, bottle of Mich, Stoli rocks." Absently, she brushed at her bangs and smiled. "Hi, Ethan."

"Busy tonight."

"Summer Saturday. Do you want a table?"

"No, this is fine."

The bartender was busy with another order, which gave her some breathing room. "Steve's got his hands full, but he'll work his way down here."

"I'm not in any hurry." As a rule, he tried not to think about how she looked in the butt-skimming skirt, those endless legs in black fishnet, the narrow feet in skinny heels. But tonight he was in a mood, and so he let himself think.

Just at that moment, he could have explained to Seth just what the big deal was about breasts. Grace's were small and high, and a soft portion of the curve showed over the low-cut bodice of her blouse.

Suddenly, he desperately wanted a beer.

"You get a chance to sit down at all?"

She didn't answer for a moment. Her mind had gone glass-blank at the way those quiet, thoughtful eyes had skimmed over her. "I, ah . . . yes, it's nearly time for my break." Her hands felt clumsy as she gathered up her order. "I like to go outside, get away from the noise." Struggling to act normally, she rolled her eyes toward the band and was rewarded with Ethan's slow grin.

"Do they ever get worse than this?"

"Oh, yeah, these guys are a real step up." She was nearly relaxed again as she lifted the tray and headed off to serve.

He watched her, while he sipped the beer Steve had pulled for him. Watched the way her legs moved, the way the foolish and incredibly sexy bow swayed with her hips. And the way she bent her knees, balancing the tray, lifting drinks from it onto a table.

He watched, eyes narrowing, as Curtis once again gave her a friendly pat.

His eyes narrowed further when a stranger in a faded Jim Morrison T-shirt grabbed her hand, tugging her closer. He saw Grace flash a smile, give a shake of her head. Ethan was already pushing away from the bar, not entirely sure what he intended to do, when the man released her.

When Grace came back to set down her tray, it was Ethan who grabbed her hand. "Take your break."

"What? I—" To her shock he was pulling her steadily through the room. "Ethan, I really need to—"

"Take your break," he said again and shoved the door open.

The air outside was clean and fresh, the night warm and breezy. The minute the door closed behind them, the noise shut down to a muffled echoing roar and the stink of smoke, sweat, and beer became a memory.

"I don't think you should be working here."

She gaped at him. The statement itself was odd enough, but to hear him deliver it in a tone that was obviously annoyed was baffling. "Excuse me?"

"You heard me, Grace." He shoved his hands in his pockets because he didn't know what to do with them. Left free, they might have grabbed her again. "It's not right."

"It's not right?" she repeated, at sea.

"You're a mother, for God's sake. What are you doing serving drinks, wearing that outfit, getting hit on? That guy in there practically had his face down your blouse."

"Oh, he did not." Torn between amusement and exasperation, she shook her head. "For heaven's sake, Ethan, he was just being typical. And harmless."

"Curtis had his hand on your ass."

Amusement was veering toward annoyance. "I know where his hand was, and if it worried me, I'd have knocked it off."

Ethan took a breath. He'd started this, wisely or not, and he was going to finish it. "You shouldn't be working half naked in some bar or knocking anybody's hand off your ass. You should be home with Aubrey."

Her eyes went from mildly irritated to blazing fury. "Oh, is that right, is that your considered opinion? Well, thank you so much for sharing it with me. And for your information, if I wasn't working—and I'm damn well not half naked—I wouldn't have a home."

"You've got a job," he said stubbornly. "Cleaning houses."

"That's right. I clean houses, I serve drinks, and now and then I pick crabs. That's how amazingly skilled and versatile I am. I also pay rent, insurance, medical bills, utilities, and a babysitter. I buy food, I buy clothes, gas. I take care of myself and my daughter. I don't need you coming around here telling me it's not right."

"I'm just saying—"

"I hear what you're saying." Her heels were throbbing, and every ache in her overtaxed body was making itself known. Worse, much worse, was the hard prick of embarrassment that he would look down on her for what she did to survive. "I serve cocktails and let men look at my legs. Maybe they'll tip better if they like them. And if they tip better I can buy my little girl something that makes her smile. So they can look all they damn well please. And I wish to God I had the kind of body that filled out this stupid outfit, because then I'd earn more."

He had to pause before speaking, to gather his thoughts. Her face was flushed with anger, but her eyes were so tired it broke his heart. "You're selling yourself short, Grace," he said quietly.

"I know exactly how much I'm worth, Ethan." Her chin angled. "Right down to the last penny. Now, my break's over."

She spun on her miserably throbbing heels and stalked back into the noise and the smoke-clogged air.

THREE

"Need bunny, too."

"Okay, baby, we'll get your bunny." It was, Grace thought, always an expedition. They were only going as far as the sandbox in the backyard, but Aubrey never failed to demand that all her stuffed pals accompany her.

Grace had solved this logistical problem with an enormous shopping bag. Inside it were a bear, two dogs, a fish, and a very tattered cat. The bunny joined them. Though Grace's eyes were gritty from lack of sleep, she grinned broadly as Aubrey tried to heft the bag herself.

"I'll carry them, honey."

"No, me."

It was, Grace thought, Aubrey's favorite phrase. Her baby liked to do things herself, even when it would be simpler to let someone else do the job. Wonder where she gets that from, Grace mused and laughed at both of them.

"Okay, let's get the crew outside." She opened the screen door—it squeaked badly, reminding her that she needed to oil the hinges—and waited while Aubrey dragged the bag over the threshold and onto the tiny back porch.

Grace had livened up the porch by painting it a soft blue and adding clay pots filled with pink and white geraniums. In her mind, the little rental house was temporary, but she didn't want it to *feel* temporary. She wanted it to feel like home. At least until she saved enough money for a down payment on a place of their own.

Inside, the room sizes were on the stingy side, but she'd solved that—and helped her bank balance—by keeping furniture to a minimum. Most of what she had were yard sale bargains, but she'd painted, refinished, re-covered, and turned each piece into her own.

It was vital to Grace to have her own.

The house had ancient plumbing, a roof that leaked water after a hard rain, and windows that leaked air. But it had two bedrooms, which had been essential. She'd wanted her daughter to have a room of her own, a bright, cheerful room. She had seen to that, papering the walls herself, painting the trim, adding fussy curtains.

It was already breaking her heart knowing that it was about time to dismantle Aubrey's crib and replace it with a youth bed.

"Be careful on the steps," Grace warned, and Aubrey started down, both tiny tennis shoes planting themselves firmly on each of the steps on the descent. The minute she hit bottom, she began to run, dragging her bag behind her and squealing in anticipation.

She loved the sandbox. It made Grace proud to watch Aubrey make her traditional beeline for it. Grace had built it herself, using scrap lumber that she meticulously sanded smooth and painted a bright Crayola red. In it were the pails and shovels and big plastic cars, but she knew Aubrey would touch none of them until she'd set out her pets.

One day, Grace promised herself, Aubrey would have a real puppy, and a playroom so that she could have friends visit and spend long, rainy afternoons.

Grace crouched down as Aubrey placed her toys carefully in the white sand. "You sit right in here and play while I mow the lawn. Promise?"

"Okay." Aubrey beamed up at her, dimples winking. "You play."

"In a little while." She stroked Aubrey's curls. She could never get enough of touching this miracle that had come from her. Before rising, she looked around, mother's eyes scanning for any danger.

The yard was fenced, and she had installed a childproof lock on the gate herself. Aubrey tended to be curious. A flowering vine rambled along the fence that bordered her house and the Cutters' and would have it buried in bloom by summer's end.

No one was stirring next door, she noted. Too early on a Sunday morning for her neighbors to be doing more than lazing about and thinking of breakfast. Julie Cutter, the eldest daughter of the house, was her much-treasured babysitter.

She noted that Julie's mother, Irene, had spent some time in her garden the day before. Not a single weed dared show its head in Irene Cutter's flowers or in her vegetable patch.

With some embarrassment, Grace glanced toward the rear of her yard, where she and Aubrey had planted some tomatoes and beans and carrots. Plenty of weeds there, she thought with a sigh. She'd have to deal with that after cutting the lawn. God only knew why she'd thought she would have time to tend a garden. But it had been such fun to dig the dirt and plant the seeds with her little girl.

Just as it would be such fun to step into the sandbox and build castles and make up games. No, you don't, Grace ordered herself and rose. The lawn was nearly ankle-high. It might have been rented grass, but it was hers now, and her responsibility. No one was going to say that Grace Monroe couldn't tend her own.

She kept the ancient secondhand lawn mower under an equally ancient drop cloth. As usual, she checked the gas level first, casting another glance over her shoulder to be certain Aubrey was still tucked in the sandbox. Gripping the starter cord with both hands, she yanked. And got a wheezing cough in response.

"Come on, don't mess with me this morning." She'd lost count of the times she'd fiddled and repaired and banged on the old machine. Rolling her protesting shoulders, she yanked again, then a third time, before letting the cord snap back and pressing her fingers to her eyes. "Wouldn't you just know it."

"Giving you trouble?"

Her head jerked around. After their argument the night before, Ethan was the last person Grace expected to see standing in her backyard. It didn't please her, particularly since she'd told herself she could and would stay mad at him. Worse, she knew how she looked—old gray shorts and a T-shirt that had seen too many washings, not a stitch of makeup and her hair uncombed.

Damn it, she'd dressed for yard work, not for company.

"I can handle it." She yanked again, her foot, clad in a sneaker with a hole in the toe, planted on the side of the machine. It nearly caught, very nearly.

"Let it rest a minute. You're just going to flood it."

This time the cord snapped back with a dangerous hiss. "I know how to start my own lawn mower."

"I imagine you do, when you're not mad." He walked over as he spoke, all lean and easy male in faded jeans and a work shirt rolled up to his elbows.

He had come around back when she didn't answer her door. And he knew he'd stood watching her a little longer than was strictly polite. She had such a pretty way of moving.

He had decided sometime during the restless night that he had better find a way to make amends. And he'd spent a good part of his morning trying to figure how to do so. Then he'd seen her, all those long, slim limbs the sun was turning pale gold, the sunny hair, the narrow hands. And he'd just wanted to watch for a bit.

"I'm not mad," she said in an impatient hiss that proved her statement a lie. He only looked into her eyes.

"Listen, Grace—"

"Eeee-than!" With a shriek of pure pleasure, Aubrey scrambled out of the sandbox and ran to him—full-out, arms extended, face lit up with joy.

He caught her, swung her up and around. "Hey, there, Aubrey."

"Come play."

"Well, I'm—"

"Kiss."

She puckered her little lips with such energy that he had to laugh and give them a friendly peck.

"Okay!" She wiggled down and ran back to her sandbox.

"Look, Grace, I'm sorry if I was out of line last night."

The fact that her heart had melted when he held her daughter only made her more determined to stand firm. "If?"

He shifted his feet, clearly uncomfortable. "I just meant that—"

His explanation was interrupted as Aubrey raced back with her beloved stuffed dogs. "Kiss," she stated, very firmly, and held them up to Ethan. He obliged, waiting until she raced away again.

"What I meant was—"

"I think you said what you meant, Ethan."

She was going to be stubborn, he thought with an inward sigh. Well, she always had been. "I didn't say it very well. I get tangled up with words most of the time. I hate to see you working so hard." He paused, patient, when Aubrey came back, demanding a kiss for her bear. "I worry about you some, that's all."

Grace angled her head. "Why?"

"Why?" The question threw him. He bent to kiss the stuffed bunny that Aubrey batted against his leg. "Well, I . . . because."

"Because I'm a woman?" she suggested. "Because I'm a single parent? Because my father considers that I smeared the family name by not only having to get married but getting myself divorced?"

"No." He took a step closer to her, absently kissing the cat that Aubrey held up to him. "Because I've known you more than half my life, and that makes you part of it. And because maybe you're too stubborn or too proud to see when somebody just wants to see things go a little easier for you."

She started to tell him she appreciated that, felt herself begin to soften. Then he ruined it.

"And because I didn't like seeing men paw at you."

"Paw at me?" Her back went up; her chin went out. "Men were not pawing at me, Ethan. And if they do, I know what to do about it."

"Don't get all riled up again." He scratched his chin, struggled not to sigh. He didn't see the point in arguing with a woman—you could never win. "I came over here to tell you I was sorry, and so maybe I could—"

"Kiss!" Aubrey demanded and began to climb up his leg.

Instinctively, Ethan pulled her up into his arms and kissed her cheek. "I was going to say—"

"No, kiss Mama." Bouncing in his arms, Aubrey pushed at his lips to make them pucker. "Kiss Mama."

"Aubrey!" Mortified, Grace reached for her daughter, only to have Aubrey cling to Ethan's shirt like a small golden burr. "Leave Ethan be now."

Changing tactics, Aubrey laid her head on Ethan's shoulder and smiled sweetly—one arm clinging like a vine around his neck as Grace tugged at her. "Kiss Mama," she crooned and batted her eyes at Ethan.

If Grace had laughed instead of looking so embarrassed—and just a little nervous—Ethan thought he could have brushed his lips over her brow and settled the matter. But her cheeks had gone pink—it was so endearing. She wouldn't meet his eyes, and her breath was unsteady.

He watched her bite her bottom lip and decided he might as well settle the matter another way entirely.

He laid a hand on Grace's shoulder with Aubrey caught between them. "This'll be easier," he murmured and touched his lips lightly to hers.

It wasn't easier. It rocked her heart. It could barely be considered a kiss, was over almost before it began. It was nothing more than a quiet brush of lips, an instant of taste and texture. And a whiff of promise that made her long, desperately, impossibly.

In all the years he'd known her, he had never touched his mouth to hers. Now, with just this fleeting sampling, he wondered why he'd waited so long. And worried that the wondering would change everything.

Aubrey clapped her hands in glee, but he barely heard it. Grace's eyes were on his now, that misty, swimming green, and their faces were close. Close enough that he only had to ease forward a fraction if he wanted to taste again. To linger this time, he thought, as her lips parted on a trembling breath.

"No, me!" Aubrey planted her small, soft mouth on her mother's cheek, then Ethan's. "Come play."

Grace jerked back like a puppet whose strings had been rudely yanked. The silky pink cloud that had begun to fog her brain evaporated. "Soon, honey." Moving quickly now, she plucked Aubrey out of Ethan's arms and set her on her feet. "Go on and build me a castle for us to live in." She gave Aubrey a gentle pat on the rump and sent her off at a run.

Then she cleared her throat. "You're awfully good to her, Ethan. I appreciate it."

He decided the best place for his hands, under the circumstances, was his pockets. He wasn't sure what to do about the itchy feeling in them. "She's a sweetheart." Deliberately, he turned to watch Aubrey in her red sandbox.

"And a handful." She needed to get her feet back under her, Grace told herself, and to do what needed to be done next. "Why don't we just forget last night, Ethan? I'm sure you meant it all for the best. Reality's just not always what we'd choose or what we'd like it to be."

He turned back slowly, and those quiet eyes of his focused on her face. "What do you want it to be, Grace?"

"What I want is for Aubrey to have a home, and a family. I think I'm pretty close to that."

He shook his head. "No, what do you want for Grace?"

"Besides her?" She looked over at her daughter and smiled. "I don't even remember anymore. Right now I want my lawn mowed and my vegetables weeded. I appreciate you coming by like this." She turned away and prepared to give the starter cord another yank. "I'll be by the house tomorrow."

She went very still when his hand closed over hers.

"I'll cut the grass."

"I can do it."

She couldn't even start the damn lawn mower, he thought, but was wise enough not to mention it. "I didn't say you couldn't. I said I'd do it."

She couldn't turn around, couldn't risk what it would do to her system to be that close again, face-to-face. "You have chores of your own."

"Grace, are we going to stand here all day arguing over who's going to cut this grass? I could have it done twice over by the time we finish, and you could be saving your string beans from being choked out by those weeds."

"I was going to get to them." Her voice was thin. They were both bent over, all but spooned together. The flash of sheer animal lust that streaked through the familiar yearning for him staggered her.

"Get to them now." He murmured it, willing her to move. If she didn't, and very quickly, he might not be able to hold himself back from putting his hands on her. And putting them on her in places they had no business being.

"All right." She shifted away, moving sideways while her heart knocked at her ribs in short rabbit punches. "I appreciate it. Thanks." She bit her lip hard because she was going to babble. Determined to be normal, she turned and smiled a little. "It's probably the carburetor again. I've got some tools."

Saying nothing, Ethan grabbed the cord with one hand and yanked it hard, twice. The engine caught with a dyspeptic roar. "It ought to do," he said mildly when he saw her mouth thin in frustration.

"Yeah, it ought to." Struggling not to be annoyed, she strode quickly to her vegetable patch.

And bent over, Ethan thought as he began to cut the first swath. Bent over in those thin cotton shorts in a way that forced him to take several long, careful breaths.

She didn't have a clue, he decided, what it had done to his usually well-disciplined hormones to have her trim little butt snugged back against him. What it did to the usually moderate temperature of his blood to have all that long, bare leg brushing against his.

She might be a mother—a fact that he reminded himself of often to keep dark and dangerous thoughts at bay—but as far as he was concerned, she was nearly as innocent and unaware as she'd been at fourteen.

When he'd first begun to have those dark and dangerous thoughts about her.

He'd stopped himself from acting on them. For God's sake, she'd just been a kid. And a man with his past had no right to touch anyone so unspoiled. Instead, he'd been her friend and had found contentment in that. He'd thought he could continue to be her friend, and only her friend. But just lately those thoughts had been striking him more often and with more force. They were becoming very tricky to control.

They both had enough complications in their lives, he reminded himself. He was just going to mow her lawn, maybe help her pull some weeds. If there was time he'd offer to take them into town for some ice cream cones. Aubrey was partial to strawberry.

Then he had to go down to the boatyard and get to work. And since it was his turn to cook, he had to figure out that little nuisance.

But mother or not, he thought, as Grace leaned over to tug out a stubborn dandelion, she had a pair of amazing legs.

⬠

Grace knew she shouldn't have let herself be persuaded to go into town, even for a quick ice cream cone. It meant adjusting her day's schedule, changing into something less disreputable than her gardening clothes, and spending more time in Ethan's company when she was feeling a bit too aware of her needs.

But Aubrey loved these small trips and treats, so it was impossible to say no.

It was only a mile into St. Chris, but they went from quiet neighborhood to busy waterfront. The gift and souvenir shops would stay open seven days a week now to take advantage of the summer tourist season. Couples and families strolled by with shopping bags filled with memories to take home.

The sky was brilliantly blue, and the Bay reflected it, inviting boats to cruise along its surface. A couple of Sunday sailors had tangled the lines of their little Sunfish, letting the sails flop. But they appeared to be having the time of their lives despite that small mishap.

Grace could smell fish frying, candy melting, the coconut sweetness of sunblock, and always, always, the moist fragrance of the water.

She'd grown up on this waterfront, watching boats, sailing them. She ran free along the docks, in and out of the shops. She learned to pick crabs at her mother's knee, gaining the speed and skill needed to separate out the meat, that precious commodity that would be packaged and shipped all over the world.

Work hadn't been a stranger, but she'd always been free. Her family had lived well, if not luxuriously. Her father didn't believe in spoiling his women with too much pampering. Still, he'd been kind and loving even though set in his ways. And he'd never made her feel that he was disappointed that he had only a daughter instead of sons to carry his name.

In the end, she'd disappointed him anyway.

Grace swung Aubrey up on her hip and nuzzled her.

"Busy today," she commented.

"Seems to get more crowded every summer." But Ethan shrugged it off. They needed the summer crowds to survive the winters. "I heard Bingham's going to expand the restaurant, fancy it up, too, to bring more people in year-round."

"Well, he's got that chef from up north now, and got himself reviewed in the *Washington Post* magazine." She jiggled Aubrey on her hip. "The Egret Rest is the only linen-tablecloth restaurant around here. Spiffing it up should be good for the town. We always went there for dinner on special occasions."

She set Aubrey down, trying not to remember that she hadn't seen the inside of the restaurant in over three years. She held Aubrey's hand and let her daughter tug her relentlessly toward Crawford's.

This was another standard of St. Chris. Crawford's was for ice cream and cold drinks and take-out submarine sandwiches. Since it was noon, the shop was doing a brisk business. Grace ordered herself not to spoil things by mentioning that they should be eating sandwiches instead of ice cream.

"Hey, there, Grace, Ethan. Hello, pretty Aubrey." Liz Crawford beamed at them even as she skillfully built a cold-cut sub. She'd gone to school with Ethan and had dated him for a short, careless time that they both remembered with fondness.

Now she was the sturdy, freckle-faced mother of two, married to Junior Crawford, as he was known to distinguish him from his father, Senior.

Junior, skinny as a scarecrow, whistled between his teeth as he rang up sales, and sent them a quick salute.

"Busy day," Ethan said, dodging an elbow from a customer at the counter.

"Tell me." Liz rolled her eyes, deftly wrapped the sub in white paper and handed it, along with three others, over the counter. "Y'all want a sub?"

"Ice cream," Aubrey said definitely. "Berry."

"Well, you go on down and tell Mother Crawford what you have in mind. Oh, Ethan, Seth was in here shortly ago with Danny and Will. I swear, those kids grow like weeds in high summer. Loaded up on subs and soda pop. Said they were working down to your boatyard."

He felt a faint flicker of guilt, knowing that Phillip was not only working but riding herd on three young boys. "I'll be heading down there myself soon."

"Ethan, if you don't have time for this . . ." Grace began.

"I've got time to eat an ice cream cone with a pretty girl." So saying, he lifted Aubrey up and let her press her nose to the glass-fronted counter that held the buckets of hand-dipped choices.

Liz took the next order, and spared a wiggling-eyebrow glance toward her husband that spoke volumes. Ethan Quinn and Grace Monroe, it stated clearly. Well, well. What do you think of that?

They took their cones outside, where the breeze was warm off the water, and wandered away from the crowds to find one of the small iron benches the city fathers had campaigned for. Armed with a fistful of napkins, Grace set Aubrey on her lap.

"I remember when you'd come here and know the name of every face you'd see," Grace murmured. "Mother Crawford would be behind the counter, reading a paperback novel." She felt a wet drip from Aubrey's ice cream plop on her leg below the hem of her shorts and wiped it up. "Eat around the edges, honey, before it melts away."

"You'd always get strawberry ice cream, too."

"Hmm?"

"As I recall," Ethan said, surprised that the image was so clear in his mind, "you had a preference for strawberry. And grape Nehi."

"I guess I did." Grace's sunglasses slipped down her nose as she bent to mop up more drips. "Everything was simple if you had yourself a strawberry cone and a grape Nehi."

"Some things stay simple." Because her hands were full, Ethan nudged Grace's glasses back up—and thought he caught a flicker of something in her eyes behind the shaded lenses. "Some don't."

He looked out to the water as he applied himself to his own cone. A better idea, he decided, than watching Grace take those long, slow licks from hers. "We used to come down here on Sundays now and then," he remembered. "All of us piling into the car and riding into town for ice cream or a sub or just to see what was up. Mom and Dad liked to sit under one of the umbrella tables at the diner and drink lemonade."

"I still miss them," she said quietly. "I know you do. That winter I caught pneumonia—I remember my mother and yours. It seemed every time I woke up, one or the other of them was right there. Dr. Quinn was the kindest woman I ever knew. My mama—"

She broke off, shook her head.

"What?"

"I don't want to make you sad."

"You won't. Finish it."

"My mother goes to the cemetery every year in the spring and puts flowers on your mother's grave. I go with her. I didn't realize until the first time we went how much my mother loved her."

"I wondered who put them there. It's nice knowing. What's being said . . . what some people are saying about my father would have got her Irish up. She'd have scalded more than a few tongues by now."

"That's not your way, Ethan. You have to tend to that business your own way."

"They would both want us to do what's best for Seth. That would come first."

"You are doing what's best for him. Every time I see him he looks lighter. There was such a heaviness over him when he first came here. Professor Quinn was working his way through that, but he had such troubles of his own. You know how troubled he was, Ethan."

"Yeah." And the guilt weighed like a stone, dead center in his heart. "I know."

"Now I have made you sad." She shifted toward him so that their knees bumped. "Whatever troubled him, it was never you. You were one strong, steady light in his life. Anyone could see that."

"If I'd asked more questions . . ." he began.

"It's not your way," she said again and, forgetting her hand was sticky, touched it to his cheek. "You knew he would talk to you when he was ready, when he could."

"Then it was too late."

"No, it never is." Her fingers skimmed lightly over his cheek. "There's always a chance. I don't think I could get from one day to the next if I didn't believe there's always a chance. Don't worry," she said softly.

He felt something move inside him as he reached up to cover her hand with his. Something shifting and opening. Then Aubrey let out a wild squeal of joy.

"Grandpa!"

Grace's hand jerked, then dropped like a stone. All the warmth that had flowed out of her chilled. Her shoulders went straight and stiff as she turned forward again and watched her father walk toward them.

"There's my dollbaby. Come see Grandpa."

Grace let her daughter go, watched her race and be caught. Her father didn't wince or shy away from the sticky hands or smeared lips. He laughed and hugged and smacked his lips when kissed lavishly.

"Mmm, strawberry. Gimme more." He made munching noises on Aubrey's neck until she screamed with delight. Then he hitched her easily on his hip and crossed the slight distance to his daughter. And no longer smiled. "Grace, Ethan. Taking a Sunday stroll?"

Grace's throat was dry, and her eyes burned. "Ethan offered to buy us some ice cream."

"Well, that's nice."

"You're wearing some of it now," Ethan commented, hoping to ease some of the rippling tension that moved in the air.

Pete glanced down to his shirt, where Aubrey had transferred some of her favored strawberries. "Clothes wash. Don't often see you around the waterfront on a Sunday, Ethan, since you started building that boat."

"Taking an hour before I get started on it today. Hull's finished, deck's nearly."

"Good, that's good." He nodded, meaning it, then shifted his gaze to Grace. "Your mother's in the diner. She'll want to see her granddaughter."

"All right. I—"

"I'll take her over," he interrupted. "You can go on home when you're ready to, and your mother'll bring her on by your place in an hour or two."

She'd have preferred he slap her than speak to her in that polite and distant tone. But she nodded, as Aubrey was already babbling about Grandma.

"Bye! Bye, Mama. Bye, Ethan," Aubrey called over Pete's shoulder and blew noisy kisses.

"I'm sorry, Grace." Knowing it was inadequate, Ethan took her hand and found it stiff and cold.

"It doesn't matter. It can't matter. And he loves Aubrey. Just dotes on her. That's what counts."

"It's not fair to you. Your father's a good man, Grace, but he hasn't been fair to you."

"I let him down." She rose, quickly wiping her hands on the napkins she'd balled up. "And that's that."

"It's nothing more than his pride butting up against yours."

"Maybe. But my pride's important to me." She tossed the napkins into a trash container and told herself that was the end of it. "I've got to get back home, Ethan. There's a million things I should be doing, and if I've got a couple hours free, I'd better do them."

He didn't push, but was surprised how strongly he wanted to. He hated being nudged and nagged to talk about private matters himself. "I'll drive you home."

"No, I'd like to walk. Really like to walk. Thanks for the help." She managed a smile that looked almost natural. "And the ice cream. I'll be by the house tomorrow. Make sure you tell Seth his laundry goes in the hamper, not on the floor."

She walked away, her long legs eating up the ground. She made certain she was well away before she allowed her steps to slow. Before she rubbed a hand over the heart that ached no matter how firmly she ordered it not to.

There were only two men in her life she had ever really loved. It seemed neither of them could want her as she needed them to want her.

FOUR

Ethan didn't mind music when he worked. The fact was, his taste in music was both broad and eclectic—another gift of the Quinns. The house had often been filled with it. His mother had played a fine piano with as much enthusiasm for the works of Chopin as for those of Scott Joplin. His father's musical talent had been the violin, and it was that instrument Ethan had gravitated to. He enjoyed the varying moods of it, and its portability.

Still, he found music a waste of sound whenever he was concentrating on a job, as he usually didn't hear it after ten minutes anyway. Silence suited him best during those times, but Seth liked the radio in the boatyard up, and up loud. So to keep peace, Ethan simply tuned out the head-punching rock and roll.

The hull of the boat had been caulked and filled, a labor-intensive and time-consuming task. Seth had been a lot of help there, Ethan admitted, giving him an extra pair of hands and feet when he needed them. Though Christ knew the boy could complain about the job as much as Phillip did.

Ethan tuned that out as well—to stay sane.

He hoped to finish leveling off the decking before Phillip arrived for the weekend, planing first on one diagonal, then across the next at a right angle.

With any luck, he could get some solid work done that week and the next on the cabin and cockpit.

Seth bitched about being on sanding detail, but he did a decent job of it. Ethan only had to tell him to go back and hit portions of the hull planking again a couple of times. He didn't mind the boy's questions, either. Though he had a million of them once he started.

"What's that piece over there for?"

"The bulkhead for the cockpit."

"Why'd you cut it out already?"

"Because we want to get rid of all the dust before we varnish and seal."

"What's all this other shit?"

Ethan paused in his own work, looking down from his position to where Seth frowned at a stack of precut lumber. "You got the sides and cabin ends, the toerail and dropboards."

"It seems like an awful lot of pieces for one stupid boat."

"There's going to be a lot more."

"How come this guy doesn't just buy a boat that's already built?"

"Good thing for us he isn't." The client's deep pockets, Ethan mused, were giving Boats by Quinn its foundation. "Because he liked the other boat I built for him—and so he can tell all his big-shot friends he had a boat designed and hand-built for him."

Seth changed his sandpaper and applied himself again. He didn't mind the work, really. And he liked the smells of wood and varnish and that linseed oil, too. But he just didn't get it. "It's taking forever to put it together."

"Been at it less than three months. Lots of people spend a year—even longer—to build a wooden boat."

Seth's jaw dropped. "A year! Jesus, Ethan."

The loud, and very normal whine, made Ethan's mouth twitch. "Relax, this isn't going to take us that long. Once Cam gets back and can put in full days on it, we'll move along. And once school's out, you can pick up a lot of the grunt work."

"School is out."

"Hmm?"

"Today was it." Now Seth grinned, wide and bright. "Freedom. It's a done deal."

"Today?" Pausing in his work, Ethan frowned. "I thought you had a couple days yet."

"Nope."

He'd lost track of things somewhere, Ethan supposed. And it wasn't Seth's style—not yet, anyway—to volunteer information. "Did you get a report card?"

"Yeah—I passed."

"Let's see how." Ethan set his tools down, brushed his hands on his jeans. "Where is it?"

Seth shrugged his shoulders and kept sanding. "It's in my backpack over there. No big deal."

"Let's see it," Ethan repeated.

Seth did what Ethan considered his usual dance. Rolling his eyes, shrugging his shoulders, adding a long-suffering sigh. Oddly enough, he didn't end with an oath, as he was prone to. He walked over to where he'd dumped his backpack and riffled through it.

Ethan leaned down over the port side to take the paper Seth held up. Noting the mutinous expression on Seth's face, he expected the news would be grim. His stomach did a quick clench and roll. The required lecture, Ethan thought with an inner sigh, was going to be damned uncomfortable for both of them.

Ethan studied the thin, computer-generated sheet, pushing back his cap to scratch his head. "*All* A's?"

Seth jerked a shoulder again, stuffed his hands in his pockets. "Yeah, so?"

"I've never seen a report card with all A's before. Even Phillip used to have some B's, and maybe a C tossed in."

Embarrassment, and the fear of being called Egghead or something equally hideous rose swiftly. "It's no big deal." He held up a hand for the report card, but Ethan shook his head.

"The hell it's not." But he saw Seth's scowl and thought he understood it. It was always hard to be different from the pack. "You got a good brain and you ought to be proud of it."

"It's just there. It's not like knowing how to pilot a boat or anything."

"You got a good brain and you use it, you'll figure out how to do most anything." Ethan folded the paper carefully and tucked it in his pocket. Damn if he wasn't going to show it off some. "Seems to me we ought to go get a pizza or something."

Puzzled, Seth narrowed his eyes. "You packed those lame sandwiches for dinner."

"Not good enough now. The first time a Quinn gets straight A's ought to rate at least a pizza." He saw Seth's mouth open and shut, watched the staggered delight leap into his eyes before he lowered them.

"Sure, that'd be cool."

"Can you hold off another hour?"

"No problem."

Seth grabbed his sandpaper and began to work furiously. And blindly. His eyes were dazzled, his heart in his throat. It happened whenever one of them referred to him as a Quinn. He knew his name was DeLauter still. He had to put it at the top of every stupid paper he did for school, didn't he? But hearing Ethan call him a Quinn made that little beam of hope that Ray had first ignited in him months before shine just a little brighter.

He was going to stay. He was going to be one of them. He was never going back into hell again.

It made it worth being called down to Moorefield's office that day. The vice principal had reeled him in an hour before freedom. It had made his stomach jitter, as it always did. But she'd sat him down and told him she was proud of his progress.

Man, how mortifying.

Okay, so maybe he hadn't punched anybody in the face in the last couple months. And he'd been handing in his stupid homework assignments every dumb day because somebody was always nagging him about them. Phillip was the worst nag in that particular area. It was like the guy was a home-work cop or something, Seth thought now. And yeah, he'd been raising his hand in class now and then, just for the hell of it.

But to have Moorefield single him out that way had been so . . . *bleech*, he decided. He'd almost wished she'd hauled his butt in to give him another dose of In-School Suspension.

But if a bunch of dopey A's made a guy like Ethan happy, it was okay.

Ethan was absolutely cool in Seth's estimation. He worked outside all day, and his hands had scars and really thick calluses. Seth figured you could practically pound nails into Ethan's hands without him even feeling it, they were so hard and tough. He owned two boats—that he'd built himself—and he knew everything about the Bay and sailing. And didn't make a big deal about it.

A couple of months back Seth had watched *High Noon* on TV, even though it had been in lame black and white and there hadn't even been any blood or explosions. He'd thought then that Ethan was just like that Gary Cooper guy. He didn't say a lot, so you mostly listened when he did. And he just did what needed to be done without a lot of show.

Ethan would have faced down the bad guys, too. Because it was right. Seth had mulled it over for a while and had decided that's what a hero was. Somebody who just did what was right.

⬥

Ethan would have been stunned and mortally embarrassed, if he'd been able to read Seth's thoughts. But the boy was an expert at keeping them to himself. On that level, he and Ethan were as close as twins.

It might have crossed Ethan's mind that Village Pizza was only a short block from Shiney's Pub, where Grace would be starting her shift, but he didn't mention it.

Couldn't take the boy into a bar anyway, Ethan mused as they headed into the bright lights and noise of the local restaurant. And Seth was bound to complain, loudly, if Ethan asked him to wait in the car for just a couple minutes while he poked his head in. Likely Grace would complain, too, if she caught on that he was checking on her.

It was best to let it go and concentrate on the matters at hand. He tucked his hands into his back pockets and studied the menu posted on the wall behind the counter. "What do you want on it?"

"You can forget the mushrooms. They're gross."

"We're of a mind there," Ethan murmured.

"Pepperoni and hot sausage." Seth sneered, but he spoiled it by bouncing a little in his sneakers. "If you can handle it."

"I can take it if you can. Hey, Justin," he said with a smile of greeting for the boy behind the counter. "We'll take a large, pepperoni and hot sausage, and a couple of jumbo Pepsis."

"You got it. Here or to go?"

Ethan scanned the dozen tables and booths offered and noted that he wasn't the only one who'd thought to celebrate the last day of school with pizza. "Go nab that last booth back there, Seth. We'll take it here, Justin."

"Have a seat. We'll bring the drinks out."

Seth had dumped his backpack on the bench and was tapping his hands on the table in time to the blast of Hootie and the Blowfish from the juke. "I'm going to go kick some video ass," he told Ethan. When Ethan reached back for his wallet, Seth shook his head. "I got money."

"Not tonight you don't," Ethan said mildly and pulled out some bills. "It's your party. Get some change."

"Cool." Seth snagged the bills and raced off to get quarters.

As Ethan slid into the booth, he wondered why so many people thought a couple hours in a noisy room was high entertainment. A huddle of kids was already trying to kick some video ass at the trio of machines along the back wall; the juke had switched to Clint Black—and that country boy was wailing. The toddler in the booth behind him was having a full-blown tantrum, and a group of teenage girls were giggling at a decibel level that would have made Simon's ears bleed.

What a way to spend a pretty summer night.

Then he saw Liz Crawford and Junior with their two little girls at a nearby booth. One of the girls—that must be Stacy, Ethan thought—was talking quickly, making wide gestures, while the rest of the family howled with laughter.

They made a unit, he mused, their own little island in the midst of the jittery lights and noise. He supposed that's what family was, an island. Knowing you could go there made all the difference.

Still the tug of envy surprised him, made him shift uncomfortably on the hard seat of the booth and scowl into space. He'd made his mind up about having a family years before, and he didn't care for this sharp pull of longing.

"Why, Ethan, you look fierce."

He glanced up as the drinks were set on the table in front of him, straight into the flirtatious eyes of Linda Brewster.

She was a looker, no question about it. The tight black jeans and scoop-necked black T-shirt hugged her well-developed body like a coat of fresh paint on a classic Chevy. After her divorce was final—one week ago Monday—she'd treated herself to a manicure and a new hairdo. Her coral-tipped nails skimmed through her newly bobbed, streaky blond hair as she smiled down at Ethan.

She'd had her eye on him for a time now—after all, she had separated from that useless Tom Brewster more than a year before and a woman had to look to the future. Ethan Quinn would be hot in bed, she decided. She had instincts about these things. Those big hands of his would be mighty thorough, she was sure. And attentive. Oh, yes.

She liked his looks, too. Just a little tough and weathered. And that slow, sexy smile of his . . . when you managed to drag one out of him, just made her want to lick her lips in anticipation.

He had that quiet way about him. Linda knew what they said about still waters. And she was just dying to see just how deep Ethan Quinn's ran.

Ethan was well aware where her eye had wandered, and he was keeping his peeled as well. For running room. Women like Linda scared the hell out of him.

"Hi, Linda. Didn't know you were working here." Or he'd have avoided Village Pizza like the plague.

"Just helping my father out for a couple of weeks." She was flat broke, and her father—the owner of Village Pizza—had told her he'd be damned if she was going to sponge off him and her mother. She should get her sassy butt to work. "Haven't seen you around lately."

"I've been around." He wished she'd move along. Her perfume gave him the jitters.

"I heard you and your brothers rented that old barn of Claremont's and are building boats. I've been meaning to come down and take a look."

"Not much to see." Where the hell was Seth when he needed him? Ethan wondered a little desperately. How long could those damn quarters last?

"I'd like to see it anyway." She skimmed those slick-tipped nails down his arm, gave a low purr as she felt the ridge of muscle. "I can slip out of here for a while. Why don't you run me down there and show me what's what?"

His mind blanked for a moment. He was only human. And she was running her tongue over her top lip in a way designed to draw a man's eyes and tickle his glands. Not that he was interested, not a bit, but it had been a long time since he'd had a woman moaning under him. And he had a feeling Linda would be a champion moaner.

"Copped top score." Seth plopped into the booth, flushed with victory, and grabbed his Pepsi. He slurped some up. "Man, what's keeping that pizza? I'm starved."

Ethan felt his blood start to run again and nearly sighed with relief. "It'll be along."

"Well." Despite annoyance at the interruption, Linda smiled brilliantly at Seth. "This must be the new addition. What's your name, honey? I can't quite recollect."

"I'm Seth." And he sized her up quickly. Bimbo, was his first and last thought. He'd seen plenty of them in his short life. "Who're you?"

"I'm Linda, an old friend of Ethan's. My daddy owns the place."

"Cool, so maybe you could tell them to put a fire under that pizza before we die of old age here."

"Seth." The word and Ethan's quiet look were all it took for the boy to close his mouth. "Your daddy still makes the best pizza on the Shore," Ethan said with an easier smile. "You be sure to tell him."

"I will. And you give me a call, Ethan." She wiggled her left hand. "I'm a free woman these days." She wandered away, hips swinging like a well-oiled metronome.

"She smells like the place at the mall where they sell all that girl stuff." Seth wrinkled his nose. He hadn't liked her because he'd seen just a shadow of his mother in her eyes. "She just wants to get in your pants."

"Shut up, Seth."

"It's true," Seth said with a shrug, but happily let the subject drop when Linda came back bearing pizza.

"Y'all enjoy, now," she told them, leaning over the table just a little farther than necessary in case Ethan had missed the view the first time around.

Seth snagged a piece and bit in, knowing it was going to scorch the roof of his mouth. The flavors exploded, making the burn more than worth it. "Grace makes pizza from scratch," he said around a mouthful. "It's even better than this."

Ethan only grunted. The thought of Grace after he'd entertained—however unwillingly—a brief and sweaty fantasy about Linda Brewster made him twitchy.

"Yeah. We ought to see if she'd make it for us one of the days she comes to clean and stuff. She comes tomorrow, right?"

"Yeah." Ethan took a piece, annoyed that most of his appetite had deserted him. "I suppose."

"Maybe she'd make one up before she goes."

"You're having pizza tonight."

"So?" Seth polished off the first piece with the speed and precision of a jackal. "You could, like, compare. Grace ought to open a diner or something so she wouldn't have to work all those different jobs. She's always working. She wants to buy a house."

"She does?"

"Yeah." Seth licked the side of his hand where sauce dripped. "Just a little one, but it has to have a yard so Aubrey can run around and have a dog and stuff."

"She tell you all that?"

"Sure. I asked how come she was busting her butt cleaning all those houses and working down at the pub, and she said that was mostly why. And if she doesn't make enough, she and Aubrey won't have a place of their own by the time Aub starts kindergarten. I guess even a little house costs big bucks, right?"

"It costs," Ethan said quietly. He remembered how satisfied, how proud he'd been when he'd bought his own place on the water. What it had meant to him to know he'd succeeded at what he did. "It takes time to save up."

"Grace wants to have the house by the time Aubrey starts school. After that, she says how she has to start saving for college." He snorted and decided he could force down a third piece. "Hell, Aubrey's just a baby, it's a million years till college. Told her that, too," he added, because it pleased him for people to know he and Grace had *conversations*. "She just laughed and said five minutes ago Aubrey had gotten her first tooth. I didn't get it."

"She meant kids grow up fast." Since it didn't look as though his appetite would be coming back, Ethan closed the top on the pizza and took out bills to pay for it. "Let's take this back to the boatyard. Since you don't have school in the morning, we can put in a couple more hours."

⟨⟨⟩⟩

He put in more than a couple. Once he got started, he couldn't seem to stop. It cleared his mind, kept it from wandering, wondering, worrying.

The boat was definite, a tangible task with a foreseeable end. He knew what he was doing here, just as he knew what he was doing out on the Bay. There weren't so many shadow areas of maybes or what ifs.

Ethan continued to work even when Seth curled up on a drop cloth and fell asleep. The sound of tools running didn't appear to disturb him—though Ethan wondered how anyone could sleep with the best part of a large sausage-and-pepperoni pizza in his stomach.

He started work on the ends and corner posts for the cabin and cockpit coaming while the night wind blew lazily through the open cargo doors. He'd turned the radio off so that now the only music was the water, the gentle notes of it sliding against the shore.

He worked slowly, carefully, though he was well able to visualize the completed project. Cam, he decided, would handle most of the interior work. He was the most skilled of the three of them at finish carpentry. Phillip could handle the rough-ins; he was better at sheer manual labor than he liked to admit.

If they could keep up the pace, Ethan calculated that they could have the boat trimmed and under sail in another two months. He would leave figuring the profits and percentages to Phillip. The money would feed the lawyers, the boatyard, and their own bellies.

Why hadn't Grace ever told him she wanted to buy a house?

Ethan frowned thoughtfully as he chose a galvanized bolt. Wasn't that a pretty big step to be discussing with a ten-year-old boy? Then again, he admitted, Seth had asked. He himself had only told her she shouldn't be working herself so hard—he hadn't asked why she insisted on it.

She ought to make things up with her father, he thought again. If the two of them would just bend that stiff-necked Monroe pride for five minutes, they could come to terms. She'd gotten pregnant—and there was no doubt in Ethan's mind that Jack Casey had taken advantage of a young, naive girl and should be shot for it—but that was over and done.

His family had never held grudges, small or large. They'd fought, certainly—and he and his brothers had often fought physically. But when it was done, it was over.

It was true enough that he'd harbored some seeds of resentment because Cam had raced off to Europe and Phillip had moved to Baltimore. It had happened so fast after their mother died, and he'd still been raw. Everything had changed before he could blink, and he'd stewed over that.

But even with that, he would never have turned his back on either of them if they'd needed him. And he knew they wouldn't have turned their backs on him.

It seemed to him the most foolish and wasteful thing imaginable that Grace wouldn't ask for help, and her father wouldn't offer it.

He glanced at the big round clock nailed to the wall over the front doors. Phillip's idea, Ethan remembered with a half grin. He'd figured they'd need to know how much time they were putting in, but as far as Ethan knew, Phillip was the only one who bothered to mark down the time.

It was nearly one, which meant Grace would be finishing up at the pub in about an hour. It wouldn't hurt to load Seth in the truck and do a quick swing by Shiney's. Just to . . . check on things.

Even as he started to rise, he heard the boy whimper in his sleep.

Pizza's finally getting to him, Ethan thought with a shake of the head. But he supposed childhood wouldn't be complete without its quota of bellyaches. He climbed down, rolling his shoulders to work out the kinks as he approached the sleeping boy.

He crouched beside Seth, laid a hand on his shoulders, and gave a gentle shake.

And the boy came up swinging.

The bunched fist caught Ethan squarely on the mouth and knocked his head back. The shock, more than the quick and bright pain, had him swearing. He blocked the next blow, then took Seth's arm firmly. "Hold it."

"Get your hands off me." Wild, desperate, and still caught in the sticky grip of the dream, Seth flailed at the air. "Get your fucking hands off me."

Understanding came quickly. It was the look in Seth's eyes—stark terror and vicious fury. He'd once felt both himself, along with a shuddering helplessness. He let go, lifted both of his hands palms out. "You were dreaming." He said it quietly, without inflection, and listened to Seth's ragged breathing echo on the air. "You fell asleep."

Seth kept his fists bunched. He didn't remember falling asleep. He remembered curling up, listening to Ethan work. And the next thing he knew, he was back in one of those dark rooms, where the smells were sour and too human and the noises from the next room were too loud and too animal.

And one of the faceless men who used his mother's bed had crept out and put hands on him again.

But it was Ethan who was watching him, patiently, with too much knowledge in his serious eyes. Seth's stomach twisted not only at what had been, but that Ethan should now know.

Because he couldn't think of words or excuses, Seth simply closed his eyes.

It was that which tilted the scales for Ethan. The surrender to helplessness, the slide into shame. He'd left this wound alone, but now it seemed he would need to treat it after all.

"You don't have to be afraid of what was."

"I'm not afraid of anything." Seth's eyes snapped open. The anger in them was adult and bitter, but his voice jerked like the child he was. "I'm not afraid of some stupid dream."

"You don't have to be ashamed of it, either."

Because he was, hideously, Seth sprang to his feet. His fists were bunched again, ready. "I'm not ashamed of anything. And you don't know a damn thing about it."

"I know every damn thing about it." Because he did, he hated to speak of it. But despite the defiant stance, the boy was trembling, and Ethan knew just how alone he felt. Speaking of it was the only thing left for him to do. The right thing to do.

"I know what dreams did to me, how I had them for a long time after that part of things was over for me." And still had them now and again, he thought, but there was no need to tell the boy he might have to face a lifetime of flashing back and overcoming. "I know what it does to your guts."

"Bullshit." The tears were burning the backs of Seth's eyes, humiliating him all the more. "Nothing's wrong with me. I got the hell out, didn't I? I got away from her, didn't I? I'm not going back either, no matter what."

"No, you're not going back," Ethan agreed. No matter what.

"I don't care what you or anybody thinks about what went on back then. And you're not tricking me into saying things about it by pretending you know."

"You don't have to say anything about it," Ethan told him. "And I don't have to pretend." He picked up the cap Seth's blow had knocked off his head, ran it absently through his hands before putting it back on. But the casual gesture did nothing to ease the tight, slick ball of tension in his gut.

"My mother was a whore—my biological mother. And she was a junkie with a taste for heroin." He kept his gaze on Seth's and his voice matter-of-fact. "I was younger than you when she sold me the first time, to a man who liked young boys."

Seth's breathing quickened as he took a step back. *No,* was all he could think. Ethan Quinn was everything strong and solid and . . . normal. "You're lying."

"People mostly lie to brag, or to get out of some stupid thing they've done. I don't see the point in either—and less in lying about this."

Ethan took his cap off again because it suddenly felt too tight on his head. Once, twice, he raked his hand through his hair as if to ease the weight. "She sold me to men to pay for her habit. The first time, I fought. It didn't stop it, but I fought. The second time, I fought, and a few times more after that. Then I didn't bother fighting because it just made it worse."

Ethan's gaze stayed level on the boy's. In the harsh overhead lights Seth's eyes were dark, and not as calm as they had been when Ethan had begun to speak. Seth's chest hurt until he remembered to breathe again. "How'd you stand it?"

"I stopped caring." Ethan shrugged his shoulders. "I stopped *being,* if you know what I mean. There wasn't anybody I could go to for help—or I didn't know there was. She moved around a lot to keep the social workers off her tail."

Seth's lips felt dry and tight. He rubbed the back of his hand over them violently. "You never knew where you're going to wake up in the morning."

"Yeah, you never knew." But all the places looked the same. They all smelled the same.

"But you got away. You got out."

"Yeah, I got out. One night after her john had finished with both of us, there was . . . some trouble." Screams, blood, curses. Pain. "I don't remember everything exactly, but the cops came. I must have been in a pretty bad way because they took me to the hospital and figured things out quick enough. I ended up in the system, might have stayed there. But the doctor who treated me was Stella Quinn."

"They took you."

"They took me." And saying that, just that, soothed the sickness in Ethan's gut. "They didn't just change my life, they saved it. I had the dreams for a long time after, the sweaty ones where you wake up trying to breathe, sure you're back in it. And even when you realize you're not, you're cold for a while."

Seth knuckled the tears away, but he didn't feel ashamed of them now. "I always got away. Sometimes they put their hands on me, but I got away. None of them ever . . ."

"Good for you."

"I still wanted to kill them, and her. I wanted to."

"I know."

"I didn't want to tell anybody. I think Ray knew, and Cam sort of knows. I didn't want anybody to think I . . . to look at me and think . . ." He couldn't express it, the shame of having anyone look at him and see what had happened, and what could have happened, in those dark, smelly rooms. "Why did you tell me?"

"Because you need to know it doesn't make you less of a man." Ethan waited, knowing that Seth would decide whether he accepted the truth of that.

What Seth saw was a man, tall, strong, self-possessed, with big, callused hands and quiet eyes. One of the weights that hung on his heart lifted. "I guess I do." And he smiled a little. "Your mouth's bleeding."

Ethan dabbed at it with the back of his hand and knew they'd crossed a thin and shaky line. "You got a good right jab. I never saw it coming." He held out a hand, testing, and ruffled Seth's sleep-tumbled hair. The boy's smile stayed in place. "Let's clean up," Ethan said, "and go home."

FIVE

G race had a morning full of chores. The first load of laundry went in at seven-fifteen while the coffee was brewing and her eyes were still mostly shut. She watered her porch plants and the little pots of herbs on her kitchen windowsill, and yawned hugely.

As the coffee began to scent the air and give her hope, she washed the glasses and bowls Julie had used the night before while babysitting. She closed the open bag of potato chips, tucked it into its place in the cupboard, then wiped the crumbs from the counter where Julie had had her snack while talking on the phone.

Julie Cutter wasn't known for her neatness, but she loved Aubrey.

At precisely seven-thirty—and after half a cup of coffee—Aubrey woke.

Reliable as the sunrise, Grace thought, heading out of the tiny galley kitchen toward the bedroom off the living room. Rain or shine, weekday or weekend, Aubrey's internal clock buzzed away at seven-thirty every morning.

Grace could have left her in the crib and finished her coffee, but she looked forward to this moment every day. Aubrey stood at the side of the crib, her sunbeam curls tangled from sleep, her cheeks still flushed with it. Grace could still remember the first time she'd come in and seen Aubrey standing, her wobbly legs rocking, her face glowing with success and surprise.

Now Aubrey's legs seemed so sturdy. She lifted one, then the other, in a kind of joyful march. She laughed out loud when Grace came into the room. "Mama, Mama, hi, my mama."

"Hello, my baby." Grace leaned over the side for the first nuzzle and sighed. She knew how lucky she was. There couldn't have been a child on the planet with a sunnier nature than her little girl. "How's my Aubrey?"

"Up! Out!"

"You bet. Gotta pee?"

"Gotta pee," Aubrey agreed and giggled when Grace lifted her out of the crib.

The toilet training was coming along, Grace decided, checking Aubrey's overnight diaper as they headed into the bathroom. It had its hits and its misses.

Aubrey hit it this time, and Grace launched into the lavish praise over bodily functions that only a parent with a toddler could understand. Teeth and hair were brushed in the closet-size bathroom Grace had brightened up with mint-green walls and awning-striped curtains.

Then the breakfast routine began. Aubrey wanted cold cereal with bananas but no milk. She plopped her hand over the bowl when Grace started to pour it on, shaking her head vigorously. "No, Mama, no. Cup. Please."

"Okay, milk in a cup." Grace filled one, set it on the high-chair tray beside the bowl. "Eat up, now. We've got lots to do today."

"Do what?"

"Let's see." Grace made herself a piece of toast while she went through the projected day. "We have to finish the laundry, then we promised Mrs. West we'd wash her windows today."

A three-hour job, Grace estimated.

"Then we have to go to the market."

Aubrey gasped in pleasure. "Miss Lucy."

"Yes, you'll see Miss Lucy." Lucy Wilson was one of Aubrey's favorite people. The supermarket cashier always had a smile—and a lollipop—for Aubrey. "After we put the groceries away, we're going to the Quinns'."

"Seth!" Milk dribbled out of her grin.

"Well, honey, I don't know for certain that he'll be there today. He may be out on the boat with Ethan, or over at his friends' house."

"Seth," Aubrey said again, very definitely, and her mouth puckered up into a stubborn pout.

"We'll see." Grace mopped up the spills.

"Ethan."

"Maybe."

"Doggies."

"Foolish, for sure." She kissed the top of Aubrey's head and gave herself the luxury of a second cup of coffee.

⚜

At eight-fifteen Grace was armed with a stack of newspapers and a spray bottle that contained a mix of vinegar and ammonia. Aubrey was entertaining herself on the grass with her Mattel See 'n Say. Every few seconds a cow mooed or a pig oinked. And Aubrey never failed to echo the sound.

By the time Aubrey had switched her affections to her building blocks, Grace had finished cleaning and polishing the outside of the windows on the front and side of the cottage and was right on schedule. She would have stayed on schedule if Mrs. West hadn't come out with tall glasses of iced tea and a desire to chat.

"I don't know how to thank you for seeing to this for me, Grace." Mrs. West, the grandmother of many, had brought Aubrey her drink in a bright plastic cup with ducks on the side.

"I'm happy to do it, Mrs. West."

"Just can't do like I used to, with my arthritis. And I do like my windows to shine." She smiled, deepening the wrinkles on her weather-scored face. "And you do make them shine. My granddaughter, Layla, said how she'd wash them for me. But I tell you the truth and shame the devil, Grace, that girl's a scatterbrain. She'd like as not start the job and end up sleeping in the vegetable patch. Don't know what's to become of that girl."

Grace laughed and scrubbed at the next window. "She's only fifteen. Her mind's on boys and clothes and music."

"Tell me." Mrs. West nodded so vigorously that her second chin wobbled with the movement. "Why, at her age I could pick a crab clean faster than you could blink. Earned my keep, and kept my mind on my work till the work was done." She winked. "Then I thought about boys."

She let out a hearty laugh before smiling at Aubrey. "That's one pretty little lamb you got yourself there, Gracie."

"The light of my life."

"Good as gold, too. Why, my Carly's youngest boy, Luke? He's not still for two minutes running and spends every waking hour looking for trouble. Just last week I caught him climbing up my parlor curtains like a house cat." Still, the memory made her chuckle. "He's a terror, that Luke is."

"Aubrey has her moments, too."

"Can't believe it. Not with that angel face. You're going to have to beat the boys off with a stick to keep them from sniffing around that sweetheart one of these days. Pretty as a picture. Already seen her holding hands with one."

Grace bobbled her spray bottle and looked around quickly to make certain her little girl hadn't grown up while she wasn't looking. "Aubrey?"

Mrs. West laughed again. "Walking on the waterfront with that Quinn boy—the new one."

"Oh, Seth." The sense of relief was so ridiculous, Grace set the bottle down and picked up her glass to drink. "Aubrey's got a crush on him."

"Good-looking boy. My young Matt goes to school with him—told me how Seth came to sock that little bully Robert a few weeks back. Couldn't help but feel it was about time somebody did. How they doing over at the Quinns?"

The question was her main purpose for coming out, but Mrs. West believed in leading up to matters.

"Just fine."

Mrs. West rolled her eyes. This pump needed more priming. "That girl Cam up and married sure is a beauty. She'll have to have quick hands, too, to keep that one in line. Always was wild."

"I think Anna can handle him."

"Went off to some foreign place to honeymoon, didn't they?"

"Rome. Seth showed me a postcard they sent. It's beautiful."

"Always puts me in mind of that movie with Audrey Hepburn and Gregory Peck—where she's a princess. Don't make movies like that anymore."

"*Roman Holiday*." Grace smiled wistfully. She had a weakness for the classic and romantic.

"That's the one." Grace looked a bit like Audrey Hepburn, Mrs. West mused. Coloring was wrong, of course, with Grace being blond as a Viking, but she had the big eyes and the cool, pretty face. Lord knew, she was skinny enough.

"Never been anyplace foreign." Which included, in Mrs. West's mind, two-thirds of the United States. "They coming back soon?"

"A couple days."

"Hmm. Well, that house needs a woman, no question. Can't imagine what it's like over there, four males in one house. Must smell like a gym sock half the time. Don't know a man on this earth who can manage to pee and hit the toilet with the whole stream."

Grace laughed and went back to her windows. "They aren't so bad. The fact is, Cam was keeping the house pretty well before they hired me to take over. But the only one of them who remembers to empty the pockets before tossing his pants at the hamper is Phillip."

"If that's the worst of it, it's not bad. I expect Cam's wife'll take over the house once they get back."

Grace's hand tightened on her wad of newspaper as her heart did a quick hitch. "I . . . She works full-time in Princess Anne."

"Most likely she'll take over," Mrs. West said again. "A woman likes her house kept her way. Best thing for the boy, I expect, having a woman there full-time. Don't know what Ray was thinking of this time around, I swear. A good-hearted man he was, but once Stella passed . . . shifted his moorings, I'd say. A man his age taking on a boy thataway. No matter what was what. Not that I believe one word of the nasty gossip you hear now and then. Nancy Claremont is the worst, flapping her lips every chance she gets."

Mrs. West waited a beat, hoping that Grace would flap hers. But Grace was frowning intently at the window.

"You know if that insurance inspector's coming around again?"

"No," Grace said quietly, "I don't. I hope not."

"Don't see how it makes a matter where the boy came from as far as the insurance company goes. Even if Ray did suicide himself—and I'm not saying it's so—they can't prove it, can they? Because . . ." She paused dramatically, as she did whenever she made the argument. "They weren't there!"

She said the last on a note of triumph, just as she had when she'd made the same statement to Nancy.

"Professor Quinn wouldn't have killed himself," Grace murmured.

"'Course not." But it did make for such interesting talk. "But the boy—" She broke off, her ears pricking up. "There goes my telephone. You just let yourself in when you want to do the inside, Grace," she said as she hurried off.

Grace said nothing, kept working steadily. But her mind was whirling. It shamed her that she couldn't concentrate on Professor Quinn. She could think only of herself and of what might happen.

Would Anna come back from Rome and want to take over the house? Would Grace lose her job there and the extra money that went with it? Worse—much worse—would she lose those opportunities to see Ethan once or twice a week? To share a meal now and then?

She'd gotten used to—even dependent on—being a part of his life, even a peripheral part, she realized. And as pathetic as it was, she loved folding his clothes, smoothing the sheets on his bed. She even allowed herself to believe that he would think of her when he found one of her little notes around the house. Or slipped between freshly laundered sheets at night.

Was she going to lose that, too—and lose the pleasure of seeing him coming in from his boat or scooping Aubrey up when she demanded a kiss, or glancing over at her and giving her that slow smile?

Was all of that going to be only pictures she tucked away in her mind now?

Her days would go on and on, without even that to look forward to. And her nights would go on and on, alone.

She squeezed her eyes tight, struggling with despair. Then opened them again when Aubrey tugged at the hem of her shorts.

"Mama. Miss Lucy?"

"Soon, honey." Because she needed to, Grace lifted Aubrey into her arms for a fierce hug.

It was nearly one by the time Grace finished putting away the groceries and fixing Aubrey's lunch. She was only half an hour behind, and she thought she could make that up without too much trouble. It just meant moving a little quicker and keeping her mind on her work. No more projecting, she ordered herself as she strapped Aubrey into the car seat. No more foolishness.

"Seth, Seth, Seth," Aubrey chanted, bouncing madly.

"We'll see." Grace climbed behind the wheel, put the key in the ignition, and turned it. The response was a wheeze and a thump. "Oh, no, you don't. No, you don't. I don't have time for this." A little panicked, she turned the key again, pumped the gas pedal, and sighed with relief when the engine caught. "That's more like it," she muttered as she backed out of the short driveway. "Here we go, Aubrey."

"Here we go!"

Five minutes later, midway between her house and the Quinns', the old sedan coughed again, shuddered, then belched out steam from under the hood.

"Dammit!"

"Dammit!" Aubrey echoed joyfully.

Grace only pressed the heels of her hands to her eyes. It was the radiator, she was sure of it. Last month it had been the fan belt, and before that, the brake pads. Resigned, she eased to the side of the road and got out to open the hood.

Smoke billowed, made her cough and step away. Resolutely, she swallowed back the knot of despair in her throat. Maybe it wouldn't be anything major. It could just be some belt again. And if it wasn't—she sighed hugely—she would have to decide if it was better to pump more money into this wreck or to worry her beleaguered budget into buying another wreck.

Either way, there was nothing to be done about it now.

She opened the passenger-side door and unbuckled Aubrey. "The car's sick again, honey."

"Awww."

"Yeah, so we're going to leave it right here."

"Alone?"

Aubrey's concern over inanimate objects made Grace smile again. "Not for long. I'm going to call the car man to come take care of it."

"Make it feel all better."

"I hope so. Now we're going to walk to Seth's house."

"Okay!" Delighted by the change of routine, Aubrey set out at a scramble.

A quarter of a mile later, Grace was carrying her.

But it was a pretty day, she reminded herself. And walking gave her a chance to look and really see. Honeysuckle was tangling along the fence that bordered a tidy field of soybeans, and the scent was lovely. She picked off a blossom for Aubrey.

By the time they skirted the marsh that edged Quinn land, her arms were aching. They stopped to study a turtle sunning on the side of the road, to let Aubrey giggle over the way its head retreated into its shell when she reached out to touch.

"Can you walk for a while now, baby?"

"Tired." With her eyes pleading, Aubrey lifted her arms. "Up!"

"Okay, up you come. Nearly there." It was past nap time, Grace thought. Aubrey wanted her nap directly after lunch every day. She would sleep for two hours, almost to the minute, then wake up ready to roll.

Aubrey's head was already a snoozing weight on Grace's shoulder when she climbed the porch and slipped into the house.

Once she had her daughter tucked onto the couch, she hurried upstairs to strip beds, gather and sort laundry. With the first load in, she made a quick call to the mechanic who did his best to keep her ailing car alive.

She rushed upstairs again, remaking the beds with fresh sheets. To save herself steps, she kept cleaning supplies on each floor. Grace tackled the bathroom first, scrubbing and rinsing in a flurry until chrome and tile sparkled.

It would be, she realized, her last full hit on the Quinn place before Cam and Anna returned. But she'd already decided, sometime during the mile walk from her broken-down car, to carve out a couple of hours for a quick polish the day they were expected home.

She had pride in her work, didn't she? And certainly another woman would notice the tidiness, the clean corners, the few extra touches she tried to add. A professional woman like Anna, a woman with a demanding career, would see, wouldn't she, that Grace was needed here?

She raced downstairs again to check on Aubrey, to drag wet clothes out of the washer into a basket and put the second load in.

She would make sure there were fresh flowers in the master bedroom when the newlyweds returned. And she'd put out the good fingertip towels. She would leave a note for Phillip to pick up some fruit so she could arrange it prettily in the bowl on the kitchen table.

She'd make time to paste-wax the hardwood floors and wash and iron the curtains.

She hung clothes on the line quickly, without any of her usual enjoyment in the task. Still, the simple routine began to calm her. Everything would be all right, somehow.

She caught herself swaying and shook her head to clear it. Fatigue had come quickly, like a punch to the jaw. If she had bothered to calculate the time she'd been on her feet and moving that day, she would have counted seven hours, on a short five hours' sleep the night before. What she did calculate was that she had another twelve to go. And she needed a break.

Ten minutes, she promised herself, and as she sometimes did on long days, stretched out right in the grass by the clothes that waved on the line. A ten-minute nap would recharge her system and still give her time to scrub down the kitchen before Aubrey woke up.

Ethan drove home from the waterfront. He'd cut his day on the water short, letting Jim and his son take the workboat out again to check the pots in the Pocomoke. Seth was off with Danny and Will, and Ethan figured on grabbing himself a quick, if delayed, lunch, then spending the next several hours at the boatyard. He wanted to finish the cockpit, maybe get the roof of the cabin started. The more he managed to do, the less time it would be before Cam could get into the finish and fancy work.

He slowed down when he saw Grace's car on the side of the road, then pulled over quickly. He only shook his head when he looked under the open hood. Damn thing was held together with spit and prayers, he decided. She shouldn't be driving something so unreliable. Just what if, he thought sourly, the goddamn thing had decided to break down when she'd been coming home from the pub in the middle of the night?

He took a closer look and hissed through his teeth. The radiator was a dead loss, and if she was entertaining the idea of replacing it, he'd just have to talk her out of it.

He would find her a decent secondhand car. Fix it up for her—or ask Cam, who knew engines like Midas knew gold, to tune it up. He wasn't having her driving around in a wreck like this, and with the baby, too.

He caught himself, took a couple steps back. It wasn't any of his business. The hell it wasn't, he thought, with an uncharacteristic flash of temper. She was a friend, wasn't she? He had a right to help out a friend, especially one who needed some looking after.

And God knew—whether or not Grace did—that she needed some looking after. He got back in his truck and drove home with a scowl on his face.

He'd nearly slammed the screen door before he saw Aubrey curled up on the couch. The scowl didn't have a chance. He eased the door shut and walked quietly over to her. Her hand was bunched into a fist on the cushion. Unable to resist, he took it gently and marveled at those tiny, perfect fingers. She had a bow around one of her curls, a little ribbon of blue lace that he imagined Grace had tied on that morning. It was lopsided now, and only sweeter for it.

He couldn't help hoping that she woke before he had to head out again.

But now, he needed to find Aubrey's mother and discuss reliable transportation.

He cocked his head, decided it was too quiet for her to be upstairs doing whatever it was she did up there. He walked into the kitchen and noted that the signs of a hurried breakfast were still in evidence. She hadn't gotten to that yet. But the washing machine was humming, and he caught a glimpse of clothes flapping in the breeze on the line outside.

The minute he stepped to the door he saw her. And hit full panic. He didn't know what he thought, only that she was lying on the grass. Terrible images of illness and injury crowded into his head as he rushed outside. He was barely one full stride away from her when he realized she wasn't unconscious. She was sleeping.

Curled up much as her daugher was inside. One fist bunched near her cheek, her breathing slow and deep and even. He gave in to his weakened knees and sat down beside her, waited for his heartbeat to return to something approaching normal.

He sat, listening to the clothes flap on the line, to the water lick the eelgrass, and to the birds chatter while he wondered what the hell he was going to do with her.

In the end, he simply sighed, rose, then bending down gathered her up into his arms.

She stirred in them, snuggled, made his blood run a little too fast for comfort. "Ethan," she murmured, turning her face into the curve of his neck and inciting the bright fantasy of rolling over that sun-warmed grass with her.

"Ethan," she said again, skimming her fingers along his shoulder. And making him hard as iron. Then again, "Ethan," only this time in a squeak of shock as she jerked her head up and stared at him.

Her eyes were dazed with sleep and bright with surprise. Her mouth made a soft O that was gloriously tempting. Then color flooded her cheeks.

"What? What is it?" she managed over a stomach-churning combination of arousal and embarrassment.

"You're going to take a nap, you ought to have as much sense as Aubrey and take it inside out of the sun." He knew his voice was rough. He couldn't do anything about it. Desire had him by the throat with gleefully nipping claws.

"I was just—"

"Scared ten years off me when I saw you lying there. I thought you'd fainted or something."

"I only stretched out for a minute. Aubrey was sleeping, so—Aubrey! I need to check on Aubrey."

"I just did. She's fine. You'd have shown more sense if you'd stretched out on the couch with her."

"I don't come here to sleep."

"You were sleeping."

"Just for a minute."

"You need more than a minute."

"No, I don't. It's just that things got complicated today, and my brain got tired."

It almost amused him. He stopped in the kitchen, still holding her, and looked into her eyes. "Your brain got tired?"

"Yeah." It nearly shut off entirely now. "I needed to rest my mind a minute, that's all. Put me down, Ethan."

He wasn't ready to, not quite yet. "I saw your car about a mile down the road from here."

"I called Dave and told him. He's going to get to it as soon as he can."

"You walked from there to here, carting Aubrey?"

"No, my chauffeur drove us in. Put me down, Ethan." Before she exploded.

"Well, you can give your chauffeur the rest of the day off. I'll drive you home when Aubrey wakes up."

"I can get myself home. I've barely started on the house. Now I need to get back to it."

"You're not walking two and a half miles."

"I'll call Julie. She'll run down and pick us up. You must have work to do yourself. I'm . . . behind schedule," she said, desperately now. "I can't catch up if you don't put me down."

He considered her. "There's not much to you."

The shimmer of need wavered into annoyance. "If you're going to tell me I'm skinny—"

"I wouldn't say skinny. You've got fine bones, that's all." And smooth, soft flesh to cover them. He set her on her feet before he forgot he intended to look after her. "You don't have to worry with the house today."

"I do. I need to do my job." Her nerves were a jittery mess. The way he was looking at her made her want to take one flying leap back into his arms and also made her want to hightail it out the back door like a rabbit. She'd never experienced such a dramatic tug-of-war on her system, and could only stand her ground. "I can do it quicker if you aren't underfoot."

"I'll get out of your way as soon as you call Julie and see if she'll come by and get you." He reached up and brushed some dandelion fluff out of her hair.

"Okay." She turned, punched in numbers on the kitchen phone. Maybe it would be best, she thought wildly as the phone started to ring, if Anna didn't want her around after she got home. It seemed she couldn't be with Ethan for ten minutes anymore without getting jumpy. If it kept up, she was bound to do something to embarrass them both.

SIX

Ethan didn't mind putting in long hours on the boat at night. Especially when he could work alone. It hadn't taken much persuasion for him to agree to let Seth camp out with the other boys in their backyard. It gave Ethan an evening alone—a rarity now—and time to work without having to tune in to questions and comments.

Not that the boy wasn't entertaining, Ethan mused. The fact was, he was firmly attached to Seth. Accepting Seth into his life had been natural because Ray had asked it of him. But the affection, the appreciation, and the loyalty had grown and solidified until it simply was.

But that didn't mean the kid couldn't wear down his energies.

Ethan kept it to handwork tonight. Even if you *felt* awake and alert at midnight, the odds were you'd be a bit sluggish, and he didn't want to risk losing a finger to the power tools. In any case, it was soothing to work in the quiet, to hand-sand edges and planes until you felt them go smooth.

They would be ready to seal the hull before the week was out, and he could start Seth on sanding the rubrails. If Cam dived right in on dealing with belowdecks, and if Seth didn't bitch too much about working with putty and caulk and varnish over the next week or two, they'd do well enough.

He checked his watch, saw that time was getting away from him, and began to put away his tools. He swept up, since Seth wasn't there to wield the broom.

By quarter after one, he was parked outside of the pub. He didn't intend to go inside anymore than he intended to let Grace walk the mile and a half home when she clocked out. So he settled back, switched on his dome light, and passed the time reading his dog-eared copy of *Cannery Row*.

Inside, it was last call. The only thing that would have made Grace happier would have been if Dave had told her that all she needed to get her car up and running was some used chewing gum and a rubber band.

Instead he'd told her it would cost the equivalent of three years' worth of both, and then she'd be lucky if the old bucket ran another five thousand miles.

It was something she would have to worry about later; at the moment, she had her hands full dealing with an overly insistent customer who was stopping off in St. Chris on his way down to Savannah and was sure Grace would like to be his form of entertainment for the night.

"I got me a hotel room." He winked at her when she stooped to serve his final drink of the night. "And it's got a big bed and twenty-four-hour room service. We could have us a hell of a party, honey pie."

"I don't do a lot of partying, but thanks."

He grabbed her hand, pulled it just enough to throw off her balance so she had to grip his shoulder or tumble into his lap. "Then now's your chance." He had dark eyes, and he aimed them leeringly at her breasts. "I got a real fondness for long-legged blondes. Always treat them special."

He was tiresome, Grace thought as he breathed one more beer into her face. But she had handled worse. "I appreciate that, but I'm going to finish up my shift and go home."

"Your place is fine with me."

"Mister—"

"Bob. You just call me Bob, baby."

She had to yank to get free. "Mister, I'm just not interested."

Of course she was, he thought, sending her a smile he knew was dazzling. He'd paid two grand to get his teeth bonded, hadn't he? "The hard-to-get routine always turns me on."

Grace decided he wasn't worth even a single disgusted sigh. "We're closing in fifteen; you're going to need to settle your tab."

"Okay, okay, don't get bitchy." He smiled widely and pulled out a money clip thick with bills. He always salted it with a couple of twenties on the outside, then filled it with singles. "You figure what I owe, then we'll . . . negotiate your tip."

Sometimes, Grace decided, it was best to keep your mouth firmly shut. What wanted to come out was vicious enough to get her fired. So she walked away and took her empties to the bar.

"He giving you trouble, Grace?"

She smiled weakly at Steve. It was just the two of them working now.

The other waitress had clocked out at midnight, claiming a migraine. Since she'd been pale as a ghost, Grace had shooed her out and agreed to cover.

"He's just another of those gifts to womankind. Nothing to worry about."

"If he's not gone by closing, I'll wait until you're locked in your car and headed home."

She made a noncommittal humming noise. She hadn't mentioned her lack of transportation because she knew Steve would insist on driving her home. He lived twenty minutes away, in the opposite direction. And had a pregnant wife waiting for him.

She cashed out tables, cleared them, and noted with relief that her problem customer finally rose to leave. He paid his $18.83 bar bill with cash, leaving $20 on the table. Though he'd managed to monopolize most of her time and attention for the past three hours, Grace was too tired to be annoyed at the pitiful tip.

It didn't take long for the pub to empty. The crowd had been mostly college students, out for a couple of beers and conversation on a weekday night. By her calculations they'd turned about ten tables no more than twice since her shift had started at seven. Her tips for the evening weren't going to make much of a dent in the new car she would have to buy.

It was so quiet, they both jumped like rabbits when the phone rang. Even while Grace laughed at their reaction, the blood drained out of Steve's face. "Mollie," was all he said as he leaped on the phone. He answered it with a stuttering, "Is it time?"

Grace stepped forward, wondering if she was strong enough to catch him if he keeled over. When he began nodding rapidly, she felt her smile spread wide.

"Okay. You—you call the doctor, right? Everything's ready to go. How far apart . . . Oh, God, oh, God, I'm on my way. Don't move. Don't do anything. Don't worry."

He dropped the phone off the hook, then froze. "She's—Mollie—my wife—"

"Yes, I know who Mollie is—we went to school together from kindergarten on." Grace laughed. Then because he looked so dear, and so terrified, she cupped his face in her hands and kissed him. "Go. But you drive careful. Babies take their time coming. They'll wait for you."

"We're having a baby," he said slowly, as if testing each word. "Me and Mollie."

"I know. And it's just wonderful. You tell her I'm going to come see her, and the baby. Of course, if you just stand there like somebody glued your feet to the floor, I guess she'll have to drive herself to the hospital."

"God! I have to go." He knocked over a chair on his way to the door. "Keys, where are the keys?"

"Your car keys are in your pocket. Bar keys are behind the bar. I'll lock up, Daddy."

He stopped, tossed one huge, electrifying grin over his shoulder. "Wow!" And was gone.

Grace was still chuckling as she picked up the chair and replaced it upside down on the table.

She thought of the night when she had gone into labor with Aubrey. Oh, she'd been so afraid, so excited. She had indeed driven herself to the hospital. There'd been no husband there to panic with her. There'd been no one to sit with her, to tell her to breathe, to hold her hand.

When the pain and aloneness had been at its worst, she weakened and let the nurse call her mother. Of course her mother came, and stayed with her, and saw Aubrey into the world. They cried together, and laughed together, and it had made it all right again.

Her father hadn't come. Not then, not later. Her mother had made excuses, tried to smooth it over, but Grace had understood she was not to be forgiven. Others had come, Julie and her parents, friends and neighbors.

Ethan and Professor Quinn.

They'd brought her flowers, pink and white daisies and rosebuds. She had pressed one of each in Aubrey's baby book.

It made her smile to remember, so when the door behind her opened, she turned with a chuckle. "Steve, if you don't get going, she'll . . ." Grace trailed off, experiencing more annoyance than fear when she saw the man step inside. "We're closed," she said firmly.

"I know, honey pie. I figured you'd find a way to hang back and wait for me."

"I'm not waiting for you." Why the hell hadn't she locked the door behind Steve? "I said we're closed. You'll have to leave."

"You want to play it that way, fine." He sauntered over, leaned on the bar. He'd been working out regularly for months now and knew the stance showed off his well-toned muscles. "Why don't you fix us both a drink? And we'll talk about that tip."

Her patience dried up. "You already gave me a tip, now I'll give you one. If you're not out that door in ten seconds, I'm calling the cops. Instead of spending the night on your big hotel bed, you'll spend it in a cell."

"I got something else in mind." He grabbed her, shoved her back against the bar, and ground himself against her. "See? You had it in mind, too. I saw the way you've been eyeing me. I've been waiting all night for some action."

She couldn't get her knee up to ram it against what he was so proudly pushing against her. She couldn't get her hands free to shove or scratch. Panic started as a tickle in her throat, then spread like a hot flood when he shot a hand under her skirt.

She was preparing to bite, scream, and spit when he was suddenly airborne. All she could do was stay pressed against the bar and stare at Ethan.

"You all right?"

He said it so quietly that her head bobbed up and down in automatic response. But his eyes weren't quiet. There was rage in them, so primal and primitive that she shuddered.

"Go on out and wait in the truck."

"I—he—" Then she squealed. It would embarrass her to remember it later, but it was the only sound that came out of her tight throat when the man rushed at Ethan like a battering ram, head lowered, fists clenched.

She watched, staggered as Ethan simply pivoted, jabbed once, twice, and flicked the man off like a fly. Then he bent, grabbed the man by the shirtfront, and hauled him up on his rubbery legs.

"You don't want to be here." His voice was steel with dangerously sharp edges. "Because if I see you here after the next two minutes, I'm going to kill you. And unless you got family or close personal friends, nobody's going to give a damn."

He tossed him away, with what seemed to Grace no more than a twist of the wrist, and the man crashed into a table. Then Ethan turned his back as if the guy didn't exist. But none of the stony fury had faded from his face when he looked at Grace.

"I told you to go wait in the truck."

"I have to— I need to—" She pressed a hand between her breasts and pushed up as if to shove the words clear. Neither of them looked as the man scrambled up and stumbled out the door. "I have to lock up. Shiney—"

"Shiney can go to hell." Since it didn't appear that she was going to move, Ethan grabbed her hand and hauled her to the door. "He ought to be horsewhipped for letting a lone woman lock up this place at night."

"Steve—he—"

"I saw that sonofabitch go flying out of here like a bomb was ticking." Ethan intended to have a nice long talk with Steve as well. Soon, he promised himself grimly as he pushed Grace into the truck.

"Mollie—she called. She's in labor. I told him to go."

"You would. Damn idiot woman."

The statement, delivered with such bubbling fury, stopped the trembling that had just begun, cut off the babbling gratitude she'd been about to express. He'd saved her, was all she'd been able to think, like a knight in a fairy tale. But the thin, romantic mist that had been shimmering over her still-reeling brain evaporated.

"I'm certainly not an idiot."

"You sure as hell are." He whipped the truck out of the lot, spitting gravel and knocking Grace back against her seat. His rare but formidable temper was in full swing, and there was no stopping it until it had blown itself out.

"That man was the idiot," she shot back. "I was just doing my job."

"Doing your job damn near got you raped. The son of a bitch had his hand under your skirt."

She could still feel it, the way it had groped at her. Nausea bubbled up to her throat and was ruthlessly swallowed down. "I'm aware of that. Things like that don't happen at Shiney's."

"It just did happen at Shiney's."

"It doesn't draw that kind of clientele usually. He wasn't local. He was—"

"He was there." Ethan swung into her drive, hit the brakes, then shut the engine off with a hard flick of the wrist. "And so were you. Mopping up some bar in the middle of the goddamn night, by yourself. And what were you going to do when you were done? Walk almost two damn miles?"

"I could have gotten a ride, except—"

"Except you're too stiff-necked to ask for one," he finished. "You'd rather limp home in those mile-high heels than ask a favor."

She had sneakers in her bag, but decided it wouldn't help to mention it. Her bag, she remembered, which was back at the unlocked pub. Now she would have to go back first thing in the morning, get her things, and lock up before the boss checked.

"Well, thank you very much for your opinion of my failings, and the lecture. And the damn ride home." She shoved at the door, only to have Ethan grab her arm and yank her back.

"Where the hell do you think you're going?"

"I'm going home. I'm going to soak my stiff-neck and my idiot-brain and go to bed."

"I haven't finished."

"*I've* finished." She jerked free and jumped out. If it hadn't been for the blasted heels, she might have made it. But he was out the opposite door and blocking her way before she'd taken three strides. "I have nothing more to say." Her voice was cold and dismissive. Her chin was high.

"Good. You can just listen. If you won't quit at the pub—which is just what you should do—you're going to take some basic precautions. Reliable transportation comes first."

"Don't you tell me what I have to do."

"Shut up."

She did, but only because she was stunned speechless. She'd never, in all the years she'd known him, seen Ethan like this. In the moonlight she could see that the fury in his eyes hadn't dimmed a bit. His face was like stone, the shadows flittering over it making it seem harsh, even dangerous.

"We'll see that you get a car you can trust," he continued, in that same edgy tone. "And you won't be closing on your own again. When you finish your shift, I want somebody walking you out to your car and waiting until you lock it and drive off."

"That's just ridiculous."

He stepped forward. Though he didn't touch her, didn't lift a hand, she backed up a pace. Her heart began to pound too fast and too loud in her head.

"What's ridiculous is you thinking you can handle every damn thing by yourself. And I'm tired of it."

She sputtered, hating herself. "*You're* tired of it?"

"Yeah, and it's going to stop. I can't do much about your working yourself half to death, but I can do something about the rest. You don't make arrangements at the pub to see you're safe, I will. You're going to stop asking for trouble."

"Asking for it?" Outrage gushed through her in such a boiling wave, she was surprised that the top of her head didn't simply blow off. "I wasn't *asking* for anything. That bastard wouldn't take no for an answer, no matter how many times I said it."

"That's just what I'm talking about."

"You don't know what you're talking about," she said in a furious whisper. "I handled him, and I would have kept handling him if—"

"How?" There was red around the edges of his vision. He could still see the way she'd been pressed up against the bar, her eyes wide and frightened. Her face had been ghost-pale, her eyes huge and sheened like glass. If he hadn't come in . . .

And because the thought of what could have been scraped raw at the center of his brain, his already slippery control shattered.

"Just how?" he demanded, in one quick move yanking her hard against him. "Go ahead, show me."

She twisted, shoved. And her pulse began to race. "Stop it."

"You think telling him to stop once he's got your scent's going to make a difference?" Lemons and fear. "Once he feels the way you fit?" Subtle curves and long lines. "He knew there was no one to stop him, that he could do anything he wanted."

Everything inside her was in a mindless rush—her heart, her blood, her head. "I wouldn't—I would have stopped him."

"Stop me."

He meant it. A part of him wanted desperately for her to stop him, to do or say something that would hold the wildness in check. But his mouth was on hers, rough and needy, swallowing her gasps, inciting more and reveling in her fast, hard trembles.

When she moaned, when her lips yielded, parted, answered his, he lost his mind.

He dragged her onto the grass, rolled with her, atop her. The thick bolt he'd kept locked on his desires exploded open, and what poured out was reckless greed and primal lust. He ravaged her mouth with the single-minded hunger of a starving wolf.

Swamped with needs so long buried, she arched against him, straining center to center, core to core. Her system stuttered with shocked pleasure, then roared into full raging life. Pumping heat, strangled moans, quivering delights.

This was not the Ethan she knew, or the one she'd dreamed would finally touch her. There was no gentleness, no care, but she gave herself to him, thrilled at the sensation of being swept away.

She wrapped long limbs around him to bind him closer, let her fingers dive into his hair, grip there. And shivered with the dark delight of knowing he was stronger.

He feasted on her mouth, her throat, while he tugged at the low, snug bodice. He was desperate for flesh, the feel of it, the taste of it. Her flesh, her flavor.

Her breast was small and firm, the skin smooth as satin against his wide, hard palm. Her heart jackhammered under it.

She whimpered, stunned at the sensation of that rough hand cupping her, kneading her, churning an echoing tug between her legs, where muscles had gone liquid and lax.

And sighed his name.

She might have shot him. The sound of her voice, the hitch of her breath, the shivers on her skin, slapped him back cold and hard.

He rolled away, onto his back, and struggled to find his breath, his sanity. His decency. They were in her front yard, for God's sake. Her baby was sleeping inside the house. He'd nearly, very nearly done worse than the man in the pub. He'd very nearly betrayed trust, friendship, and vulnerability.

This beast inside of him was precisely the reason he'd sworn never to touch her. Now by loosing it, he'd broken his vow and ruined everything.

"I'm sorry." A pitiful phrase, he thought, but he didn't have any other words. "God, Grace, I'm sorry."

Her blood was still flowing hot, and that wonderful, terrifying need aroused to screaming. She shifted, reached out to touch his face. "Ethan—"

"There's no excuse," he said quickly, sitting up so she wasn't touching him—tempting him. "I lost my temper and I stopped thinking straight."

"Lost your temper." She stayed where she was, sprawled on the grass that now seemed too cold, her face lifted to the moon that now shone too bright. "So you were just mad," she said dully.

"I was mad, but that's no excuse for hurting you."

"You didn't hurt me." She could still feel his hands on her, the rough, insistent press of them. But the sensation then, the sensation now, wasn't one of pain.

He thought he could handle it now—looking at her, touching her. She would need it, he imagined. He couldn't have lived with himself if she was afraid of him. "The last thing I want to do is hurt you." As gentle as a doting parent, he tidied her clothes. When she didn't cringe, he stroked a hand over her tousled hair. "I only want what's best for you."

She didn't cringe, but she did, suddenly and sharply, slap his hand aside. "Don't treat me like a child. A few minutes ago you were treating me like a woman easy enough."

There'd been nothing easy about it, he thought grimly. "And I was wrong."

"Then we were both wrong." She sat up, brushing briskly at her clothes. "It wasn't one-sided, Ethan. You know that. I didn't try to make you stop because I didn't want you to stop. That was your idea."

He was baffled, and abruptly nervous. "For Christ's sake, Grace, we were rolling around in your front yard."

"That's not what stopped you."

With a quiet sigh, she brought her knees up, wrapped her arms around them. The gesture, so purely innocent, contrasted sharply with the tiny skirt and fishnet stockings and made his stomach muscles tie themselves into hot, slippery knots again.

"You'd have stopped anyway, wherever it happened. Maybe because you remembered it was me, but it's harder for me to think that you don't want me now. So you're going to have to tell me you don't if you want things to go back to the way they were before."

"They belong back where they were before."

"That's not an answer, Ethan. I'm sorry to press you about it, but I think I deserve one." It was hard, brutal, for her to ask, but the taste of him still lingered on her lips. "If you don't think about me that way, and this was just temper pushing you to teach me a lesson, then you have to say so, straight out."

"It was temper."

Accepting the fresh bruise to her heart, she nodded. "Well, then, it worked."

"That doesn't make it right. What I just did makes me too close to that bastard in the bar tonight."

"I didn't want him to touch me." She drew in a long breath, held it, let it out slowly. But he didn't speak. Didn't speak, she thought, but moved back. He might not have shifted an inch, but he'd moved away from her in the way that counted most.

"I'm grateful to you for being there tonight." She started to rise, but he was on his feet ahead of her, offering a hand. She took it, determined not to embarrass either of them any further. "I was afraid, and I don't know if I could have handled it on my own. You're a good friend, Ethan, and I appreciate you wanting to help."

He slid his hands into his pockets, where they would be safe. "I talked to Dave about another car. He's got a line on a couple decent used ones."

Since screaming would accomplish nothing, she had to laugh. "You don't waste any time. All right, I'll talk to him about it tomorrow." She glanced toward the house where the front porch light gleamed. "Do you want to come in? I could put some ice on your knuckles."

"He had a jaw like a pillow. They're fine. You need to get to bed."

"Yeah." Alone, she thought, to toss and turn. And wish. "I'm going to come by on Saturday for a couple hours. Just to spruce things up before Cam and Anna get home."

"That'd be nice. We'd appreciate it."

"Well, good night." She turned, walked across the grass toward the house.

He waited. He told himself he just wanted to see her safely inside before he left. But he knew it was a lie, that it was cowardice. He'd needed the distance before he could finish asnwering her question.

"Grace?"

She closed her eyes briefly. All she wanted now was to get inside, crawl into bed, and indulge in a good, long cry. She hadn't let herself have a serious jag in years. But she turned back, made her lips curve. "Yes?"

"I think about you that way." He saw, even with the distance, the way her eyes widened, darkened, the way her pretty smile slid away so that she only stared. "I don't want to. I tell myself not to. But I think about you that way. Now go on inside," he told her gently.

"Ethan—"

"Go on. It's late."

She managed to turn the knob, to step inside, shut the door behind her. But she turned quickly to the window to watch him get back in his truck and drive away.

It was late, she thought with a shiver that she recognized as hope. But maybe it wasn't too late.

SEVEN

"I appreciate you helping me out, Mama."

"Helping you out?" Carol Monroe tsk-tsked the thought away as she knelt to tie the laces on Aubrey's pink sneaker. "Taking this cube of sugar home with me for the afternoon is pure pleasure." She gave Aubrey a chuck under the chin. "We're going to have us a time, aren't we, honey?"

Aubrey grinned, knowing her ground. "Toys! We got toys, Gramma. Dollbabies."

"You bet we do. And I might just have a surprise for you when we get there."

Aubrey's eyes grew huge and bright. She sucked in her breath to let out a sharp squeal of delight as she jumped down from the chair to race through the house in her own version of a victory dance.

"Oh, Mama, not another doll. You spoil her."

"Can't," Carol said firmly, giving her knee a push to help herself straighten. "Besides, it's my privilege as a granny."

Since Aubrey was occupied running and shouting, Carol took a moment to study her daughter. Not sleeping enough, as usual, she decided, noting the shadows smudged under Grace's eyes. Not eating enough to feed a bird either, though she'd brought over Grace's favorite homemade peanut butter cookies to try to put some flesh on her girl's delicate bones.

A child not yet twenty-three ought to paint her face a little, put some curl in her hair, and go out kicking up her heels a night or two instead of working herself into the ground.

Since Carol had said as much a dozen times or more and had been ignored on the subject a dozen times or more, she tried a different tack. "You got to quit that night work, Gracie. It doesn't agree with you."

"I'm fine."

"Good hard work's necessary for living, and admirable, but a person's got to mix in some pleasure and fun or they dry right up."

Because she was weary of hearing the same song, however the notes might vary, Grace turned and scrubbed at her already spotless kitchen counter. "I like working at the pub. It gives me a chance to see people, talk to them." Even if it was just to ask them if they'd like another round. "The pay's good."

"If you're low on cash—"

"I'm fine." Grace set her teeth. She'd have suffered the torments of hell before she would admit that her budget was strained to breaking—and that solving her transportation problems was going to mean robbing Peter to pay Paul for the next several months. "The extra money comes in handy, and I'm good at waitressing."

"I know you are. You could work down at the cafe, have day hours."

Patiently, Grace rinsed out her dishcloth and hung it over the divider of the double sink to dry. "Mama, you know that isn't possible. Daddy doesn't want me working for him."

"He never said that. Besides, you help out with picking crabs when we're shorthanded."

"I help you out," Grace specified as she turned. "And I'm happy to do it when I can. But we both know I can't work at the cafe."

Her daughter was as stubborn as two mules pulling in opposite directions, Carol thought. It was what made her her father's daughter. "You know you could soften him up if you tried."

"I don't want to soften him up. He made it plain how he feels about me. Let it be, Mama," she murmured when she saw her mother preparing to protest. "I don't want to argue with you, and I don't want to put you in the position ever again of having to defend one of us against the other. It's not right."

Carol threw up her hands. She loved them both, husband and daughter. But she'd be damned if she could understand them. "No one can talk to either of you once you get that look on your face. Don't know why I waste breath trying."

Grace smiled. "Me, either." Grace stepped close, bent down and kissed her mother's cheek. Carol was six inches shorter than Grace's five feet eight. "Thanks, Mama."

Carol softened, as she always did, and combed a hand through her short, curly hair. It had once been as blond by nature as her daughter's and granddaughter's. But nature being what it was, she now gave it a quiet boost with Miss Clairol.

Her cheeks were round and rosy, her skin surprisingly smooth, given her love of the sun. But then, she didn't neglect it. There wasn't a single night she climbed into bed without carefully applying a layer of Oil of Olay.

Being female wasn't just an act of fate, in Carol Monroe's mind. It was a duty. She prided herself that though she was coming uncomfortably close to her forty-fifth birthday, she still managed to resemble the china doll her husband had once called her.

They'd been courting then, and he'd taken some trouble to be poetic.

He usually forgot such things these days.

But he was a good man, she thought. A good provider, a faithful husband, and a fair man in business. His problem, she knew, was a soft heart too easily bruised. Grace had bruised it badly simply by not being the perfect daughter he'd expected her to be.

These thoughts came and went as she helped Grace gather up what Aubrey would need for an afternoon visit. Seemed to her children needed so much more these days. Time was, she would stick Grace on her hip, toss a few diapers into a bag, and off they'd go.

Now her baby was grown, with a baby of her own. Grace was a good mother, Carol thought, smiling a bit as Aubrey and Grace selected just which stuffed animal should have the privilege of a visit to Grandma's. The fact was, Carol had to admit, Grace was better at the job than she had been herself. The girl listened, weighed, considered. And maybe that was best. She herself had simply done, decided, demanded. Grace was so biddable as a child, she'd never thought twice about what unspoken needs had lived inside her.

And the guilt stayed with her because she had known of Grace's dream to study dance. Instead of taking it seriously, Carol passed it off as childish nonsense. She hadn't helped her baby there, hadn't encouraged, hadn't believed.

The ballet lessons had simply been a natural activity for a girl child as far as Carol had been concerned. If she'd had a son, she'd have seen to it that he played in the Little League. It was . . . just the way things were done, she thought now. Girls had tutus and boys had ball gloves. Why did it have to be more complicated than that?

But Grace had been more complicated, Carol admitted. And she hadn't seen it. Or hadn't wanted to see.

When Grace came to her at eighteen and told her she had her summer job money saved, that she wanted to go to New York to study dance, and begged for help with the expenses, she'd told her not to be foolish.

Young girls just out of high school didn't go haring off to New York City, of all places on God's Earth, on their own. Dreams of ballerinas were supposed to slide into dreams of brides and wedding gowns.

But Grace had been dead set on following her dream and had gone to her father and asked that the money they'd put aside for her college fund be used to pay tuition to a dance school in New York.

Pete had refused, of course. Maybe he'd been a little harsh about it, but he'd meant it for the best. He was just being sensible, just looking out for his little girl. And Carol had agreed wholeheartedly. At the time.

But then Carol watched as her daughter had worked tirelessly, saved every penny, month after month. She'd been bound and determined to go, and seeing it, Carol had tried to nudge her husband into letting her.

He hadn't budged, and neither had Grace.

She was barely nineteen when that slick-talking Jack Casey came around. And that was that.

She couldn't regret it, not when Aubrey had come from it. But she could regret that the pregnancy, the hasty marriage and hastier divorce, had driven a thicker wedge between father and daughter.

But what was couldn't be changed, she told herself and took Aubrey's hand to lead her to the car. "You're sure this car Dave has for you runs all right?"

"Dave says it does."

"Well, he ought to know." He was a good mechanic, Carol thought, even if he had been the one to hire Jack Casey. "You know you could borrow mine for a while—give yourself more chance to shop around."

"This one will be fine." She hadn't even laid eyes on the secondhand sedan Dave had picked out for her. "We're going to do the paperwork on Monday, then I'll have wheels again."

After securing Aubrey in the car seat, Grace slipped in while her mother took the wheel.

"Go, go, go! Go, fast, Gramma," Aubrey demanded. Carol flushed when Grace cocked a brow.

"You've been speeding again, haven't you?"

"I know these roads like the back of my hand, and I haven't had a single ticket in my life."

"Because the cops can't catch you." With a laugh, Grace strapped herself in.

"When do the newlyweds get home?" Not only did Carol want to know, she preferred to have the conversation veer away from her notoriously heavy foot.

"I think they're due in about eight tonight. I just want to give the house a buff, maybe put something on for dinner in case they're hungry when they get here."

"I imagine Cam's wife'll appreciate it. What a beautiful bride she was. I've never seen lovelier. Where she managed to get that dress when the boy gave her so little time to plan a wedding, I don't know."

"Seth said she went to D.C. for it, and the veil was her grandmother's."

"That's fine. I have my wedding veil put aside. I always imagined how pretty it would look on you on your wedding day." She stopped, and could cheerfully have bitten her tongue.

"It would have looked a little out of place in the county courthouse."

Carol sighed as she pulled into the Quinns' driveway. "Well, you'll wear it next time."

"I'll never get married again. I'm not good at it." While her mother gaped at the statement, Grace climbed quickly out of the car, then leaned in the window and kissed Aubrey soundly. "You be a good girl, you hear? And don't let Grandma feed you too much candy."

"Gramma has chocolate."

"Don't I know it! Bye, baby. Bye, Mama. Thanks."

"Grace . . ." What could she say? "You, ah, you just call when you're done here and I'll come by and pick you up."

"We'll see. Don't let her run you ragged," Grace added and hurried up the steps.

She knew she'd timed it well. Everyone would be at the boatyard working. She was determined not to feel awkward about what had happened the night before last. But she did—she felt miserably awkward and she wanted time to settle before she had to face Ethan again.

This was a home that always felt warm and welcoming. Caring for it soothed her. Because she knew that a large part of her motivation for working on it that afternoon was self-serving, she put more effort into the job. The results would be the same, wouldn't they, she thought guiltily as she ran the old buffer over the hardwood floors to make the wax gleam. Anna would come home to a spotless house, with the scents of fresh flowers, polish, and potpourri perfuming the air.

A woman shouldn't have to come home from her honeymoon to dust and clutter. And God knew the Quinn men generated plenty of both.

She was needed here, damn it. All she was doing was proving it.

She spent extra time in the master bedroom, fussing with the flowers she'd begged off Irene, then changing the position of the vase half a dozen times before she cursed herself. Anna would put them where she wanted them to be anyway, she reminded herself. And would probably change everything else while she was at it. More than likely, she would want new everything, Grace decided as she pressed the curtains she'd washed until not the tiniest wrinkle showed in the thin summer sheers.

Anna was city-bred and probably wouldn't care for the worn furniture and country touches. Before you knew it, she'd have things decked out in leather and glass, and all Dr. Quinn's pretty things would be packed up in some box in the attic and replaced with pieces of sculpture nobody could understand.

Her jaw tightened as she rehung the curtains, gave them a quick fluff.

Cover the lovely old floors with some fancy wall-to-wall carpet and paint the walls some hot color that made the eyes sting. Resentment bubbled as she marched into the bathroom to put a bunch of early rosebuds in a shallow bowl.

Anybody with any sense could see the place only needed a little care, a bit more color here and there. If she had any say in it . . .

She stopped herself, realizing that her fists were clenched, and her face, reflected in the mirror over the sink, was bright with fury. "Oh, Grace, what is *wrong* with you?" She shook her head, nearly laughed at herself. "In the first place you don't have any say, and in the second you don't know that she's going to change a single thing."

It was just that she could, Grace admitted. And once you changed one thing, nothing was quite the same again.

Isn't that what had happened between her and Ethan? Something had changed, and now she was both afraid and hopeful that things wouldn't be quite the same.

He thought of her, she mused and sighed at her own reflection. And what did he think? She wasn't a beauty, and she'd never filled out enough to be sexy. Now and then, she knew, she caught a man's eye, but she never held it.

She wasn't smart or particularly clever, had neither stimulating conversation nor flirtatious ways. Jack had once told her she had stability. And he'd convinced them both, for a while, that that was what he wanted. But stability wasn't the sort of trait that attracted a man.

Maybe if her cheekbones were higher or her dimples deeper. Or if her lashes were thicker and darker. Maybe if that flirty curl hadn't skipped a generation and left her hair straight as a pin.

What did Ethan think when he looked at her? She wished she had the courage to ask him.

She looked—and saw the ordinary.

When she had danced she hadn't felt ordinary. She'd felt beautiful and special and deserving of her name. Dreamily, she dipped into a plié, settling crotch on heels, then lifting again. She'd have sworn her body sighed in pleasure. Indulging herself, she flowed into an old, well-remembered movement, ending on a slow pirouette.

"Ethan!" She squeaked it out, color flooding her cheeks when she saw him in the doorway.

"I didn't mean to startle you, but I didn't want to interrupt."

"Oh, well." Mortified, she snatched up her cleaning rag, twisted it in her hands. "I was just . . . finishing up in here."

"You always were a pretty dancer." He'd promised himself he would put things back the way they'd been between them, so he smiled at her as he would a friend. "You always dance around the bathroom after you clean it?"

"Doesn't everyone?" She did her best to answer his smile, but the heat continued to sting her cheeks. "I thought I'd be done before y'all got back. I guess the floors took longer than I figured on."

"They look nice. Foolish already had a slide. Surprised you didn't hear it."

"I was daydreaming. I thought I'd—" Then she managed to clear her brain and get a good look at him. He was filthy, covered with sweat and grime and God knew what. "You're not thinking of taking a shower in here?"

Ethan lifted a brow. "It crossed my mind."

"No, you can't."

He shifted back because she'd taken a step forward. He had a good idea just how he smelled at the moment. That was reason enough to keep his distance, but worse, she looked so fresh and pretty. He'd taken a solemn vow not to touch her again, and he meant to keep it.

"Why?"

"Because I don't have time to clean it up again after you, or the bath downstairs, either. I still have to fry the chicken. I thought I'd make that and a bowl of potato salad so you wouldn't have to worry about heating anything up when Cam and Anna get home. I have to deal with the kitchen after, so I just don't have time, Ethan."

"I've been known to mop up a bathroom after I've used one."

"It's not the same. You just can't use it."

Flustered, he took off his cap, dragged a hand through his hair. "Well, then, that's a problem because we've got three men here who need to scrape off a few layers of dirt."

"There's a bay right outside your door."

"But—"

"Here." She opened the cabinet under the sink for a fresh bar of soap. Damned if she'd have them use the pretty guest soaps she'd set out in a dish. "I'll get you towels and some fresh clothes."

"But—"

"Go on now, Ethan, and tell the others what I said." She shoved the soap into his hand. "You're already scattering dust everywhere."

He scowled at the soap, then at her. "You'd think the Royal Family was dropping by for a visit. Damn it, Grace, I'm not stripping down to my skin and jumping off the dock."

"Oh, like you've never done it before."

"Not with a female around."

"I've seen naked men a time or two, and I'm going to be too busy to take Polaroids of you and your brothers. Ethan, I've just spent the best part of my day getting this house to shine. You're not spreading your dirt around."

Disgusted, because in his experience arguing with a woman's made-up mind was as painful and fruitless as banging your head against a brick wall, he shoved the soap in his pocket. "I'll get the damn towels."

"No, you won't. Your hands are filthy. I'll bring them out."

Muttering to himself, he went downstairs. Phillip's reaction to the bathing arrangements was a shrug. Seth's was pure glee. He darted outside, calling for the dogs to follow, and sent shoes, socks, shirt, scattering as he raced for the dock.

"He'll probably never want to take a regular bath again," Phillip commented. He sat on the dock to remove his shoes.

Ethan remained standing. He wasn't taking off a blessed thing until Grace delivered the towels and clothes and was back in the house. "What are you doing?" he demanded when Phillip pulled his sweat-stained T-shirt over his head.

"I'm taking off my shirt."

"Well, put it back on. Grace is coming out."

Phillip glanced up, saw that his brother was perfectly serious, and laughed. "Get a grip, Ethan. Even the sight of my amazing and manly chest isn't likely to send her over the edge."

To prove it, he rose and shot Grace a grin as she crossed the lawn. "I heard something about fried chicken," he called out.

"I'm about to get to it." When she reached the dock, she set the towels and clean clothes in neat piles. Then she straightened, smiling out to where Seth and the dogs splashed. She imagined they'd scared every bird and fish away for two miles. "This arrangement suits them just fine."

"Why don't you take a dip with us?" Phillip suggested and swore he heard Ethan's jaw crack. "You can scrub my back."

She laughed and picked up the clothes that had already been discarded. "It's been a while since I've gone skinny-dipping, and as appealing as it sounds, I've got too much to do to play right now. You give me the rest of your clothes, I'll get them washed before I go."

"Appreciate it." But when Phillip reached for his belt buckle, Ethan jabbed an elbow into his ribs.

"You can wash them later if you're set on it. Go in the house."

"He's shy." Phillip wiggled his brows. "I'm not."

Grace only laughed again, but she headed back to the house to give them privacy.

"You shouldn't tease her that way," Ethan muttered.

"I've been teasing her that way for years." Phillip peeled himself out of his work-stained jeans, delighted to be rid of them.

"Now it's different."

"Why?" Phillip started to slip out of his silk boxers, then caught the look in Ethan's eye. "Oh. Well, well. Why didn't you say so?"

"I got nothing to say." Because Grace was in the house now and he couldn't imagine her pressing her nose to the window, he pulled off his shirt.

"It's her voice that always got me."

"Huh?"

"That throaty sound," Phillip continued, pleased to be able to rile Ethan about something. "Low and smooth and sexy."

Gritting his teeth, Ethan pried off his work boots. "Maybe you shouldn't listen so hard."

"What can I do? Can I help it if I have perfect hearing? Perfect eyesight, too," he added, judging the distance between them. "And as far as I can see, there's nothing wrong with the rest of her either. Her mouth's particularly attractive. Full, shapely, unpainted. Looks tasty to me."

Ethan took two slow breaths as he tugged off his jeans. "Are you trying to irritate me?"

"I'm giving it my best shot."

Ethan stood, gauged his man. "You want to go in headfirst, or feetfirst?"

Pleased, Phillip grinned. "I was going to ask you the same thing."

Both waited a beat, then charged, grappled. And with Seth's rousing cheers ringing, wrestled each other into the water.

Oh, my, Grace thought with her nose pressed up against the window. *Oh, my.* If she'd ever seen two more impressive examples of the male form, she couldn't say when. She'd only intended to sneak a quick glance. Really. Just one innocent little peek. But then Ethan had peeled off his shirt and . . .

Well, damn it, she wasn't a saint. And what harm did it do to anyone just to look?

He was just so beautiful, inside and out. And God, if she could get her hands on him again for just five minutes, she thought she could die a happy woman. Maybe she could, since he wasn't indifferent—the way she'd always assumed he was.

There'd been nothing indifferent in the way his mouth had crushed down on hers, or the way his hands had rushed over her.

Stop, she ordered herself and stepped back from the window. The only thing she was going to accomplish this way was to get herself all worked up. She knew how to channel her more intimate needs, and that was to work until they passed away again.

But if her mind wasn't completely on her chicken, who could blame her?

She had the potatoes cooling for the salad and the chicken frying when Phillip came back in. Gone was the image of the sweaty laborer. In its place was the smooth, the gilded, the casually sophisticated. He winked at her. "Smells like heaven in here."

"I made extra so you can have it for lunch tomorrow. You just put those clothes in the laundry room, and I'll see to them in a minute."

"I don't know what we'd do without you around here."

She bit her lip and hoped everyone felt the same. "Is Ethan still in the water?"

"No, he and Seth are doing something to the boat." Phillip went to the refrigerator and took out a bottle of wine. "Where's Aubrey today?"

"With my mother. In fact she just called and wants to keep her a little longer. I guess one of these days I'm going to have to give in and let her stay overnight." She glanced down blankly at the glass of cool golden wine he offered her. "Oh, thanks." What she knew about wine wouldn't fill a thimble, but she sipped because it was expected. Then her brows lifted. "This isn't anything like what they serve down at the pub."

"I wouldn't think so." He considered what they called the house white down at Shiney's one shaky step up from horse piss. "How are things going there?"

"Fine." She gave serious attention to her chicken, wondering if Ethan had mentioned the incident. Unlikely, she decided when Phillip didn't press. She relaxed again and let Phillip entertain her while she worked.

He was always full of stories, she mused. Of easy, even careless conversation. She knew he was smart and successful and had slipped into city living like a duck in water. But he never made her feel inadequate or silly. And in a cozy way, he made her feel just a little more feminine than she had before he'd come into the room.

That was why Grace's eyes were laughing and her mouth prettily curved when Ethan came in. Phillip sat, sipping wine while she put the finishing touches on the meal.

"Oh, you're making that up."

"I swear." Phillip held up a hand in oath and grinned as Ethan came in. "The client wants the goose to be the spokesperson, so we're writing dialogue. Goose Creek Jeans, fine feathers for everyday living."

"That's the silliest thing I ever heard."

"Hey." Phillip toasted her. "Watch them sell. I've got a few phone calls to make." He rose, deliberately rounding the table to kiss her and make Ethan seethe. "Thanks for feeding us, darling."

He strolled out, whistling.

"Can you imagine, making a living writing words for a goose." Amused, Grace shook her head as she tucked the bowl of potato salad into the refrigerator. "Everything's done, so you can eat when you're hungry. Your clothes are in the dryer. You don't want to leave them sitting in there after it's done or they'll be wrinkled."

She moved around, tidying the kitchen as she spoke. "I'd wait and fold them for you, but I'm running a bit behind."

"I'll drive you home."

"I'd appreciate it. I'm dealing with the car on Monday, but until then . . ." She lifted her shoulders and saw with one last glance that she had nothing left to do. Still, she eyed every nook and corner as she walked through the house to the front door.

"How are you getting to work?" Ethan demanded when they were in his truck.

"Julie's taking me. Shiney's taking me home himself." She cleared her throat. "When I explained what happened the other night he was upset. Not mad at me, but really upset it had happened. He was set to skin Steve, but under the circumstances—they had a boy, by the way. Eight and a half pounds. They're calling him Jeremy."

"I heard," was Ethan's only comment

Now she drew a bolstering breath. "About what happened, Ethan, I mean afterward—"

"I've got something to say about that." He'd worked it out carefully, word by word. "I shouldn't have been mad at you. You were scared and I spent more time yelling at you than making sure you were all right."

"I knew you weren't really mad at me. It was just—"

"I've got to finish this," he said, but waited until he'd turned into her driveway. "I had no business touching you that way. I'd promised myself I never would."

"I wanted you to."

Though the quiet words caused his stomach to clench, he shook his head. "It's not going to happen again. I've got reasons, Grace, good ones. You don't know, and you wouldn't understand."

"I can't understand if you don't tell me what they are."

He wasn't going to tell her what he'd done, or what had been done to him. And what he was afraid still lurked inside him ready to spring out if he didn't keep that cage locked. "They're my reasons." He shifted to look at her because it was only right to say what he had to say facing her. "I could have hurt you, and I nearly did. That's not going to happen again."

"I'm not afraid of you." She reached out to touch, to stroke his cheek, but he grabbed her hand and held her off.

"You're never going to have to be. You matter to me." He gave her hand a quick squeeze, then released it. "You always have."

"I'm not a child anymore, and I won't break if you touch me. I want you to touch me."

Full, shapely, unpainted lips. Phillip's words echoed in his head. And now Ethan knew, God help him, exactly how tasty they were. "I know you think you do, and that's why we're going to try to forget that the other night happened."

"I'm not going to forget it," she murmured, and the way she looked at him, her eyes soft and full of need, made his head swim.

"It's not going to happen again. So you stay clear of me for a while." Desperation tinged his voice as he leaned across and shoved open her door. "I mean it, Grace, you just stay clear of me for a while. I've got enough to worry about."

"All right, Ethan." She wouldn't beg. "If that's what you want."

"That's exactly what I want."

This time he didn't wait until she was in the house but backed out of the drive the minute she closed the truck's door.

For the first time in more years than he could count, he thought seriously about getting blind drunk.

EIGHT

Seth kept watch for them. His excuse for being in the front yard as the shadows grew long was the dogs. Not that it was an excuse, exactly, he thought. He was trying to teach Foolish not just to chase the battered, well-chewed tennis ball but to bring it back the way Simon did. The trouble was that Foolish would race back to you with the ball, then expect you to play tug-of-war for it.

Not that Seth minded. He had a supply of balls and sticks and an old hunk of rope that Ethan had given him. He could toss and tug as long as the dogs were willing to run. Which was, as far as he could tell, just about forever.

But while he played with the dogs, he kept his ears tuned for the sound of an approaching car.

He knew they were on their way home because Cam had called from the plane. Which was just about the coolest thing Seth could think of. He couldn't wait to tell Danny and Will how he'd talked to Cam while Cam had been flying over the Atlantic Ocean.

He'd already looked up Italy in the atlas and found Rome. Had traced his finger back and forth, back and forth across that wide ocean from Rome to the Chesapeake Bay, to the little smudge on Maryland's Eastern Shore that was St. Christopher's.

For a little while he'd been afraid they wouldn't come back. He imagined Cam calling and saying they'd decided to stay over there so he could race again.

He knew Cam had lived all over the place, racing boats and cars and motorcycles. Ray had told him all about it, and there was a thick scrapbook in the den that was filled with all kinds of newspaper and magazine pictures and articles about how many races Cam had won. And how many women he'd fooled around with.

And he knew that Cam had won this big-deal race in his hydrofoil—which Seth wished he could ride in just once—right before Ray had run into the telephone pole and died.

Phillip had finally tracked him down in Monte Carlo. Seth had found that place in the atlas, too, and it didn't look all that much bigger than St. Chris. But they had a palace there and fancy casinos and even a prince.

Cam had come home in time to see Ray die. Seth knew he hadn't planned to stay very long. But he had stayed. After they'd had sort of a fight, he'd told Seth he wasn't going anywhere. That they were stuck with each other and he was staying put.

Still, that was before he'd gotten married and everything, before he'd gone back to Italy. Before Seth had started to worry that both Cam and Anna would forget about him and the promises they'd made.

But they hadn't. They were coming back.

He didn't want them to know he was waiting for them or that he was excited that they would be home any minute. But he was. He couldn't understand why he was all pumped up about it. They'd only been gone a couple of weeks, and Cam was a pain in the ass most of the time anyway.

And once Anna was living there, everybody would say how he had to watch his language because there was a woman in the house.

A part of him worried that Anna would change things. Even though she was his caseworker, she might get tired of having a kid around. She had the power to send him away. More power now, he thought, because she was doing it with Cam all the time.

He reminded himself that she'd played it straight with him, from the minute she'd pulled him out of class and sat down with him in the school cafeteria to talk.

But working on a case and living in the same house with that case was different, wasn't it?

And maybe, just maybe, she'd played straight with him, she'd been nice to him, because she'd liked having Cam poke at her. She'd wanted to get married to him. Now that she was, she wouldn't have to be nice anymore. She could even write in one of her reports that he'd be better off somewhere else.

Well, he was going to watch, and he was going to see. He could still run if things got sticky. Though the idea of running made his stomach hurt in a way it had never done before.

He wanted to be here. He wanted to run in the yard, throwing sticks to the dogs. To crawl out of bed when it was still dark and eat breakfast with

Ethan and go out on the water crabbing. To work in the boatyard or go down to Danny and Will's.

To eat real food whenever he was hungry and sleep in a bed that didn't smell like somebody else's sweat.

Ray had promised him all of that, and though Seth had never trusted anyone, he'd trusted Ray. Maybe Ray had been his father, maybe he hadn't. But Seth knew he'd paid Gloria a lot of money. He thought of her as Gloria now and not as his mother. It helped to add more distance.

Now Ray was dead, but he'd made each of his sons promise to keep Seth in the house by the water. Seth figured they probably hadn't liked the idea, but they'd promised anyway. He'd discovered that the Quinns kept their word. It was a new and wonderful concept to him, a promise kept.

If they broke it now, he knew it would hurt more than anything had hurt him before.

So he waited, and when he heard the car—the not-quite-tamed roar of the Corvette—his stomach jittered with excitement and nerves.

Simon woofed twice in greeting, but Foolish set up a din of wild, half-terrified barking. When the sleek white car pulled into the drive, both dogs raced toward it, tails waving like flags. Seth stuck hands that had gone sweaty into his pockets and strolled over casually.

"Hi!" Anna shot him a brilliant smile.

Seth could see why Cam had gone for her, all right. He himself had sketched her face a number of times in secret. He liked to draw above all else. His fledgling artist's eye appreciated the sheer beauty of that face—the dark, almond-shaped eyes, the clear, pale-gold skin, the full mouth, and the exotic hint of cheekbones. Her hair was windblown, a dark, curling mass. Her wedding ring set glinted, diamonds and gold, as she stepped out of the car.

And caught him unprepared in a laughing, bone-crushing hug. "What a terrific welcome party!"

Though the embrace had surprised him into wanting to linger there, he wiggled free. "I was just out fooling with the dogs." He looked over at Cam, shrugged. "Hey."

"Hey, kid." Lean and dark, and just a little dangerous to the eye, Cam unfolded his length from the low-riding car. His grin was quicker than Ethan's, sharper than Phillip's. "Just in time to help me unload."

"Yeah, sure." Seth glanced up, noted the small mountain of luggage strapped to the roof of the car. "You didn't take all that crap with you."

"We picked up some Italian crap while we were there."

"I couldn't stop myself," Anna said with a laugh. "We had to buy another suitcase."

"Two," Cam corrected.

"One's just a tote—it doesn't count."

"Okay." Cam popped the trunk, pulled out a generous dark-green suitcase. "You carry the one that doesn't count."

"Putting your bride to work already?" Phillip crossed to the car, waded through the dogs. "I'll take that, Anna," he said and kissed her with an enthusiasm that had Seth rolling his eyes at Cam.

"Turn her loose, Phil," Ethan said mildly. "I'd hate for Cam to have to kill you before he even gets in the house. Welcome home," he added and smiled when Anna turned to give him as enthusiastic a kiss as Phillip had given her.

"It's good to be home."

⨳

The tote, it turned out, contained gifts, which Anna immediately began to dispense, along with stories of each one. Seth only stared down at the bright-blue-and-white soccer shirt she'd given him. No one had ever gone on a trip and brought him back a present. The fact was, if he thought about it, he could count the gifts he'd been given—something for nothing—on the fingers of one hand.

"Soccer's big over in Europe," Anna told him. "They call it football, but it's not like our football." She dug deeper, then pulled out an oversized book with a glossy cover. "And I thought you might like this. It's not as good as seeing the paintings. It really grabs you by the throat to see them in person, but you'll get the idea."

The book was filled with paintings, glorious colors and shapes that dazzled his eyes. An art book. She'd remembered that he liked to draw and had thought of him.

"It's cool." He muttered it because he couldn't trust his voice.

"She wanted to buy everyone shoes," Cam commented. "I had to stop her."

"So I only bought myself a half a dozen pair."

"I thought it was four."

She smiled. "Six. I snuck two by you. Phillip, I stumbled across Maglis. I could have wept."

"Armani?"

She sighed lustily. "Oh, yeah."

"Now I'm going to cry."

"You can sob over fashion later," Cam told them. "I'm starving."

"Grace was here." Seth wanted to try on his shirt right away but thought it would be too lame. "She cleaned everything—made us wash up in the Bay—and she fried chicken."

"Grace made fried chicken?"

"And potato salad."

"There's no place like home," Cam murmured and headed for the kitchen. Seth waited a few seconds, then followed.

"I guess I could eat another piece," he said casually.

"Get in line." Cam pulled the platter and bowl out of the fridge.

"Don't they give you stuff to eat on the plane?"

"That was then, this is now." Cam heaped a plate with food, then leaned back against the counter. The kid looked tanned and healthy, he noted. The eyes were still wary, but his face had lost that rabbit-about-to-run look. He wondered if it would surprise Seth as much as it had himself to know he'd missed the smart-mouthed brat. "So, how's it been going?"

"Okay. School's done, and I've been helping Ethan out on the boat a lot. Pays me slave's wages there and at the boatyard."

"Anna's going to want to know what you got on your report card."

"A's," Seth muttered around a mouthful of drumstick, and Cam choked. "All?"

"Yeah—so what?"

"She's going to love that. Want to make more points with her?"

Seth jerked a shoulder again, narrowing his eyes as he considered what he would be asked to do to please the woman of the house. "Maybe."

"Put the soccer shirt on. It took her damn near half an hour to pick out the right one. Major points if you wear it the same night she gives it to you."

"Yeah?" As easy as that? Seth thought and relaxed into a grin. "I guess I can give her a thrill."

⟨∞⟩

"He really liked his shirt," Anna said as she meticulously tucked away the contents of one suitcase. "And the book. I'm so glad we thought of the book."

"Yeah, he liked them." Cam figured the next day, even next year, was soon enough to unpack. Besides, he liked stretching out on the bed and watching her—watching his wife, he thought with an odd little thrill—fuss around the room.

"He didn't freeze up when I hugged him. That's a good sign. And his interaction with Ethan and Phillip is easier, more natural, than it was even a couple of weeks ago. He was anxious to see you again. He's feeling a little threatened by me. I change the dynamics around here just at the point where he was getting used to how things worked. So he's waiting, and he's watching for what'll happen next. But that's good. It means he considers this his home. I'm the intruder."

"Miz Spinelli?"

She turned her head, arched a brow. "That's Mrs. Quinn to you, buster."

"Why don't you turn off the social worker until Monday?"

"Can't." She slipped one of her new shoes out of its bag and nearly cooed at it in delight. "The social worker is very pleased with the status of this particular case. And Mrs. Quinn, the brand-new sister-in-law, is determined to win Seth's trust, and maybe even his affection."

She slipped the shoe back into the bag and wondered how long she should wait before asking Cam to customize their closet. She knew just what she had in mind, and he was good with his hands. Considering, she studied him. Very, very good with his hands.

"I suppose I could finish unpacking tomorrow."

He smiled slowly. "I suppose you could."

"I feel guilty about it. Grace has this place so spotless."

"Why don't you come over here. We'll work on that guilt."

"Why don't I?" She tossed the shoe over her shoulder and, with a laugh, jumped him.

"She's coming along."

Cam studied the boat. It was barely seven in the morning, but his internal clock was still set to Rome. Since he'd awakened early, he hadn't seen the point in letting his brothers sleep the day away.

So the Quinns stood, under the hard, bright lights of the boatyard, contemplating the job at hand. Seth mimicked their stance—hands in pockets, legs spread and braced, face sober.

It would be the first time the four of them had worked on the boat together. He was wildly thrilled.

"I figured you could start belowdecks," Ethan began. "Phillip estimates four hundred hours to finish the cabin."

Cam snorted. "I can do it in less."

"Doing it right," Phillip put in, "is more important than doing it fast."

"I can do it fast *and* right. The client'll have this baby under sail and the galley stocked with champagne and caviar in less than four hundred hours."

Ethan nodded. Since Cam had come through with another client, who wanted a sport fishing boat, he dearly hoped that was true. "Then let's get to work."

And work kept his mind off things his mind had no business being on. The brain had to be focused to use the lathe—if you were fond of your hands. Ethan turned the wood slowly, carefully, forming the mast. Ear protectors turned the hum of the motor and the hot rock blasting from the radio into a muffled echo.

He imagined there was conversation going on behind him, too. And the occasional ripe curse. He could smell the sweet scent of wood, the sting of epoxy, the stench of tar used to coat bolts.

Years ago, the three of them had built his workboat. She wasn't fancy, and he couldn't claim she had a pretty face, but she was sound and she was game. They'd built his skipjack as well because he'd been determined to dredge oysters in the traditional craft. Now the oysters were nearly gone, and his boat joined the other handful in the Bay, pulling in extra money during the summer by giving tours.

He rented it to Jim's brother during tourist season, because it helped them both and was the practical thing to do. But it bothered him some to see the fine old vessel used that way. Just as it bothered him some to know other people lived and slept in the house that was his.

But when push came to shove, money mattered. Seth's laugh snuck through his ear protectors and reminded him why it mattered now more than ever.

When his hands cramped from the work, he turned off the lathe to give them a rest. Noise filled his ears when he took off the protectors.

He could hear the pounding of Cam's hammer echoing from belowdecks. Seth was coating the centerboard with Rust-Oleum so the steel plate gleamed with wet. Phillip had the nastier job of soaking the inside of the centerboard case with creosote. It was good old-growth red cedar, which should discourage any marine borers, but they'd decided not to take chances.

A boat by Quinn was built to last.

He felt a stir of pride watching them and could almost imagine his father standing beside him, big hands fisted on his hips, a wide grin on his face.

"It makes a picture," Ray said. "The kind your mother and I loved to study. We had plenty of them put aside, to take out and look over again once you all grew up and went off your own ways. We never really had the chance because she left first."

"I still miss her."

"I know you do. She was the glue that kept us all together. But she did a good job of it, Ethan. You're still stuck."

"I guess I'd have died without her, without you. Without them."

"No." Ray laid a hand on Ethan's shoulder, shook his head. "You were always strong, heart and mind. You came out the other side of hell as much because of what's inside you as what we did. You should remember that more often. Just look at Seth. He handles things differently than you did, but

he's got a lot of the same qualities inside him. He cares, deeper than he
wants to. He thinks deeper than he lets on. And his wants go deeper than
he'll admit even to himself."

"I see you in him." It was the first time Ethan had allowed himself to say
it, even to himself. "I don't know how to feel about it."

"Funny, I see each one of you in him. The eye of the beholder, Ethan."
Then he gave Ethan a quick slap on the back. "That's a damn fine boat coming along there. Your mother would have gotten a kick out of this."

"Quinns build to last," Ethan murmured.

"Who're you talking to?" Seth demanded.

Ethan blinked, felt his head go light, filled with thoughts thin as strands
of cotton. "What?" He pushed a hand up his forehead, into his hair, knocking his cap back. "What?"

"Man, you look weird." Seth cocked his head, fascinated. "How come
you're standing here talking to yourself?"

"I was . . ." Asleep on my feet? he wondered. "Thinking," he said. "Just
thinking out loud." Suddenly the noise and smells seemed to roar into his
dizzy brain. "I need some air," he muttered and hurried out through the
cargo doors.

"Weird," Seth said again. He started to say something to Phillip, then
was distracted as Anna came through the front door carrying an enormous
hamper.

"Anybody interested in lunch?"

"Yeah!" Always interested, Seth made a beeline. "Did you bring the
chicken?"

"What's left of it," she told him. "And ham sandwiches thick as bricks.
There's a cooler of iced tea in the car. Why don't you go haul it in?"

"My hero," Phillip said, wiping his hands on his jeans before relieving
her of the hamper. "Hey, Cam! There's a gorgeous woman out here with
food."

The hammering stopped instantly. Seconds later, Cam's head popped up
through the cabin roof. "My woman. I get first dibs on the food."

"There's plenty to go around. Grace isn't the only one who can put
meals together for a bunch of hungry men. Though her fried chicken's a gift
from the gods."

"She's got a way with it." Phillip agreed. He set the hamper down on a
makeshift table fashioned out of a sheet of plywood laid over two sawhorses.
"She cooked for Ethan regularly when you two were away." He dug out a
ham sandwich. "I get the feeling something's happening there."

"Happening where?" Cam wanted to know as he jumped down to ex-
plore the hamper.

"With Ethan and Grace."

"No shit?"

"Mmm." The first bite made Phillip close his eyes in pleasure. He might have preferred French cuisine served on fine china, but he could appreciate a well-built sandwich balanced on a paper plate. "My deathless observation skills have homed in on certain signs. He watches her when she's not looking. She watches him when he's not looking. And I got some interesting gossip from Marsha Tuttle. She works down at the pub with Grace," he explained to Anna. "Shiney's adding a security system and has a new policy that none of the waitresses are to close up alone."

"Did something happen?" Anna asked.

"Yeah." He looked over to be certain Seth hadn't come back in. "A few nights ago some bastard came in after closing. Grace was alone. He put his hands on her and, according to Marsha, would have done more. But it just so happened Ethan was outside. Interesting coincidence if you ask me, when we're talking of our early-to-bed, early-to-rise brother. Anyway, he put some dents in the guy." He took another healthy bite.

Cam thought of slender, fine-boned Grace. Thought of Anna. "I hope they were nice deep dents."

"I think we can assume the guy didn't walk off whistling. Of course, in typical Ethan style, he doesn't mention it, so I have to hear it from Marsha over the fresh produce at the market Friday night."

"Was Grace hurt?" Anna knew all too well what it was to be trapped, to be helpless, to be faced with what a certain kind of man would do to a woman. Or a child.

"No. Must have shaken her up, but she's like Ethan there. Never mentioned it. But there were several long, silent looks between them yesterday. And after Ethan ran her home, he came back sizzling." Remembering, Phillip chuckled to himself. "Which for Ethan is saying something. Got himself a couple of beers and went out in the sloop for an hour."

"Grace and Ethan." Cam considered it. "They'd fit." He saw Seth come in and decided to give the topic a rest. "Where is Ethan, anyway?"

"He went outside." With a grunt, Seth set the cooler down and nodded toward the cargo doors. "He said he needed some air, and I guess he did. He was standing there talking to himself." Thrilled with the bounty, Seth dived into the hamper. "He was, like, carrying on a conversation with someone who wasn't there. He looked weird."

The back of Cam's neck prickled. Still, he moved casually, dumping food on a plate. "I could use some air myself. I'll just take him a sandwich."

He saw Ethan standing out on the end of the pier, staring out at the water. The shore of St. Chris with all its pretty houses and yards was on either side, but Ethan looked straight out, over the light chop to the horizon.

"Anna brought some food out."

Ethan folded up his thoughts and glanced down at the plate. "Nice of her. You hit lucky with her, Cam."

"Don't I know it." What he was about to do made him a little nervous. But, after all, he was a man who lived for risks. "I still remember the first day I saw her. I was pissed off at the world. Dad was hardly buried, and everything I wanted seemed to be somewhere else. The kid had given me plenty of grief that morning, and it occurred to me that the next part of my life wasn't going to be racing, it wasn't going to be Europe. It was going to be right here."

"You gave up the most. Coming back here."

"It seemed like it at the time. Then Anna Spinelli walked across the yard while I was fixing the back steps. She gave me my second jolt of the day."

Since the food was there, and Cam seemed inclined to talk, Ethan took the plate and sat on the edge of the dock. An egret flew by, silent as a ghost. "A face like hers is bound to give a man a jolt."

"Yeah. And I was already feeling a little edgy. Not an hour before, I'd had this conversation with Dad. He was sitting in the back porch rocker."

Ethan nodded. "He always liked sitting there."

"I don't mean I remembered him sitting there. I mean I saw him there. Just like I'm seeing you now."

Slowly, Ethan turned his head, looked into Cam's eyes. "You saw him, sitting in the rocker on the porch."

"Talked to him, too. He talked to me." Cam shrugged, gazed out over the water. "So, I figure I'm hallucinating. It's the stress, the worry, maybe the anger. I've got things to say to him, questions I want answered, so my mind puts him there. Only that's not what it was."

Ethan stepped carefully onto boggy ground. "What do you figure it was?"

"He was there, that first time and the others."

"Other times?"

"Yeah, the last was the morning before the wedding. He said it would be the last because I'd figured out what I needed to figure out for now." Cam rubbed his hands over his face. "I had to let him go again. It was a little easier. I didn't get all the questions answered, but I guess the ones that mattered most were."

He sighed, feeling better, and helped himself to one of the chips on Ethan's plate. "Now you'll either tell me I'm crazy or that you know what I'm talking about."

Thoughtfully, Ethan tore one of the sandwiches in half, handed a share to Cam. "When you follow the water, you get to know there's more to things than you can see or touch. Mermaids and serpents." He smiled a little. "Sailors know about them, whether they've ever seen them or not. I don't think you're crazy."

"Are you going to tell me the rest?"

"I've had some dreams. I thought they were dreams," he corrected himself, "but lately I've had a couple when I was awake. I guess I have questions, too, but I have a hard time pushing somebody into answers. It's good to hear his voice, to see his face. We didn't have enough time to really say good-bye before he died."

"Maybe that's part of it. It's not all of it."

"No. But I don't know what he wants me to do that I'm not doing."

"I imagine he'll stick around until you figure it out." Cam bit into the sandwich and felt amazingly content. "So, what does he think of the boat?"

"He thinks it's a damn fine boat."

"He's right."

Ethan studied his sandwich. "Are we going to tell Phil about this?"

"Nope. But I can't wait until it happens to him. What do you bet he'll think about heading to some fancy shrink? He'll want one with lots of initials after his name and an office on the right side of town."

"Her name," Ethan corrected and began to smile. "He'll want a good-looking female if he's going to lie down on a couch. It's a pretty day," he added, suddenly appreciating the warm breeze and the flash of sun.

"You've got another ten minutes to enjoy it," Cam told him. "Then your ass goes back to work."

"Yeah. Your wife makes a damn good sandwich." He angled his head. "How do you think she'd do at sanding wood?"

Cam considered, liked the image. "Let's go talk her into letting us find out."

NINE

Anna was thrilled to have the afternoon off. She loved her job, had both affection and respect for the people she worked with. She believed absolutely in the function and the goals of social work. And she had the satisfaction of knowing she made a difference.

She helped people. The young single mother with nowhere to turn, the unwanted child, the displaced elderly person. Inside her burned a deep and bright desire to help them find their way. She knew what it was to be lost, to be desperate, and what one person who offered a hand, who refused to snatch that hand back even when it was slapped or snapped at, could change.

And because she had been determined to help Seth DeLauter, she'd found Cam. A new life, a new home. New beginnings.

Sometimes, she thought, rewards came back to you a hundredfold.

Everything she'd ever wanted—even when she hadn't known she wanted it—was tied up in that lovely old house on the water. A white house with blue trim. Rockers on the porch, flowers in the yard. She remembered the first day she'd seen it. She'd traveled along this same road, with the radio blaring. Of course, the top had been up then, so the wind wouldn't tug her hair free of its pins.

That had been a business call, and Anna had been determined to be all business.

The house had charmed her, the simplicity of it, the stability. Then she walked around the pretty two-story house by the water and saw an angry, uncooperative, and sexy man repairing the back porch steps.

Nothing had been quite the same for her since.

Thank God.

It was her house now, she thought with a smug grin as she drove fast along the road flanked by wide, flat fields. Her house in the country, with the garden she'd imagined . . . and the angry, uncooperative, sexy man? He was hers, too, and so much more than she'd ever imagined.

She drove along that long, straight road with Warren Zevon howling about werewolves in London. But this time, she didn't care if the wind tugged at her once tidily pinned hair. She was going home, so the top was down and her mood was light.

She had work to do, but the reports she needed to complete could be done on her laptop at home. While her red sauce simmered on the stove, she decided. They'd have linguini—to remind Cam of their honeymoon.

Not that this particular event seemed to be over, even if they were back on the Shore rather than in Rome. She wondered if this wild and wicked passion they had for each other would ever ease.

And hoped not.

Laughing at herself, she zipped into the drive. And nearly rammed her pretty little convertible into the rear of a dull gray sedan with a rusted bumper. Once her heart had bumped back down into its proper place, she puzzled over it.

It certainly wasn't Cam's kind of car, she decided. He might like to tinker with engines, but he preferred the fast and the sleek body to go around them. This aged and sturdy body looked anything but fast.

Phillip? She let out a snort. The fastidious Phillip Quinn wouldn't have placed his Italian-loafer-shod foot on the worn floorboard of such a vehicle.

Ethan, then. But she found herself frowning. Pickups and Jeeps were Ethan's style, not compact sedans that had fenders still painted with gray primer.

They were being robbed, she thought with a jolt that turned her heartbeat into a jackhammer. In broad daylight. No one ever thought to lock the doors around here, and the house was sheltered from its neighbors by trees and the marsh.

Someone was inside, picking through their things, right now. Eyes narrowed, she slammed out of the car. They weren't getting away with it. It was her house now, damn it, and her things, and if any half-baked burglar thought he could . . .

She trailed off as she looked into the sedan and saw the big pink rabbit. And the car seat. A house burglar with a toddler in tow?

Grace, she realized with a sigh. It was one of Grace Monroe's cleaning days.

City girl, she chided herself. Put the city instincts away. You're in another place now. Feeling monumentally foolish, she returned to her own car and hefted her briefcase and the bag of fresh produce she'd picked up on the way home.

As she stepped onto the porch, she heard the monotonous hum of the vacuum, underscored by the bright tinkle of a commercial on TV. Good domestic sounds, Anna thought. And she was more than delighted that she wasn't the one running the vacuum.

Grace nearly dropped the wand when Anna came through the door. Obviously flustered, she stepped back, tripping the foot switch to turn the machine off. "I'm sorry. I thought I'd be finished before anyone got home."

"I'm early." Though her arms were full, Anna crouched in front of the chair where Aubrey sat manically scribbling purple crayon on a picture of an elephant in her coloring book. "That's beautiful."

"It's a phant."

"It's a terrific phant. Prettiest phant I've seen all day." Because Aubrey's nose just seemed to demand it, Anna gave it a quick kiss.

"I'm nearly done." Nerves danced down Grace's spine. Anna looked so professional in her business suit. The fact that her hair was tumbling out of its pins only made her seem . . . professionally sexy, Grace decided. "I finished upstairs, and in the kitchen. I didn't know . . . I wasn't sure what you'd like, but I made up a casserole—scalloped potatoes and ham. It's in the freezer."

"Sounds great. I'm cooking tonight." Anna rose and jiggled her bag cheerfully. She nearly stepped out of her shoes but then stopped herself. It didn't seem right to start cluttering things up when Grace was still in the middle of cleaning.

She'd wait until later.

"But I won't get off early tomorrow," she continued. "So it'll come in handy."

"Well, I . . ." Grace knew she was a little sweaty, a little grimy, and she felt miserably outclassed by Anna's crisp blouse and tailored suit. And oh, those shoes, she thought, doing her best not to make her survey obvious. They were so pretty, so classic, and the leather looked soft enough to sleep on.

Her toes curled in shame inside her frayed white sneakers. "The laundry's nearly done, too. There's a load of towels in the dryer. I didn't know where you wanted me to put your things, so I folded everything and left it on the bed in your room."

"I appreciate it. Catching up after a couple of weeks away takes forever." Anna caught herself before she squirmed. She'd never had a housekeeper in her life, and she wasn't quite sure of the proper procedure. "I should put these away. You want something cold to drink?"

"No, thanks. No. I should finish up and get out of your way."

Curious, Anna thought. Grace had never seemed cool or nervous before. Though they didn't know each other well, Anna had felt they were friendly. One way or the other, she decided, they had to come to terms. "I'd really like to talk to you if you have the time."

"Oh." Grace ran her hand up and down the metal wand of the vacuum. "Sure. Aubrey, I'm going in the kitchen with Mrs. Quinn."

"Me, too!" Aubrey scrambled up and raced ahead. By the time her mother caught up, she was sprawled on the floor, intently creating a purple giraffe.

"That's her color this week," Grace commented. Automatically she went to the refrigerator and took out the pitcher of lemonade she'd made. "She tends to settle on one until she wears the crayon down to a nub, then she picks another."

Her hand froze on the glass she'd been about to take from a cupboard. "I'm sorry," she said stiffly. "I wasn't thinking."

Anna set her bag down. "About what?"

"Making myself at home in your kitchen."

Aha, Anna thought, there was the problem. Two women, one house. They were both a little uneasy about the situation. She took a plump tomato from the bag, examined it, then set it on the counter. Next year she was going to try to grow her own.

"You know what I liked about this house from the first time I stepped into the kitchen? It's the kind of place where it's easy to make yourself at home. I wouldn't want that to change."

She continued to unload her bag, setting carefully chosen vegetables on the counter.

Grace had to bite her tongue to keep from mentioning that Ethan didn't care for mushrooms when Anna set a bag of them beside the peppers.

"It's your home now," Grace said slowly. "You'll want to tend to it your own way."

"That's true. And I am thinking of making some changes. Would you mind pouring that lemonade? It looks wonderful."

Here it comes, Grace thought. Changes. She poured two glasses, then took the plastic cup from the counter to fill for Aubrey. "Here, honey, now don't spill."

"Aren't you going to ask me what changes?" Anna wondered.

"It's not my place."

"When did we get to have places?" Anna demanded with just enough annoyance to put Grace's back up.

"I work for you—for the time being, anyway."

"If you're about to tell me you're quitting you're really going to spoil my day. I don't care how much progress women have made, if I'm alone in this house with four men, I'll end up doing ninety percent of the housework. Maybe not at first," she continued, pacing now, "but that's just how it'll end up. It won't matter that I have a full-time job on top of it, either. Cam hates housework, and he'll do anything he can to get out of it. Ethan's neat enough, but he has a habit of making himself scarce. And Seth, well, he's ten, so that says it all. Phillip only lives here on weekends, and he'll make the argument that he didn't make the mess in the first place."

She whirled back. "Are you telling me you're quitting?"

It was the first time Grace had seen Anna under full steam, and she was both impressed and baffled. "I thought you just said you were going to make some changes and you were going to let me go."

"I'm thinking about getting some new pillows and having the sofa re-covered," Anna said impatiently, "not losing the person I already realize I'm going to depend on for my sanity around here. Do you think I didn't know who made sure I didn't come home to a houseful of dishes and laundry and dust? Do I look like an idiot to you?"

"No, I . . ." The beginnings of a smile flirted at Grace's mouth. "I worked my tail off so you'd notice."

"Okay." Anna let out a breath. "Why don't we sit down and start over?"

"That'd be good. I'm sorry."

"For?"

"For all the nasty things I let myself think about you over the last few days." She smiled fully as she sat down. "I forgot how much I liked you."

"I'm outnumbered around here, Grace. I could sure use another woman. I don't know exactly how these things are done, and since I'm the outsider here—"

"You're not an outsider." Grace all but gaped in shock. "You're Cam's wife."

"And you've been a part of his life, of all their lives, a great deal longer." She turned her hands palms up, smiled. "Let's get this one thing out of the way so we can forget it. Whatever you've been doing around here works just fine for me. I appreciate knowing you're doing it so I can concentrate on my marriage, on Seth, and on my job. Are we clear there?"

"Yeah."

"And since my instincts tell me you're a kind, understanding person, I'm going to confess that I need you a lot more than you need me. And throw myself on your mercy."

The quick, easy laugh made shallow dimples flicker in Grace's cheeks. "I don't think there's anything you couldn't do."

"Maybe not, but I swear to God I don't want to be Wonder Woman. Don't leave me alone with all these men."

Grace nibbled on her lip for a moment. "If you're going to have the living-room sofa redone, you'll need new curtains."

"I was thinking priscillas."

They beamed at each other, in perfect accord.

"Mama! Gotta pee!"

"Oh." Grace sprang up and scooped a frantically dancing Aubrey into her arms. "We'll be right back."

Anna had a good chuckle, then rose, stripped off her jacket, and prepared to start her sauce. This kind of cooking—the familiar, the dependable—relaxed her. And since she had no doubt that it would earn her points with the Quinn men when they got home, she intended to enjoy herself.

It pleased her as well that she'd cemented a basis of friendship with Grace. She wanted that benefit of small towns and country living—the neighbors. One of the reasons she'd been restless during her time in D.C. was the lack of connection with the people who lived and worked around her. When she'd moved to Princess Anne she'd found something of the old-neighborhood ease she'd grown up with in her grandparents' well-established section of Pittsburgh.

And now, she thought, she had the opportunity to become good friends with a woman she admired and believed she would enjoy.

When Grace and Aubrey came back into the room, she smiled. "You hear stories about toilet training being a nightmare for everyone involved."

"There are hits and misses." Grace gave Aubrey a quick squeeze before setting her down. "Aubrey's such a good girl, aren't you, sweetie?"

"I didn't wet my pants. I get a nickel for the piggy bank."

When Anna roared with laughter, Grace winced good-naturedly. "And bribery works."

"I'm all for it."

"I should finish up."

"Are you in a hurry?"

"Not really." Cautious, Grace glanced at the kitchen clock. By her judgment, Ethan shouldn't be back for at least an hour.

"Maybe you could keep me company while I put this sauce together."

"I suppose I could." It had been . . . she couldn't remember how long it had been since she'd just sat in the kitchen with another woman. The simplicity of it nearly made her sigh. "There's a show that Aubrey likes to watch that's just coming on. Is it all right if I settle her down with it? I can do the rest of the vacuuming when it's over."

"Great." Anna slid her tomatoes into the pot to let them simmer and soften.

"I've never made spaghetti sauce from scratch," Grace said when she came back in. "I mean, all the way from fresh tomatoes."

"Takes more time, but it's worth it. Grace, I hope you don't mind, but I heard what happened the other night at the bar where you work."

Surprise made Grace blink and forget to memorize the ingredients Anna had set out. "Ethan told you?"

"No. You have to pull on Ethan's tongue to get him to tell anything." Anna wiped her hands on the bib apron she'd put on. "I don't want to pry, but I have some experience with sexual assault. I want you to know you can talk to me if you need to."

"It wasn't as bad as it could have been. If Ethan hadn't been there . . ." She trailed off, discovered that thinking about it still made her cold inside. "Well, he was. I should have been more careful."

Anna had a quick flash of a dark road, the bite of gravel against her back as she was shoved to the ground. "It's a mistake to blame yourself."

"Oh, I don't—not that way. I didn't deserve what he tried to do. I didn't encourage him. The fact is, I made it clear I wasn't interested in him or his hotel bed. But I should have locked up after Steve left. I wasn't thinking, and that was careless."

"I'm glad you weren't hurt."

"I could have been. I can't afford to be careless." She glanced to the doorway where the bright music and Aubrey's brighter laughter came through. "I've got too much at stake."

"Single parenting's hard. I see the problems that can come out of it all the time. You're brilliant at it."

Now it wasn't surprise, but shock. No one had ever called her brilliant at anything. "I just . . . do."

"Yes." Anna smiled. "My mother died when I was twelve, but before that she was a single parent. When I look back and remember, I see that she was brilliant at it too. She just did. I hope I'm half as good at 'just doing' as both of you when I have a child."

"Are you and Cam planning on it?"

"I'm good at planning," Anna said with a laugh. "I want to give just being married a little time, but yes, I want children." She looked out the window to where the flowers she'd planted were blooming. "This is a wonderful place to raise kids. You knew Ray and Stella Quinn?"

"Oh, yes. They were wonderful people. I still miss them."

"I wish I'd known them."

"They'd have liked you."

"Do you think?"

"They'd have liked you for yourself," Grace told her. "And they'd have loved what you've done for the family. You helped bring them back together. I think they got a little lost for a while—after Dr. Quinn died. Maybe they all had to go their own way, just like they had to come back."

"Ethan stayed."

"He's rooted here—in the water, like eelgrass. But he drifted, too. And spent too much time alone. His house is around the bend that the river takes away from the waterfront."

"I've never seen it."

"It's tucked away," Grace murmured. "He likes his privacy. Sometimes on a quiet night if I went walking, when I was carrying Aubrey, I could hear him play his music. Just catch the notes on the air if the wind was right. It sounded lonely. Lovely and lonely."

Eyes that were dazzled by love saw some things with perfect clarity. "How long have you been in love with him?"

"Seems like all my life," Grace murmured, then caught herself. "I didn't mean to say that."

"Too late. You haven't told him?"

"No." At even the thought of it, Grace's heart clutched in panic. "I shouldn't be talking about this. He'd hate it. It'd embarrass him."

"Well, he's not here, is he?" Amused and delighted, Anna beamed. "I think it's terrific."

"It's not. It's awful. It's just awful." Horrified, she pressed a hand to her mouth to hold back a sudden and unexpected rush of tears. "I ruined it. Ruined everything, and now he doesn't even want to be around me."

"Oh, Grace." Flooded with sympathy, Anna abandoned her chopping to wrap her arms tight around Grace's stiff form, then nudged her toward a chair. "I can't believe that."

"It's true. He told me to stay away." Her voice hitched, mortifying her. "I'm sorry. I don't know what's got into me. I never cry."

"Then it's time you broke tradition." Anna tore off a couple of sheets of paper towels and offered them. "Go ahead, you'll feel better."

"I feel so stupid." With the dam broken, Grace sobbed into the paper towels.

"There's nothing to feel stupid about."

"There is, there is. I made it so we can't even be friends anymore."

"How did you do that?" Anna asked gently.

"I was pushing myself at him. I guess I thought—after the night he kissed me . . ."

"He kissed you?" Anna repeated, and immediately began to feel better.

"He was mad." Grace pressed her face into the towel, breathing deep until she could regain some control. "It was after what happened at the pub. I've never seen him like that. I've known him most of my life and never knew he could be like that. I'd have been scared if I hadn't known him—the way he tossed that man aside like he was a bag of feathers. And he had this look in his eyes that made them hard and different, and . . ." She sighed and admitted the worst. "Exciting. Oh, it's horrible to think that."

"Are you kidding?" Anna reached over and squeezed her hand. "I wasn't even there and I'm excited."

With a watery laugh, Grace mopped at her face. "I don't know what came over me, but he was yelling at me. It got my back up, and we had a fight when he took me home. He was saying that I should quit my job and talking to me like I'd lost every working brain cell in my head."

"Typical male reaction."

"That's right." Abruptly angry all over again, Grace nodded. "It was just typical, and I never would have expected that from him. Then we were rolling around on the grass."

"You were?" Absolutely delighted, Anna grinned.

"He was kissing me, and I was kissing him back, and it was wonderful. All my life I'd wondered how it would be, and then there it was and it was better than anything I'd ever imagined. Then he stopped and said he was sorry."

Anna closed her eyes. "Oh, Ethan, you idiot."

"He told me to go inside, but just before I did he said he thought about me. That he didn't want to, but he did. So I hoped that things would start to change."

"I'd say they'd changed already."

"Yes, but not the way I'd hoped. The day you and Cam came back, I was here when he got home. And it seemed like, maybe . . . but he took me back to my house. He told me he'd thought it through and he wasn't going to touch me again and I was to steer clear of him for a while." She let out a long breath. "So I am."

Anna waited a moment, then shook her head. "Oh, Grace, you idiot." When Grace frowned, Anna leaned across the table. "Obviously the man wants you and it scares the hell out of him. You have the power here. Why aren't you using it?"

"The power? What power?"

"The power to get what you want if what you want is Ethan Quinn. You just need to get him alone and seduce him."

Grace snorted. "Seduce him? Me seduce Ethan? I couldn't do that."

"Why couldn't you?"

"Because I . . ." There had to be a simple and logical reason. "I don't know. I don't think I'd be good at it."

"I bet you'd be great at it. And I'm going to help you."

"You are?"

"Absolutely." Anna rose to fuss with her sauce and to think. "When's your next night off?"

"Tomorrow."

"Good, that's just enough time. I'd keep Aubrey for you overnight, but that might make it too obvious, and we'd better be subtle. Is there someone you'd trust with her?"

"My mother's been wanting to take her overnight, but I couldn't—"

"Perfect. You might feel inhibited with the baby in the house. I'll figure out how to get him over there."

She turned around, studied Grace. Cool, classic looks, she mused. Big, sad eyes. The man was already a goner. "You'll want to wear something simple but feminine." Considering, she tapped a fingertip against her teeth. "Pastel would be best, a fragile color, soft green or pink."

Because her head was starting to spin, Grace put a hand to it. "You're going too fast."

"Well, someone has to. At this rate, you and Ethan will still be circling each other when you're sixty. No jewelry," she added. "Just the bare minimum of makeup. Wear your usual scent, too. He's used to it, it'll say something to him."

"Anna, it doesn't matter what I wear if he doesn't want to be there."

"Of course it matters." As a woman who had a long-term love affair with clothes, she was very nearly shocked at the suggestion. "Men don't think they notice what a woman wears—unless it's next to nothing. But they do, subconsciously. And it helps click the mood or the image."

Lips pursed, she added fresh basil to the sauce and got out a skillet for sautéing onions and garlic. "I'm going to try to get him over there close to sunset. You should light some candles, put on music. The Quinns like their music."

"What would I say to him?"

"I can only take you so far here, Grace," Anna said dryly. "And I'm betting you'll figure it out when the time comes."

She was far from convinced of that. While new scents began to romance the air, Grace worried her lip. "It feels like I'd be tricking him."

"And your point would be?"

Grace chuckled. And gave up. "I have a pink dress. I bought it for Steve's wedding a couple years ago."

Anna glanced over her shoulder. "How does it look on you?"

"Well . . ." Grace's lips curved slowly. "Steve's best man hit on me before they cut the cake."

"Sounds like a deal."

"I still don't—" Grace stopped as her mother's ear caught the tinkling music from the living room. "That's the end of Aubrey's show. I have to finish up in there."

She rose quickly, panicked at the thought of Ethan coming home before she was gone. Surely everything she felt must show on her face. "Anna, I appreciate what you're trying to do, but I just don't think it's going to work. Ethan knows his own mind."

"Then it won't hurt him to come around to your house and see you in a pink dress, will it?"

Grace blew out a breath. "Does Cam ever win an argument with you?"

"On the rare occasion, but never when I'm at my best."

Grace edged toward the door, knowing that Aubrey's sit-and-behave time was nearly up. "I'm glad you came home early today."

Anna tapped her wooden spoon on the lip of her pot. "Me, too."

TEN

The following day as sunset approached, Grace wasn't certain she was glad at all. Her nerves were stretched so tight she could feel them straining and bubbling under her skin. Her stomach continually jumped in quick little rabbit hops. And her head was beginning to throb in a sharp, insistent rhythm.

It would be just perfect, she thought in disgust, if Anna managed to get Ethan over, and she simply pitched forward, ill and babbling, at his feet.

That would be seductive.

She should never have agreed to this foolishness, she told herself as she paced through her little house yet again. Anna had thought so quickly, made up her mind so fast and put everything in motion so smoothly, that she'd been swept along before she could calculate the pitfalls.

What in the world would she *say* to him if he came? Which he probably wouldn't, she thought, caught between relief and despair. He probably wouldn't even come and then she'd have sent her baby away for the night for nothing.

It was too quiet. There was nothing but the early-evening breeze rustling through the trees for company. If Aubrey had been there—where she belonged—they'd have been reading her bedtime story now. She would have been all scrubbed and powdered and curled up under Grace's arm in the rocker. Snuggly and sleepy.

When she heard her own sigh, Grace pressed her lips tightly together and marched to the small stereo system on the yellow pine shelves in the living room. She selected CDs from her collection—an indulgence that she refused to feel guilty over—and let the house fill with the weeping and romantic notes of Mozart.

She walked to the window to watch the sun drop lower in the sky. The light was going soft, slipping away shade by shade. In the ornamental plum that graced the Cutters' front yard a lone whippoorwill began to sing to the twilight. She wished she could laugh at herself, silly Grace Monroe standing by the window in her pink dress waiting for a star to wish on.

But she lowered her forehead to the glass, closed her eyes, and reminded herself that she was too old for wishes.

A nna thought she would have done very well in the espionage game. She had kept her plans locked tight behind closed lips—no matter how desperately she'd wanted to spill out everything to Cam.

She had to remind herself that he was, after all, a man. And he was Ethan's brother, which was another strike against him. This was a woman thing. She thought she was very subtle about keeping her eye on Ethan as well. He wasn't going to escape somewhere directly after dinner, as was his habit, nor would he have a clue that his sister-in-law was keeping him on a short rein.

The ice cream idea had been a brainstorm. She'd picked up a gallon on the way home and now had all three of her men, as she liked to think of them, settled on the back porch downing bowls of Rocky Road.

Timing and execution, she told herself, and rubbed her hands together before she stepped out on the porch. "It's going to be a warm night. It's hard to believe it's nearly July already."

She wandered to the porch rail to lean over and scan her flower beds. Coming right along, she thought with a sense of righteous satisfaction. "I thought we could have a backyard picnic on the Fourth."

"They have fireworks on the waterfront," Ethan put in. "Every year, half hour after sunset. You can see them from right here on the porch."

"Really? That would be perfect. Wouldn't it be fun, Seth? You could have your friends over and we'd cook burgers and dogs."

"That'd be cool." He was already down to scraping his bowl and calculating how to finesse seconds.

"Have to dig out the horseshoes," Cam decided. "Do we still have them, Ethan?"

"Yeah, they're around."

"And music." Anna shifted just enough to rub her husband's knee. "The three of you could play. You don't play together nearly often enough to suit me. I'll have to make a list. You'll have to tell me who we should invite—and the food. Food." She thought she feigned flustered irritation very well as she pushed away from the porch rail. "How could I have forgotten? I promised Grace to trade her my recipe for tortellini for hers for fried chicken."

She dashed inside to retrieve the index card that she'd neatly written the recipe on—something she'd never done before in her life—then dashed back out again. All apologetic smiles.

"Ethan, would you run this over to her?"

He stared at the little white card. If he hadn't been sitting down, his hands would have jumped into his pockets. "What?"

"I promised I'd get her this today and it completely slipped my mind. I'd run it over myself, but I still have a report to finish. I'm just dying to try out that fried chicken," she went on quickly, pushing the recipe card into his hand, then all but dragging him to his feet.

"It's kind of late."

"Oh, it's not even nine o'clock." Don't give him time to think, she warned herself. Don't give him a chance to pick out the flaws. She pulled him into the house, used smiles and fluttering lashes to move him along. "I really appreciate it. I'm so scatterbrained these days. I feel like I'm chasing my own tail half the time. Tell her I'm sorry I didn't get it to her sooner and to be sure to let me know how it turns out once she tries it. Thanks so much, Ethan," she added, rising up to give him a quick, affectionate peck on the cheek. "I love having brothers."

"Well . . ." He was baffled, closing in on miserable, but the way she said that, the way she smiled when she did, left him helpless. "I'll be right back."

I don't think so, Anna thought with a wisely controlled chuckle as she cheerily waved him off. The second his truck was out of sight, she dusted her palms together. Mission accomplished.

"Just what the hell was that?" Cam demanded, making her jolt with surprise.

"I don't know what you mean." She would have sailed past him and into the house, but he stepped out, blocked her path.

"Oh, yeah, you know what I mean." Intrigued, he angled his head. She was trying to look innocent, he decided, but couldn't pull it off. Too much pure glee in her eyes. "Exchanging recipes, Anna?"

"So what?" She lifted a shoulder. "I'm a very good cook."

"No argument there, but you're not the recipe-emergency type, and if you'd been so hell-bent on giving one to Grace, you'd have picked up the phone. Which is something you didn't give Ethan a chance to point out, since you were so busy batting your lashes at him and cooing like some empty-headed twit."

"Twit?"

"Which you're not," he continued, slowly backing her up until she was trapped against the porch rail. "At all. Shrewd, savvy, sharp." He laid his hands on either side of her hips to cage her. "That's what you are."

It was, she supposed, a fine compliment. "Thank you, Cameron. Now I really should get to that report."

"Uh-uh. Why'd you con Ethan into going over to Grace's?"

She shook back her hair, aimed a bland look dead into his eyes. "I'd think a shrewd, savvy, sharp guy like you ought to be able to figure that out."

His brows drew together. "You're trying to get something going between them."

"Something *is* going between them, but your brother is slower than a lame turtle."

"He's slower than a lame turtle with bifocals, but that's Ethan. Don't you think they should muddle through this on their own?"

"All they need is five minutes alone, and that's all I did—work it out so they'd have a few minutes alone. Besides"—she slipped her arms up and around his neck—"we deliriously happy women want everyone else to be deliriously happy, too."

He cocked a brow. "Do you think I'm going to fall for that?"

She smiled, then leaned over to nip his bottom lip. "Yeah."

"You're right," he murmured and let her convince him.

E than sat in his truck for a full five minutes. Recipes? That was the dumbest damn thing he'd ever heard of. He'd always thought Anna was a sensible woman, but here she was, sending him off to deliver recipes, for Christ's sake.

And he wasn't ready to see Grace just yet. Not that his mind wasn't made up about her, but . . . even a rational man had certain weaknesses.

Still, he didn't see how he was going to get out of it, as he was already here. He'd make it quick. She was probably putting the baby to bed, so he'd just get it done and get out of her way.

Like a man condemned, he dragged himself out of the truck and to her front door. Through the screen he could see the flickering lights of candles. He shifted his feet and noticed that music was playing, something with weeping strings and soaring piano.

He'd never felt more ridiculous in his life than he did standing there on Grace's front porch holding a recipe for a pasta dish while music slid around the warm summer night.

He knocked on the wood frame, not too loudly, as he worried about waking Aubrey. He gave serious thought to sticking the card in the door and hightailing it, but he knew that would be cowardice, plain and simple.

And Anna would want to know why he hadn't brought her the instructions for Grace's fried chicken.

When he saw her he wished to God Almighty he'd taken the coward's way.

She walked out from the kitchen, at the back of the house. It was a tiny place, had always made Ethan think of a dollhouse, so she didn't have far to travel. To him it seemed he watched her walk through that music, that light for hours.

She wore pale, fragile pink that skimmed down to her ankles, with a row of tiny pearl buttons from the hollow of her throat to the hem that flowed around her bare feet. He had rarely seen her in a dress, but now he was too thunderstruck by the sight of her to question why she was wearing it.

All he could think was she looked like a rose, long and slim and just ready to bloom. And his tongue tangled up in his mouth.

"Ethan." Her hand trembled lightly as she reached down, opened the screen. Maybe she hadn't needed a star to wish on after all. For here he was, standing close and watching her.

"I was . . ." Her scent, familiar as his own, seemed to wrap around his brain. "Anna sent you—she asked me to bring this by."

Mystified, Grace took the card he held out. At the sight of the recipe she had to bite the inside of her cheek to keep from laughing. Her nerves backed off just enough that her eyes smiled when she lifted them to his. "That was nice of her."

"You got hers?"

"Her what?"

"The one she wants. The chicken thing."

"Oh, yes. Back in the kitchen. Come on in while I get it." What chicken thing? she wondered, nearly giddy from suppressed laughter that she knew would come out well on the hysterical side. "The, um, casserole, right?"

"No." She had such a tiny waist, he thought. Such narrow feet. "Fried."

"Oh, that's right. I'm so scatterbrained lately."

"It's going around," he mumbled. He decided it was safer to look anywhere but at her. He noted the pair of fat white candles burning on the counter. "You blow a fuse?"

"Excuse me?"

"What's wrong with your lights?"

"Nothing." She could feel the heat rise into her cheeks. She didn't have a recipe for fried chicken written down anywhere. Why would she? You just did the same as you always did when it came time to make it. "I like candle-light sometimes. It goes with the music."

He only grunted, wishing she would hurry up so he could get the hell away. "You already put Aubrey to bed?"

"She's spending the night with my mother."

His eyes, which had been steadfastly studying her ceiling, shot down and met hers. "She's not here?"

"No. It's her first overnight. I've already called over there twice." She smiled a little, and her fingers reached up to fiddle with the top button of her dress in a way that made Ethan's mouth water. "I know she's only a few miles away, and as safe as she'd be in her own crib, but I couldn't help it. The house feels so different without her here."

"Dangerous" was the word he'd have used. The pretty little dollhouse was suddenly as deadly as a minefield. There wasn't any little girl innocently sleeping in the next room. They were alone, with music sobbing and candles flickering.

And Grace was wearing a pale-pink dress that just begged to have those little white buttons undone, one by one by one.

The tips of his fingers began to itch.

"I'm glad you stopped by." Holding tight to her courage, she took a step forward and tried to remember that she had the power. "I was feeling a little blue."

He took a step back. More than his fingertips was itching now. "I said I'd be back directly."

"You could stay for . . . coffee or whatever?"

Coffee? If his system got any more wired than it was at that moment, it would have jumped right through his skin to dance the hornpipe. "I don't think . . ."

"Ethan, I can't steer clear of you the way you asked me. St. Chris is too small, and our lives are too tangled up together." She could feel the pulse in her throat pounding against her skin in hard, insistent little knocks. "And I don't want to. I don't want to steer clear of you, Ethan."

"I said I had my reasons." And he could think of what they were if she'd just stop looking at him with those big green eyes. "I'm just watching out for you, Grace."

"I don't need you to watch out for me. We're all grown up, both of us. We're alone, both of us." She stepped closer. She could smell his after-work shower on him, but under it, as always, was the scent of the Bay. "I don't want to be alone tonight."

He edged back. If he hadn't known her better, he'd have sworn she was stalking him. "I've made up my mind on this." But damn it, it wasn't his mind working overtime, it was his loins. "Just stay back, Grace."

"It seems like I've been staying back forever. I want to move forward, Ethan, whatever that means. I'm tired of staying back or standing still. If you don't want me, I'll live with that. But if you do . . ." She moved closer, lifted a hand to lay it on his heart. And discovered that his heart was pounding. "If you do, then why won't you take me?"

He backed hard into the counter. "Stop it. You don't know what you're doing here."

"Of course I know what I'm doing." She snapped it out, suddenly furious with the pair of them. "I'm just not doing a good job of it, since you'd rather climb up my kitchen wall than lay a finger on me. What do you think I'd do, shatter into a million pieces? I'm a grown woman, Ethan. I've been married, I've had a child. I know what I'm asking you, and I know what I want."

"I know you're a grown woman. I've got eyes."

"Then use them, and look at me."

How could he do otherwise? Why had he ever believed he could? There, standing in shadow and light, was everything he yearned for. "I'm looking at you, Grace." With my back to the wall, he thought. And my heart in my throat.

"Here's a woman who wants you, Ethan. One who needs you." She saw his eyes change at that, sharpen, darken, focus. On an unsteady breath, she stepped back. "Maybe I'm what you want. What you need."

He was afraid she was, and that telling himself he could and would do without had been an exercise in futility. She was so lovely, all rose and gold in the candlelight, her eyes so clear and honest. "I know you are," he said at length. "But that wasn't supposed to change anything."

"Do you have to think all the time?"

"It's getting hard to," he murmured. "Right at the moment."

"Then don't. Let's both stop thinking." Even as the blood pounded in her brain, she kept her gaze locked on his. And lifted her hands, trembling hands, to the top button of her dress.

He watched her unfasten it, staggered at how that single, simple gesture, that tiny inch of exposed skin, could electrify him. He felt his lungs clog, his blood sizzle, and his needs, all the long-denied needs, beg for release.

"Stop, Grace." He said it gently. "Don't do that."

Her hands fell back to her sides in defeat, and she shut her eyes.

"Let me do it."

Her eyes blinked open, stared stunned at his sober gaze as he stepped to her. She took in one shaky breath and held it.

"I've always wanted to," he murmured and slipped the next tiny button free.

"Oh." The breath she held came out in a hitch and a sob. "Ethan."

"You're so pretty." She was already trembling. He lowered his head to brush a kiss over her lips and soothe. "So soft. I've got rough hands." Watching her, he skimmed his knuckles down her cheek, over her throat. "But I won't hurt you."

"I know. I know you won't."

"You're shaking." He undid another button, then another.

"I can't help it."

"I don't mind." Patiently he eased the buttons free to her waist. "I guess I knew, deep down, if I walked in here tonight, I wouldn't be able to walk away again."

"I've been wishing you'd walk in here. I've been wishing it a long time."

"So have I." The buttons were so tiny, his fingers so big. Her skin, where the dress parted, where the edge of his thumb slid up, was so soft and warm. "You tell me if I do something you don't like. Or if I don't do something you want."

The sound she made was part moan, part laugh. "I'm not going to be able to talk in a minute. I can't get my breath. But I wish you'd kiss me."

"I was getting to it." He nibbled gently, teasingly, because he hadn't taken his time the first time he'd tasted her. Now he would linger, sample, find a rhythm that suited them both. When her sigh filled his mouth, it was sweet. He loosened more buttons and let the long, deepening kiss spin out.

Touched her nowhere else, not yet. Only mouth against mouth with flavors mixed. When she swayed, he lifted his head, looked into her eyes. Clouded now, heavy and aware.

"I want to see you." Slowly, inch by inch, he slipped the dress from her shoulders. They were sun-kissed, strong, gracefully curved. He'd always thought she had the prettiest shoulders, and now he indulged himself by tasting them.

The hum in her throat told him she was both surprised and pleased by the attention. He had a great deal more to give her.

She'd never been touched this way, as if she were something rare and precious. What that touch stirred in her was so new and warm. Her skin seemed to soften and sensitize under the brush of his lips, the blood beneath to go thick and lazy. She only sighed as her dress slid down to pool at her feet.

When he eased back again, she could only stare up at him in wonder. Her lashes fluttered, her pulse skipped when he stroked his fingers lightly over the swell of her breast above her simple cotton bra. She had to bite her lip to hold back the groan when he flicked open the hook, when he gently cupped her breast in his palms.

"Do you want me to stop?"

"Oh, God." Her head fell back, and this time the groan escaped. His workingman's thumbs were skimming slowly, rhythmically over her nipples. "No."

"Hold on to me, Grace." He spoke quietly, and when her hands came to his shoulders and gripped, he brought his mouth to hers again, drawing more this time, asking more until she went limp.

Then he lifted her into his arms. He waited until her eyes opened again. "I'm taking you, Grace."

"Thank God, Ethan."

He had to smile when she pressed her face into the curve of his shoulder. "I'll protect you."

For a moment as he carried her off, she thought of dragons and black knights. Then the more practical meaning got through. "I—take the Pill. It's all right. I haven't been with anybody since Jack."

He'd known that in his heart, but hearing it only added to his steadily rising need.

She'd lighted candles in the bedroom as well. Slim tapers there that lanced up out of tiny white shells. The white of her iron headboard glowed in the soft light. White daisies sprang out of a clear glass vase on the small table beside the bed.

She thought he would lay her down, but instead he sat, cradling her, holding her, drugging her with those slow, endless kisses until her pulse beat thickly, grew sluggish. Then his hands began to move.

Everywhere he touched a small fire fanned into flame.

Callused hands, slipping, sliding over her skin. Long, rough-edged fingers stroking, pressing. There, oh, yes, just there.

The day-long stubble of beard rubbed the sensitive curve of her breasts as his tongue circled, then flicked. And always, always, his mouth coming back to hers for one more, just one more endless, mind-reeling kiss.

She tugged at his shirt, hoping to give back some of the pleasure, some of the magic. Found the scars and the muscle and the man. His torso was lean, his shoulders broad, the flesh warm under her seeking fingers. The breeze whispered through the open window, the call of the whippoorwill chasing after it. And the sound no longer seemed so lonely.

He eased her back, settled her head on the pillow, then bent to pull off his boots. Pale-gold candlelight swayed against shadows the color of smoke. Both shades shimmered over her. He watched as her hand snuck up to cover her breast, and he paused long enough to take it and kiss the knuckles.

"I wish you wouldn't," he murmured. "You're such a pleasure to look at."

She hadn't thought she'd feel shy, knew it was foolish, but she had to order herself to let her hand fall onto the bed. When he slipped out of his jeans she had to struggle with her breathing all over again. No fairy-tale knight had ever been built more magnificently or borne scars more heroically.

Desperate with love, she held out her arms in welcome.

He slipped into them, careful not to press his full weight onto her. She was fragile, he reminded himself, so slim and so much more innocent than she believed.

As the rising moon slanted its first light through the window, he began to show her.

Sighs and murmurs, long, slow caresses, quiet sips and tastes. His hands aroused, devastated, but never hurried. Hers explored, admired, and forgot to hesitate. He found where she was most sensitive, the underside of her breast, the back of her knee, the sweet, shallow, seductive valley between her thigh and her center.

So focused on her was he that his own rising need took him by surprise, flashing once, hard and strong and dragging out his moan when he took her breast into his mouth.

She arched, shuddering at the edgier demand.

And the rhythm changed.

With his breath growing ragged, he lifted his head, his eyes intent on her face. His hand slid between her thighs, pressed there against the heat. Found her already wet.

"I want to see you go over." He played his fingers over her, in her, as her breath quickened. Pleasure, panic, excitement all raced over her face. He watched her climb, closer, closer, with her breath tearing, then releasing on a strangled cry as she peaked.

She tried to shake her head to clear it, but the delicious dizziness continued to spin. The familiar room revolved, hazed, so that only his face was clear, was real. She felt drunk and dazed and unspeakably aroused.

This, finally this, was love as she'd dreamed it would be.

Her skin quivered as he slid slowly up her body, his mouth laying a warm, damp trail.

"Please." It wasn't enough. Even this wasn't enough. She craved the mating, the union, the final intimacy. "Ethan." She opened for him, arched. "Now."

His hands cupped her face, his lips covered her lips. "Now," he murmured against them and filled her.

Their long, groaning sighs blended, that first endless shudder of pleasure as he buried himself inside her rocked them both. When they began to move, they moved together, smoothly, silkily as if they'd only been waiting.

Desire was fluid, its current steady. They rode it, thrilling to the pace, to the deep, resonant pleasure of each long, slow stroke. Grace swirled close to the edge, felt the orgasm build, slide through her system like velvet ribbon so that she rose up, farther up, wallowed in the glow, then floated down into weightless wonder.

He pressed his face into her hair, and let himself follow.

⟨∞⟩

He was so quiet it worried her. He held her, but he would have known she'd need him to. Still he didn't speak, and the longer the silence stretched the more she feared what he would say when he broke it.

So she broke it first.

"Don't tell me you're sorry. I don't think I could stand it if you told me you were sorry."

"I wasn't going to. I promised myself I'd never touch you like this, but I'm not sorry I did."

She rested her head on his shoulder, just under his chin. "Will you touch me like this again?"

"Right this minute?"

Because she caught the lazy amusement in his voice, she relaxed and smiled. "I know better than to rush you on anything." She lifted her head because it was vital that she know. "Will you, Ethan? Will you be with me again?"

He traced a finger through her hair. "I don't see talking either one of us out of it after tonight."

"If you started to, I'd have to try to seduce you again."

"Yeah?" A smile crept over his face. "Then maybe I should start talking."

Thrilled, she rolled over him and hugged hard. "I'd be better at it the next time, too, because I wouldn't be so damned nervous."

"Nerves didn't seem to get in your way. I nearly swallowed my tongue when you walked to the door in that pink dress." He started to nuzzle her hair, stopped, narrowed his eyes. "What were you doing wearing a dress to sit around at home?"

"I don't know . . . I just was." She turned her head, ran kisses along his throat.

"Hold on." Knowing just how quickly she could distract him, he took her shoulders and lifted her up. "A pretty dress, candlelight . . . it's almost like you were expecting me to come along."

"I'm always hoping you will," she said and tried to kiss him again.

"Sending me off with a recipe, for Christ's sake." In a smooth and easy move he plopped her on her butt beside him, then sat up. "You and Anna got your heads together on this, didn't you? Set me up."

"What a ridiculous thing to say." She tried for indignant, but could only manage guilty. "I don't know where you get these ideas."

"You never could lie worth spit." Firmly, he took her chin in one hand, holding it until her eyes shifted to his. "It took me a while to figure it, but I've got it now, don't I?"

"She was only trying to help. She knew I was upset about the way things were between us. You've got a right to be mad, but don't take it out on her. She was only—"

"Did I say I was mad?" he interrupted.

"No, but . . ." She trailed off, drew in a careful breath. "You're not mad?"

"I'm grateful." His grin was slow and wicked. "But maybe you ought to try to seduce me again. Just in case."

ELEVEN

In the dark, while an owl still hooted, Ethan shifted, easing out from under the arm Grace had wrapped around his chest. In response she snuggled closer. The gesture made him smile.

"Are you getting up?" she asked in a voice that was muffled against his shoulder.

"I've got to. It's after five already." He could smell rain on the air, hear it coming in the rising wind. "I'm going to get a shower. You go back to sleep."

She made a sound that he took for assent and burrowed into the pillow.

He moved lightly through the dark, though he had to check himself a couple of times on the way to the bathroom. He didn't know her house as well as his own. He waited until he was inside before turning on the light so the backwash of it wouldn't spill into the hall and disturb her.

The room was scaled to match the rest of the house, so small he could have stood in the center and touched each side wall with his hands. The tiles were white, the walls above them papered in a thin candy stripe. He knew she'd hung the paper herself. She rented from Stuart Claremont, and the man wasn't known for his generosity or his sense of decor.

He had to grin at the orange-billed rubber duck nested on the side of the tub. One sniff at the soap made him realize why Grace always smelled faintly of lemons. While he appreciated the fragrance on her, he hoped sincerely that Jim wouldn't notice the citrus scent on him.

He ducked his head under what he thought of as a piss-trickle of spray. She needed a new showerhead, he decided, and as he rubbed a hand over his face, noted that he needed a shave. Both would have to wait.

But it was likely that now that things had changed between them, she would let him take care of a few things around the house for her. She'd always been so blessed stubborn about accepting help. It seemed to him that even a proud woman like Grace would be less stiff about taking help from a lover than a friend.

That's what they were now, Ethan reflected. No matter how many promises he'd made to himself. It wouldn't end with one night. Neither one of them was built that way, and it had as much to do with heart as it did with loins. They'd taken the step and that step involved commitment.

That's what worried him most.

He would never be able to marry her, have children with her. She would want more children. She was too fine a mother, had too much love to give not to want them. Aubrey deserved brothers or sisters.

There wasn't any point in thinking about it, he reminded himself. Things were the way things were. And right now he had a right, and a need, to live in the moment. They would love each other as much as they could for as long as they could. That would be enough.

It took him barely five minutes to discover that Grace's hot water heater was as small as the rest of the house. Even the miserly trickle of water turned cool, then cold, before he'd managed to rinse away all the lather.

"Cheap bastard," he muttered, thinking of Claremont. He switched off the spray and wrapped one of the bright-pink towels around his waist. He intended to go back and dress in the dark, but when he opened the door, he could see the light from the kitchen and hear Grace's still sleep-husky voice singing about finding love, just in the nick of time.

While the first drops of rain pattered against the windows, he stepped into the scent of bacon frying and coffee brewing. And the sight of Grace wrapped in a short cotton robe the color of spring leaves. His heart gave such a hard bounce of joy he was surprised it didn't simply leap out of his throat and land quivering in her hands.

He moved quick and quiet, so that when he wrapped his arms around her, pressed his lips to the top of her head, she jolted in surprise.

"I told you to go back to sleep."

She leaned back against him, closing her eyes and absorbing the lovely thrill of a kitchen embrace. "I wanted to fix you breakfast."

"You don't have to do things like that." He turned her around. "I don't expect things like that. You need your rest."

"I wanted to do it." His hair was dripping, his chest gleaming with wet. The sparkling gush of lust both delighted and shocked her. "Today's special."

"I appreciate it." He bent, intending to give her one soft morning kiss. But it deepened, lengthened until she was on her toes straining against him.

He had to pull himself back, block off the rushing need to tug off the robe and take her. "The bacon's going to burn," he murmured, and this time pressed his lips to her forehead. "I'd better get dressed."

She turned the bacon briskly to give him time to cross the room. Anna had been right, she thought, about having power. "Ethan?"

"Yeah?"

"I've got an awful lot of need for you stored up." She glanced over her shoulder, and her smile was smug. "I hope you don't mind."

The blood danced gleefully out of his head. She wasn't just flirting, she was challenging. He had a feeling she knew she'd already won. The only safe answer he could think of was a grunt before he retreated to the bedroom.

He wanted her. Grace did a quick dance and spin. They'd made love three times, three beautiful, glorious times during the night, had slept wrapped around each other. And he still wanted her.

It was the most beautiful morning of her life.

⬭

It rained all day. The water was rough as the tongue of a shrew and just as likely to lash. Ethan fought to keep the boat on course and was glad he hadn't let the boy come with them. He and Jim had worked in worse, but he imagined Seth would have spent a good portion of the day hung over the rail.

But foul weather couldn't spoil his mood. He whistled even as rain slapped his face and the boat pitched under him like a rodeo bronc.

Jim eyed him sideways a few times. He'd worked with Ethan long enough to know the boy was the friendly, good-natured sort. But a whistling fool he wasn't. He smiled to himself as he hauled up another pot. Looked like the boy did something more energetic than reading in bed last night, if you asked him.

About time, too—if you asked him. By his reckoning, Ethan Quinn was round about thirty years of age. A man should oughta be settled down with a wife and kids by that time of life. A waterman was better off going home to a hot meal and a warm bed. A good woman helped you through, gave you direction, cheered you up when the Bay got stingy. As God knew it could.

He wondered who this particular woman might be. Not that he stuck his nose in other people's business. He minded his own and expected his neighbors to do the same. But a man had a right to a little curiosity about things.

He pondered on how to bring the subject around when an under-the-limit she-crab found a tiny hole in his glove and snapped before he could toss her back.

"Little bitch," he said with a wince but without much heat.

"She get you?"

"Yeah." Jim watched her splash back into the waves. "I'll be back for you before the season's over."

"Looks like you need new gloves there, Jim."

"The wife's picking me up some today." He shoved the thawing alewives they used for bait into the trap. "Sure helps matters to know you got a woman to do for you some."

"Uh-huh." Ethan shoved the steering stick with one hand, picked up the gaff with the other, and timed the chop and the distance.

"A man spends the day working on the water, it's a comfort to know his woman's waiting for him."

A little surprised that they were having a conversation, Ethan nodded. "I suppose. We'll just finish up this line, Jim, then head in."

Jim culled the next pot, let the silence settle between them. A few gulls were having what Jim thought of as a pissing match overhead, screaming and diving and threatening each other over loose fish parts.

"You know, me and Bess, we'll be married thirty years come next spring."

"Is that so?"

"Steadies a man, a woman does. You wait too long to marry up, though, you get set in your ways."

"I guess."

"You'd be around thirty now, wouldn't you, Cap'n?"

"That's right."

"Don't want to get set in your ways."

"I'll keep that in mind," Ethan told him and shot out the gaff.

Jim merely sighed and gave up.

⟨⟨⟩⟩

When Ethan wandered into the boatyard, Cam was at the skill saw and three young boys were sanding the hull. Or pretending to.

"You hire a new crew?" Ethan asked as Simon trotted over to investigate.

Cam glanced to where Seth chattered away with Danny and Will Miller. "It keeps them out of my hair. You give up on crabs today?"

"Pulled in enough." He pulled out a cigar and lit it while he gazed thoughtfully out the open cargo doors. "Rain's coming down pretty hard."

"Tell me about it." Cam sent an accusing scowl toward the streaming windows. "That's why those three were in my hair. The little one'll talk your ears blue. And if you don't have the others doing something to keep them busy, they make trouble out of thin air."

"Well." Ethan puffed out smoke, watched the kids send Simon into ecstasy with rough rubs and scratches. "At the rate they're going, they'll have that hull sanded down in ten or twenty years."

"That's something we have to talk about."

"Hiring on those kids for the next two decades?"

"No, work." It was as good a time as any to take a break. Cam stooped and pumped iced tea out of the cooler. "I got a call from Tod Bardette this morning."

"The friend of yours who wants the fishing boat?"

"That's right. Now, Bardette and I go back a ways. He knows what I can do."

"He offer you another race?"

He had, Cam mused, cutting the dust in his throat with the sweet tea. Turning it down had stung, but the sting had eased more quickly this time around. "I made a promise here. I'm not breaking it."

Ethan tucked a hand in his back pocket and looked toward the boat. This place, this business, had been his dream, not Cam's, not Phillip's. "I didn't mean it that way. I guess I know what you put away to pull this off."

"We needed it."

"Yeah, but you're the only one who's given up anything to make it happen. I haven't bothered to thank you for it, and I'm sorry for that."

Every bit as uncomfortable as his brother, Cam stared at the boat. "I'm not exactly suffering here. The business is going to help us get permanent guardianship of Seth—and it's satisfying on its own account. Of course, Phil's bitching about our cash flow every time you turn around."

"That's his strength."

"Bitching?"

Ethan grinned around the cigar clamped in his teeth. "Yeah, and cash flows. You and me, we could never pull this off without him nagging us about the details."

"We may have more for him to nag about. That's what I started to tell you. Bardette has a friend who's interested in a custom catboat. He wants fast and he wants pretty, fitted out and sailing by March."

Ethan frowned and worked timetables in his head. "It's going to take us another seven or eight weeks to finish this one, and that puts us into end of August, beginning of September."

Calculating, he leaned back against the workbench, his eyes narrowed against the smoke. "Then we got the sport's fisher. I can't see us finishing her off before January, and that's pushing. That doesn't give us enough time to deliver."

"No, not the way things are. I can give it full-time and after crab season's over, I imagine you'll put in more hours here."

"Oystering isn't what it was, but—"

"You'll have to decide if you can juggle more time off the water, Ethan, and in here." He knew what he was asking. Ethan didn't just live on the water, he lived for it. "Phil's going to have to make some hard decisions before much longer, too. We're not going to have the cash to hire on laborers for a while yet." He blew out a breath. "Unless we count a couple of kids. This friend of Bardette's isn't ready to commit. He's going to come down and take a look at the place, and us, and what we've got here. I figure we make sure Phillip's around to sweet-talk him into a contract and a deposit."

Ethan hadn't expected it to happen so soon, to have one dream grow and steal from the other. He thought of the chill winter months spent dredging, the rise and fall of the skipjack over hard chop, the long, often frustrating search for oyster, for rockfish, for a living.

A nightmare for some, he supposed. But hope and glory for him.

He took the time to look around the building. The boat, nearly finished, waiting for willing and able hands under the hard overhead lights. Seth's drawings were framed on the wall and spoke of dreams and sweat. Tools, still shiny under a coating of dust, stood silent, waiting.

Boats by Quinn, he mused. If you wanted to grab ahold of one thing, you had to let go of another.

"I'm not the only one who can captain the workboat or the skipjack." He saw both the question and the understanding in Cam's eyes and jerked a shoulder. "It's just juggling time where it needs to be spent most."

"Yeah."

"I guess I could work up a design for a cat."

"And have Seth do the drawing," Cam added and laughed when Ethan grimaced. "We all have our strengths, pal. Art isn't yours."

"I'll think about it," Ethan decided. "And we'll see what happens next."

"Good enough. So . . ." Cam drained his cup. "How'd the recipe exchange go?"

Ethan ran his tongue around the inside of his cheek. "I'm going to have a talk with your wife about that."

"Be my guest." Smiling, Cam plucked the cigar from Ethan's fingers and took a trio of careless puffs. "You sure look . . . relaxed today, Ethan."

"I'm relaxed enough," he said evenly. "And I'd think you might have seen fit to mention to me that Anna had some plot to improve my sex life for me."

"I might have, if I'd known about it. Then again, since your sex life needed some improvement, I might not." On impulse, Cam grabbed Ethan in a headlock. "Because I love you, man." He only laughed when the elbow plowed into his stomach. "See? It even improved your reflexes."

Ethan shifted, angled his weight, and reversed their positions. "You're right," he said and rubbed his knuckles hard on the top of Cam's head for good measure.

Since it was his night to cook, Ethan added an egg to a bowl of ground beef. He didn't mind cooking. It was just one of those things you did to get through. He'd harbored a small, selfish, and purely chauvinistic hope that Anna would take over the kitchen duties as woman of the house.

She'd squashed that hope like a bug.

Of course, having her around did spread out the chore. But the worst of it, as far as he was concerned, was figuring out the menu. It was different from cooking for himself. He'd learned quickly enough that when you cooked for a family, everybody was a critic.

"What is that?" Seth demanded when Ethan shook oatmeal into the mix.

"Meat loaf."

"Looks like crap to me. Why can't we have pizza?"

"Because we're having meat loaf."

Seth made a gagging sound as Ethan dumped some tomato soup into the mix. "Gross. I'd rather eat dirt."

"There's plenty of it outside."

Seth shifted from foot to foot, rose up on his toes to get a closer look at the bowl. The rain was driving him crazy. There was nothing to *do*. He was starving to death, he had six million mosquito bites, and there was nothing but kid crud and news on TV.

When he listed this litany of complaints, Ethan merely shrugged. "Go bug Cam."

Cam had told him to go bug Ethan. Seth knew from hard experience that it took much longer to bug Ethan than Cam.

"How come you put all that crap in there if it's called meat loaf?"

"So it doesn't taste like crap when you eat it."

"I bet it does."

For a kid who only months before hadn't known where his next meal was coming from, Ethan thought darkly, Seth had gotten mighty particular. Instead of saying so, he aimed a single, sharp dart. "Cam's cooking tomorrow."

"Oh, man. Poison." Seth rolled his eyes dramatically, grabbed his throat, and staggered around the room. Ethan might have been mildly amused if the dogs hadn't gotten into the act by scrambling in and barking wildly.

By the time Anna walked in, Ethan had the meat loaf in the oven and was dumping aspirin into his palm.

"Hi. Miserable day. Traffic was filthy." She raised an eyebrow as Ethan downed the pills. "Headache, huh? All-day rain can sure give you one."

"This one's named Seth."

"Oh." Concerned, she poured herself a glass of wine and prepared to listen. "There's bound to be periods of stress and difficulties. He has a tremendous amount to overcome, and his belligerence is a defense."

"Did nothing but complain for the last hour. My ears are still ringing. Doesn't want meat loaf," Ethan muttered and snagged a beer from the fridge. " 'Why can't we have pizza?' He ought to be grateful somebody's putting food in his belly. Instead he's saying it looks like crap and will likely taste worse. Then he gets the dogs all fired up so I can't even work in peace for five damn minutes. And . . ."

He trailed off, steely-eyed, when he saw her grinning. "Easy for you to be amused by it."

"I am, I'm sorry. But I'm even more pleased. Oh, Ethan, it's so wonderfully normal. He's behaving just like an annoying ten-year-old after a rainy day. A couple of months ago he'd have spent that time sulking in his room instead of giving you a headache. It's such tremendous progress."

"He's progressing into being a pain in the ass."

"Yes." She felt tears of delight sting her eyes. "Isn't it marvelous? He must have been really annoying if it was enough to try your unflappable patience. At this rate he'll be a terror by Christmas."

"And that's a good thing?"

"Yes. Ethan, I've worked with children who haven't faced nearly the miseries Seth has, and it can take them so much longer to adjust, even with counseling. You and Cam and Phillip have done wonders for Seth."

Cooling off, Ethan sipped his beer. "You had a hand in it."

"Yes, I did, which makes me as happy on a professional level as I am on a personal one. And to prove it, I'll give you a hand with dinner." So saying, she shrugged out of her jacket and began to roll up her sleeves. "What did you have in mind to go with the meat loaf?"

He'd planned on sticking some potatoes in the microwave because they didn't require any fussing, and maybe digging some frozen peas out. But . . .

"I thought maybe some of those cheese noodles you make would go nice as a side dish."

"The alfredo? Cholesterol city, added to meat loaf, but what the hell. I'll fix them. Why don't you sit down until the headache passes?"

It already had, but it seemed smarter not to mention it.

He sat, prepared to enjoy his beer—and fix his sister-in-law's wagon. "Oh, Grace said I should thank you for the recipe. She'll let you know how it turns out for her."

"Oh?" Turning to hide her satisfied smile, Anna reached for an apron.

"Yeah, I got the fried chicken makings for you—stuck it in the cookbook." He hid his own smile with his beer when her head swiveled.

"You . . . oh, well . . ."

"I'd have given it to you last night, but it was late when I got back, and you were in bed. I ran into Jim when I left Grace's."

"Jim?" Puzzled annoyance showed clearly on her face.

"Went on over to his place to help him tune up this outboard that's been giving him trouble."

"You were at Jim's last night?"

"Stayed later than I meant to, but there was a ball game on. The O's were playing out in California."

She could have cheerfully smashed him over the head with his own beer bottle. "You spent last night working on an engine and watching a ball game?"

"Yeah." He sent her an innocent look. "Like I said, I got in kinda late, but it was a hell of a game."

She huffed out a breath, yanked open the refrigerator to get out cheese and milk. "Men," she muttered. "All of them idiots."

"What's that?"

"Nothing. Well, I hope you had a fine time watching your baseball game." While Grace was home alone, miserable.

"I can't remember enjoying myself more. Went into extra innings." He was grinning now, just couldn't help it. She looked so flustered and furious and was trying desperately to hide it.

"Well, hot damn." Fuming, she shifted to get the fettuccine out of the cupboard and saw his face. She turned slowly, holding the package of pasta. "You didn't go over to Jim's to watch a ball game last night."

"Didn't I?" He lifted a brow, glanced thoughtfully at his beer, then sipped. "You know, come to think of it, you're right. That was some other time."

"You were with Grace."

"Was I?"

"Oh, Ethan." With clenched teeth she slammed the package down. "You're making me crazy! Where were you last night?"

"You know, I don't believe anyone's asked me that since my mother died."

"I'm not trying to pry—"

"You're not?"

"All right, all right, I am trying to pry and you make it impossible to be subtle about it."

He leaned back in his chair, studying her. He'd liked her, almost from the first—even when she made him uneasy. Wasn't it funny, he mused, to realize that sometime over the last few weeks, he had come to love her. Which meant that teasing her was, well, required.

"You're not asking me if I spent the night in Grace's bed, are you?"

"No. No, of course not." She snatched up the pasta, then set it down again. "Not exactly."

"Were the candles her idea, or yours?"

Anna decided it was a good time to get out a skillet. She just might need a weapon. "Did they work?"

"Yours, I imagine; probably the dress, too. Grace's mind doesn't work that way. She's not what you'd call . . . sneaky."

Anna hummed and prepared to make her cheese sauce.

"And it was sneaky, underhanded, meddling, to send me over there that way."

"I know it. But I'd do it again." More skillfully next time, she promised herself. "You can be annoyed with me all you want, Ethan, but I've never seen anyone more in need of some meddling."

"You're a pro at it. I mean, being a social worker, you make a living meddling in people's lives."

"I help people who need it," she said, firing up the skillet. "God knows you did." She yelped when his hand dropped on her shoulder. She half expected him to give her a quick shake, so when he kissed her cheek she could only blink at him.

"I appreciate it."

"You do?"

"Not that I'd care to have you do it again, but this once, I appreciate it."

"She makes you happy." Everything inside Anna softened. "I can see it."

"We'll see how long I can make her happy."

"Ethan—"

"Let it stand." He kissed her again, as much in warning as affection. "We'll take it a day at a time for a while."

"All right." But her smile bloomed. "Grace is working at the pub tonight, isn't she?"

"Yeah. And just so you don't have to bite your tongue in half to keep from asking, I'm thinking of going by for a while after dinner."

"Good." More than satisfied, Anna got to work. "Then we'll eat soon."

TWELVE

It was like walking wide awake into a dream, Grace thought, where you couldn't be sure what was going to happen next, but you just knew it would be wonderful. It was living inside a familiar world that had been polished into a constant state of anticipation and excitement.

Days and nights were still filled with work, responsibilities, small joys and petty annoyances. But for now, with this full rush of love, the joys seemed huge, the annoyances minute.

Everything she'd ever read about love was true, she discovered. The sun shined brighter, the air smelled fresher. Flowers were more colorful, the songs of birds more musical. Every cliché became her reality.

There were stolen moments—an embrace outside the pub during her break that left her jittery and delighted and unable to sleep long after she went home. A slow, intense look filled with awareness if she managed to linger long enough at the Quinn house to see him. It seemed she was in a constant state of yearning, only more acute now that she knew what could be.

What would be.

She wanted to touch and be touched, to take that long, slow ride into pleasure and passion again. Side by side with the yearning was the endless frustration that life constantly intruded on dreams.

There was never enough time to be alone, to simply be.

She often wondered if Ethan felt the same edgy need dogging his heels throughout his day. She thought it must be something inside her, some long-hidden sexual greed—and she didn't know whether to be delighted by it or mortified.

She only knew that she wanted him constantly, and that with every day that want passed into another night alone, that want increased. She wondered if he would be shocked, worried that he would be.

She needn't have.

He only hoped he'd timed it right, and that his excuses to Jim for taking in the catch before checking all the pots weren't as ridiculously transparent as they'd seemed. He wasn't going to let guilt eat at him either, Ethan promised himself as he secured his boat at his home dock.

He would work a couple extra hours that evening in the boatyard to make up for leaving Cam on his own that afternoon. If he didn't have one hour alone with Grace, if he didn't release some of this pressure that was building up, he'd go crazy. Then he'd be no good to anyone.

And if she'd already finished up at the house and left, well, he'd just have to hunt her down, that's all. He had enough control left not to scare her, or shock her, but he just couldn't get through another day without her.

His grin began to spread when he came through the back door and saw that the morning untidiness had yet to be cleared away. The washer was rumbling in the laundry room. She hadn't finished. He started into the living room, looking for signs of her.

The cushions were all smoothed and plumped, the furniture dust-free and shining. And as the floor above his head gave a quiet creak, he glanced up.

At that moment, he thought Fate was the most beautiful woman he'd ever known. Grace was in his bedroom, and what could be more perfect? It would be much easier to lure her into a daytime bed without jolting her sensibilities if she was already close by one.

He started up the stairs, delighted when he heard her humming.

Then his system suffered a sizzling lightning bolt of lust when he saw she wasn't just close by his bed, she was all but in it. She leaned over, smoothing and tucking fresh sheets, her long legs showcased in ragged cutoffs.

His blood raced, a roar of speed that left him breathless, that turned the low ache he'd learned to live with into a sharp and gnawing pain. He could see himself springing forward, dragging her onto the bed, pulling and tearing at her clothes until he could hammer himself inside her.

And because he could, because he wanted to, he made himself stand where he was until he was certain his control was firmly in place.

"Grace?"

She straightened, whirled, pressed a hand to her heart. "Oh. I . . . oh." She couldn't speak, could barely think coherently. What would *he* think, she wondered giddily, if he knew she'd been fantasizing about rolling naked and sweaty over those crisp clean sheets with him?

Her cheeks had gone pink, charming him. "Didn't mean to sneak up on you."

"That's all right." She let out a long breath, but it did nothing to calm her racing heart. "I didn't expect anyone to . . . what are you doing home so

early in the day?" Quickly she clasped her hands together because they
wanted to grab at him. "Are you sick?"

"No."

"It's not even three o'clock."

"I know." He stepped into the room, saw her press her lips together,
moisten them. Take it slow, he reminded himself, don't spook her. "Aubrey's
not with you?"

"No, Julie's minding her. Julie got a new kitten and Aubrey wanted to
stay, so . . ." He smelled of the water, salt, and sun. It made her light-headed.

"Then we've got some time." He came a little closer. "I wanted to see
you alone."

"You did?"

"I've been wanting to see you alone since we made love that night." He
lifted his hand, gently encircled the nape of her neck. "I've been wanting
you," he said quietly and lowered his mouth to hers.

So soft, so tender, her heart seemed to turn one long, loose somersault in
her chest. Her knees went weak. They trembled even as she threw her arms
around him, as she answered that tentative kiss with a flash of heat. His fingers dug into her skin, his mouth bruised hers. For one wild and wicked moment, she thought he would take her where they stood, fast and frantic and
free.

Then his hands gentled, smoothed over her. His lips softened, cruising
over hers now. "Come to bed with me," he murmured. "Come to bed with
me," even as he lowered her, covered her.

She arched against him, wanting and willing, impatient with the clothes
that separated her flesh from his. It seemed like years since she had last
touched him, had last felt those hard planes, those iron muscles. Moaning
his name, she tugged up his shirt, let her hands possess, and possessing, they
aroused.

His breath came raggedly, burning his throat. Her movements under him
urged him to hurry, hurry, but he was afraid he would bruise her if he didn't
take time, didn't take care. So he fought to slow the pace, to taste rather
than devour, to caress rather than demand.

But whereas she had once seduced him, she now destroyed him.

He tugged off her shirt, found her naked beneath it. She saw his eyes
flash, turn to a burning blue that all but scorched her skin. He was careful,
so careful not to bruise, not to frighten. Slow, to slow the pace even while
the brutal desire to take, take more, take swiftly, swarmed into him.

Then his mouth was on her, sucking her in with a desperate hunger that
threatened to consume them both. She threw her arm back, reached, but
there was nothing to hold on to except empty air. He dragged her up, his

mouth streaking down her torso, teeth scraping, until, gasping for air, she folded herself around him.

He couldn't wait, knew it would kill him to wait. The only thought in his head was now, it had to be now, and even that was wrapped in the rusty edges of primal need. He tugged at her shorts, cursing, then plunged his fingers inside her.

She bucked, cried out, came. He watched her eyes go opaque, her head fall back so that the long line of her throat was there for him to feast on. Battling the violent urge to drive himself into her, he continued to taste until the sharp void was filled.

Then he freed himself from his jeans and slipped into her. She cried out again, her muscles clamping tight around him.

And he lost his mind.

Speed and heat and force. More. He shoved her knees up and stroked deeper, harder, darkly thrilled when her nails bit into his shoulders. He plunged inside her, quivering with raw, blind greed.

Sensations swamped her, scraped at her, stripped her into one shuddering mass of need. She thought she might die from it. When the next orgasm slammed into her, a hard, hot fist, she thought she had.

And went limp, her hands sliding from Ethan's damp shoulders, the silver flash of energy draining to leave her exhausted. She heard his long, low groan, felt his body plunge, then stiffen. When he collapsed on her, panting, her lips curved in a smile of pure female satisfaction.

The sunlight dazzled her eyes as she stroked her hands down and over his hips. "Ethan." She turned her head to kiss his hair. "No, not yet," she murmured when he started to shift. "Not yet."

He'd been rough with her, and he cursed himself for allowing the knot on his control to slip. "Are you all right?"

"Mmmmmm. I could lie here all day, just like this."

"I didn't take the time I meant to."

"We don't have as much as most people."

"No." He lifted his head. "You wouldn't even tell me if I'd hurt you." So he looked for himself, carefully studying her face. And he saw in it the sleepy satisfaction of a woman well, if hurriedly, loved. "I guess I didn't."

"It was exciting. It was wonderful knowing you wanted me so much." Lazily, she twirled a lock of his sun-tipped hair around her finger and hugged the gorgeously wicked sensation of being naked in bed with him in the middle of the day. "I'd been worried that I wanted you more than you could ever want me."

"You couldn't." To prove it, he kissed her long and slow and deep. "This isn't the way I want it for you. Cramming minutes alone between chores. And using those minutes to jump into bed because it's all we've got."

"I've never made love in the middle of the day before." She smiled. "I liked it."

On a long breath, he lowered his brow to hers. If it had been possible, he would have spent the rest of the day right there, inside her. "We're going to have to figure out a way to find a little more time now and again."

"I've got tomorrow night off. You could come by for dinner . . . and stay."

"I ought to take you out somewhere."

"There's nowhere I want to go. I'd like it if we could have dinner in." Then her smile spread. "I'll make you some tortellini. I just got this new recipe."

When he laughed, she threw her arms around him and chalked up another of the happiest moments of her life. "Oh, I love you, Ethan." She was so giddy with it that it took her a moment to realize he was no longer laughing, had gone very still. Her wildly bounding heart slowed, and chilled.

"Maybe you don't want me to say that, but I can't help feeling it. I don't expect you to say it back, or feel obligated to—"

His fingers pressed lightly against her lips to silence her. "Give me a minute, Grace," he said quietly. His system had flooded, rising tides of joys, hopes, fears. He couldn't think past them, not clearly. But he knew her, knew that what he said now, and how he said it, would be vitally important.

"I've had feelings for you for so long," he began, "I can't remember when I didn't have them. I've spent just as long telling myself I shouldn't have them, so all of this is taking me some time to get used to."

When he shifted this time, she didn't try to stop him. She nodded, avoided his eyes and reached for her clothes. "It's enough that you want me, maybe even need me a little. It's enough for now, Ethan. This is all so new for both of us."

"They're strong feelings, Grace. You matter to me more than any woman ever has."

She looked at him now. If he said it, she knew he meant it. Hope began to beat in her heart again. "If you had feelings for me, strong feelings, why didn't you ever let me know?"

"First you weren't old enough," He pushed his hand through his hair, knowing that that was an evasion, an excuse, and not the core of it. He couldn't tell her the core of it. "And I wasn't real comfortable having the kind of thoughts and feelings for you I was having when you were still in high school."

She could have leaped up on the bed and danced. "Since I was in high school? All this time?"

"Yeah, all this time. Then you were in love with somebody else, so I didn't have any right to feel anything but friendship."

She let out a careful breath, because it would be a confession that shamed her. "I was never in love with anybody else. It was always you."

"Jack—"

"I never loved him, and everything that went wrong between us was more my fault than his. I let him be the first man to touch me because I never thought you would. And about the time I realized how foolish that was, I was pregnant."

"You can't say it was your fault."

"Yes, I can." To keep her hands busy, she began to tidy the bed. "I knew he wasn't in love with me, but I married him because I was afraid not to. And for a while I was ashamed, angry and ashamed." She lifted a pillow, tucked it into its case. "Until one night when I was lying in bed thinking my life was over, and I felt this fluttering inside me."

She closed her eyes, pressed the pillow against her. "I felt Aubrey, and it was so . . . so huge, that little flutter, that I wasn't ashamed or angry any-more. Jack gave me that." She opened her eyes again and carefully laid the pillow on the bed. "I'm grateful to him, and I don't blame him for leaving. He never felt that flutter. Aubrey was never real to him."

"He was a coward, and worse, for leaving you weeks before the baby was born."

"Maybe, but I was a coward, and worse, for being with him, for marry-ing him when I never had a fraction of the feeling for him that I did for you."

"You're the bravest woman I know, Grace."

"It's easy to be brave when you have a child depending on you. I guess what I'm trying to tell you is that if I made a mistake, it was in going so long without letting you know I loved you. Whatever feelings you have for me, Ethan, are more than I ever thought you would have. And that's enough."

"I've been in love with you for the best part of ten years, and it's still not enough."

She'd picked up the second pillow, and now it slipped out of her hands. When tears swam into her eyes, she closed them, squeezed tight. "I thought I could live without ever hearing you say that. Now I need to hear you say it again so I can get my breath back."

"I love you, Grace."

Her lips curved, her eyes opened. "You sound so serious, almost sad when you say it." Wanting to see him smile again, she held out a hand. "Maybe you should practice."

His fingers had just touched hers when the screen door slammed downstairs. Feet pounded on the stairs. Even as they jerked apart, Seth raced down the hall. He skidded to a halt at the door to his room, then stood, stared.

He glanced at the bed, the sheets not quite smoothed out, the pillow on the floor. Then his gaze shifted, and filled with a bitter fury that was much too adult in his young face.

"You bastard." There was loathing in the tone as he snapped at Ethan, then disgust as his eyes locked on Grace. "I thought you were different."

"Seth." She took a step forward, but he turned on his heel and ran. "Oh, God, Ethan." When she started to rush after the boy, Ethan took her arm.

"No, I'll go after him. I know what he's feeling. Don't worry." He gave her arm a squeeze before walking out. Still, she followed him to the steps, worried sick. She'd never seen such dark hate in the eyes of a child.

"Damn it, Seth, I told you to hurry up." Cam slammed in the front door just as Ethan hit the bottom of the steps. Cam glanced up, saw Grace, and felt a grin tug at his mouth. "Oops."

"I don't have time for lame jokes," Ethan shot back. "Seth just took off."

"What? Why?" It struck him even before the word was out. "Oh, shit. He must have gone out the back."

"I'm going after him." He shook his head before Cam could protest. "It's me he's pissed off at right now. It's me he figures let him down. I have to fix it." He glanced up to where Grace sat on the steps. "Look after her," he murmured to Cam and headed for the back door.

Ethan knew Seth would have headed into the woods, and he had to trust that the boy wouldn't run too far into the marsh. He was a survivor, Ethan thought. But relief shimmered through him when he heard the rustle of brush and old leaves.

It was simple enough to spot where Seth had veered off the path. Ethan pushed through tangled vines, the prickle of briars, and followed. The leaves on the trees that arched overhead blocked the glare and the worst of the sun's heat. But the humidity was immense.

Sweat ran down Ethan's back, dripped into his eyes, as he patiently walked, and waited. He was well aware that Seth was evading him, keeping a few yards ahead. Finally he sat on a fallen log, deciding it would be easier to let the boy come to him.

It took ten long minutes, with gnats swarming in clouds and mosquitoes sniffing for blood, but finally Seth emerged from a thicket and faced him.

"I'm not going back with you." He all but spat it out. "If you try to make me, I'll just run again."

"I'm not going to make you do anything." From his seat on the log, Ethan studied him. Seth's face was filthy, streaked with dirt and sweat, flushed with heat and fury. His legs and arms were thoroughly scratched from pushing through briars.

They were going to sting like fury, Ethan knew, when Seth cooled off enough to notice.

"You want to sit down and talk this out?" he asked mildly.

"I don't believe anything you say. You're a liar. You're both fucking liars. You gonna try to tell me you weren't screwing each other?"

"No, that's not what we were doing."

Seth flew at him so fast, Ethan was thrown off guard enough to take the first fist solidly in the jaw. He would think later, much later, that the kid threw a fine punch. But at the moment it took all his concentration to wrestle Seth to the ground.

"I'll kill you! You bastard, I'll kill you as soon as I get a chance." He wiggled and struggled and fought and waited for the rain of blows.

"Just hold on." Frustrated as the slick, sweaty arms kept sliding out of his grip, Ethan gave Seth a quick shake. "You're not getting anywhere this way. I'm bigger than you are, and I'll just pin you down till you run out of steam."

"Take your hands off me." Seth set his teeth and snarled. "Son of a whore."

It was a blow harder, and more sharply aimed, than the fist had been. Ethan caught his breath and nodded slowly. "Yeah, that's what I am. That's why you and I know each other. You can run when I let you up, Seth. You can spill filth all over me. That's what people expect from sons of whores. I'm going to figure you want better for yourself than that."

Ethan eased back, sat on his heels and wiped the blood off his mouth. "That's the second damn time you've punched me in the face. You try it again, and I'm going to wallop your ass so you don't sit for a month."

"I hate your fucking guts."

"Fine. But you're going to have to hate them for the right reasons."

"All you wanted was to get between her legs, and she spread them for you."

"Watch it." In a lightning move, Ethan grabbed Seth by the shirt and hauled him up to his knees. "Don't you talk about her that way. You had sense enough to recognize right off what kind of person Grace was. That's why you trusted her, why you cared about her."

"I don't give a shit about her," Seth claimed and had to swallow hard before the hot tears poured out.

"If you didn't, you wouldn't be so mad at both of us. And wouldn't be feeling like we let you down."

He let Seth go, then rubbed his hands over his face. He knew how miserably inept he could be at explaining emotions. Especially his own. "I'm going to talk to you straight." He dropped his hands. "You're right about what went on before you came home, you're just wrong about what it meant."

Seth's lips quivered into a snarl. "I know what fucking means."

"Yeah, the way you know it it's ugly sounds in the next room, fast gropes in the dark, sour smells, money changing hands."

"Just because you didn't pay her doesn't—"

"Be quiet," Ethan said patiently. "I used to think that's all it was, or the only kind there was. Hard and heartless, sometimes mean. All you want from the other is what you can get for yourself. So that makes it selfish, too. You get some release, pull your pants up and walk away. It's not always wrong. If it doesn't matter to either one of you, if it gets you through the night, it's not always wrong. But it's not the only way, and it sure as hell isn't the best way."

He remembered now thinking that he hoped someone else would explain such things to the boy when the time came. But it appeared that the time was now and he was in charge.

He couldn't say it all with a grin and a wink as Cam might, or smooth and fancy as Phillip surely would. He could only speak from the heart and hope it was right.

"Sex can be the same as eating. Just filling a hunger. Sometimes you pay for a meal, sometimes you trade something, and if it's fair you're giving as much as you're taking."

"Sex is just sex. They just pretty it up to sell books and movies."

"Do you figure that's all there is between Anna and Cam?"

Seth moved his shoulders, but he was thinking.

"They've got something that matters, and lasts, that lives get built on. It's not what you've grown up with, or what I spent the first part of my life with—that's why I can tell you straight."

Ethan pressed his fingers to his eyes and ignored the swarm of bugs and the sweat. "It's different when you care, when the other person isn't just a face or a body that's convenient and willing. I've had that. Most people do along the way. It's different when it's just that one person who matters, who makes it right. When it isn't all hunger pushing at you. When you want, more than anything, to give back more than you take. I never had with anyone what I have with Grace."

Seth shrugged and looked away, but not before Ethan saw the misery on his face. "I know you've got feelings for her, and that they're real and strong and important. Maybe part of you wanted her to be perfect, not to have the needs other women do. I think a bigger part of you wanted to protect her, to make sure nobody hurt her. So I'm telling you what I just finished finally telling her. I love her. I've never loved anybody else."

Seth stared off into the marsh. He hurt all over, but the worst of it was shame. "Does she love you back?"

"Yeah, she does. Damned if I can figure out why."

Seth thought he knew why. Ethan was strong, and he didn't put on a big show. He did what had to be done. What was right. "I was going to take care of her when I got older. I guess you think that's pretty lame."

"No." He suddenly, urgently, wanted to pull the boy against him, but he knew the timing was wrong. "No, I think that's pretty great. It makes me proud of you."

Seth's gaze flicked up, then quickly away again. "I kind of, you know, love her. Sort of. Not like I want to see her naked or anything," he added quickly. "Just—"

"I get it." Ethan clamped down on the tip of his tongue to stifle the chuckle. The quick surge of amused relief tasted finer than an icy beer on a hot day. "Kind of like she was a sister, like you wanted the best for her."

"Yeah." And Seth sighed. "Yeah, I guess that's it."

Thoughtfully, Ethan sucked air between his teeth. "It's got to be tough for a guy to walk in and see that his sister's been with some guy."

"I hurt her. I wanted to."

"Yeah, you did. You'll have to apologize if you want to put things right with her."

"She'll think I'm stupid. She won't want to talk to me."

"She wanted to come after you herself. By this time, I'd say she's pacing around the backyard, worried sick."

Seth sucked in a breath that was too close to a sob to suit either of them. "I razzed Cam until he brought me home for my ball glove. And when I . . . I saw you in there, it made me think of how I would come back to wherever Gloria was living, and she'd be doing it with some guy."

Where sex was a business, Ethan thought, both ugly and mean. "It's hard to put those things aside, or let yourself believe there's a different way." Since he was still working on it himself, Ethan spoke carefully. "That making love, when you care, when it matters, when things are right, it's clean."

Seth sniffled, wiped at his eyes. "Gnats," he muttered.

"Yeah, they're a bitch out here."

"You should've slugged me, for saying that shit."

"You're right," Ethan decided after a moment. "I'll slug you next time. Now, let's go home."

He rose, brushed off his pants, then held out a hand. Seth stared up at him, saw kindness, patience, compassion. Qualities in a man he might have sneered at once because he'd found so little of them in anyone who had touched his life.

He put his hand in Ethan's and, without realizing it, left it there as they walked down the path. "How come you didn't hit me back even once?"

Little boy, Ethan thought, you've had too many hands raised against you in your short life. "Maybe I was afraid you could take me."

Seth snorted, blinking furiously at tears that still wanted to come. "Shit."

"Well, you're small," Ethan said, taking the cap from Seth's back pocket and snugging it down on Seth's head. "But you're a wiry little bastard."

Seth had to take long breaths as they came close to where the sunlight struck the edge of the woods, slanting white light.

He saw Grace, as Ethan had predicted, in the yard, hugging her arms as if she were chilled. She dropped them, took a quick step forward, then stopped.

Ethan felt Seth's hand flex in his and gave it a quick encouraging squeeze. "It'd go a long way to making things up to her," Ethan murmured, "if you were to run up and hug her. Grace is big on hugs."

It was what he'd wanted to do, what he was afraid to risk. He looked up at Ethan, jerked a shoulder, cleared his throat. "I guess I could, if it'd make her feel better."

Ethan stood back, watched the boy race across the lawn, watched Grace's face light with a smile as she threw open her arms to take him in.

THIRTEEN

If you were going to have to work over a long holiday weekend, Phillip figured, it might as well be at something fun. He loved his job. What was advertising, anyway, but a knowledge of people and of which buttons to push to nudge them into opening their wallets?

It was, he often thought, an accepted, creative, even expected twist on picking those wallets. For a man who had spent the first half of his life as a thief, it was the perfect career.

On this day before the celebration of America's independence, he put his skills to use in the boatyard, schmoozing a potential client. He much preferred it to manual labor.

"You'll forgive the surroundings." Phillip waved a well-manicured hand, encompassing the enormous space, the exposed rafters and hanging lights, the yet-to-be-painted walls and scarred floors. "My brothers and I believe in putting our efforts into the product and keeping our overhead minimal. Those are benefits that we pass along to our clients."

At which time, Phillip thought, they had exactly one—with another in the box and this one nibbling at the line.

"Hmmm." Jonathan Kraft rubbed his chin. He was in his mid-thirties and fortunate enough to be a fourth-generation member of the pharmaceutical Krafts. Since his great-grandfather's humble beginnings as a storefront pharmacist in Boston, his family had built and expanded an empire on buffered aspirin and analgesics. It allowed Jonathan to indulge in his great love of sailing.

He was tall, fit, tanned. His hair was mink-brown and perfectly styled to showcase his square-jawed, handsome face. He wore buff-colored chinos, a navy cotton shirt, and well-broken-in Top-Siders. His watch was a Rolex, his belt hand-tooled Italian leather.

He looked exactly like what he was: a privileged, wealthy man with a love of the outdoors.

"You've only been in business a few months."

"Officially," Phillip said with a flashing smile. His hair was a rich, deep bronze, styled to make the most of a face that the angels had gifted with an extra kiss of pure male beauty. He wore fashionably faded Levi's, a green cotton shirt, and olive-drab Supergas. His eyes were shrewd, his smile charming.

He looked exactly like what he'd made himself into: a sophisticated urbanite with an affection for fashion and the sea.

"We've built or worked on teams that built a number of boats over the years." Smoothly, he guided Jonathan toward the framed sketches hanging on the wall. Seth's artwork was displayed rustically, as Phillip felt suited the ambience of a traditional boatyard.

"My brother Ethan's skipjack. One of the handful that still goes under sail every winter to dredge for oysters in the Chesapeake. She's had over ten years in service."

"She's a beauty." Jonathan's face turned dreamy, as Phillip had suspected it would. However a man chose to pick wallets, he had to gauge his marks. "I'd like to see her."

"I'm sure we can arrange that."

He let Jonathan linger before nudging him gently along. "Now, you may recognize this one." He indicated the drawing of a sleek racing skiff. "The *Circe*. My brother Cameron was involved with both her design and her construction."

"And she beat my *Lorilee* to the finish line two years running." Jonathan grimaced good-naturedly. "Of course, Cam was leading the team."

"He knows his boats." Phillip heard the buzz of a drill from where Cameron worked belowdecks. He intended to bring Cam into this shortly.

"The sloop currently under construction is primarily Ethan's design, though Cam added some points. We're dedicated to serving the client's needs and wishes." He led Jonathan over to where Seth continued his hull sanding. Ethan stood on deck, attaching the rubrails. "He wanted speed, stability, and some luxuries."

Phillip knew the hull was a brilliant show of smooth lap construction—he'd put in plenty of sweaty hours on it himself. "She's built for show as well as function. Teak from stem to stern, at the client's direction," he added, knocking his knuckles cheerfully against the hull.

Phillip wiggled his brows at Ethan. Recognizing the signal, Ethan bit back a sigh. He knew he was going to hate this part, but Phillip had pointed out that it was good business to bring the potential client into the fold.

"The joints are wedged and married, without glue." Ethan rolled his shoulders, feeling as though he were giving an oral school report. He'd always hated them. "We figured if the old-time boat builders could make a joint last a century or so without glue, so could we. And I've seen too many glued joints fail."

"Hmmm," Jonathan said again, and Ethan took a breath.

"The hull's caulked in the traditional way—stranded cotton. Planking's tight, wood to wood on the inside. We rolled two strands of cotton in most of the seams. Hardly needed the mallet. Then we payed them with standard seam components."

Jonathan hummed again. He had only a vague idea what Ethan was talking about. He sailed boats—boats that he'd bought fresh and clean and finished. But he liked the sound of it.

"She appears to be a fine, tight boat. A pretty pleasure craft. I'll be looking for speed and efficiency as well as aesthetics."

"We'll see that you get it." Phillip smiled broadly, waving a finger at Ethan behind Jonathan's head. It was time to pull out the next round.

Ethan headed belowdecks, where Cam was fitting out the framing for an under-the-bunk cabinet. "Your turn up there," he muttered.

"Phil got him on the string?"

"Couldn't tell by me. I gave my little speech, and the guy just nodded and made noises. You ask me, he didn't know what the hell I was talking about."

"Of course he doesn't. Jonathan hires people to worry about maintaining his boats. He's never scraped a hull or replanked a deck in his life." Cam rose from his crouch, worked the stiffness out of his knees. "He's the kind of guy who drives a Maserati without knowing dick about engines. But he'd have been impressed with your salty waterman's drawl and rugged good looks."

As Ethan gave a snorting laugh, Cam elbowed past him. "I'll go give him my push."

He climbed topside and managed to look credibly surprised to see Jonathan onboard, studying the gunwales. "Hey, Kraft, how's it going?"

"Fast and far." With genuine pleasure, Jonathan shook Cam's hand. "I was surprised when you didn't show at the San Diego regatta this summer."

"Got myself married."

"So I hear. Congratulations. And now you're building boats instead of racing them."

"I wouldn't count me out of racing entirely. I'm toying with building myself a cat over the winter if business slacks off any."

"Keeping busy?"

"Word gets out," Cam said easily. "A boat by Quinn means quality. Smart people want the best—when they can afford it." He grinned, fast and slick. "Can you afford it?"

"I'm thinking of a cat myself. Your brother must have mentioned it."

"Yeah, he ran it by me. You want light, fast, and tight. Ethan and I have been modifying a design for what I had in mind for me."

"That's bullshit," Seth murmured, only loud enough for Phillip to hear.

"Sure." Phillip winked at him. "But it's Class A bullshit." He leaned a little closer to Seth as Cam and Jonathan launched into the lure of racing a catboat. "Cam knows that while the guy likes him fine, he's competitive. Never beat Cam in a head-to-head race. So . . ."

"So he'd pay buckets of money to have Cam build him a boat that not even Cam could beat."

"There you go." Proud, Phillip gave Seth a light punch on the shoulder. "You got a quick brain there. Keep using it, and you won't be spending all your time sanding hulls. Now, kid, watch the master."

He straightened, beamed up. "I'd be happy to show you the drawings, Jonathan. Why don't we go into my office? I'll dig them out for you."

"Wouldn't mind taking a look." Jonathan climbed down. "The problem is, I need this boat seaworthy by March first. I'll need time to test her, work out the kinks, break her in before the summer races."

"March first." Phillip pursed his lips, then he shook his head. "That might be a problem. Quality comes first here. It takes time to build a champion. I'll look over our schedule," he added, dropping an arm over Jonathan's shoulder as they walked. "We'll see what we can work out—but the contract's already in place, and the worksheets tell me May is the soonest we can deliver the top-quality product you expect and deserve."

"That's not going to give me much time to get the feel of her," Jonathan complained.

"Believe me, Jonathan, a boat by Quinn is going to feel fine. Just fine," he added, glancing back at his brothers with a quick and wolfish grin before he nudged Jonathan inside the office.

"He'll buy us till May," Cam decided, and Ethan nodded.

"Or he'll make it April and skin the poor bastard for a bonus."

"Either way." Cam clamped a hand on Ethan's shoulder. "We're going to have ourselves another contract by end of day."

Below, Seth snorted. "Shit, he'll wrap it up by lunchtime. The guy's toast."

Cam tucked his tongue in his cheek. "Two o'clock, soonest."

"Noon," Seth said, peering up at him.

"Two bucks?"

"Sure. I can use the money."

"Y̶ou know," Cam said as he dug out his wallet, "before you came along to ruin my life, I'd just won a bundle in Monte Carlo."

Seth sneered cheerfully. "This ain't Monte Carlo."

"You're telling me." He passed the bills over, then winced when he saw his wife come into the building. "Cool it. Social worker heading in. She's not going to approve of minors gambling."

"Hey, I won," Seth pointed out, but he stuffed the bills in his pocket. "You bring any food?" he asked Anna.

"Oh, no, I didn't. Sorry." Distracted, she dragged a hand through her hair. There was a sick ball in the pit of her stomach that she did her best to ignore. She smiled, a curve of lips that didn't quite manage to reach her eyes. "Didn't you all pack lunch?"

"Yeah, but you usually bring something better."

"This time I've been pretty tied up putting food together for the picnic tomorrow." She ran a hand over his head, then left it lying on his shoulder. She needed the contact. "I just . . . thought I'd take a break and see how things were going around here."

"Phil just nailed this rich guy for a ton of money."

"Good, that's good," she said absently. "Then we should celebrate. Why don't I spring for ice cream? You think you can handle picking up some hot fudge sundaes at Crawford's?"

"Yeah." His face split into a grin. "I can handle it."

She dragged money out of her purse, hoping he didn't notice that her hands weren't quite steady. "No nuts on mine, remember?"

"Sure. I got it. I'm gone." He raced out, and she watched him, heartsick.

"What is it, Anna?" Cam put his hands on her shoulders, turned her to face him. "What happened?"

"Give me a minute. I broke records getting here, and I need some time to settle." She blew out a breath, drew one in, and felt marginally steadier. "Go get your brothers, Cam."

"Okay." But he lingered, rubbing his hands over her shoulders. It was rare for her to look so shaken. "Whatever it is, we'll fix it."

He walked to the cargo doors, where Ethan and Phil stood outside arguing over baseball. "Something's up," he said briefly. "Anna's here. She sent Seth off. She's upset."

She was standing by a workbench, with one of Seth's drawing books open, when they came in. It made her eyes sting to see her own face, carefully, skillfully sketched by the young boy's hand.

He'd been more than a case file, almost from the start. And now he was hers, as much as Ethan and Phillip were hers. Family. She couldn't stand to think that anything or anyone would hurt her family.

But she was steadier when she turned, scanned the quiet and concerned faces of the men who'd become essential to her life. "This came in today's mail." Her hand no longer trembled as she reached into her purse and pulled out the letter.

"It's addressed to 'The Quinns.' Just 'The Quinns,'" she repeated. "From Gloria DeLauter. I opened it. I thought it best, and well, my name's Quinn now, too."

She offered it to Cam. Saying nothing, he took out the single sheet of lined paper and passed the envelope to Phillip.

"She mailed it from Virginia Beach," Phillip murmured. "We lost her in North Carolina. She's sticking with the beaches, but coming north."

"What does she want?" Ethan stuffed hands that had curled into fists into his pockets. A low, simmering rage was already pumping through his blood.

"What you'd expect," Cam answered shortly. "Money. 'Dear Quinns,'" Cam read. "'I heard how Ray died. It's too bad. You might not know that Ray and me had an agreement. I think you'll want to make good on it since you're keeping Seth. I guess he's pretty settled in there in that nice house. I miss him. You don't know what a sacrifice it was for me to give him up to Ray, but I wanted what was best for my only son.'"

"You ought to have your violin," Phillip muttered to Ethan.

"'I knew Ray would be good to him,'" Cam continued. "'He did right by the three of you, and Seth's got his blood.'"

He stopped reading for a moment. There it was, in black and white. "Truth or lie?" He looked up at his brothers.

"That's to deal with later." Ethan felt the ache begin around his heart and move in to squeeze. But he shook his head. "Read the rest."

"Okay. 'Ray knew how much it hurt me to part with the boy, so he helped me out. But now that he's gone, I'm starting to worry that it might not be the best place for Seth there with you. I'm willing to be convinced. If you're set on keeping him, you'll keep up Ray's promise of helping me out. I'm going to need some money, like a sign that you've got good intentions. Five thousand. You can send it to me, care of General Delivery here in Virginia Beach. I'll give you two weeks, figuring the mail's kind of unreliable. If I don't hear back, I'll know you don't really want the kid. I'll come get him. He must be missing me something awful. Be sure to tell him his mom loves him, and might be seeing him real soon.'"

"Bitch," was Phillip's first comment. "She's testing us out, trying her hand at a little more blackmail to see if we'll fall for it the way Dad did."

"You can't." Anna put a hand on Cam's arm, felt the quiver of rage. "You have to let the system work. You have to trust me to see that she doesn't do this. In court—"

"Anna." Cam shoved the letter into the hand Ethan had held out. "We're not going to put that boy through a court case. Not if there's another way."

"You don't mean to pay her. Cam—"

"I don't mean for her to have one fucking cent." He prowled away, struggling to fight off fury. "She thinks she's got us by the balls, but she's wrong. We're not one lone old man." He whirled back, eyes blazing. "Let's see her try to get through us to lay hands on Seth."

"She was pretty careful how she worded things," Ethan commented as he scanned the letter again. "Doesn't make it less of a threat, but she's not stupid."

"She's greedy," Phillip put in. "If she's already angling for more after what Dad paid her, she's testing the depth of the well."

"She sees you as her source now," Anna agreed. "And there's no predicting what she'll do if she knows that source isn't easily tapped." Pausing, she pressed her fingers to her temples, ordered herself to think. "If she comes back into the county and attempts to make contact with Seth, I can have her detained, legally barred—at least temporarily—from direct contact with him. You have guardianship. And Seth is old enough to speak for himself. The question is, will he?"

She lifted her hands, frustrated, let them fall. "He's told me very little about his life before he came here. I'll need specifics in order to block any custody attempt on her part."

"He doesn't want her. And she doesn't want him." Ethan resisted, barely, crumpling the letter into a ball. "Unless he's worth the price of another fix. She let her johns try for him."

Anna shifted to face him, kept her eyes calm and direct on his. "Did Seth tell you that? Did he tell you there had been sexual abuse and she'd been a party to it?"

"He told me enough." Ethan's mouth went hard and grim. "And it's up to him if he wants to tell anybody else and see it put in some goddamn county report."

"Ethan." Anna laid a hand on his rigid arm. "I love him, too. I only want to help him."

"I know." He stepped back because the anger was too fierce and too likely to spew on everyone. "I'm sorry, but there are times the system makes it worse. Makes you feel like you're being swallowed up." He struggled to block out the echo of pain. "He's going to know he's got us, with or without any system, to stand with him."

"The lawyer needs to know she made contact." Phillip took the letter from Ethan, folded it, and tucked it back into the envelope. "And we have to decide how we're going to handle it. My first impulse is to go down to Virginia Beach, dig her out of her hole, and tell her in a way she'd understand just what's going to happen to her if she comes within fifty miles of Seth."

"Threatening her won't help . . ." Anna began.

"But it would feel damn good." Cam bared his teeth. "Let me do it."

"On the other hand," Phillip continued, "I think it might be very effective—and look very good if it ever comes to a legal battle—if our pal Gloria got an official letter from Seth's caseworker. Outlining the status, the options, and the conclusions reached. Contacting or attempting to contact a birth mother who may be rethinking giving up custody of her child—a child who's in your files—would come within the parameters of your job, wouldn't it, Anna?"

She mulled it over, knowing it was a fine line and expert balance would be required to walk it. "I can't threaten her. But . . . I may be able to make her stop and think. But the big question is, do we tell Seth?"

"He's afraid of her," Cam murmured. "Damn it, the kid's just starting to relax, to believe he's safe. Why do we have to tell him she's poking her finger back into his life?"

"Because he's got a right to know." Ethan spoke quietly. His temper had leveled off, and he was able to think clearly again. "He's got a right to know what he might have to fight. If you know what's after you, you've got a better chance. And because," he added, "the letter was addressed to the Quinns. He's one of us."

"I'd rather burn it," Phillip muttered. "But you're right."

"We'll all tell him," Cam agreed.

"I'd like to do the talking."

Both Cam and Phillip stared at Ethan. "You would?"

"He might take it easier from me." He looked over as Seth came through the door. "So let's find out."

"Mother Crawford put on extra hot fudge. Man, she just poured it on. There's about a million tourists up on the waterfront, and . . ."

His excited chatter trailed off. His eyes went from gleeful to wary. Inside his chest, his heart began to drum. He recognized trouble, bad trouble. It had its own smell. "What's the deal?"

Anna took the large bag from him and turned to set the plastic-topped dishes of ice cream out. "Why don't you sit down, Seth?"

"I don't need to sit down." It was easier to get a head start running if you were already on your feet.

"There was a letter that came today." It was best, Ethan knew, if hard news was delivered fast and clean. "From your mother."

"She's here?" The fear was back, sharp as a scalpel. Seth took one quick step in retreat, going stiff as a board when Cam laid a hand on his shoulder.

"No, she's not here. But we are. You remember that."

Seth shuddered once, then planted his feet. "What the hell did she want? Why's she sending letters? I don't want to see it."

"Then you don't have to," Anna assured him. "Why don't you let Ethan explain, then we'll talk about what we're going to do."

"She knows Ray's dead," Ethan began. "I gotta figure she's known right along, but she's taken her time getting to it."

"He gave her money." Seth swallowed hard to gulp down the fear. Quinns weren't afraid, he told himself. They weren't afraid of anything. "She took off. She doesn't care that he's dead."

"I don't suppose she does, but she's hoping for more money. That's what the letter's about."

"She wants me to pay her?" Fresh and bright fear exploded in Seth's brain. "I don't have any money. What's she writing to me for money for?"

"She wasn't writing to you."

Seth took a ragged breath and concentrated on Ethan's face. The eyes were clear and patient, the mouth firm and serious. Ethan knew, was all he could think. Ethan knew what it was like. He knew about the rooms, the smells, the fat hands in the dark.

"She wants you to pay her." Part of him wanted to beg them to do it. To pay her whatever she wanted. He would swear in blood that he would do anything they asked of him for the rest of his life to honor the debt.

But he couldn't. Not with Ethan watching him, and waiting. And knowing.

"If you do, she'll just come back for more. She'll keep coming back." Seth rubbed the back of a sweaty hand over his mouth. "As long as she knows where I am she'll keep coming back. I have to go someplace else, someplace where she can't find me."

"You're not going anywhere." Ethan crouched so they were closer to eye level. "And she's not going to get any more money. She's not going to win."

Slowly, mechanically, Seth shook his head back and forth. "You don't know her."

"I know pieces of her. She's smart enough to know we're set on keeping you with us. That we love you enough to pay." He saw the flash of emotion in Seth's eyes before the boy lowered them. "And we would pay if that would end it, if that would ease things. But it won't end or ease it. It's like you said. She'd just come back."

"What are you going to do?"

"It's what we're going to do now. All of us," he said and waited for Seth's gaze to settle on his face again. "We'll go on as we've been going on, mostly. Phil will talk to the lawyer so we got that end covered."

"You tell him I'm not going back with her," Seth said furiously, shooting a desperate look at Phillip. "No matter what, I'm not going back."

"I'll tell him."

"Anna's going to write her a letter," Ethan continued.

"What kind of letter?"

"A smart one," Ethan said with the hint of a smile. "With all those fifty-dollar words and that official-sounding stuff. She'll be doing it as your case-worker, to let Gloria know we've got the system and the law behind us. It might give her pause to think."

"She hates social workers," Seth put in.

"Good." For the first time in more than an hour, Anna smiled and meant it. "People who hate something are usually afraid of it, too."

"One thing that would help, Seth, if you can do it—"

He turned back to Ethan. "What do I have to do?"

"If you could talk to Anna, tell her how things were before—as close to exact as you can manage."

"I don't want to talk about it. It's over. I'm not going back."

"I know." Gently, Ethan put his hands on Seth's trembling shoulders. "And I know talking about it can be almost like being there again. It took me a long time to be able to tell my mother—to tell Stella. To say it all out loud, even though she already knew most of it. It started to get better after that. And it helped her and Ray get the legal crap handled."

Seth thought of *High Noon,* of heroes. Of Ethan. "It's the right thing to do?"

"Yeah, it's the right thing."

"Will you come with me?"

"Sure." Ethan rose, held out a hand. "We'll go home and talk it through."

FOURTEEN

"Ready? Mama? Time to go?"

"Almost, Aubrey." Grace put the finishing touches on her potato salad, sprinkling paprika on to give it zest and color.

Aubrey had been asking her the same question since seven-thirty that morning. Grace decided the only reason she hadn't run out of patience with her daughter was because she felt just as anxious and eager as a two-year-old herself.

"*Maaamaaa.*"

At the deep frustration in Aubrey's voice, Grace had to swallow a chuckle. "Let me see." Grace tucked the clear wrap tidily around the bowl before she turned and studied her little girl. "You look pretty."

"I have a bow." In a purely female gesture, Aubrey lifted a hand and patted the ribbon Grace had threaded through her curls.

"A pink bow."

"Pink." With a smile, Aubrey beamed up at her mother. "Pretty Mama."

"Thanks, baby." She hoped Ethan thought so. How would he look at her? she wondered. How should they behave? There would be so many people there, and no one—well, besides the Quinns—no one knew they were in love.

In love, she thought with a long, dreamy sigh. It was such a marvelous place to be. She blinked when little arms wrapped around her legs and squeezed.

"Mama! Ready?"

Laughing, Grace hauled her up for a big hug and kiss. "All right. Let's go."

No general in the hours before a decisive battle ever ordered his troops into action with more authority and determination than Anna Spinelli Quinn.

"Seth, you set those folding chairs up under the shade trees over there. Isn't Phillip back with the extra ice yet? He's been gone twenty minutes. Cam! You and Ethan are putting those picnic tables too close together."

"Minute ago," Cam said under his breath, "they were too far apart." But he walked backward, hauling the table another foot.

"That's good. That's fine." Armed with bright red, white, and blue striped cloths, Anna hurried across the lawn. "Now you can move the umbrella tables, nearer the water, I think."

Cam narrowed his eyes. "You said you wanted them over by the trees."

"I changed my mind." She scanned the yard as she spread the tablecloths.

Cam opened his mouth to protest, but caught Ethan's warning shake of the head in time. His brother was right, he decided. Arguing wasn't going to change a thing.

Anna had been on a tear all morning, and when he said as much to Ethan as they moved out of earshot, it was with the irritation of the baffled.

"We're talking about a practical-minded, organized woman here," Cam added. "I don't know what's gotten into her. It's just a damn picnic."

"I guess women get that way over things like this," was Ethan's opinion. He remembered the way Grace had refused to let him take a shower in his own bathroom just because Cam and Anna were coming home. Who knew what went on in a female mind?

"She wasn't this bad over the wedding reception."

"I expect she had her mind on other things then."

"Yeah." Cam grunted as he picked up one of the round umbrella tables—again—and began to cart it toward the sun-dazzled water. "Phil's the smart one. He got the hell out of the house."

"He's always had a knack for it," Ethan agreed.

He didn't mind moving tables, or setting up chairs, or any of the dozens of chores—small and large—that Anna came up with. It helped keep his mind off weightier matters.

If he let himself think too much, he started to get a picture of Gloria DeLauter in his head. Because he'd never seen her, the image his brain conjured up was a tall, fleshy woman with tangled straw-colored hair, hard eyes smeared with sooty makeup, a mouth lax from too many trips to the bottle, too many matings with the needle.

The eyes were blue, like his own. The mouth, despite its slick coat of lipstick, shaped like his own. And he knew it wasn't Seth's mother's face he was seeing. It was his own mother's.

The picture wasn't dim and fuzzy as it had become over time. It was sharp and clear as yesterday.

It still had the power to ice his blood, to churn a sick animal fear in his stomach that was kin to shame.

It still made him want to strike out with bruised and bloodied fists.

He turned slowly as he heard the squeal of joy. And saw Aubrey racing over the lawn, her eyes bright as sunbeams. And saw Grace, standing by the porch steps, her smile warm and just a little shy.

You've got no right, the nasty little voice in his head hissed. *No right to touch something so fine and bright.*

But, oh, he had a need, one that swamped him like a storm surge and left him floundering. When Aubrey launched herself at him, his arms reached down, swung her up and around as she shrieked in delight.

He wanted her to be his. With a bone-deep longing, he wanted this perfect, this innocent, this laughing child to belong to him.

Grace's knees wobbled as she walked to them. The picture they made flashed into her mind, into her heart, where she knew it would imprint itself. The lanky man with big hands and a serious smile and the golden-bright child with a pink bow in her hair.

The sun poured over them as full and rich as the love that poured from her heart.

"She's been ready to come over since she opened her eyes this morning," Grace began. "I thought we could come a little early and I'd give Anna a hand." He was watching her so intently, so quietly, her nerves did a rapid dance under her skin. "There's not much left to do, but—"

She broke off because his arm had snaked out, wrapped around her fast and hard to pull her against him. She had time to draw in one startled breath before his mouth came down on hers. Rough and needy, it shot bolts of heat into her blood, sent her startled brain into a dizzying spin. Dimly she heard Aubrey's happy squeal.

"Kiss, Mama!"

Oh, yes, Grace thought, sprinting to catch up to this frantic pace he'd set. Please. Kiss me, kiss me, kiss me.

She thought she heard some sound from him, a sigh perhaps, that came from someplace too deep inside to make a sound. His lips softened. The hand that had clutched the back of her shirt like a man gripping his own life opened, stroked. This gentler, sweeter emotion that shimmered from him was no calmer than that first whip of greed; it only gilded the edges of the yearning he'd stirred.

She could smell him, heat and man. She could smell her daughter, powder and child. Her arms circled them both, instinctively making them a unit, holding there when the kiss ended and she could press her face into his shoulder.

He'd never kissed her in front of anyone. She knew Cam had only been a few feet away when Ethan had taken hold of her. And Seth would have seen . . . and Anna.

What did it mean?

"Kiss me!" Aubrey demanded, patting her hand against Ethan's cheek and puckering up.

He obliged her, then nuzzled at her neck where it would tickle and make her laugh. Then he turned his head and brushed his lips over Grace's hair. "I didn't mean to grab you that way."

"I was hoping you did," she murmured. "It made me feel you've been thinking about me. Wanting me."

"I've been thinking about you, Grace. I've been wanting you."

Because Aubrey was wiggling, he set her down and let her run off toward Seth and the dogs. "I meant I didn't mean to be rough with you."

"You weren't. I'm not fragile, Ethan."

"Yes, you are." When he saw Aubrey fall on Foolish so they could wrestle in the grass, he looked back at Grace, into her eyes. "Delicate," he said softly, "like the white china with pink roses we only use on Thanksgiving."

It made her heart flutter pleasantly that he would think so, even if she knew better. "Ethan—"

"I was always afraid I'd pick it up wrong, break it in half from being clumsy. I never really got used to it."

He skimmed his thumb lightly across her cheekbone, where the skin was warm and soft and silky. Then he dropped his hand to his side. "We'd better pitch in before Anna drives Cam over the edge."

⚭

Grace's stomach continued to flutter with nervous delight even when she went about the chore of carting food from the kitchen out to the picnic table. She would catch herself stopping, a bowl or platter in hand, to watch Ethan drive the horseshoe stakes into the ground.

Look how his muscles ripple under his shirt. He's so strong. Look at the way he shows Seth how to hold the hammer. He's so patient. He's wearing the jeans I washed just the other day. The cuffs have gone white and they're starting to fray. There was sixty-three cents in the right front pocket.

See how Aubrey climbs up on his back. She knows she'll be welcome. Yes, he reaches back, gives her a little hitch to secure her there, then goes back to work. He doesn't mind when she steals his cap and tries to put it on her own head. His hair's gotten long, and the ends glint in the sun when he shakes it back out of his eyes.

I hope he keeps forgetting to go to the barber for a while yet.

I wish I could touch it, right now. Make those thick, sun-bleached ends curl around my finger.

"It's a nice picture," Anna murmured from behind her and made Grace jolt. With a quiet laugh, Anna set down the enormous bowl of pasta salad. "I do the same thing with Cam sometimes. Just stand and watch him. The Quinns are very watchable men."

"I think I'm just going to take a quick glance, then I can't stop looking." She grinned when Ethan rose, Aubrey still clinging to his back, and turned slow circles as if trying to find her.

"He has a wonderful, natural way with children," Anna commented. "He'll make a wonderful father."

Grace felt heat rise up into her cheeks. She'd been thinking the same thing. It was hard to believe that only a few weeks before she'd told her own mother she would never marry again. And now she was thinking, and wondering. And waiting.

It had been easy to put all thoughts of marriage aside when she hadn't believed she could ever have a life with Ethan. She made a poor job of marriage before because her heart had belonged to someone other than her husband. That was her fault, and she accepted the responsibility for the failure.

But she could make marriage shine with Ethan, couldn't she? They could build a home and a family and a future based on love and trust and honesty.

He wouldn't move quickly, she mused. It wasn't his way. But he loved her. She understood Ethan well enough to know that marriage would be the next step.

She was already poised to take it.

⬡

The smell of burgers smoking on the grill, the yeasty tang of beer pumped from a cold keg. The sounds of children laughing and adult voices lifted in bright conversation or lowered in juicy gossip. The low roar of a boat zipping over the water, with the thrilled shouts of its teenage occupants, the metallic clang of a horseshoe striking home.

There were scents and sounds and sights. There was the snappy red, white, and blue of the cloths covering the tables that were crowded with bowls and plates and platters and casseroles.

Mrs. Cutter's cherry pie. The Wilsons' shrimp salad. What was left of the bushel of corn the Crawfords had brought along. Jell-O molds and fruit salad, fried chicken and early vine tomatoes. People were spread out and gathered. On chairs, on the lawn, down at the dock, and on the porch.

Several men stood with hands on hips, watching the horseshoe match, their faces sober in the way men had when they kibitzed a sporting event. Babies napped in carriers or willing arms while others wailed for attention. The young splashed and swam in the cool water, and the old fanned themselves in the shade.

The sky was clear, the heat immense.

Grace watched Foolish nosing along the ground in search of dropped food. He'd found plenty, and she imagined he'd be sick as a—well, a dog—before the day was over.

She hoped it was never over.

She waded into the water, gripping Aubrey firmly despite the colorful floats wrapped around her arms. She dipped her daughter down, laughing when Aubrey's little legs began to kick with delight.

"In, in, in!" Aubrey demanded.

"Honey, I didn't bring my bathing suit." But she eased out a little more, until the water lapped at her knees, so she could let Aubrey splash.

"Grace! Grace! Watch this!"

Obliging, Grace squinted against the sun and watched Seth take a running leap off the dock, tucking knees, wrapping arms, and hitting the water like a bomb so that it shot it up in a glittering fountain. And all over her.

"Cannonball," he announced proudly when he surfaced. Then he grinned. "Gee, you got all wet."

"Seth, take me." Straining, Aubrey held out her arms. "Take me."

"Can't, Aub. Got bombs to blow." When he swam off to join the other boys, Aubrey began to sniffle.

"He'll come back and play later," Grace assured her.

"Now!"

"Soon." To ward off what Grace knew could turn into a fine temper, she tossed Aubrey up, catching her as she hit the water. She let her paddle and splash, then let her go, biting her lip as Aubrey reveled in the freedom.

"Swimming, Mama."

"I see that, baby. You're a good swimmer. But you stay close."

As Grace expected, the sun and water and excitement combined to tire the child out. When Aubrey blinked and widened her eyes as she did when she fought sleep, Grace drew her in. "Let's get a drink, Aubrey."

"Swimming."

"We'll swim some more. I'm thirsty." Grace lifted her, braced for the minor battle that was bound to come.

"What you got there, Grace, a mermaid?"

Mother and daughter looked up onto the wet slope and saw Ethan.

"She sure is pretty," he said, smiling into Aubrey's mutinous face. "Can I have her?"

"I don't know. Maybe." She leaned close to Aubrey's ear. "He thinks you're a mermaid."

Aubrey's lip trembled, but she'd nearly forgotten why she'd wanted to cry. "Like Ariel?"

"Yes, like Ariel in the movie." She started to climb out, then Ethan's hand was there, clasping hers firmly. And when she gained her balance, he plucked Aubrey out of her arms.

"Swimming," she told him, rather pitifully, then buried her face in the curve of his throat.

"I saw you swimming." She was cool and wet and curled against him. He reached out, took Grace's hand again and pulled her to level ground. This time, his fingers twined with hers and held. "Looks like I've got two mermaids now."

"She's tired," Grace said quietly. "It makes her cross sometimes. She's wet," she added and started to take Aubrey from him.

"She's fine." He released her hand only because he wanted to skim his over Grace's damp and shining hair. "You're wet, too." Then he slipped an arm around her shoulders. "Let's walk in the sun for a while."

"All right."

"Maybe around the front of the house," he suggested, smiling a little as Aubrey's breath fluttered against his skin, evening out into sleep. "Where there aren't so many people."

With surprise and a low surge of pleasure, Carol Monroe watched Ethan take her daughter and granddaughter walking. With a woman's eyes she saw more than a neighbor and friend strolling with a neighbor and friend. Impulsively, she tugged on her husband's arm, distracting him from his absorption in the current round of horseshoes.

"Hold on, Carol. Junior and I are playing the winners of this round."

"Look, Pete. Look at that. Grace is with Ethan."

Vaguely annoyed, he flicked a glance around, shrugged. "So what?"

"*With* him, Pete, you knothead." It was said with exasperation and affection. "Like a boyfriend."

"Boyfriend?" He snorted, started to dismiss it—Christ knew, Carol had the screwiest ideas from time to time. Like when she was all het up to take a cruise down to the Bahamas. As if he couldn't take a sail any damn time of the day or night right in his own backyard. But then he caught—something—in the way Ethan leaned his body toward Grace, the way she tilted her head up.

It made Pete shift his feet, scowl, look away. "Boyfriend," he muttered, and didn't know how the hell he was supposed to feel about that. He didn't poke his nose in his daughter's life, he reminded himself. She'd already gone her own way.

He scowled hard into the sun because he remembered what it had been like to have his little girl rest her head on his shoulder the way Aubrey was doing right then and there with Ethan Quinn.

When they were little like that, he thought, they trusted you and looked up to you and believed what you told them even if you told them thunder was just angels clapping.

When they got older they started to tug away. And to want things that didn't make a damn bit of sense. Like money to live in New York City, and your blessing to marry some sneaky bastard who wasn't half good enough for them.

They stopped thinking you were the man with the answers, and they broke your damn heart. So you had to put it back together as best you could, with a lock on it so it couldn't happen again.

"Ethan's just what Grace needs," Carol was saying in a low voice—just in case any of the fuddy-duddies, who thought tossing a horseshoe at an iron peg was an exciting way to spend the day, had sharp ears. "That's a steady man, and he's got gentleness in him. He's a man she could lean on."

"Won't."

"What?"

"She won't lean on nobody. She's too proud for her own good, and always has been."

Carol merely sighed. If it was true, Grace had gotten every stubborn ounce of that pride from her father. "You've never even tried to meet her halfway."

"Don't you start on me, Carol. I've got nothing to say." He shifted away from her, ignoring the guilt because he knew the gesture would hurt her. "I want a beer," he muttered and stalked away.

Phillip Quinn and some of the others were gathered around the keg. Pete noted with an amused snort that Phillip was flirting with the Barrow girl, Celia. He couldn't blame the boy—she was built like a Playboy pinup and not afraid to show it off. It wasn't something a man stopped noticing even if he was old enough to be her father.

"Want me to pull you one, Mr. Monroe?"

" 'Preciate it." Pete nodded toward the celebrants in the backyard. "Got you a crowd here, today, Phil. Fine spread, too. I remember how your folks'd throw a picnic most every summer. It's nice you're keeping up the tradition."

"Anna thought of it," Phillip told him, handing Pete a foaming beer in a tall plastic cup.

"Women do, more'n men, I suppose. If I don't get the chance, you tell her I appreciate the invite. I gotta get back to the waterfront in an hour or so, set up for the display."

"You always put on a good one. Best fireworks on the Shore."

"Tradition," Pete said again. It was a word that mattered.

Carol Monroe hadn't been the only one to notice the way Ethan and Grace had walked off together. Speculation and sly grins started to spread over the potato salad and steamed crabs.

Mother Crawford wagged her fork at her good friend Lucy Wilson. "You ask me, Grace is going to have to put her foot down if she wants Ethan Quinn to come up to snuff before that baby's old enough for college. Never seen a man moved so slow."

"He's thoughtful," Lucy said loyally.

"Not saying different. Just saying slow. Seen them moony-eyed over each other since before that boy got his own workboat. Has to be nearly ten years passed. Stella and I—bless her soul—had a conversation over it a time or two."

Lucy sighed over her fruit salad, and not just because she was watching her calories. "Stella knew her boys inside and out."

"That she did. I said to her one day, 'Stella, your Ethan's got cow's eyes for the young Monroe girl.' " And she laughed, said how he had himself a hard case of puppy love, but that sometimes it was the best way to start the real thing. Never could figure why Ethan didn't step forward a bit before Grace got herself tangled up with that Jack Casey. Never did like him much."

"He wasn't a bad sort, just weak. Look there, Mother," Lucy said, lowering her voice like a conspirator. She nodded toward Ethan and Grace, as they walked back around the side of the house, hands linked, the baby sleeping on his shoulder.

"Nothing weak about that one." Mother wiggled her brows and leered at her friend. "And slow can be a fine thing in bed, can't it, Lucy?"

Lucy hooted. "It can, Mother. That it can."

Blissfully unaware of the speculation buzzing about a quiet walk around the house on a hot summer afternoon, Grace stopped to pour some iced tea. Before she'd half filled the first glass, her mother was bustling over, beaming smiles.

"Oh, let me hold that precious girl. Nothing so soothing as sitting with a sleeping baby." She'd slipped Aubrey out of Ethan's arms while she talked, her voice low and quick. "It'll give me a fine excuse to sit in the shade a while and be quiet. I swear, Nancy Claremont's been talking both my ears off. You young people should be off enjoying yourself."

"I was going to lay her down," Grace began, but her mother just waved it away.

"No need, no need. I don't get nearly enough chances to hold her when she's still. Go on and finish your walk. Ought to get out of the sun, though. It's brutal."

"It's a good idea," Ethan mused as Carol hurried off, cooing to the sleeping Aubrey. "A little shade and a little quiet wouldn't hurt."

"Well . . . all right, but I've only got another hour or so before I have to leave."

He'd been tugging her gently toward the trees, thinking that he could find a sheltered spot, a private spot, and kiss her again. He stopped at the verge and frowned at her. "Leave for what?"

"For work. I'm on at the pub tonight."

"It's your night off."

"It was—that is, it usually is, but I'm putting on some more hours."

"You work too many hours already."

She smiled, distracted—then relieved when the shade she walked into cut the intense heat in half. "It's just a few more. Shiney was good about helping me out so I can make up what I had to pay for the car. Oh, this is nice." She closed her eyes, breathed deep of the moist, cool air. "Anna said you and your brothers were going to play later. I'll be sorry to miss that."

"Grace, I told you if money was a problem, I'd help you out."

She opened her eyes again. "I don't need you to help me out, Ethan. I know how to work."

"Yeah, you know how. It's damn near all you do." He paced away from her, paced back as if trying to shake off what was biting at his gut. "I hate you working down there."

Her spine stiffened—she could feel it go hard and straight, vertebra by vertebra. "I don't want to fight with you about that again. It's a good job, honest work."

"I'm not fighting with you, I'm saying it." He stalked toward her, the swirling temper in his eyes surprising enough that she backed up against a tree.

"I've heard you say it before," she said evenly. "And it doesn't change the facts. I work there, and I'm going to go on working there."

"You need looking after." It scraped him raw that he couldn't be the one to do it.

"I don't."

Hell she didn't. There were already tired smudges under those change-able green eyes, and now she was telling him she'd be carting trays until two in the morning. "Did you pay Dave for the car yet?"

"Half." It was humiliating. "He was good enough to give me until next month to pay him the rest."

"You won't pay him." That, at least, was something he could do. Would do, by Christ. "I will."

She forgot about humiliation. Her chin came up, sharp and fast as a bullet. "You will not."

Another time he would have persuaded, cajoled. Or simply done the deed on the quiet. But something was bubbling up in him—something that had been there, simmering, since he'd turned that morning and seen her. It wouldn't let him think, only feel and act. With his eyes on hers he slipped a hand up, over her throat.

"Be quiet."

"I'm not a child, Ethan. You can't—"

"I'm not thinking about you like a child." Her eyes were bright and sharp. They were heating the something that was inside him to a boil. "I stopped being able to do that, and I can't go back to it. Do what I want this time."

She didn't know when her breath had started to back up or her skin to shiver. Dimly she felt the rough bark of the tree bite into her hands as she pressed them against it. She didn't think he was talking about her accepting a few hundred dollars for a car any longer.

"Ethan—"

His other hand was on her breast. He hadn't meant to put it there, but it covered her and his fingers began to flex and knead. Her shirt was still damp, just a little damp. He could feel her skin go hot under it. "Do what I want this time," he repeated.

Her eyes were huge. He was falling into them, drowning in them. Her heart was pounding against his hand, as if he held it beating in his palm. His mouth crushed down on hers with a violent greed that he was for once help-less to stem. He heard her shocked cry muffled against his assaulting mouth. And it only thrilled him darkly.

The heat swarmed from him, stunning her. His teeth nipped roughly into her lip, making her gasp, opening herself to the swift and skillful invasion of his tongue.

Sensations flew too quickly to separate one from the other, but all were dark and keen and compelling. His hands were everywhere, tugging up her shirt, claiming her breasts, scraping those deliciously rough palms over her. She felt him quiver, gripped his shoulders to balance them both.

Then he was yanking at her shorts.

No! Part of her mind drew back in shock, all but screamed it. He couldn't mean to take her, here, like this, only yards away from where people sat and children played. But another part of her simply moaned in shocked excitement and whispered yes.

Here. Now. Like this. Exactly like this.

When he drove into her, her scream would have carried some of both, but it was swallowed by his mouth, lost in his ragged breaths.

He thrust hard, fast, deep, his body surging into hers, his hands biting into her tight, round bottom as he plunged. His mind was wiped clean of everything but this one desperate need. When she came, exploding over him, around him, in him, his thrill was dark and primal and coated his skin with sweat.

His own climax had claws, hot-tipped, razor-sharp, that ripped through him brutally, so that his vision went red.

Even when it cleared he continued to shudder, to pant. Gradually he became aware of what was. He heard the wild drumming of a woodpecker deeper in the woods, the tinkle of laughter from beyond the trees. And Grace's sobbing breaths.

He felt the breezing cooling his skin. And her trembles.

"Oh, God. Goddamn it." His curse was quiet, vicious.

"Ethan?" She hadn't known, would never have believed anyone could have such a need inside them. For her. "Ethan," she said again and would have lifted her weak arms around him if he hadn't stepped back.

"I'm sorry. I—" There weren't words. Nothing he could say would be right, would be enough. He bent, slipped her shorts back up, fastened them. With the same deliberate care, he straightened her shirt. "I can't offer you an excuse for that. There isn't any."

"I don't want an excuse. I don't ever need one for what we do together, Ethan."

He stared at the ground while a sick pounding began in his head. "I didn't give you a choice." He knew what it was not to have a choice.

"I've already made my choice. I love you."

He looked at her then, everything that lived inside of him swirling into his eyes. Her mouth was swollen where he'd ravished it. Her eyes were enormous. Her body would carry bruises from his hands. "You deserve better."

"I like to think I deserve you. You made me feel . . . desired. That's not even the word." She pressed a hand to her still speeding heart. "Craved," she realized. "Craved. And now I'm sorry . . ." Her gaze flicked away from his. "I'm sorry for any woman who's never known what it is to be craved."

"I scared you."

"For a minute." Mortified, she blew out a breath. "Damn it, Ethan, do I have to tell you that I liked it? I felt helpless and overpowered and it was so exciting. You lost control, and you have this incredibly unshakable control most of the time. I liked knowing that something I did, or something I am, snapped it."

He pulled his hand through his hair. "You confuse me, Grace."

"I don't mean to. But I don't think that's such a bad thing, either."

He let out a sigh, then stepped forward just enough that he could smooth her tousled hair into place. "Maybe the trouble is we've been thinking we know each other so well. But we don't have all the pieces." He picked up her hand, studied it with that thoughtful frown she loved. Then he kissed her fingers in a way that made her lashes flutter.

"I don't ever want to hurt you. In any way." But he had, and he would.

He kept his hand in hers as he walked her back toward the sunlight. He would have to tell her about those pieces of himself soon. So she would understand why he couldn't give her more.

FIFTEEN

"So, I don't know if I'm going to go out with him anymore because he's getting way too possessive, you know? I don't want to hurt his feelings, but you gotta live, right?"

Julie Cutter crunched into the shiny green apple she'd plucked out of the fruit bowl in Grace's kitchen. She felt every bit as much at home there as she did next door. Comfortable, she hitched herself up to sit on the counter while Grace folded laundry on the table.

"Plus," Julie went on, gesturing with her apple, "I met this incredibly cute guy. He works at the computer store at the mall? He wears these little metal-frame glasses and has the sweetest smile." She grinned, lighting up her pretty heart-shaped face. "I asked him for his phone number, and he blushed."

"You asked him for his phone number?" Grace was listening with only half an ear. She loved it when Julie came over just to visit. She was always so full of fun and talk and energy. But today it was hard to concentrate. Her mind was so full of what had happened between her and Ethan in those shady woods. What had leapt out of him to devour her—and why had it left him so distant afterward?

"Sure." Julie cocked her head, her brown eyes full of humor. "Didn't you ever ask a guy out? Come on, Grace, we're at the dawn of the next millennium here. Most of them really like it when the woman takes the initiative. Anyway . . ." She shook back her long fall of straight-as-a-pin brown hair. "Jeff did—the sexy computer nerd? He got all flustered at first, but then he gave it to me, and when I called him I could tell he was happy about it. So we're going out Saturday, but I have to break up with Don first."

"Poor Don," Grace murmured, and glanced over absently as Aubrey knocked over the block tower she'd been building, then applauded its destruction.

"Oh, he'll get over it." Julie shrugged. "It's not like he's in love with me or anything. He's just used to having a chick."

Grace had to smile. A few months earlier, Julie had been wild about Don, rushing over to tell Grace every detail of their dates. Or, Grace suspected, at least an edited version of their dates. "You told me Don was the one."

"He was." Julie laughed. "For a while. I'm not ready for the *only* one yet."

Grace went to the refrigerator to pour the three of them a drink. At Julie's age—nineteen—she'd been pregnant, married, and worried about paying bills. She was only three years older than Julie, but it might as well have been three hundred. "You're right to look around, to be sure." She handed Julie a glass, held her gaze for a moment. "To be careful."

"I'm careful, Grace," Julie assured her, touched. "I'd like to be married one day. Especially if it means having a baby as beautiful as Aubrey. But I want to finish college, then see some of the world. Do . . . things," she added, gesturing widely. "I don't want to find myself tied down, changing diapers and working at some dead-end job because I let some guy talk me into . . ."

She trailed off, suddenly and sincerely appalled at herself. Eyes huge and apologetic, she slid off the counter. "God, I'm sorry. I can be so thick sometimes. I didn't mean that you—"

"It's all right." She gave Julie's arm a quick squeeze. "That's exactly what I did, exactly what I let happen to me. I'm glad you're smarter."

"I'm a moron," Julie murmured, very close to tears. "I'm an insensitive clod. I'm hateful."

"No, you're not." Grace gave a light laugh and picked up a pair of Aubrey's rompers from the basket. "You didn't hurt my feelings. I'd hate to think we weren't friends enough for you to be able to say what you think."

"You're one of my best friends. And I've got a big mouth."

"Well, you do." Grace chuckled at Julie's wince. "But I like it."

"I love you and Aubrey, Grace."

"I know you do. Now stop worrying about it, and tell me where you're going with Jeff the cute computer guy?"

"Safe date. Movies and pizza." Julie let out a soft sigh of relief. She'd have . . . shaved her head and dyed it purple, she decided, before she'd do anything to hurt Grace. Hoping to make up, just a little, for her insensitivity, she beamed a smile.

"You know, I'd be happy to keep Aubrey on your next night off if you and Ethan want to go out."

Grace had finished folding the rompers and started on socks. She stopped, staring, with a tiny white sock trimmed in yellow in each hand. "What?"

"You know—catch a movie, go to a restaurant, whatever." She wiggled her brows on the "whatever," then fought to bite back a grin at Grace's expression. "You're not going to stand there and tell me you're not seeing Ethan Quinn."

"Well, he's . . . I'm . . ." She looked helplessly down at Aubrey.

"If it was supposed to be a secret, he should be parking his truck somewhere other than your driveway on the nights he sleeps over."

"Oh, God."

"What's the problem? It's not like you're having this illicit affair—like Mr. Wiggins has been having with Mrs. Lowen on Monday afternoons at the motel on Route 13." At Grace's strangled sound, Julie just shrugged. "My friend Robin's working there and taking night classes at the college, and she says how he checks in every Thursday morning at ten-thirty while she waits in her car. Anyway—"

"What must your mother think?" Grace whispered.

"Mom? About Mr. Wiggins? Well—"

"No, no." Grace didn't want to think about the portly Mr. Wiggins's weekly motel romp. "About . . ."

"Oh, you and Ethan. I think she said something about 'high time.' Mom's not an idiot. He's such a *hunk*," Julie said with feeling. "I mean, the way he fills out a T-shirt is awesome. And that smile. It takes, like, ten minutes for it to finish moving over his face, and by then, man, you are *drooling*. Robin and I went down to the waterfront every day for a month last summer just to watch him offload his catch."

"You did?" Grace said weakly.

"We both built a real case on him." She reached into the white stoneware cookie jar and found two oatmeal raisin cookies. "I flirted with him, big-time, whenever I got the chance."

"You . . . flirted with Ethan."

"Mmm." She nodded, swallowing cookie. "Really put some effort into it, too. Mostly I think it embarrassed him, but I got a couple of great smiles out of him." She smiled sunnily when Grace kept staring. "Oh, I'm way over it now, so don't worry."

"Good." Grace picked up the drink she'd neglected and drank deeply. "That's good."

"Still, he's got a terrific butt."

"Oh, Julie." Grace bit her lip to keep from giggling and sent a meaningful look toward her daughter.

"She's not listening. So, anyway, how'd I get started on this? Oh, yeah, I'll keep Aubrey for you if you want to go out."

"I, well, thanks." She was trying to decide if she wanted to get well off the subject of Ethan Quinn, or linger on it, when she heard a knock and saw him standing at her front door.

"Like magic," Julie murmured, and romance bloomed in her heart. "You know, why don't I take Aubrey over to see Mom for a while? I'll just keep her and feed her dinner."

"But I don't have to leave for work for nearly an hour yet."

Julie rolled her eyes. "So make good use of the time, pal." Then she scooped Aubrey up. "Want to come to my house, Aubrey? See my kitty cat?"

"Oooh, kitty. Bye, Mama."

"Oh, but—" They were already sailing out of her back door, with Aubrey calling for the kitty and waving madly. She looked at Ethan again, staring at his face through the screen, then lifted her hands.

He decided to take it as an invitation and stepped inside. "Was that Julie who ran off with Aubrey?"

"Yes. She's going to let Aubrey play with her kitten and have dinner over there."

"It's nice you have someone like Julie to look after her."

"I'd be lost without Julie." Puzzled, Grace angled her head. He was standing awkwardly, a hand tucked behind his back. "Is something wrong? Did you hurt your hand?"

"No." What an idiot he was, Ethan thought, offering her the flowers he had held behind him. "I thought you might like some." He wanted, desperately, to find ways to make up to her for the way he'd treated her in the woods.

"You brought me flowers."

"I stole some here and there. You may not want to mention it to Anna. I got the tiger lilies off the side of the road. They're blooming thick this year."

He'd picked her flowers. Not store-bought flowers but ones he'd stopped and selected and plucked with his own hands. On a long, trembling sigh, she buried her face in them. "They're beautiful."

"They made me think of you. Almost everything does." And when she lifted her head, when he saw that her eyes were stunned and soft, he wished he had more words, better ones, smoother ones. "I know you only have the one night off now. I'd like to take you to dinner if you don't have any plans."

"To dinner?"

"There's a place Anna and Cam like up in Princess Anne. Suit-and-tie place, but they claim the food's worth it. Would you like to?"

She realized she was nodding her head like a fool and made herself stop. "I'd like that."

"I'll come by for you. About six-thirty?"

There went her head, bobbing again like a spring robin drunk on worms. "Fine. That'd be fine."

"I can't stay now because they're expecting me at the boatyard."

"That's all right." She wondered if her eyes were as huge as they felt. She could have devoured him with them. "Thanks for the flowers. They're lovely."

"You're welcome." And with his eyes open, he leaned over, laid his lips on hers very gently, very softly. He watched her lashes flutter, watched the green of her irises go misty under those tiny flecks of gold. "I'll see you tomorrow night, then."

Her muscles had turned to putty. "Tomorrow," she managed and breathed out a long, long sigh as he walked away and out her front door.

He'd brought her flowers. She clasped the stems in both hands, held them out and waltzed through the house with them. Beautiful, fragrant, soft-petaled flowers. And if some of those petals drifted to the floor as she danced, it only made the scene more romantic.

They made her feel like a princess, like a woman. She sniffed them lavishly as she circled back into the kitchen for a vase. Like a bride.

She stopped abruptly, staring at them. *Like a bride.*

Her head went light, her skin hot, her hands trembly. When she realized she was holding her breath, she let it out with a whoosh, but it caught and stumbled as she tried to pull air in again.

He'd brought her flowers, she thought again. He'd asked her to dinner. Slowly, she pressed a hand to her heart, found that it was pumping light and fast, very fast.

He was going to ask her to marry him. *To marry him.*

"Oh, my. Oh." Her legs wanted to fold, so she sat down, right on the floor of the kitchen with the flowers cradled in her arms like a child. Flowers, tender kisses, a romantic dinner for two. He was courting her.

No, no. She was jumping to conclusions. He would never move that quickly to the next step. She shook her head, picked herself up, and found an old wide-mouthed bottle for a vase. He was just being sweet. He was just being considerate. He was just being Ethan.

She turned on the faucet and filled the bottle. Just being Ethan, she thought again, and found her breath gone a second time.

Being Ethan, he would think and he would do things in a certain manner. Struggling for calm, for logic, she began to arrange the precious flowers, stem by stem.

They'd known each other for . . . she could hardly remember not knowing him. Now they were lovers. They were in love. Being Ethan, he would consider marriage the next step. Honorable, traditional. Right. He would believe it right.

She understood that but had expected it to be months yet before he drifted in that direction. Yet why would he wait, she asked herself, when they'd already waited for years?

But . . . She had promised herself she would never marry again. She made that vow as she signed her name on the divorce papers. She couldn't fail so miserably at something ever again, or risk putting Aubrey through the misery and trauma. She'd made the decision that she would raise Aubrey alone, raise her well, raise her with love. That she herself would provide, would build the home, tend it, where her daughter could grow up happy and safe.

But that was before she had let herself believe Ethan would ever want them, would ever love her the way she loved him. Because it had always been Ethan. Always Ethan, she thought, closing her eyes. In her heart, in her dreams. Did she dare break her promise, one she had made so solemnly? Could she risk being a wife again, pinning her hopes and her heart on another man?

Oh, yes. Yes, she could risk anything if the man was Ethan. It was so right, so perfect, she thought, laughing to herself as her head and heart went light with joy. It was the happy-ever-after that she'd stopped letting herself yearn for.

How would he ask? She pressed her fingers to her lips, and those lips trembled and curved. Quietly, she thought, with his eyes so serious, so intent on hers. He would take her hand, in that careful way of his. They'd be outside with moonlight and breezes, with the scents of night all around them and the musical lap of water close by.

Simply, she thought, without poetry or fuss. He would look down at her, saying nothing for a long moment, then he would speak, without hurry.

I love you, Grace. I always will. Will you marry me?

Yes, yes, yes! She spun herself in giddy circles. She would be his bride, his wife, his partner, his lover. Now. Forever. She could give her child to him knowing, without hesitation, that he would love and cherish, would protect and tend. She would have more children with him.

Oh, God—Ethan's child growing inside her. Overwhelmed by the image, she pressed her hands to her stomach. And this time, this time, the life that fluttered inside her would be wanted and welcomed by both who'd made it.

They would make a life together, a wonderfully, thrillingly simple life.

She couldn't wait to begin it.

Tomorrow night, she remembered, and in a sudden panic, pushed at her hair. Dropped her hands to look at them in utter despair. Oh, she was a mess. She needed to look beautiful.

What would she wear?

She caught herself laughing, the laughter full of joy and nerves. For once she forgot work and schedules and responsibility and raced to her closet.

◈

Anna didn't notice the stolen flowers until the next day. Then she noticed them with a shout.

"Seth! Seth, you come out here right now." She had her hands on her hips, her sassy straw hat askew, her eyes snapping and dangerous.

"Yeah?" He came out, munching on a handful of pretzels, though dinner was simmering on the stove.

"Have you been messing with my flowers?" she demanded.

He slid a glance down to the mixed bed of annuals and perennials. And snorted. "What would I be messing with stupid flowers for?"

She tapped her foot. "That's what I'm asking you."

"I never touched them. Hey, you don't even want us to pull up weeds."

"That's because you don't know the difference between a weed and a daisy," she snapped. "Well, somebody's been in my flower beds."

"Wasn't me." He shrugged, then rolled his eyes in glee as she stormed past him into the house.

Somebody, Seth thought, was in for it big time.

"Cameron!" She stomped upstairs and into the bathroom where he was washing up from work. He glanced over, lifting a brow as water dripped from his face into the sink. She scowled for a moment, then shook her head. "Never mind," she muttered, slamming the door.

Cam would no more fiddle with her gardens than Seth, she decided. And if he was picking flowers for anyone, it damn well better be his loving wife, or she'd just murder him and be done with it.

Her eyes narrowed on the door to Ethan's room. And she made a low, threatening sound in her throat.

She did stop to knock, though it was only three staccato raps before she simply pushed open the door.

"Christ, Anna." Mortified, Ethan snatched up the slacks that lay on his bed and held them in front of him. He was wearing nothing but his briefs and a pained expression.

"Just save the modesty, I'm not interested. Have you been into my flowers?"

"Into your flowers?" Oh, he'd known this was coming. The woman had eyes like a cat when it came to her posies. But he hadn't expected the moment to come when he was half naked. Half, hell, he thought and clutched the slacks more firmly.

"Somebody's snapped off more than a dozen blooms. Snapped them right off." She advanced on him, her eyes scanning the room for evidence.

"Oh, well . . ."

"Problem?" Cam leaned on the doorjamb, tongue in his cheek. It was an amusing sight after a hard day's work, he decided. His well-riled wife stalking around his all-but-bare-assed brother.

"Somebody's been in my garden and they stole my flowers."

"No kidding? Want me to call the cops?"

"Oh, shut up." She whirled back to Ethan, who took a cautious and cowardly step in retreat. She looked fit to murder. "Well?"

"Well, I . . ." He'd intended to confess, throw himself on her mercy. But the woman glaring at him out of dark, furious eyes looked several quarts low on mercy. "Rabbits," he said slowly. "Probably."

"Rabbits?"

"Yeah." He shifted uncomfortably, wishing to Christ he'd at least gotten his pants on before she burst in. "Rabbits can be a problem with gardens. They just hop up and help themselves."

"Rabbits," she said again.

"Could be deer," he added, just a little desperately. "They'd graze over and eat every damn thing down to stubs." Counting on pity, he shot a look at Cam. "Right?"

Cam weighed the situation, knew Anna was city girl enough to buy it. Oh, Ethan would owe him for this, he decided and smiled. "Oh, yeah, deer and rabbits, big problem." Which having two dogs running tame pretty much eliminated, he mused.

"Why didn't anybody tell me!" She whipped off her hat, rapped it against her thigh. "What do we do about it? How do we make them stop?"

"Couple ways." Guilt stung, just a little, but Ethan rationalized that deer and rabbits *could* be a problem, so she should take precautions anyway. "Dried blood."

"Dried *blood*? Whose?"

"You can buy it at the garden store, and you just dump it around. It'll keep them away."

"Dried blood." Her lips pursed as she made a mental note to buy some.

"Or urine."

"Dried urine?"

"No." Ethan cleared his throat. "You just go out and . . . you know, around so they smell it and know there's a meat eater in the vicinity."

"I see." She nodded, satisfied, then whirled on her husband. "Well, get out there then and pee on my marigolds."

"Could use a beer first," Cam said and winked at his brother. "Don't worry, darling, we'll take care of it."

"All right." Calmer, she huffed out a breath. "Sorry, Ethan."

"Yeah, well, hmmm." He waited until she'd hurried out, then lowered himself to the edge of the bed. He slanted a look at Cam, who continued to lean against the door. "That wife of yours has a streak of mean in her."

"Yeah. I love it. Why'd you steal her flowers?"

"I just needed a few of them," Ethan muttered and pulled on his pants. "What the hell are they out there for if you get your head cut off for picking them?"

"Rabbits? And deer?" Cam began to hoot with laughter.

"They're garden pests right enough."

"Pretty brave rabbits who hop between two dogs and right up to the house to select a few flowers. If they got that far, they'd mow the whole garden down to the ground."

"She doesn't have to know that. For a while. I appreciate you backing me up. I thought she was going to punch me."

"She might have. Since I saved your pretty face, I figure you owe me."

"Nothing comes free," Ethan grumbled and stalked to the closet for a shirt.

"You got that right. Seth needs a haircut, and he's already outgrown his last pair of shoes."

Ethan turned, shirt dangling from his fingertips. "You want me to take him to the mall?"

"Right again."

"I'd rather have the punch in the face."

"Too late." Cam hooked a thumb in his front pocket and grinned. "So, why'd you need the flowers?"

"Just thought Grace would like them." Muttering, Ethan shrugged into his shirt.

"Ethan Quinn stealing flowers, going out—voluntarily—to a jacket-and-tie restaurant." Cam's grin widened, his eyebrows wiggled. "Serious business."

"It's a usual thing for a man to take a woman out to dinner, bring her flowers now and then."

"Not for you it isn't." Cam straightened, patted his flat belly. "Well, I guess I'll go choke down that beer so I can be a hero."

"Man's got no privacy around here," Ethan complained when Cam sauntered away. "Women come right on into your bedroom, don't even have the courtesy to leave when they see you don't have your pants on."

Scowling, he dragged one of his two ties out of the closet. "People ready to skin you alive over a few flowers. And the next thing you know, you're at the goddamn mall fighting crowds and buying shoes."

He wrestled the tie under his collar and began to deal with the knot. "Never had to worry when I was in my own place. I could walk around buck ass naked if I wanted to." He hissed at the tie that refused to cooperate. "I hate these fuckers."

"That's because you're happier tying a sheepshank."

"Who the hell wouldn't be?"

Then he stopped, his fingers freezing on the tie. His gaze stayed on the mirror, where he could see his father behind him.

"You're just a little nervous, that's all," Ray said with a smile and a wink. "Hot date."

Taking a careful breath, Ethan turned. Ray stood at the foot of the bed, his bright-blue eyes merry, the way Ethan remembered they would sparkle when he was particularly tickled about something.

He was wearing a squash-yellow T-shirt that sported a boat under full sail, faded jeans, and scuffed sandals. His hair was long, past his collar, and shining silver. Ethan could see the sun glint on it.

He looked exactly like what he was—had been. A robust and handsome man who appreciated comfortable clothes and a good laugh.

"I'm not dreaming," Ethan murmured.

"It was easier for you to think so at first. Hello, Ethan."

"Dad."

"I remember the first time you called me that. Took you a while to come to it. You'd been with us almost a year. Christ, you were a spooky kid, Ethan. Quiet as a shadow, deep as a lake. One evening when I was grading papers, you knocked on the door. You just stood there for a minute, thinking. God, it was a marvel to watch your mind work. Then you said, 'Dad, the phone's for you.'" Ray's smile went bright as sunlight. "You slipped right out again, or you'd have seen me make a fool of myself. Sniffled like a baby and had to tell whoever the hell it was on the phone I was having an allergy attack."

"I never knew why you wanted me."

"You needed us. We needed you. You *were* ours, Ethan, even before we found each other. Fate takes its own sweet time, but it always finds a way. You were so . . . fragile," Ray said after a moment, and Ethan blinked in surprise. "Stella and I were worried we'd do something wrong and break you."

"I wasn't fragile."

"Oh, Ethan, you were. Your heart was delicate as glass and waiting to be shattered. Your body was tough. We never worried about you and Cam pounding on each other those first months. Thought it did both of you good."

Ethan's lips twitched. "He usually started the pounding."

"But you never were one to back off once your blood was up. Took some doing to get it up," he added. "Still does. We watched you watch and settle and think and consider."

"You gave me . . . time. Time to watch and settle, to think and consider. Everything I've got that's decent came from the two of you."

"No, Ethan, we just gave you love. And that time, and the place."

He wandered over to the window, to look out on the water and the boats that swayed gently at the dock. He watched an egret sail across a sky hazed with heat and plumped by clouds.

"You were meant to be ours. Meant to be here. Took to the water like you'd been born in it. Cam, he always just wanted to go fast, and Phillip preferred to sit back and enjoy the ride. But you . . ."

He turned back again, his gaze thoughtful. "You studied every inch of the boat, every wave, every turn of a river. You'd practice tying knots for hours, and nobody had to nag you into swabbing the decks."

"It came easy for me, right from the start. You wanted me to get a college degree."

"For me." Ray shook his head. "For me, Ethan. Fathers are human, after all, and I went through a time when I thought my sons needed to love schooling as much as I did. But you did what was right for you. You made me proud of you. I should have told you that more often."

"You always let me know it."

"Words count, though. Who would know that better than a man who spent his life trying to teach the young the love of them?" He sighed now. "Words count, Ethan, and I know some of them come hard for you. But I want you to remember that. You and Grace have a lot to say to each other yet."

"I don't want to hurt her."

"You will," Ray said quietly. "By trying not to. I wish you could see yourself as I do. As she does." He shook his head again. "Well, fate takes its time. Think of the boy, Ethan, think of Seth—and what pieces of yourself you see there."

"His mother—" Ethan began.

"Think of the boy for now," Ray said simply, and he was gone.

Sixteen

There wasn't a hint of rain on the breezy summer air. The sky was a hot, staggering blue, an unbroken bowl that held a faint haze and fragile clouds. A single bird sang manically, as if mad to complete the song before the long day was over.

She was as nervous as a teenager on prom night. The thought of that made Grace laugh. No teenager had ever dreamed of nerves like these.

She fussed with her hair, wishing she had long, glossy curls like Anna's—exotic, Gypsy-like. Sexy.

But she didn't, she reminded herself firmly. And never would. At least the short, simple crop showed off the pretty gold drop earrings Julie had loaned her.

Julie had been so sweet and excited about what she'd termed the Big Date. She'd launched straight into a what-to-wear-and-what-to-wear-with-it routine—and naturally had deemed the contents of Grace's closet a total loss.

Of course, letting Julie drag her off to the mall had been sheer foolishness. Not that Julie had to yank very hard, Grace admitted. It had been so long since she'd shopped simply for the simple pleasure of shopping. For the couple of hours they'd spent swarming through the shops, she'd felt so young and carefree. As if nothing was really more important than finding the right outfit.

Still, she'd had no business buying a new dress, even if she did get it on sale. But she couldn't seem to talk herself out of it. Just this one little indulgence, this one little luxury. She so desperately wanted something new and fresh for this special night.

She'd yearned for the sexy, sophisticated black with its shoestring straps and snug skirt. Or the boldly sensuous red with the daringly plunging neckline. But they hadn't suited her, as she'd known they wouldn't.

It had been no surprise that the simple powder-blue linen had been discounted. It had looked so plain, so ordinary, hanging on the rack. But Julie had pressed it on her, and Julie had an eye for such things.

She'd been right, of course, Grace thought now. It was simple, almost virginal, with its unadorned bodice and graceful lines. But it looked pretty on, with the color cool against her skin, and the skirt floating around her legs.

Grace traced a finger over the square neckline, faintly amazed that the bra Julie had nagged her into buying actually did gift her with a hint of cleavage. A miracle indeed, Grace thought with a little laugh.

Concentrating, she leaned close to the mirror. She'd done everything Julie had instructed with the borrowed makeup. And her eyes did look bigger and deeper, she decided. She'd done her best to blot away the signs of fatigue and thought she had succeeded. Maybe she hadn't managed more than a wink of sleep the night before, but she didn't feel in the least tired.

She felt energized.

She reached out, and her hand hovered over the samples of perfumes they'd been given at the cosmetics counter. Then she remembered that Anna had told her to wear her own scent for Ethan before. That it would say something to him.

Choosing that instead, she closed her eyes and dabbed it on. With her eyes closed, imagining that his lips might brush here, brush there, linger and taste where her pulse beat that fragrance into life.

Still dreaming, she picked up a little ivory evening bag—another loan—and checked its contents. She hadn't carried such a small purse since . . . well, before Aubrey was born, she thought. It was so odd to look inside and see none of the dozens of mother things she was used to carrying. Only women things now, she mused. The little compact she'd splurged on, a tube of lipstick she rarely thought to use, her house key, a few carefully folded bills, and a tissue that wasn't thin and ragged from wiping a sticky face.

It made her feel feminine just to look at it, to slip her feet into impractical heeled sandals—oh, she'd be scrambling to pay off her charge card when the bill came—to turn in front of the mirror and watch her skirt follow the movement.

When she heard his truck pull up outside, she dashed across the room. Made herself stop. No, she wasn't going to race to the door like an eager puppy. She would wait right here until he knocked. And give her heart a chance to beat normally again.

When he did knock, it was still thundering in her ears. But she stepped out, smiled at him through the screen, and moved toward the door.

He remembered watching her walk to the door like this before, on the night they'd made love the first time. She'd looked so lovely, so lonely with the candlelight flickering around her.

But tonight she looked . . . he didn't think he had words for it. Everything about her seemed to glow—skin, hair, eyes. It made him feel awkward, humble, reverent. He wanted to kiss her to be certain she was real, and yet was afraid to touch.

He stepped back as she opened the screen, then took the hand she held out carefully. "You look different."

No, it wasn't poetry. And it made her smile. "I wanted to." She pulled the door closed behind her and let him lead her to his truck.

He wished immediately that he'd borrowed the 'Vette.

"The truck doesn't suit that dress," he said as she climbed in.

"It suits me." She swept her skirts in to be certain they didn't catch in the door. "I may look different, Ethan, but I'm still the same."

She settled back and prepared for the most beautiful evening of her life.

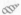

The sun was still up and bright when they arrived in Princess Anne. The restaurant he'd chosen was in one of the old, refurbished houses where the ceilings were high and the windows tall and narrow. Candles yet to be lighted stood on tables draped in white linen, and the waiters wore jackets and formal black ties. Conversations from other diners were muted, as in church. She could hear her heels click on the polished floor as they were led to their table.

She wanted to remember every detail. The way the little table sat snug by the window, the painting of the Bay that hung on the wall behind Ethan. The friendly twinkle in the waiter's eyes when he offered them menus and asked if they'd like a cocktail.

But most of all she wanted to remember Ethan. The quiet smile in his eyes when he looked across the table at her, the way his fingertips continued to brush hers on the white linen.

"Would you like to have some wine?" he asked her.

Wine, candles, flowers. "Yes, that would be nice."

He opened the wine list, studied it thoughtfully. He knew she preferred white, and one or two of the types were familiar. Phillip always kept a couple of bottles chilling. Though God knew why any reasonable man would pay that much money on a regular basis for a drink.

Grateful that the selections were numbered and he wouldn't have to attempt to pronounce any French, he gave the waiter the order, privately pleased when he saw his choice met with approval.

"Hungry?"

"A little." She wondered if she'd be able to swallow a crumb around the delight in her throat. "It's just so nice to be here like this, with you."

"I should've taken you out before."

"This is perfect. There hasn't been much time for this."

"We can juggle some time." And it wasn't so bad, he discovered, wearing a tie, eating in a place surrounded by other people. Not when he got to look at her across the table. "You look rested, Grace."

"Rested?" The laugh bubbled out, making him smile uncertainly. Then her fingers squeezed his affectionately. "Oh, Ethan. I do love you."

⊘

The sun dipped lower, and the candles were lighted as they sipped wine and enjoyed a perfectly prepared meal served with flair. He told her about the progress of the boat, and of the new contract Phillip had finessed.

"That's wonderful. It's hard to believe you only started the business this spring."

"I'd thought about it for a long time," he told her. "Had a lot of the details worked out in my head."

He would have, of course, she thought. Thinking things through was innate with Ethan. "Even so, you're making it work. Really making it work. I've thought about coming by dozens of times."

"Why haven't you?"

"Before . . . If I saw you too often or in too many different places, it worried me." She loved being able to tell him, to watch his eyes change when she did. "I was sure you'd be able to see the way I felt about you—how I wanted to touch you, and have you touch me."

The blood hummed in his fingertips as they grazed hers. And his eyes did change, just as she'd wanted, deepening as they stared into hers. "I'd talked myself out of you," he said carefully.

"I'm glad it didn't stick."

"So am I." He brought her fingers over, touched his lips to them. "Maybe you'll come by the boatyard one of these days, and I'll look at you . . . and I'll see."

She angled her head. "Maybe I will."

"You could drop in some hot afternoon and . . ." His thumb cruised lazily over her knuckles. "Bring fried chicken."

Her laugh was quick and easy. "I should've figured that's what really attracted you to me."

"Yeah, it tipped the scales. A pretty face, sea-goddess eyes, long legs, a warm laugh—they don't mean much to a man. But you add a nice batch of southern fried chicken, and you've got something."

Delightfully flattered, she shook her head. "And here I was thinking I wouldn't get any poetry out of you."

His gaze skimmed over her face, and for the first time in his life he wished he had a talent for composing odes. "Do you want poetry, Grace?"

"I want you, Ethan. Just the way you are." With a long, contented sigh, she looked around the restaurant. "And you add an evening like this now and then . . ." She shifted her gaze back to him and grinned. "And you've got something."

"Sounds like a deal, since I like being out with you, like this. I like being anywhere with you."

She curled her fingers into his. "A long time ago. It seems like a long time, I used to dream about romance. The way I hoped it would be one day. This is better, Ethan. Real turned out to be better than the dream."

"I want you to be happy."

"If I was any happier, I'd have to be two people for it all to fit." Her eyes sparkled with the laugh as she leaned toward him. "And then you'd have to figure out what to do with two of me."

"One's all I need. Do you want to take a walk?"

Her heart soared. Would it be now? "Yes. I think a walk would be perfect."

The sun was nearly gone as they strolled along the pretty streets, casting shadows lovely and deep. In a sky dazzled by hot color, the moon was starting its rise. It wouldn't be full, Grace noted, but it didn't matter. Her heart was.

When he turned her into his arms just at the edge of the splash of light from a streetlamp, she melted into the long, slow kiss.

Different, Ethan thought again as he let himself take the kiss just a shade deeper. She felt softer, warmer, yielding against him, though he could feel faint tremors rippling through her.

"I love you, Grace." He said it to soothe both of them.

Her heart bounded straight into her throat, making her voice shaky. Stars were blinking to life overhead, brilliantly white points of light. "I love you, Ethan." She closed her eyes, held her breath in anticipation of the words.

"We'd better start back."

She blinked her eyes open. "Oh. Yes." Let out her breath. "Yes, you're right."

Foolish of her, she decided as they walked back to his truck. A man as careful and thorough as Ethan wouldn't propose to her on a street corner in Princess Anne. He would wait until they got back, until Julie had gone home and Aubrey had been checked on.

He'd wait until they were alone, private, in familiar surroundings. Of course, that was it. So she beamed a smile at him as he started the engine. "It was a wonderful dinner, Ethan."

※

There was moonlight, just as she'd imagined. It slanted through the window and slipped gently over Aubrey in her crib. Her baby dreamed happy dreams, she thought. And how much happier they would all be in the morning when they'd taken the next step toward becoming a family.

Aubrey already loved him, Grace thought as she stroked her daughter's hair. Just a short time ago, she had resolved to raise her child alone, to make certain that she was enough. All that was changing now. Ethan would be a father to her daughter, a loving parent who would watch over her.

One day they'd tuck Aubrey in together. One day they would stand over a crib watching another child sleep. With Ethan she could share the joy of a simple moment like that—that quiet moment in the moonwashed dark when you looked in and saw your child asleep and safe.

There was so much he could give them, she thought. And that she could give to him.

A man like Ethan, she knew, would feel that first flutter of life in his heart just as she would feel it in her womb. They could share that, and a lifetime of simple moments.

She moved quietly into the living room and saw Ethan standing, gazing through the screen door. She had an instant of panic. He wasn't going? He couldn't be leaving. Not now. Not before . . .

"Do you want some coffee?" she said it quickly, her voice rising before she could control it.

"No, thanks." He turned. "She sleeping all right?"

"Oh, yes, she's fine."

"She looks so much like you."

"Do you think?"

"Especially when she smiles. Grace . . ."

He watched her eyes fix on his, glow in the low light of the lamp. For a moment it seemed to him that nothing had come before, nothing would come after. It could be the three of them, there together on quiet nights just like this, in the little dollhouse. It could be his future. He wanted to believe it could be his life.

"I'd like to stay. I'd like to be with you tonight, if you want."

"I want. Of course I want." She thought she understood. He needed to show her love first. More than willing, she held out a hand. "Come to bed, Ethan."

He took care to be tender, to stroke her gently to peak. Holding her there, holding until her body bowed up, a trembling bridge of sensations. To make her float and sigh. He watched the moonlight dapple her skin, followed its shifting shadows with his fingertips, with his lips. Pleasured her.

Love surrounded her. It cradled her. It rocked her with a rhythm as gentle as a quiet sea. Gliding on it, she offered it back to him, a shimmering reflection.

His tenderness moved her to tears. She knew now that his needs could be ripe and raw and reckless. And that thrilled her. Yet this part of him, this compassionate, sensitive, and most generous part of him touched her heart at the core. She fell fathoms deeper into that wide well of love.

When he slipped into her, when they were joined, his mouth moved over hers to capture each sigh. She glided up, trembled on that silk-covered peak, holding, holding until he was trembling with her and they could catch each other on the slow tumble down.

After, he shifted her so that she curled into the curve of his arm. And stroked her. Her eyes grew heavy. Now, she thought as she began to drift. He would ask her now while they were both still glowing.

Waiting, she slid into sleep.

⚉

He was ten, and the last beating she'd given him had left his back a maze of purpling bruises and scarlet pain. She never hit him in the face. She'd learned quickly that most clients didn't care to see black eyes and bloody lips on the merchandise.

She'd stopped using her fists, mostly. She found a belt or a hairbrush more effective. She liked the thin, circular brushes that were all hard bristles. The first time she'd used one on him, the shock and pain had been so unspeakable that he'd fought back and it had been her lip that had been bloody. She'd used her fists then until he'd found escape in unconsciousness.

He was no match for her, and he knew it. She was a big woman and strong with it. When she was drunk, she was stronger yet and more ruthless. It didn't help to plead, it didn't help to cry, so he'd stopped doing both. And the beatings weren't as bad as the other. Nothing was.

She'd gotten twenty dollars for him the first time she'd sold him. He knew because she told him, and promised to give him two dollars for himself if he didn't make a fuss about it. He hadn't known what she was talking about. Not then. He hadn't known, not until she left him in the dark bedroom with the man.

Even then he didn't know, didn't understand. When those big, damp hands were on him, the fear was so blinding bright, the shame so dark, the terror so loud, as loud as his screams.

He'd screamed until nothing could crawl through his throat but a guttural whimper. Even the pain of being raped couldn't push more out of him.

She even gave him the two dollars. He burned it, there in the dirty sink in the horrible bathroom that stank of his own vomit, he watched the money curl up black. And his hate for her was just as black.

He promised himself, staring at his own hollow eyes in the spotty mirror, that if she ever whored him again, he would kill her.

"Ethan." Her heart tripping in her throat, Grace scrambled onto her knees to shake his shoulders. The skin under her hands was like ice. His body was rigid as stone, but trembling. It made her think wildly of earthquakes, volcanos. Boiling violence under a hard layer of rock.

The sounds he made had wakened her. They'd made her dream of an animal caught in a trap.

His eyes flew open. She could see only the glint of them in the dark, but they looked blind and wild. For a moment she was afraid that the boiling violence she sensed would break through and batter her.

"You were having a dream." She said it firmly, certain that that was what was needed to put Ethan back into those staring eyes. "It's all right now. It was a dream."

He could hear his breath rasping. More than a dream, he knew. It had been the cold-sweated flashback he hadn't had in years. But the result was the same. Nausea curled sickly in his stomach, his head pounded and swam with the pathetic echo of a young boy's scream. He shuddered once, violently, under the gentle hands on his shoulders.

"I'm okay."

But his voice was rough, and she knew he lied. "I'll get you some water."

"No, I'm okay." Not even water would settle on his jumping stomach. "Go back to sleep."

"Ethan, you're shaking."

He would stop it. He could stop it. It would only take a little time and concentration. He saw that her eyes were huge, more than a little frightened. He was both sick and furious that he had brought even the memory of that horror to her bed.

Dear God, had he let himself believe, for even an instant, that it could be different for him? For them?

He forced himself to smile. "Just spooked me, that's all. Sorry I woke you."

Reassured because she saw a shadow of the man she loved come back into his eyes, she stroked his hair. "It must have been awful. Scared both of us."

"Must've been. Don't remember." The next lie, he thought, abominably weary. "Come on, lie back down. Everything's all right now."

She snuggled up beside him, hoping to comfort, and laid a hand over his heart. It was still racing. "Just close your eyes," she murmured as she would have to Aubrey. "Close your eyes and rest now. Hold on to me, Ethan. Dream of me."

Praying for peace, he did both.

⊄⊃

When she woke to find him gone, Grace tried to tell herself that the weight of her disappointment was out of proportion. He hadn't wanted to disturb her so early, so he hadn't said good-bye.

Now that the sun was up, he would already be out on the water.

She rose, slipped on a robe, and padded in to make coffee and to grab those few minutes of alone time before Aubrey roused.

Then she sighed and stepped out on her little back porch. She knew her disappointment didn't stem from finding him up and gone when she woke. She'd been sure, so sure he was going to ask her to marry him. All the signs had been there, the scene set, the moment perfect. But the words hadn't come.

She'd all but written the script, she thought with a grimace, and he hadn't followed it. This morning was supposed to begin the next phase of their lives. She'd imagined running over to Julie's and sharing the joy of it, of calling Anna and babbling, begging for wedding advice.

Of telling her mother.

Of explaining it all to Aubrey.

Instead, it was a quiet morning.

After a beautiful night, she scolded herself. A lovely night. She had no business complaining about it. Annoyed with herself, she went back inside to pour the first cup of freshly brewed coffee.

Then she began to chuckle. What had she been thinking of? This was Ethan Quinn she was dealing with. Wasn't this the same man who'd waited—by his own admission—nearly a decade to so much as kiss her? At the rate he took things, it could be another one before he brought up the subject of marriage.

The only reason they'd moved from that first kiss to where they stood now was because she . . . well, she'd thrown herself at him, Grace admitted. Plain and simple. And she wouldn't have had the guts to do that if Anna hadn't shoved her along.

Flowers, she thought, turning so that she could smile at them, bright and pretty on her kitchen counter. Candlelight dinner, moonlit walks, and long, tender lovemaking. Yes, he was courting her—and would likely continue to do so until she went mad waiting for him to take the next step.

But that was Ethan, she admitted, and just one of the things she adored about him.

She sipped coffee, bit her lip. Why did he have to take the step? Why shouldn't she be the one to move things along? Julie had told her men liked it when a woman took the initiative. And hadn't Ethan liked it when she finally worked up the courage to ask him to make love with her?

She could do some courting herself, couldn't she? And she could move it along at a faster pace. God knew she was an expert at getting things done on schedule.

It would only take the courage to ask him. She blew out a breath. She'd have to find that, but she would dig inside herself until she did.

⚓

Temperatures soared, and the humidity thickened in a syrupy morass that Cam not so cheerfully dubbed "fumidity." He worked belowdecks, trimming out the cabin until the heat sent him topside desperate for fluids and one stingy breeze.

Though he rarely complained about the working conditions, Ethan was—like Cam—stripped to the waist. Sweat poured as he patiently varnished.

"That's going to take a week to dry, it's so goddamn damp."

"Decent storm might blow some of it out."

"Then I wish to Christ we'd have one." Cam grabbed up the jug and glugged water straight from the lip.

"Close weather makes some people edgy."

"I'm not edgy, I'm hot. Where's the kid?"

"Sent him for some ice."

"Good idea. I could take a bath in it. There's no fucking air down there."

Ethan nodded. Varnishing was a miserable enough job in this weather, but working below in the little cabin where even the big fans couldn't reach was probably kin to working in hell. "Want to switch off for a while?"

"I can do my own goddamn job."

Ethan merely lifted a sweaty shoulder. "Suit yourself."

Cam gritted his teeth, then hissed. "Okay, I am edgy. The heat's frying my brain, and I keep wondering if that alley cat's gotten Anna's letter yet."

"Ought to. It went out Tuesday as soon as the post office broke the holiday. It's Friday now."

"I know what day it is, Ethan." Disgusted, Cam swiped sweat off his face and scowled at his brother. "Aren't you worried a damn bit about it?"

"It won't make any difference if I am or not. She'll do what she's going to do." His gaze flicked up to Cam's and was hard as a bunched fist. "Then we'll handle it."

Cam paced the deck, caught a whiff of air from the fans, paced back. "I never could understand how you can stay so calm when things go to hell."

"Practice," Ethan murmured and kept on varnishing.

Cam rolled his aching shoulders, drummed his fingers on his thigh. He had to think of something else or he'd go crazy. "How'd the big date go the other night?"

"Well enough."

"Jesus, Ethan, do I have to get the pliers?"

A smile moved over Ethan's mouth. "Had a nice dinner. Drank some of that Pouilly Fuisse Phil's so wild about. Tastes fine enough, but I don't see what the big fuss is about."

"So, you get laid?"

Ethan flicked up another glance, took in Cam's wide grin, and decided to take the question in the spirit it was asked. "Yeah—did you?"

Entertained, if no cooler, Cam threw back his head and laughed. "Damn, she's the best thing that ever happened to you. I don't just mean the sex, though that's got to be part of what's perked you up around here lately. The woman fits you like the proverbial glove."

Ethan paused, scratched his belly where sweat dribbled and itched. "Why?"

"Because she's rock-steady, pretty as a picture, patient as Job, and she's got enough humor about life to tickle out yours. I guess we'll be sprucing up the yard for another wedding before long."

Ethan's fingers tightened on his brush. "I'm not going to marry her, Cam."

It was the tone as much as the statement that made Cam's eyes narrow. Quiet despair. "I guess I could be reading you wrong," Cam said slowly. "I figured, the way things were moving, you were serious about her."

"I am serious, about Grace. About a lot of things." He dipped his brush again, watched the clean gold varnish drip. "Marriage isn't something I'm looking for."

Ordinarily Cam would have let a subject such as this drop. He'd have walked away from it with a shrug. Your business, brother. But he knew Ethan too well, had loved him too long to walk away from the pain. He crouched by the rail so their faces were closer.

"I wasn't looking for it either," he murmured. "Scared the hell out me. But when the woman comes into your life, *the* woman, it's scarier to let her go."

"I know what I'm doing."

The dug-in-at-the-heels look didn't stop Cam. "You always figure you do. I hope you're right this time. I sure as hell hope this isn't some shit that goes back to that ghost-eyed kid Mom and Dad brought home one day. The one who used to wake up screaming at night."

"Don't go there, Cam."

"Don't you go there, either. Mom and Dad did better by us than that."

"It has nothing to do with them."

"It all has everything to do with them. Listen—" He broke off with a mild oath as Seth came running in.

"Hey, this shit's already melting."

Cam straightened, scowled over at Seth out of habit rather than heat. "Didn't I tell you to find an alternate word for 'shit'?"

"You say it," Seth pointed out, shifting the bag of ice.

"That's beside the point."

Knowing the routine, Seth dumped the ice into the cooler. "Why?"

"Because Anna's going to have my ass if you keep it up. And if she has mine, pal, I'll have yours."

"Oh, now I'm scared."

"You oughta be."

They continued to bicker, Ethan continued the varnish. Tuning them out, concentrating on the job at hand, he locked his unhappiness away.

SEVENTEEN

It was going to be perfect. It was so obviously right, Grace wondered that she hadn't thought of it before. A sunset sail on calm seas with skies going pink and gold in the west was a custom-made backdrop for both of them. The Bay was part of their lives, what it offered and what it took.

She knew it was more than a place where Ethan worked. It was a place he loved.

It had been easy to arrange. All she'd had to do was ask. He looked surprised, then he smiled. "I'd forgotten you love to sail," he said.

She was touched when he'd simply expected that Aubrey would come with them. There would be other times, she thought. A lifetime for the three of them. But this warm and breezy evening would be for the two of them only.

Giddy laughter continued to rise up in her as she imagined his reaction when she asked him to marry her. She could see it so clearly, the way he would stop, stare at her with surprise in those wonderful blue eyes. She would smile, hold out her hand to him as they glided along with soft wind and dark water. And she would tell him everything that was in her heart.

I love you so much, Ethan. I always have and always will. Will you marry me? I want us to be a family. I want to live my life with you. To give you children. To make you happy. Haven't we waited long enough?

Then, she knew, that would be the moment his smile would begin. That slow, beautiful smile that moved degree by degree over the planes and shadows of his face, into his eyes. He would probably say something about how he'd intended to ask her. That he'd been getting to it.

They would both laugh, and they would hold each other as the sun dropped red beyond the shore. And their lives together would really begin.

"Where are you sailing off to, Grace?"

She blinked, saw Ethan smiling back at her from the wheel. "Daydreaming," she told him, chuckling at herself. "Sunset's the best time for daydreams. It's so peaceful."

She rose, nestled herself under his arm. "I'm so glad you can take a few hours off so we can do this."

"We're going to have the boat trimmed out within the month." He nuzzled his face in her hair. "Couple weeks ahead of schedule."

"You've all worked so hard."

"It's going to be worth it. The owner was here today."

"Oh?" This was part of it, too, she mused. The easy talk about their days. "What did he say?"

"Hardly shut up, so it's hard to know what he said half the time. Spouted off the latest this and that he'd read in his boating magazines, asked enough questions to make your head ring."

"But did he like it?"

"I figure he was pleased with her, since he grinned like a kid on Christmas morning the whole afternoon. After he left, Cam wanted to bet me that he would run her aground first time out on the Bay."

"Did you take the bet?"

"Hell, no. He likely will. But you haven't really sailed the Bay until you've run aground."

Ethan wouldn't, she mused, watching his big, competent hands on the wheel. He sailed clean.

"I remember when you and your family were building this sloop." She trailed her fingers over the wheel. "I was helping out at the waterfront the first time y'all took her out. Professor Quinn was at the wheel and you were working the lines. You waved at me." Chuckling, she angled her head to look up at him. "I was thrilled that you noticed me."

"I was always noticing you."

She leaned up and kissed his chin. "But you were careful not to let me notice you noticing." On impulse she gave his jaw a teasing nip. "Until lately."

"I guess I lost my knack for it." He turned his head until his mouth found hers. "Just lately."

"Good." With a quiet laugh, she laid her head on his shoulder. "Because I like noticing you notice me."

They weren't alone on the Bay, but he stayed well clear of the zipping motorboats out for a summer-evening cruise. A flock of gulls frantically swooped and swirled around the stern of a skiff where a young girl tossed out bread. Her laugh carried, high and bright, to mix with the greedy calls of the birds.

The breeze rose up, filling the sails and whisking away the wet heat of the day. The few clouds drifting in the west were going pink around the edges.

Almost time.

Odd, she realized, she wasn't a bit nervous. A little giddy perhaps, because her head felt so light, her heart so free. Hope, so long buried, was golden bright once freed.

She wondered if he would slip into one of the narrow channels where the shade would be thick and the water the color of tobacco. He could thread past the bobbing buoy markers to a quiet place, one without even the gulls for company.

He was so content with her beside him, Ethan let the wind choose the course. He should make adjustments, he thought. The sails would reef before long if he didn't. But he didn't want to let her go—not quite yet.

She smelled of her lemon soap, and her hair was soft against his cheek. This could be their lives, he thought. Quiet moments, evening sails. Standing together. Building little dreams into big ones.

"She's having the time of her life," Grace murmured.

"Hmmm?"

"The little girl there, feeding the gulls." She nodded in the direction of the skiff, smiling as she imagined Aubrey, a few years from now, laughing and calling to the gulls from the stern of Ethan's boat. "Uh-oh, here comes her little brother to demand his share." She laughed, charmed by the children. "They're nice together," she murmured, watching as the two of them heaved bread high into the air for eager beaks to snatch. "Company for each other. There're more lonely times for an only child."

Ethan closed his eyes a moment as his own half-formed daydream shattered. She would want more children. Deserve them. Life wasn't all pretty sails on the Bay.

"I need to trim the sails," he told her. "Do you want to take the wheel?"

"I'll trim them." She grinned at him as she ducked under his arm to move to port. "I haven't forgotten how to handle lines, Cap'n."

No, he thought, she hadn't forgotten. She was a good sailor, as at home on deck as she was in her own kitchen. She ran the rigging with the same skill that she showed when she served drinks to a crowd at the pub.

"There's not much you can't do, Grace."

"What?" She glanced up, then laughed. "It's not hard to know how to use the wind when you grow up with it."

"You're a natural sailor," he corrected. "A wonderful mother, a fine cook. You know how to make people easy around you."

Her pulse went from calm to frantic. Would he ask her now, after all, before she had the chance to ask him? "Those are all things I enjoy," she said, watching him watch her. "Making a home here in St. Chris contents me. You do the same, Ethan, because it contents you."

"I've got a need for this place," he said softly. "It's what saved me," he added, but he'd turned away and she didn't hear.

Grace waited another moment, willing him to speak, to tell her, to ask her. Then with a shake of her head, she crossed the deck again.

The sun was sinking, coming close, so close to that long nightly kiss of the shore. The water was calm, little wavelets waltzing against the hull. The sails were full and white.

The moment, she thought with a leap of heart, was now.

"Ethan, I love you so much."

He lifted an arm to bring her against his side. "I love you, Grace."

"I've always loved you. I always will."

He looked down at her then, and she saw the emotion come into his eyes, deepening the blue. She lifted a hand to his cheek, held it there as she drew in the next breath.

"Will you marry me?" She saw the surprise, as she'd expected, but she didn't notice the way his body went stiff as she rushed on. "I want us to be a family. I want to live my life with you. To give you children. To make you happy. Haven't we waited long enough?"

And she waited now, but she didn't see the slow smile slip across his face, into his eyes. He only continued to stare at her, with something she thought might be horror. Bony wings of panic fluttered in her stomach.

"I know you might have planned to do this differently, Ethan, and me asking you is a surprise. But I want us to be together, really together."

Why didn't he say something? her mind screamed. Anything. Why did he just stare at her as if she'd slapped him?

"I don't need courting." Her voice hitched and she stopped to try to steady it. "Not that I don't love things like flowers and candlelight dinners, but all I really need is for you to be there. I want to be your wife."

Afraid he would shatter if he looked into those hurt and baffled eyes another instant, he turned away. His hands white-knuckled on the wheel. "We have to come about."

"What?" She jerked back, staring at his set face, at the muscle that worked in his jaw. Her heart was still pounding, but no longer in anticipation. Now it was with dread. "You have nothing to say to me except that we have to come about?"

"No, I've things to say to you, Grace." His voice was as controlled as his heart was wild. "We have to go back so I can."

She wanted to shout at him to say them now, right now. But she nodded. "All right, Ethan. Come about."

The sun was gone when they docked. Crickets and peepers sent up their nightly chorus, filling the air with shrill, too-bright music. Overhead a few stars blinked through the haze and a three-quarter moon shimmered.

The air had cooled quickly, but she knew that wasn't the reason she was cold. So cold.

He secured the lines himself, silently. Just as he'd sailed home, silently. He stepped back into the boat, sat across from her. The moon was still low, just riding the tops of the trees, but the early stars sprinkled down enough light for her to see his face.

There was no joy in it.

"I can't marry you, Grace." He spoke the words carefully, knowing they would hurt. "I'm sorry. I can't give you what you want."

She gripped her hands together tightly. She didn't know whether they wanted to ball into fists and pound or hang limp and shaking like an old woman's. "Then you lied when you said you loved me?"

It might be kinder to tell her so, he thought, then shook his head. No, it would only be cowardly. She deserved the truth. All of the truth. "I didn't lie. I do love you."

There were degrees of love. She wasn't fool enough to think differently. "But not the way you need to love a woman you'd marry."

"I couldn't love any woman more than I love you. But I'm—"

She held up a hand. Something had just occurred to her. If it was his reason for turning her away, she didn't think she could ever forgive him. "Is it because of Aubrey? Because I had a child with another man?"

He moved fast so rarely, it took her by surprise when he snatched her hand out of the air and squeezed it hard enough to rub bone against bone. "I love her, Grace. I'd be proud for her to think of me as her father. You have to know that."

"I don't have to know anything. You say you love me, and you love her, but you won't have us. You're hurting me, Ethan."

"I'm sorry. I'm sorry." He released her hand as if it had burned his palm. "I know I'm hurting you. I knew I would. I had no business letting things come to this."

"But you did," she said evenly. "You had to know I'd feel this way, that I'd expect you would feel the same."

"Yeah, I knew. I should have been honest with you. I've got no excuse for it." *Except I needed you. I needed you, Grace.* "Marriage isn't something I'm looking for."

"Oh, don't treat me like a fool, Ethan." She sighed now, too battered to be angry. "People like us don't have relationships, we don't have affairs. We get married and raise families. We're simple and basic, and as amusing as that might be to some, that's just who we are."

He stared down at his hands. She was right, of course. Or would have been. But she didn't know he wasn't simple or basic. "It's not you, Grace."

"No?" Hurt and humiliation tangled inside her. She imagined Jack Casey would have said the same thing, if he'd taken the time to say anything before he left her. "If it's not me, who is it? I'm the only one here."

"It's me. I can't raise a family because of what I come from."

"What you come from? You come from St. Christopher's on the southern Eastern Shore. You come from Raymond and Stella Quinn."

"No." He lifted his gaze. "I come from the stinking slums of D.C. and Baltimore and too many other places to count. I come from a whore who sold herself, and me, for a bottle or a fix. You don't know what I come from. Or what I've been."

"I know you came from a terrible place, Ethan." She spoke gently now, wanting to soothe the brutal pain in his eyes. "I know your mother—your biological mother—was a prostitute."

"She was a whore," Ethan corrected. " 'Prostitute' is too clean a word."

"All right." Cautious now, for she saw more than pain, she nodded slowly. There was fury as well, just as brutal. "You lived through what no child should ever have to live through before you came here. Before the Quinns gave you hope and love and a home. And you became theirs. You became Ethan Quinn."

"It doesn't change the blood."

"I don't know what you mean."

"How the hell would you?" He shot it at her like a bullet, hot and dangerously sharp. How would she know? he thought furiously. She'd grown up knowing her parents, and their parents, never once having to question what they had passed on to her, what she'd taken from them.

But she would, before he was done, she'd know. And that would end it. "She was a big woman. I get my hands from her. My feet, the length of my arms."

He looked down at those arms now, at those hands that had bunched into fists without his being aware of it. "I don't know where I get the rest from because I don't think she knew who my father was any more than I did. Just another john she had bad luck with. She didn't get rid of me because she'd already had three abortions and was afraid to risk another. That's what she told me."

"That was cruel of her."

"Jesus Christ." Unable to sit any longer, he rose, leaped onto the dock to pace.

Grace followed more slowly. He was right about one thing, she realized. She didn't know this man, the one who moved in fast, jerky steps with his fists clenched as if he would use them viciously on anything that moved into his path.

So she stayed out of it.

"She was a monster. A fucking monster. She beat me senseless for the hell of it as often as when she figured she had a reason."

"Oh, Ethan." Helpless to do otherwise, she reached out for him.

"Don't touch me now." He wasn't sure what he might do if he put his hands on her just then. And it frightened him. "Don't touch me now," he repeated.

She let her empty arms fall to her sides, battled back the tears that wanted to come.

"She had to take me to the hospital once," he continued. "I guess she was afraid I was going to die on her. That's when we moved from D.C. to Baltimore. The doctor asked too many questions about how I fell down the steps and gave myself a concussion and a couple cracked ribs. I used to wonder why she didn't just leave me behind. But then, she got some welfare money because of me and had a live-in punching bag, so I guess that was reason enough. Until I was eight."

He stopped pacing and stood still, stood facing her. There was so much rage inside him he could all but feel it searing his pores. And the bitter rise of it stung his throat. "That was when she figured I'd better start earning my keep. She'd been in the life long enough to know where to go to find men who didn't much care for women. Men who would pay for children."

She couldn't speak, even when she pressed a hand to her throat as if to push words, any words, out. She could only stand there, her face bone-white in the light of the rising moon and her eyes huge and horrified.

"The first time, you fight. You fight like your life depends on it, and part of you doesn't believe it's really going to happen. It just can't happen. Doesn't matter that you know what sex is because you've been around the ugly edge of it all your life. You don't know what this is, can't believe it's possible. Until it's happening. Until you can't stop it from happening."

"Oh, Ethan. Oh, God. Oh, God." She began to weep, for him, for the little boy, for a world where such horrors could exist.

"She made twenty dollars, gave me two. And made a whore of me."

"No," Grace said, helpless and sobbing. "No."

"I burned the money, but that didn't change anything. She gave me a couple of weeks, then she sold me again. You fight the second time, too. Harder even than the first, because now you know, and now you believe. And you keep fighting, every time, over and over through the same nightmare until you just give up. You take the money and you hide it because one day you'll have enough. Then you'll kill her and get out. God knows you want to kill her maybe even more than you want to get out."

She closed her eyes. "Did you?"

He heard the raspiness in her voice, took it for disgust rather than the sick fury it was. A fury for him, underscored with a vicious hope that he had. Oh, that he had.

"No. After a while it's just your life. That's all. Nothing more, nothing less. You just live it."

He turned away now to stare toward the house, where the lights glowed in the windows. Where music—Cam on guitar—carried by the breeze played a pretty tune.

"I lived it until I was twelve and one of the men she'd sold me to went a little crazy. He knocked me around pretty hard, but that wasn't so unusual. But he was flying on something and he went after her. They tore the place apart, made enough trouble that a couple neighbors who'd made it their business to mind their own got riled enough to beat on the door.

"He had his hands around her throat," Ethan remembered. "And I was sprawled on the floor, looking up, watching her eyes bulge, and I was thinking, Maybe he'll do it. Maybe he'll do it for me. She got her hand on a knife, and she jammed it into him. She jammed it into his back just as the people beating on the door busted it in. People were shouting and screaming. She pulled the son of a bitch's wallet out of his pocket while he was bleeding on the floor. And she ran. She never even looked at me."

He shrugged, turned back. "Somebody called the cops and they got me to a hospital. I'm not clear on it, but that's where I ended up. Doctors and cops and social workers," he said quietly. "Asking questions, writing things down. I guess they went looking for her, but they never found her."

He lapsed into silence so that there was only the lap of water, the call of insects, the echoing notes of a guitar. But she said nothing, knowing he wasn't finished. Not yet finished.

"Stella Quinn was at some medical conference in Baltimore, and she was doing guest rounds. She stopped by my bed. I guess she'd looked at my chart, I don't remember. I just remember her being there, putting her hands on the bed guard and looking down at me. She had kind eyes, not soft but kind. She talked to me. I didn't pay any attention to what she said, just her voice. She kept coming back. Sometimes Ray would be with her. One day she told me I could come home with them if I wanted."

He fell silent again, as if that was the end. But all Grace could think was that the moment when the Quinns had offered him a home had been the beginning.

"Ethan, my heart breaks for you. And I know now that as much as I loved and admired the Quinns all these years, it wasn't enough. They saved you."

"They saved me," he agreed. "And after I decided to live, I did everything I could to be something that honored that, and them."

"You are, and always have been, the most honorable man I know." She went to him, wrapped her arms around him, and held tight despite the fact that his arms didn't enfold her in return. "Let me help," she murmured. "Let me be with you. Ethan." She lifted her face, pressed her mouth to his. "Let me love you."

He shuddered, broke. His arms came round her now, fiercely. His mouth took the comfort she offered. He swayed there, holding on to her, a lifeline in a thrashing sea. "I can't do this, Grace. It's not right for you."

"You're right for me." She clung when he would have eased her away. "Nothing you've said changes what I feel. Nothing could. I only love you more for it."

"Listen to me." His hands were steady, but they were firm as they gripped her shoulders and pushed her back. "I can't give you what you need, what you want, what you should have. Marriage, children, family."

"I don't—"

"Don't tell me you don't need them. I know you do."

She drew in air, let it out slowly. "I need them with you. I need a life with you."

"I can't marry you. I can't give you children. I promised myself I'd never risk passing on to a child whatever pieces of her are in me."

"There's nothing of her in you."

"There is." His fingers tightened briefly. "You saw it that day in the woods when I took you against a tree like an animal. You saw it when I yelled at you over working in a bar. And I've seen it too many times to count when someone pushes me the wrong way once too often. Holding it back doesn't mean it's not there. I can't take vows with you or make a child with you. I love you too much to let you believe it's ever going to happen."

"She scarred more than your body," Grace murmured. "It's your heart she really abused. I can help you heal it the rest of the way."

He gave her a quick, gentle shake. "You're not listening to me. You're not hearing me. If you can't accept the way things have to be between us, I'll understand. I'll never blame you for stepping back and looking for what you want with someone else. The best thing for you is for me to let you go. And that's what I'm doing."

"Letting me go?"

"I want you to go home." He released her and stepped back. Felt as if he'd entered a huge, dark void. "Once you think this all through, you'll see it my way. Then you can decide if we should go on seeing each other the way we have been or if you want me to leave you be."

"I want—"

"No," he interrupted. "You don't know what you want right now. You need time, and so do I. I'd rather you went on. I don't want you here right now, Grace."

She lifted a hand to her temple. "You don't want me here?"

"Not now." He set his jaw when he saw the hurt swim into her eyes. For her own good, he reminded himself. "Go home and leave me be for a while."

She took a step back, then another. Then turned and ran. Around the house rather than through it. She couldn't bear having anyone see her with tears on her cheeks and this awful tearing pain in her heart. He wouldn't have her, was all she could think. He wouldn't let her be what he needed.

"Hey, Grace! Hey." Seth abandoned his pursuit of the lightning bugs that flickered and flashed through the dark and raced after her. "I've got about a million of these suckers." He started to hold up a jar.

Then he saw the tears, heard them in her ragged breathing as she fumbled with the door handle on her car. "What's wrong? Why are you crying? Did you get hurt?"

She sobbed out a breath, pressed a hand to her heart. Oh, yes, oh, yes, I'm hurt. "It's nothing. I have to go home. I can't—I can't stay."

She tore open the car door, stumbled inside.

Seth's eyes went from puzzled to grim as he watched her drive away. Hot with fury, he stormed around the side of the house, slapping the bright jar on the edge of the porch. He saw the shadow on the dock and strode toward it with fists clenched for battle.

"You bastard. You son of a bitch." He waited until Ethan turned, then rammed his fist as hard as he could into his gut. "You made her cry."

"I know I did." The fresh and physical pain jolted through him, and joined the rest. "This isn't your business, Seth. Go on in the house."

"Fuck you. You hurt her. Go on, try to hurt me. It won't be so easy." Teeth bared, Seth swung again, and again, until Ethan picked him up by collar and seat and held him dangling over the end of the dock.

"Cool off, you hear, or I'll toss you in." He added a hard, threatening shake, but his heart wasn't in it. "You think I wanted to hurt her? You think I got any pleasure out of it?"

"Then why did you?" Seth shouted, struggling like a baited fish.

"There wasn't any choice." Suddenly abominably weary, Ethan dropped Seth to his feet on the dock. "Leave me alone," he murmured and sat on the edge. Giving in, he put his head in his hands, pressed his fingers to his eyes. "Just leave me alone."

Seth shifted his feet. It wasn't just Grace who was hurt. He hadn't really understood that a grown man could be, not this way. But Ethan was. Tentatively, he stepped forward. He stuck his hands in his pockets, pulled them out. Shuffled. Sighed. Then sat.

"Women," Seth said in a level and considering voice, "make a man want to shoot himself in the head and be done with it." It was something he'd heard Phillip say to Cam, and he thought it might be appropriate. He was rewarded when Ethan let out a short laugh, even if it wasn't a happy one.

"Yeah, I guess they can." Ethan draped an arm around Seth's shoulders, pulled the boy close to his side. And took a little comfort.

EIGHTEEN

Anna weighed her priorities—and took the day off. She couldn't be sure what time Grace would be by to tend the house, and she couldn't risk missing her.

She didn't give a good damn what Ethan said—or didn't say. There was a crisis.

If she'd believed they'd simply had a spat or misunderstanding, she would have been sympathetic or amused, whichever was most called for. It wasn't a misunderstanding that had put misery into Ethan's eyes. Oh, he had a way of hiding it, she mused as she slowly and ruthlessly tugged out weeds that threatened her begonias in the front-yard bed. And he hid his more personal feelings very well. It just so happened she was a professional at filtering through to emotion.

Too bad for him that he'd inherited a social worker for a sister-in-law.

She'd poked at Seth a bit. There was no doubt in her mind the boy knew something. But she'd run straight into unwavering male loyalty. All she got out of him was a Quinn shrug and a zipped lip.

She could have wheedled it out nonetheless. But she hadn't had the heart to put a chip in that lovely bond. Seth could keep his loyalty to Ethan.

Anna would work on Grace.

She was positive they hadn't seen each other for days. It was pathetically easy to keep tabs on Ethan. He was out on the water every morning, in the boatyard every afternoon and through the evening. He poked at his dinner, then retreated to his room, where she'd seen the light slanting under his door well into the night on several occasions.

Brooding, she thought with an impatient shake of her head. And if he wasn't brooding, he was looking for a fight.

She had broken up what would certainly have been bloodshed over the weekend when she walked in on the three brothers going nose to nose in the boatyard, Seth looking on with avid interest.

Whatever had caused it remained a mystery as she'd bounced straight off that same united male wall. Shrugs and snarls were all she got for her trouble.

Well, it was going to stop, she decided, and attacked some chickweed with enthusiasm. Women knew how to share and discuss. And if she had to bang Grace Monroe over the head with her garden spade, Grace was damn well going to share and discuss.

It was with pleasure that she heard Grace's car pull in. Anna tipped back her hat, rose, and offered a welcoming smile. "Hi, there."

"Hello, Anna. I thought you'd be at work."

"Took a mental health day." Oh, yes, misery here as well, she mused. And not quite as well coated as Ethan's. "You didn't bring Aubrey with you."

"No. My mother wanted her today." Grace ran a hand up and down the strap of the oversized bag over her shoulder. "Well, I'll get started and let you get back to your gardening."

"I was just looking for an excuse to take a break. Why don't we sit down on the porch a minute?"

"I really should get the first load of laundry in."

"Grace." Anna laid a gentle hand on her arm. "Sit down. Talk to me. I count you as one of my friends. I hope you count me as one of yours."

"I do." Grace's voice wavered. She had to take three breaths to steady it. "I do, Anna."

"Then let's sit down. Tell me what's happened to make you and Ethan so unhappy."

"I don't know if I can." But she was tired, bone-tired, so she sat down on the steps. "I guess I made a mess of everything."

"How?"

She'd cried herself dry, Grace thought. Not that it had helped. Maybe it would help to talk things over with another woman, one she was beginning to feel close to. "I let myself assume," she began. "I let myself plan. He picked me flowers," she said with a helpless lift of her hands.

"Picked you flowers?" Anna's eyes narrowed fractionally. Rabbits, my butt, she thought, but filed it away for later retribution.

"And he took me to dinner. Candles and wine. I thought he was going to ask me to marry him. Ethan does things stage by stage, and I thought he was leading up to proposing."

"Of course you did. You're in love with each other. He's devoted to Aubrey and she adores him. You're both nesters. Why wouldn't you think it?"

Grace stared for a moment, then let out a long breath. "I can't tell you what it means to hear you say that. I felt like such a fool."

"Well, stop. You're not a fool. I'm not, and I certainly thought it."

"We were both wrong. He didn't ask me. But he loved me that night, Anna. So tenderly. I never believed anyone would feel so much for me. He had a nightmare later."

"A nightmare."

"Yes." And she understood it now. "It was bad, very bad, but he pretended it wasn't. He told me not to worry and brushed it off. So I didn't think any more about it. Then." Thoughtfully, she rubbed a faint bruise on her thigh that she'd given herself bumping into a table at Shiney's.

"The next day I decided if I sat around waiting for Ethan to do the asking, I'd have gray hair on my wedding day. Ethan doesn't exactly rush through life."

"No, he doesn't. He gets things done in his own time, and gets them done well. But he could sure use a poke now and then."

"He does, doesn't he?" She couldn't stop the warm, wistful smile. "Sometimes he just thinks things to death. And I thought this was going to be one of those times, so I made up my mind to do the asking myself."

"You asked Ethan to marry you?" Anna chuckled, leaned back on the steps. "Atta girl, Grace."

"I had it all worked out. Everything I wanted to say and how to say it. I thought, on the water where he's most content, so I asked him to take me out for an evening sail. It was so lovely, with the sun setting and the sails bright and full of wind. And I asked him."

Anna slipped a hand over Grace's. "I gather he turned you down. But—"

"It was more than that. If you'd seen his face . . . He went so cold. He said he'd explain things to me when we got back. And he did. I don't feel right telling you, Anna, because it's Ethan's business. But he said he can't marry me, won't marry me or anyone. Ever."

Anna didn't speak for a moment. She was Seth's caseworker, which meant she'd had full access to the files on the three men who would stand as his guardians. She knew their pasts nearly as well as they did. "Is it because of what happened to him as a child?"

Grace's gaze flickered, then she stared straight ahead. "He told you?"

"No, but I know about it, most of it. It's part of my job."

"You know . . . what his mother—that woman—did to him, let other people do to him? He was only a little boy."

"I know that she forced him to have sex with clients for several years before she abandoned him. There are still copies of the medical reports in his file. I know that he was raped and beaten before Stella Quinn found him in the hospital. And I know what that kind of trauma, that kind of consistent abuse can do. Ethan could very well have become an abuser himself. It's a miserably common cycle."

"But he didn't."

"No, he became a thoughtful, considerate man with nearly unflappable control. The scars are there, under it. It's likely that his relationship with you has brought some of them closer to the surface."

"He won't let me help. Anna, he's got it into his head that he can't risk having children because he's got her blood in him. Bad blood that he would pass on. He won't marry because marriage means family to him."

"He's wrong, and he has the best example of how wrong in his own mirror. He not only has her blood but he spent the first twelve years—the most impressionable years—with her in an environment that could warp any young mind. Instead, he's Ethan Quinn. Why should his children—children that come from the two of you—be any less than he is?"

"I wish I had thought to say that," Grace murmured. "I was so shocked and sad and shaken." She closed her eyes. "I don't think it would have mattered if I had. He wasn't going to listen. Not to me," she said slowly. "He doesn't think I'm strong enough to live with what he's lived with."

"He's wrong."

"Yes, he's wrong. But his mind's made up. He won't want me now. He says the choice is mine, but I know him. If I say I can accept this and we go on as we are, it'll eat at him until he pulls away."

"Can you accept it?"

"I've asked myself that, thought about that for days now. I love him enough to want to, maybe to settle for it, at least for a while. But it would eat at me, too." She shook her head. "No, I can't accept it. I can't accept only one part of him. And I won't ask Aubrey to accept anything less than a father."

"Good for you. Now, what are you going to do about it?"

"I don't know that there's anything I can do. Not when we both need different things."

Anna let out a huff of breath. "Grace, you're the only one who can decide. But let me tell you, Cam and I didn't just float to the altar on gossamer wings. We wanted different things—or thought we did. And to find out what we wanted together, we hurt each other, we got in each other's faces and we dealt with it."

"It's hard to get in Ethan's face about anything."

"But it's not impossible."

"No, it's not impossible, but . . . He wasn't honest with me, Anna. Underneath it all, I can't forget that. He let me spin my daydreams, all the time knowing he was going to cut the threads of them and let me fall. He's sorry for it, I know, but still . . ."

"You're angry."

"Yes, I guess I am. I had another man do that to me. My father," she added, coolly now. "I wanted to be a dancer, and he knew I was pinning my hopes on it. I can't say he ever encouraged me, but he let me go on taking lessons and wishing. And when I needed him to stand up and help me try for that dream . . . he cut the threads. I forgave him for it, or tried to, but things were never the same. Then I got pregnant and married Jack. I guess you could say that cut his threads, and he's never forgiven me."

"Have you tried to resolve things there?"

"No, I haven't. He gave me a choice, too, just like Ethan did. Or what they seem to think of as a choice. Do this their way. Accept it, or do without them. So I'll do without."

"I understand that. But while it may buffer your pride, what does it do to your heart?"

"When people break your heart, pride's all you've got left."

And pride, Anna thought, could turn cold and bitter without heart. "Let me talk to Ethan."

"I'll talk to him, as soon as I can work out what needs to be said." She blew out a breath. "I feel better," she realized. "It helps to say it all out loud. And there was no one else I could say it to."

"I care about both of you."

"I know. We'll be all right." She gave Anna's hand a squeeze before she rose. "You helped me stop feeling weepy. I hate feeling weepy. Now I'm going to work off some of this mad I didn't realize was in there." She managed to smile. "You're going to have a damn clean house when I'm done. I clean like a maniac when I'm working off a mad."

Don't work it all off, Anna thought, as Grace went inside. Save some of it for that idiot Ethan.

It took two and a half hours for Grace to scrub, rinse, dust, and polish her way through the second floor. She had a bad moment in Ethan's room, where the scent of him, of the sea, clung to the air, and the small, careless pieces of his daily life were scattered about.

But she drew herself in, calling on the same core of steel that had gotten her through a divorce and a painful family rift.

Work helped, as it always had. Good, strenuous manual labor kept both her hands and her mind busy. Life went on. She knew it firsthand. And you got through from one day to the next.

She had her child. She had her pride. And she still had dreams—though she'd come to the point that she preferred to think of them as plans.

She could live without Ethan. Not as fully perhaps, not as joyfully, certainly. But she could live and be productive and find contentment in the path she forged for herself and her daughter.

She was finished with tears and self-pity.

She started on the main floor with the same single-minded fervor. Furniture was polished until it gleamed. Glass was scrubbed until it sparkled. She hung out wash, swept porches, and battled dirt as if it were an enemy threatening to take over the earth.

By the time she got to the kitchen her back ached, but it was a small and satisfying pain. Her skin wore a light coat of sweat, her hands were pruny from wash water, and she felt as accomplished as a corporate president after a major business coup.

She checked the clock, measured time. She wanted to be finished and gone before Ethan came in from work. Despite the purging wrought by labor, there was a small, simmering ember of anger still burning in her heart. She knew herself well enough to understand that it would take very little to fan it to full flame.

If she fought with him, if she said even a portion of the things that had careened through her head over the last few days, they would never be able to be civil again, much less friends.

She wouldn't force the Quinns to take sides. And she wouldn't risk putting her precious and vital relationship with Seth at risk because two adults in his life couldn't mind their tempers.

"I won't lose my job over it, either," she muttered as she went to work on the countertops. "Just because he can't see what he's throwing out of his life."

She hissed out a breath, scooped her fingers through her hair, which the heat and her exertion had dampened at the temples. And calmed herself by giving the drip pans on the ancient range a good scouring.

When the phone rang, she snatched it up without thinking. "Hello?"

"Anna Quinn?"

Grace glanced out the window, saw Anna puttering happily among the back garden. "No, I'll—"

"I got something to say to you, bitch."

Grace stopped, two steps from the screen door. "What?"

"This is Gloria DeLauter. Who the hell do you think you are, threatening me?"

"I'm not—"

"I got rights. Do you hear me? I got fucking rights. The old man made a deal with me, and if you and your bastard husband and his bastard brothers don't live up to it, you're the ones who'll be sorry."

The voice wasn't just hard and harsh, Grace realized. It was manic, the words shooting out so fast that one ran into the back of the other. This was Seth's mother, she thought as more abuse rang in her ear. The woman who'd hurt him, who frightened him. Who'd taken money for him.

Sold him.

She wasn't aware that she had twisted the phone cord around her hand, that it was so tightly wrapped it bit into the flesh. Struggling for calm, she took a deep breath. "Miss DeLauter, you're making a mistake."

"You're the one who made the goddamn mistake, sending me that fucking letter instead of the money you owe me. You fucking *owe* me. You think I'm scared 'cause you're some asshole social worker. I don't give a shit if you're the goddamn Queen of goddamn England. The old man's dead, and if you want things to stay like they are you're going to deal with me. You think you can hold me off with words on paper? You're not going to stop me if I decide to come back and take that boy."

"You're wrong," Grace heard herself say, but her voice sounded far away, echoing in her head.

"He's my flesh and blood and I got a right to take what's mine."

"Try it." Rage tore through her like a storm surge. "You'll never put your hands on him again."

"I can do what I like with what's mine."

"He's not yours. You sold him. Now he's ours, and you're never going to get near him."

"He'll do what the hell I tell him to do. He knows he'll pay for it otherwise."

"You make one move toward him, I'll take you apart myself. Nothing you've done to him, however monstrous, is close to what I'll do to you. When I'm finished, they'll barely have enough left to scrape up and toss in a cell. That's just where you'll go for child abuse, neglect, assault, prostitution, and whatever it is they call a mother who sells her child to men for sex."

"What kind of lies has that brat been telling? I never laid a finger on him."

"Shut up. You shut the hell up." She'd lost track, mixed Seth's mother and Ethan's into one woman. One monster. "I know what you did to him, and there isn't a cage dark enough to lock you in to suit me. But I'll find one, and I'll shove you in it myself if you come near him again."

"I just want money." There was a wheedle in the voice now, both sly and a little scared. "Just some money to help me through. You've got plenty."

"I don't have anything for you but contempt. You stay away from here, and you stay away from that child, or you'll be the one who pays."

"You better think again. You just better think again." There was a muffled sound, then the clink of ice against glass. "You're no better than me. I'm not afraid of you."

"You should be afraid. You should be terrified."

"I'm . . . I'm not finished with this. I'm not done."

The click of the disconnect was loud. "Maybe not," Grace said in a soft and dangerous voice. "But neither am I."

"Gloria DeLauter," Anna murmured. She stood just on the other side of the screen door, where she'd been for the last two minutes.

"I don't think she's human. If she'd been here, if she'd been in this room, I'd have had my hands around her throat. I'd have choked her like an animal." She began to shake now, fury and reaction crashing against each other inside her. "I'd have killed her. Or tried."

"I know how it feels. It's hard to think about someone like her as a person and not a thing." Anna pushed the door open, her eyes on Grace. She would never have expected to see that white-hot rage in such a mild-tempered woman. "I see it all too often in my work, but I never get used to it."

"She was foul." Grace shuddered. "She thought I was you when I answered the phone. I tried to tell her at first, but she wouldn't listen. She just shouted and threatened and swore. I couldn't let her get away with it. I couldn't stand it. I'm sorry."

"It's all right. From the end of the conversation I could hear, I'd say you handled it. You want to sit down?"

"No, I can't. I can't sit." She shut her eyes, but still only saw that blinding red haze. "Anna, she said she'd come back and get Seth if you didn't give her money."

"That's not going to happen." Anna moved to the refrigerator, pulled out a bottle of wine. "I'm going to pour you a glass of this. You're going to drink it, slowly, while I get my notebook. Then I want you to try to tell me what she said, as close as possible to exactly what she said. Can you do that?"

"I can. I can remember."

"Good." Anna glanced at the clock. "We're going to want to document everything. If she does come back, we're going to be ready."

"Anna." Grace stared down into the wine Anna had given her. "He can't be hurt anymore. He shouldn't have to be afraid anymore."

"I know it. We'll make sure he's not. I'll only be a minute."

Anna took her through the conversation twice. As she went through it the second time, Grace found herself unable to sit. She rose, leaving her glass of wine half full, and got a broom.

"The way she said things was every bit as vile as what she said," she told Anna as she began to sweep. "She must use that same tone on Seth. I don't know how anyone can speak to a child that way." Then she shook her head. "But she doesn't think of him as a child. He's a thing to her."

"If you were called on to testify, you'd be able to swear under oath that she demanded money."

"More than once," Grace agreed. "Will it come to that, Anna? Will you have to take Seth into court?"

"I don't know. If it heads in that direction, we should be able to add extortion to the list of charges you reeled off. You must have scared her," she added with a small, satisfied smile. "You'd have scared me."

"Things just come flying out of my mouth when I get worked up."

"I know what you mean. There are things I'd like to say to her, but in my position, I can't. Or I shouldn't," she said with a long sigh. "I'll type this up for Seth's file, then I suppose I'll have to compose another letter to her."

"Why?" Grace's fingers tightened on the handle of the broom. "Why do you have to have any contact with her?"

"Cam and his brothers need to know, Grace. They need to know exactly what Gloria DeLauter and Seth were to Ray."

"It's not what some people are saying." Grace's eyes flashed as she yanked a dustpan out of the broom closet. She couldn't seem to sweep away the simmering anger inside her. "Professor Quinn wouldn't have cheated on his wife. He was devoted to her."

"They need to have all the facts, and so does Seth."

"I'll give you a fact. Professor Quinn had taste. He wouldn't have looked twice at a woman like Gloria DeLauter—unless it was with pity, or disgust."

"Cam certainly feels the same way. But another thing people say is that when they look at Seth they see Ray Quinn's eyes."

"Well, there's another explanation for it, that's all." Her own eyes were hot as she shoved the broom and dustpan away, yanked out a bucket and a mop.

"Perhaps. But it may have to be faced and dealt with that the Quinns hit a rocky patch in their marriage, as people often do. Extramarital affairs are distressingly common."

"I don't give a damn about all the statistics you hear on television or read in magazines about how three out of five men—or whatever it is—cheat on their wives." Grace dumped cleanser in the bucket, dropped it into the sink, and turned the water on full blast. "The Quinns loved each other, and they liked each other. And they had an admiration for each other. You couldn't be around them and not see it. They were tied only tighter together because of their sons. When you saw the five of them together, you were seeing family. Just the way the five of you are family."

Touched, Anna smiled. "Well, we're working on it."

"You just haven't had as many years as the Quinns did." Grace hauled the bucket out of the sink. "They were a unit."

Units, Anna thought, often broke down. "If something had happened between Ray and Gloria, would Stella have forgiven him?"

Grace thrust the mop into the bucket and gave Anna a cool, decisive look. "Would you forgive Cam?"

"I don't know," Anna said after a moment. "It would be hard to because I'd have killed him. But I might, eventually, put flowers on his grave."

"Exactly." Satisfied, Grace nodded. "That kind of betrayal doesn't swallow down easily. And it follows that if the Quinns had that kind of tension between them, their sons would have known it. Children aren't fools, no matter how many adults might think so."

"No, they're not," Anna murmured. "Whatever the truth is, they need to find it. I'm going to type up my notes," she said as she rose. "Will you take a look at them, see if there's anything you want to add or change before they go into the file?"

"All right. I've still got some wash to hang out, then I'll be . . ."

They heard it at the same time, the wildly happy barking of dogs. Grace's reaction was pure distress. She'd lost track of the time, and Ethan was home.

Going on instinct, Anna slipped her notebook into a kitchen drawer. "I want to talk to Cam about this before we tell Seth about the phone call."

"Yes, that's best. I . . ."

"You can go out the back, Grace," Anna said quietly. "Nobody could blame you for not wanting another emotional hit today."

"I have wash to hang out."

"You've done more than enough for one afternoon."

Grace straightened her shoulders. "I finish what I start." She turned into the laundry room and the lid of the washer clanged as she tossed it up. "Which is more than can be said of some people."

Anna lifted a brow. Ethan was in for a surprise, she decided. And wasn't it handy that she was around to see him get it?

NINETEEN

When he saw her car in the driveway, Ethan had to force himself not to rush into the house just for a look at her. A quick glimpse, just one. He could take all of her into his mind with just one look.

He hadn't known it was possible to miss a woman—to miss anything—the way he was missing Grace.

The way, he thought, that left him empty and achy and edgy every hour of every day until he was desperate to fill the void. Until he laid awake at night listening to the air breathe.

Until he thought he was losing his mind.

The control he'd kept in place for so many years where she was concerned seemed constantly shaky these days. The walls of that control had already been breached, were tumbled at his feet so that he could swear he was choking on their dust.

He supposed once a man let it go, it was hard to build it back up again.

But he'd left the choice in her hands, he reminded himself. Since she hadn't made a move in his direction in days, he was afraid he knew which choice she'd made.

He couldn't blame her for it.

She would find someone else—someone she could make a life with. The thought burned in his gut as he loitered by his truck, but he refused to let it pass. She deserved to have what she wanted out of life. That was marriage and children and a pretty home. A father for Aubrey, a man who would appreciate both of them for the treasures they were.

Another man.

Another man who would slip his arms around her waist, rub his mouth over hers. Hear her breath quicken, feel her bones go soft.

Some faceless son of a bitch who wasn't good enough for her would turn to her in the night, sink inside her. And smile every goddamn morning because he knew he could do it again.

Christ, Ethan thought, it was making him crazy.

Foolish bumped into his legs, a ratty tennis ball clamped hopefully in his mouth, his tail wagging persuasively. In a habitual move, Ethan tugged the ball free and tossed it. Foolish bounded after it, yapping furiously when Simon darted like a bullet from the left and intercepted.

Ethan only sighed when Simon pranced back, sat, and waited for the game to continue.

It was as good an excuse as any to stay outside, Ethan decided. He would fool with the dogs, go fiddle with his boat, stay out of Grace's way. If she had wanted to see him, she could have found him.

The dogs worked him around the side yard, and taking pity on the slower, less skilled Foolish, Ethan found a stick to toss along with the ball. It lightened his mood a little to watch them bash into each other, wrestle, fetch, and retrieve.

You could depend on a dog, he thought, giving the ball a higher, harder toss that sent Simon bounding in pursuit. They never asked for more than you could give them.

He didn't see Grace until he was well around the house. Then he simply stood.

No, one look, one quick glimpse, wasn't enough. Would never be enough.

The sheet she lifted to the line flapped wetly in the breeze as she pegged it. The sun was on her hair. As he watched, she bent to the basket, took out a pillowcase, gave it a quick snap, then clipped it beside the sheet.

Love flooded into him, swamped him, left him weak and needy. Small details hammered him—the curve of her cheek in profile. Had he ever noticed how elegant her profile was? The way her hair sat on her head, feathered at the back of her neck. Was she letting it grow? The way the trim cuff of her shorts skimmed her thigh. She had such long, smooth thighs.

Foolish rapped his head against Ethan's leg and snapped him back.

Abruptly nervous, he wiped his hands on his work pants, shifted his feet. It was probably best, he decided, if he just slipped back around the front, went into the house and upstairs. He took the first step back, then pulled up short when she turned. She gave him a long look, one he couldn't read, then bent to take out another pillowcase.

"Hello, Ethan."

"Grace." He tucked his hands in his pockets. It wasn't often he heard her voice quite so cool.

"It's foolish to go all the way back around to the front of the house just to avoid me."

"I was . . . going to check something on the boat."

"That's fine. You can do that after I talk to you."

"I wasn't sure you'd want to talk to me." He approached her cautiously. Her tone of voice took the blistering heat right out of the day.

"I tried to talk to you the other night, but you weren't inclined to listen." She reached into the basket, apparently unperturbed that she was now hanging his underwear. "Then I needed a little time to myself, to settle everything in my head."

"And have you?"

"Oh, I think so. First, I should tell you that what you told me about what you went through before you came here shocked me, and it hurt me, and I have nothing but pity for that little boy and rage about what happened to him." She glanced at him as she secured the next clothespin. "You don't want to hear that. You don't want to think that I have feelings about it, that it touched me."

"No," he said evenly. "No, I didn't want it to touch you."

"Because I'm so fragile. Because I'm so delicate of nature."

His brows drew together. "Partly. And—"

"So you hoarded that nasty little seed all for yourself," she went on, calmly working her way down the clothesline. "Even though there's nothing in or of my life that you don't know. It's the way it should be, in your opinion, that I'm an open book and you're a closed one."

"No, it wasn't that. Exactly."

"What could it have been exactly?" she wondered, but he didn't think it was a question and wisely formed no answer. "I've been thinking about that, Ethan. I've been thinking about a number of things. Why don't we go back a ways first? You like to do things in neat, logical steps. And since you like things to be done your way, we'll just be neat and logical."

The dogs, sensing trouble, retreated to the water. Ethan found himself envying them.

"You told me you've loved me for years. Years," she said with such quick fury that he nearly stumbled back. "But you don't do anything about it. You don't once, not once, come up to me and ask me if I'd like to spend some time with you. One word from you, one look from you, would have thrilled me. But oh, no, not Ethan Quinn, not with his broody mind and incredible control. You just kept your distance and let me pine over you."

"I didn't know you had those kind of feelings for me."

"Then you're blind as well as stupid," she snapped.

His brows drew together. "Stupid?"

"That's what I said." Seeing the outrage cross his face was balm to her battered ego. "I would never have looked twice at Jack Casey if you'd given me anything to hope for. But I needed someone to want me, and it sure as hell didn't appear it was ever going to be you."

"Now just a damn minute. I'm not to blame for you marrying Jack."

"No, I take the blame. I take the responsibility, and I don't regret it because it gave me Aubrey. But I blame you, Ethan." And those gold-flecked green eyes blazed with it. "I blame you for being too pigheaded to take what you wanted. And you haven't changed a damn bit."

"You were too young—"

She used both hands, and all the force of her temper went into the shove. "Oh, shut up. You had your say. Now I'm having mine."

In the kitchen, Seth's eyes went hot. He made a dash for the door, only to be brought up short by Anna, who was eavesdropping as hard as she could.

"No, you don't."

"He yelled at her."

"She's yelling, too."

"He's fighting with her. I'm going to stop him."

Anna cocked her head. "Does she look like she needs any help?"

His mouth set, Seth glared through the screen. Then reconsidered when he saw Grace shove Ethan back a full step. "I guess not."

"She can handle him." Amused, she gave Seth a scrubbing pat on the top of the head. "How come you don't leap to my defense when Cam and I argue?"

"Because he's afraid of you."

Anna rolled her tongue into her cheek, enjoying the idea. "Oh, really?"

"Half afraid, anyway," Seth said with a grin. "He never knows what you'll do. And besides, you guys like to argue."

"Observant little brat, aren't you?"

He shrugged, cheerful now. "I see what I see."

"And know what you know." Laughing, she edged closer to the door with him, hoping for a better view.

"Let's move to the next step, Ethan." Grace shoved the empty basket out of her way with her foot. "Fast-forward a few years. Think you can keep up?"

He took a long breath because he didn't want to yell at her again. "You're pissing me off, Grace."

"Good. I mean to, and I hate to fail at something I'm working on."

He wasn't sure which emotion came out on top, annoyance or bafflement. "What's gotten into you?"

"Oh, I don't know, Ethan. Let's see—could it be the fact that you think I'm some brainless, helpless female? Yes, you know . . ." She jabbed her index finger into his chest like a drill into wood. "I bet that's just what's gotten into me."

"I don't think you're brainless."

"Oh, just helpless, then." Even as he opened his mouth she was rolling over him. "Do you think a helpless woman can do what I've been doing the last few years? Do you think—what was it you called me once—delicate, like your mama's good china. I'm not china!" she exploded. "I'm good solid stoneware, the kind you can drop and it rattles around on the floor. It doesn't shatter. You have to *work* to break good stoneware, Ethan, and I'm not broken yet."

She punched a finger into his chest again, darkly pleased when his eyes flashed a warning. "I wasn't so helpless when I got you into my bed, was I? Which is just where I wanted you."

"You didn't get me anywhere."

"Hell, I didn't. And *you're* brainless if you think differently. I reeled you in like a goddamn rockfish."

It gave her pleasure, oh, such vivid pleasure, to see both fury and frustration race over his face. "If you think a statement like that flatters either of us—"

"I'm not trying to flatter you. I'm telling you straight out, I wanted you and I went after you. If I'd left the matter up to you, we'd have been pinching each other's butts in a nursing home."

"Jesus, Grace."

"Just be quiet." There was no stopping now, whatever the consequences, not with this roaring sea crashing in her head. "You just think about that, Ethan Quinn. You give that some good long thought and don't you *dare* call me fragile again."

He gave her a slow nod. "It's not the word that's coming to mind at the moment."

"Good. I haven't needed you or anyone to help me build a decent life for my baby. I used muscle, and I used guts to do what needed to be done, so don't you tell me I'm china."

"You wouldn't have had to do it all alone if you weren't too damn proud to settle things with your father."

The truth of that put a hitch in her step. But she balled her fists and rushed on. "We're talking about you and me. You say you love me, Ethan, but you don't for one minute understand me."

"I'm starting to agree with that," he muttered.

"You've got some ego-ridden male idea in your head that I need to be taken care of, protected, coddled—when what I need is to be needed and respected and loved. And you'd know that if you paid attention. You ask yourself this, Ethan, who seduced whom? Who said 'I love you' first. Who proposed marriage? Are you so nearsighted you can't see I've had to take every step first with you?"

"You make it sound like you've been leading me by the nose, Grace. I don't care for that."

"I couldn't lead you by the nose if I jabbed a fish hook in it. You go exactly where you want to go, Ethan, but you can be so infuriatingly slow. I love that about you, and I admire it, and now I understand it more. You had a terrible period in your life when you had no control, now you take care not to lose it. But you can slip from control into stubbornness in one short step, and that's just what you've done."

"I'm not being stubborn. I'm being right."

"Right? It's right for two people to love each other and not build a life out of it? It's right to pay all your life for what someone else did to you when you were too young to defend yourself against it? Is it right for you to say you can't and won't marry me because you're . . . stained and you made some ridiculous promise to yourself never to have a family of your own?"

It sounded off when she said it like that. It sounded . . . stupid. "It's the way it is."

"Because you say so."

"I told you how it is, Grace. I gave you the choice."

Her jaw hurt from clenching it. "People like to say they've given somebody a choice when what they're really saying is 'do this my way.' I don't like your way, Ethan. Your way only takes into account what was and doesn't add what is, or what could be. You think I don't know what you expected? You'd take your stand and sweet, delicate Grace would just fall in line."

"I didn't expect you to fall in line."

"Then crawl off, wounded, and pine after you for the rest of my life. You're getting neither. I'll give you a choice this time, Ethan. You straighten yourself out, you go on and think things through for the next eon or two, then you let me know what conclusions you've come to. Because my stand is this. It's marriage or it's nothing. I'll be damned if I'll spend the rest of my life pining over you. I can live without you." She tossed back her head. "Let's see if you're man enough to live without me."

She whirled around and stalked off, leaving him fuming.

"U pstairs," Anna hissed at Seth. "He's coming inside. Now it's my turn."

"Are you going to yell at him, too?"

"Maybe."

"I want to watch."

"Not this time." She all but shoved him out of the room. "Upstairs. I mean it."

"Hell." He stomped to the stairs, waited a moment, then slipped back down the hallway.

Anna was pouring herself a homey cup of coffee when Ethan slammed the back door. Part of her wanted to go over and give him a big, sympathetic hug. He looked so miserably unhappy and confused. But the way she figured it, there were times when it was best all around to kick a good man when he was down.

"Want some?"

He flicked a glance at her and kept walking. "No, thanks."

"Hold it." She smiled sweetly when he stopped, when she all but saw the jittery waves of impatience shimmering around him. "I need to talk to you for a minute."

"I'm about talked out for the day."

"That's all right." Deliberately she pulled a chair out from the table. "You sit down and I'll talk."

Women, Ethan decided as he dropped into the chair, were the bane of his existence. "I guess I'll take the coffee, then."

"All right." She poured him a mug, brought him a spoon so he could dump his customary heaps of sugar into it. She sat, folded her hands neatly, and continued to smile.

"You stupid jerk."

"Oh, Jesus." He rubbed his hands over his face, left them there. "Not another one."

"I'm going to make it easy on you at first. I'll ask a question, you answer. Are you in love with Grace?"

"Yes, but—"

"No qualifications." Anna cut him off. "The answer is yes. Is Grace in love with you?"

"Hard to say just now." He shifted his hand to nurse the point on his chest where she'd all but bored a hole in him.

"The answer is yes," Anna said coolly. "Are you both single, otherwise unattached adults?"

He could feel himself sinking into a sulk, and detested it. "Yeah—so?"

"Just laying the groundwork, gathering the facts. Grace has a child, correct?"

"You know damn well—"

"Correct." Anna lifted her cup, took a sip of coffee. "Do you have feelings of affection for Aubrey?"

"Of course I do. I love her. Who wouldn't?"

"And does she have feelings of affection for you?"

"Sure. What—"

"Wonderful. We've established the emotions of the parties involved. Now let's move on to stability. You have a profession, and a new business. You appear to be a man with skill, who's willing to work and has the capability of earning a good living. Have you incurred any large, outstanding debts you believe you'll have difficulty meeting?"

"For God's sake!"

"No offense intended," she said brightly. "I'm simply approaching this matter the way I assume you would, calmly, patiently, step by tedious step."

He narrowed his eyes at her. "Seems to me people are having major problems with how I do things lately."

"I love the way you do things." She reached across the table and gave his tense hand an affectionate squeeze. "I love you, Ethan. It's wonderful for me to have a big brother at this stage of my life."

He shifted in his chair. He was touched by the obvious sincerity in her eyes, but he had a feeling she was tenderizing him in preparation for the roasting to come. "I don't know what's going on around here."

"I think you'll figure it out. So, we'll say you're financially sound. Grace, as we know, is well capable of earning a living. You own your own home, and a one-third share in this one. Shelter certainly isn't an issue. So, we'll move on. Do you believe in the institution of marriage?"

He knew a trick question when he heard one. "It works for some people. Doesn't work for others."

"No, no, do you believe in the institution itself? Yes or no."

"Yes, but—"

"Then why the hell aren't you down on one knee with a ring in your big, clumsy hand, begging the woman you love to give your fat head another chance?"

"I'm a patient man," Ethan said slowly, "but I'm getting tired of insults."

"Don't you dare get out of that chair," she warned when he started to scrape it back. "I swear I'll belt you. God knows I want to."

"That's another thing that's going around." He subsided only because it seemed easier to get it all over with at once. "Go ahead then, say what you have to say."

"You think I don't understand. You think I can't relate to what's eating you up inside. You're wrong. I was raped when I was twelve years old."

Shock jolted his heart, pain squeezed his soul. "Jesus, Anna! Jesus, I'm sorry. I didn't know."

"Now you do. Does it change me, Ethan? Aren't I the same person I was thirty seconds ago?" She reached for his hand again, held it this time. "I know what it is to be helpless and terrified and want to die. And I know what it is to make something of your life, despite that. And I know what it is to have that horror in you always. No matter how much you've learned, no matter how much you've come to accept it and know it was never, ever your fault."

"It's not the same."

"It's never the same, not for any two people. We have something more in common as well. I never knew who my father was. Was he a good man or a bad one? Tall or short? Did he love my mother, or did he use her? I don't know what parts of him were passed to me."

"But you knew your mother."

"Yes, and she was wonderful. Beautiful. And yours wasn't. She beat you, physically and emotionally. She made you a victim. Why are you letting her keep you one? Why are you letting her win even now?"

"It's me now, Anna. There has to be something twisted, something sour inside a person to make them the way she was. I came from that."

"Sins of the fathers, Ethan?"

"I'm not taking on her sins, I'm talking about heredity. You can pass on the color of your eyes, your build. Weak hearts, alcoholism, longevity. Those things can run in families."

"You've given this a lot of thought."

"Yeah, I have. I had to make a decision, and I made it."

"So you decided you could never marry or have children."

"It wouldn't be fair."

"Well, then, you'd better talk to Seth before too long."

"Seth?"

"Someone has to tell him he's never going to be able to have a wife and children. It's best if he knows that early, so he can try to protect himself from becoming emotionally involved with a woman."

For a trio of heartbeats he could only gape at her. "What the hell are you talking about?"

"Heredity. We can't be sure what bad traits Gloria DeLauter passed down to him. God knows she's got something twisted inside her, just as you said. A whore, a drunk, a junkie, from all accounts."

"There's nothing wrong with that boy."

"What difference does that make?" She met Ethan's furious stare blandly. "He shouldn't be allowed to take chances."

"You can't mix him in with me this way."

"I don't see why. You both come from similar situations. In fact, there are far too many cases that come through social services nationally that slip into parallel categories. I wonder if we can pass a law to prevent children of abusers from marrying and having children of their own. Think of the risks we'd avoid."

"Why don't you just geld them?" he said viciously.

"That's an interesting concept." She leaned forward. "Since you're so determined not to pass on any unhealthy genes, Ethan, have you considered a vasectomy?"

The instinctive and purely male cringe nearly made her laugh. "That's enough, Anna."

"Is that what you would recommend to Seth?"

"I said that's enough."

"Oh, it's more than enough," she agreed. "But answer this last question. Do you think that bright, troubled child should be denied a full and normal life as an adult because he had the bad luck to be conceived by a heartless, perhaps even evil woman?"

"No." His breath shuddered out. "No, that's not what I think."

"No buts this time? No qualifications? Then I'll tell you that in my professional opinion, I couldn't agree with you more. He deserves everything he can grab, everything he can make, and everything we can give him to show him that he's his own person and not the damaged product of one vile woman. And neither are you, Ethan, anything but your own man. Stupid, maybe," she said with a smile as she rose. "But admirable, honorable, and incredibly kind."

She went to him, put an arm around his shoulders. When he sighed, turned his face to press it against her midriff, tears stung her eyes.

"I don't know what to do."

"Yes, you do," she murmured. "Being you, you'll have to think about it for a while. But do yourself a favor this time, and think fast."

"I guess I'll go down to the boatyard and work until I get it clear in my head."

Because she was feeling suddenly maternal toward him, she bent and kissed the top of his head. "Do you want me to pack you some food?"

"No." He gave her a squeeze before he rose. When he saw that her eyes were damp, he patted her shoulder. "Don't cry. Cam'll have my head if he finds out I made you cry."

"I won't."

"Well, then." He started out, hesitated, then turned back briefly to study her as she stood in the kitchen, her lashes wet, her hair tangled from being out in the breeze. "Anna, my mother—my real mother," he added, because Stella Quinn was in his mind all that was real—"would have loved you."

Hell, Anna thought as he walked away, she was going to cry after all.

Ethan kept going, particularly when he heard Anna's sniffle. He needed to be alone, to clear out his head and let the thoughts gather again.

"Hey."

With his hand on the door, he looked over his shoulder and saw Seth on the stairs—where the boy had dashed like a skillful rabbit seconds before Ethan had started out of the kitchen.

"Hey what?"

Seth started down, slowly. He'd heard everything, every word. Even when his stomach had begun to pitch, he had stayed and listened. As he studied Ethan now, owlishly, he thought he understood. And he felt safe.

"Where you going?"

"Back to the boatyard. I got some things I want to finish up." Ethan let the door ease closed again. There was something in the boy's eyes, he thought. "You okay?"

"Yeah. Can I go out on the workboat with you tomorrow?"

"If you want."

"If I went with you, we'd finish sooner and be able to work on the boat with Cam. When Phil comes down on the weekend, we can all work on her together."

"That's how it goes," Ethan said, puzzled.

"Yeah. That's how it goes." All of them, Seth thought with a flash of pure joy, together. "It's hard work because it's hot as a bitch in heat."

Ethan bit back a chuckle. "Watch the mouth. Anna's in the kitchen."

Seth shrugged, but aimed a wary glance behind him. "She's cool."

"Yeah." Ethan's smile spread. "She's cool. Don't stay up half the night drawing or bugging your eyes out at the TV if you're working with me in the morning."

"Yeah, yeah." Seth waited until Ethan was outside, then snatched up the bag sitting beside the chair. "Hey!"

"Christ, boy, are you going to let me out of here before tomorrow?"

"Grace forgot her purse." Seth pushed it into Ethan's hand and kept his face bland and innocent. "I guess she had something on her mind when she left."

"I guess." Brows knit, Ethan stared down at it. Damn thing weighed ten pounds if it weighed an ounce, he thought.

"You ought to take it over to her. Women go nuts if they don't have their purses. See you."

He raced back inside, pounded up the stairs and straight to the first window that faced the front of the house. From there he could watch Ethan scratch his head, shove the purse under his arm like a football, and walk slowly to the truck.

His brothers sure could be weird, he thought. Then he grinned to himself. His brothers. Letting out a whoop, he raced down the steps to head for the kitchen and nag Anna for something to eat.

TWENTY

Grace intended to cool off and calm down before she stopped by her parents' house to pick up Aubrey. When she was this emotionally churned up, there was no hiding it from anyone, much less from a mother or a very perceptive child.

The last thing she wanted was questions. The last thing she felt capable of giving was explanations.

She'd said what needed to be said and done what needed to be done. And she refused to feel sorry for it. If it meant losing a long-standing friendship, one that she had always treasured, it couldn't be helped. Somehow she and Ethan would manage to be adult enough to be polite when in public and not to drag anyone else into their battles.

It certainly wouldn't be an easy or happy situation, but it could work. The same arrangement had worked for three years with her father, hadn't it?

She drove around for twenty minutes, until her fingers were no longed gripping the wheel like a vise and the reflection of her face in the rearview mirror was no longer capable of frightening children and small dogs.

She assured herself that she was now perfectly under control. So under control that she thought she'd take Aubrey out to McDonald's for a treat. And on her very next evening off, she was taking them both to Oxford for the Firemen's Carnival. She certainly wasn't going to stay around the house moping.

She didn't slam the door of her car, which she felt was an excellent sign of her now placid mood. Nor did she stomp up the steps of her parents' tidy Colonial. She even paused for a moment to admire the pale-purple petunias spilling out of a hanging planter near the picture window.

It was just bad luck and bad timing that her gaze shifted a few inches past the blooms and that she spotted her father through that picture window, lounging in his recliner like a king on his throne.

Temper geysered and blasted her through the door like a sharp-edged pebble from a well-aimed slingshot.

"I have a few things to say to you." She let the door slam at her back and marched up to where Pete rested his feet. "I've been saving them up."

He goggled at her for the five seconds it took for him to arrange his face. "If you want to speak to me, you'll do it in a civilized tone of voice."

"I'm through being civilized. I've had civilized up to here." She made a sharp slashing motion with her hand.

"Grace! Grace!" Cheeks flushed, eyes huge, Carol hustled in from the kitchen with Aubrey on her hip. "What's gotten into you? You'll upset the baby."

"Take Aubrey back to the kitchen, Mama. And it won't traumatize her for life to hear her mother raise her voice."

As if to prove arguments were inevitable, Aubrey threw back her head and sent up a wail. Grace stifled the urge to grab her, run out of the house with her, and smother her face with kisses until the tears stopped. Instead she stood firm. "Aubrey, stop that now. I'm not mad at you. You go on in the kitchen with Grandma and have some juice."

"*Juice!*" Aubrey sobbed it, at the top of her lungs, straining away from Carol with her arms held out to Grace and fat tears trembling on her cheeks.

"Carol, take the child in the kitchen and calm her down." Pete clamped down the exact urge as Grace's and waved a hand at his wife impatiently.

"Child hasn't shed a tear all day," he muttered, with an accusing look at Grace.

"Well, she's shedding them now," Grace snapped back, adding layers of guilt onto frustration as Aubrey's sobs echoed back from the kitchen. "And she'll forget them five minutes after they're dry. That's the beauty of being two. You get older, you don't forget tears as easily. You made me cry plenty of them."

"You don't get through parenthood without causing some tears."

"But some people can get through it without ever knowing the child they raised. You never looked at me and saw what I was."

Pete wished he was standing. He wished he had shoes on his feet. A man was at a distinct disadvantage when he was kicked back in a recliner without his damn shoes on. "I don't know what you're talking about."

"Or maybe you did—maybe I'm wrong about that. You looked, you saw, and you put it aside because it didn't fit in with what you wanted. You knew," she continued in a low voice that nonetheless snapped with fury. "You knew I wanted to be a dancer. You knew I dreamed of it, and you let me go right on. Oh, taking the lessons was fine with you. Maybe you grumbled about the cost of them from time to time, but you paid for them."

"And a pretty penny it came to over all those years."

"For what, Daddy?"

He blinked. No one had called him Daddy in nearly three years and it pinched at his heart. "Because you were set on having them."

"What was the point if you were never going to believe in me, never going to let go enough or stand by enough to let me try to take the next step?"

"This is old business, Grace. You were too young to go to New York, and it was just foolishness."

"I was young, but not too young. And if it was foolishness, it was my foolishness. I'll never know if I was good enough. I'll never know if I could have made that dream real, because when I asked you to help me reach for it, you told me I was too old for nonsense. Too old for nonsense," she repeated, "but too young to be trusted."

"I did trust you." He jerked his chair up. "And look what happened."

"Yes, look what happened. I got myself pregnant. Isn't that how you put it at the time? Like it was something I managed all by myself just to annoy you."

"Jack Casey was no damn good. I knew it the first time I laid eyes on him."

"So you said, over and over again until he took on the gleam of forbidden fruit and I couldn't resist sampling it."

Now Pete's eyes flashed and he rose out of the chair. "You're blaming me for getting yourself in trouble?"

"No, I'm to blame if there has to be blame. And I won't make excuses. But I'll tell you this—he wasn't nearly as bad as you made him out to be."

"Left you high and dry, didn't he?"

"So did you, Daddy."

His hand shot up, shocking both of them. It didn't connect, and it trembled as he lowered it. He'd never done more than paddle her bottom when she was a toddler, and even then he'd suffered more than she had because of it.

"If you'd hit me," she said, struggling to keep her voice low and even, "it would be the first real feeling you've shown me since I came to you and Mama and told you I was pregnant. I knew you'd be angry and hurt and disappointed. I was so scared. But as bad as I thought it would be, it was worse. Because you didn't stand by me. The second time, Daddy, and the most important of all, and you weren't there for me."

"A man's daughter comes in and tells him she's pregnant, that she's gone on and been with a man he took trouble to warn her away from, it takes him time to deal with it."

"You were ashamed of me, and you were angry thinking of what the neighbors were going to say. And instead of looking at me and seeing that I was scared, all you saw was that I'd made a mistake you were going to have to live with."

She turned away until she was sure, absolutely sure, there wouldn't be tears. "Aubrey is not a mistake. She's a gift."

"I couldn't love her any more than I do."

"Or me any less."

"That's not true." He began to feel sick inside and more than a little scared himself. "That's just not true."

"You stepped back when I married Jack. Stepped back from me."

"You did some stepping back yourself."

"Maybe." She turned around again. "I tried to make it once without you, putting my money away for New York. I couldn't do it on my own. I was going to make my marriage work without any help. But I couldn't do that, either. All I had left was the baby inside me, and I wasn't going to fail there, too. You never even came to the hospital when I had her."

"I did." Groping, he picked up a magazine from the table, rolled it into a tube. "I went up and looked at her through the glass. She looked just like you did. Long legs and long fingers and nothing but yellow fuzz on her head. I went and looked in your room. You were asleep. I couldn't go in. I didn't know what to say to you."

He unrolled the magazine, frowned at the fresh-faced model on the cover, then dropped it back on the table. "I guess it made me mad all over again. You'd had a baby, and you didn't have a husband, and I didn't know what to do about it. I've got strong beliefs about that kind of thing. It's hard to bend."

"I didn't need you to bend very much."

"I kept waiting for you to give me the chance to. I thought when that son of a bitch ran out on you, you'd figure out you needed some help and come home."

"So you could have told me how right you were about everything."

Something flickered in his eyes that might have been sorrow. "I guess I deserve that, I guess that's what I would've done." He sat down again. "And damn it, I was right."

She gave a half laugh, weary around the edges. "Funny how the men I love are always so damn right where I'm concerned. Am I what you'd call a delicate woman, Daddy?"

For the first time in too long to remember she saw his eyes laugh. "Hell, girl, about as delicate as a steel rod."

"That's something, anyway."

"I always wished you had a little more give in you. Instead of coming once, just once, and asking for help, you're out there cleaning other people's houses, working until all hours in a bar."

"Not you, too," she murmured and moved to the window.

"Half the time if I see you down on the waterfront you've got shadows under your eyes. 'Course, the way your mother's jabbering, that'll change before long."

She glanced over her shoulder. "Change?"

"Ethan Quinn's not a man who'll let his wife wear herself to the bone working two jobs. That's the kind of man you should have been looking at all along. Honest, dependable."

She laughed again, pushed a hand through her hair. "Mama's mistaken. I won't be marrying Ethan."

Pete started to speak again, closed his mouth. He was smart enough to learn by his mistakes. If he'd pushed her toward one man by pointing out his flaws, he might also push her away from another by listing his virtues.

"Well, you know your mother." He let it go at that. Trying to fit the words in his head, he plucked at the knee of his khakis. "I was afraid to let you go to New York," he blurted out, then shifted when she turned from the window to stare at him. "I was afraid you wouldn't come back. I was afraid, too, that you'd get yourself hurt up there. Hell, Gracie, you were only eighteen, and so damn green. I knew you were good at dancing. Everybody said so, and you always looked pretty to me. I figured if you got yourself up there and didn't get your head bashed in by some mugger, you'd find you wanted to stay. I knew you couldn't manage it unless I gave you the money to start you out, so I didn't. I thought you'd either stop wanting to go so damn bad, or if you didn't, it'd take you a year or two to put by enough."

When she said nothing, he sighed and leaned back. "A man works hard all his life building something, and while he's doing it he thinks that someday he'll pass it on to his child. My daddy passed the business on to me, and I always figured I'd pass it on to my son. Had a daughter instead, and that was fine. I never wanted to change that. But you never wanted what I was planning on giving you. Oh, you'd work. You were always a good worker, but anybody could see you were only doing a job. It wasn't going to be a life. Not your life."

"I didn't know you felt that way."

"Didn't matter how I felt. It wasn't for you, that's all. I started to think that you'd get married one day and maybe your husband would come into the business. That way I'd still be passing it on to you, and to your children."

"Then I married Jack, and you didn't get your dream, either."

His hands rested on his knees, and he lifted his fingers, let them fall.

"Maybe Aubrey'll have an interest in it. I'm not planning on retiring any-time soon."

"Maybe she will."

"She's a good girl," he said, still looking down at his hands. "Happy. You . . . you're a fine mother, Grace. You're doing a better job than most un-der hard circumstance. You've made a good life for both of you, and done it on your own."

Her heart trembled and ached. "Thank you. Thank you for that."

"Ah . . . your mother would like it if you'd stay for dinner." Finally he looked up, and the eyes that met hers weren't cool, weren't distant. In them was both plea and apology. "I'd like it, too."

"So would I." Then she simply walked over, climbed into his lap and buried her face in his shoulder. "Oh, Daddy. I missed you."

"I missed you, Gracie." He began to rock and to weep. "I missed you, too."

<hr />

Ethan sat on the top step of Grace's front porch and put her purse down beside him. He had to admit he'd been tempted several times to open it and poke inside to see just what a woman carted around with her that was so damned heavy and so indispensable.

But so far he'd managed to resist.

Now he wondered where she could be. He'd driven by her house nearly two hours earlier before going to the boatyard. Since her car wasn't in the drive, he didn't stop. Odds were, her door was unlocked and he could have set her purse inside the living room. But that wouldn't have accomplished anything.

He'd done some hard thinking while he worked. Some of that thinking centered on how long it was going to take her to cool off from snarling mad to mildly irritated.

He figured he could deal with mildly irritated.

He decided it was probably best that she wasn't home quite yet. It gave them both more time to settle down.

"Got it all figured out yet?"

Ethan sighed. He'd smelled his father before he heard him, before he saw him sitting comfortably on the steps, feet crossed at the ankles. It was the salted peanuts in the bag Ray had in his lap. He had always had a fondness for salted peanuts.

"Not exactly. I can't seem to think it through so it gets clear."

"Sometimes you have to go with the gut instead of the head. You've got good instincts, Ethan."

"Following instinct's what got me into this. If I hadn't touched her in the first place . . ."

"If you hadn't touched her in the first place, you'd have denied both of you something a lot of people look for all their lives and never find." Ray rattled into the bag and pulled out a handful of nuts. "Why regret something that rare and that precious?"

"I hurt her. I knew I would."

"That's where you went wrong. Not in taking love when it was offered but in not trusting it for the long haul. You disappoint me, Ethan."

It was a slap. The kind that both knew would sting the most. Because it did, Ethan stared hard at the thirsty little pansies going leggy beside the steps. "I tried to do what I thought was right."

"For whom? For a woman who wanted to share your life, wherever that would take you? For the children you may or may not have? You're on dangerous ground when you second-guess God."

Annoyed, Ethan slanted a narrow look at his father's face. "Is there?"

"Is there what?"

"Is there a God? I figure you ought to know, seeing as you've been dead the last few months."

Ray threw back his big head, let out his wonderful rolling laugh. "Ethan, I've always appreciated your understated wit, and I wish I could discuss the mysteries of the universe with you, but time's passing."

Munching on nuts, he studied Ethan's face, and as he did, Ray's wickedly amused grin softened, warmed. "Watching you grow into a man was one of the greatest pleasures of my life. You've got a heart as big as your Bay. I hope you'll trust it. I want you to be happy. There'll be trouble coming for all of you."

"Seth?"

"He'll need his family. All his family," Ray added in a murmur, then shook his head. "There's too much misery in the short time we spend living, Ethan, to turn away happiness. You remember to value your joys." Then his eyes twinkled. "I'd brace myself, son. Your thinking time's over."

Ethan heard Grace's car, glanced toward the road. He knew without looking that his father was no longer beside him.

When Grace saw Ethan sitting on her front porch steps she wanted to lay her head on the steering wheel. She wasn't sure her heart could handle yet another trip through an emotional wringer.

Instead, she climbed out of the car and went around to unstrap the sleeping Aubrey from her car seat. With Aubrey's head heavy on her shoulder, she walked to the house and watched Ethan unfold his long legs and rise.

"I'm not willing to go through another round with you, Ethan."

"I brought your purse by. You left it at the house."

Startled, she frowned when he held it out to her. It showed just how jumbled her mind had been that she hadn't even realized she'd been without it. "Thank you."

"I need to talk to you, Grace."

"I'm sorry. I have to put Aubrey to bed."

"I'll wait."

"I said I'm not willing to talk about this again."

"I said I need to talk to you. I'll wait."

"Then you can just wait until I'm good and ready," she told him and sailed into the house.

It appeared she hadn't quite gotten down to mildly irritated, he decided. But he sat again. And he waited.

∽

She took her time, stripping Aubrey down to her training pants, covering her with a soft sheet, tidying the bedroom. She went into the kitchen and poured herself a glass of lemonade she didn't want. But she drank every drop of it.

She could see him through the screen door, sitting on the steps. For a moment, she considered simply going to the door, closing it, and tossing the bolt to make her point. But she discovered she didn't have quite enough mad left to be that petty.

She opened the screen, let it close quietly.

"Is she down for the night?"

"Yes, she's had a long day. So have I. I hope this won't take long."

"I guess it doesn't have to. I want to tell you I'm sorry for hurting you, for making you unhappy." Since she didn't come down and join him on the steps, he stood and turned to her. "I went about it wrong, and I wasn't honest with you. I should have been."

"I don't doubt you're sorry, Ethan." She walked to the rail, leaned out, looked over her little patch of yard. "I don't know if we can be friends the way we were before. I know it's hard to be at odds with someone you care about. I made up with my father tonight."

"Did you?" He stepped forward, then stopped because she'd shifted away. Just a little, just enough to tell him he no longer had the right to touch. "I'm glad."

"I suppose I have you to thank for it. If I hadn't been so mad at you, I wouldn't have let myself be mad at him and get everything out. I'm grateful for that, and I appreciate your apology. Now I'm tired, so—"

"You said a lot of things to me today." She wasn't going to brush him off until he'd finished.

"Yes, I did." She shifted again, met his gaze straight on.

"Some of it was right, but not all. Not acting on how I felt about you before . . . it's the way it had to be."

"Because you say so."

"Because you couldn't have been more than fourteen when I started loving you, and wanting you. I was close to eight years older. I was a man when you were still a girl. It would have been wrong to touch you then. Maybe I waited too long." He stopped, shook his head. "I did wait too long. But I'd had time to think it through and I'd promised myself I wouldn't get you tangled up with me. You were the only one who I wanted enough that it mattered. Part of it was for me because I knew if I ever had you I wouldn't want to let you go."

"And you'd already decided that you would."

"I'd decided that I was going to live my life pretty much alone. I was managing that well enough until recently."

"You see it as a noble sacrifice. I see it as ignorance." She lifted her hands, knowing she was heating up again. "I guess we'd better leave it at that."

"You know damn well that if we were to get married you'd want more children."

"Yes, I would. And while I'll never agree with your reasoning for not making them together, there are other ways to make a family. You of all people should know. We could have adopted children."

He stared at her. "You . . . I figured you'd want to get pregnant."

"You figured right. I would want it because I would treasure your child living inside me, and knowing you were there with us. But that doesn't mean I couldn't find another way. What if I couldn't have children, Ethan? What if we were in love and planning to be married, and we found out I couldn't have babies? Would you stop loving me because of it? Would you tell me you couldn't marry me?"

"No, of course not. That's—"

"That's not love," she finished. "But it's not a matter of can't. It's a matter of won't. And I could have tried to understand your feelings if you hadn't kept them from me. If you hadn't turned me away when all I wanted was to help you. And I won't compromise on everything. I won't be with a man who doesn't respect my feelings and who won't share his problems with me. I won't be with a man who doesn't love me enough to stay. To make a promise to me to grow old with me and to be a father to my child. And I won't spend my life having an affair with you and then having to explain to my daughter why you didn't love and respect me enough to marry me."

She stepped toward the door.

"Don't." He shut his eyes, fought down panic. "Don't turn away from me, Grace."

"I'm not doing the turning away. Don't you see, Ethan? You've been doing the turning away all along."

"I've ended up right back where I started. Looking at you. Needing you. I'm never going to be able to stop now. I made so many promises to myself about you. I keep breaking them. I let her put her hands on this, too," he said slowly. "I let her put her mark on what we have. I want to clear that mark away, if you give me the chance."

He lifted his shoulders. "I've been doing some thinking."

She nearly smiled. "Well, there's news."

"Do you want to hear what I'm thinking now?" Following instinct, listening to his heart, he started up the stairs. "I'm thinking it's always been you, Grace, and only you. It's always going to be you, and only you. I can't help it if I want to take care of you. It doesn't mean I think you're weak. It's only because you're precious to me."

"Ethan." He would make her give in. She knew it. "Don't."

"And I'm thinking I'm not going to be able to give you the chance to live without me after all."

He took her hands, holding them when she tried to tug them free. And keeping his eyes on hers, he drew her out and down the steps to catch the last gilded light of the setting sun.

"I'll never let you down," he told her. "I'll never stop needing you to stand beside me. You make me happy, Grace. I haven't valued that enough, but I will from now on. I love you."

He touched his lips to her brow when she trembled. "The sun's setting. You said that was the best time for daydreams. Maybe it's the best time to pick the dream you want to hold on to. I want to hold on to this one. I need you to look at me," he said softly and lifted her face to his. "Will you marry me?"

Joy and hope blossomed within her. "Ethan—"

"Don't answer yet." But he'd seen the answer, and overcome with gratitude, he brought her hands to his lips. "Will you give Aubrey to me, let me give her my name? Let me be her father?"

Tears began to swim in her eyes. She willed them back. She wanted to see him clearly as he stood watching her with his face so serious, lit by the last quiet light of the day. "You know—"

"Not yet," he murmured and this time touched his lips to hers. "There's one more. Will you have my children, Grace?"

He saw the tears she'd been struggling to hold back spill over and wondered that he could ever have thought to deny them both that joy, that right, that promise.

"Make a life with me, one that comes from love, one that I can watch grow in you. Only a fool would believe that what comes from what we have together would be anything but beautiful."

She framed his face with her hands, took that picture into her heart. "Before I answer, I need to know that this is what you want, not just for me but for yourself."

"I want a family. I want to build what my parents built, and I need to build it with you."

Her lips curved slowly. "I'll marry you, Ethan. I'll give you my daughter. I'll make children with you. And we'll take care of each other."

He drew her close, just to hold, while the sun slipped away and the light shimmered into evening. Her heart beat quick and light against his. Her single quiet sigh echoed seconds before the whippoorwill began to sing in the plum tree next door.

"I was afraid you weren't going to be able to forgive me."

"So was I."

"Then I figured, hell, she loves me too much. I can get around her." The laugh rumbled out as he nuzzled her throat. "You're not the only one who can reel somebody in like a damn rockfish."

"Took you long enough to bait the hook."

"If you take your time about things, you end up with the best at the end of the day." He buried his face in her hair, wanting the scent and the texture. "Now, I've got the best. Good, solid stoneware."

Laughing, she leaned back so she could see his eyes. The humor there, she thought, was aimed at both of them. "You're a smart man, Ethan."

"Few hours ago you said I was stupid."

"You were." She pressed a noisy kiss on his cheek. "Now you're smart."

"I missed you, Grace."

She closed her eyes and held tight, thinking it was a day for forgiveness. And hope. And beginnings. "I missed you, Ethan." She sighed, then gave the air a puzzled sniff. "Peanuts," she said and snuggled against him. "That's funny. I could swear I smell peanuts."

"I'll explain it to you." He tilted her head up for one soft kiss. "In a little while."